The
TRANSFORMER
TRILOGY

By
M. A. FOSTER

The Book of the Ler
Omnibus:
THE GAMEPLAYERS OF ZAN
THE WARRIORS OF DAWN
THE DAY OF THE KLESH

The Transformer Trilogy
Omnibus:
THE MORPHODITE
TRANSFORMER
PRESERVER

M. A. FOSTER

The TRANSFORMER TRILOGY

DAW BOOKS, INC.

DONALD A. WOLLHEIM, FOUNDER
375 Hudson Street, New York, NY 10014
ELIZABETH R. WOLLHEIM
SHEILA E. GILBERT
PUBLISHERS
http://www.dawbooks.com

DAW Books Collectors No. 1384.
DAW Books are distributed by the Penguin Group (USA) Inc.

First Trade Printing, November 2006
1   2   3   4   5   6   7   8   9

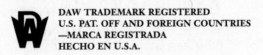

DAW TRADEMARK REGISTERED
U.S. PAT. OFF AND FOREIGN COUNTRIES
—MARCA REGISTRADA
HECHO EN U.S.A.

PRINTED IN THE U.S.A.

The Morphodite

Dedicated to:
Judith

1

Evening in Symbarupol

SYMBARUPOL, IN LISAGOR, ON OERLIKON:
4 CHAND 22 PAVILON CYCLE 7:

TWO MEN AT their ease relaxed on the terrace of one of the many bland, pastel buildings which composed the city outline, and observed the fall of night over the subtle outlines of Symbarupol. One was still, and watched the scene to the east without gesture or movement, as if completely at rest. The other, shorter and stouter, fidgeted and moved constantly, sometimes looking about the terrace, sometimes staring at the city as if it contained some vital secret. The taller and quieter of the two was silver-haired and distinguished in appearance, with long, thoughtful features which under certain circumstances might be called mournful or dolorous; the other was florid, excitable, and nervous, a worrier.

The taller man, obviously the senior of the two, seated himself in a chair and continued to muse over the soft outlines of the city, with its ranks of superimposed buildings—offices, factories, dormitories, habitats, all made in the same basic box shape, unadorned by slogans or signs or extraneous stylistic detailing. He liked it. His name was Luto Pternam, and he was the senior member of an organization which provided the guardians of public order with their raw material, and in addition disposed of the recalcitrant.

His associate was known as Elegro Avaria, and he was Pternam's confidant, executive secretary, henchman, and general man Friday. Avaria was nervous because he was expecting visitors, and he looked out over the evening-dimming cityscape as if he expected them to materialize at any moment.

Pternam said, almost idly, "Surely you don't expect them so soon, or that they'd walk right up the road as if they worked here?"

Avaria scratched his head, looked again, and shook his head. "No. For a fact, if they come tonight, it'll be late. Still . . ."

"You're sure about the date?"

"As sure as anyone could be, dealing with people like those. I spoke with their contact-man, Thersito Burya, when the last arrangements were made. He was definite: the Triumvirate was interested in our proposal and would come in person to investigate. Today, on this very date."

Pternam mused, "Odd they wouldn't send Burya. The files suggest that he does all their contact work. Or perhaps that other fellow, Mostro Ahaltsykh."

Avaria corrected his chief respectfully. "Personally, I did not expect Ahaltsykh. What he seems to do is more in the enforcement line: muscle, you know."

Pternam answered equably, "I suppose you are right; were I to judge this, I would not wish to agree to anything like this on the judgment of anyone less than you or I, and would probably think long on a recommendation by you alone."

Avaria agreed. "Rightly so."

Pternam continued, "Still, all three? That's dangerous work, exposing the three most important heads of an underground that isn't supposed to exist, all at once, in the same place. Surely they suspect we might have treachery in mind."

"Thersito Burya suggested that our proposal was important enough to be worth the risk. They have a replacement Triumvirate in the wings, should we prove false."

Pternam thought for a moment, and then said, "Yes, important. I imagine it would be: we offered them something from the very bowels of our organization—a perfect assassin, one that can find the target, select the method, execute the assignment, and then vanish by changing its identity. They have revolutionary zeal, but they can't produce that."

Avaria nodded briskly. "Right! And when they have committed to the thing that we will give them, and he makes his stroke, which you and I know to be a sham, they'll all pop out of the woodwork, and we'll have them all, the Changemonger scum, and we . . ."

Pternam completed the sentence, ". . . will be rewarded for the fine work we've done; I will move to the Central Group, and you will take my place here."

Avaria added, "Might put both of us in it."

Pternam smiled into the dim, soft evening light. "They might, at that. Yes, a possibility, Elegro."

The light was almost gone. Avaria looked about nervously and said, "It is about time I set out to meet them."

Pternam nodded. "Go ahead, then. We will wait for you here. Everything is ready for them."

"Including the one we've prepared?"

"Yes. Tiresio is ready. It is all ready. The moment of truth is here."

Avaria turned to go. "I suppose you know it will be late."

"How could it be otherwise? Go on—it will work out right."

Avaria nodded and set out across the terrace resolutely, turning into an alcove and disappearing.

For a long time Luto Pternam sat and looked out over the city in its evening light—surely something worth striving for. Symbarupol, a city of blocky plain buildings by day, became magic in the light of evening. What seemed by day to be impersonal and abstract became then something soft and lovely beyond words, its colors cyan, magenta, old rose, as the star Gysa sank into the Blue Ocean far to the west, beyond Clisp.

For all his relaxed manner, he felt inside himself a furious excitement building, the culmination of years of effort. The failures they had had, the making up of a suitable vehicle, even after the parts of the theory had been tested. And then, with the one specimen they had succeeded with, the long and difficult training, which had been as painful for the instructors as it had been for the trainee . . . All the arts of the assassin, and at the end of it, the loose control they had over it. And the terrifying power of Change the creature had. And the last, convincing it that what he knew to be a crackpot theory was in fact a lost science, that only he, Tiresio, could rediscover. . . . And they gave him some concepts, and turned him loose, and after a time he had said, "I can do it." Nonsense, of course, but it was of course important that Tiresio believe that he could do it.

No, this was not a trap for that pitiful Triumvirate: Merigo Lozny, Pericleo Yadom, Porfirio Charodei. Oh, no. Pternam reflected that by the time this had run its course, they would have them all, even to the farthest corners of Lisagor, the Alloyed Land.

Oerlikon was a planet with a singular history, quite unlike any other's: it had been discovered by accident, as a ship had dropped out of transit-space for minor repairs in the midst of a desolate region, which, while not as empty as the famous Purlimore Canyon, or the equally well-known B'tween-The-Arms, was indeed devoid of notable features. There, to their astonishment, the crew saw displayed on their instruments a single dwarf star, one planet, and an irregular collection of asteroids— the planetesimals. The star, a yellow-orange body, appeared to be exceptionally stable, and the single planet gave all the indications of being habitable. There were no nearby bright stars, and all the known O and B giants were far, far away. The region was populated solely by a thin and scattered collection of G, K and/or main-sequence stars, and a few white dwarfs.

While the ship was making repairs, the crew closed on the isolated little system and took a closer look. The star was smaller than the usual for a habitable system; the single planet orbited at roughly the orbital distance of Venus from Sol. The star they named Gysa, and dutifully noted its position and coordinates. The planet they named, with a small ceremony, Oerlikon. Sometime afterwards, when someone attempted to track down the source of the names, they found that the discovering ship, the Y-42, was a small Longline ship with an under-strength crew, and that apparently "Gysa" had been a legend printed on a shirt belonging to one of the crew, supposedly a sports association somewhere, and that "Oerlikon" had been the brand name of an inexpensive pocket tape machine used to reproduce the popular music of the day. They could recall no other names they had wished to use. And of such incidents are names fixed forever to pieces of real estate such as float about tenantless.

A gig from the Y-42 landed, and reported that all was well, if a bit bland. The view of the sky was uninspiring and uninteresting: the atmosphere was thick and hazy, and at night what stars could be seen arranged themselves into random patterns which suggested nothing whatsoever even to the most imaginative.

Oerlikon was moonless, and rotated slowly with a small axial tilt, so that the effect of the seasons was small. Moreover, its orbit about Gysa was astonishingly low in eccentricity. It turned out to have the lowest orbital eccentricity ever recorded for a habitable planet. The day was long, about thirty standard hours. It was also a watery world, with deep, abysmal ocean basins. The landing party observed only two continent-sized masses, one Asia-sized, an irregular oval high up in the subarctic, and a smaller, kite-shaped mass around the curve of the planet to the west, and south, partly temperate, partly tropical. A loose association of islands arcing south from the smaller continent across the equator completed what could be seen of land masses.

The larger continent they humorously named Tartary, but they found little on it of interest. Glaciation, geologically recent, had polished it flat, and crustal measurements indicated that it was drifting slowly south. For now, and the next million years, it would be cold and barren and cruel.

The smaller continent was much more interesting. The main part of it was shaped rather like a kite in flight. It had low mountains, rivers, and a complete, if rather limited, flora and fauna. The east, north, and western shores were mountainous, although none rose to great heights. In the west, the chains formed an outline of a discus thrower, or javelin hurler, while the eastern ranges formed a concave curve open to the east and trailing off in the islands of the south. An interior range, a spur of the eastern range, enclosed a broad valley that connected with the interior in the north. The rest of the interior was a vast grassy plain. And far in the west, as if hanging off the bent leg of the javelin thrower, a small subcontinent was attached, joined to the mainland by a narrow mountainous isthmus. It seemed pleasant and habitable, and was so reported when the Logline freighter Y-42 reached settled regions again.

As always the case with a new planet, at first the explorers and settlers came, although Oerlikon attracted no great numbers owing to its isolation and the reluctance of star-captains to make planetfall at such an out-of-the-way place. Once there, these early immigrants were able to see for themselves that there were normal quantities of metals, a biosphere of no great novelty, although some of the forms were odd, and the oceans well-stocked. The large continent, Tartary, was severe in climate and sparse in vegetation, and only the hardiest souls went there, prospectors and herdsmen, hermits and misanthropes, where they built sod huts on the treeless steppes, or erected frowning castles of the native shield granite, and remained to brood under the iron-gray skies.

Others, more sociable, moved on to the smaller continent, and settled places soon appeared, including a fishing and trading center which grew in the delta of the great river of the interior, and soon became a sprawling, disorderly city, which the locals called Marula, from one of the notable early explorers, Esteban Marula. Oerlikon had a city, and to the northwest of Marula, between the marshy land of the delta and the bones of the hills, even a spaceport of sorts.

But Oerlikon was not popular, and the immigrants were few, a mere trickle. The land available was not great, the climate bland, in short it was a world too much like the ones they left behind. For a fact, Oerlikon would have remained a bare, underpopulated world, had it not been for a certain sect hearing of it, and deciding that this empty little world and its isolation suited their desires exactly. These were the peoples who later became known as "The Changeless."

Who were The Changeless? They gave allegiance to no flag, for they came from every sort of state, principality, crank empire, and gimcrack commonwealth and idealistic union. Nor were they a single race: every color, hue, and possible physiognomy was represented. Their tongues were Babel, and their home cultures as diverse as fish in the sea. But for all their disunity, they all held one thing in common with a belief that would not die, that the rate of change that was the pace of Time had run out of control, and they knew the present was inferior to the past, and growing more so daily, and they wanted no part of a future they neither understood, liked, nor profited by. And when they heard of Oerlikon, they knew they had found El Dorado, an obscure planet in an obscure region of space, where they could go and let Time pass them by forever.

And so they came, settled, and many survived; Oerlikon was neither rigorous nor poisonous within the smaller continent, nor on the tropical islands of the southeast cape, which they called the Pilontary Islands. And little by little, they gathered strength, were soon a majority, and the ships began to call less often, and then rarely, and soon not at all, save an occasional tramp trader from the remotest regions. No one went to Oerlikon. And no one left.

In a sense heavy with irony, which The Changeless neither understood nor appreciated, it was only with the arrival of The Changeless that history can be said to begin on Oerlikon. For, before the arrival of The Changeless, the smaller continent had only known isolated settlements, hunters and prospectors, and leagues of wild lands. But the newcomers, full of boundless zeal, quickly established growing and highly organized enclaves, and slowly excluded the old settlers, who either went further into the wild, or began drifting toward the subcontinent far to the west, or to Marula.

They ignored the wilds of Tartary as too stern a land, but moved in force onto the smaller continent and the Pilontary Islands. Their growing enclaves became autonomous regions, and developed names.

Now for some time, the smaller continent had been known as Karshiyaka, which meant, more or less, in Old Turkish, The Opposite Shore. But early on, The Changeless invented their own language to make sense among themselves, and they preferred their own names, some in echoing evocations of places they had once been to, and some in the harsh sounds of the new way of speaking.

North of the mountains (that formed the arms of the javelin thrower), the lands enclosed by spur ranges became Grayslope, rugged slopes and defiles covered with silvergrass falling to the gray turbulence of the polar seas. East of the thrower's left arm, there was a still sterner land that they called Severovost. In the west, facing the blue waters of evening, along the right arm and down the trunk was the land Zefaa, from its winds; and from the place where the ranges divided, and formed the legs of the thrower, the right leg became The Serpentine, a narrow isthmus connecting the continent with a smaller land somewhat farther west, called Clisp.

Between the legs was Zolotane, the land of gold, an arid country. The Delta became Sertsa Solntsa, the "Heart of the Sun," and the inside of the long point to the southeast became Priboy—"The Surf." The rest of the peninsula was Zamor, and all the east coast was Tilanque, save a tiny enclave in the northeast, which retained the old name of Karshiyaka for itself.

And in the interior there were three lands. The strip between the parallel ranges, the hidden land, was Puropaigne. Across the north along the south slopes of the mountains was Akchil, the Dales. And all the rest, so goes the saying, was Crule The Swale.

Of large cities there were only three: Marula, renamed Marulupol; Symbar, renamed Symbarupol, between Puropaigne and The Swale; and in Clisp, Marisol.

For a time, each area retained some identity, but a powerful process was at work among the stern and relentless Changeless; for one of their main drives was naturally toward orthodoxy and uniformity, and so a gradual pressure upon the old settlers began, and increased, and the more sensitive to it began moving away, drifting out of the old lands and into fringe areas: Clisp, in the far west, arid and mountainous. The tropical Pilontary Islands, where life was too easy to worry about doctrine. And Marula, which had always been a gathering-place for the riffraff of all Karshiyaka. A few hardy souls set up exile regimes in Tartary.

The impetus for unification emerged from the center—The Swale and Puropaigne, joined shortly by the men of Akchil. Once these areas were cleared, things moved swiftly, and with a small action that wasn't a war, and wasn't a coup, but was something of both and of neither, and which of The Changeless called "The Rectification," all Karshiyaka, save only Clisp, became one land, a nation its inhabitants named Lisagor— The Alloyed Land. Then, too, was when they renamed Tartary Makhagor—The Lawless Land. Clisp, free and full of ferment, remained independent for almost two cycles* longer, until it, too, fell, and was re-named, with malice aforethought, Vredamgor—The Conquered Land.

With vast relief, Anibal Glist departed the communal mess and made his way down the winding exterior stairs to the Level, which functioned more or less as the Lisagorian equivalent of a street. Glist stepped off the last of the narrow, whitewashed masonry stairs into the cool dark-ness of the street, and caught himself reflecting that now he only rarely thought in terms of "equivalents." He had been on Oerlikon for a long time, and was well on the way to becoming native in his patterns of habit and thought. His retirement would be not far off, and more than once he had considered taking his retirement here. Staying. Not entirely impossible. Novel, perhaps, but not impossible. He had grown to like it, this impossible planet and this even more improbable country which dominated it, Lisagor.

    The one Custom he found hardest to get used to were the commu-nal meals, served to the tune of popular songs, sung badly out of key and time, but sung together nonetheless. The food, at least, was good. Next, of course, he would return to his cell, essentially an apartment built on an artificial hill, reached by means of the winding stairs. Liask towns were clusters of these hills, connected by narrow streets made as level as pos-sible without regard to the curves this might produce. How did one get from one part of town to another? Afoot, or on ludicrous variations of bicycles called velocipedes, in which the rider sat on a triangular truss

---

* Cycles: Time on Oerlikon was computed on an arbitrary calendar which used the ancient Mayan computation as a model. The "Years" thus com-puted had no relationship with the orbital period of Oerlikon or any other known planet, but instead were an elegant construction of four Prime Fac-tors, twenty-three, eleven, thirteen, and thirty-one, which provided, vari-ously, a Ritual year of 253 days, and a Great Year of 403 days, which cycled together to produce a Cycle of 101,959 days—253 Great Years. Time was counted from the day when Lisagor was proclaimed. The present, within this story-frame, is within the seventh Cycle.

framework between the wheels, low to the ground, and pedalled with the legs held horizontally out in front. Odd, and with little outrigger wheels to help get started, which were retracted once balance was attained, but fast and little work. They were expensive, though, and distinctly a luxury item.

At the velocipede rack, while unentangling his own vehicle, Glist happened to find himself next to a young woman engaged in a similar task. Glist knew her, of course—she was one of his student observers, by name Aril Procand. But as far as the Liasks about him might know, she was only someone who had been at this particular mess hall, and by chance was near him at the velocipede rack.

Glist spoke casually: "A fine speech tonight by Primitivo Mercador, the First Synodic for Trade and Equity; almost as good as if the Prime Synodic, Simonpetrino Monclova himself, had been with us."

The young woman disengaged her velocipede and nodded politely, adding, "Monclova is more restrained, but of course sees further. Still, it is an honor to have Mercador." Her motions with the velocipede brought her fractionally closer to Glist, and she said quickly, in a much quieter tone, "Enthone Sheptun tells me he has an item for you which is most urgent. He will follow you, and meet you along your way to your cell, on the Level."

Glist nodded, and said no more. He did not have direct relations with Aril Procand, a fact which disappointed him as he risked an appreciative glance at the young woman's slender figure and curly brown-gold hair. A shame. Glist evaluated her reports, of course, and knew her to be a fine young operative, a keen observer of events on this peculiar planet. Oh well, he thought ruefully, someone younger will doubtless be having a covert affair with her—most likely Sheptun, a romantic fool. Glist continued readying his velocipede for riding, as Aril mounted hers with youthful nonchalance and sped away into the night, the soft night of Symbarupol.

The news set something uneasy stirring in Glist; Sheptun was one of his more deeply buried operatives, not a mere observer, like Procand, and also unlike her, not on student-probationary status. Sheptun also reported much, as part of his duties here, and the reports were always quite good. If he continued, there was no doubt he'd have Discretionary Authority before long. Not his successor, of course: that was already arranged, and it would be Cesar Kham, who was now working on something in Marisol, in Clisp. Verdamgor, he corrected himself.

Glist settled into the machine, prepared himself, and set off onto the Level, retracting his outriggers and turning on the lamps, working up through the gears into a comfortable pace. Still, he wondered what Sheptun could have on his mind. Although contact of any sort was discouraged among the members, other than through the channels already established, it was not prohibited, provided certain assumptions were always borne in mind, the most important being that the Lisaks must not, under any circumstances, learn that there was in their midst a sizable body of off-planet visitors engaged in studying and manipulating their odd, retrogressive society.

He had not proceeded far along the Level, when, in the light evening traffic, another velocipede joined up with him and proceeded alongside in formation. Glist recognized Enthone Sheptun immediately, and followed him without comment, when Sheptun pedalled ahead, and turned into a narrower side-level which ended in a teahouse and a reside-hill across from a Dragon Field.* Sheptun stopped, extended the outriggers on his machine, and went into the teahouse, and Glist, slightly behind, did the same, as if he had happened to be going that way.

Inside the teahouse, a bluish haze in the air from the charcoal heaters and the water pipes which the patrons enjoyed blurred the atmosphere, and Glist had to squint to find Sheptun. Also, the place was crowded; a Dragon game must have recently broken up. By luck, Sheptun had found a table with two empty seats, in a far corner, and the constant hubbub and drone of conversation would bury their conversation. Glist made his way across the floor to the corner.

The Waiter brought tea, the commonplace Mixture #79, without comment, and left them, returning to the kitchen. Glist looked about, a little nervously, and said, in a low voice which he hoped would not carry far, "Student Procand alerted me, and so I was awaiting contact. This doubtless will refer to something which could not be forwarded through the usual channels?"

Sheptun, an alert young man of some years, blinked rapidly and answered. "Much remains to be said through the normal reports, but I felt you needed to be alerted. I have just uncovered something you need to know, perhaps even advise the Policy Group about."

"Go on—expound at will, although you may not mention that group again in here. You are reckless."

"You will understand." Sheptun spoke without heat, calmly. Then, "For the last few days, I have been engaged in verifying a very strange

* Dragon: the sole public physical sport played in Lisagor and Lisak-dominated areas.

tale: to the point, there is a weapon of some sort about to be released which will change everything here."

Glist carefully controlled his body movements, and his expressions. He looked musingly at the teacup and said, tonelessly, "What is the nature of this alleged weapon, and who is intended to use it?"

Sheptun adopted the same tonelessness, and the same blank expression, and said. "The nature of it remains unknown."

"You could not find out what?"

"The sources I tap do not know themselves. As to who will use it—presumably the Heraclitan Society."

"The so-called Underground, that favors normalization of the way of life here?"

"The same. Although, there is inexactitude there, too."

"Inexactitude? In what way? Do they intend to use it, or do they support someone who will use it in their stead?"

"This may be hard to believe, but it's more as if it's something uncontrollable will be released, and they will be the prime beneficiaries of it. I cannot find its source."

"Or what it is. A Bomb? A Revolutionary Tract? That's difficult to imagine, for there is no widespread dissatisfaction for that to trigger."

"Just so are my conclusions; nevertheless, all my sources were certain, and very apprehensive. I tested them, all unaware on their part, and by Scandberg's Second Speech Reduction, they believe in it."

"But you have been unable to determine what it is . . ."

"As I said, they don't have any idea. But whatever it is, it is coming to realization fast. That they know. And what they call it is significant, too."

"What's that?"

"They call it, 'The Angel of Death'."

Glist finished his tea and made ready to leave. "I fail to become alarmed. I do not doubt your conviction, but we need more hard data. More facts. You understand I can't act on night-fogs like this."

"Your pardon, Ser Glist, but my intention was not to request action, but to bring a matter to your attention, so that when the facts come, as I am certain they will, you can proceed in the best manner."

Glist nodded, agreeably. "Just so . . . I will be on the lookout for this, although I have seen nothing to date . . ."

"Perhaps you can obtain verification by contacting . . . you know . . . that deep-sensor."

Glist continued to look ahead, but he said, in a low tone, "That is something else that should not be spoken of."

"Can you?"

"It is not wise. That is perilous, that one. I would not now risk it upon no more than I have."

Sheptun said, "I feel you will hear from him soon. There is supposed to be something afoot that he will have high probability of having access to."

Glist stood up and prepared to leave. "Perhaps. I trust when he does, he will have occasion to be more specific."

Sheptun looked down, feeling a sly reprimand, and said, "You of all people should understand field conditions here, and know how difficult it is to obtain hard data."

"I understand very well how things are. But nonetheless, however they disguise it, at the core of every functioning society there is a social entity which knows and acts upon the facts. Even here. If a thing has a real existence, we can derive its nature by the traces and echoes it leaves, most especially if in use or preparatory to use. The motion of a thing is its reality, and the motion is what leaves the traces. Probe deeper."

"That in itself is becoming difficult."

"Remember the Credo of the Institute: *There is no such thing as a problem: there are many opportunities for outstanding solutions.* Your learning of these distinctions, these subtleties, will certainly result in advancement; otherwise . . ." Glist did not have to continue the threat. At best, he could have Sheptun removed from Oerlikon, and there were several other options he could use. He could, if circumstances required it, have Sheptun killed and disposed of, to protect the integrity of the net. Glist had done this before, and did not have pangs of conscience over it, then or now. It was a matter of protecting one's livelihood, and the way of life of uncounted numbers involved in the Watch of Oerlikon, by the Institute of Man, on Heliarcos.

Then he left the teahouse, and did not spend much more thought on the matter. Except much later, when he was climbing the stairs to his cell, negotiating the eccentric curves and twists and landings, that something floated back, of the conversation he had had with Sheptun. Odd: but Sheptun had said they had called it "The Angel of Death." Indeed, an odd name for a weapon. Still, he doubted if it would come to much. Because since the Liasks were so much against change, they were no great threat in the technological sense, and so it was unlikely they could produce much of a secret weapon that would make any difference. These things always kept coming up, these superstitions, in many societies, but there was nothing like reality to dispel the shadows.

2

Midnight in the Mask Factory

IN THE CONVENTIONS of the Mayan-like calendar which measured time on Oerlikon, the next day commenced at sundown, at precisely the moment of absolute darkness. And so, though Luto Pternam had waited only a short time for the return of his henchman, the counters in the Horologium had already changed over to the symbols for the next day.

The organization over which Pternam presided had an official title: The Permutorium. Its name, however, was less meaningful than what it actually did, which was dire enough. The Permutorium took in persons adjudged to be of either criminal or changist tendency, the distinction in Liask custom being slight, and transformed them, by a number of techniques, into units of an army which would always be utterly trustworthy because all its soldiers had been totally conditioned to unquestioning obedience. Naturally, there was a tradeoff: their reactions were relatively slow, and the "units" retained little or no initiative, but neither did they flinch from pain, nor from unpleasant orders.

A considerable part of the energy expended within this department was devoted to a continuing program of research and development, which could in loose terms be considered quasi-medical, involving as it did the specifications of the human body and all its subsystems. Much had been done, which had borne fruit in other areas, but most in the area of what might be called the techniques of psychological control of a population.

Persons who were processed in this facility might reappear, but never in the lineaments of their old forms. Part of the program involved manipulation of the hormone systems, so that physiognomy aligned with function. This change was the reason why the office had a jargon name in the streets, which was never pronounced openly: "The Mask Factory."

Just so, it had been during the course of these researches that Pternam and Avaria had happened, during review of the reports of routine experiments, to suspect a particular line of work, which no one had followed up. This they did, at first only curious, but later realizing what a weapon the line might lead them to. And so it was that a certain person had come into existence, under the long tutelage of Pternam, and a special cadre of assistants, carefully primed on half-truths and threats, a person who, in the terms usually referenced in Lisagor, literally did not exist. But in other terms, exist he did. And, as Pternam reflected on his creation, it was with a certain baleful purpose.

Pternam, feeling a chill in the night air, had returned to the inside of the residence, and was there now speaking with Orfeo Palastrine, his chief guard over the subject, over an antique communicator set into an alcove in the plain whitewashed walls.

"Palastrine? Yes. Pternam here. How goes it with Rael?"

"Normal. He's up and about, working at his studies, but not at a real furious pace. Took a short nap after supper, he did. A fat job, may I say so."

"You wouldn't want it if you knew some of the things he'll have to do. This one pays his dues afterwards, instead of the usual case before." Then he inquired, "Is the sexual orientation still holding? No evidence of overlay?"

"None that we can see . . . He asked for a woman last night, and so we took a chit down to the local happy-house, and got him one, with whom he was reported to disport himself in the usual manner."

"Do they report anything?"

"This last one was debriefed without anything being noted. As a fact, if anything is out of the ordinary . . ."

"Yes?"

"Well, it's not so odd. They all say they would rather come here for this service than take their chances. They say . . . well, he's kind and considerate, and, ah, how do they say it . . . 'shows them a good time.' Funny to hear that from whores."

"And no trace of overlay from another personality."

"Not that we can observe. Straight as a string is old Rael; he just addresses himself to one of those double-breasted mattress-thrashers and goes straight on."

"Naturally these are still being recorded."

"Of course. I view them personally."

"See anything?"

"Nothing outstanding. Standard male responses. No problems. I might say his frequency seems a little low, and he seems to want to keep them over the period allowed."

"You don't let him have them?"

"No. Straight by the book, Director. We signal when time's up, and he gives them up without a fuss."

"Good. You know what your instructions are in case he appears to have gained control over one of those women?"

"Yes, exactly. We flood the chamber with monoxide gas, and then incinerate what is left with oxy-acetylene. I know the drill: we check the reserve gas cylinders daily."

"I have some news . . . there may be some visitors tonight down there. No interference, no interruption. Avaria and I will be in there with them, and him."

"Begging your pardon, but . . ."

"I know the danger. The rules are still in force. Rael is supremely dangerous and must not be allowed to leave the chambers before his time. However, if all goes well, after this visit, he may be released in the future; possibly tonight, possibly much later. The use for which he has been trained may be at hand."

"Do you intend to pattern another one like this?"

"Decision has not yet been made. We lean toward not doing it again."

"Understandable. It is a fearsome creature, so the manual alleges."

"Rightly so. This is not something one would do casually . . . we can use the facilities for other purposes, and your people will of course be rewarded for this difficult service—just what they deserve."

"Ah, now, Director, that's fine to hear that. You know, some of the lads have chafed a bit at the secrecy and the isolation. Not the usual sort of duty."

"You still have security over your force?"

"Exactly. Positive control, all the way. No leaks. I know that."

"Good. We're depending on you. I'll call down later."

"We'll be here."

Pternam replaced the receiver in its receptacle and turned away with no particular destination in mind. He stopped and practiced an exercise he had often used, that of Confronting the Hidden Antagonist: he understood thereby that his anxiety was commonplace and related solely to waiting for his visitors. Would Avaria find them? Would they come with him? More importantly, would they accept what was being offered here, something of high order indeed? Yes. That was the real issue, the one that would be resolved only as things developed out of the flux.

The doorward, a lobo especially trained for the post, by name Tryono Ektal now, padded softly up the stairs from the lower level, taking, to a person with normal reactions, an excessively long time to assure himself that Pternam was in the room. Finally he said, in a measured, carefully paced monotone, "Ser Pternam, the respectable Avaria approaches through the outer barrier in company with three persons whose aspect is not known to me."

Pternam said, equally carefully, "All are expected. You may return to your cells and sleep. Your duty has been done this day. Go in peace."

Ektal nodded solemnly and turned and left. As he left the dim room, a rustle at the lower doorway indicated the approach of Avaria and three others. That would be them, doubtless. He faced away from the landing.

When he turned about again, there they were. Elegro, of course. And with him . . . Pternam knew the descriptions well enough. It was the three he wanted.

Avaria said, to the three, "We are secure here, throughout the Residence. You may speak as you will." As an afterthought he added, "Absolutely. We would not have anyone hear what we ourselves might say here."

One said, in a low, growling mutter, "Absolute control over a space? Unheard-of, it is. What would Monclova say? Or Femisticleo Chugun, our well-loved Synodic of Law and Order? This makes for islands of individuality, as they say."

Pternam recognized the speaker as Merigo Lozny: low of brow, head densely furred with bristly, unruly hair the color of cast iron. The nose and chin, however, were sharp, and the eyes glittered and flashed like cursed jewels. The torso was barrel-like, and the legs short and bowed. He looked grotesque, and stupid as well, but Pternam knew very well that Lozny was exceptionally smart, and could be extremely difficult, even among his fellows.

There was a tall, rather athletic man with them. That would be Pericleo Yadom, the ostensible public figure, the front man, the one who spoke for those who manipulated the strings offstage. Were it not for the intense strain lines on his face, he could have been called handsome, and certainly once was. The other, an older man would be Porfirio Charodei;

if Lozny was the executive officer of the Underground, and Yadom the front man, then Charodei would fill the position of ideologue. That one had somewhat of the air and manner of a professor, off on an excursion outside his own proper field. But here, Pternam was not fooled, either: he knew from many reports that of all of them, Charodei was by far the most alert and the most dangerous. Yadom would be easy. Lozny would be won over by a logical argument that moved a little too fast for him. But Charodei would be the key to it. Pternam expected the real objection to come from that way.

Avaria said, conversationally, "We are late. Our contact point was to be a Dragon-Field, and of course, we had to mix it up a little."

Pternam said, "I am surprised no one accosted you. These visitors are not without enemies."

Yadom said, "It was arranged. Most of those present were our people, mixed with a few genuines."

Pternam thought, to himself, *So they used a Dragon-Field as cover, did they? That damned anarchic game. That would be another hiding place they'd shut off for good after they'd flushed all the insects out.*

They did not make polite introductions, for they were known to each other. But Lozny said, "You know what we are. My question is, 'What are you, that we should come here?'"

Pternam answered, as if feeling his way along the lines of an ancient ritual, "I am the alchemist who found the perfect solvent, and now lacks the proper container for this ferocious substance which attacks everything. I have brought the Angel of Death to Paradise Unending."

Lozny said, "It may be contained by Will and Idea. We have those."

Charodei added, "This thing we have heard distant rumors of: may it be seen?"

Pternam said, "There is no reason to wait. Come with me." And without looking to see if they were following, he turned and set off through the halls and corridors of the Residence, eventually leading them downwards, via stair-wells of narrow aspect and precipitous turns, to a much lower level.

Yadom remarked, "You bury it deep; tell me, why would your organization offer the gift of a perfect assassin to those whom you know will use it without restraint?"

Pternam, leading the way, said back over his shoulder, "Avaria and I have seen what must be, for the greatest good of the greatest numbers. Of the world—this world. We have lived in a dream far too long."

"But you would not use it yourself . . . ?"

"By giving it to you, I do use it. I place it where it will do the most good. So that you know it. But you will see; there is much we have to say here which will clarify things."

Pternam had conducted them deep under the Residence, and now they were at one of the lowest levels, in a dim landing. Before them was the confinement facility, a house within a house, so to speak. It was not crude, or hastily constructed. Here, everything was made and finished as well as the rest of the Residence. After they had all collected, he led them into a small antechamber, facing a large window of one-way glass. The view inside was of a large room, furnished for many activities— work, rest, relaxation. It was a cage, but it did not look like one. And in- side the room, they could see a man, or what appeared to be a man, seemingly working at a desk, as if performing some study, occasionally writing short notes, or formulas in a commonplace notebook. This was the Morphodite.

Pternam stood back from the window and let them look, but he really didn't know what they had expected to see. Perhaps some scowling and grimacing savage, more brutish than the wildest Makhak? Or, a golden god-man, wearing a cape and striding back and forth like some frenzied orator? The Morphodite was certainly none of these; as a fact, he seemed to be so ordinary that the sight was disappointing. What they did see through the window appeared to be a mature man, no longer young, slightly worn around the edges, but above average height and with a slim frame that argued agility and self-discipline. His face was so ordinary it was difficult to remember it. He had lank dark hair, loose skin of a sallow-olive color. Except for the interest he showed in his work, he could easily have been one of the lobotomized trusties one often observed in the simple menial positions which were too easy for the labor pool.

After a moment, Lozny asked, "Can it hear us?"

Pternam answered, "No. Nor can he see who is here. But I may add that we have trained him to be extremely sensitive, and sometimes he is aware of observation . . . As in many cases of this sort, where one reaches into the unknown with both hands, the subject seems to be a bit more than planned." As if to underline Pternam's comments, the fig- ure at the desk gave a quick, flickering glance at the window, almost too fast to be seen, a mere motion of the eyes, and then returned to his stud- ies, turning slightly more away from the window, as if desirous of a deeper concentration. The three visitors glanced uneasily at one another: the glance had held an instant of direst malevolence, of a glittering regard which reduced them all to something considerably less than human.

Lozny asked, "What is he doing in there now?"

Avaria volunteered, "Continuing to refine his main discipline, adding depth to the field we set him upon to study."

Lozny continued, "Which is? We have little enough time for dilettante intellectuals, as you may well know."

Pternam explained, not apologetically, but slightly sternly, "This is no idler, but an artisan, a craftsman, of a most subtle art. Here I must make my first exposition; you may have heard something of this, but only a little, for we could not let much of it out."

Charodei said, "Continue."

"Very well: throughout human history, or as much of it as we can reach here through the archives, the view has always been that key individuals are the shapers of history, that they hold a society together, make the special decisions that shape the pattern of events. Naturally, it has always been assumed that those key people are the leaders, and therefore the assassin's trade—that by removing the key leader, they could change the flow, divert the stream. But despite this belief, and the efforts of assassins, somehow things rarely changed according to those acts . . . in fact, a sober examination will reveal that assassins rarely have a better rate of success than ordinary murderers in changing societies— ordinary crime. This suggests an error in the view, and so we studied it, and arrived at this startling idea: that there are key people, but that they never show on the surface, that they are almost never the obvious leaders. Unseen, unknown men and women, who unknowingly acted out the ritual mythos of an era."

Lozny had been growing restive, and now he blurted out, "Nonsense! The masses make history! Currents move in the people, and those currents shape the destiny of the leaders, who are called into being by these currents—and dismissed by them as well."

"No. The absolute key parts, the balance-points, are hidden within the organism, within the machinery. There has been no way to get to them, or even find them. It is as if the social organism, the machine, is deliberately designed to avoid tampering. But. Ah, yes, but. This individual has been shaped, inculcated, indoctrinated to this new theory. He has followed the initial idea out, and found the ways to make it work: you may view this as a precision tool to determine the identity of the key figures, and how to remove them, using the method calculated to be of maximum effectiveness. I will not enumerate all the forms of training he has had. I will say that he had to take what was a wild idea and carry it far beyond the bounds of what we thought we knew, what we suspected. This was self-training. He works at it yet. He is so far beyond us in this area that I find his explanations totally incomprehensible. So do the rest of us, who have been involved with training him. But hear me: we know for an undeniable fact that whatever he does, it works with a precision beyond our wildest dreams, and he does as he says he will do. He is absolutely dependable."

Charodei said, "You have tested him?"

"You may recall an incident a while back . . . in Vredam. There was a spectacular murder, I believe, which caused the surfacing and dissolution of a peculiar organization known as the Acmeists . . . That is a sample."

Yadom whispered, "The Acmeists were not of us, but they were valuable allies. That event evoked much distress."

Pternam stood his ground. Now was no time for apologies. "We could not risk using the weapon untested. And most certainly we would not have offered it to you."

Lozny snorted, "Hmf. Clispic scumbags, one and all. We are better purged of such trash. Pternam here, did us a favor. We would have made their eyes water ourselves, after we'd got the mileage out of them."

Charodei thought for a moment, and said, "I agree in part with Merigo, although I would not say it so definitively." And to Pternam he said, "How did you know to limit the test . . . or keep the results confined?"

"Those were the instructions we gave to the weapon."

Yadom said, "All right. So much is true. Still, it was a dangerous game that was played there. Pternam, if he's that good, why wouldn't you just use him yourself . . . you could even turn him loose on us!" Yadom already knew that Pternam wouldn't, because he hadn't. But the question was to uncover why.

Pternam answered, "True. We could do just that. But some of us wish change, too, and if we turned him loose on you, then there would be no opposition at all worthy of the name. No. But more importantly, I have no vision of the world I would build, and I am not experienced in guiding others in such tasks. Tear down? Yes, we would help there, but no one has much of an idea for rebuilding. You have this, and have for a long time. There: I speak directly."

Lozny said, quietly, "So you offer him to us, because you know we'll use him. And we would, if he's half what you say he is. I understand. You came late to the truth. And you must know that there will be little use for an organization such as this, afterwards . . ."

Yadom said, "You must have used him to foresee things we cannot. If you are as high in the counsels of the State as we think you are, then you must know our fortunes have been poor the last few years, great and small."

Pternam said, "It is because of some of his insights that we conceived the idea to present him to you in the first place."

Charodei said, "In other words, you foresee through his program that whatever our present fortunes are, we have something like time on our side, and you want to make sure you are supporting the winning side."

"Not entirely. There is an element of chance here, and of choice."

Charodei was not satisfied, but he continued: "The words were whispered in the night, and the winds carried it. Night-things spoke of it, and in the darkness we also heard. And so also we heard rumors—that societies are founded on hidden, secret balance-points: unknown people, the crucial hinges. Pull them out and the structure falls."

Pternam corrected him, "Pull them out and the structure adjusts to a new pattern of stresses."

Charodei persisted, "Very well, Consider the theory as if it were true. Why not give us the theory, and let us use it—train our own people? Why do we need this dire creature of the night? Just give us the concept, and we'll take it from there; we have the material to do it with."

Pternam said, "It is not something I can give anyone, because I have not been able to comprehend it. It is alien to our most basic thought-patterns. I have tried, and failed. None of the other workers associated with this has been able to make any more of it. No: we told him, 'Here it is—develop it.' And he's done it, but he can't tell us how. He's so far into it that he would have to train us over from scratch so that we could understand it. This came early, and so we then trained him to the rest, so someone could implement it . . . all the arts of violence, mayhem, pain, death and disfigurement. And the best of all, that he can totally change his identity with the proper stimulus, and thus vanish after the deed."

Lozny said, "We heard somewhat of this. How so? Change? In what way—disguises are susceptible to penetration, as we have found out."

"Not disguise, but change. It came out of our studies of the hormone system. We have known for some time that certain aspects of exterior forms of the body are controlled by hormone secretions—the shape of certain muscle groups, certain fatty areas, the distribution of patterns of facial and body hair. But there is more—the whole body is under these controls. It's just a matter of finding the key to the system. It's a little disturbing to understand it, but as real as you seem to yourself, you are not a fixed reality, but a wave in Time; every two thousand days, the cells in your body have changed, and so you are different. We found a way to uncouple this process from the memory and the controls built in, and reset the master control, as it were. You change, constantly, held in precarious balance . . . we found a way to speed the process up, to what you might call catastrophic change."

Charodei asked, "What kinds of time are we talking about?"

"Most can't do it, so we have to screen for those who can, and then train them to the degree of concentration required. At the extremes we have the subject attain, I have to refer to the state of consciousness as an intense trance state, something on the order of self-hypnosis, or yogic concentration . . . The process won't work at all if the time involved in the change is more than three or four days, and the release of metabolic by-products which poison the organism limits its shorter end to about a day—this is for the ones who can live through it. At the end of it, even the genetic code is changed, and the sex of the subject changes as a by-product, and the age as well, or rather the appearance of age. In fact, we have succeeded with only one. This one is the only one, and he's only gone through one change."

Yadom exclaimed, "Sex?"

"Everything." Pternam gestured at the Morphodite. "*That* was originally a woman, an old derelict we selected out of the sloggers of the Labor Pool last-leggers. She was far gone, but somehow she responded."

Charodei breathed, "Woman! And now it's a man?"

Pternam said, "That was Jedily Tulilly, who is officially listed as being deceased. That is now an unregistered adult male whom we call Tiresio Rael."

Charodei said, "Tiresio! You dared name him that, or did you know?"

Pternam said, "The name was picked, so far as I know, at random."

Charodei explained, "In Hellas, on Earth, there was an oracle who was called Tiresias, who was said to have been both man and woman. And this Tiresio . . . Ah, I see, a most perilous weapon, I think I see. But go on. We are your guests."

Pternam reiterated, "This was a woman. Now it's a man."

Yadom asked, incredulously, "In every way?"

"As far as form goes, yes. He has all the requisite appurtenances, spigots, tubes and valves. Why not? All tissues are the same in either sex—they are controlled differently by the hormone system."

Yadom continued, "To the sexual level?"

"To the DNA level! That's a man. There is no way to connect that with Jedily Tulilly—not by fingerprints, retinal scan, or DNA breakdown."

Lozny asked, "How . . . ?"

"Hypnosis, operant conditioning, severe stress, Will and Idea. We send it where we dare not go, and there it sets the Change off. And it also loses a substantial fraction of age, too. Tissue samples tell us that this man is about twenty of the old biological years younger than the old woman. The Change process apparently resets the timer running in the body. As I say, It has only undergone one Change, so we don't know how it goes after that."

Charodei exclaimed, "Then it's effectively immortal!"

Lozny added, "That's more important than revolution! Gehenna with changing things! Give us the secret of that and we'll outlive them!" He cast a burning, lustful glance at Yadom and Charodei, who nodded in agreement.

Pternam said, "Wait, before you ask for it. Consider that it is a gift you may not want: for one thing, it is painful beyond imagination. That one lost a third of its body weight while growing a fourth taller. That was in the first day. And there is a lot of memory loss, or blockage. That one remembers nothing of its life as Jedily, whatever that was . . . Of course, we help it, because we did not want it to know. It knows that it can change, but it can't remember anything of its old life. And you . . . perhaps you would no longer be revolutionaries. And of course the Change makes it sick for a time. And consider what we know of this—we do not elect to serve as subjects. Not a one. Think on that."

Charodei said, "Subjectively, then, to it . . ."

"Subjectively, the old woman died. And far below the level of anything we would understand as consciousness, *something* survived, and on that we built a personality . . . eventually, we were able to build a functioning persona, and of course we taught it much . . . but as far as the theory it operates under, it taught itself, and has done all the original work itself, and there is so much in that which is alien to us that it doesn't inhabit the same universe we do, conceptually."

Charodei said, "You mean it doesn't agree with us?"

"I mean we have a bargain with it, and its word is good—we've tested that, too. But it doesn't understand why what we've trained it to do is so important to us."

"But will it change?"

"Voluntarily? Yes. No doubts. Although that is another thing which separates us, because of course the process is a sort of death . . . it's immortality is not escape from death, but the acceptance of many deaths, none of them pleasant."

Lozny mused, "Why is the ability of it to change so important?"

"Because it doesn't matter if they track it down and find it afterwards! There is no link between the two persons. Its origins can't be traced. It doesn't matter how public its act is. And rest assured we've given it an extreme education in avoidance."

Yadom asked, "And in what else?"

"All the tools of the trade for assassins. That one can brew poison from drinking water, make a pistol from trash, sabotage any machine made, live in the wild, maim with a gesture you can't even see, and use most conceivable weapons to a high level of accuracy, in addition."

"Why?"

"It told us that in the system it uses to identify its targets, it gets method as an inseparable part of the answer. It says that the assassins of old were wrong in target *and* method, and that it must have the ability to implement the answer it gets out of its calculations."

"There is some sort of formula?"

Pternam said, "Yes. It makes no sense to anyone we've shown it to. Apparently it is using some underlying understood mathematical and logical concepts we haven't discovered yet, or can't imagine, blocked conceptually from them by what we already know."

Charodei interrupted, "You say, 'implement the answer.' You were speaking of method, but I sense there is more . . . the Target. Then we don't assign it a target, is this correct?"

"Exactly. All you have to do is agree—and we release it."

"It selects the subject, the method . . . ?"

Pternam said, "And the time to act. All of it. Remember, it sees our society as an extended schematic."

Yadom shook his head. "We heard tales, but this is even more fearsome. I feel as if I were comparing brushfires to surgery, our methods to its. Incredible! And what governs its loyalty to us?"

Pternam said, slowly, "You are to take advantage of the shift it creates. It is programed to remove the pin that holds this society in its present form. That is all. It doesn't understand what we would put in its place, or that we could. Only that it can do this. Neither you nor I have the option of controlling it once it is released. We can choose to release it, having given you advance warning, or we could destroy it . . . for we who created it fear it, too. My question is, do you think that you can take advantage of its release?"

Yadom didn't speak, but held his face immobile. Charodei looked away from the window, and also from the group. But Lozny, after a moment, solemnly nodded. "We can handle it."

Charodei said, thoughtfully, "You could have another choice, and set it loose on us . . ."

Pternam answered carefully, "No. That would require more retraining than we can do. Possibly we could pattern such a person, similarly to the way this one was done, but I frankly do not know. In the case of the Acmeists in Clisp, there were special circumstances involved. It told us of that situation; actually of three we could have tested, but we could use only one of them. It says that its actions disturb its own equations. In any event, I do not intend to use one against you. We went too far with this one, and we fear it also. There are serious restraints on this area. We simply do not take chances with it."

"Well," said Charodei. "Let's go visit with your fabulous beast, before we decide. I'd like to talk with it."

3

Meetings by Night

ANIBAL GLIST WAS not the name he had been born with, nor had his subsequent upbringing and education known that name; however, it was the one he had been known by for so many years that it sometimes slipped his mind what the old one was. He actually had to stop and make an effort to recall it.

Glist had made his way back to his cell, but he did not rest, as he had intended to. At first he had dismissed the alarming report by Sheptun as nothing more than fancy; for this was a common enough trait among new operatives assigned to Project Oerlikon/Lisagor. They saw shadows everywhere. The trouble was that there was never any shortage of shadows, so that the problem became to discriminate between the real problems and the false starts, of which Lisak society was overloaded. Who would believe a monolithic totalitarian state still could erect itself and exist, and even prosper after its own fashion, in these times? It was a tribute to some perverse human vice from the farthest reaches of the squalling past.

But the more he thought on it, pacing back and forth in his small cell, the more he felt uneasy. There was something about this, some lunatic flavor that he had learned to associate, by dint of long experience on this planet, with some furtive glimmer of truth. And so it was that after a time, Glist, donning a night cloak against the autumnal chill in the late night air, set forth again, negotiating the narrow walkways, stairs, and balustrades of his hill to the place of another of his associates.

This was a woman, Arunda Palude, who served as the archivist for the Symbarupol Central Group. Having no contact with the operatives, and insulated from all communications save certain specified ones, she concentrated on retaining data, for the reporting officials of their group to use. Most of her files were in her head: she was a trained mnemonicist, so that in case of emergency, there would be no damaging records found to link their group with anyone off-planet. She did not make reports herself.

As he laboriously climbed up a particularly steep masonry stairwell to her cell, Glist did not worry too much about being seen, or his presence commented upon, for another of the endless wonders of Lisagor was that despite constant antisexual propaganda by the government, and total absence of any public media stimulation, the major concern of Lisaks seemed to be devoted to the maintenance of numerous affairs, and exotic practices associated with them. He smiled to himself. Rather than resent, or even take note of his visit, any ordinary Lisak would probably admire his verve, and consider Glist's example as another goad to personal excesses.

At the cell door, Palude let him in without ceremony or comment, closing the door and bolting it. Once inside, she did not waste time or effort with pleasantries, but addressed Glist directly. She was a woman of mature but graceful aspect, tall and slender, with dark hair, streaked with gray, tied into a loose bun at the back of her neck.

She said, "Something would bring you out at night and over here directly; you're not known for lechery, and all the Dragon games have ended by now, so something's bothering you. What is it?"

"Direct as ever, I see. Well, I have heard some odd things tonight, and I thought I would stop by and check with you to see if you could make a tie to any of it."

"Go on."

Glist gave, in summarized form, a loose account of the incident in which Student Procand and Student Sheptun had collaborated in reporting odd circumstances to him. For a time, Arunda did nothing but listen, with a rather expressionless, passive face. Then she looked up and went to a small cupboard, from which she took a pad of paper and pen and wrote down short phrases.

Glancing at the list she had written, she began, "I have some items that may or may not connect with the information relayed by Sheptun. One. The Heraclitan Society central committee has been unusually active in recent weeks, doing a lot of moving around. Our contact has been sporadic and tenuous. There are indications that they have made contact with some other group, which has not been identified yet. Two. Vigilance was instituted, but the usual sources report negative. Other clandestine organizations associated with HS in the past are disorganized and passive, and the Synodic of Law and Order, Ministry of

Femisticleo Chugun, currently has no provocative actions in effect, except a very minor one operative in Marula, which appears to be unconnected."

She continued, "Three. Cesar Kham is working on this personally. There is an incident in Marisol, Clisp, which has very odd aspects. A very minor fringe underground group calling itself the Acmeists, was recently brought to light in the aftermath of a murder, and the group completely fell apart. They are hunting down the survivors now, but the group is considered completely purged."

Glist interrupted, "What is so odd about that? Chugun unearths one every other week. They don't amount to much."

Palude answered, "That's the odd part. Chugun didn't do it. It was brought into the open by an odd, motiveless murder, and at that of a very minor clerk of the group. The killing has all the marks of a very professional assassination, and naturally, the assassin has not been located. Chugun is not worrying much about the killer, since he's had so much fun rounding up the Acmeists. Another odd thing was that they were not really very secret, or very effective, or much of a threat. They had no known enemies among other factions, and were in fact rather useful as a sort of sounding-board. The usual sources in Marisol and throughout Clisp all report no contact, and in fact, all the local cabals are very busy denying it. They were all well covered, so the fall of the Acmeists hurt no one except their own people, nevertheless, it caused a lot of nervousness, since no one seems to know where the incident that set it off came from. Kham went there personally to see if he could make sense of it. His last report is that it's as if something came out of the night and struck, and left the scene immediately. Kham also says that his investigation shows that this particular victim, although unknown and obscure, seemed to provide just the right impetus so that the internal weaknesses of the Acmeists caused them to fall apart in public. Chugun has written it off as a fortunate accident, and proceeded to clean up whatever was left of it. Kham suspects conscious motivation and direction behind the incident, but cannot identify the organization."

Glist thought for a moment, and then asked, "Is there coincidence in time between the activity of the Heraclitans and this incident in Clisp?"

Palude thought about it, and then said, "The Clisp incident was first. The activity commenced about ten days later. Also Kham notes that the Acmeists were the only group in Clisp with no active connections with any other group. He plainly suspects a sort of demonstration, since they were relatively open and isolated, but by whom and for whom?"

"Kham suspects? If half of what he thinks is true, there's a finer control afoot than we've seen here."

Palude said, thoughtfully, "My material on the Acmeists is current, via Laerte Ormolu, and confirms their general harmlessness. This is why Kham is investigating. Somebody wiped them out, and they are manifestly not dangerous—there are much more alarming groups active in Clisp, and also in the Serpentine, which Femisticleo Chugun views as almost as bad as Clisp itself."

Glist reflected, "If a demonstration, it reveals extremely fine intelligence—that bothers me. We have Chugun pretty well covered, as well as the central organization under Monclova. If not from them, then who? Past reports indicate that there are few with that level of ability, or the networks to support the data base. Outside the police under Chugun, and the Heraclitan Society, everything else is local and pretty much ineffective."

Palude nodded. "I have one more item. Thersito Burya has been acting as a go-between with a person or persons unknown, this also after the Clisp incident. This activity is rated as unusual, and highly secretive. Well, and I should add that since the HS became active, they are no longer working out of Marula, but on the move."

"Not to Clisp?"

"Not noted there. Burya made a brief visit, but was gone in a day."

"Coincident?"

A pause. "Yes. Definitely possible."

Glist sat down on the edge of the bed and pondered for a moment. Then he said, "I suppose some watchfulness is warranted. If you can associate with this, advise me. I will try to scare up some data for you."

She said, "Glist, I know I am here to record these reports, but I have had an idea about all this."

"Speak freely."

"With that fine a control, do you suppose whoever it was could also *see* us—I mean, our mission, here? That's . . ."

"I agree. We've never been compromised, or even seriously threatened. During the last testing period we ran our existence wasn't even suspected. We're clean with Chugun, and also with the HS. We had always assumed that they lacked the sophistication to penetrate our screen. Still, it's that fine control that bothers me. I will put the net on defensive alert until we can determine what this element is." He stood up and started for the door. "Tonight."

At the door, Pternam hesitated, for here indeed was the point they had worked for, but it also was a point of no return. There was also in this an air of chance. Rael *was* unpredictable, and he knew well how dangerous. Once they were in there with him . . . Still, this had to go on. There could be no stopping it now. He took a deep breath. "Are you quite certain that you wish to go on with this? I mean, once we penetrate the security system, we'll be in there with it, locked in, whatever happens."

Yadom said, "You have him under such tight security?"

"Indeed we do. This is the tightest security system in all Lisagor. There is none tighter."

"You fear it, then?"

"We had, past a certain point, to secure his active cooperation. To that end, we have a certain bargain with him, the details of which need not be told now, save this: if he's the man for the job, and if you are ready to live with the consequences, then we release him. If not we'll keep him in there."

Yadom reflected, "You mean if we don't want him, then you keep him in there . . . why?"

"Because he can do what he says he can—what we say he can. Absolutely. And I will not release him knowing that the main underground group cannot rebuild from the ruins he will leave. And because once we turn it loose, there's no way to recall him. Or catch him. We trained him to be invincible and invisible." And here, closer than any other time during the evening's visit, Pternam was approaching the truth. They did not know for a fact that they could get Rael back, or stop him, if released. They had plans, but for this kind of contingency they had never been tested, not even in simulation.

"And he picks the victim! That's turning the whole program over to him!" Charodei was for once beside himself with agitation.

"You can waste your finest people and murder every member of the Council of Synodics, and not get the job done; he can do it with one stroke. In fact, an actual killing may not be necessary, so he has explained it to me. But this is putting things where they belong: you claim to have a better way for Oerlikon. So, then. He's the thing that sets it off."

Charodei and Yadom lapsed into silence. Pternam continued, "I advise you to have a care with him, for I cannot predict his reactions to you; he does not perceive relationships as you and I do."

Lozny inquired, "It is rational? Does it talk?"

"Very well, on both counts."

Charodei said, to his associates, "Perhaps it might be better if I phrased our discussions with it . . ."

Yadom agreed. "By all means. Do we need to wait further?"

Pternam said, quietly, "No." And he opened a small panel by the window and removed a handset, which he spoke into. "Tiresio Rael."

The bland figure at the desk did not look at the window, but spoke into the air, which they heard through the handset. "Yes?" The voice was husky and a little rough around the edges, but also it sounded curiously flat, unemphasized, distant, almost uninterested.

Pternam said, briskly. "I have some visitors who would speak with you, before committing themselves further. Is the time in phase for such discussions?"

The figure in the room leaned back from the desk, paused, and said, "The modes are aligned in an acceptable configuration . . . for many ventures. Not all, but more than is usually the case. I will admit four, no more, no less, and make no restriction of subject matter, even to Life and Death." Then he stood up and walked to a small panel in the wall beyond the desk.

Pternam replaced the handset, hurriedly, and said, "We are in luck! Things are not always so easy, where any but myself are involved. And of course, Avaria will remain outside . . . Elegro, you know what to do." The last was a statement, not a question.

Avaria looked grim and resolute, a vast departure from his normal choleric self. He said nothing, but nodded quickly, a slight, clipped gesture. And to the three visitors, there was something menacing in that brief exchange. Pternam added, admonishing them, "I will warn you only once: do not hector, or appear to threaten him. Say what you must, but do not expect a servant."

Pternam went around to the entrance side, and, motioning the guards away, manipulated a series of intricate locking devices according to an order with which he seemed familiar; and after a moment, the door opened, and they entered the chamber, where Rael waited for them, standing in front of the desk, and holding one hand in the other in front of his spare frame. Pternam pushed the door shut after they had all come in, and they heard faint mechanical noises, as of precision machinery, as Avaria manipulated the locks. Rael nodded pleasantly to them, and made some adjustments to the panel at his left.

Pternam felt a sense of danger, now as he always did when he came in here, which was seldom. But it was low tonight. He glanced at the three leaders of the Underground; they looked uncomfortable. For a certainty, they would feel trapped here, totally at the mercy of a creature they couldn't begin to understand.

Rael said, in that same distant, husky voice they had heard earlier, "There are chairs: please use them, that we may integrate as equitants. This is always pleasant, is it not?"

There was a faint irony to his greeting, but the meaning was clear enough: here, now, equals would negotiate. No one would give orders. Charodei understood this in the words, and the full implications of it. He said pleasantly, "Of course. Come, my associates; be seated, We are guests." And starting with himself, he introduced them all.

Rael started the conversation, "We have heard somewhat of your ideas."

Charodei answered, "We have also heard of you through our mutual friend, here, as a teacher might speak of a student who surpassed him. We would speak with you to learn how your expertise might help us achieve our goals, if possible. We might speak of your studies; perhaps it could be that we could ask for your assistance."

Rael began, "I have modesty and make few claims, however, there are few who can speak well of the things I have studied, so I must needs blow my own horn, as there is no one else to blow it for me. And you should speak plainly of the things you desire, as well."

Yadom said, suavely, "Men came to the world Oerlikon to turn their backs on the flux and pressure of the normal human universe, to stop things as they were, or as they thought they should be. We believe they were in error, and have harmed us all, and wish to remedy that defect."

Lozny said, "Generations of Lisaks have worked to this aim, but therein is no accomplishment. They have built an impervious system to which we have not found a key."

Charodei said, "We wish to rejoin the human community, whatever it is now, which is rumored yet to exist out among the stars. To participate, to be. Our people are skilled and conscientious, and surely most of them would find a welcome."

To each one, Rael listened respectfully and attentively, nodding and moving his body slightly to the flow of the words. At the end, he said, "Is that all?"

Yadom began, "The People—"

Rael interrupted, "The People? The People will suffer more from the change you have in mind that they have suffered in all the cycles since the Rectification. Can this be a gift: suffering and death and violent change? No. Let us not speak of the people, but of ourselves, for that is what we are here about. We will do this . . . for ourselves."

Charodei asked, "Of us, then. And what will you have of it?"

Rael answered, after a moment, "I will be free of a debt which I owe. One more transition, and then I will live out the life of the one who will come after me, innocent. Understand, I do not wish to destroy, but it is the only way I know in this mode. It is a weight."

"I understand. Then your cooperation is voluntary?"

"Yes."

"What can you do for us?"

"I can locate the keystone of the arch of civilization, break it and escape. I can dissolve this perfectly closed system. And they will never understand that what they find . . . could not have done the things they all saw me do. I will be changed."

Charodei said, perceptively, "There are to be witnesses, then?"

"There must be witnesses."

Charodei said, "There will be phocorders which will capture the image of Rael; can he be traced? Can they backtrack to us, or to Pternam?"

"Acceptable records are already in place for this contingency."

Lozny asked, "Why do you need the identity-change? Once you do it, it will all be over for the old way."

Rael said patiently, "There is a delay factor in time. The old will move for a time under inertia. There is a transition period which has duration. During that period, I am vulnerable. That is why the change."

Yadom asked, "Do you know who you will be, or is that blind to you?"

"The process I undergo involves manipulation of the genetic code. I become an ancestor, in effect. I have computed this ancestor. I know this identity, and have already had suitable papers drawn up for the contingency."

Porfirio Charodei could not restrain himself. "You will actually change, permanently? This grows more incredible each moment. This is a thing all our experience denies. Not even by miracle or thaumaturgy do men pervolve into women!"

The Morphodite acknowledged his amazement and said, "The obvious differences that you perceive are simple: by a readjustment of glandular balances, a reordering of hormone progressions, and a shifting of tissue structure, the process is accomplished. There is a penalty to the act, however—I lose the ability to form reproductive cells, and so cannot perpetuate my kind. A small loss, actually, which I do not bemoan excessively."

Charodei said, "And you know who you will be! That is also unbelievable!"

"I . . . ah, calculate the essential uniqueness of that identity in a similar manner to that by which I compute the identity of the target personality. It is a similar process," he said, emphasizing the word similar, "but in the case of my own identity, considerably more difficult. But I did so; it would seem logical to wish to know."

"Of course, of course. And so, having been appraised of what we need, you already know who it must be?"

"Of course." Here, the Morphodite allowed his features to settle into a complacent saturnine leer, an effect which Charodei felt disconcerting and threatening. He continued, "I know who it is to be, where, when, and by what method. Indeed, I can *see* it. After the act of calculation, it comes to me as if it were a memory, a remembrance. I call it premembering. There are some differences, which you need not know unless you would like to enroll in Dr. Pternam's program . . . I see you do not wish to, an excellent choice."

Charodei paused, thought, and asked delicately, "Is it permitted to ask . . . ?"

Rael shrugged. "One can ask anything. Anything at all. But one would not get answers. No hints, no oracles, no parables, no nothing. Absolute zero. I have been given the assay of the task, and I can do it: I *know* precisely what has to be done. Do you wish it done?" He paused. "It changes in time, of course, so that if too much time passes, it will have to be recalculated. . . ."

Yadom said, muttering, "This is a madman, and Pternam with him. How can we direct a sentence of execution when we do not know the identity of the condemned? Or when? Or how? We cannot mobilize our supporters . . ."

Pternam interjected, "When we made contact, your people said that the only thing you lacked was a suitable circumstance. A key to unlock the bound gate. We have a key. This much is simple and demonstrable. Does the key have to be used at your signal? Or are you, as your people have averred, ready to rush through the door once it's been opened?

But if your resolve is in doubt, then let us await a better day, or perhaps less hesitant revolutionaries. . . ."

Charodei motioned Yadom to silence, and said, "You have a potent talisman here. One that could be turned to many purposes."

Both Rael and Pternam nodded solemnly.

Charodei continued, "Therefore a threat to us as well, infinitely more perilous than those ham-handed clowns commanded by Chugun. But yet you risked the peril of fervent idealists to show us this. Do you understand risks?"

Pternam was not alarmed, and yawned. "If I were sure three men could contain Rael, I would have them in here with us, and they would be armed. But no, we lock the door and surround this chamber with monoxide gas, and then oxygen and acetylene. I have no fears on that score whatsoever, and feel no anxiety."

Rael glanced at the three representatives and said languidly, "I am not aware of any threat you can offer to me. Here, or elsewhere. Now, or otherwhen. Perhaps you imagine to know something I do not. Perhaps. But they are not good odds upon which to gamble. I know you, but you do not know me. Thereby proceed with care."

Charodei breathed audibly and changed the subject. "Pternam, do you know who it will be?"

"No. Rael tells me that information contaminates the results. In fact, he tells me that the act of calculation makes the identity of the target somewhat unstable. And that to reveal anything about the execution of the mission to anyone causes a rapid shift in the identity. A tricky, slippery business! So I know nothing of who it is to be. There are, so I am told, cases in which identity shift does not occur, but the other parameters change, such as time, or place. The more that is known, the more it, the knowledge, smears the result out."

Lozny said, "Then this is a form of knowing the future?"

Rael answered, "I would more properly describe it as a form of knowing the nature of things. Time as you look at it is not really a measure— in fact, you cannot do what I do because of the way you look at Time. And I cannot explain that further to you unless you become as I."

Lozny suddenly said, "But what if the target is one of us? We don't know! What if it's Pternam? Or someone else we value?"

Rael said, "This society you wish to bring down: if I can find the one person who is essential to the upholding of that society, would you not agree to go ahead, no matter who it is? Otherwise you do not wish a change. . . ."

Charodei turned to Pternam. "What if we don't take Rael?"

Pternam leaned back in his chair and said reflectively, "Nothing. We approached your group because you seem to have the clearest alternative course, and the organization to take up where the old left off. Somebody has to make the decisions. But if you don't want to act, then we'll use Rael in some other way. I have no plan for using him against your group, because the way things stand now, you are locked out and represent no threat to me." At this, Lozny glared, but Pternam added, equably, "As for normal assassins, I have quite adequate defenses."

"Then Rael is not for sale to the highest bidder, then?"

"Rael is not for sale to anyone for any price, including you. It is a possibility that I could have him redirect his calculations into the contingency that we would proceed without your group, entirely, and do it anyway."

Rael added, "In that circumstantial pattern, this group is not only locked out, but is precluded."

Yadom said, "Meaning?"

Rael explained, "When a society has a given orientation, the way it's assembled, it makes some alternative courses or structures either difficult to attain, or even impossible. The way things are now, and here, your group and its sympathizers are effectively prevented from assuming more than a nuisance value; if I go without you, the conditions that permit your organization to exist at all will fade, and there will be no Heraclitan Society. No violence. You'll just fade. The individuals involved won't even know why. It just won't work any more."

Charodei said, "But there's no decision on this alternative?"

Pternam said, "No. Certainly not now. To be frank, we did not anticipate you'd have such cold feet, so no studies have been done, other than a preliminary scan by Rael. Certainly nothing strong enough upon which to base a decision about something of this magnitude."

Yadom stood up. "Very well. I'm satisfied. We'll take him. Lozny? Charodei?"

Lozny nodded, not without dour frowns, but he nodded assent. Then he growled, "I like it not, but let's get on with it. And once he does it, it will shift to us?"

Charodei thought that the remark was extremely perceptive for Lozny, and made an immediate reassessment of the man. He said, "Yes, I came to the same conclusion. Pternam?"

"That is correct. This was set up, as it were, not just in the 'What if' mode, but, 'To tilt in your favor.' Rael likens the process somewhat to the chopping of a tree—one can influence the way the bole will fall, sometimes with great precision."

Rael said, "With defensive-mode sociodromes such as this one, the analogy is particularly apt. This one can be caused to fall in a number of directions." Here, he paused, and smiled at Pternam. "Even to produce a successor even more defensive and highly structured than this one."

Pternam said, before he had time to cut the thought off, "You never told us that!"

Rael shrugged and said, "You never asked."

Charodei asked Rael, "May we know who you will be, afterwards?"

Rael nodded. "The information affects nothing. This I will tell: In Marula, a younger woman called Damistofia Azart will come to your people for a position, after she recovers from a mysterious fever. You will see that she obtains a suitable position, not demanding, not in the public eye. She will be harmless. You have no fear of her." Here Rael rummaged through the papers on the desk, and shortly produced a pencil drawing of a woman's face and upper body, dressed. The picture was simply done, but skillful enough so that she could easily be recognized. "Here is something of her aspect."

Charodei took the proffered drawing and looked intently at it, then passing it to other two. The woman depicted was substantially younger than Rael now appeared to be, and did not resemble him in the least. This one was of slight stature and subtle figure, pleasant enough, but not beautiful. The drawing suggested dark hair and pale skin. The face was crisp and well-defined. The eyes were large, dark, and slightly protuberant, suggesting an imbalance of the thyroid. She would be nervous, active. He said, finally, "This is to be you . . . ?"

"Exactly. That is about as close as I can get in a drawing. Of course, like anyone else, she will shift her appearance slightly with mood and circumstance. Diet as well. And she will come to you after recovering from an unknown disease. She will be slightly disoriented, understandable after her terrible struggle, and will need care and rehabilitation."

Charodei understood. He said, "Damistofia won't remember much, eh?"

Pternam said, "Ask him now what he remembers of Jedily Tulilly."

Rael said, unbidden, "Nothing. I know that such a condition was, but I do not remember it. I know more about her, Damistofia, now. Premembering . . ."

Charodei said, with some satisfaction, "Then it's a onetime weapon . . ."

Rael answered, "Once is all you need, isn't it? And as for me, I don't fancy going through Change every three months or so as your resident repairman. Once I'll do, to earn my freedom. Not again."

Charodei said, "Very well. I agree. Let's do it. When does it commence?"

Rael considered, and said after a time, "There will be an event you can't mistake. On that event, you move. When you see me again, you'll know."

"There's no signal . . . ?"

"The act itself is informative."

"And when?"

"Not disclosable. I pick the time, and I don't tell you in advance. Attempt nothing before that. Remain in your present configuration. If I sense that you are anticipating me, I'll recompute for it, because otherwise it won't work. And if you move too much, it can slip beyond my power to do it and influence it to your way. You understand how this is to work?"

The three conspirators nodded, almost as if they were operated by the same will, the same brain.

Rael said, getting to his feet, "Well, then, enjoy the remainder of the night." He turned away from them and began manipulating the locks of the room, to let them out.

Those inside the room shortly heard the slight sounds Avaria made, unlocking the outer locks, and afterward the door opened. Rael made no motions at all, but Pternam politely led the rest, after glancing at Rael, who made no attempt to follow them. After the door closed upon Rael, Pternam said, "Avaria can show you the way. We will not meet again, but remember how this was done."

They agreed, and Avaria led them away through the catacombs of Pternam's headquarters.

4

Night's Transition into Day

EXCERPT FROM A routine report submitted by Anibal Glist to On-planet Operations Director, Project Oerlikon, in Dorthy on Heliar-cos, dated (Lisak Calendar) 3 Gul 11 Quillion Cycle Seven*:

Dragon: File under Games, Sports and other Rituals.

1. Manislav's Conjecture states that the Organization of games and sports takes an opposing structure to that of the society pro-viding the players. Individualistic societies valuing excellence and competition favor highly structured team sports directed along military lines, while collectivist societies select sports of individual striving. With this in mind, we must consider the ramifications of the single sport known within Lisagor and Liask-dominated areas as Dragon. (The name appears to be traditional and does not ap-pear to have other symbolic connotations.—AG)

2. Dragon is a member of the tag family, which is rarely ob-served outside children's groups. Reflecting this relationship, it re-tains much of the lack of sophistication associated with children's games. In practice in Lisagor, however, there is nothing childish about it; indeed, it is played with a violent abandonment and lack of scruple not observed elsewhere. Dragon is the only sport played by adults.

3. Dragon is played generally in areas which have no use other-wise, or partial utility. No special areas are set aside, as arenas, col-iseums, etc. The most common sites are vacant lots, dumps, junkyards, eroded and waste areas. The more irregular and broken

---

* In standard dating, this is approximately fifteen years prior to the events in this tale.

the ground, the more it is used as a site. Places with suitable cover spots are preferred, *i.e.*, those with small tangles of vegetation, trash piles, brush dumps, or other refuse such as might be found in junkyards (which are especially popular). A group contemplating play will come to agreement on a site, go there, and demarcate the field with great exactitude. Anyone leaving the bounds is out of the game and may not return. Next, the group divides itself into "judges," "spectators," and "players," and money is collected and put up for the game, in the ratio (as listed above) 2:3:1.

4. The sole implement of the sport is a narrow, weighted leather sack with a grip handle at the narrow end, called "The Scorpion." The first Dragon (or lead player) is selected by scrimmage, the players linking arms and trying to reach the scorpion which has been placed in the center of the huddle. The winner of this free-for-all then displays the scorpion for all to see, delivering a monologue describing his or her qualifications and past triumphs, or virtues. During this speech, a harangue, judges take up positions, spectators gather in strategically placed huddles, and players attempt to conceal themselves or get as far as possible from the Dragon. At the conclusion of the monologue the Dragon attacks whomever he pleases with the object of striking another player with the scorpion, either thrown or as a blow, whereupon that player then becomes the next Dragon.

5. Dragon is played in all cases in the evening or night, and play continues until all players have had an opportunity to be the Dragon. Each Dragon is authorized a monologue, the most take advantage of the opportunity, but only the first Dragon is required to make it. The same rules apply as with the first: free movement is permitted during the speech.

6. There is no preferred mode of attack: the scorpion may be wielded or thrown. However, if thrown and missed, the intended target may capture the scorpion without becoming a Dragon, and may do anything with it: he may throw it away, or hide it, or keep it as long as he can.

7. Individual style is all-important: some prefer stealth and subtlety, sneaking up on their targets and laying the scorpion on them gently, while others pursue their targets belligerently, screaming invective and curses, and then batter them to the earth. There are no rules here and no fouls and no penalties. The Dragon may act solely as he sees fit. Serious injury is not uncommon, and death not all that rare.

8. At the end of the game, agreed by mutual consent, the stake is distributed to players, judges and spectators, in the ratio (as listed) 3:2:1: Those players who were Dragons often are awarded bonuses, which are taken from the spectators' shares.

9. No one is barred or refused. There are no membership rules, save a desire to participate in the risk of the game. Neither age nor sex is a factor. The only crime in the game is to enter and then leave the field, which event is regarded with scorn and ostracism, which may extend to real-life activities.

10. The alteration of personality upon entering a Dragon game is marvelous to behold. Quite often, the local bully will become meek and skulking, while a civil servant of impeccable exactitude may rush about applying homicidal violence to anyone he may meet.

11. Certain individuals become well known as masters of the game or else as trustworthy judges. Others become equally famous for avoiding the scorpion, whereupon they are known as squids (traditional usage) and considered equally honorable. Another curious facet of the game is that despite the rigid organization of Lisak society, prominent public personages also play, and indeed, there appears to be a correlation such that the intangible esteem level of the player translates into major position within society.

12. Some of the operatives assigned to this project have entered the game and found it, especially in the context of Lisak society, pleasurable and exhilarating. However, in the light of its anarchic violence and irresponsibility, we cannot recommend its introduction in the Homeworlds.

With respect: A. Glist—Symbarupol.

Outside the Residence, Charodei, Yadom and Lozny all felt exposed and vulnerable. They had felt the risk was worthwhile before and so ignored their danger instincts; but now that the business was done, and the decision made, they felt, as one, disoriented and deflated, and so their previous feeling rose again; this was, after all, Symbarupol, the nerve center nexus of that which they would demolish and replace with a better world. They walked along the dark, curving walkway which led to the Residence, all wishing to have the last words said and be on their separate ways, to the ends of the world.

Yadom hissed, "Well, tell me: can we depend on this?"

Charodei said, "Improbable as it sounds, there's that insane ring of unspeakable truth to it. . . ."

Lozny said, a low muttering, "Hum. Likely so. But I'm going to ask us: with such a weapon, why does the owner of it give it away? Nobody gives anything away!"

Charodei answered, "Well said! But consider that he did not give Rael to us but wished to know if we would take advantage of a possible release."

Lozny snorted, "Dialectical hair-splitting. Rampant squidism."

"Ah, no—not acting the squid, but the squum*, for in the distinction lies the germ of it. No doubt Pternam's got all sorts of oddities and freaks in there, some projects that never came to anything, others that failed too many times, transformations too difficult. But this one, against the odds, worked: a fearsome thing. Yet how would he employ it? It is a destroyer."

Yadom said, "He would take it to Clisp or the Serpentine."

Lozny huffed, "Wrong. Even Pternam is perceptive enough to know how tight a rein Chugun keeps on those places. No, it would not come from a *place*, but something spread throughout the system, as we are. And certainly, there is no other group who can claim to have the contact we do with all parts of Lisagor."

Charodei said, "No group we know of."

"Do you know of one?"

"No. But that does not delimit all possibilities. I say this because Pternam may have had alternate courses in mind. *He* may know of one."

Yadom said, "I think not. There was a do-or-die element to the proceedings."

Lozny said, "So we would believe."

Charodei said, "You don't trust it. Well, neither do I, but all the same, I am for preparedness."

Yadom agreed. "Just so. We wait, and then move. This may well be the chance we need. The improbable ally. Stranger things have happened. Who knows what his motivations are? And, for that matter, who cares? It will all be moot when we get control, because The Mask Factory will be the first thing to go."

Lozny nodded with grim satisfaction. "Right. And what do we do with the Azart woman? Leave her on the loose? I don't buy at all that line about not remembering. Perhaps the first time—all right. That one

* Dragon jargon: one who demonstrably invites attack, to become Dragon.

forgotten under trauma. But the second, when he's already predicted what he's going to turn into and can draw a picture of her? No. With that kind of control, he's built a fortress, so there will be something left over to achieve whatever it is he wants. And we definitely don't want something like that lying around self-controlled. What if she decides she doesn't like our way, and starts tinkering with our new order?"

Yadom said, "A dreary, dismal business, but those things can be arranged, as you know. After the change, she will be sick, and require care. . . ."

Charodei said, "But with the training it's had, and even partial retention by the subsequent persona, Azart, it could be dangerous to approach it, to attack it. It would have to be something other than a frontal attack."

Yadom purred, "I have just the thing in mind. We have a young fanatic in Marula, one Cliofino Orlioz, who, in addition to a most murderous disposition, is something of a celebrity among the ladies."

Lozny concurred at once. "Exactly! He has the face of a poet, the body of a young athlete, and the mind of a war criminal. We shall install young Cliofino as an orderly in the Marula Palliatory."

". . . A physical therapist. He will seduce her, of course. That way he can get close enough, I would suppose."

Lozny said, "Leave the details to me! We can handle it! I'll see he has backup, too."

"Not too many. We'll need them elsewhere, you know."

"As you say . . . And the signal can come from him, too: because whatever Rael does, if he appears as Azart, there's no doubt. Nobody can mistake that. So we'll have Cliofino give the alert too. Very good! So it shall be!"

Charodei suggested, "And now to our separate paths."

Yadom said, "Yes, separate. And Lozny . . . Make sure. If this is what is going to give it to us, we don't want it left for anyone else to use . . . and especially not itself. Let it do it, but afterwards, kill it! Under no circumstances must that creature run free!"

"As you order it, that's how it will be. Until next time."

Luto Pternam had returned to the chamber after the others had left. Orfeo Palastrine, his Commander of Guards in the section below the Residence, had tried, politely but insistently, to persuade him otherwise, but Pternam had insisted on returning. The danger, so he thought, was almost over. Most certainly, the time for release of the Morphodite was drawing near; perhaps was now. At any rate, he wanted to have a small talk with Rael before things became set in concrete.

In the chamber, there was a sense of tension departed: a relaxation and a fatigue, overlain with a wariness, a mistrust. Pternam heard the locks click into place behind him and observed that Rael this time did not lock the chamber from the inside.

Observing this, he said, plainly, "I see you do not lock the door."

Rael nodded, slowly. "This is correct; agreement has been reached, has it not? So I no longer restrain myself."

Pternam thought a moment, then said, "It is your wish that we open the way?"

"Yes."

"There is haste?"

"Were there haste, I would not be here now, asking."

Pternam thought of the massive building above their heads, the system of deadfalls, the guards, the cylinders of toxic gases and inflammables in readiness. Surely this . . . creature did not think he could simply walk out if he wanted. Yet he spoke plainly, like one stating a simple fact. Pternam ruefully considered that there was probably more in this Angel of Death than they had put into him, her, it. He moved his head once, as if to concur, and said, "Explain. You have trod strange paths since we first met."

Rael said, "And you have remained on the broad thoroughfare. No matter. I will explicate: Power consists of four components, which are in order of importance, Will, Timeliness, Skill, and Strength, weighted so that in that order, it is $4 + 3 + 2 + 1 = 10$, which is the Whole. The Strength a person has, his force, his resources: that is the least part of it— even Timeliness outweighs it. Here, you have arranged things so that my Strength is low compared with yours. But in all other things I have more. Some of that you gave by intent, some by accident, and some came of my own devising. Let it be so, for I have done what you asked, and made cause with the revolutionaries, as asked, and now comes the rest of it."

"Yes, my part of the bargain. Very well. . . ." Pternam made a hand signal to the observers outside, and when he heard no response, made it again, more emphatically. Then he heard the locks release. He said, "The way is now open."

"That is good."

"Indulge my curiosity: do you wish to leave tonight out of a sense of urgency, of Timeliness?"

"I appreciate your question, but cannot answer it. To answer is to contaminate the computation; to answer is to violate a basic fact of life, indeed all existence: things happen in their own time. If one has to hasten, it is already too late, is it not?"

"If you so aver."

Rael continued, "This computation I do is difficult, and complex and recursive: by that, I mean that there are stages in the process which cannot be compressed or jumped. A computer could do it faster, but not better. I would say that this would be wrong, inasmuch as the act of computation itself is included within the system of computation: how it is performed influences the result. In the end of it, it gives me a four-dimensional answer: place, time, method, circumstance, identity. I study the symbols, and by the knowledge of interpretation and isomorphism of this system, I come to *see* it, as a fact: premembering."

"It is not easy, then? I mean, practice with it has not made it easier to do?"

"The more you do it, the harder it gets. This contradicts common experience, yes, but that is how it is. You *see* more and more, and then the overriding problem becomes to stop the pattern . . . it just keeps on going, into deeper and deeper levels. No, I would not use a computer to do this; the speed of the computation . . . ah . . . makes it harder to disengage. I would fear for the safety of the machine, and for the fabric of local space-time—it induces strains. I suspect that at the maximum computational speeds, you would be *manipulating* the future—not just seeing it come to be, but changing it directly."

"That's magic, such as certain old legends speak of."

"I can comprehend that if you do it a certain way, what would occur would look like magic to an outside observer—there would be change without apparent reason. Things would appear without cause. Disappear, too. I know of no way to do this and protect oneself from the field, if I may call it that."

"Some would call what you do magic of the direst sort."

"All call things they don't understand magic—usually evil magic. Especially the way of knowing."

"Interesting. I would like to explore this."

"I do not desire that you know it. One like me is quite enough for this corner of the universe."

Pternam felt a sudden surge of alarm as Rael spoke. Could this *thing* see that they had tried once before and failed, in this very part, and that the subject had evaded them. Harmless, true. It was a creature somewhat like Rael, but it had not been able to understand what they wanted of it. Could he see the past, too?

He said, "Can you see the past as well?"

"I do not choose to look at it; no matter, for the past is embedded in the present. The present contains it entirely. I know this is a disturbing notion."

"Indeed."

Rael paused, and then said, "I must say one more thing, and then the time will have arrived."

"Say as you will."

"I normally would not, but there is something here I do not understand entirely, because I did not have the time to follow out the implications; I could *see* a certain condition, but not where its roots led. I think it is something about your world-line that you do not know about. Your actions indicate a blindness to it. Therefore I must inform you."

"Continue."

"A . . . condition of existence is a balancing of forces, a tension. I would expect a bipolar field for this place, this time. That is what the theory I have worked out calls for. But here, there is a third field, extremely subtle, but I sense power behind it, at a great distance. This makes the field here tripolar."

"Does that change what you do?"

"No. I act at the point where the three sets intersect. But hear me: something on this world maintains it, that is not of this world. I have not determined what it is. It is masked very well here, and extremely difficult to see. I understand that I will see it later, but for the now, I would have to run a special series to capture it."

"This maintaining set: it opposes us?"

"That is the odd part: it supports. Were such a thing to exist, I would think it weighted on the side of opposition, but this is not so—it maintains. Supports Lisagor as it is. You may wish to look into this."

Pternam said, "Why? By releasing you, I unleash Change upon the world."

"Just so—even the names of places will change." And then he said, "I have not determined your motives yet—that is another set of exercises I have not had the time or given the priority to do. Yet things are not as they seem to you, and you may wish to take some action or initiate a search."

Pternam shrugged and said, "You will change things. It matters not."

"Very well. Release me." Rael stood up, and began to arrange the papers and tablets on his work desk.

Pternam said, "What will you take with you?"

"My knowledge. I leave you my notes; you may study them at your leisure."

"Aren't you afraid that we'd learn how to do this ourselves?"

Rael gave a slight chuckle. "Not at all. If you understand what's in those notes, you won't dare. And besides, giving you this has no effect on things. Or not giving: it makes no difference. A rare find, I assure you, when it makes no difference."

"Very well. The door is unlocked, and the troops are advised. It is appropriate to wish you luck?"

Rael said, "I can appreciate the sentiment expressed." He looked at Pternam directly. "But in a sense, which I perceive, there really is no such thing as luck. Remember my equation of Power? Therein was no mention of luck . . . Enjoy your studies."

And with no more than that, Tiresio Rael went to the door, stepped through it as it was opened for him, and turned the corner. He was now loosed.

Pternam remained for a time in the chamber, gathering up in a slow, bemused fashion the notes, notebooks, and scratch pads which Rael had left behind; artifacts of some unknown process, whose validity Pternam seriously doubted. Still, he was certain that Rael would do something, however irrational it was. But he, Pternam, knew better. The basic idea they had fed Rael was false, and he had erected a science upon a totally worthless proposition; no matter—they had this world under control, and Rael was the last decoy. His key to the Inner Council, and with that the Central Committee. . . . He glanced down at the pile of papers he was gathering, and leafed idly through them, thinking to himself that they would make an interesting study for that section which specialized in delusions. Excellent material! But it caused him a peculiar emotion for which he had no name when his eye struck upon a short phrase close to the margins of one of the formulae-covered sheets.

It said, in Rael's meticulous printing, "It makes absolutely no difference whether one approaches the universe from an initial position of truth or falsity; it all comes out, if pursued far enough. And the Answer astounds either origin equally.—TR"

Anibal Glist was not accustomed to receiving visitors at late hours; he was one to retire early and leave alley-skulking to others of more ambitious bent. Therefore it was somewhat of a surprise to him to be awakened by a hurried knocking at his door, sometime, he imagined, in the hours between midnight and morning. He could not recall afterward what time it had been. But the subject soon made itself most memorable.

The visitor, meeting a very sleepy and out-of-sorts Glist, was Arunda Palude, the recorder. As soon as Glist opened the door and admitted her, she slipped in, motioning him to silence.

"Secure?"

Glist nodded assent, still half asleep.

"I'll be brief. I have had short-form communication with the inside man. A major assault in the works; agent, a human supposedly deep-trained in some kind of assassination science, target unknown, location to be Marula. Reference Acmeists in Clisp. Time unknown, to be associated with initiation of underground effort. I have recognition coordinates*, but although they are in stage-five form, there's a tag line attached that says they are changeable or tentative."

Glist now began to wake up. "That's a risk, sending all that."

"He was quite concerned. Action Flash, Priority Grave—survival of mission at stake. So he said. I came immediately."

"You have the recognition coordinates?"

"Yes. Do you want them?"

"No. Take them to Sheptun, now, tell him to go to Marula and stop this person by any means available, and capture alive for shipment. He can take a few with him, if he wants. We don't want this thing to occur."

"No, we do not. But do you have an idea of what you are sending and what he will have to face?"

"I would send Kham, but I can't get to him, and even if I could, I don't know he could get there in time—we don't know when it is. Besides . . . we can't send this kind of thing to our people in Marula until Sheptun gets there. That's one place outside Clisp they keep a close eye on. Marula, they say, a necessary evil, but evil nonetheless."

"It's the only real city they have. . . ."

"Yes and they distrust it mightily. No. We don't dare try to communicate direct. I prohibit it. Send Sheptun and tell him to recruit, and do it quietly. We don't want to set this off ourselves."

"As you say . . . right now?"

---

* A technique of verbal description of a person utilizing that section of the brain devoted to recognition of facial patterns. Used when photographs or drawings would be impractical or dangerous, as for espionage operations. Use widespread off Oerlikon, unknown there by natives.

"Yes. Now. And tomorrow . . . I'll come to your place, and we'll translate those RCs into a picture and I'll see that it gets to Chugun's people."

"Won't that contradict our sending Sheptun? I mean, won't that create a confusion?"

"Possible. But I trust the Insider to set priorities accurately. He's no wolf-cryer, so much I know. I want everything working on this, so it can be stopped. Chugun will grind Marula to a powder, and he may flush something for Sheptun."

"I know the structure is in place, but you know we've never shipped a Lisak off-planet before. If Sheptun captures this thing, whoever it is, trying to get it off-planet may be more difficult than the plan has envisioned. There's a risk of exposure there. I feel an uneasiness about that."

"Risk, yes. But if the insider calls for action, then it must be something extraordinary. We need to have that person examined on Heliarcos, where we have proper facilities for testing."

"If he gets him, what will we do with him? The assassin?"

"Find out how he was trained and who trained him. Then dispose of him. Then dismantle the apparatus here. That's what I'll recommend, and at the moment I expect no difficulty with Control. The prime directive is to protect the mission here *no matter what.*" At the last words, Glist's voice shifted tone, to emphasize the words. *No matter what.* That was the key. Glist nodded, as if agreeing with himself, and he said, "Now go on; do it. And we'll meet tomorrow morning for the rest."

Arunda adjusted the hood of her night cloak and departed without further word. Glist closed the door behind her and returned to his bed. But he did not sleep for a long time, and he felt an odd emotion he could not recall ever feeling before, something to which he could not put a proper name. He considered several conditions before it dawned on him that the emotion was fear.

Elegro Avaria met Luto Pternam outside the chamber in which Rael had been housed. He said, excitedly, "I saw him leave!"

Pternam felt weary, bone-tired. He said, "Yes. It's done now. And now we wait. I'll arrange to have a small talk with Monclova about impending activity among the underground factions in Marula."

"You can't."

"Why not?"

"He's already there. Went down there to have that big public celebration marking the Liberation of Sertse Solntsa."

"What bad luck! Well, who's left behind?"

"He always leaves Odisio Chang to mind the store when he's out motivating the people, as he calls it."

"Chang's a shadow, that's all. He doesn't cast his own. Worthless for our purposes. We have to register it that we forwarned them. Chang is so busy covering himself that if he acted at all, he'd say it came from himself . . . look into this, will you? We have to find somebody now who will act for us."

"You are not worried that Rael will get Monclova?"

"Not at all. According to Rael, Monclova is the least one he'd be interested in. No—he says he's looking for someone ordinary, obscure, someone nobody knows, a slogger . . . No, I have no fear for Monclova."

"Very well. I will set to it in the morning. I'm sure we can find someone left behind."

"Good. And take these, will you . . . send them over to R&D Delusion Section and let them break a few computers on it." Pternam handed Avaria the sheaf of papers he had taken from Rael's quarters. "Also have housekeeping put some trusties in there and clean the place out. I want every scrap of paper; otherwise, strip it down to the bare walls and seal it off."

"Not going to try again?"

"No. It's just a feeling, but I think we came quite close enough this time. If this doesn't work . . . well, we'll try something else."

"I understand. And what about the guards?"

"They should be retrained, of course."

"All of them?"

"I can't think of any reason to make an exception. Them, the same way as the ones who set Rael up in that method of taking command of his own hormone system."

"As you say. That's a lot of people to put through the process, though."

"But there's nothing to connect him here, and that's the way we want it."

Avaria sighed deeply, shaking his head. "I'll see to it, and all the records and logs as well. Nice and clean."

"Good. See me tomorrow . . . about who we can place a hint to so they'll remember."

"I'll do it. Want a feedback from R&D, on those notes?"

"Only if they make any sense other than delusional." Pternam laughed at this. "Which I doubt greatly."

And with that last remark, they parted company, Avaria to his errands, and Pternam to bed. Before Avaria saw to the room and the guards, however, he made a short side trip to the Research section, in particular the computational facility, where he left the package of notes off, with a casual instruction to the night operator to "make some sense of it if you can." Avaria told the operator that the papers were some things done up by one of the subjects undergoing reorientation, and they wanted to know if any of the material was valid, by chance. Then he set about initiating another sequence of events.

Luto Pternam greeted the new day's daylight considerably sooner than he had hoped or expected, by being awakened by the earnest, excitable voice of Avaria at the bedside communicator. Its buzzing was soft, but insistent, and Pternam answered it with reluctance.

"Pternam."

"Avaria. I have a report to make."

"Make it, then."

"In person."

"Can it wait?"

"No. At least, so much I think. I urge haste."

"Come up, then—I'll be ready." And he closed the unit down with both disgust and foreboding. He hated being bothered after the events of the night before, but in the same manner, he knew that Avaria would probably not assay to bother him with senseless trivia. In a peculiar state of emotion, he found himself wishing that it was some trivial problem.

By the time Pternam had dressed, Avaria had appeared, with a disturbed look to him and an air of someone who was also awakened too early. And the report was by no means trivial.

Avaria came into Pternam's private chambers and did not wait nor did he pass conversational pleasantries before beginning; "The Computational Facility advised me early on this morning that the material in the Rael folder remains incomprehensible to them but that the machine considers it valid, coherent data which can be assembled into a system. They wish to know if you want it translated."

"Translated?"

"It is built of concepts which are alien to our present state of reference, and there is a program of re-education involved. So they are advised by the machine. It will take translation to make it comprehensible to us. Such a process is possible, but it will disrupt the operating schedule."

Pternam reflected and said, "No. So inform them. Return the material to me immediately, and purge the computer of all associations. We will destroy this."

Avaria, pausing for Pternam to permit him to use the room communicator, which he did with a slight inclination of the head, went to the unit and spoke rapidly into it. Then he turned back to Pternam and said slowly, "Done. Coming by messenger. Do you . . . ?" The question was unthinkable and unaskable. And as he had started to ask it, Avaria had realized that it was also unanswerable.

Pternam said, "Go on. No offense."

". . . They don't know what it is. It went directly to the delusion section, and was read out by the machine. So we can snuff that out easily enough. But about Rael . . ."

"This means, Avaria, that Rael is in possession of valid knowledge of how to do the thing we thought impossible—a delusion."

"That is my conclusion. And we have already released him, holding now an active weapon, not an imaginary one. I comprehend our error, but I don't understand how it could have been otherwise. Who would have thought such a thing: to attack the smallest and change the nature of a whole world."

Pternam said, "You are extraordinarily calm for such a disaster."

"I assume you know something I do not, that you have a program in reserve you did not advise me of. Such are the ways of one's superiors; otherwise they would not be superiors. Anything else is unthinkable."

Pternam's mind was racing at top speed, considering possibilities, but he did not miss the weight of the sarcasm Avaria had laid upon him, and of course the veiled threat behind it. He understood. This plan had entangled itself in its own nets of subtlety. And now they had a real problem on their hands. Onrushing, the future unthinkable was rushing to meet them, in the mind and hands of Rael the changeling, Rael the Morphodite who could vanish into another identity. Avaria was saying that Pternam was not fit for the position. But of course he had alternatives. They were not subtle, and they lacked imagination, but there was a chance they would work.

He said, "We aren't completely out of control yet; consider—we know Rael will do it in Marula, and we know he'll reappear as Azart afterwards. We may also deduce that it will be soon, hence he'll have to get there."

Avaria stroked his plump chin and said, "We can't very well count on the revolutionaries anymore—besides, what could we tell them? That our lie has become true? No. And as for Rael, you and I know him well enough, so I do not take him for a fool. Azart he may become, unless he lied, but I would not wait for him to present himself or herself to them."

Pternam said, "We'll notify Chugun that a prisoner from Reprocessing has escaped, believed headed for Marula to settle a grudge, highly dangerous, no remand."

"Shoot on sight."

"Something like that. But that's not all. We've some retrainees here who would carry out a hazardous assignment. . . ."

Avaria looked at Pternam hard. He said, "You haven't got anybody that good, to go one-on-one against Rael. I supervised that phase of his training; in that, at least, he's highly dangerous."

"I don't expect them to win; just slow him down, enough for Chugun's goons to catch up with him. He's like a queen in chess, but even a queen may have a pause to destroy pawns placed in the way."

"Do you have any feel for how long we have to stop him?"

"No. But I do feel that we have some time, if we act now."

"Very well. I will see to it. I know the subjects you mean. We'll ready them, prime them and send them out."

"Use all of those in readiness state."

"All? Just so. And Chugun?"

"I'll do that."

"Fair enough. But there's something about this sequence of events I find makes me uneasy."

"Go on."

"Rael left the papers behind for you. And he said he wouldn't tell us anything that would make any difference. So by that, he's telling us he doesn't care if we know. That we can't stop him."

"You are filled with happy prospects today."

"Yes. Hindsight is wonderful; but there are things you can't know, it seems, until you reach for them in reality."

"And everything else he told us in the end?"

"That, too. Well, to work." And Avaria turned and left Pternam's private quarters.

Pternam, now alone, waited a bit before calling Chugun. For a time, he thought bleak and private thoughts, his mind still racing. And in rehearsing exactly what he was going to tell Chugun, he quite forgot one thing Rael had told him. It hadn't seemed important at the time, and was even less so now. Something about an unseen party maintaining the Lisak world. It hovered, this thought, just out of sight. Something important, but not right now.

And when he had finished his call to the offices of Femisticleo Chugun, a nagging thought kept ticking away at the corner of his mind that there was something else he should have said, but he couldn't quite place exactly what it was. No matter. The forces were now in motion, for better or worse.

5

Tiresio

SECONING. RAEL READ the signboard and paused a moment to allow some sense of spatial orientation to assert itself. He had come in the night, using these first few hours of freedom to put distance between himself and Pternam. But on foot there was not much he could do except disappear, which he could do well enough. Seconing. This was a distant suburb to the south of Symbarupol, a small and sleepy townlet concentrating on small manufactures, small crafts shops. Here, the buildings were more functional, and smaller, and the streets narrower. They favored plain wooden buildings here with large windows of many small panes, which now in the darkness showed only the dim glow of watchlamps. The streets were empty, shiny-damp with dew, colored with a bluish tint from the shops and streetlamps; Seconing tumbled down the last slope to the plains of Crule in pleasant disorder, with the hills close behind to the east. Far off out on the plains, he could hear in the quiet the passing of a beamliner running on its elevated I-beam, a rhythmic, steady, muffled sound.

The beamliner passed to the south. An express, it did not approach or stop at places like Seconing. Now he listened again, and heard, farther off, eastwards, deep in the hills, the night-cries of bosels, indigenous creatures of unpredictable habit. The calls had the odd quality of sounding profoundly artificial to the human ear, as if made electronically. There was a monotonous three-syllable call, starting on one note, then one higher, sliding to the original tone, repeated rhythmically several times. Another was a tinkling, tumbling sequence of no apparent order, and still another was a long wail, suggestive of profound loneliness. No one knew if that was what it really expressed; bosels were alien, wild, and erratic enough to be regarded as demons by more conservative country folk. At night they prowled and called back and forth, sometimes making astonishing collations of sound, which the Lisaks wisely shut their windows to.

Rael quickened his pace through the dark streets, among the shops, avoiding the residential hillocks and their attendant racks of velocipedes, all set neatly in rows. Bosels were not unknown in towns like this in the night, so his recent education informed him, and against them his equations seemed to have no power. They were approximately man-sized, and could be dangerous; Rael felt no fear, but he did not wish to meet one. That was not within the desirable sequence of events, and would attract some onlooker. Not now.

There were short ramps connecting the levels of the curving streets, hardly more than alleyways, which Rael followed downwards, to the edge of the plains. At the bottom, he found his view to the west obscured by an untidy tangle of I-beams in sturdy metal posts: the local beamer switching yards, now mostly quiet, although here he could sense the suggestion of active life. He followed the lines farther south, not entering them, but staying in the street, until the local terminal building appeared; this a plain, workshoplike structure with a small windowed cupola at each end. Empty, dark as the rest, with a small lamp inside making only a weak glimmer. Closed for the night. Across the street there was a glimmer of light and movement, a small rest-place halfway under the overhang of one of the buildings fronting the yards and the station. A warehouse or storage depot. Rael detached himself from the shadows and walked slowly toward the rest, falling easily into the movement pattern of one who had nothing to do but wait. An easy walk, passing time, while inside he heard time running steadily, inexorably.

Around him, there was quiet, and, muffled and distorted by the buildings of the town, he heard a last call of a bosel, somewhere up in the hills on the other side: a long, rising, reedy tone, leveling out and collapsing at the end into a descending series of short titters. Eerie music. It bothered him that he heard it so clearly, for he knew that the humans on Oerlikon ignored or avoided the native life forms as much as possible. *Nerves*, he thought. After all, this, now was really where he emerged into the stream of the world. Now. Rael stepped out of the shadows into the glow of the overhanging streetlights and went directly to the rest-house, down a short flight of stone stairs, smelling of damp woolen clothing and stale beer.

Inside, it was a small, cramped room with benches around the walls, and a counter along one wall backed by a fading mirror. It was early in the morning; predawn, and there was no tipsy night gaiety. The proprietor sat lumpishly on a stool and stared off into nothing. The room was crowded, but curiously empty in feeling. As if the people were there, but not in spirit. They filled the benches, their bundles piled beside them, waiting for the local beamer that was always late. Rael looked briefly at them, and then into the fading mirror, at the unrecognizable stranger who was the only one standing in the room, who looked back at him with an alien face whose set conveyed no meaning to him whatsoever. He caught the weak attention of the counterman and ordered a mug of hagdrupe, which was presently passed across the counter, reeking with the acrid flavor of the boiled potion. Rich in an alkaloid similar to caffeine, hagdrupe served the settlers of Oerlikon in place of coffee, which they had left behind. This was vastly overboiled and rancid, but he sipped at it anyway, passing one of the coins from his meager store across the counter.

Rael found the place subtly disturbing, familiar. Not that he had been in one before; not as Tiresio Rael. Perhaps as someone else who had been, once. He blinked. He could not remember Jedily; but the association set him to reflecting. He knew this world well, despite his loss of the other life which he had been, so they had told him. It felt familiar, all the sad nothingness of it, the sour flavor of the arguments the lifers* used to bolster their endless justifications to the poor sloggers*. He fit into it perfectly, and he did not know why in any direct sense. The logical explanation was that Jedily was familiar with this sort of life, and that there were ingrained habits even The Mask Factory could not erase, did not know of. Rael knew of one he had saved, hidden carefully from them, although it was covered openly in the notes he had left Pternam. Small chance, there.

What did Rael know? Rael's system of computation was paradoxical, like all good science, ambiguous, fleeting. He thought, *Science and Art are exactly alike in that. Ambiguity, a shimmering mirage.* It considered, on the one hand, that human faces were unique to a terrifying degree, even when broken down into component parts, and that a large section of the brain was devoted solely to the recognition of those unique patterns. It considered, equally, that music shared the same sort of uniqueness; that what the uninitiated saw as a single persona was in reality a highly organized group of disparate personalities gathered under the one roof of the body. And that whole societies acted as these complex entities, and that certain highly specialized statistical methods led one,

* The slang terms for the two main classes of Lisak society.

by a crooked trail, into understanding, which integrated Time into the picture, a continuum that one could follow one's way through, with discipline and will.

He looked at the figure in the mirror: a thin, saturnine person, some slogger down on his luck, perhaps, insignificant, unworthy of notice. He looked . . . resigned, used to it by now. Oerlikon was the place where the Changeless gained power, and they had locked it into place for all time. To one tied within that perception, there was no hope, no possibility of change. But Rael had seen how it could be done within the holistic pattern his formulae had revealed, and he had seen much more there than he had told Pternam. Pternam! They had done something to him . . . not once, but many times. There had been pain and fear, later fading but never completely gone. They could always bring it back, if they wished. And as they had perceived a pattern emerging, so it had suited them to see that Rael could at least convince some that the incredible idea might be true. But they of course did not believe it. He saw that, understood it from the beginning; that made him all the more determined to make it real, make it work. And work it would.

It was exactly as Pternam had told the revolutionaries. That much. But there was more to it. Once he did it, the world would change, obeying its own laws about the speed of the reaction, but not as any of them imagined it. No. In the new alignment, there would be no Pternams, and the Heraclitan Society could not exist, would fade and be a curious note in the histories, if any were written. Those in the future, they would look back in astonishment, in gaping, slack-jawed wonder. And in this set of the world, Rael felt the pressure: he was not supposed to *be*. The orientation of a world that set a premium on Changelessness did not include one who could stand partly outside it, outside the *mythos*, and reset the balance point of the reflected pyramid so that it assumed a new set, a set in which Rael, or rather what he would become, would live openly, buried. Rael would make the act that would begin the Change, but not for Pternam or the revolutionaries, but to create a Set of World in which he could exist. It would be, of course, as Damistofia. It was fitting, he thought, for somehow he felt that Jedily had been pushed to the edge as well, in her own time, without knowing why, pushed to the edge and beyond, and would return to peace in a world he would make for one who would come.

*   *   *

Now he allowed the composition of the group in the nasty little godown to seep onto him, carefully, so that they were not aware of his attention. He heard fragments of small talk, small sounds of half-awake people trying to arrange themselves comfortably. He let his eyes wander, seeing what they would, careful not to allow the lingering of attention, anything which might alert some watcher who might be spotted in this group. The owner was harassed and overworked. To him the faces that pressed upon him daily were just papers in the wind, faded petals on a rain-wet branch; a handful of traveling reps of the trade guilds, or contact men for the small factories that were the mainstay of small suburbs like this. A couple of farmers from back in the country, scared of bosels by night and city sharpers by day, but on the way to Marula no less, where they expected to be cheated; one recognizable Proctor, one who was tasked with uncovering Change and arresting it. This one was old and tired and waiting for his pension after an uneventful lifetime of snooping and offering Pollyanna-pap advice, usually unsolicited, which never worked for those who needed it most. The Proctor was not even aware of him, and the rest were totally uninterested. He had picked a good group, bound for the distant City, one they hated and feared, Marula, vast, sprawling, trashy, fecund Marula, the City-as-Beast in the warmth of the southern province of Sertse Solntsa.

Rael relaxed into the disciplines of his craft, and began to read the group identity; this one was weak, but it was there for the initiate to understand: a minimum of awareness and coherence. As he *read* the group, he felt a sudden constriction, a knotting, a small awakening. He visualized it as an abstract plane surface with random undulating waves of low amplitude, which developed a bunching: he followed it, and understood that the beamer was coming. They had heard it before they were consciously aware they had heard anything. He levered himself out of this state and perceived normally: he saw someone get up and stretch, while others began stirring, although it would be some time yet before time came to board.

They were rising, now, one by one, moving slowly, joints stiffened from inactivity. One seemed to be having considerable difficulty with an unwieldy bundle which resisted all efforts to gather it for lifting. He looked closer, something catching his attention. Yes. Under the shapeless plain garments of a wandering agricultural worker, he thought he could recognize a girl or woman. She turned so her face showed: Rael saw that she was not particularly attractive, and no one seemed to pay her any attention at all—indeed, they seemed to avoid her. Could he contact her? He took a quick moment to *read*, and saw that he could, but that it would lower his position, such as it was. What was she? With her plain looks, she certainly was not one of the inhabitants of one of the happy-houses. He made as if to leave the room, and as if on an impulse, turned back and approached the girl, and asked, "You need help with that bundle?"

For a flicker of an instant, she registered fear, looking back to him, but this faded, and after a moment she said, "Yes. Please; it was fine until I set it down."

Rael bent and grasped the bundle, and after a few tries, found it to be indeed uncooperative. He sat back on his haunches and said, "It doesn't work so well for me, either; what's in here?"

The girl continued to struggle with the bundle, and said, without looking up, "Cured fleischbaum pod."

He understood better why the rest ignored her. The fleischbaum, a scraggly, ragged tree, produced a pod whose fibers, properly cured, were of the flavor and protein content of meat. The problem was that the trees would not grow close to one another, which made orchards and plantations impossible, and the gathering was done from wild trees scattered through the wild. And for reasons which Rael did not completely understand, this was considered the lowest occupation one could take. He said, neutrally and as politely as he could, "You're a gatherer."

"Yes."

He said, "By the feel of it, it may take two to manage this bundle; it's shifted inside badly. Did you carry it here alone?"

She brushed a strand of curly, mouse-brown hair out of her face, now shiny with sweat. "Yes. For the markets. In Marulupol." Gatherers were the most solitary and taciturn of people, people of the open, the empty places, the stony wildernesses, people who heard their own thoughts in the silences, and who often had to run for their lives: from bosels, and from occasional bands of more integrated people who delighted in harassing solitaries, knowing there could be no retribution when none but the victim knew of the crime. Rael looked at her again. She was not a beauty, but there was no ugliness on her face. He could read it. Fear and despair and loneliness she had known, but not envy, impatience, rage, frustration, the marks of societal people.

He got a grip on the bundle at last, and lifted it. It was surprisingly heavy, and he felt more respect for the girl for managing to carry it alone; it was a load that would have taxed a strong man, yet somehow she had managed alone. He said, "I've got it, but it won't stay; it'll take both of us."

She picked up her end. "I had it packed just so—it wasn't hard. Now if we stop to retie it, I'll miss the beamer. . . . Are you certain you won't feel shame associating with a gatherer?"

"Will it disturb you to associate with a stranger?"

"What are you, that you would call yourself stranger?"

"I am Tiresio. Let us say that things have changed somewhat for me. Fortune, as it were. However it is, I now find myself looking for a new life of sorts, and in a land where things remain as they were, this can be difficult."

Now she smiled a little. As if she understood. Yes. Rael was someone who had been through Correction. Attitude Adjustment. He saw her in the light coming in from the street, seeing an open face free of guile or plot. Well-formed, though plain. She said, "And so you would take up with a gatherer, or a lonely woman? No matter—I need the help, so it would seem. Have a care, though: I'm an egg-stealer, too, and I've grappled bosels more than once and come away alive, and they don't volunteer for it."

Now that she was standing, he could see more of her shape and configuration; she was shorter than he, stocky and sturdy. He noticed that she moved well, confidently, with balance and no small amount of grace. He read truth in her words. She was extraordinarily self-possessed. She was exactly what she said she was. He said, "Very well, that is fair to say. And you know me as Tiresio. How are you called?"

She half turned away from him, shyly. "Meliosme."

Still grappling with the load, Rael made an artificially polite face. "Meliosme. May I accompany you to Marula?"

She gave him a wry smile, saying, "If you will help me get this thing to the fleischbaum bazaar, I will not complain, nor will I eat stinkhorns in front of you. But there remains a thing—which is what must I do. You can see that I can pay little or nothing, and . . ."

"I will be grateful for the company. I know no one now. Until Marula; I have affairs there."

"You could have one prettier, no doubt, if for hire, from the happyhouse."

"Perhaps." Here he raised one index finger dramatically. "True. But *they* will not ride the beamer to Marula. Moreover I have little enough in the way of money. . . . And last, you are by no means homely or fearsome, or one to be called a bagger."*

"Gallant as well! And with the words as well. Are you a fugitive?"

"Not yet."

"So. Very well, then. But few seek such as I, and I'll sully your reputation, such as it is. Others may sneer. It's said that when a slogger associates with a gatherer, it's the gatherer who's in bad company, for who would stoop so low . . ."

"I accept. Let's go."

They were the last of the group to leave the dim little godown. The proprietor remained behind the bar, glum and absorbed in his own concerns, and ignored them and the irregular bundle they were struggling with. Outside, a weary daylight was seeping into the adyts of the world, like a winter sunrise through frosted glass, although winter was by no means near yet.

The beamer was still moving along its elevated track, very slowly, but the rest of the people were gathering at locations which they suspected from long practice would be where the doors were when the machine stopped. Unlike the express models which ran at high speeds out on the plains of Crule, the locals made no rhythmic, driving sounds evocative of motion and power but emitted noises of mechanical, electrical and pneumatic protest: the electric motors hummed and throbbed irregularly and joints squealed with friction; likewise, the air brakes emitted vulgar flatulent moans, ventings and hisses. With a last moan, the beamer stopped, and the passengers began crowding at the doors.

Meliosme said, "No need to hurry; we won't get a seat with a sack full of fleischbaum with us, anyway."

"The baggage section, then?"

"Where else? But I accept it with resignation—at least I don't have to endure the lifers up in the fine compartments, or the sloggers on the benches with their envy. No—it's all just plain stuff back with the tramps and the thieves. All fools together. Never worry—they won't bother us. What I am can't be helped and you don't seem to have

* Slang. Homely women were called "baggers" by the men, allegedly on the premise that they were so ugly they would have to put a bag over their head in order to have a liaison with someone. Even more extreme were the so-called two-baggers, in which cases the man would also put a bag over his head, in case hers came off.

anything worth stealing . . . or else you're hiding well. Either way, you're not worth a risk. We'll have an easy bit of it."

Rael cast Meliosme a wintry glance from his end of the sack. "You inspire one to excellence with your compliments."

"I mean that you should trust me, for this seems new to you. There is something . . . out of place with you."

Rael said, "I would not say why, but I am as confident in my own resources as you are in yours. Let not the aspect deceive you."

She smiled, like a child. "Oh, I am not. Otherwise I would not have let you come with me. What I do, out there; it makes one sensitive to the quick judgment of people. I mean that you cannot de-egg a bosel's creche in the company of idle boasters; that kind of stuff shortens lives. You, now: I think you could do it, but you never have. You don't move like one who has done a sprightly step with a bosel buck, or better yet a great mother bosel in oestrus, but you are wary—a good thing to be. So come along now; never fear—I will not betray your direness, which hangs about you like a thundercloud. So long as it does not involve me."

Rael did not have to look. This was not his quarry. He said, "It does not." And then they were boarding, wrestling the sack through a door which had seemed big enough, but at the crucial moment wasn't. And after they had negotiated that problem, there were others to attend to, until at last they found an open spot no one else had claimed, and there set the sack down, and themselves leaning up against it from opposite sides. For the while, they said nothing, and presently they felt the jerky, erratic motions that signaled the movement of the beamer.

Rael sat in silence beside Meliosme and reflected on how fortunate he had been to meet one such as her. For however much he knew about the pattern of deed which he must do, it was in no way a revelation of the whole future to come. Meliosme had arrived by luck—pure aleatory hazard, a happening, a fortune; and by this hazard he had picked someone who was infinitely more real than those pallid phantoms moving about who thought they were people. And as an outcast type, herself, she would be acutely sensitive to the whims of the groups they passed through: a most excellent antenna tuned to the present, and an odd, intriguing mind as well. Now, for the first time since he had computed this course, since he'd *seen* this way, he felt like he could relax for a little. And he thought, as he relaxed, that he sincerely hoped that he could disengage from his cover, Meliosme, when things began in earnest.

*   *   *

The beamliner started up again, and moved out onto the elevated trackage leading south along the edge of the hills to the next small town, somewhere out of sight. It rode roughly; the beams were uneven and aligned poorly. Nevertheless, Rael saw, sneaking a quick glance out of the corner of his eye, that Meliosme was cat-napping, taking little short naps, broken by a slight movement, then relaxation again. It looked effortless, and Rael envied her the skill; he would like to have that ability himself. He needed rest, now. The moment of action was not all that far away.

Rael tried to compose himself by imagining how one could know parts of the future. He did not question the techniques he had been taught and had added to himself, so much as he failed, as everyone else did, to integrate such momentary flashes into a coherent theory of how the universe worked. He knew about prescient dreams, and visions people had under one circumstance or another. His method, while controlled, non-mystical, scientific, all that negated mystery, only opened up deeper layers, and was no less ambivalent, contradictory, incomprehensible. He asked a coherent system for answers, and it gave them. But only that. There was no linking; the answers were as unique as the stars, as a piece of music, as a face. *Do this at this moment and it changes.* He had free choice: he could refuse, or pass. *It did not matter: such chances to alter the lines of this world occurred over and over again. It was a matter of finding the next one, finding the next act, or non-act.* But he could feel this moment coming, and this one was special, different from the others in the way that all such instants were: they had different reaches of influence. And this moment coming at him at the speed the beamliner was running was one in which he could reach all the phases that controlled Oerlikon. And as he thought about it, he saw something else he'd not realized before: that in reaching all phases, there would be a backlash here that would reach into the incomprehensible third phase, and institute change there, too, although he couldn't see that, or how it would be. Only that it would be.

The sun rose and morning began fading into forenoon. Small towns passed, and the line of the hills began curving off to the east. Now the stops were out on the plains, which were becoming flatter and more watery, although they were a good ways yet from Marula. Once Meliosme went forward and returned with some buns, which she shared with Rael. They were hard and crusty, but good. He was hungry. And sharing them made them better.

After one long halt at a place called Orgeon, the beamer started up again, and as soon as it was trundling along out in the open country, he stood up, stiff from long sitting.

Meliosme glanced at him. "Where are you going?"

"Want to move about. I'm getting stiff. Is there water somewhere forward?"

"All the way up."

She fumbled a moment, and handed Rael a small metal flask. "Bring me some, please."

Rael nodded, and leaned to take it. A motion of the car moved him off-balance, and he caught himself on the sack of fleischbaum, feeling for something he knew would be there. A pin in the fabric, holding a place together that did not matter much. A sharp pain met his palm, and he grasped the pin out and palmed it. Meliosme did not notice. As the car steadied, Rael took the flask.

Meliosme said, "Be careful between cars; they can pitch you out in the swamp. This is one place you don't want to walk it, especially nursing bruises or worse."

Rael said, "Bosels?"

She said, grimly, "No. Not here. They're hill-creatures, or at least they prefer firmer ground. Upper Crule. Here, you'll have Letomeres, Sentrosomes. Maybe Kidraks."

"I'll watch out." As if to emphasize his words, the car gave another lurch, which this time did not throw him off-balance.

Meliosme said, "Well, you seem to be getting the hang of it . . ." And she shifted her attention. Rael turned about and started forward along the length of the car, toward the front of the beamliner, somewhere unseen far ahead, negotiating the ill-set elevated beams which guided the train. Now. Between Orgeon and the next halt, Inenda. It was a long passage, the last long stretch between here and Marula. Now. He could feel apprehension pounding the blood in his ears. Now. He permitted himself a nervous little chuckle, thinking about Pternam and the revolutionaries, all curious, all certain that he would do it in Marula, because he had told them that Damistofia would be there. All wrong. Not in Marula. Before Marula. Now.

Rael made his way forward through the swaying cars slowly, deliberately, like one who had never been on one before, lurching, leaning, holding on as he went. In part, this was wholly natural, and also in part it was a careful motional disguise, which effectively made him invisible to those around him. In this way he passed through four of the cars before he found what he was looking for: one of the wooden bench seats, occupied by a single young man, who was now looking out the window at the dreary passing landscape, a passing panorama of sloughs, marshes, expanses of territory neither land nor water but an uncomfortable hybrid of both, dotted by random clumps of spikegrass in the water proper, and brackberry tangles covering the land portions with their stiltlegged arachnid stance.

He had not known which car it would be, but he premembered the scene perfectly, just as it was: the light from Gysa coppering the marshes with its afternoon slants, the clear aqua-blue of the sky, by which he knew that the seasons had changed. Now it was autumn. It would be cooler now. And the young man sitting on the bench.

Rael leaned forward and said, "Seat taken?"

The young man shook his head absently, thoughts clearly elsewhere. Rael sat down, softly, so as not to attract any attention. No one had noticed him. The young man placed an arm on the windowsill and propped his head up, leaning forward slightly.

Rael said, "Excuse me," and leaned over behind him, as if reaching to place something on the shelf over the windows, and with a motion that did not seem to deviate from those normal lurchings caused by the swaying of the car, drove the pin he had taken into the base of the young man's brain.

Rael felt the body stiffen, and then relax, as he resumed his own seat. The body did not slump or fall, but remained in position, propped up; it would remain that way, the muscles locked, until someone moved him, which doubtless would not be until the last stop in the Marula transit yards. Rael sat back, blending into the background with the rest of the sloggers, reflecting, feeling conflicting emotions. He felt a pain deep in his heart, an emotion he could put no name to. It was without doubt that it was an evil thing to dispatch this young man into the darkness so coldly, not even in the heat of an argument, not in conflict, but coldly. Without warning, without anticipation. Yet at the same time he could see this figure as a nexus of powerful forces, himself obscure, a nobody, but paradoxically the carrier of the weight of the whole world. This was the one. This was, without doubt, the enemy. Rael did not understand, but he could see it clearly. This was the one. And he could see the rest of it as well, how he would place a slip of paper in the boy's hand, with one word printed on it: "Rael." They would have to know who had done this. Rael printed the word on the paper and placed it in the boy's free hand, now cool. Rael looked carefully at the face; the eyes were closed, as if the boy were napping along the way. Exactly the way it was supposed to go.

And the rest: Rael got out of the seat and caught the attention of one sitting nearby, who had also been woolgathering, studiously trying not to see others or be seen by them, and to this one he said, "Pardon, but my friend is sleeping. He's very tired, and will not need to get off until Marulupol."

The other nodded. "Right. Up all night with a lady before his trip to the big city, eh? Well, no harm there; it's not a flaw to nap on the way."

Rael agreed, the man continued, "He seemed to be looking for someone, a bit earlier . . . was he to meet someone on the way?"

Rael thought, and answered, "Perhaps he was. Maybe they'll see him when he gets to Marula."

The other nodded, and began sinking back into his own thoughts, already dismissing the incident. Rael began turning away, letting him sink back. That was fine. He would almost forget it, until incidents at the station caused him to remember. No matter. By then, Rael would be long gone, or so he planned to be. The deed was done now, in the only time-slot open for it. Now the clock was running. When the beamer reached Marula, there would be a confusion over the body, but sooner or later they would sort things out, and then the hunt would be on. Rael figured that to make a successful *change*, he had to get at least a full day ahead of his pursuers, better yet a day and a half. He started forward, to get the water for Meliosme.

6

Marula

THE OUTSKIRTS OF Marula slid by, mostly beneath the level of the elevated beamer. In the baggage car, Meliosme glanced out the window from time to time, but did not keep a close eye on the city. Rael, on the other hand, watched intently, for to his knowledge it was a place totally strange to him. From his training, he knew in a rough sort of way how Marula was laid out, if that phrase could apply to an organism which constantly changed, as variable as the channels of the sluggish inland river whose delta formed its foundation.

To the Lisaks with the most correct attitude orientation, Marula was something of a necessary evil, but withal a place to be avoided if at all possible. It changed. And its people survived from day to day by managing, so the saying went, with changing channels, docks whose approaches silted up overnight, roads which sank into the soft muck without a trace, elevated beamlines which leaned crazily to either side of center, and were propped up with ropes and stumps. Unlike the other cities of Lisagor, there was no area within the complex which could be called a city center, a built-up area in which authority resided. Authority, such as it was, moved about according to where the action was. No one bothered to erect anything resembling a permanent structure; instead, they threw up temporary buildings which became semi-permanent by force of habit, some part of them in constant repair.

With so much change about, it was natural that the inhabitants would take on some of its aspects; to this end, large numbers of the infamous Pallet-Dropped Troopers were settled there in garrison, and were paraded through the streets often. Those who missed their attentions did not complain, but expressed a sigh of relief that they had not been given over to the mercies of the troopers. There were also numerous officials, proctors, attitude patrols, informers, spies, and investigators, the result of which was that Marula, for all its diversity and sprawl, was effectively and tightly controlled.

Perhaps it was controlled, but it was not run very well. Marula was chaotic and disorganized, a fact Rael hoped to use to his advantage. Here, even with modern communications, things proceeded slowly; slowly enough so that if Rael could get away cleanly from the beamer, he could count on being able to gain the lead on them he needed.

Here, they did not bother to build the little hills on which the living-quarters grew which were traditional with other Lisak cities; the land wouldn't support them. Instead, they fashioned small enclaves resembling labyrinths in which one-, two- and three-story buildings proliferated. Inside the enclaves the streets were hardly more than alleys. Low walls separated the enclaves from the rest of the land, which was given over to other uses, mostly industrial.

Rael said, "Where are we now?"

It was evening, and the sky was becoming overcast from the southwest, washing the outlines of the city with a soft, weak light that obscured much of its harshness. It seemed, in this light, slightly magical, strange, exotic, a place where odd events might succeed.

Meliosme said, "This district is called Sango; the beamer won't stop here. The next named place is Semora, which is where I leave."

"It's close to the markets you have to go to?"

"Closest for this beamline. Got to walk a bit more."

"You'll still need help. . . ."

Meliosme looked sidelong at him, an odd coy look. "Still?"

"I'll trade you that for you telling me a place I can go and be unknown for, say, two days. After that . . . it won't matter."

Some light in her face faded. She said, "Plenty of places like that in Marula, in fact, if you're willing to move, you can keep ahead of them very well indefinitely . . . I know of something that might do, near the markets, if they haven't torn it down, which they often do here, but it will probably do. I'll trade."

"What will you do after you sell your fleischbaum?"

"What else? Go out again for more."

"Back to the Symbar area?"

"No, I'm a wanderer. I'll probably go on over into Tilanque, more southerly than Symbarupol. Winter's coming on, cold nights and the like, and I flow with it. You wouldn't catch me working Grayslope or Severovost in the cold season, no. . . . And what are your plans?"

"After a day or so, I'll seek out a position here for the time. That will be enough."

"You wouldn't care to wander?"

"Not now."

"You look as if you could, and there's not many I'd say that to."

Rael chuckled, half to himself. "Not now, but if I came later, how would I find you?"

"Not out in the field! But if you visited the markets, you'd likely catch word of me. . . ." She looked thoughtful, an attitude that made her plain face seem full of light and animation. "Mind, I offer little in the way of bennies*, but on the other hand, neither would you have to endure a preachy lifer, either. To be free . . ."

"You don't have trouble with the authorities?"

She shrugged. "People want fleischbaum, and it's a lot of trouble to get it, so they leave it to people like me. Why not? We offer no Change to the sloggers. They wouldn't leave if they could."

Rael said. "They might have to, some day."

Meliosme frowned. "I know. I've heard too, but it's just talk; it'll come to nothing, all that. They'll throw out Monclova and Chugun, but who'll come along but someone just as vile, with the same kind of bosel-dung, promising, promising, but the end of it is that there'll still be lifers running things and spouting slogans, and millions of sloggers keeping them afloat, all idiots. At any rate, they won't do a night-trot with a bosel, and so much for them." She looked at Rael again. "Surely you aren't after all that."

Rael answered her straightly, more honestly than he knew. "I need now some time to think, to wait. But after that, well I might come, at least for a while."

She looked at him critically. "Need to put some weight on you, and some sun for that dungeon tan you wear on your hide." But she smiled shyly as she said it.

Rael agreed. "That wasn't a seaside resort I was in, that's a fact."

The beamer went through an alarming series of junctions which felt rubbery and insecure, and began slowing down. Meliosme glanced through the window quickly and said, "Semora coming up."

---

* Bennies: "Benefits," *i.e.*, of accepting an income from State Service as opposed to making your own living. These included food, clothing, housing and job security, all of which demanded a careful attention to one's allegiances and remarks.

"Does the beamer have stops after Semora?"

. "Beyond? Yes. It goes to the yards, to the shops. The old terminal used to be there, and many people still go all the way in. Did you change your mind?"

"No. Just curious." Rael turned away from her and pretended to look out the window on the opposite side, to conceal the relief he felt.

The beamer slowed to a groaning crawl and proceeded through a district, so it seemed, down the middle of a broad street. To either side were drab, low buildings of many sizes and styles, but they all had that shanty atmosphere which seemed to characterize Marula. There were a lot of people about, most on foot, strolling about in the evening air, which was thick and flavored with many odd substances so close to the ocean and the marshes, and with so many different industrial operations. Yet they displayed a certain swagger, a furtive elan, which distinguished them from the rest of Lisaks, who generally favored uniformity and anonymity.

The beamer aligned itself in the platform area and stopped with a series of alarming noises, and finally a bump, which made Rael wince, as he thought of someone precariously propped on an elbow four cars forward. But he got to his feet calmly, and began working with Meliosme to grapple the awkward bundle, and eventually they got it up between them and struggled to the door.

Together they made their way through the streets where Meliosme went with an unerring sense of familiarity. Near the station, on the main thoroughfare, there had been crowds, who fastidiously gave them room, but as they left the station area the crowds thinned and grew less deferential although no one bothered them. They negotiated a series of narrow alleys poorly lit, and at last came to a cavernous shed which seemed to be abandoned but wasn't; there was a sleepy night watchman, who let them pass inside without comment, almost without notice.

Inside the shed there was a dim light from lanterns set at intervals along the walls, none of them bright. Meliosme picked a place by a dimmer spot along one wall and there they set the bag down. Rael now took time to look around. Scattered all over the floor of the shed were others with various-sized bundles, some large and apparently unmanageable, others hardly worth the effort of dragging them here. Most of the others appeared to be gathers like Meliosme, all rather ragged, most catnapping, or conversing in small groups, very quietly in low tones so as not to disturb the others. Now and then one might go out for some food, or a bottle of spirits. In contrast to the lively, wary activity outside on the streets, here was quiet and a sense of peace, in which he felt some irony, for these were the outcasts of Lisak society, the gatherers.

Meliosme arranged the bag, and settled down next to it, motioning to Rael to sit beside her. This he did, half-leaning against the wall behind them. In the semidarkness, with the soft mumble of distant slow conversations all around them, he was conscious of the solid warmth of her body next to his, and she did not move away. He said, after a time, "You stay here?"

Meliosme nodded. "This is the fleischbaum bazaar. The selling will commence at dawn. That is why you see little in the way of rowdying and roistering. You have to be awake then, or you'll wake up with little or nothing for a month's trip in the wild. No one, besides, wants a gatherer in their hostel or inn, so we stay here. You sell, and then you leave. I expect to make a good bundle this trip. . . ."

"What do you do with it?"

"Replace worn clothes, boots, a new knife . . . If there's much left over, I'll get a place for a few days and enjoy some luxuries, like a hot bath; cold streams are fine, but everyone likes a little laziness now and then." She relaxed a little, softening. "You could stay here tonight without fear. In the morning, I'll show you how it's done and then I'll set you on the righteous path of being free."

"How do you know I could?"

She shrugged. "I don't *know*. You might work out badly—who knows? There are more women gatherers than men, why I don't know. But you have an air about you of one worth a chance. You are an outcast, that much I can see with my own eyes, no matter which Silver City* you were a guest in; and not so much one who'd make a good little slogger, not here in Marula. No! You've got to snuffle up to the old bung smartly here to get along. And you'll not do it well. Admit it."

Rael found himself liking immensely this rough woman. He put his arm about her shoulders, and she did not move away. "It's true what you say, and I admit I'm tempted to go your way. . . ."

A noise from outside intruded on his train of thought, and interrupted his words. It was a sound of wheels, and a thudding, rhythmic

* Silver City: The exercise yard of a confinement camp, fenced in with a tinny-bright metal mesh, electrified, hence the slang term.

compression, and a piercing little whistle, repeated at intervals. The noise grew, and then faded. Rael had never heard anything like it, but he noticed that Meliosme listened to it intently, and many others in the warehouse also listened closely to it. As the sound faded, he asked, "What was that?"

She said, quietly, "Police van. Something's happened. Sounded like somewhere near the station . . . not so good."

"Why so?" Rael whispered, so others wouldn't hear.

Meliosme sighed, "Anything happens, they sift the gatherers. We are always suspect, you know. And you and I were on the beamer. If it's something on the train, they'll be along presently . . . I guess we'll have to wait."

"You are not in danger . . . ?"

"No." But Rael suddenly thought of a pin, and that it might well be a common type used by gatherers. They had been seen together, and this was the place where gatherers congregated. He felt a sudden constriction of alarm.

"Meliosme?" He fumbled in his clothing and extracted a hidden wallet. "How much would you expect to get for your sackful, there?"

"What?"

He extracted some currency notes and showed them to her. "Take what you think the sack's worth. I can't explain it now, but we have to leave this place now and hide. Separately."

For a moment she hesitated. Rael hissed, "Take it. I trusted you: now you trust me. I know danger."

Reluctantly, she peered at the money in the dim light, at last selecting some notes, which she took and stuffed into her breast. Rael said, "I am sorry to have caused you this, but we must get out of here. And you must tell me how to get a place I can hide."

She stood up, and Rael stood with her. She said, "I don't know, but I'd guess you don't want to be caught, and if they see you, they'll know you. Did you escape?"

"In a manner of speaking. . . . Where do we go?"

Meliosme glanced at the large sack with some regrets, and hesitated. Then she turned to him, face straight and matter-of-fact. "Come along. I know the way, and with all the coming and going, no one will notice." She led him back to the entrance, where a group of gatherers was just coming in, and two were trying to get out, causing a confusion with which the watchman was unsuccessfully coping. In a moment, depending on the respect and good manners the gatherers showed one another, they were through the gate and into the heavy night.

Then they set off in another direction, traversing narrow ways and crossing broad streets, rapidly crossing several small districts, and the only thing Rael could tell about their route was that it seemed that they were headed away from both the station and the bazaar, to the unknown. They saw no one who looked at them twice; there were few out. But at last they came to a more habited place, a sort of neighborhood of small shops, taverns and inns, and a few walk-up dwellings. It looked rough, but far removed. Meliosme took them to a small, three-story hostel and engaged a room for them without comment, nor did the night man make any. Lisaks were as they were about their affairs, even in Marula. Night-clerks did not comment upon whom they rented rooms to.

When they had gotten the key and climbed the stairs to the room, they found it a little bare, but serviceable. And it had its own bath. Meliosme smiled at the single bed, and at the bath, and said, "Well, it's sooner than I planned, but looks like I get my hot tub."

Rael gently took her by the shoulders and looked in her eyes. "No. Believe me, I did not intend to have you in this; you must not stay here."

She smiled at him, exposing white, even teeth. "No matter. This is a good hideout. They'll never find us."

Rael shook his head. "There is something you don't understand, but which you must take and accept. For your life, you have to leave, and by a different way than we came in."

"No problem there. . . . If you didn't want me . . ."

"That is the problem right now. I do want you: that is why I am telling you to leave. They will catch me. I only need to be ahead of them for about a day, and then it doesn't matter. But you can't stay."

"Why?" She set her feet, preparing to stay.

"Something is going to happen to me which I will not have you see . . . and which will entangle you in something unimaginably bad. If you love your freedom, leave me while you can, now."

She relaxed, incomprehension on her face. She said slowly, "Are you going to be killed . . . or changed?"

"I may, both. I didn't want you in it . . . but I stayed because I felt good with you. But because of that I now ask you to leave and save yourself."

"I believe you . . . but I don't understand. Can you escape? Can you meet me somewhere else after this blows over?"

Rael knew he had won. He said, "I can escape, but it has to be alone. I will seek you out, no matter where you are, but I may look different. Would you still have me?"

"Would it be only the looks that changed?"

"I don't know. I think it's only that, if this works. . . . Go back to the wild, tonight. Marula's not safe for you this trip, but it will be later."

"Would you really come looking for me?"

"I think so now."

"You'd never find your way around Tilanque . . . I'll go from here northwest, into the hills between Zolotane and Crule. You know those?"

"No better than Tilanque."

"At any rate, it's closer, and you can find me better, I think. I'll go there for my next trip, work north toward the Serpentine. But how will I know you?"

"I'll come to you and tell you who I am, what we did . . . or almost did."

"Would you have?"

"I would have liked to very much . . . more than anything in the life I can remember."

"Very well . . . Good-bye, Tiresio."

"Good-bye, Meliosme. Good fortune to you."

"And to you. I think you need the wish more than I." She took his face in her hands swiftly and brushed her lips on his, ever so shortly. And then she turned quickly and left the little flat, closing the door behind her.

For a long time, Rael stood in silence and waited, counting his heart-beats, feeling the pressure of time. While he waited, he did a quick, shallow reading of circumstances, according to his art, and concluded that he probably had some time, but not as much as he had hoped to have. He breathed deeply, went to the door, opened it, and looked out. No sign of Meliosme, and the hall was quiet. Rael retreated into the flat, locked and barred the door. He looked about the room coldly. It wasn't much. A window. A single narrow bed. A table with a washstand. A bathroom, an unheard-of luxury. . . . Still, a shabby little room. He nodded, as if confirming something to himself. It would have to be here, then.

Rael felt hungry, but he knew that didn't matter now. He went to the window, looked out on the street below for a few moments, and then went to the bed and wearily lay down on it, placing his hands behind his head, and staring at the dim ceiling. He thought for a long moment, considering whether he had any regrets. After some thought, he determined that there were indeed some regrets, but that they could not make any difference. The thing would go forward, as he had both planned and dreaded.

Now he thought about what he had to do: that in itself was an odd, half-process—he knew with the certainty of long-practiced, perfected motions *what* he must do. The problem was that he couldn't recall anything about what happened as a result of it, even though he knew he had done it successfully once before. Nor could he imagine it. All the same, there was a somber sense of dread, of fear, of—yes, a special kind of horror—which he felt associated with the Change. Rael knew very well that the gaps in his memory were deliberate omissions purposely installed by Pternam and friends, when he did this before. They wanted him to forget as much as possible. But now he was aware of that problem, and had found ways around it. This time, he would retain something. One never knew, safety or not as promised for Damistofia, for since when on any planet had revolutionaries ever kept their word?

He began the exercise, by relaxing, as if preparing for sleep, consciously feeling each muscle group, becoming aware of its tension, and deliberately untensing it, one by one, starting with the feet and working upward along the body. But as he felt the rhythms of sleep, he carefully shunted them aside into another state, a concentrated focus of psychic energy that seemed to magnify his self and reduce everything beyond that to a meaningless fog. He felt the brightening and the dimming of the other, and now slowly began to increase the contrast between the two, brightening the self locked somewhere behind the eyes, probably at the pineal junction, dimming the exterior, the outside, the body, everything. Sensations faded, became meaningless, and then vanished entirely. Rael was functionally blind and deaf, lacking sense of smell and taste, and finally touch. The outside faded, faded . . . and went out. The core brightening further, became painful, unreachable, unstable, a burning pinpoint flux, a tight coil of glowing threads, all moving, writhing. He could *see* it, but only gaps, short flashes. The motion was still too fast for him. He held on, brightening it more, racing now with the unimaginable time pace underlying the perception. The motions became more coherent, the matching moments longer now, recognizable now as short flickers of motion which he *saw* directly; and longer still. The concentration was intense. (A part of him still left rational reminded him that if he failed to synchronize with that painful bright motion, he would not be able to attempt it again for days, which was too late.) He made an effort he didn't think he really could, and matched with the flow, riding with it in time, and the bundle of bright worms at the center of his consciousness slowed, slowed, and stopped.

Now. There was a certain configuration there, which he had to change, while moving in this current, which he did, slowly, feeling a hot wash of dread and loathing as he did so. One of the threads had to go *this way*, instead of *that way*. Dangerous, subtle work. He turned it, feeling it resist, feeling resistance from the rest, but after an effort, it turned, and locked into position with a rubbery snapping sensation. Rael turned it loose and let it go, and fell away weakly. The center leapt into instant motion, writhing and squirming as before, and as it whirled away from him, he relaxed the hold he had on the center and let the brightness fade, feeling the outside lighten up again, come back. He let it come, feeling nothing but a vast fatigue, and a great sadness for something he couldn't quite understand.

One by one, his senses came back to him, and the intense self-awareness faded. He looked down. He could see, he could move, although he felt weak, and he thought, *I don't feel any different; perhaps the whole thing is just another sham cooked up by Pternam. Nothing is going to happen at all. Nothing. I'll stay here for a while, and then they'll come for me.* He sat up on the small bed, and ran his hands through his hair, wearily. He took a deep breath, and stood up, placing his right hand on the windowframe for support. Other than a feeling of weakness, he felt nothing out of order, nothing different. Rael took a step, and then moved forward more confidently, first to the washstand where he picked up the metal pitcher, and then to the bathroom, where he drew some water from the tap. He came back into the room and sat the pitcher down, looking about uncertainly for a glass.

It was then that he did notice something not quite right. He found the glass, but only by looking away from it: there was a small hole in the center of his vision, in which there was *nothing*, not blackness, not patterns of light. Nothing. As if there was nothing there. Rael stopped, as if listening. Nothing else was happening. He breathed deeply. Probably some transient effect, an aftershock of the concentration, something similar to a migraine visual pattern. He poured himself a glass of water, and drank it, feeling a sudden thirst. He drank a second glass, wondering how he had become so thirsty. Then he stood by the window and looked out into the dark streets below. There was nobody there. It seemed an unreal, empty city. There were lights but no life. He started to move toward the bed, for he felt very tired, when suddenly he felt a sharp pang of intense nausea; he ran to the bathroom instinctively, opened the water-closet lid, and vomited instantly in powerful heaves that felt as if he were trying to tear his insides out.

When his stomach had stopped heaving, Rael sat back on the floor, shaking. He tried to stand up, and found that his legs wouldn't hold him: they felt rubbery, unstable, unhinged, as if he were being unboned before his own eyes. There was also a dizzy vertigo. He thought, *I'm sick. I have to get to the bed.* He tried again to stand and fell back, weakly. Undaunted, he placed his hands on the floor and began crawling, a little uncertain, but making progress. He managed to get about halfway there, to the middle of the bedroom, when the second attack came. A sudden sharp pain which felt just like someone had kicked him exactly halfway between the testicles and the prostate. Rael fell over, groaning, biting his hand to keep from crying out, tears starting from his eyes. He rolled over into a fetal position and grasped his organs which felt white hot, glowing. Then came a third; suddenly his body jerked, and he felt as if every nerve in his body had shorted out at once. There was a buzzing in his ears, his eyes transmitted a view of a flickering random black-and-yellow checkerboard, his skin burned, and he smelled and tasted unimaginable things: burnt flesh, a sweet-pungent gas, like acetylene, and his limbs contorted into odd, rigid positions. His hands were like shrunken claws. Then there was another attack of nausea, and this time he didn't make it. In fact, he didn't even try. It was all he could do just to breathe.

After a time, the attack faded somewhat, and he was aware of things again, but in an altered way, as if he hallucinated. He could not move; his muscles were totally uncoordinated. He had chills. Then it eased a little, and he could move, although only enough to shift his position a bit. His skin was crawling, and he was sweating. He managed to have a short space of lucid thought: *This is Change—it actually worked. It will probably get a lot worse. I will lose consciousness. I might die here without help. Got to get clothes off. It'll be messy. Nasty. I'm going to lose about a third of my body weight in the next half day. I premember Damistofia: she's small, graceful, almost petite. No other way—catabolism, destructive distillation, excretion by all available orifices and surfaces.*

Fumbling with his pants, Rael managed to get them partially off. He stopped and forced himself to look at his organs. Already they were swollen, painful, covered with a milky secretion. He fell back, gasping for air. And then the real attack set in, and the worst part of it was that he did not lose consciousness. Time expanded, engulfed him, and the seconds loomed like adamantine monuments stretching across the world. And it got a lot worse.

Thedecha was a word which described the unrolling intricate recursive calendar of Oerlikon, and also, not by chance, was the proper name of the immense long river which drained all parts of the continent Karshiyaka save those that sloped directly to the oceans. West of Symbarupol, out in the plains of Crule The Swale, it was lost in the limitless flat distances, or sometimes the hint of a shimmer on the horizon, a lightness in the air, a memory. Thedecha water described a large counterclockwise loop around the end of the mountains separating Innerland Puropaigne from Crule, and far to the southeast in the mountains of Far Zamor it began. And sometimes one could catch sight of it east of the city as it flowed into the north, before the turn.

This was such a morning; beyond the bulky stark structures of Symbarupol and the sun Gysa was rising in a clear sky, and between the blank faces of the structures gold flashes could be seen out in the valley. Pternam always rose early, but clear, cool mornings he would stroll about on the terrace and look across the city for sight of that fugitive glimmer. And he was not disappointed when he went out on the terrace, for in the shadows and illuminations he could see it. Soon, though, some ground mists rose and obscured the view. Still, he considered it worthwhile. And he added to himself, if they managed to get through this problem, he'd try to arrange that they built a capital closer to the water. Surely there was something about water in a great city that could soothe one.

Not long after, one of the house bondsmen brought breakfast, and he had hardly cleared the entrance to the terrace when Avaria hurried in, face florid, manner agitated, more or less as usual. Avaria was never calm about anything. Pternam nodded politely to him and continued with his breakfast. Avaria understood that he was to remain quiet, but his constant motions and nervousness finally chipped a path through Pternam's studied lack of attention.

"Heard anything yet?"

"Yes. I got up early and strolled over by Chugun's place to see. There's no secret about it—they were free enough with me."

"Therefore, what?"

"Rael made his move: killed a young fellow on the local beamer, near Marula, apparently, and then tried to fade into the city. They are . . ."

"Did they get him?"

"No, but they aren't concerned; they have sealed the city and are doing area searches, eliminating areas one at a time. They know what part of the city he's probably in and they seem to think they'll ground him by evening. They aren't using the troopers, but very quiet methods, so as not to scare him until they have him penned in. It was odd, though—he left a calling card with the body. Signed it 'Rael,' as if he wanted someone to know. A subtle job, apparently done right under the noses of the passengers."

"Who was the victim?"

"Didn't get his name . . . but Chugun is looking into that, too. I mean, the job has all the marks of an assassination, but it doesn't seem to connect to anything. But the fellow Rael . . . ah, killed, has them hopping. They ran some routine checks to see if they could determine a reason, and this fellow's not supposed to exist."

"Enlighten me."

"He had identification and normal position-rights papers, but they don't relate to any real records on file. Chugun's people think the victim may prove to be more a problem than Rael, because they feel certain they can eventually get Rael, but this youngster . . . what was he? Ostensibly somebody's agent, with a cover that would look perfect—so good no one would try to verify it."

"Certainly not Clisp or the Serpentine; that's not their way."

"That's the tone of what I heard over there. Doesn't feel Clispish, as it were. They already have determined that he's not with any known Lisak group."

"Could he be with the Heraclitan Society?"

"I don't know. Possible, but according to Chugun's people, not very likely. They have no links, at any rate. They think something further out—some obscure sect in the Pilontary Islands, or maybe Tartary."

Pternam commented, "There are some curious groups in the Far Pilontaries, but Tartary . . . ? Not likely, unless . . . If this fellow was from Tartary, it would show up in his body parameters; the natives have taken on some adaptations to the severe climate. We haven't studied them much because we don't often get a specimen from there, so we don't know much. But enough to identify him as one, if in fact he is." Pternam reflected for a moment, and then added, "Rael said something, just before he left, about a 'third faction,' or something like that. What was it? He said, 'The field that maintains Lisagor is tripolar, subtle but powerful, probably the most powerful force. . . . Something not of this world.'

Yes. It didn't make a great deal of sense then, and no more now. Surely he couldn't have been talking about agents from Tartary infiltrating Lisagor with that kind of sophistication; man, they can't even agree among themselves. Tartary is, for all practical purposes, anarchy, and being anarchistic keeps them from being either of interest or a threat."

"Did he tell you what this third force was?"

"No, and I'm afraid I didn't give it much thought at the time; I was convinced that the line we fed him was just that—a line, nothing more, and so I didn't follow it. He might not have answered had I asked."

Avaria rubbed his chin and said, "No, I think that if you had asked him, he would have told you, at least as much as he could calculate of it within his system. He always gave straight answers if he answered at all; that was his way."

"Hm. Well, my guess is that Chugun's people won't get him; he's probably found a hidey-hole and initiated Change. They won't find anyone like Rael. They will probably find Damistofia, treat her, rough her up a little, and release her, she won't connect."

"Exactly . . . should we try to get her ourselves? I mean, sir, that she may remember . . . and if we can get her we can scrub her clean. As long as that relic lives, someone will know what part we played."

Pternam sat back and gazed into the distances of the east. "I would normally be tempted," he began. "But we don't want to show any interest at all to Chugun's people. I don't like this unearthing they are doing, and I definitely don't want them looking this way. You see, we can't get her, ourselves. We're blocked. They would want to know why we want her right off, instead of having her remanded to us after all the interrogations."

"We still have our own people looking for Rael. They are still under controls, and could be reaimed."

"Blocked there, too. They are not well covered, and shortly after they got her someone would ask, why does The Mask Factory intervene in a case it's supposed to know nothing about? And once they ask one, they'll ask some more. And ask and ask, and there won't be enough we could say that would end it there. Oh, no. But I will have them ordered to make contact, observe and report. No action, though—make that certain. And they are not to be seen themselves. Valuation: if the mission would be compromised, break off contact with the girl. We can follow her through Chugun somewhat, if we have to."

"Aye. So it will be done, as you ordered. And what about the revolutionaries?"

"I've heard nothing. If they know it, they are sitting tight."

"They wouldn't tell us anyway."

"No."

Pternam reflected again for a moment, and Avaria sensed that it was not time to leave, just yet.

Pternam said, "Take the best one of those we have on Rael's scent, and have him stand by, well back out of sight. If they let her go, we might have a chance."

Avaria said, "I see. . . . Bring her in?"

Pternam smiled, an unpleasant facial gesture he rarely used. "Oh, no. Not to bring her here, or anywhere. If we can, kill her. We still don't want something like that lying around uncontrolled. She may remember something from Rael. . . . We put it through Change before, but we had the control, and we made sure he remembered nothing of Jedily."

"You don't want to try to reestablish control?"

"I want that thing eliminated as soon as practically possible with the minimum commotion."

"As you say. I will set to it immediately."

"Avaria?"

"Yes."

"I feel a pressure here, of distant events unseen or at least unreported. . . . I wonder why Chugun's group is so swift to respond to this one boy . . . surely he was insignificant."

"As I understand it, they got an anonymous tip that something was about to happen in Marula. They couldn't very well prevent anything given the vagueness of the tip, but they were prepared to hop right onto whatever materialized out of the night, as it were."

"Of course they got a tip! From us!"

"Not from us is this one they're talking about. Somewhere else."

"But . . . that could hardly be, could it? There was only us. . . . Oh, yes, I see. The Heraclitan Society knew about it. That raises more issues still; why would they tip off Chugun?"

"Begging your pardon, sir, but it seemed obvious to me, that's why I didn't say anything. . . . They will have a couple of sleepers, you know, passives, buried in Chugun's department, and so they would alert Chugun so they could tell by the reaction when it happened. They might miss it, otherwise. Or at least so goes my suspicion."

"What's their reaction to this tip?"

"They are trying to find out where it came from, and they are looking into some odd corners indeed. Not to worry, we're not involved at all. Clear as the morning air. As a fact, they are rather more interested in the tip than in the assassination."

"Wouldn't that inconvenience the Revolutionaries? On the other hand, Rael did say it would go their way. . . ."

"Begging your pardon again, sir, but that isn't what he said. He just said that it would change. The rest of the interpretation was added on by us. He didn't contradict it, but neither did he confirm; I asked him several times, and he said, 'no comment.' That was all."

Pternam stroked his chin and looked off a moment thoughtfully. He mused. "Then that would indicate that, all things considered, the process Rael envisioned is already under way. . . ."

"So it would appear. But the world seems as solid as ever."

7

Morning in Symbarupol

ARUNDA PALUDE HURRIED through the same morning streets of the same city, Symbarupol, but her motions were not those of one at ease, as had been Avaria and Pternam, but those of one with a concern on her mind. She made her way to Glist's settlement and negotiated the stairs and walks almost at a run. There were few abroad to see her, yet.

When she reached the quarters of Anibal Glist, there was further delay while he woke up through her knocking at the door, and took his own time about getting there. She swore under her breath, thinking bitterly that Glist had, after all, been here too long, entirely too long: he was becoming just like the damned natives. He didn't care about Time.

Eventually, Glist opened the door a crack, saw that it was Arunda, and let her in. He closed the door, a heavy timber door affected more for aesthetic reasons than practical ones, and said, "You seem agitated. Surely it could have waited?"

"No. You had to be informed immediately: my evaluation."

"Continue, then. Deliver your report."

"I have reports from Laerte and Foleo, and . . ."

"Laerte is in Marula, yes? And Foleo is currently in Symbarupol?"

"Yes, and yes. You sent Sheptun to Marula, yes? To capture that changeling? Something went wrong—Sheptun was killed on the way to Marula!"

"Killed?"

"Apparently by the creature he was supposed to find. He never knew who did it. There was a calling card with it. The creature's name was on it: Rael. That was all, of that."

"That's not good."

"The rest is worse: his documents didn't check. At all. They are now working on finding out who Sheptun was. And there was a tip planted with Chugun's people. . . ."

Glist interrupted her: "I did that."

"No matter who. They are now assuming Sheptun was connected with whoever sent the tip, and . . . They took Aril Procand."

"How?"

"Checking, they found out she was Sheptun's girlfriend, and went looking for her. Got her early this morning. Her papers don't check, either."

"Damn it, I told those idiots more than once to fix those temporary papers . . . they *knew* that stuff the organization makes up on Heliarcos wouldn't stand a real check—it's just supposed to look good, that's all."

"Nevertheless . . . Foleo had to disengage, but he had it on good report that Chugun was interrogating her himself. He thinks he's uncovered something bigger than a murderer. . . ."

"Chugun himself . . . Well, that's not so bad. He's a blusterer, and Aril was trained to resist that approach."

"Perhaps. But they have patience, and more than Chugun—he has assistants, helpers, flunkies, henchmen."

"Evaluation?"

"Lost. These people are raised on a diet of conspiracy from birth, and they rule all of Oerlikon that matters, and as they see it they don't share that with anybody. Our cover here is fragile; eventually, they'll get something out of her."

"Now?"

"Not as of last contact, which was about . . . an hour ago, I think. They are not in a hurry, because they don't know what they have, so I would estimate at least a full day."

Anibal Glist turned away from Arunda Palude and stared blankly at the wall. Still facing it, he said, "We'll have to contact Transport, and arrange for our people to be picked up."

Palude said softly, "We have too many down here to make pickup without revealing ourselves; besides, it will take days . . . even if we could. What about Kham, in Clisp? I can't contact him until he calls me, and he's not scheduled to for a tenday. Besides . . ."

"Go on."

"We have no comm with Central. We're out of position for it: Oerlikon is on the wrong side of Gysa for the relay station. The only ship is the one that brought the last group in, the one Sheptun and Procand were on. They are well out of range now, without the Comus Relay."

"Then effectively, we are stranded. We should have comm back in twenty days . . ."

"In twenty days, if they are sharp, they could have all of us in The Mask Factory, and then we'd find out for sure what goes on in that place. So far all they have is one fellow whose papers don't check, and a girl who doesn't know much."

"She knows me; she knows you. She knows Foleo. Any one of the three of us . . ."

"I know, I know. All right. I give the order: Initiate the Pyramid Course, commence sanitization of mission. Have all the operatives vanish into the background—whatever they have to do. We all get this in Indoctrination as a possible course. . . ."

"But nobody ever thought it would come to this."

"True. But when you don't contact Central, on time, after Oerlikon comes back into contact position, they will know something's gone wrong, and so they will activate the alternate plan—contact through Tartary."

"When I first came here, I missed a contact; it was so hard to compute orbital years from this insane calendar they use here, that Mayan gibberish. And so I missed it, and when I finally did set up again, I was terrified because I knew the plan—that if there was no contact after a clearing, they would come get us."

"What happened?" Glist quite forgot to scold her for it.

"Nothing. They didn't seem to have noticed. As for now . . . it might occur to them after a time, because once we sanitize, we won't have comm with Central or anybody. But personally I don't think they will risk it; Oerlikon is a bit out of the way. So there's something final in this."

Glist continued looking at the wall. "Yes, I suppose so."

Palude went to the door, and paused, just before opening it. "I will initiate the pyramid, and sanitize, as you said. You had better leave here, as well. No point in making it easy for them. They'll come for you first, if Procand fails."

"Yes, of course. Where are you going?"

"Under sanitization, you are not to know."

"Yes, quite correct." Arunda opened the door, and Glist called to her as she was leaving, "What should I have done?"

She paused on the step, and said, "Everything was set with clear choices, of which you took the rational path. I may not criticize actions I would have done exactly the same way. You made the best choices—

indeed, the only choices. It's as if it were fixed: you didn't have Kham, you had something you couldn't evaluate, and Sheptun never fixed his papers. Then no comms. It has a flow. If we were vulnerable, it would be now. Something out there could see us, and he struck exactly where his blow would topple things—where and when. And with our mission gone, I can't say what will happen here. Save yourself."

And then she was gone. Glist started moving, slowly at first, but then faster, arranging things, picking up things, putting others down, things he wouldn't need anymore. He was ready to go in a remarkably short time, and about that, at least, he felt good. Clean, crisp. The tie severed. All these years of work: ended. And one last thought crossed his mind as he left his Spartan little apartment: that Palude had not said one single word that could have been thought of as anything personal. Nothing. The loss of the mission seemed something less by contrast.

He had thought he would go mad; stark, raving mad. It would have been, in its own way, a release, an escape. He hadn't. He also had thought he would die, that the vast dark night of death would be the end of it. That night never came. He forgot as much of it as he could, winning a victory over each microsecond as it came, and then meeting the next, which was usually worse, never better, or if the same, in a new place. Rael discovered new levels of pain, to an extent that he had left words far behind. His own body was undergoing self-initiated destructive distillation, catabolism, and yet through it all, there was something that watched, monitored, did not let go and did not take him to the breaking point. Up to it, within an angstrom of it—but not through it. His lungs erupted fluids, his bowels constricted spasmodically, violently, his stomach heaved; and also he wept, and his skin wept fluids, and then sloughed off in great, raw patches that felt like burns, and wept some more. His hair fell out early—first the body hair, then the pubic hair, and then the hair on his head. All went. But after that, through the changes, the head hair began to return, growing abnormally fast.

The night made transition into day, a sodden gray, overcast day, which he knew in some corner of his mind, but did not reflect on. In brief moments of lucidity he remained on the floor, waiting for the next attack, the next wave. That was all he knew. And the whole of the day passed that way: the gray light pressing at the windows.

But when the light had dimmed and the room was almost dark again, he noticed that it seemed that the stages of the attacks were not so strong, that they were shorter, and that they were coming further apart. During one of the quiet periods he actually caught himself thinking about moving, of trying to move his limbs again. And if he could move, he could perhaps begin to think about cleaning up the floor before they came for him. Rael had been lying on his side, in a compressed foetal position. He tried, experimentally, to straighten a bit. With great effort, he managed a little, and rolled over onto his stomach. It was painful, and it made him light-headed, but it worked. The only problem was that his body felt wrong, but he couldn't quite say exactly in what way it felt wrong. Just wrong. The muscles worked, he rolled on one hip, but it didn't feel right. He didn't think about it deeply, just then, because another attack started, and he concentrated on fighting pains that flickered over his body like summer lightning.

Later, there was a more lucid period, in which he felt much more confident, although very weak and very sick. He struggled for some moments, fighting a profound sense of strangeness which affected every move he made, however small, and at last attained a sitting position, legs sprawled. He managed enough coordination to look down at his body: he expected to see a riddled, tumorous, burned wreck.

It was not exactly that way. His feet were smaller, and not so angular as he remembered them. The legs were shorter, more rounded, and the skin was smooth and, under the filth, the color of pale cream. The knees were delicate, the thighs following the outlines of the rest, a smoother shape. He looked directly at his crotch. There was nothing there.

Rael looked again. Nothing? No, not quite nothing. There was a little fleshy sprig where his penis should have been, and below that, a fold still swollen, but obviously containing no testicles. His mind was dulled, insensitive; he saw, but it did not register. He looked more closely, down at his chest, his belly. There was no hair on his chest or belly, and in place of hard pectorals and small, non-functional nipples, there were soft swellings, and the nipples were much larger, darker. A wave of dizziness passed over him, and painfully he tried to walk. His legs felt rubbery, and the hips felt *wrong*, looser, more articulated, the muscles hard to control. But one step at a time, he managed it; he crawled into the bathroom, and climbed up, pulling on every available handhold, until he could look in the mirror.

Rael looked into the reflection, and he saw there a softer, younger face, with a small, delicate chin, a wide, blurred mouth, a sharper and larger nose, deep chocolate eyes whose whites were still swollen and red. It was the face of a stranger, and yet it was also a face he knew well enough to draw, although he was not especially skilled at drawing. The face belonged to Damistofia Azart. The next attack came then, but he could sink down to the cold floor slowly, and this time he slept a little, or fainted; he was not sure. She could not say.

Achilio Yaderny, Team Leader of Marula Squad Forty-Two, Bureau of Remandation, looked about the small and shabby room with a nagging sense of irritation and incompletion. Certainly this was the place where the murderer had to be: Rael. They had traced him to this building, and through the terrified night-man to this very room. There could be no mistake. And yet there was no Rael. Instead, there was a girl with no papers who was extremely ill, with God only knew what sort of disease. Give her credit: she had half cleaned the place up, but you could tell it had been rough.

And her story, what they could make of it, during the occasional lucid moments she had, would be impossible to check. She met him, and agreed to meet him here: he let her in and then left. She had been sick then, coming down with it, whatever it was. He hadn't come back. He'd taken her clothes, too. Small chance he'd use them as a disguise, because according to the description they had, this Rael was tall and gaunt, whereas this girl was small; and as wasted as she was, she looked even smaller. All probable, no doubt, and so there would be a report back to the prefecture, and there would be no end to it—a royal pain in the arse, up all day and all night, too, trying to figure out where the bastard got to.

Yaderny glanced at his men with a weary gesture, raising his eyebrows and glancing at the ceiling, and removed his communicator, inserting the earplug, and pressing the Headquarters Call button.

"Yaderny here.

"Yes, we are there. No suspect. We have a girl whom he picked up on the way, but she was sick when she met him here, and he left and took her clothes and papers.

"Yes, she still has something, although she says the worst of it has already been. No, she doesn't appear to know anything about him, or where he might have gone."

Yaderny rolled his eyes and made sputtering motions without sound before replying. "Yes, of course. Definitely. We will bring her in, but she should be put in the palliatory for observation until it can be determined if she's contagious or not—we don't want the whole city down with diarrhea—Marula's not that high above sea level.

"No. No trace whatsoever. He didn't leave anything here. No one saw him leave . . . but that doesn't mean much in itself. We will check the rest of the building, it's not large, but I'm sure we won't find him. This taking the room was a decoy operation, as obviously was the girl as well.

"Yes. Send a medical team to move her, she's not in walking condition."

There was a moment during which Yaderny listened intently to the communicator, and then, shaking his head, he replied, "Yes, we could, but as I said, I don't know what she has, and I don't know if we can move her without losing her. She's not much good to us, but she's no good at all dead.

"Fine, then. I'll wait. I'll personally watch her, and send the rest out in the building. We'll be in shortly. Out."

Yaderny kept his distance from the girl and looked at her. She was asleep now, or unconscious, at any rate. Sick as she was, he didn't think she looked like much. Pale, and very thin, with a metallic sheen to her skin that spoke of recurring high fever. Poor kid, someone who was looking for a little fun, and met up with a cold-blooded maniac who killed with a pin, and then vanished, leaving her. She was in a tight spot, no doubt about it. No papers, no clothes, sick, probably a stranger—yes, she said she wasn't from Marula. Came here to die. Well, probably not die. She was breathing evenly enough. He turned to his men and told them what more they would have to do while he waited for the medical team to come for the girl, and they nodded, not complaining, because their patience was endless, and they were thorough, and they obeyed. And they filed out of the room quietly.

Yaderny went to the window and looked out onto the street, where one of his outside men was waiting. That one looked up and saw Yaderny, and made a small sign, signaling that everything was quiet on the street that no one had come or gone. Good. At least they could depend on that for a fact.

After a time, Yaderny's men came back, silent and glum, shaking their heads. Yaderny did not rage and rant at them; it would do no good. No—they had looked, and they had found nothing. No trace. That meant that somehow Rael had slipped out of the building sometime between the time he had come here and the time when they had traced him to this place. That wasn't much and it meant that he'd still be in the city, unless he could make contact with someone who could smuggle him out.

Not likely, but still possible. But Yaderny was a long-time squad leader, he had instincts, and this one told him strongly that Rael had not left Marula. Indeed, he was sure that Rael was somewhere nearby, hiding, after leaving them the dummy trail to run to and cover up the real scent with their own tracks. Yes, he was certain: Rael was close by, probably within hearing of a speech-projector.

Yaderny shivered with anticipation at what the captain would·say— that it was all a lot of superstitious nonsense, that they had missed the assassin and that was that. But Yaderny would argue, and eventually he'd agree to send a team back to this neighborhood. But by then, dammit, it would be too late. That was what the bastard was waiting for. Now! They had him pinned down somewhere, somewhere close, damn close! So close he couldn't move until they left. And they'd told him to come back to headquarters! Yaderny took the communicator out again and put the earplug in once again, noticing as he did that the medical team was arriving to pick up the girl. Good. He keyed the Headquarters relay.

"Yes. Yaderny here. We didn't turn him up in the building, but I'm certain he's not left the neighborhood. We covered it too well.

"Yes, it's my instinct again, but I could tell you how many times that's been right, or nearly. . . .

"You say stay and do house-to-house? Thank you, sir. I will do it. Please seal this area off. . . . You already have? Good. I'll need some more troops, have them report to me directly, I'll turn the locator on so you can trace me. Good, and thank you again. Yaderny out."

By this time the medical team was at the door carrying a stretcher. Yaderny turned to them, pocketing his communicator. "This girl we believe to be associated with an assassin, and so she is under remandation." Yaderny produced an ID card which the medics acknowledged by nodding agreement. He continued, "She has no papers, also. She claims to bear the name Damistofia Azart. She has had some sort of attack, of what we don't know. She'll need quarantine, and isolation, and guard."

One of the medics said, "Your people, or the Palliatory staff?"

Yaderny thought a moment, and replied, "Yours, until we have something else on her. Right now, she is a low-grade suspect. Keep her confined. I think that whatever she had, the worst of it seems to have passed, but I'm no medical, I don't know what she has. Fever, vomiting, diarrhea. . . ." He made a gesture as of picking something loose out of his pocket and handing it to them, as if for their choice. "With those symptoms, it could be anything: Mercani's Ague, Bosel Fever, Chory-lopsis, Battarang, Vyrygnenia, Nasmork, Tifa. . . . I assume you can find out there."

They nodded, and the one who had spoken before said, "Hope it's not Tifa; but doesn't look like it. We'll keep her locked up good, never worry." And they went to the bed and took Damistofia from it, wrapping her up in the sheet she was already covered with, laying her on the stretcher carefully, almost tenderly. And they took her out without further ceremony. As they were taking her out, it seemed that she awakened for a moment and looked at Yaderny briefly, but it was an unfathomable expression, one Yaderny himself could assign no meaning to.

After that, he told his men what they were going to do, and they left the shabby little room in the rooming house and rejoined the men they had left outside, on the street. Soon they were met by the first of the new troops, and Yaderny threw them into the search immediately, with the elan and verve of one who knew that they would pick up the trail again, very soon. There was great excitement as they began, spreading out. Yaderny threw himself into the chase wholeheartedly, not content to let the underlings do all the work while he stood back and supervised.

In fact, he didn't slow down until they had gotten a couple of blocks away. They had just cleared a small commercial building, with unused warehousing facilities on the upper floors, and they had come out in the street to take a short break. Yaderny sat down on a curbstone, just pausing for a moment to think where to hit next, and then his instinct suddenly rose within him again, quite out of nowhere, for no special reason, but he knew. He *knew* that somehow Rael, the assassin, had escaped them, that their search would turn up nothing. It came to him with the utter certainty he had always known and employed when he could, with a general pattern of success. That was why he was a Squad Leader, not just one of the foot soldiers. *But he knew it.* Rael was gone. He sat still for a moment, thinking. They would continue, of course; foolish to recall the teams now that they were already working. But he already knew the outcome: their quarry had moved, and was now outside the area they had under control.

One of the team members, long accustomed to the moods and intuitions of the boss, noticed a change in Yaderny's general demeanor, and stepped close, to speak to him. "Something wrong?"

Yaderny said, "Yes. I think we've missed him. The trail's cold now."

"We haven't covered much, and that area back there is still sealed. He can't have gotten out of it."

"Yes. You're right . . . but I don't think it was like that, that he was there and we missed him, and when we left, he moved. No, nothing so simple. No. We moved a certain way, and our move made it clear for him. And you know what?"

"What's that, boss?"

"I think it's for good."

"But you felt sure back there; you thought . . ."

"I *was* sure. He *was* close. Damn close. Or somewhere we could have seen if we had only looked. But not now. No. Rael, whoever he was, is gone, and we'll not find any more trail."

The squad member reflected, "All's not lost: we have the girl, Azart."

Yaderny replied, without heat, "What do we have in her? Not much, I'll bet; oh, I'll have her checked, but not hard. You see, we already know she wasn't on the Beamer with Rael, or at least as far as we can determine. No we'll hear her story, and they'll probably give her some correction for losing her papers, but she doesn't know anything: she was part of the decoy setup he arranged. We would spend enough time with her, just enough a delay, for him to get in position, and then when we moved, then he'd move. I'm sure that's the way of it. Too bad. I'd like to get a handle on this one—there are a lot of problems with this case."

"Yes, so goes the rumor. And as far as the girl having no papers; that's not all that uncommon, either. There's quite a few of them wandering around, you know. . . . I'll bet she didn't figure on running into this, or us."

Yaderny added, "Or getting sick, either. Now under guard, in isolation, and under quarantine. Poor kid! But that's the way it works out: you never know what's going to crawl out from under a rock and bite your arse, do you?"

The squadman chuckled. "No, no."

Yaderny said, "Let's get on with it, for the sake of form; take your men and work that shop across the street. Take your time. We aren't going to catch him, or see any trace of him."

"You don't think we'll pick him up from another job, later on?"

"No. He's gone, that's all. Just vanished. I don't know how, but he did."

"What about the other guy, the one who Rael cooled on the beamer? The higher-ups going to work on that?"

Yaderny said, "I hear they are working on that with a will. In fact, it wouldn't surprise me to see them turn on that more than this; that's the sort of talk I've heard."

"Yes, me as well. But now . . . we'll go do it." And picking up his partner, the squadman walked across the street to search the place there. But Yaderny knew it was all over. Too late. And what bothered him was that he had been so certain they were close to him, once. *Close.*

For Damistofia, Time, once a string of crystalline beads, now mutated into an undifferentiated grayness, which displayed random and subtle variations that communicated no meaning to her whatsoever. She was taken somewhere, across Marula, so she thought, but it all looked the same to her. There was a place that was quieter, removed from the street noise, and there, things were done to her, which she did not resist; they were not especially gentle things, but she sensed there was no deliberate intent to cause pain, and the rough treatment seemed to help, after its own fashion. She slept. She was fed and washed and examined under the guidance of what passed for medical arts in Marula, in Lisagor.

There was a doctor who came and examined her, and talked with her some, and who eventually told her that her case had them baffled, that she had apparently contracted some factor which had caused her to, as he put it, "purge herself completely." And that, save from some drowsiness and temporary confusions, she was completely healthy, and would need only time to recover. That she was vague about her past they wrote off to amnesia, and after a few desultory attempts to penetrate it, they gave up, and recommended that upon discharge from the Marula Main Palliatory she be assigned to retraining and given some simple task to do, along with a suitable probationary period.

The police came and talked with her a few times, but as Yaderny's assistant had remarked, when everything was considered, the loss of papers wasn't the most serious event in the world of law enforcement, in fact, they did have much more pressing problems than an unidentifiable girl who had had a momentary association with a mysterious assassin. What these problems were, they did not say, and Damistofia did not ask, although a part of herself she kept under rigid control thought she knew. For a time, Yaderny seemed to show an interest in her, but more and more he delegated his work to assistants, progressively lower in the police chain of command, and at last, she was talking with either disinterested flunkies or confused students, neither of which profited by the experience. They pursued things as far as their priorities permitted them to, and then they quietly gave up on her and instructed the Identification Bureau to issue her new papers in the name she claimed to be her own, in the full form favored by the Bureau, Damistofia Leonelle Azart i Zharko, Resident, Marulupol, Sertse Solntsa, Lisagor.

They moved her from the largely empty violent ward to a more relaxed part of the Palliatory, still somewhat isolated, where she had a small cubicle of her own, and where she spent the days attending retraining, eating and sleeping, and exercising; they had insisted on the last, because of the condition she had been in.

Her appearance, at first curiously mutable, soon stabilized; after that she began to gain weight and take on an appearance of more health and normalcy: a slender young woman somewhere in her late twenties or perhaps early thirties, slight and graceful, with pale skin and dark hair and eyes. The face was oval, with large, slightly protuberant eyes, which lent her an intensity she did not, on acquaintance, seem to have.

Internally, she practiced on herself a self-willed amnesia almost as thorough as the one they thought she had; this was necessary to make a clean transition from Rael to Damistofia, because she soon discovered that thinking as Rael, which she tended to do without being aware of it, brought her into conflict with the realities of the body she inhabited: there were too many discrepancies. The weight and mass of Damistofia's slight body was distributed differently from that of the lanky but powerful Rael. Thinking as Rael, she wanted to swing her shoulders more, and walking was a problem because of the feel of the placement of the thighs and hips. Men walked spraddle-legged, compared to women, because their hip joints were closer together and they needed to leave space for the genitals. Women walked with their feet together, and did not need to counterbalance the heavy legs with motions of the upper body. This was something normal people learned unconsciously, or instinctively, but Damistofia had to practice it constantly until it became routine.

Another problem, which showed less but bothered her more, was sex, or more precisely, sense-of-sex. Rael had learned, whatever he had been before, to enjoy women, and sex. This sense of desire, part of the psyche, made the transition with Damistofia, but the realization of it was a constant difficulty. It was difficult for her to grasp, especially in the location of the impulse. She experimented a bit, to get the feel of it, touching herself, trying to imagine . . . It was like, and unlike. Desire was as strong, when she encouraged it, but curiously diffused, unspecific, unlocalized; more, it didn't drive her to assertive motion, even though she could recall that clearly enough; rather, it made her lethargic, with an odd undertone of tension that would often culminate in a headache. And she tried to reach back further, to Jedily, whoever she had been, but there was simply nothing there. Whatever they had done to the original subject at The Mask Factory, their work had been complete: Rael could not remember Jedily, and now Jedily was even farther away. Damistofia knew, fatalistically, that whatever sexual orientation she settled on, she would have to do it on her own.

In the wing where she was assigned, there were others about, men and women, girls and boys, patients and employees, and those she watched closely, trying to build an identity by using the hints of their reactions to her; equally importantly, she worked at erasing old patterns which were Rael's habits, and learning new ones, but that was also hard.

But, little by little, it began to form. She thought that she would carry it as far as she could in this place, and then, outside, on her own, develop it fully. Because she knew that to vanish completely into the anonymity of the population, she would have to become what she seemed to be; she did not wish to be singled out for any deviation, however insignificant. For she knew very well that the machinery that was Lisagor might be inattentive from time to time, but it could be roused into full alertness very quickly. Rael's odd science: she still had that, and his martial and survival skills, but she hoped that she would not have to use them. She wanted most of all to be left alone, and vanish.

And she wanted to forget what Rael's price had been, what he had had to do, that he could see from the beginning. She felt shame and regret, even though she still knew completely that Rael's target had been the right one, the pivot point, at that moment. It helped her to feel a guilt about a cold, calculated murder of an attractive young man, and not as the breaking of a connection holding Lisagor together through the imposition of a third force she had not bothered to trace out, although this lay within the limits of the science Rael had devised.

News from the outside world was particularly difficult to get, which suggested that her wing was a sort of mental ward; they kept it that way on purpose. Reasonable enough, considering that most of the patients there would have been retreating from the outside reality anyway, and being led back to it was a subtle, gentle task, at which they took their own time.

Nevertheless, there were hints that something wasn't quite right outside. Often, and then more often, she would surprise the normally reserved orderlies, engaged in heated discussion, not the less energetic for being conducted in whispers, which would stop as soon as they caught sight of her. She tried to read it, but the data was too thin for her to build an image: Rael's science built answers like holograms, reconstructing virtual images from the interference of wave fronts. But unlike a hologram, there was a lower threshold limit for assembly, and what she was receiving in the Palliatory was below that limit. Still, it teased her because it seemed to have a particularly dire import for those who talked about it so earnestly. Whatever it was, it seemed to mean some kind of trouble, outside, and it wasn't getting any better.

It was about this time that they changed her routine, and put her on outside work, in the landscaped gardens surrounding the Marula Main Palliatory. That was a pleasant change, although it was growing somewhat chill and damp early in the mornings, and in the late afternoons.

One day, under a high, silvery overcast, she had been working with a small group, finishing a planting set in an odd and random grouping of cast concrete pipes and pipe-junctions. The larger plants had already been set in, and the tubs filled with soil by a detachment from the local labor pool, so that now all that remained was the planting of ornamental creepers and small accent plants, mostly evergreens. Damistofia enjoyed the activity, and being outside; she felt almost normal, although most of her associates seemed to be a dispirited group, with minimal motivation.

Some she knew by sight; others, not at all. But as she worked, she also watched the others, trying to imagine what circumstances might have brought them here, and what their ultimate fate might be. It saddened her to comprehend that most of those working on the planting didn't have much of a future: they were withdrawn, passive and resigned to their lot, which was to remain here, doing odd jobs, until some use was found for them, either in the labor pools for the most stultifying jobs, or else material for The Mask Factory, where they would be purged and made faceless servants of the Alloyed Land. That reflection motivated her a bit more, and so she worked more diligently.

By afternoon, the others on the crew had become familiar to her, so that she knew them as separate personalities, even though she was not interested in them. But one, an older man, she worried about. This one retained some traces of a former high position, but he was the most severely withdrawn of all of them, often talking to himself inaudibly. None of the others seemed to pay any attention to him, and his contribution to the planting seemed to be minimal. When she asked about him, she was told by the more communicative that they knew nothing about him, save that he'd been picked up after a disturbance near the docks, dazed, wandering in the streets, mumbling all things about getting to Tartary, and raving about his agents. They said that he claimed to be the leader of a group of spies, representing vast powers from the Void, but he couldn't explain how his position had led him to be picked up and unceremoniously assigned to the Marula Palliatory, Deranged Section. They ignored him.

It was customary to have a midday rest in Marula, and the custom was allowed for the inmates as well, and so, after lunch, they all spread out a little to find sunny spots beside walls or large ornamental rocks, to stretch out, and perhaps to nap a bit under the eyes of the distant supervisors. Damistofia saw something different about this one man, something she needed to do; he was clearly not on a course that would encourage survival. And so after she had eaten the buns they had brought out for lunch, she found the older man, and sat down beside him. She didn't know exactly what she wanted to do, but she thought if perhaps someone paid a little attention to him, he would come back to himself.

He paid little attention to her when she sat down, still mumbling disjointedly, and gazing longingly at the low wall that separated the park from the streets of Marula, a wall that might as well have been as high as the sky, as far as getting over it successfully went. She tried to talk to him, but he didn't respond, so she let him go along as he would, and gradually he seemed to notice her and turn his remarks more toward her.

". . . the only hope was to get to Tartary, but that's gone, now, too . . . all gone . . . everything . . ." he said. And, ". . . The fools, they are overreacting, just as we knew they would, and it's going critical now, feeding on itself, injustice and revenge upon injustice and revenge . . . I tell you, I know these things, once the people get revenge in their heads, nothing but the deaths of millions will get it out. . . . We could stop it, the fools, they won't listen. . . ."

Damistofia said, softly intruding, "Stop what?"

The man glanced at her with the hunted expression of an animal at bay, and then said, "Listen; this is a world whose people undertook an impossible task—they set their task to totally stop change, evolution of society. They failed, of course—for nothing will stay the same, but they slowed it! They slowed it to a negligible amount! Now all that pressure has been building up for generations. . . ."

Damistofia thought she had his attention now, and so she prodded him a little: "I know, I'm from these parts myself. We don't change; that's the way we made this world when we came here. Every child in the schools knows that. Why does it fail now?"

"They had help! That's what. Help. For a long time. Some people from far away came here to see if it worked, and it was close, but not enough, and so they helped a little, influencing here, pressing there, dampening this influence out here. And then the worst possible combination of chance happened, and we were cut out as neatly as by a scalpel, and now human nature takes its course."

"Why don't you tell the higher-ups? Surely they don't want change."

The man shook his head. "Only worked as long as we were unseen. When we intervene openly, it changes the balance, and we ourselves became part of the process of change."

She looked curiously at the man now. And she remembered, as Rael, sitting in a cell poring over odd equations that identified a third source of power on Oerlikon, in Lisagor, a hidden, concealed power. And here it was, right in front of her, somehow scooped up off the street and lodged in the Deranged section. She asked, "Why would these people want to help us achieve our goal of changelessness? What could it be to them? If they wanted to live like we do, why couldn't they just come and *be* us. I know no one's done it for a long time, but the immigration laws are still open . . ."

He said, after some thought, "I'm not sure I could explain that; these people, you see, they didn't really want to live here. This is in many ways a primitive little world. It was . . . we developed an interest here, for ourselves. As long as Lisagor stayed changeless, then we who were in the project had something. And if it changed, then we no longer had a place. . . ." He stopped, and lowered his face to his hands, and after a bit, mumbled, "I've told you too much, and besides, you don't believe me any more than they did in there."

Damistofia said softly, "If I did believe, what could I do about it."

"Nothing, nothing. It's too late for us, that's all. Too late! Nothing can salvage the mission here: that's gone forever." He looked at her craftily. "You could help me escape."

She shook her head. "I've been unable to escape myself."

The man looked away, now, and seemed to withdraw internally from her, although he still continued to talk. "Well, so much for that; but it just drives me almost crazy to think that some crazed assassin came out of the darkness and struck in just precisely such a way that it sliced us out of it, and now they're calling him a hero."

Damistofia became suddenly very alert. She said, cautiously, "I heard there was a murder, that they were hunting for an unknown assassin. But is this the same person?"

"That's right. You wouldn't have heard so much in here, if you've been here a bit. No, at first they hunted him, but now they call him a great hero, and they seek him out, to honor him. That's a laugh; when he struck, he pulled more than one world down! They grabbed a couple of our weakest links and they talked enough to get a purge started. We had started withdrawing, of course, knowing what would come, but some were still in place when Chugun's men came for them."

"Who were you?"

"Here, on this world, I was Anibal Glist, and I was the head of the Oerlikon Project."

"It is dangerous that you tell me this—I could identify you. Surely they are looking for you."

He shook his head again. "They don't seem to care about us, now. I have hidden, to be sure, but you? You are in as much trouble as I am; why I don't know, but you are here and that's enough for me. And they have much more dire things to worry about besides defunct spy organizations: Clisp is seething with secessionists, Marula is crawling like a maggot pile, daily the ideologues of the inland provinces call for more ruthless measures of expostulation. No, they don't really want me now. They have their hands full."

She said, "You can get out, eventually, if you do what they want you to; and they'll find a place for you. That is what they are doing for me— I think I'll be out soon."

"You don't believe me. . . ."

"No, that doesn't matter, that I believe or not. You've fallen, wherever you came from, into a different trap, and now you have to get out of it and live on."

Glist shook his head and looked away. Clearly, the choices before him were almost too much to bear.

Damistofia discreetly excused herself, seeing that Glist didn't notice her leaving, and went back to the group at the planter. Outwardly, she was quiet, just as she had been all along since she had found herself in this place, but inside, her mind was working furiously. Rael now called a hero of the people! What a blow: to have gone through so much to escape detection, and now this one says they are calling the unknown assassin a hero. Who would have thought it? But she remembered that in Rael's analysis of the timing and necessity of the act of waiting for honors. One could get killed waiting for honor, and neither Rael nor Damistofia wanted honors when they came posthumously.

But in the way that things would influence her, she passed that information up. It didn't matter to her; she was already on the safe course plotted long ago, and she had survived so far. What did interest her was the confirmation of the third force operating in Lisagor, unseen, unknown, generally on the side of those who wanted no change whatsoever. And that it was now inoperative, allowing nature to take its course, whatever that would be. Confirmation! And Rael had been guessing, or hardly more than that. That she could remember: one could feel the third unknown there, but couldn't identify it, without an exhaustive search. It had been vague, subtle, weak . . . but enough to tip the balance, and allow such monstrosities as The Mask Factory to exist. And, she added, for their cruel work to produce one such as herself.

And *something* was working out there: either Glist was a hopeless basket case, or else it was true—Lisagor was coming apart, unraveling from the weakest points: Clisp and the Serpentine, vast Marula, and the ravings of the intolerant Inlanders. What else, which he couldn't see, or catch rumor of? And that led straight to the next conclusion, flowing like smooth water—she had to get herself released from the Palliatory and out of Marula. Soon. A vast, massive organism was shifting its weight to another center, and she wanted very much to be as much out of the way as possible. If possible.

8

Marula Nights

THE DAY'S RATION of work was over and Damistofia was walking back to her building alone. The silvery half-overcast had slowly evolved to a dense bluish overcast that promised rain; there was a scent of brackish water from the invisible estuary, a sea-wind, mixed with the odors of the city, the usual ones, too many people, dusty streets, odd chemical odors, and—something else, a faint sour reek she seemed to know but couldn't quite identify. A smoky odor that seemed to alarm her without her knowing why. Deep in her own thoughts, and pondering the odd odor, she failed to notice that someone was moving along the same walk, from behind her, and catching up, until he was quite close. When she turned to see who it was, he raised his right hand, as if in greeting, and so she stopped.

She had seen this one before, but never close. He was a young man of the Palliatory, judging by his clothing, which was the pale off-white of the staff. She didn't know his name, but she had noticed him; slender and muscular, he was quick and nervous, but also very precise, qualities that suggested an alert, predatory nature. His face was oddly delicate for a young man, almost girlish, very finely shaped, and he affected an odd sort of mustache that seemed to grow only at the corners of his mouth. He also wore spectacles, very large ones which seemed to magnify his eyes, which were a pale gray color.

He said, "I wanted to talk with you before you retired for the night."

"I've seen you, but I don't know you."

He gestured at himself. "Sorry. Cliofino Orlioz, Exercisist and Disciplinarian. I haven't worked with your group, either, but I have been observing you—part of the job, you see; we always keep an eye out for indications in our guests that indicate something exceptional."

She thought: He'll be one who watches for those who think they can fool the system.

He paused and went on, "Not what you may think. My job is to watch for those we can release . . . or perhaps use here. There is need of experienced people."

Damistofia laughed a little. "That's good! You will use recent loonies to help the real ones back to their feet after they've fallen."

Cliofino smiled, "And why not? Who better knows the condition? And who would wish to be more successful? All such a person needs is some proper training, and they find a rewarding position here. It is better, it need not be said, than going through the Placement Bureau and getting the luck of the draw. . . . But I diverge; I race ahead, I pass the real point: they watched you working with that old fellow this afternoon, and they noted how he responded to you, something we've not been able to do. He actually responded. They've not been able to get him to do that since he's been here. And so the suggestion is that you might be worth considering. . . . What would you say to that?"

"You're not serious."

"Oh, yes—indeed I am so."

"I know nothing of such matters . . . I acted by instinct, if you will; no one seemed to care for that man, who has the most remarkable delusion. . . ."

"We know his delusion; thinks he's an offworlder, in charge of some great windy plot. No matter. Forget about him. There are others who need Reality Orientation much more."

"How can you be sure I would do it well? After all, you might very well assign me to someone I would hate, or feel nothing for, or someone I might abuse."

"You'd be surprised how many in a place like this abuse them all with great random abandon; if you only abused every other one, you'd be an improvement over some we have on the staff!"

Again she laughed. "Come on! I've been treated well enough."

Cliofino grew more somber, which caused his odd mustache to droop comically. He said, after a moment, "Actually, that's for other reasons; your illness still hasn't been identified, nor have you, but in the absence of positive indications of anything, they are not looking closely at that. We don't know what happened to you . . ."

". . . Neither do I."

"Just so. At any event, you do not appear to be demented, but a victim of someone else's plot. The theory is now that you were drugged."

She said, "I have no recollection of what happened. I remember only some of it. . . . The earliest thing I can recall is that they took me from a room and brought me here."

Cliofino continued, "The police have lost interest in your case, although it is not closed. You understand that they have, shall we say, higher priorities now. So we can do this; actually easier than releasing you to general assignment or the labor pool."

Her mind raced, as she looked away, trying to hide the hope and the anticipation. Was this the way out? She said, she hoped with the proper shyness, "I don't know, now. This is sudden."

"Of course. That much I well comprehend. But you will consider it?"

"Yes."

"Good. Exemplary! I've taken the liberty of having myself assigned to work with you, so we'll have more contact, and we can discuss this more. And in the meantime, I can work with you on some exercises; they say you aren't completely well yet."

"Well, no . . . I tire easily yet, it seems. I don't know why."

"Lack of the proper exercises, lack of motivation. It's all easy enough. We could start tonight, if you're so minded. . . ."

Behind the easy words and the logical progression, Damistofia sensed a subtle pressure; nothing definite, but a pressure she couldn't recall feeling as Rael. Was he attempting to seduce her? She didn't have enough experience so that she could remember to tell if that was what he was after. She decided to be cautious, and said, "Tonight? Let me think on it. I am tired after today. Could we not work it in the regular exercise period?"

A momentary flash of annoyance flickered in his eyes, but he replied, pleasantly enough, "I'm still working those details out, shifting assignments, and that sort of thing. I do have others to work with I can't just let go."

She said, "I understand. Well, tomorrow I have no work assignment, and so I could do it after the regular day."

"Very good! We'll do it that way, then. I'll come after regular hours."

"You won't be getting into any trouble, will you?"

"Oh, no. And you won't, either. Just a little overtime."

"I want to ask you something . . ."

"Yes. Ask on."

"What is that peculiar burnt smell in the air?"

He looked off into the distant sky, and then said, "Burnt housing. And now is not the time to talk about that."

"You know about it?"

"Yes. Tomorrow. This is not the place."

"All right, then. Tomorrow. . . . And what do I call you?"

"Say nothing to your usual people; they would be offended. But Cliofino, if you're so minded."

She smiled at the informality, and reminded herself to watch him more closely, to see what he looked at. She said, "Good enough; and so I will be Damistofia, as opposed to Patient Azart. And so good evening."

Cliofino nodded politely and turned back to the way he had come. And Damistofia set out again for her own building in the dusk, now with a fine mistiness in the air that said, beyond a doubt, that the rain was here.

And later, after supper and a bath, she lay in her little cubicle in the dark and listened to the rainwater running and gurgling in the downspouts and guttering, lying awake for a long time, trying to understand the significance of what had happened to her today; she sensed hidden motivation behind Cliofino's words, which were reasonable enough, in themselves. And what if he wanted to seduce her? At first consideration the idea seemed odd and a little perverse, but she understood that as arising from her thinking as Rael. And she wasn't Rael anymore, was she? She ran her hands over her body under the covers. No, most certainly she wasn't Rael. And she caught herself thinking, *This wasn't quite the way I planned it, but after all, why not. I will have to learn to live completely in this disguise, which is permanent.* And, thinking about it some more, she concluded that Cliofino wasn't unattractive at all, and that if he could be used to get her out of here, it might be well worth the trouble of adjusting to the new experience. And on that note she slept.

The day opened gray and drizzly, with a damp chill in the air that seemed to soak in and make itself at home; an intimation of the winter of this southerly but not tropical city. Nothing definitely cold; just chilly and unpleasant. Damistofia went through her routines of the day absentmindedly, trying to keep warm in the drafty halls and rooms. In her free time, it was no better—her own wing was no less chilly than the rest of the place.

Toward afternoon, she caught a whiff in the air of the same odor of burnt rags she had smelled the day before, but when she tried to see out the window to see where it might be coming from, she saw little or nothing she could identify. There was a plain, unadorned brick wall around the Marula Palliatory which shut out almost all the view of the world outside, except the tops of the taller buildings and some industrial chimneys. Certainly nothing nearby seemed to be burning.

And later, while that was still in her mind, late in the afternoon, actually in the early evening, she heard in the distance some very odd sounds; there was a mechanical droning, as of a large number of engines, which grew out of nothing, but didn't seem very close. The noise level stayed about the same for a time, and then faded, followed by another set of sounds that seemed to alarm her without her knowing why—a noise as of a large crowd of people in confusion, but it, too, was distant, and faded away. The droning came back for a short time, and faded away entirely. And with the dark, there came on the night air another odor of burning, this mixed with a sharp, sweetish chemical odor—something inflammable. The attendants put the more excitable to bed early.

No one seemed to bother with her, and so she wandered after supper to the dayroom, where there were a few late-stayers and persons as bored and apprehensive as she was, reading magazines and playing cards and dominoes to pass the time. Here, she settled in a corner under a dim lamp with a travel brochure about the Pilontary Islands, a place far to the southeast that she could reasonably hope never to see.

Damistofia felt the attention of someone watching her closely, staring; she looked up, and saw Cliofino across the room. When she looked up, she saw that he looked away, as if he did not want her to know he had been watching her. He was just a shade too slow. And just a shade too practiced on acting as if he had just seen her; but again, with him, she felt a confusion on trying to interpret his intentions. For a second, she felt like Rael, and felt like screaming, "Dammit, I can't make the assumptions women do because I don't know how to be one yet! And so what's this Cliofino's game? Why is he so interested in me? It can't be ravishing beauty—I'm ordinary and plain at best—as a fact, I wouldn't give me a second look." The frustration passed, and she nodded to him, that she'd seen him, and he came across the room to her.

She saw that he was dressed differently from his workday uniform; he wore dark clothing, dull and plain, except on one shoulder there was the emblematic figure of a dragon worked into the material in a low-contrast pattern of some different material. Again, she felt as if she were groping in the dark; the emblem was obviously intended to symbolize something, but it meant nothing to her at all. He was also damp, and there were rain sparkles on his clothing and hair—he had been outside, somewhere.

He said, "I signed out the gym for a while, if you'd like."

Damistofia put the brochure back in its rack and stood up. "Yes. I could stand some motion, some movement. I need activity, some kind of challenge."

He nodded agreeably and said, "That's right! Most of the duds are content with the routine, and they stay that way! But I thought it would be a good idea for us to go there, and have you work out a little; I want to see how dexterous you are, and check your reflexes, before we get too far into this. You might conceivably need to work on your general body tone before we can go on."

"I hardly need an examination to tell that; I already know it."

He looked closely at her. "But you don't remember what you were before . . . ?"

"No. But I'm not in the shape I could be in . . . and I'd like to have my figure back, at least, for what life I've got left to live."

He looked at her again, with an odd, guarded intensity that Damistofia found disconcerting. "There's nothing in general wrong with the figure you have now—nothing at all."

"You couldn't prove that by me, or my mirror, as I see it, but if you say so, that gives me some hope all was not lost. Well! Lead on."

Without further word, Cliofino turned and led the way out of the dayroom into the dim hallways and set out for the Gymnasium, which was located some distance away in another building. They traversed long corridors, now mostly untenanted, and then outside, for the most part passing under covered walkways from whose eaves the rainwater dripped into puddles. Only once they had to pass from one covered walk to another, and Damistofia felt the rain on her face, and in the air there were still traces of the smoke she had smelled.

She asked casually, "What's burning?"

Cliofino looked at her sharply, and waited a moment before replying. Then he said, "Settlement areas, squattertowns. There had been some trouble, and they've had a couple of pallet drops."

Damistofia shook her head, not understanding what he was referring to. "Please. Say again. I don't understand."

He reiterated patiently, as if recalling that he was talking to a woman who had lost a large part of her knowledge of how things were, "One thing led to another, and there was a riot among the people of some habitats. They restored order by landing several platoons of Pallet-Dropped Heavy Troopers on them."

Damistofia walked on for a minute, and then said, "And what do they do?"

"They hit the ground shooting; they are a force whose sole mission is to terrify and subdue. They carry sawed-off shotguns, flamethrowers, grenade launchers, and chainsaws, which they use as swords. Rumor has it they are recruited in a place called 'The Mask Factory' where they have parts of their minds removed to make them amenable to heinous orders, and then given glandular injections to bring their mass up. In this series of actions, of course they were successful and things have quieted down, but it is uneasy. They have gone too far, of course, and who can tell if the measures will work. It seems that people no longer restrain themselves."

He was clearly disturbed by the events, as he told them. Something of this showed in his voice. Damistofia said, "You say this as one who does not approve."

"Who could?" he asked passionately. "Many were killed, two habitats completely leveled, a third damaged so badly it will have to be pulled down and rebuilt. I mean, everyone knew that there was such a corps as the Pallet-Dropped Heavy Troopers, but they were never actually used against the people."

Damistofia said, "If one has a weapon. I would guess time comes to use it."

"Mind, we present-day people don't know if they ever did. They say they loosed them before, but all we saw was the parades in the streets. That was enough. Now they have used them in actuality; and they destroy everything. . . ."

"I do not remember what my feelings were before this, and I have not been allowed outside, so I cannot approve or condemn on the face of it; still, it would seem to be excessive. What brought that on?"

Cliofino said, "There are disturbances everywhere now, and they feel they cannot be slack with Changemongers, and so they strike at will—here, there. I know that long ago our ancestors came to Oerlikon to escape the relentless pressure of Change, but their desires built a system that cannot respond, and so resentment and pressure build up. There is no feeling of compromise, of finding the way that will work. The people say, 'we need,' and they say, 'no.' And when they gather to demonstrate, then come the troops. This is happening all over."

They had arrived at the gym door and now stopped before it. Damistofia said, "And what is your place in this? Or am I asking too much on so short an acquaintance?"

Cliofino opened the door for her, and said, "Something has gone wrong, and we must right it, to maintain the vision of old, that we came to this planet for."

Damistofia nodded, not speaking, and stepped into the darkness, which Cliofino banished by turning the lights on. He looked around, and then said, "And now we must work. How do you feel?"

"Good enough, I suppose; a little restless. . . . What do you want me to do?"

"I will show you—mostly some simple tumbling, and some light defensive methods I will show you. I will be judging your reflexes, your speed in learning."

She said, "I see. This is a test. I will see more if I pass. And if I do not?"

He said, in a low voice deliberately restrained, "That you ask that is your admission to continue."

They located some loose floor mats and put them together, and then Cliofino led Damistofia through a series of motions and short exercise routines that seemed ridiculously easy at first, something like dancing, but steadily grew more difficult. Still, she took on the activity and did as well as she could; she needed to capture the dynamic feel of her body, and this was an excellent opportunity. And moving, exerting a little, told her things more quiet routines had suggested—that she was now very different from Rael. Her center of gravity was lower, and she was more supple, once she ironed the kinks of inactivity out. And putting all of herself into the exercise helped her feel more at home in her body, and it began to feel more right, more herself, less an intrusion. And as this feeling of lightness increased, she found herself becoming more aware of Cliofino, who moved with her easily and with complete confidence. Their close proximity, moving together, brought forth responses from her body itself, and less and less she found them strange and frightening. And doing so, she found that it lessened some internal tension and made things easier.

Cliofino showed and demonstrated a couple of easy defensive techniques, and then stopped. He was breathing hard. He said, "Enough for now, I think. This will stretch muscles you haven't used. To the showers! Hot water, and then cold."

She sat on the floor and sprawled out awkwardly. "I am already stretched. Tomorrow I will be sore. And I must tell you that my clothes are all sweaty and I shouldn't want to wash and then put them back on to walk back."

"A good idea, that. Well—we can do it that way."

"I to my room, and you to yours. Where do you stay?"

"I have several places. I move around a lot. I would like to come with you, if I may ask."

She smiled at him archly. "You see me at my worst, which is not how I might have it."

He said, "There isn't anything wrong with your looks. You are fine. Act with confidence."

"Is this also part of the testing?"

Now he smiled. "No. For now, you pass." And he extended his hand and helped her to her feet. They put the floor mats back where they had found them, and turned out the lights. In the dark, illuminated only by the night-glow coming from the doors. Cliofino took her hand, and with an odd excitement she did not suppress, she did not turn it loose. And on the way back to the dormitory, she did not turn it loose, either, although they said nothing and he attempted nothing more.

The night air felt cooler now, almost chilly, as they walked along. Damistofia thought many things to herself; in one set of arguments, she sensed a powerful current of danger associated with Cliofino, an out-of-place-ness that bothered the old Rael instincts profoundly. Still she could not work these things out in her head. She would have to write things down, ensymbolize, compute, to determine the answers she needed. The likely computation was that he was a spy of some sort— but for what side? On the other hand, she felt this whole encounter as another test of sorts, one she was conducting on herself.

She asked, "Now, what about the more that's assumed to be? Who are you?"

"A simple worker here, who has associates who believe that we can set things on the correct path . . . someone who has need of a trusty and agile friend. I would not say much more yet; but on that, would you want to leave, to get out before we go deeper?"

Damistofia breathed deeply, and then said, "No, I would like to see more. They have given me little enough here, that I would rely on it alone. That's just it; they don't seem to care very much what happens to me."

"Exactly. You cause them no problems, and the police are no longer interested. They have much more alarming cases to worry about, and so you languish. If it turns out that we will be able to work together, then I believe that I can get you out of here. And I think you should consider getting out of Marula; this is becoming a hazardous place to reside, what with the troubles, and the responses."

"Where could I go?"

"Lisagor is large, and it's not the whole world."

"But Clisp . . . say. That would be worse, I'd think. They will be bearing down hard in places like that."

"I will tell you a secret. The trouble came to Clisp first, and although there are still incidents there, they have written it off. They have trouble here they can't ignore. Don't worry about where, just yet. That can be arranged. What I want you to think of is wanting to leave here."

"And what of my old life? Perhaps someone waits for me to return."

Cliofino said, "They found you with Rael the assassin. There were no reports of missing young women. Therefore the assumption is held that however you came to be there, you came on your own. No one has come searching for you. Whatever your old life was, you seem to have left it behind voluntarily, and if there were others, they let you go. I would say not to worry about the past, but act as you see the best path."

She nodded. "There seems to be no future here."

"Exactly. I can help, if you allow it."

They reached the dormitory building and slipped inside. There was no one about, and they passed through the halls without sound. When they reached Damistofia's room, and went in, she said, "It's late and no one is up. All are fast asleep."

"Leave the lights off. We don't want to attract attention."

"How will we see?"

"You know your way around. There's some glow from outside, the city lights in the clouds. We'll manage." Wordlessly, with her heart pounding, she went through the dark to the bath and set the shower running. After a time, she said, "At least the hot water is on tonight."

"Is it ready?"

"Yes."

"Can we do it together?"

"Yes . . . if you promise to scrub my back."

"I promise." Then he started pulling his clothes off and hanging them on a peg on the back of the door. After a moment, Damistofia did the same, saying softly, "I feel awkward; I haven't done this for a long time . . . I can't remember it."

He said, "Don't worry. Do you want to go on?"

"Yes."

"Then don't look back." Then he took her hand again and helped her into the running water.

In the hot water of the shower, in the dark, they spent the first moments washing, scrubbing, washing the sweat and fatigue away, and it was only after they were rinsing the soap off that he touched her, and brushed her face lightly with his mouth, and kissed her. It was odd only for an instant, and then it felt right, and she did what her instincts told her to.

They finished rinsing, and now shyly stepped out of the bath, where they dried each other off. He touched her, and she felt his bare nakedness against her. Cliofino led her back to the small bedroom, turned down the sheets, and gently laid her down on her stomach, kneeling over her and firmly but deftly massaging her back and shoulders. She felt hard, hairy knees gripping her hips, the pressure of his hands, and she let herself go to the feeling, and when at last she could stand it no longer, and rolled over to face him and hold him, it felt perfectly right and good and she enclosed him within herself and held him tightly to her until it was the best, and that went away slowly; and before they parted and slid beside one another to sleep, she felt indeed as if she had passed a test she had set for herself, and there was a real sense of accomplishment in that. Rael faded a great deal. And Damistofia stretched, and felt warm inside, and said to herself that she liked what she had become, that at least in this there was nothing to fear. She could do it.

Luto Pternam no longer spent the evening hours lounging on his terrace, looking over the soft outlines of Symbarupol, but instead worked long hours into the night, trying to keep up with the demands put on his organization. Not only him, but Avaria as well was pressed and they seldom saw each other save in passing.

The situation was essentially simple: for cycle upon cycle, the specialized product of The Mask Factory had been paraded, displayed, threatened with use, but actually used seldom. Now they were in constant use, somewhere in Lisagor, and their use required replacements. The Pallet-Dropped Heavy Troopers, lobotomized goon squads in uniforms, were dropped into action on cargo pallets with only drogue parachutes to slow their descent down a little, and from landing alone they could expect as much as a ten percent casualty rate, never mind the numbers that fell in their suicidal disregard for their own lives. In recognition of this terrible decimation, survivors of five operations were awarded a golden bolt to wear in their free hand; those few who survived ten got a gold bolt in their heads, all installed with all due surgical nicety.

Lisagor was crawling with incidents, and no area seemed to be free of them. The Innerlands and Crule The Swale were the quietest; Clisp, the

Serpentine, and Sertse Solntsa the worst. And so Pternam had little time
to wonder about revolutionaries, save to note that they seemed to be
having great successes, which caused him to have dark thoughts indeed
about the wisdom of the plan he had concocted. The operatives he had
sent off to Marula had either been swallowed up in the chaos reigning
there, or reported back with negative results; they were unable to get
near the place where Rael-Damistofia had gone to earth.

But late one night, when Pternam and Avaria were pausing in one of
their rare occasions of camaraderie, they were interrupted by a signal
from the door, which Avaria went to investigate. Shortly he returned
with two individuals, to Pternam's surprise, one the redoubtable Porfirio
Charodei, accompanied by a heavily built individual with beetling black
hair and enormous hands whom he knew to be the equally fearsome
Mostro Ahaltsykh.

Ahaltsykh took up a position at the door to the study they met in,
and Charodei joined Pternam by the occasional table. Avaria waited a
respectable moment, and then joined Ahaltsykh by the door, saying
nothing.

Charodei started out, waving aside the usual pleasantries. "I have
come on an errand which may sound like nonsense to you, but none the
less it must be done: if there is any help your organization can give us,
we would be most desirous of having it."

Pternam said, "If you mean that we should contribute to the revolution, it hardly seems necessary—your people are enjoying a singular success. The fact is, word is now from the Council of Syndics that they
expect to wind up from this brawling with considerably less Lisagor
than they started with. And losing it all is not out of the realm of possibility, either. We are examining several escape options along those lines
already."

Charodei reasserted, "To the contrary. This 'brawling,' as you call it, is
not of our doing. It is apparently spontaneous, and uncontrolled. In the
few cases where our people have been able to foment a rising, they can't
control it and lose it. In other cases, we have been able to take advantage of a situation, but it seems that we lose control of those as well. No.
The Heraclitan Society is far behind things. We know you loosed that
Rael among us, but we had no idea it would lead to this. We have
thought that perhaps you had something like him left over, that we
could use as an antidote, or some leavening agent."

"Not so. We tried to stop him, after release, when we realized he was
more powerful than we had originally imagined." Pternam choked on

the lie, but after he said it, it went a little smoother. "We sent operatives to detain him, but they were too late. We also sent assassins to catch up with the remnant, the woman Azart, but they also have failed to date. At any rate, what we had here in reserve did not work out, and we have been hard-pressed since."

"We also put a man on Azart. The best. And according to reports, he's got contact."

Pternam sat up stiffly. "Contact? What is he waiting for? My permission? Kill the insect immediately!"

Charodei held up a hand. "A moment, if you will. He had to be sure before he acted, and to date he's not completely convinced. After all, Azart is still in detention, under surveillance by the police. To be sure, it's light but nonetheless there is considerable risk to our man, and we told him not to move unless he's sure, because if he strikes down the wrong woman, there's a good chance he'll be caught, and we don't want him risked on a nobody."

"What does he report?"

"He has contact with a woman who meets the general specifications; there are some minor discrepancies, but none major."

"I still ask: what is he waiting for?"

"Orlioz reports that the woman Azart responds as a woman in all pertinent matters, but that her reflexes are abnormally fast. He tested her under the pretext of physical therapy. In short, he doesn't know if he can. He has arranged a sexual liaison with her at the moment, but he claims that she's quick enough still that if she divined his purpose, she could probably defend herself well enough to endanger him. He has asked for clarification instructions."

Pternam shook his head. "This is your best? No wonder you needed Rael-Damistofia. You send an assassin in there, he gets a little sugar, and now he's got cold feet."

Charodei said stiffly, "I don't think that's the case at all."

Pternam said, "Well, there isn't much we can do to help him. I mean, he's there and we're here. He has her; he will have to make the critical decision alone. We agree on this: Azart must be killed. We don't know what she is capable of."

"Orlioz said in his report that her movements under stress revealed a concealed level of control . . . a level he thought higher than his own. He said further that this ability seems to come and go, as if she were not completely sure of herself, or was half-asleep. He fears the consequences if he initiates any series of actions which would alert her completely, or awaken her to her full potential. Apparently, under the stress of changing genders, she is attempting to bury Rael and *become* Damistofia Azart in reality. In the light of what Rael has proven capable of, and that by way of a simple agreement, we are not certain we wish to see what Damistofia Azart might try to do motivated by emotions like revenge."

Pternam said, silkily, "We are not convinced that what Rael did is the proximate cause of these internal problems."

Charodei responded, "We are! We need no convincing; we know."

Pternam looked narrowly at Charodei. "How so?"

Charodei said, beginning slowly, cautiously, "There was an element in Lisagor which acted as a dampening agent on the pressures within this society—the impetus to change, and the resistance to that which was so strong here. No one imagined that this was the keystone holding Lisagor and Oerlikon together, but Rael struck at it, and through a series of coincidental events, which we believe he could somehow perceive, he neatly sliced that element out of the picture, which allowed the contending forces to come into direct contact. They will continue to work against one another until another stable amalgam is attained. The prospectus now is that of a number of semi-independent states, some hostile to others . . . the unique conditions here will not reappear; in fact, they have already gone."

Pternam commented, "There is some truth in what you say; I know for a fact that Clisp is already loose, however much they disguise the fact. Much of the Serpentine as well, and also Karshiyaka, of all places. *They* have brought the mercenaries from Tartary. But aside from all that, I find your, ah, viewpoint, as it were, a little odd. You speak almost as an outsider, with a clinical detachment I cannot manage. How is this so?"

"I have some truth to deliver, and you must take it as you will."

"Speak on—we have need of it."

Charodei said, "The element that dampened: those people were not natives, but were from the old worlds, let us conjecture."

"Go on. Why would they care?"

"Originally, let us say that they wanted to see how a change-resistant system of society would work, because elsewhere they don't. But as they stayed here longer, they gained a vested interest in keeping things as they were."

Pternam swore, "Hellation! They were filthy spies, laughing at us."

Charodei demurred gently. "No, they may seem that way, but they were not. They were in fact mere academics, students, if you will, who wanted to maintain what they found. Change was building up pressure here, as elsewhere. And so they acted to deflect the impetus for those changes, to keep Oerlikon as it was."

Pternam was still skeptical. "Why should they care?"

"They, such people, would have to train exhaustively for such a mission, learn the modes of speech, the customs, the laws, also which are more followed, and what outlets does the system allow, or encourage. In doing so, one would become used to thinking like a native; some might come to like it, after all, everyone on every planet sometimes remarks about the 'good old days.' We all share the fear that things will not remain as we left them, that the change of values makes us ciphers, nothing, insignificances. And frankly, I think that some of those watchers would also prefer this kind of work to other occupations they might be doing, for in a lot of ways, the mission would be a soft job, and they would want the conditions that called the Oerlikon project into existence to continue, so they would have a place, however obscure. Let us further say that the tour here would last, say, twenty-five standard years, so that one could do a trip here and go home and have a pension. Not a bad life, eh?"

Pternam said softly, "And these people from the void; they would have been here a long time, yes?"

"From the beginning. Many—indeed, the vast majority, were insignificant people who were never noticed. Some rose to high position. One or two ruled."

Pternam thought about something Rael had told him, something about a third force. And here was this Charodei describing the same thing, although it was much more fearsome than he imagined. "How would they come and go?"

"Spaceships, naturally. The locals have no incentive to travel space in the local system, and the nearest inhabited systems are too far. Also, Lisagor has no competition, hence, no enemy to watch for. And Lisagor early turned away from space—it is a powerful motive for change. Most landings took place at sea; a few in Tartary."

Pternam said, "Why should you voice such conjectures to me?"

Charodei smiled mildly, "To accustom you to the idea. Most Lisaks would find the idea insupportable, but you seem receptive to ideas of this sort, and your business here involves change in a profound way. You would react the most reasonably."

Pternam glanced at Avaria, then said, "Could I make one of my own conjectures? That you might be one such person?"

Charodei hesitated, as if weighing minutiae, and said at last, "In the light of what we have said, the assumption would seem to follow."

Pternam said, not missing a fraction of the beat of the conversation, "Then one could also assume Ahaltsykh would be one as well; one would hardly reveal such a secret before a mere idealist."

"That is correct."

Pternam nodded. "I understand. This is valuable tender to reveal. We have heard, of course, of such a thing, from Femisticleo Chugun and his henchmen, lackeys, and minions. But also Monclova is taken with the idea. I had considered it nonsense. But then, you must desire something of me. You may speak of it."

It was Charodei who flinched. He had evaluated Pternam correctly, of course, but the quickness and ruthlessness of his response took him aback. He cleared his throat and said, "Rael struck during a period when we could not communicate, and our infrastructure here was destroyed by him. Those of us who survive would like to return to our home-worlds. You are high enough to have constructed a suitable apparatus so that we can arrange for pickup with our monitor ship. Then we depart."

Pternam said briskly, "Difficult that would be, especially in such times. . . ." He glanced at Charodei. "But not totally impossible. We have a certain secrecy here, and a certain tether. . . . But what can you provide in exchange? I have no irrational hatreds against your people, but I am pressed now. Lisagor is in great danger, and with it, all of us who have ruled it. I do not care to have a mob uncover all that was here, in the pits and training cribs."

Charodei said, "One of the first native casualties of the unrest was the Heraclitan Society; it disintegrated into a score of ideological and terri-torial factions. Certain survivors have come together, and taken over some of the larger surviving fragments. This movement is now under the effective control of a council of four persons, two of whom are here now."

"The other two?"

"Cesar Kham and Arunda Palude. Kham was acting bureau chief for Clisp and the Serpentine, Palude was central integrator."

Pternam said, "Those are not your real names, the ones you had at birth?"

"No, but what matter? I am Porfirio Charodei now. But to the point: we are trying to salvage a core here in the inland provinces; Crule The Swale, Puropaigne, Akchil, part of Grayslope. The Lisak central govern-ment will of course be discredited and will fall as a matter of course, but something will take its place. We offer our expertise in arranging things to fall your way. We will work with those people you designate."

"There are details to be worked out. . . ."

"Yes. This is detail-work of no great importance. What we need early on is a sign of commitment that we may proceed."

"What would you do otherwise?"

"Just vanish into the masses. We can do so."

Pternam nodded, "And who knows who else you'd make such an offer to? Doubtless there's someone somewhere who'd stand still for it, besides us here. Yes. Very well. Proceed. I will arrange to have the proper components brought here and assembled. You have an expert to coordinate this?"

"One will be provided."

"And your end?"

"We will commence immediately. The resultant state which emerges cannot be guaranteed as to physical extent, but you and such associates as you designate will be at the head of it."

"And we'll be rid of you."

"Yes."

"Very well. Our motives seem to coincide. Is there anything else we need to discuss?"

"Yes. Rael; or more properly, Damistofia. We would like to take her with us. He, she, is a unique being, and we would desire to study this creature under controlled conditions."

"Is Orlioz one of you?"

"No. He is a Lisak. A real one, if somewhat deviant. He has asked for clarification before proceeding. Capture would be simple, relatively. We would also ask for the experimental notes and records, and some person from your staff who participated in such training."

"You would take such a monster back to your own worlds? Alive? I might, were I you, take it back, a certified corpse, encased in a ton of glass. But you have no idea what you are dealing with. It is supremely dangerous, and must—I say *must*—be eliminated. I insist. Rael must die."

Charodei began, "We must look beyond revenge—"

Pternam interrupted, "That creature possesses an ability to disrupt entire worlds. I am not thinking revenge, but protecting my own world from further disruption. And probably yours as well."

Charodei said confidently, "We think we can isolate it suitably there—we have devices and methods . . ."

"Yes. Devices, methods, spaceships and telephones that speak across the void. But you couldn't make a Morphodite. We did that. And I reiterate: you have no idea how dangerous that thing, that insect, really is, fully awakened. We simply cannot take the chance. I say have it killed, or . . . I'd reconsider."

"How much of a reconsideration?"

"Come, come, my good Charodei, let us not fall to threats and promises of dire events. Nothing is more boring than the fool who claims, 'I intend to do so-and-so,' when one can be certain that such claimers will in fact do nothing, or cannot. I prefer to speak of accomplishments, of facts, of deeds, of 'I shall.' We made Rael. We know now how dangerous he is. He must be killed."

Charodei looked at Ahaltsykh, who nodded. Charodei said, "Very well. Done. I will have Orlioz so instructed."

"Tonight. And put some backup in with him. Don't miss; it may charge if it's only wounded."

"Have no fears. Orlioz is expert."

"Does he know what he's really dealing with?"

"To my knowledge, no. He's been told what to look for—Damistofia Azart—and to verify certain things about her. As far as I know he operates under the assumption that he is to dispatch a dangerous operative."

"Make sure he understands that if he misses, he won't get a second chance."

Pternam let that admonition rest a moment, and then added, "And for a fact, we won't get one, either."

9

Marula: The Far Side of Now

MARULA WAS A place, to Damistofia's perception of it, limited though that was, which seemed to lend to its inhabitants little or no consciousness of any aspect of nature, save perhaps the verminous life forms which infested the docks and warehouses and as well the poorer habitats. In Marula, as Damistofia heard it, they did not speak of the sky, or of plants, or of animals, or winds; they did speak to excess to a degree she found incomprehensible, of relationships between people, for which they invariably used slang and jargon all of which carried strong overtones of envy, jealousy, and general resentment, as well as a well-loaded cargo of sexual allusions which left no doubt as to what people did in Marula to amuse themselves.

At least in this much, she was thankful of this, because it enabled her to become fractionally more invisible, against the day when she should be let out of the Palliatory.

The relationship with Cliofino continued, although it seemed with fits and starts, and odd hesitations. But as far as his skill as a lover, she had no complaints, for he was both passionate and considerate, and although she sensed that there was no permanence to the relationship, she let her new emotions and pleasures take her where they would, and afterward, when they lay quietly together, saying nothing but feeling the echoes of each other's passages ring through themselves, she admitted to herself that she felt warm and good, and full of life.

Still, something eluded her, and much of that vague absence she marked down to her severance from her original past. Old Jedily; now she would have known exactly what to do, how to feel, what to suppress and what to loose, and when to cry out and make animal noises. But that was gone and Damistofia had no way to get it back. She knew that she would have to take what was worthwhile of Rael and discard the rest, and with her own experiences make her life now.

But something still nagged at her, which all her explanations to herself and her allowances could not complete. She knew very well what her problem was; there was something bothering Clio as well, and as time passed, it bothered her more and more.

She sensed, weakly at first, and then stronger, that he was holding something back, something he wouldn't share, no matter what their transports. And when he went with her and paced her in her exercises, which were limbering up her body into a finely balanced supple instrument that responded in its slender, graceful economy of muscle and soft flesh much better than Rael's awkward heavy lengths of limbs, she could catch him watching her closely, more so than she felt was motivated by lust or love or interest, but by something else. He was measuring her carefully, *and what he saw he feared. He feared her!* And to her knowledge he had no reason to.

Here, she was absolutely on her own. They had known this from the beginning, when her training began, when she had been Rael, but they had counted on what she seemed to be to shield her from the worst until she could get her own bearings. So even yet she had no outside source of information she could tap, to verify what Clio said he was. And as yet, she had no reason to doubt him, and yet she did, in the dark nights when he was not with her, and she had time to think about it.

This was such a night. The disturbances, which had seemed to be growing, had faded, and now one only heard distant hushed rumors of thwarted uprisings, or else marches and protests, which sprang up and then faded away. Nothing nearby. The weather was no longer made up of the clear bright days of summer, but the rainy season of fall. Perhaps that had calmed them down. The Marula natives were long on talk, but as far as she could see, short on positive action.

But she could not sleep, and so she turned on the light, which was weak as is usually the case at night, and sat in her soft chair, which Clio had brought her, and thought, clearly.

She had been trying to forget Rael for weeks, now, months. And it was hard to try to bring back the old formulas by which Rael had plied his deadly trade, the only one he knew. The ideas swirled in her head like leaves in a street-gutter drain-mouth. It was all there, but it was fragmented and fading; the matrix of order was almost gone from it. Still, she thought that perhaps in that arcane and bizarre formulation of reality, perhaps there was insight, and so she tried harder, trying to remember, and as she did, feeling the strangeness of the female flesh that she wore now. The ideas, the very ideas, did not seem to fit well in Damistofia's head as they had in Rael's.

She had no notes, no reminders, but it worked, after all, with a specific code of logic, and there were axioms and postulates, and then developmental proofs, simple proven bases, and upon that foundation one erected Operations, which were statements about reality. She reviewed the logic, and found she could recall it; then the axioms and assumptions, each with its name and title, according to some caprice of trickery of Rael: The First Noble Truth, Godel's Refutation, Heisenberg's Trinity, Asimov's Law, and then, for no reason, Number Five. There were a score of others, and, one by one, they fell back into place. Then the basic exercises in manipulating the symbols, which at first felt clumsy and often threw her into errors, but she began to make them work properly for her, and the symbols for the Arbitrary Exercise Answers began to come in proper order.

She warmed up to it, feeling the same thrill as had Rael when he had first built this system: it was neither mystical nor mysterious but clear and logical and scientific. It did not reveal the future, but only extremely narrow sections, as related to specific problems. The more specific the inputs were, the narrower and brighter became the Searchlight. Yes. That was a good way to look at it: a searchlight beam, illuminating something, or showing you that nothing was there. In the manipulations she could also choose the angle of illumination.

And so, one datum at a time, she began substituting elements she knew into the progress of the formulas, turning them back onto themselves, building resonances, harmonic derivatives, orders of probability. It went like music, only music always stopped too soon, and this, abstract, alive on its own, did not, but kept on building to the final phrase. She exhausted the small sheaf of papers she had hurriedly grabbed, and absentmindedly got some more, and continued, and the Answer came, with difficulty, dim, and somewhat blurred, but it came, and she knew it was Truth: *Cliofino is an assassin and you are his target.*

There was a verification subroutine, and she ran it without hesitation, suspecting the Answer, yet feeling no emotion but a sense of achievement and triumph, and it was clear: *Cliofino is an assassin and you are his target.* Hard as diamond, adamantine and poised, it hung in her mind in the dance of symbols and formulae and was itself. Damistofia was so far into the routine that she hardly paused, muttering aloud only, "Thought something wasn't right," and continued, now using this formulation as a base, and building it into a more difficult phase, now asking "why?"

And in a shorter time, now, she also had the answer: *Because he knows what you are, and those who order him have so directed, and he will obey.*

Now she sat back, feeling clammy sweat on her body, and noticing that her palms were damp. All this time, working out together in the gym, wrestling with one another, bodies conjoined, interpenetrated, one, in the throes of love and desire; he had had a thousand opportunities, and had not tried. Why? She didn't need the system of Rael to tell her that: because he senses or comprehends that her reactions may be faster and to try would be deadly peril—to him, and he might not succeed. She could defend, merely, or defend-attack. What was the course? Here was a problem Rael's system could easily handle. She thought, and then began coding in the symbols and sequences to derive the answer she sought. The first thing that came clearly was the element of Time. *Soon.* As she would have explained it to someone who had no knowledge of the system, "at the far side of Now." And what was the correct action for her? Again she bent to the pencil and paper, again she frowned in concentration, and the answer came almost too easily: *You must kill him when he tries it. That is the only course open.*

The rest of it was anticlimactic, and tiring, and she felt sleepy. But she remembered from Rael that it was only right and only correct to carry the operation out to the last place, to derive the whole answer, for only in that way could one sense the awful chasms that lay on either side, even if they were not described. And at last she finished, knowing what she had to do, and feeling the correctness of it, however painful it was to think of it. And after she had torn the paper into shreds and flushed them down the commode, and went back to bed, she thought long on it: *And I asked, I did, if I could save him, because he is so good, so young, and so nice a lover, so pretty, so muscular and graceful, and it said there was no way.* And then, looking at the light beginning to bleed wanly into her single window toward the east, she allowed her heart to ache and a small tear formed at the outer corners of her eyes, and she sniffled once, and went to sleep at last.

The Far Side of Now. It came late the next day, toward evening, a gray and cheerless day, of damp, cold winds off the invisible estuary, but at least the rain had stopped. Cliofino appeared, quite out of nowhere, and announced that he had at last obtained a work-release for her and had secured a small place in a habitat far enough away from the Palliatory for her to forget it.

He added, "And we'll wait a bit, and then just not report back, and they'll forget about you entirely, among the much more alarming problems they have here."

"And I'll be free, with correct papers, and everything . . ."

"Everything. It's all taken care of. All it has to do is unwind."

"How did you do it?"

"Ah, some persuasion here, some chicanery here, and in a couple of cases, outright bribery." He handed Damistofia a thin wallet, which contained her new identity papers.

She took them, and said, "This is what you have been working on all along?"

"Well, in a manner of speaking, yes."

"Tell me the real reason. You, of course, are not one of these people."

Cliofino did not hesitate. "You have been recruited. We have need for operatives who are both agile and mentally alert . . . and who can be extracted from the matrix of the people with the minimum of disturbance."

"I see. All of it was that?"

"No, not all. Sometimes extra things happen . . . sometimes they don't, or perhaps you wouldn't want them to. No, that which went between us was real enough, and I hope it might continue."

She nodded, as if overwhelmed by the information, but smiled, and began gathering up her things, which were very few. She thought, *I travel light now.*

They walked through the grounds and out the main gate, and no one seemed to care, or make any gesture toward them. This surprised Damistofia, and she asked Cliofino, as they stepped outside the wall into the street and began walking down it, "They didn't even care! How did you do that?"

"I convinced them I was a deep cover agent of Femisticleo Chugun, the head of the, ah, secret state police. Of course, I have help in maintaining this disguise, but in these times, as long as one seems on the side of order, few questions are asked. I have recruited here before, and they are a little relaxed in their vigilance, and so . . ."

"But you are not that."

"Not for Chugun. We hope to see him over a slow fire."

They walked along for a while, beside the wall still, which seemed to go on and on, and at last she saw the end of it. "I suppose you'll tell me more when we get where we're going."

"Yes, more."

"And I don't really have much choice in this, do I?"

He looked at her sidelong, with an engaging smile. "Choice? Of course you'll have choice. We are not like those who have held it so long here. I'll tell you how things are, and then you make up your own mind."

"Should I not want to work with your . . . group?"

"Read your papers. Go on, open them."

Damistofia removed the wallet from her bundle while she walked, and opened the wallet. There was, inside, a standard Lisak Identification card, listing name, residence, province and the like, and at the bottom, in the block marked "Occupation," it said, *"Landscaping Inspector, Beautification Section, Not Restricted."* She shook her head, and said, "I don't understand this at all. I know little or nothing about plants or landscaping."

Clio laughed. "Neither do the inspectors, as a rule. It's a fat patronage job. All you have to do is travel around and fill out forms. Nothing is ever done wrong, of course, unless it's by someone you don't like. So I'll tell you what we want you to do, and if you don't want to, then go and inspect; I'll arrange an appointment with your new boss. Your initial assignment will be the South Coast sector, which is to say, in Sertse Solntsa, Zolotane, and Priboy. If you are nice to the Head Inspector here in Marula, he'll post you off to the Pilontaries where you can really vanish."

"You are serious?"

"Absolutely. Although . . . I'd hate to see you go. I have to stay here in the Marula area."

They were beyond the wall, now, but there seemed to be nothing in particular near the Palliatory. A few deserted buildings, vacant lots, old warehouses. The street was broad and straight, and veered off toward the west where, farther down, there seemed to be something, an untidy jumble of buildings she could not identify. Overhead, the sky was overcast, but in the far west there was an immense pearly flare of clouds, backlit by the westering sun, now setting somewhere out to sea beyond Clisp. She walked, and stared at the bright western sky until her eyes grew weary and blurred, and then she looked back to the thoroughfares of Marula. She saw around her empty, uninhabited and unused spaces, abandoned, rusting machinery and odd parts of old buildings left behind, and trash blowing in the vacant lots. It was the most desolate and forbidding thing she could remember seeing in that part of her life she

could remember, and it filled her with an aching longing to be elsewhere, now, immediately, somewhere . . .

Damistofia turned to Cliofino and said, "Why is there nothing here,
next to the Palliatory?"

"Cleared it off a while back. No reason, that I know of. They were
going to build something else, and then they never got around to it, and
so it stayed the same."

"The smoke and . . . all that; where did that come from?"

Cliofino pointed vaguely southwest. "Over there was the nearest one.
That's what you probably smelled. South Mernancio District."

"There were others?"

"Oh, yes . . . many more. Three in Marula so far." He paused and
added, "We've not seen the end of it yet. There'll be more before it's
over."

"There must be a better way for people to live together."

"You will hear our ideas." He took her hand shyly and they walked on
into the dusk.

The untidy jumble of buildings came nearer as they walked, and the
light grew more uncertain. Damistofia thought they had walked about
half an hour, or less. Not very far. She felt no fatigue. As they came near
the first buildings, they saw motion in an open field, behind an untidy
fence long since gone to ruin, vandals, and wood-stealers. Soft, low,
melodious calls, running, quick, darting shadows in the failing light.

Cliofino gestured toward the dim figures. "In the midst of chaos, they
still find time to have a round of Dragon."

"Can we watch? I often heard them talking about Dragon, back
there."

"I suppose so. We have nothing to do tonight, except find a place to
eat, and find your new place."

Damistofia squeezed his hand, "And of course we'll have to try it
out?"

"Oh, yes. Mind, I've already been there, and it's in a quiet corner."

"Good." While they walked up to the fence, a few late arrivals approached on velocipedes, pedaling madly in the uncertain light, swerv-
ing and stopping and recklessly throwing themselves off their machines,
to slip through the fence, and pausing for a moment to size things up,
leap immediately into the action, which was at a high peak.

The newcomers quickly found places of concealment in what appeared to be an abandoned junkyard. Hardly had they vanished into the shadows when the current reigning Dragon returned from another part of the field, trotting effortlessly, glaring here and there, and carrying the scorpion meaningfully limp, ready for instant use. Here he stopped, and called out, "Latecomers, show yourselves! Skulk not in the shadows like bezards and wisants. Come forth, come forth! I am somewhat tired from overexertion, and will lay my friend on your shoulder as a comrade." The spectators tittered among themselves, and glanced at one another.

Cliofino leaned close and whispered, "Judging by the crowd, this one's a famous liar. He'll wait for one to show and then pound him down. Just you watch!"

All remained quiet, however, from distant parts of the field came, at intervals, odd half-calls, subvocalized and unintelligible—obviously, the other players taunting the Dragon. Damistofia thought she could sense movement back there, players risking little swift lunges and darts. They did not like a waiting game.

The Dragon walked about, as if uncertain, peering here and there like a stage villain, an act which seemed to fool no one. At last he stopped, and mopped his brow with his sleeve. He called out, "Come, my children, bear my heavy burden."

One of the shadows erupted into a running form that seemed to reach his top speed instantly, as if shot from a gun. He passed directly in front of the Dragon, hooting as he ran, wildly, almost like the cry of a bosel. The Dragon was not caught off-guard. When the runner had emerged, the Dragon had been slightly out of position, but in an astonishing display of virtuosity, shifted the scorpion to the other hand and neatly, almost effortlessly, backhanded the runner between the shoulder blades, a motion that seemed light, almost easy, until one saw the runner pitched over headfirst by the force of the blow, landing rolling awkwardly, while the former Dragon now dusted his hands off, and began walking off the field. He said, to no one in particular, "Told you I was tired. Now take up the scorpion and demonstrate excellence to the laggards by the fence." And with that, he joined the spectators there, but made no further move to leave. He passed near Damistofia and Cliofino, and she heard him breathing hard. He was an older man, and overweight. Yet he had entered this anarchic game and plunged into the action, chasing younger sprites.

The new Dragon, somewhat shaken, now got to his feet, and returned for the scorpion; picking it up, he waved it about to get the feel of it, for there was no standard model. This one seemed heavy, weighted, a vicious weapon, and it moved in his hands like some live thing, wriggling, twisting. It was his privilege to give a short address if he wished, and this one chose to do so. Gathering his breath, he said, "I will now speak. Night creatures, make your moves; the demon avenger is upon you! True, we came late to this gathering of nobles, we rushed, we fretted. Would we be on time? But now we are here, and the waiting is over."

Those along the fence made fretful motions, moving slightly into positions of better advantage. They were in fact not immune to the Dragon, should he decide to attack them. Everyone was fair game.

The Dragon now swaggered, feeling the sense of power come to him. He strolled closer to Damistofia and Cliofino, still orating, "But where would we start? The far fields, where they hide in security? Or here along the fence, where they think to watch others sweat, as they stand in immunity. No immunity, I assure you. All are equal on the field."

Damistofia watched the Dragon, and Cliofino, who watched with glittering attention. The Dragon paraded back and forth, and suddenly stopped, right in front of them, and gallantly handed the scorpion to Damistofia, saying as he did, "Here's a switch in the game of surprises! I hand it off without mayhem or malice aforethought. I say, here's a young lady with her bravo, walking along to an evening rendezvous! Wonder what she'd really do? Will she clout him over the head like Thelonia* and her rolling pin?"

Damistofia took the instrument, numbly. Now had become NOW. This scorpion was a soft, still leather, rather heavy toward the large end, a bit longer than her forearm. She swung it, experimentally, as if trying to make up her mind. As a newcomer who had just walked up, she could hand it back to him if she wished.

As if trying to read her mind, Cliofino hissed, "You don't have to take it! Hand it back!"

She stiffened, and said, "No, I will take it." She stepped out onto the field, through the ruinous fence, and looked back at the crowd in the dusk. She said, "People! I have not played before, but I know what to do!" The erstwhile Dragon smiled broadly, winked at her, and sidled off into the shadows, to find a place to hide. Damistofia continued. "I am small and a poor imitation for Thelonia, so I will try to attain

---

* A famous character of Lisak folklore, an immense fat woman always waylaying unlucky men with a rolling pin and a venomous tongue.

hard-headed Caldonia, who cannot be dissuaded once her mind is made up." The crowd of idlers murmured their approval. Caldonia was another mythical woman who was notorious for being hard-headed and suspicious, and a shrew to boot. She went on, "Today is a day when I celebrate my new liberty, and what better way than to play here, to know choice and cunning, fierce pride and the thrill of the chase." This was good stuff, the crowd thought, and out on the field, many of the players made hand signs to each other, also approving. She was small, they thought, and not so dangerous. There would be action.

Without further hesitation, Damistofia turned and loped out onto the field, opening her eyes wide to take in as much as she could. For a moment, Cliofino hesitated, uncertain, and then also stepped through the fence, watching her carefully. She called out, in the manner of Dragons from time immemorial. "Come, my pretties, my bulls, my bosel bucks! Who will dare the arm and aim of a small woman? I will tempt you further—he whom I strike, I will sleep with . . . if he's able!"

Hoarse hoots greeted this announcement from various parts of the field, voices in the dusk, heedless that they would give their position away. One called, "Take me!" Another said, "Try me! Then you'll really get a thrashing!" One said, "I'm a credit to my gender!" Another sung, simply, "Forget the scorpion and sit on my face!"

Cliofino followed uncertainly, not sure which way to turn. This had suddenly taken a radical turn for the worse. What the hell was she doing, egging them on like that? Could she have seen him? And if she had, what would she do? Attack him with the scorpion? Nonsense. He had played Dragon since he had been a mere lad, and he was fairly certain she knew little about the evasions an experienced player could make. He could run her ragged. He thought he knew: she would try to escape in the dim light and confusion of the game. Well, he had an answer for that, too . . . Dimness and confusion abetted many things, and here was as good a place as any. Yes. Here. He looked for Damistofia, and suddenly she wasn't there. Damn. He loped off onto the field, senses alert, watching for the sudden motion out of the corner of his eye.

Ahead, where he thought she went, he heard running feet, harsh panting. A voice called out, "Not there, over here! Celebrate with me. I didn't see your face, but we've a sack for that!" Another voice added, "Maybe you'll need two bags—one for you if hers comes off." He heard Damistofia reply, "Come and see for yourself!" She was somewhere not far ahead; he thought he saw her slight figure, moving by a dark place, checking if anyone was in it. She had worn soft gray clothing, a loose tunic top and pants, and he thought that the lightness of her clothing would have made her show up better, but apparently it didn't, but instead, in the failing light, it made her fade in and out of visibility like a ghost.

Those who never played Dragon saw the play as a lot of waiting, broken by sudden noise and alarms, quick scuffles, rare, random violence, but now Cliofino, an old player of the game, knew this to be an illusion. Quiet? The dimness was electric and alive with the eyes of hidden watchers; currents of anticipation flowed over it like night in the wildest jungles. All his senses were alert, as he pressed further into the back reaches of this field, alert for the flickering gray shadow, which now seemed to have disappeared. No matter. She'd have to show herself—she had the scorpion, and she had to get rid of it. Ahead, he noted an obstruction, which seemed too small and insignificant to offer concealment, nevertheless, he made a detour around it, watching ahead. And aha! There was the soft pad of running feet to his left, a little behind him. He turned to look, and caught a tremendous blow on the right temple that knocked him completely off his feet. He twisted with the force of it, technicolor sparkles flashing in checkerboard patterns before his eyes and fell heavily on his face, and he tasted dry dirt and blood where he had split his lip.

He tried to get up, but fell back, fearing he'd lose consciousness completely. He felt nauseated, disoriented. Had that been Damistofia? He couldn't imagine her getting enough force behind the scorpion to deliver a blow like that. He sat up and looked around, still dazed, and now feeling a fine, hard and hot anger rising in him, a delayed chain reaction. Groping about, he found the scorpion nearby, dropped in contempt. And around him, the players called out the timeless insult and invective of the anarchic game:

"Off your dead arse and on your dying feet!"

"Up and claim your prize, lunker! She said she'd sleep with you!"

"He thinks she will anyway. Not likely, after taking him down like that!"

A woman's voice, not Damistofia's said, from nearby, "You had it coming, you roach, or else she would have come after us!"

"What is this, a rest-station on the Symbar pilgrimage? Up and demonstrate your excellence, else we'll take it from you."

This last was cruel, for Dragons who were considered slack in their action were often ganged up on, beaten, and the scorpion taken from them. No more ignominious fate could be imagined. Cliofino, still somewhat dazed, felt he could handle himself well enough, one-on-one, but against the onslaught of half a dozen local bullies, with their women on the field to egg them on, that would be questionable. He stood up and glared about, swinging the scorpion meaningfully, and saying, in a low growl, "Come and take it, if you're able!" The hoots and catcalls faded, and he noted small flickering motions out of the corners of his eyes, as the new round started and the players took up strategic positions, or made themselves secure in their old ones.

The anger he had felt before was now rising like an ancient god from the bottom of the sea. He had hesitated to do his duty, though he knew what he had to do. It would have been quick; it would have had to be. But he would have done it with compassion and mercy. A monster, they had said. Kill it. And so he would. Here. Now. No one would question a casualty of a game that produced them regularly. And then he'd vanish into the night, and make the connections to the trip to Marisol, in Clisp, that they'd promised him. No more Marula.

Cliofino made a quick tour of the area he was in, looking swiftly, sure she wouldn't be close by. His swift and methodical search flushed several, who would burst out of concealment like birds and race off, legs pumping mightily. Those he left, to the amusement of those farther off, who continued to hoot at him:

"Revenge! That's the stuff!"

But they kept their distance, knowing that in his mood, he could easily injure someone else before he found her. So they all knew he was looking for her. It didn't matter.

He went back toward the street a little, hoping to catch sight of her in the brighter lighting from the streets, and ahead he thought he saw her; she stepped out from behind a rusty hulk, as if waiting for him, joined by others, who seemed to grow out of the earth like phantoms. Cliofino shook his head, wondering if he was hallucinating, seeing double. Ahead, not a dozen paces, there were four, no, six, all in gray, although they looked different, moving nervously, but staying more or less in place, as if waiting for him, dancing, inviting. Which one was Damistofia? One he selected, and he made a rush at that one, but he or she scampered off, and he saw that it was an adolescent, hardly more than a child, trying the field out a little, and a soft voice said beside him, "No, not that one. Here!"

And she stood still, long enough for him to recognize it was truly her. He checked, a little unsteadily, and turned after her, but now she ran, close in among the obstacles and dumps and hiding-places, running with incredible agility, more than he had seen her display yet. But he was catching up: he switched the scorpion to the position of readiness. First he'd knock her off her feet, and then . . . She ducked under a low beam, and he plunged in behind her almost close enough to touch her, close, too close to swing the scorpion for the felling blow, and he ran into an upright post that stunned him, knocking the breath out of him, as he fell back, gasping for air. No one was around. They were completely hidden. Frustration rose in his throat like a burning gall, rage, he thought, "I'll tear her apart . . ." but something moved in the close darkness, and he felt a tremendous blow on his throat, which cut off his air. He choked, panicked, struggled, but all that would come were distant gargling noises, and as his sight dimmed and he fought the darkness rising around him like a wave, he felt soft fingers moving over his face, a lover's intimacy, over his ears, under them, and there was a pressure, and time stopped.

Damistofia sat back on her haunches, still holding her fingers tightly pressed on Cliofino's carotid arteries, until the jumping, leaping pulse in them slowed, became irregular, and stopped. And she still waited, counting her own loud heartbeats, until she was certain. Even then, after she released her pressure, she went back and felt for it again. Nothing. She felt over the body, felt carefully for other places, felt there for a pulse. There was none. No breathing. It was done.

She sat back in the cool darkness, feeling the heat radiate off her face, breathing deeply, trying to fill her lungs, not just pant. *In the end*, she thought, *he betrayed himself and was a fool, after all*. He could have waited and done it his way, no doubt while they were lying abed, but he had to follow her onto the field. The idiot. Dragon had been part of Rael's education, too, and the computation had showed her that was the way to do it. And now that link was cut. No one here knew her.

She stepped out into the night, now, feeling the cold of the air, the sea-damp. Around her, voices were calling out, nervously, bantering, vulgar. She answered, calling out, "Here, over here. The fellow who was Dragon. He ran into a post and hurt himself. He won't get up." In the dark, on the field, no one would examine the body closely. They'd see the bruises and scrapes from the scorpion and the post, and that would be that. And as soon as they left her alone, she'd *Change*, and there would, after a day of terror and pain, be nothing left. No Cliofino, no Damistofia.

Soon, hesitantly at first, and then with greater resolve, they came, to find Damistofia sitting by one who would not rise, still grasping the scorpion tightly. One of them pried his fingers loose.

That one said softly, "Miss, I think he's dead."

Another asked, "What happened?"

She answered, forcing her voice, slowly, "He was pursuing me, here, and went in there and ran into that post, and fell back."

"Were you bonded?"

"We were just friends, you know. Not especially close. Just friends. This was insane. . . ."

Another said, "It's no matter. It happens; part of the game. He played like one who knew what he was about—we could see that. He knew the risks. And tonight was omened badly—Abelio was hurt earlier, and they carried him off. By the way, has anyone gone to see what became of him?" There was muttering and discussion in hushed tones in the back of the crowd that had gathered, and someone said that Abelio was at home, resting, and had sworn off Dragon for the duration.

Several men volunteered to carry the body down to the Palliatory, for the night-clerk to settle, and she told them that his name had been, or so he said, Alonzo Durak, and they nodded solemnly, exchanging knowing glances. Uh-huh. He gave her a false name. Happens all the time; well, Alonzo Durak or Jaime Kirk, it was all one—they had a body to move, and so to it, lift, here, and off they went.

Damistofia remained where she was, and after a time, the spokesman for the group pronounced the game closed, and suggested that they all repair to a tavern they knew of, not too far away, and they would there pause and consider their losses of the night, although someone ventured that, shocking as it was, at the least the accident had not happened to one of their own, and no one commented on this seeming cruelty, for that was the way of Dragon, and would the young lady come with them, and she said shakily that she would, and so, in a crowd, Damistofia left the field and walked with the others off toward the west, toward a certain tavern they knew of. She thought that she was free of the threat of Cliofino, but she was not out of danger yet, nor could she initiate *Change* in the midst of a crowd. But they would soon drink, and tell yarns, and grow sleepy, and somewhere there'd be a place she could hide, and change.

10

Deserted Cries of the Heart

THE CROWD MARCHED along the deserted streets in clusters, all talking among themselves, discussing the events of the evening: a well-known Dragon player injured, and another, who seemed to know what he was doing, was dead, seemingly, from carelessness. And the times were odd and perilous as well. Who could know such things? At any event, what was now needed was a tavern with plenty of the rank beer of Sertse Solntse to guzzle, and all of this could then be arranged in its place. That was the way things went, and the way they sorted out. Beer. What they did not speak of, and did not consider, was how much their group, a crowd from a Dragon game, resembled a mob on their way to a mischief.

Lisagor was in truth coming apart, the uneasy amalgam unraveling under the stresses brought into conflict by the removal of the neutralizing agent, the leaven that had kept it stable. In parts of the continent, in fact, there was no more Lisagor, although these people could not know that and did not know it. And, more importantly, to the segment of Lisagor-the-Entity that survived, it did not know it, by choice. And that entity had sensors, ordinary eyes of informers, and electronic devices, and those sensors and eyes saw an irregular band of people moving with seeming purpose toward a more populous part of the city, and that entity responded with the measures that had worked for it in the past, the threat-become-real: A Pallet-Dropped Trooper force was launched without delay, reacting. A mob simply could not be allowed to reach the city proper and ignite the hysteria which waited there.

Damistofia walked along with the crowd, with them, in their midst, and yet now mostly ignored by them. Perhaps they sensed her agitation, and thought it a kind of grief, and wished to leave her alone with it. Some of the women walked beside her, saying nothing, but providing a presence. But she felt acute danger; some sixth sense was still working. But it was odd, that. Rael was almost gone, despite the exercise she had forced herself to recall. Now, after everything, she felt *herself.* Right as what she was. The walk felt natural, and the ebb of the excitement of the game in the crowd, and the sensations she knew. She was Damistofia, completely. As if Cliofino had freed her.

Nevertheless, danger. Very close. She rationalized it—it would have to be that the ones who sent Cliofino would have backup behind him, someone she could not see. And that would mean that this crowd was only an apparent safety, that somewhere the reserve was moving into active position, and so she would have to find a place to start Change soon. Odd, but as she thought it, it seemed correct, but not with that absolute certainty she had known about the formulations she could perform from Rael's science. *I was correct, but not yet correct enough.*

Another thought also worked in her mind, and that had to do with the consequences of the killing of Cliofino. With the first one, that she remembered well, there were consequences to that, and she had known them, as Rael. But now, she had not worked the figures that way, so that part of it had been blind to her. *She didn't know anything at all about the results of killing Cliofino.* And there was here neither time nor place to sit down and perform the long calculations necessary to work the answer out. No way to know. She reflected as she walked that it did not really matter: she had taken the path she had to for survival, and that was sufficient. She doubted if Cliofino had the Power-That-Supported. He was much too ordinary, too much the climber, to fit into that schema. *She had probably rid the world of one who had, for all his motion and activity, no measurable effect on the world. It was not the people who were replaceable at will, but the politicians and climbers.*

Slowly, she let the crowd pass her, as she imperceptibly drifted to the rear of the formation by simply slowing down a little. Some of those who walked with her stayed for a while, but then speeded up to the crowd's pace and left her behind. Now she began looking for a place to hide, some dark corner. Another thought crossed her mind, a dark thought indeed; *This time I'm jumping blind. I don't know what I'll be, as Rael knew he'd become me. That's one of the longest operations in the system. And I shouldn't initiate so soon, either, because this body's still not ready for that yet—it's not completed, the old Change. But so much I know: I'll be male, I'll remember, and I'll be younger.* Another odd thought

crossed her mind: *I don't know what I'll call myself, then.* The answer
came, as if a personal demon had entered her mind and placed the answer there: *Phaedrus. Very well, Phaedrus it is.*

She stopped and sat down on a curb, as the last part of the crowd
from the game passed her by, some casually calling out to her to hurry
along and catch up, that surely there would be a tavern open not far
down the thoroughfare, closer in to the city; while others passed without noticing her at all. She sat, as if weary beyond endurance, folded her
arms on her knees and lowered her head to the arms as if resting. She
was seeking the state of consciousness within herself, the odd combination of self-hypnosis and yogi trance in which she could initiate Change.
The street faded, and the noises of the crowd died away, although they
were only just past her, a lonely figure resting on the curb for a moment.
No matter, she'd catch up. And it came surprisingly easy to her, much
easier than she remembered it from when she had been Rael. She
reached the state of darkness, and the outside world was gone, and
there, in the center, was the bright wormlike coiling of the threads,
black-and-yellow checkerboard color washing over them, moving impossibly fast, impalpable, inconceivable, and she aligned something in
herself to them, and they slowed, and slowed, and stopped, in an uneasy
stasis, and she reached into that network and changed a thread, the one
that controlled this process, and quickly let go and began falling out of
the trancelike state, as fast as possible. The structure resumed its frantic
writhing motions, and began fading to bright fog, and was gone, and
after a moment her senses began filtering back to her.

Wrong, wrong. She heard the sounds of running feet, and cries, and
the droning roar of motors overhead. She opened her eyes, still dazed
by the aftereffects of the trance state she had just gone into so quickly,
and she could not at first make sense of it. Before, the Dragon crowd
had been moving south; now they were running north in disorder, while
overhead motors roared and bright flares fell in slow-acting arcs too
bright to look at. What had happened?

One of the running figures passed her, stopped, came back, and
dragged her to her feet. One of the men she had been walking with before, when they had just started here. He was out of breath, but pulled
her to her feet, shouting over the noise and confusion, "Come on, girl,
you can't rest here, run!"

Damistofia stood up, feeling normal, and hypersensually alert, but also
knowing what dread timer was running inside her now, that it would
probably be only moments before she had the preliminary attack.

She stammered, "I . . . don't understand! What's happening?"

The man shouted back, "Pallet drop! Thought we were a riot about to happen, I guess. No matter now, run, save yourself! They go after everyone standing once they ground!" He took her hand and pulled her roughly, and she started out with him, running, her heart pounding. And she thought, *What is this exertion going to do to Change?* But she couldn't complete the thought, because there was a powerful roaring drone low overhead, a rattling, a pause and then a hard crash behind her, not too far. She heard staccato sounds, then, and another odd sound, a piercing hissing. A voice, choked with running, cried, "Now leg it good, the first wave's down, and most made it!"

She wanted to see what they were running from, but others urged her on. "No! No looking. Run!" Behind her she heard a dull explosion, and something rattled around her on the street and buildings, and some around her fell. The hissing sound increased, drawing into a deeper timbre, and there was a yellow light back there now making dancing shadows ahead of them. A voice cried in terror, "Plasma cutters!" And behind her she heard heavy steps, and a mechanical snarling, and there was another explosion, with more immediate peppery rattling around her, and some more fell, and she increased the pace, hearing another voice, strangling, gargling, "Chainsaws and flamethrowers and sawed-off shotgun pistols in this bunch!" And she ran on. There was another droning overhead, and another crash not far behind her, and the sounds started up again. Now ahead there were lights in the sky suddenly, blinding searchlights, and where they pointed, sudden rivers of fire lanced down in brief bursts, and where the fire went, runners went down like grass. And there were crashes to the side as well, now. Dimly, she sensed they were being surrounded, by the lobotomized troopers on three sides, and ahead, slow-moving aircraft armed. It was at that moment that she felt the first presence of Change. A sudden pain cramped her abdomen, and she doubled over, grasping her stomach, and the man who had taken her hand tugged at her. "Come on, you can't stop now!"

She fell over, coughing, and managed to gasp out, "Can't run, I'm hit. Go on!"

She saw him hesitate a moment, glancing at her, and at those advancing behind them, and then he turned and ran off, with the others who were still on their feet, and behind her she heard, with monstrous clarity, the sounds of chainsaws and flamethrowers, and an occasional boom of a shotgun pistol, fired into the crowd at random. And then she didn't hear any more, because a terrific constriction took her and firmly and irresistibly tried to bend her in two, and her consciousness faded. She sank into darkness, thinking, *I have failed, they will carve me up now with the others.* But after that she did not think anymore. Change commenced, and it was far more drastic than the first time. She had been right in one thing: this body had not been ready for the ordeal of Change—it had not yet completed all phases of its own Change.

Cliofino had been undoubtedly correct about one aspect of life in Marula, that being that the police had things on their minds vastly more important than worrying about exactly who Damistofia Azart was, or had been. For one thing, they were used by the distant authorities as a cleanup force after the depredations of the Pallet-Dropped Troopers, a task they did not relish, but one which occupied much of their time now.

Achilio Yaderny surveyed the street in the bright light of a clear morning, and shook his head wearily. Bad, bad. No good would come of this, none whatsoever. He saw a street, which would now in normal circumstances be busy with folk on their errands, empty of every sign of life except the body-recovery teams. And, of course, the bodies. In this case, they were spared much of the worst; it appeared that most of the victims had fallen to gunshots, rather than the other traumas which the Troopers were capable of inflicting. Small piles of discarded clothing— that's what they looked like. And of course, the pallets. They always left them where they lay, along with the Troopers who didn't make it on the landing. There were a few of those—something near the expected ten percent. But there weren't any Trooper bodies anywhere else.

The body-recovery teams were sorting through the victims, recording the appearance of them with bulky devices on wheeled carriages, for later comparison with the identification records. Incidentally, and only incidentally, they were also searching for rare survivors of the purge, but they did not expect many; survivors of Trooper raids were usually few.

Yaderny's assistant, a wiry and energetic young man who went by the name of Dario Achaemid, came along from out of a side alley, carrying a small notebook, to which he was adding notes. Yaderny called to him, "Find anything?"

Achaemid consulted his notes, and looked up briskly, after the manner of an overly thoughtful athletic coach, and said as he approached, "Not so much; on the other hand, quite a bit that makes little or no sense."

Yaderny, who was used to these odd excursions, by which

circumlocutious fits and starts Achaemid attempted to seduce reality into revealing herself, sighed and said, "You may explicate if you will."

Achaemid looked owlishly at his notes, and said, "This habitat is hard by an area in which the Bureau of Remandation has little, or no, favor. The general attitude is negative at best, and graduates up through several degrees of hostility, which I will not enumerate, as you are doubtless familiar with them all. Nevertheless," he said portentously, "Some facts emerge: this was not an assemblage of rioters, but the aftermath of a large Dragon game, which took place somewhat to the north of here."

"A costly mistake."

"Correct. On the other hand, they were more adept at escaping because of it. Not so many casualties."

"Now that you mention it, there do seem to be fewer."

"And so there will be much fewer of the type we'd be interested in: criminals, revolutionaries, rabble-rousers and the like."

"I see. Then you do not recommend intense search."

"I could not see any particular reason for it. Let the recording teams run routine ID procedures, and catalogue the victims. The bodies can be hauled off in the usual manner, for sanitization purposes."

"Anything else?"

"We might notify Symbarupol that they are too quick on the trigger. This will not win friends here. Marula is already a very large problem."

"Your reasoning is faultless, although the tact and discretion which I have had to cultivate in my position suggest that it might be wiser to edit such remarks severely, or perhaps not utter them at all. I say that not out of fear, but out of a consideration that no effect will result. They are not listening any more."

"Ah! Truth must yield to manners, as always."

"True! But what are discretions but the glue that binds us? Well, see to it, will you? I think I will return to Headquarters, and from there try to word something that will pass through. The problem here is so far out of hand that we are not dealing with ordinary criminals at all, and they are gaining entirely too much liberty. I fear much more of this and the city may go."

"I have thought the same; and heard much more alarming things."

"I have heard them as well; you understand, somewhat fainter, but yet I still hear them."

"Very well! It will be as you say. I will clean this up, and have the remains dumped. Where should these go? The last bunch overfilled the burial site."

"Are there other places?"

"Very far out, to the northwest; the Old City ruins, in fact, was what I had in mind. These should be transported far away, to lessen morbid curiosity."

"The old spaceport?"

"Yes."

"Aren't there some stragglers lurking thereabouts?"

"Renegades, tramps, thieves, and the like. The Troopers often use the area for training exercises, and so the inhabitants are scarcely in evidence. At any rate, they will issue no challenges, neither martial nor legal. The Old City is technically not there. . . ."

"Not all that good, but I suppose it will have to do."

"I'll be back in tomorrow. This will be unpleasant and extended work."

"I understand, Achaemid. Go ahead."

And so they parted company, Achilio Yaderny to return to his office and try to say something fundamentally unsayable, and Achaemid to his unpleasant task of disposing of the bodies of the fallen.

As the body-handling teams worked their way along the street, they soon fell into a routine; after they had made a desultory search for still-living persons among the fallen and scattered heaps, they would arrange the bodies to be recorded, and afterward, bring small, three-wheeled electric wagons alongside, in which the bodies would be piled, as neatly as possible to maximize the load. Then the trucks would set off on the poorly maintained road which still led to the Old City, although few went there now for any purpose.

The members of the Bureau of Remandation who were working with the teams saw little to pass on of special interest to Achaemid; dead folk were, after all, dead, and that was that. But near the end of the street, they did find one thing, which they duly reported to the assistant, but who in turn dismissed it. They had found a young man, in fact, probably a late-adolescent, who had no wounds or evidence of trauma, but who appeared to have been afflicted by a violent disease. Achaemid examined the body, which was severely emaciated and covered with filth, although he kept his distance, and the team handled the body with tongs. It seemed as cold and stiff as the rest. Achaemid said, "What about this one?"

"No marks, no injuries. Looks like some kind of plague or fever."

"Any others like that?"

"No. Not a one."

"He couldn't have walked around like that, without someone noticing him."

"We doubt it."

"Put him in the pile with the rest. I'll see what I can uncover. If there are more, we may want to come back for him later, but I don't think we'll find any more; everyone I've spoken with said nothing about disease. . . . Any identification on the body?"

"To be truthful, Ser, we haven't looked; you know . . ."

"Understandable. Distasteful job, this. Well, be sure it's recorded with the rest. Not to worry. Everyone will be identified, sooner or later."

"There is one other thing about this one . . ."

"What's that?"

"Has on woman's clothing, or something cut for a woman, so it seems."

Achaemid chuckled, an odd note among the somber horrors of the scene, the bright morning sunlight suffusing into the cool street shadows, innocent, clean, while squads of men in disposable overalls gingerly stacked bodies into small trucks with three wheels. He said, "That is not so great a surprise, considering this crowd and what they were doing. I remember a case in South Marula, near the docks, which was my first assignment: there was a fire in one of those transient hostels, you know? One of those old firetraps. But they had time, with this one, and everything was going right. Up came the fire squad and the pumpers, and the water mains were all up to pressure. Everything was going right, impossibly. And of course, all the Information Services people were there, recording like crazy. Inside the building, you could see all these people running back and forth, but they wouldn't come out, even though they could! Finally, in desperation, the Chief formed up a shock brigade of us, and we went in there and dragged them all out! Saved them all! Turned out the reason they wouldn't come out was that they were all transvestites, dressed up in women's clothing. And oh, there were some famous ones in the crowd, you can be sure. The scandal went on for weeks, but eventually quieted down. This is probably something similar. In a Dragon game, I wouldn't be surprised. In fact, I'm surprised you haven't turned up more."

The spokesman for the team said, laughing, "We will exercise more diligence! But how do we tell?"

"Never mind! And be careful handing that one, will you? That looks contagious, at the least!"

"No fear! We will not touch it!"

"Fine—carry on." And Achaemid strolled off to another part of the street, to supervise another team at their sad work.

The body, lying with others in the little truck, soon set out along the broken and disused concrete road to the Old City, and after a long ride, of which none of the cargo was aware, reached a ravine by the Old City, a rugged tumble of irregular blocks, and was rolled off, with the rest, where it lay quietly.

There was one peculiarity about this particular body which no one noticed at the time. That was that it seemed to lack some of the stiffness and rigidity of the others. And another odd characteristic, hard to see in the fading light among the gullies and chasms of the ravine, was that it was more limber than its associates, when rolled off onto the pile. But the drivers were not interested in looking overly much at what was already a dreary business. If they had looked closely, after the body had stopped rolling, they might have seen some movement in it: a hand clenched, spasmodically, and a leg stiffened, but they were small motions, and the light was uncertain, and they weren't looking for movement; and to an equally placed observer, there were no more motions, at any rate. At any event, none that could be seen.

There were a few more loads, but they hurried more, owing to the nature of the work, and they placed their cargoes somewhat off to the side of this particular body, and left hurriedly, for they heard odd sounds in the ruins, and in the distance, the hooting and calling of bosels, and they thought it better to leave. At least, there were no more to bring.

Achaemid made meticulous notes, and from them, assembled a report, complete with cross-references and footnotes, which was complete and magnificently documented, and which reached Yaderny's desk, along with sections of the reports of others. There was a long roster from Identification, listing the positive matches they had made, along with an abbreviated resume of the person so identified. To Yaderny's general disgust, the list totally lacked known criminals or notorious deviants, although there were a few low-grade rowdies and tavern brawlers among the listings.

What did catch his attention, was a most singular fact; there were two on the list who were totally unidentifiable. One had been found at the site of the earlier Dragon game, and the other among the casualties in the street, apparently a victim of an odd and loathsome wasting disease. Something clicked in his detective's mind, but it took him a bit to reason it all out. A case in which he had seen something similar to the recordings ID had sent along. There had been that girl, what had been her name? Dovestonia? No. Damistofia. Azart.

Yaderny started to call the Palliatory on the Comm, but stopped in mid-action, and decided to visit the place. When he arrived, he was most disturbed to discover that the lady Azart had departed, just the night before, in the company of a fellow who was part of the Internal Security Organization, or so they felt. Yaderny produced a record of the body they had found at the Dragon field, and that was him. But of Damistofia there was no trace. The Palliatory had a Communications Center with all the customary facilities, although they were hardly used, and these Yaderny now applied to attempt to identify the young man, by transmitting a facsimile print of the ID recording to Symbarupol, to Chugun's own office.

To his surprise, they were polite and cooperative, but they could offer no help on the young man supposed to have been one of theirs. In fact, their Chief of Personnel was definite, and stated categorically that the young man was not one of theirs, and they could not claim him. Chugun's office was so definite and so sincere, that Yaderny could not bring himself to believe otherwise: they were telling the truth, for a change and dealing directly with a minor officer in a local police department.

Yaderny made some notes, to follow this up later, because there was something peculiar about this all which disturbed his sense of rightness, an instinct he always listened to. And for a fact, he would have investigated it in depth, but on the next day, there were urgent matters to attend to, involving a section over in Southeast Marula in which a Pallet-Dropped Heavy Trooper strike was narrowly averted, and there was an increase in looting and general unrest, which took all his time, and then came some desertions among his men, and somehow or other he never quite got around to it, and Damistofia vanished from the little awareness of Lisagor which she had been a small part of.

In Symbarupol, there were those who were very interested in the whereabouts of Damistofia Azart, and her fate, as well as that of Cliofino Orlioz, and they were not happy to discover that their own assassin had been found dead, with Damistofia vanished, but some among them conjectured that she had tried to escape, and died somewhere in the uprisings of Marula, but Luto Pternam was not among these. He remembered Rael, and his nights grew more sleepless than they had been, thinking about a mutable person, a chameleon, who suddenly could no longer be seen. Something changeable vanishes: one cannot, from that date, assume termination. Only that the target can no longer be seen. And that worried Pternam, and subsequently Avaria, more than many of their other problems, because they were now sure that whatever Rael had become, he would someday, if alive, return to extract a horrible revenge for what they had done to him; and what more they had tried to do. Pternam added guards to his staff, as well as some special experimental projects from the lab, hulking lobos who were more dangerous than the Pallet Troopers, but he ruefully considered that he did not know who he was looking for. Or waiting for.

11

The City of the Dead

FIRST, THERE WAS a dream about singing, which came and went in unknown intervals. This singing made no sense whatsoever, and there were no words in it, and the melody didn't register, either. That was no problem: Lisaks were not particularly fond of music and the only music ever heard was hardly more than childish jingles, monotonous and repetitive. This was different, complex harmonies, all high sweet voices that made the heart ache. But for what? There was no knowing.

Then there was singing, and it was clearer and did not fade. There was a sense of clarity to it, and a sense of stability. A sense of ego, of being, of consciousness of being part of a body that did not drift and fade in and out of existence. There was a room with a low ceiling and large patches of light and darkness, sense of movement, presence. A lot of people, perhaps. And the self. What self? *Am I Damistofia, or . . . something else? Someone else?*

There was movement nearby, to the side, and a woman's voice spoke. It was definitely a woman's voice, but low and harsh. "Are you awake?"

"Yes." The word came easily enough, and not in the clear, high voice of Damistofia. The sounds were low, ragged, probably from disuse. There was a moment of panic while weak limbs were moved, and the outlines of a body felt out under a rough homespun blanket. *He! I am he!* He felt the realization run through him, and for a moment his consciousness faded a little, a delicious feeling. *I lived through it.* Then solidity returned, and now full consciousness.

He was weak, and could not sit up, although he tried. He could look around. Yes, there was a room, although the shape was not quite regular. Low ceiling, apparently made of broken slabs of concrete braced with timbers. The room was really two sections joined by a short hall. This side was large, and dim, with the illumination coming from candles.

The other side was brighter, and the singing came from there, although now it was stopped. There were low voices there, in the part he could not see. Squatting on her haunches beside his pallet was a tall, strongly built woman whose features were in detail concealed by the half-light. She asked again, "Well, are you going to stay with us this time?"

He waited, and then said, "I think so."

"We had a time with you. They threw you out with a body-dump from the city. We found you there. You were moving, crawling, or trying to. Krikorio said leave you, that you were gone and didn't know it, but I thought not. We cleaned you up and brought you here."

"Where am I?"

"In the dead city. Refugees live scattered in the ruins, hiding. . . . You were more dead than alive, and much of the time out of your head. We were very afraid that you had some unknown disease, but it seemed to cure itself, and at any rate none of us caught it. You talked a lot . . . about Damistofia, and Rael, and Jedily. Who were they?"

"They were some people I used to know. Gone now. Never mind them. We cannot bring them back. And for disease . . . you can't catch it. Neither can I, anymore. I think I'm cured."

"Well, that's good! What you had I wouldn't give to a bosel!" She laughed, a rich, throaty laugh. "Hah! I wouldn't even give that to a Temple-bolter, and I've seen plenty of them, you can bet."

"What is this place?"

"A refuge of sorts, although . . . there're some who found it not so nice."

"I don't understand."

"This is no-man's land, where they train the Troopers. They practice on us, and so one has to be well-hidden, and strong. You live alone, they sniff you out. All sorts of conditions exist here, in the ruins. I have an alliance with Krikorio, whom you will presently meet. . . ."

"You are espoused?"

"We have an alliance. I fight, he fights. We protect each other. We are not friends, nor lovers. You understand, this just works for us. Kriko follows his star, and I attempt to find one."

"Why don't you leave?"

"It has not been possible." She shook her head, implying that she wished to say no more, but after a moment, she continued, "You may not understand it . . . wait a while, before you judge. At any rate, we can't leave now, with the turmoil outside, and . . . things are unfinished. Just unfinished. Krikorio hunts, and when he finds what he's looking for, then there will be a celebration, a consummation. Then, maybe, I can leave. Now I watch over his girls, and keep them safe."

"Girls? I thought I heard singing."

"They are the singers. They are also the Brides of Krikorio, whose wedding we await. I will tell you now, so you will know it: leave them alone, no matter what they do or say. You understand? Don't look, and especially don't feel. They belong to him."

"Who are you?"

"Call me Emerna. That is enough of it. How do you call yourself?"

He had to think a moment. He caught himself wanting to say "Damistofia." But it wouldn't come. After a moment, he said, "Phaedrus."

She nodded. "Fine, Phaedrus. Now you rest. Don't try too much at first. We'll feed you up a bit, and then you can help me some." She stood up now, and he could see how large she was. She towered over him like some heraldic figure out of mythology, from the forgotten worlds. Tall, heavily built, powerful, deep-breasted. She called into the other part of the shelter, "Lia! Bring some brew from the pot! He's awake!" She looked down at him. "We've had the girls taking care of you since you've been here. I guess now that'll have to stop. But this time, I'll do it for them. You can start looking after yourself."

After a few moments, there was a rustle from the other part of the shelter, and presently a girl appeared, carrying a crude bowl of something hot. He sat up, the better to take it, and saw the girl in the flickering light from the other room, the bright room. This one was slender and graceful as a reed, very young, but also nubile and beautiful, with long pale hair that reflected the highlights of the fire behind her. Her beauty was heart-stopping, impossible. She set the bowl down beside him, with a quick, burning glance at him, and then vanished quickly.

Emerna sat down beside him, folding one leg under her, and offered him a spoonful of something that smelled odd, but made his stomach rumble. She said, in a low voice, "I know. They're all like that. Pretty little things. Krikorio collects them, he does. Come the occasion, and he says he's going to take them all in one night. A real marathon! And they are not for you, although they will provoke you to madness if you let them. You must not. You understand. That is the one rule here."

Phaedrus nodded, gulping at the hot broth, which was painful to swallow, but good, despite its odd taste. "Yes. None of the girls. Do they all wear white gowns, like . . . Lia?"

"Yes. That, and they sing, and together they weave Krikorio's cloak, in which he will go out when all is done. For now, though, you eat, sleep, gather your strength. I will tell you as we go, how things are, and you can decide for yourself, allowing that, of course, Krikorio will let you decide."

He ate, but it was with apprehension. Nothing made any sense, here. He couldn't find his proper place. Something clearly wasn't right. However, some truths emerged, which while perhaps not great universals, at least seemed workable: Emerna saved him, and was keeping him; and he was to leave Krikorio's girls alone. It wasn't much, but he thought he could live with it until he knew what he had fallen into.

Outside, it was winter now. That much Phaedrus could determine by watching Emerna dress to go out, which she did, although for much shorter periods than Krikorio, who seemed to be gone all the time, making only rare appearances, and then only to sleep. Outside, winter, but in the shelter it was tolerably warm. He did not go outside; he was not invited.

What little he saw of Krikorio astounded him, for he was very much like Emerna; large, powerful, an enormous man with heavy black hair and a luxuriant beard which hid most of the contours of his face. For Krikorio's part, he avoided Phaedrus completely, although something suggested that he approved, at least tentatively. Krikorio stayed in his end of the shelter with the girls, who fussed about him like exotic birds. He seemed to treat them offhand, like children, or pets, but now and again, when his wandering gaze drifted across one of the girls, there was fire in the half-hidden eyes, a feral glint which Phaedrus understood. He had no difficulty complying with the unstated rule of the shelter, although the girls seemed to go out of their way to tease and provoke him, without ever making any gesture whatsoever which was a clear invitation. After some time of this, Phaedrus was firmly convinced that the girls, whose number he could not ever seem to ascertain exactly, were as aberrant as Krikorio and Emerna. Nothing seemed normal, or leading toward anything, save day-to-day survival. And he could not build a coherent picture of events outside; the girls he would not talk to, Krikorio he could not, and Emerna was as opaque as obsidian. True: they had saved him, after their own fashion. But for them, he would really belong in the body dump with the rest. In the weakened condition after Change, he would have died of nothing more elaborate than exposure—loss of vital body heat.

Little by little, he regained his strength, and Emerna saw to it that he had plenty to do, working him in the household chores; which he hated, and yet exulted in, because he was moving again. And because he knew that if he could escape this place, he would be truly free of all his pursuers at last. He also took stock of his new body, which was completely new to him. It was odd, because he remembered both Rael and Damistofia clearly, but this body was lean and wiry, somewhat like Rael, but much lighter, shorter, and without Rael's sallow saturnine color. It felt like this body wasn't completely finished yet. From what he could discover about himself, he estimated that this Change had taken him almost as far as the Change from Rael to Damistofia, and that he feared very much trying it again. If it worked out as he suspected, the next Change would place him in the body of a preadolescent girl, which he rated with low survival odds in the times they were in. It was true what Pternam had told about him—that through the changes was a kind of immortality. But it was a perilous kind of immortality, one in which you had to pass through the process of death in order to live; to live forever entailed an infinite number of agonizing deaths. He could not remember the first time: that belonged to Jedily. But the other Changes he had initiated at least had clear reasons for them. Now he knew that it would become progressively harder to face each time, until he would reach the point at which he could not face it, and yet after all those lives, would not be able to face final termination, real death, either. It was as exquisite a trap as the one he was in, in the shelter.

There was, of course, another problem, which was growing: Emerna. Krikorio had his harem, even if for unknown ritual reasons he had abstained from their supple young bodies. Now Emerna was echoing that, or so Phaedrus felt. He could feel the pressure, although she did not make it apparent openly to him, as such. And of course, Emerna had no reason to wait. Phaedrus could perceive her three ways, from three views, of the egos he had known. None of the three ways seemed to build any excitement in him, although he realized by doing so how disabled and fragmented Rael had been. In fact, Rael had been only barely functional, like something pieced together. Only with Damistofia had there been any sense of integration, and that had just been a spark, a tiny flame, before it had been snuffed out. Now . . . it would be in this body that he lived, and he felt Emerna's attention on him, as well as a deep requirement of his deepest self to engage himself with her, to build a lasting persona out of the encounter. That was the only way it could be done—by becoming involved/integrated with others. He reflected that he had a poor choice to begin with.

From fragmented accounts from Emerna, he built up a slow and patchy image of the past, how they had come to be here, and the way they were. It wasn't a pretty story. Krikorio had found Emerna, a dazed survivor of some nameless atrocity, and together they had found this place. She had been a gawky, awkward adolescent, then, too tall for her age, angular and bony. Krikorio was half-crazy himself, but she didn't mind: he brought firewood, and wild meat, and other food which he stole in the long treks northeastwards into the wide farmlands of Crule The Swale, and he defended her, and took no liberties. He explained his dream, which she did not understand, but helped him with it, collecting the girls, who were also fleeing, always fleeing. The first ones had come from the west—Clisp and the Serpentine and Zolotane, but of late they had come from Sertse Solntsa, and Marula. Children, running from catastrophe, from murder and mayhem, spared by chance.

What was he waiting for? He had dreamed he would contend with the white bosel for mastery of the world, that this magic white bosel was in fact the demon of the world Oerlikon, whose intemperate and chaotic spirit ruled the planet, and he Krikorio, would triumph, and then and only then would this world be truly a human world. He would be the Emperor-High-Priest, and the girls would be his maidens, through them he would breed and raise assistants, his spawn, to spread the word throughout the world, even to far Tartary. They would tear down the derivative civilization the old men had brought from the stars, contaminated, useless, life-hating, and they would build a more natural world.

Phaedrus listened to the fragments, second-hand from Emerna, as it gradually unfolded, and reflected that all in all, it wasn't entirely insane. Only a little far-fetched, and a step backward into the trackless dark forests of Original Man of legendary long ago, on the homeworld. In a normal world, people like Krikorio would be helped to rationality, or at least to art, where they could relive their dreams in some measure of sanity . . . or adjustment. Here? For a moment, Phaedrus cursed the settlers of Oerlikon and their hatred of Change, that led them to build this flawed, broken society. But, then, on second reflection, what he had seen of the product of the worlds where Change held sway without stint or let, the brainless careerists who had manipulated this world to give themselves a job and not much more than that, that did not cheer him either, or lead him to rush pell-mell into that camp. Lisagor was finished, although it would doubtless stagger on for a time. The old worlds, wherever and whatever they were, offered nothing better. He lay back on his pallet and smiled to himself. Nothing to be done but wait for the moment, and try to understand the conditions outside he would have to cope with.

The days passed; at first Phaedrus could not discern any notable differences among them, save the distant hints of weather. But he gradually became aware that there was a change evolving in the shelter, and through these things he came to understand that things were moving forward to their conclusion. He resisted the temptation to work the formulas of Rael, to see what the conclusion would be. He wanted to be free of it, of all things the most.

The first thing he noticed was that Krikorio was staying out for longer and longer periods, and when he did appear, he wore on his dark and malign face a growing expression of unspeakable triumph. The girls were becoming quieter, more solemn, and soon ceased to sing. Also, they avoided him pointedly, save Lia, who seemed to watch from an infinite distance away, observing something she neither understood nor wanted, but powerless to deflect it.

Emerna also was changing. As he felt himself gaining back his health, he felt her eyes on him more and more, and her behavior moved between a rough truculence and an embarrassing solicitude. He knew what was coming; the only question remained to answer was when it would occur.

Emerna told him that Krikorio's moment of triumph was near; the mysterious white bosel had been sighted for some time, and though eluding him with its indescribable mixture of craft and irrational randomness, Krikorio was closing in on it, and she expected him to succeed soon.

"Then what? I mean, I know from what you've told me that he will then celebrate by having an orgy with the girls, but . . ."

"I never said this before, even to myself; but this is blank; unknown; he has this idea of what he will dare to do, and I cannot find myself in those plans. Neither are you in them."

"Of course."

"I had always thought that things wouldn't come to this—that he would never achieve what he wanted. I mean, I didn't even believe in the beast he hunts with such fervor. A white bosel! Whoever heard of such a thing? And so this would just . . . go on and on. We have a functioning life here, hazardous as it is. Many others have not done so well. Yet now; I don't know."

"You saved me from the dump; I owe you."

"This is so."

"I have seen little of this, but I think you and I should not stay here when it happens."

"I have so thought. But consider this—we could not leave before him—he is a superb tracker, and a worse foe than those who hunt us. Besides, he can't make it alone with the girls—they are hopeless outside. He has raised them that way."

"It would be a matter of timing, then—to find the right moment?"

Emerna said, without hesitation, "Yes." And Phaedrus thought that perhaps the worst part, getting her to accept that she would have to leave, was over. She added, "You are now in some danger from him. When you were ill and unconscious all the time, you weren't real to him. Sick and recovering, also you didn't matter much. But now . . . ?" She let the idea hang in the air, unfinished.

Phaedrus said, after a moment, "I'm a rival, whether I behave or not."

"Of course you are. And no matter how they sing and weave and chatter about the day to come, they are all, to a girl, terrified of Krikorio—they have no idea what he will do with them. They see more of him than you have. More than I, although I have seen many things which lead me to make alliance with him and not oppose. You understand, I would fear, too, were I one of them."

"I must leave, then."

"There is an alternative, for the time."

Phaedrus nodded, indicating that she should go on. She said, thoughtfully, "If I take you as a lover, and you sleep with me, then according to the way he sees things, you will not matter any more, and he will forget you."

It was said matter-of-factly, without a trace of emotion, even a little grudgingly, but underneath this exterior he saw the second truth of it as well as the first, which was exactly as stated. The second was that in entering into this odd relationship with Krikorio, Emerna had also walked into a trap built of Krikorio's disordered fantasies, and traded off what femininity she had for physical prowess and survival skills. He, Krikorio, saw her as a neutral partner, and in accepting that, she had blocked off anything else. Seeing this, Phaedrus could feel some real compassion for Emerna, who had become enmeshed in a trap as vile as his own, and with that realization, he felt an emotion for her he could not have approached from any other direction. He said, "We can do that, I think." And he saw the light begin to flicker, ever so slightly in her eyes, which he now noticed were a light greenish-blue, an indeterminate agate color. He added, "We have time . . . let it happen."

She nodded and got to her feet abruptly. "I will go have the girls scrub me down. Lia will bring you a basin." She smiled now, an odd little half-smile he had not seen on her face before, and her face softened a little from the hard set she habitually wore. She added, "I don't know what you were about before we found you; as for me, I have not known much of this save in the hungers for it. We will be inept, I think."

Phaedrus said, kindly, "It has been a long time; I also plead a lack of expertise with which I will take no offense."

She nodded. "Then we must manage as we may; but at the least we will warm each other." And she turned and walked into the other section of the shelter, where she began issuing orders to the girls, in a softer voice than he could remember hearing her use. And presently there were sounds of water splashing, and Lia shyly, eyes downcast, brought him a basin of hot water, and left quickly. He wanted to say something to the girl, but the words did not come. Perhaps there weren't any.

It was much later, deep in the night, that he dreamed of singing again, and shuddering with the thought of what he had passed through the last time he heard singing, he awakened and listened carefully. Beside him, he heard Emerna's breathing change rhythm, and she grew very quiet. Glancing at her, he saw by the light from the other part of the shelter that her eyes were open. There was revelry and singing and uproarious noise, chatter, giggling. On the wall between the sections was a shapeless thing that had not been there before, something pale and fur-like. They heard Krikorio's heavy laughter, drunken-sounding, and she whispered, "Not a sound, on your life."

Phaedrus turned to her and put his arm across her ribs, curling closely to the heavy, hot body next to him. She breathed deeply, and pulled the cover over them, shutting the light out, and after a few moments they no longer heard any noises.

When Phaedrus awoke, he thought something was wrong, because there was a routine in the shelter to morning, even if no daylight filtered into the deep place in which it was built. The shelter was dark and lifeless. Emerna was not beside him. He started up, and looked carefully about, listening. There was a faint odor of fire that had gone out, and only one oil lamp was still burning. The pelt on the wall was gone.

He got up and found his clothes, and rummaged about, through all sections of the shelter: there was no one there. Krikorio, the girls, Emerna . . . all gone. He heard steps outside the door he had never gone through, and a familiar fumbling with the catch, and Emerna opened the door, wearing her heavy winter overclothing, which made her look even larger and heavier than she actually was.

He said, "Where is everybody?"

She shook her head, as if dazed. "Gone. Left before dawn, all of them. Krikorio dressed them all up in the outside clothes they had never worn, and drove them out. They didn't understand. I saw him, and he saw me watching, but I dared not speak. He was . . . completely gone. I wouldn't dare even ask. Such was the cast of his eye. Wearing his white-bosel cloak, he was, like some savage. I went out just now to see if I could still see them. . . ."

Her face was blank, devoid of any expression. Phaedrus looked slowly along the heavy structure of her face, trying to read something in it. "What was it?"

Her eyes cleared, as if she had just become aware of him. "Oh? No, there isn't anything we can do. They are gone, that's all."

"Then we are free."

She nodded, absentmindedly. "Yes, free. To stay or go as we would. I suppose you will want to leave, too."

Phaedrus put his hands on her shoulders, which were as wide as a man's. "You can't stay here alone."

"I never thought about it. It's been this way so long . . . What?"

"It is time to leave this refuge and trust to our own selves. This may have worked, but it's insane to stay. You don't have to. The old world is breaking up. We can't be far from Zolotane, and from there we can get to Clisp. . . ."

He broke off and waited, sensing that this was a balanced moment. Whatever adjustment to misfortune they had made here, she was at the end of it, and was now calculating chances. If she decided to stay, and tried to hold him there, he knew he could not prevent it, at least for a while. Finally, she looked down at the floor, breathed deeply once and said, in a soft, barely audible voice, "Yes, it's time to go, now. We'll need to get some things together. It's cold now, and we've a long walk."

"Why not just straight west? It shouldn't be so far . . ."

"Closed off. Too close to the city. We'd go north, along the Hills of the

Left Leg, to about the Knee, and then turn west. Two can sneak where they could not force a way."

Phaedrus said, frankly, "And you do not know what I can do."

"True . . . at least I do not know about how you handle conflict and strife. I do know something now I didn't know yesterday, and that part . . . seems to work well enough."

Phaedrus smiled, and squeezed her arm. "We seemed to manage in that. We will do as well in this."

He said, "Never mind why, but last night . . . was more a trial for me than you realize. I think I can do well enough outside."

She smiled at him, saying, "So you say! You are a cityman. I sense it. And there you may well do as you say. But we are going into the wild, now, and it's different. Besides, you didn't fare so well, there either."

Phaedrus agreed, adding, "Cruel but true. But I remember the circumstances and the odds against me, too."

"They do not seem so good, even now, for either of us."

He said, "They are better now than they ever have been. That much I know. I will take my chances with the outside and you."

Emerna gave him a quick hug, and then shifted to her old, commanding self again. "Here now! We'll need these things; bring them here and we'll sort them out as to who carries what." And she began naming things and telling him where they would be found within the shelter, and Phaedrus gathered them up, willingly, feeling a growing excitement within him at the prospect of leaving. Even though he sensed some of her disquiet about it. Not for nothing had they hid here, in the dead city, hardly venturing out, save for quick raids and adventures. Yet he felt closer to freedom than he could ever remember feeling; the pressure and the tangled webs of obligation and treachery were gone, and he was dealing with a now-world, free of the past.

12

The Knee Hills

EMERNA MADE UP packs for them, and they loaded each other's, turning away alternately; Phaedrus felt his own load grow heavier, and he piled the things she indicated on until she muttered, "Enough." Even with the weight of it, there wasn't much—most of it was bedding and shelter cloths against the night wind, weapons and ammunition. She thought it might take them four days to reach the Knee and turn west across that tumbled and trackless wilderness, a day or so there, and one more day to the coast of Zolotane, where they could expect no more than small fishing villages along the coast; Zolotane was a bare and empty land.

She wasted little time, and as soon as they were loaded, opened the door to the passageway and started into the darkness, with Phaedrus following. There was a narrow, lightless tunnel, full of odd turns and slants, up and down as well, barely wide enough for Emerna's broad figure to fit through with her load, but the floor was free of rubble. Like the shelter itself, the tunnel seemed to be made of odd pieces and slabs of concrete, fitted together crudely.

To Phaedrus's heightened perceptions, the way seemed to be long, extremely so for a hiding-place, and he said as much. She said back, over her shoulder, "There are many blind turns and odd corners here, as well as deadfalls, which I have disarmed as I came in before. This place is safe! They never came near it, although they tried hard enough." Then she resumed walking on, not varying the pace.

After a time, a weak light showed around a corner, and Emerna here slowed her pace, and motioned to Phaedrus for him to be silent. Together, they crept forward, making no sound, in a silence so profound he could hear his clothing rasping, and his heartbeat. There was no sound from the outside at all, that he could hear. Emerna stopped and knelt, listening carefully for a moment, and then slowly moving into the lighter part of the tunnel, which seemed to end in a random pile of concrete rubble, open to the sky. She whispered, "Can you hear anything?"

He listened. Then he said, "Aircraft, maneuvering, but not getting closer. They sound far off. Also something else, but I can't make it out; maybe gunfire, or just noise."

"Your hearing is very acute. I wasn't sure."

"Do you hear anything near?"

"No. I'll have a look. Wait here." She looked again, and then went out into the pit, and climbed upward, all the time looking about nervously. Finally he heard her whisper, "Come on." And he followed, clambering over the rough and tilted blocks with difficulty, also watching, but not seeing anything but an irregular circle of sky which grew larger, opening up.

The sky was high and cold and far away, deep blue and streaked with cirrus in broad smears and filaments, the sun low on the horizon and colorfully diffused by the clouds. For a moment, he couldn't decide if it was morning or afternoon, but as the distant horizon came into view, he saw that below the sun was the wavy outline of distant hills and low mountains, and on the opposite side of the sky there was only a dark line, very far away: that would be the east, across the lower parts of Crule The Swale. All around them were tumbles of shapeless landforms, broken blocks, tilted slabs, enigmatic shapes that could not be recognized. They seemed to be an irregular hill, whose slopes gradually descended to a plain, flattish to the east, south and north, but not far to the west, broken by more rolling terrain of ridgelines and shallow valleys.

Emerna said, "Safe for now. And so now you see the Dead City, or what's left of it. You were right about the aircraft, too—look toward Marula, south."

Far off in the south he could see specks moving in the sky, which behind them, colored by clouds, was a pale orange. They were moving in a low, slow oval, and they seemed to be moving very slowly. She said, "They won't be back today; that's something real they are working over there, although they may very well fly back this way. We had better be moving."

She stood up in the open and reached back to offer Phaedrus a hand up. When he stood beside her, he looked long over the desolate landscape. "What was here? What kind of city?"

Emerna started off toward the north, and said back, in the wind which he now felt to have a sullen bite to it, "Was a spaceport, so I'm told. After a while, the ships stopped coming, and people moved away, save a few renegades. *They* broke it up for practice, and for the thrill of the hunt, so I would guess."

He stopped, to have a last look at the dreary landscape, all around the circle of the horizon. Something caught his eye, south, still well within the ruins; something white fluttering in the wind. He stepped a little closer, as if to see if he could make it out. There was something familiar about that white fluttering, but he couldn't quite recognize it. Something tugged at a fugitive memory. Emerna stopped and looked back, and said softly, "You don't want to see that."

Phaedrus shook his head, and glanced back at her, and then turned back to the south, walking slowly. Behind him, Emerna stopped and waited, but said no more. He walked slowly toward the white fluttering, and saw that it was not all that far, just a little ways down the gentle slope but getting there required several detours around obstructions, some pits, others blocks tilted at crazy angles. But he was able to keep the goal in sight most of the time, and finally reached it, looked at the ground for a long time, and then abruptly turned away with a sharp motion, biting his fist. He looked back once, and farther off, to where the aircraft were now circling higher, now, not maneuvering, and returned to where Emerna was waiting for him.

He stood by her and did not say anything, but the wind was cold as it blew in his face. Finally she said, "Told you not to go."

Phaedrus said, in a low, clear voice, pronouncing each word as if each one were the only word in the universe, "Lia. Somebody cut her throat. That isn't Trooper work."

Emerna nodded. "If you want revenge, look back toward Marula; that was them, there. He's getting his now, or has already had it."

"And the girls, too."

"Maybe not. When I was out, I saw signs that he'd taken some of the others around here with him . . . perhaps the girls would have run off."

Phaedrus took a deep breath, and felt a nameless horror flow through him, but he said only, "What a waste." He said nothing else, but obediently followed Emerna when she set off, after a long pause, toward the north, where the sky was a nameless dark color, and the wind blew in their face and was cold, and they did not speak for a long time, and there were cold streaks of wetness along the outside corners of his eyes, and Emerna wisely did not speak to him of it, nor make any gestures to him, but walked along steadily, picking the trail out through the broken ground until they were well out on the plain. But he fixed an image deep in his mind of the face he had seen, eyes open to the cold sky, blank and empty, a broken doll abandoned and forgotten. They had been clear, pale eyes, and her mouth soft and gentle. He walked on, and thought only of steps forward, and wind in the face.

The luminous unlight of the northern sky guided them as the day faded into blue tones, and then violet, with a clear patch of sky that showed a glowing turquoise color, which was an open part of true sky unblemished by the swirls of clouds flowing across the high heavens. They walked on in a silence that was not broken, Emerna leading, Phaedrus following, placing one foot in front of the other, concentrating on the discipline of that.

As the cold darkness grew and spread from the well of the east, they heard around them, some far, some farther, the haunting evening cries of bosels, each one anarchic and expressing some demonic emotion known only to the individual creature. Far, far off to the east, there were a few scattered lights, and in the south they could see a faint glow from Marula; but here, going north hard against the hills of the Left Leg, there was no road and there were no settled places, and the land seemed as empty and free as when men first set foot on Oerlikon.

After a time, the distant, hallucinating cries began to bother Phaedrus, and he asked Emerna, "Is there any danger from the creatures?"

She stopped, turned, and said, "No, not from bosels, at least not in this season."

He ventured, "From men?"

"Not so much so from organized bands, such as the Arms of the Amalgam. But from wanderers . . . best be wary. We have passed several already; they sensed us, and I them, and we kept distance. No one trusts another now, not around these parts of The Swale, and, for all I know, so it is throughout the rest of Lisagor. People do things and blame 'the Troubles' for them, and every person's hand is turned against another's. I have learned that to hold power is the only way to fix this. You must lead, or find one who will, and stick by that, gathering others. Thus I came to Krikorio, and now it is just you and I."

An odd flash crossed Phaedrus's mind, listening to her, and after a few more steps; he said, "That doesn't change anything, does it? It just raises the level of violence . . . It is still one hand against another. I sense that down that road is the road to hell, in fact, we have already walked it, we Lisaks."

She thought a moment, walking on, and finally said, "Perhaps. But one must do something; try."

"It's too much trying that makes it stir. The way out is to let go. Do what one must, but stop trying to make something that won't be made. We say Krikorio was insane, do we not? Then his insanity lay in that he was divided, planning, desiring his great dream of power and force, but also doing what he knew was right: he hid and waited. Had he accepted the one, he could have seen the foolishness of the other."

"You would have wasted yourself had you said so to him."

"I see that. The evidence he left was clear."

She scoffed, "Ha! You say let go; what then? Isolated individuals who fall to the strongest hand! You'd be prey in a heartbeat. Press gangs would catch you and you'd find out what The Mask Factory is like; and you'd obey orders."

"I know. But wait . . . did you say 'press gangs'? I thought only the criminal were sent there."

"So did I. But we captured one of the Troopers once, badly injured and dying, but incoherent, and we pieced it together from him. No criminals, but whoever they can catch—the young and ignorant, and those too old or slow to escape. You were there, too."

Phaedrus stopped. "Yes."

Emerna also stopped, and turned to face him, an intense watchfulness in her face, and a loose, awkward stance to her large, powerful body. She said, in a careful, measured way, "You remember it?"

Phaedrus shook his head. "Not what they did to me as I was before. I remember the latter parts, when I was whole again."

Emerna still held the same stance, and the same intense regard. Phaedrus saw and understood the signs correctly, that at this moment was great peril. She said softly, "And they sent you forth with secret instructions in mind, horrid deeds."

He sighed, and half-turned from her, knowing that relying on his recollection of Rael he stood a good chance of taking her. He said, "No. They only instructed me in some things, and let me figure the rest out, and when I had gotten deep in it, they released me to do what I wanted to do, what I thought was right. They did not understand what they created. And I have no horrid instructions: I have already done it, and am free of them, a wanderer of no more consequence than yourself." He turned away from her, making the decision then and there to turn from the path of control, and let be what would.

Emerna did not ask him what he did, but instead, "I suspected, but only now did I know. What is it you want?"

The answer came easily, although he had not thought of it so much before. "To be free of wanting; to just be, as I am now. I know there is no going back, not an inch. No, just to become, to be nobody."

"You can't forget."

"But I can refuse to act, knowing that it does no good."

With his senses sharpened, he *heard* her relax; the slight motions of her body within its clothing. She said, after a time, "Let us be moving on; this is not a good place, but I think a bit farther on there are some abandoned farms where we might find a refuge."

He nodded, readjusted his pack, and turned to follow her. She said, "I believe you would have let me kill you, just then; that was what convinced me . . . I will take you to Zolotane, and from there you can lead. As you will."

Again, he nodded silently. Then he said, "Yes, that will be soon enough." And then they set forth again, walking now a little more confidently in the cold night.

Darkness fell slowly, nevertheless it fell, and the wind increased and grew colder. They walked on into the dark, steadily, and they did not speak for a long time. At last, however, triggered by something Phaedrus did not notice, Emerna stopped, a little uncertainly, listening, looking intently into the darkness. He had been following some distance behind her, and now he approached and stood close. He ventured, after a while, "What is it?"

She whispered, "If I remember right, we should now have an old place in sight, even in the dark, but I see it not."

"Could you have navigated wrongly?"

"No. The signs are right; something isn't right. Change."

Phaedrus sniffed at the cold air, testing it. "I smell fire, ashes. Very faint. Old fire, old ash. What would we be looking for?"

"House, barn. They had a commune here, long ago, but they failed and went away. House remained . . . This was a place where wanderers came; there was a well. Many people know of this place. Be wary, now."

Phaedrus started to say, "I think . . ." but he stopped, hearing a sudden rustle and pounding feet. Emerna heard it also, and began wriggling out of her heavy pack. Phaedrus shed his instinctively, reaching for the first weapon that came to hand—and what met his hand was one of the odd shotgun-pistols from the Troopers. He said, grimly, "Let them come! I've got something that'll water their eyes!"

Emerna raised something metallic; there was a sharp report, and a bright streak fled to the zenith, where it blossomed in fire: a flare. The darkness faded and they could see: a band of ragged tramps, armed, so far as they could see, with a random collection of odd things which only had marginal use as weapons: scythes, pitchforks, staves and clubs. Still; there were about a score of them, and they rapidly fanned out to surround the two before they had time to seek shelter. Keeping his eye on them, Phaedrus drew close to Emerna, who, watching the band, hissed at him, "Can you use what we brought?"

Phaedrus grinned and risked a quick glance at her. "I can use it all. Call them, ask them to leave off. I want no more killing."

She hesitated, but called out, "You, there, parley!"

The leader, a slight, furtive person who remained somewhat back, called back, weakly, "No parley. No quarter asked, none given."

She called out, "We have no money!"

The answer came, "Don't want money. Want fresh meat for the pot!" The voice was neither angry nor heated, and it had a thin, reedy whine to it that was more chilling than what it said. Emerna glanced at Phaedrus, and said, "Kill or be killed."

He replied, "All of them."

The circle was almost complete, and the flare went out. Emerna took aim and fired the flare pistol again, this time at one of the figures, the slim one who had spoken. A bright light flashed across the distance between them and lodged in the speaker's midsection, burning with a bright white light, and then it went out as he apparently fell on it, but it flared up again, reaching its flare stage. Phaedrus recalled instincts he had learned as Rael, and listened, aiming by feel, and pulled the trigger six times, feeling the heavy explosive canisters slam and buck as they fired, and each time one fired, another of the would-be attackers fell back, flailing the air or grasping at its head. He threw the shotgun-pistol down, now emptied and useless for this kind of work, and reached for the pack. Emerna fired two more flares, hitting with one. A third she fired at the sky. When it exploded, they could see that half the attempted circle was gone, and there were gaps in the half that remained.

She called out again, "Now it evens up! Will you stop while you can?"

They heard a strangled voice call back, "No quarter," and by the light of the flare they could see the remaining members of the band still coming on, fatalistically. Phaedrus said, "These are fools! Break free and leave them."

She said back, in a low harsh whisper, "Close your eyes and cover them, quick!"

He glanced at the band, and did as she commanded, throwing his arm up, but he was almost too late: there was a searing bright flash that shone through the flesh of his arm. Afterwards, he heard moans and pitiful calls in the dark, which had become permanent for those who had sought them. Emerna said, "Open your eyes now."

"What was that?"

"Light-bomb. These won't bother any more wayfarers, nor roast limbs for the pot—they can't kill what they can't see. Closing your eyes is no good against it—it can blind even through eyelids."

"What about the survivors?"

Emerna bent to her pack, and began rearranging things. "It would be merciful to dispatch them, cruel to leave them alone. You left injured and maimed, too."

Phaedrus felt a sudden heat, and said, "Let them grope for each other and gnaw in the dark like worms."

"Just so: you have made judgment. But now I say we should check their stronghold before we leave; there may be more of them, one or two."

"I would not have survivors tracking us; you are right. But we cannot remain here."

"No. I wouldn't stay here, now, unless we cut all their throats, and even then I wouldn't. There may be outriders, scouts. No. We would best move on. But first we will see what we can."

She withdrew a large knife from the pack and sidled up to one of the blinded attackers, who was crawling about aimlessly and blinking his eyes, occasionally stopping to rub them. Phaedrus saw her kneel close beside him, and lean close, as if whispering. The man started violently, as if struck, and grabbed at her. She pulled his head up by the hair and cut his throat, and went to the next. After he had listened, he grew still for a moment, and then rushed up with an inarticulate cry and ran blindly off into the night until a sodden thump and a last cry revealed that he had run headlong into a pit. Emerna called to Phaedrus wearily, "This is hopeless! All these folk are mad! Totally mad!"

And he thought, *by an act of mine was all this brought to pass, these vile men and their vile end, none better than the other. One cries for the power to change a world, and I had, have that power, and used it, and this is the result. This, and who knows what miseries elsewhere? Lia, staring sightless at the winter sky, her beautiful pale limbs moving gracefully no more. Cliofino, bringing no more of the incomparable release and joy that he brought to the women he casually seduced, and thought nothing of. A hundred people looking for a tavern and taken for a riot by the overreactive governors of Lisagor, and had set upon them the relentless killers.* But he said, "We will probably have to look on our own. Do you remember anything about the lay of this place?"

Emerna came back to him, and said softly, "There was a large communal house, and some barns and outbuildings. I do not see any of them left standing."

"Yet these robbers and cannibals would have some place to hide."

She said impatiently, "Just so. Come, we will look. There would be a cellar somewhere . . . Also let us be quiet."

They moved first toward the place where the leader of the band had stood, reasoning that they had issued forth from a spot near there. They found the body, burned nearly in half by the action of the flare, smelling of burned flesh and still smoking. From there, they spread out a little, going over the ground carefully, looking for something, a mark, that would show a concealed entrance. Emerna found a blinded sentry some distance beyond the leader's body, moaning on the ground. He would have been close to the entrance, watching what he could see of the action.

The burned-out timbers of a barn loomed behind the groping figure, and close by the foundations was a low, slanted door, one of its leaves still open. Inside, there was no sound. Emerna shed her pack and, gripping the knife, peered into the dark opening, and then quickly stepped over the sill and into the darkness. Phaedrus half expected to see some struggle, but in another moment, she reappeared and motioned for him to follow her. He followed, carefully setting his pack on the ground beside the door.

Inside it was pitch-dark and musty-smelling, flavored with a rancid fatty odor that cut through the lingering stench of burned wood from the barn. Emerna whispered, "It goes on under the old barn. They'll have dug a place out, and made light-baffles. They'd have to, for that big a band."

She turned and began moving slowly along the tunnel, which was low enough so that they had to stoop in places, and in others gave a suggestion of large open space. After what seemed a long walk, they saw a dim glimmer of light ahead and a bit to the left. And as Emerna went forward to draw closer to the light, Phaedrus heard a sudden scrape from behind him and above and felt a weight about his shoulders, grasping and feeling for his chin. He stumbled forward under the weight, and bent over and ran hard, for he had seen Emerna duck, silhouetted against the light. He felt an impact, cushioned by whatever had fallen on him, and the struggles stopped for a moment. He fell flat onto the floor, and then stood upright with all his strength, feeling the impact of the roof again. Stunned, his attacker went limp, and Phaedrus threw him off and knelt by him for a moment, feeling along the unkempt head for the right place, and then he sent this one into the darkness to join the others they had killed. After a moment, there was no surge of pulse.

He looked up and sensed the bulk of Emerna close beside him. She said, "Clever, that. You look innocent, but you act like a man who knows woman, and you kill with precision, like one who knows what he is doing."

He said, "Seeming other than I have been has saved my life, has it not?"

"So far."

"Then observe that there is much else you have not seen, and allow things to pass as if they were just as they seem, save that I guard your flank well."

"Is that all you want?"

"No, but what I want you cannot give me."

"Hah! Fame, fortune, power, beauty?"

"No. Leave it, and let us see within. Others may lurk."

She turned abruptly and set off toward the light. After a short traverse through a zigzag part of the tunnel, they emerged into a large room with a series of corridors radiating from it. In this room were lanterns, burning a greasy oil which bubbled and smoked, and a pit in the center, which was used for a roasting fire, but which now was very low. Along the walls were various devices, whose purpose did not seem clear until Phaedrus reflected that here, with such a large crowd to feed, they would shackle one victim close to hand while they were working on the other—no point in having to carry them any distance, and in addition, their lamentations would doubtless provide a macabre entertainment. A shiver rippled across his spine, and a hot fluid rose in his throat, a gall of disgust.

Emerna called out, "Is anyone left in here? Throw down your arms and come out and walk away free." That was what she said, but she stood alertly and held the knife at readiness.

No one responded, at least not anyone of the band, but from one of the corridors, they heard a voice call out weakly, "Release us! There are prisoners!"

Emerna looked at Phaedrus, and then grasped a lamp from its wall bracket, and entered one of the corridors. Not far down it, they found a large pen, or cell, in which were kept women, about half a dozen of them, mostly unkempt and filthy, and most withdrawn, with much horror on their faces. They stared blankly as Emerna and Phaedrus approached their cell, and manipulated the crude latch that secured it, and stepped inside. Phaedrus looked over the group with wonder and horror alike; most looked as if they had once, not long ago, been young and pretty, or at least plain. Now, they looked otherwise. Only two responded with any animation. One, a ragged young girl who was very dirty and skinny, but who had retained some kind of animal sense of survival. The other looked familiar, somehow, but Phaedrus couldn't quite place the girl's face, although it seemed that he should.

The ragged waif's name was Janea, and she was telling Emerna a tale of horror and abuse, about why they had kept a pit of women inside, although they could have guessed as much by themselves. What interested him, in hearing the tale, was that Janea told them that the familiar girl had resisted them long, and in fact had proven so obstinate and uncooperative that they were planning to roast her the next day. Emerna moved, so that the weak light of the lamp shone on the girl's face somewhat better. It was a dirty face, to be sure, but it looked more familiar yet, and it came to Phaedrus who this girl was: Meliosme, the wandering gatherer, whom he had met as Rael, long ago. Phaedrus wanted to grasp her, for she had been kind to him, as an old friend, but he dared not, because here, in his present body, he was no more than a stranger to her.

13

Meliosme

THEY DID NOT waste any time lingering over the possessions of the robbers; those were scant loot from poor travelers. Nor did they attempt to find or use any food they might have found. There were some cured pieces, but they would have none of it. And last, there was nothing like a place to clean the survivors, so they gathered them up, one by one; some they had to work with more than others, and guided them back through the tunnels and corridors to the night outside, by the slanted door, by which the blinded guard was still moaning and making scrabbling motions with his hands at the dirt and ashes. As they emerged into the night, which had more light than the reeking tunnel, one of the women who had been passive and withdrawn, suddenly came alive, and spoke earnestly with Emerna, who presently gave her a small knife from her pack, and then went back to the others and began guiding them off, away from the place. The woman who had taken the knife dropped down on her hands and knees, and crawled to where the moaning guard lay. The rest of them moved off, Emerna motioning them in agitation, Phaedrus bringing up the rear, looking about warily. Presently they were well away from the barn, and still the woman did not join them. But they heard a sudden sharp cry, followed from the same throat by more hoarse calls, entreaties, remonstrances, confessions, and finally, sounds that bore no resemblance to a human voice at all. These sounds were still going on as they trudged away, and never quite ended, but merely faded from the distance increasing between them.

Phaedrus joined Emerna, at whom he questioned, "What did you let her do?"

Janea, who was walking nearby, volunteered, in her bratty voice, "The one who was guard was a favorite with us, and especially Lefthera; she has some instruction for him, and for those others who survive and grope as well."

As if to bear her words out, they noted that the distant sounds were silent, indeed. But in a moment, behind them, they could hear another start up, at first sounding manlike, but rapidly rising in pitch and frenzy and finally reaching extremes even bosels did not often attain.

Emerna added, "She told me she would rather settle with them than be sheltered, and that her home was not far, in any event. She would return when she had done what she had to do. She told me what they did and I gave her the knife: she has the right, if she does nothing else. It is fitting for them, although they seem to be protesting more than their former victims."

Janea said, "They aren't taking their medicine as well as they handed it out: how they laughed and joked! For just a little I'd go back and help her, but for the fact that she's selfish and wouldn't share one, not even one."

Phaedrus asked, "Are there any more like that around here?"

Janea answered, "No. Not one band. This one either killed or ate them all. I hear it's clear up north all the way to Akchil Sunslope, or so they bragged."

Nevertheless, they all fell silent, and waited for the next series of screams to begin, and they did not have to wait very long: it was short, hoarse, and ended abruptly. For a time they stood in the empty dark spaces and listened for something else—perhaps approaching footsteps—but there were no more sounds, save that of the wind, and Emerna turned to the north and started walking, and the rest, after hesitating a little, drifted off, following her, more or less. Phaedrus let the survivors string out into an irregular line and brought up the rear, listening into the dark warily, but he heard no more sounds, not even those of bosels.

Apparently, Emerna had decided to walk on through the darkness; either she knew some place farther on, or decided to leave the immediate area. As they walked, he noticed a curious thing happening; each time he looked up at the band, the number of people in it seemed to dwindle. He did not see the women leave, or wander off, but somehow they did, drifting off silently into the darkness, one by one, presumably starting back for wherever they had come from, or resuming their journey. The only one he watched closely was Meliosme, and she did not waver, but trudged on, tiredly but steadily. By the time light was coming

up from the east, they were well into the hill country between Crule
The Swale and Zolotane, and there were only four of them left: Emerna,
Janea, Meliosme and Phaedrus.

This was dry country, but their way crossed and recrossed water
courses, at first as dry as the land around them and marked only by
gravel beds and brushy tangles along the sides, but soon showing some
water in them as they went higher up.

In the shadow of a steep bank, Emerna stopped uncertainly, looking
about her wearily. Meliosme joined her, and Phaedrus came up to them
in a moment. Emerna wanted to stop and rest, but was uncertain about
the place; she was now well out of the area she knew well and additionally had turned into the hills too soon, and admitted she did not
know the area. Meliosme glanced about, almost off-handedly, and told
her that the place was safe enough, and sat down against a large rock
over which a bare and scraggly tree hung, and closed her eyes. Emerna
found another place not too far off, and Janea followed her, and they
settled down together. Phaedrus watched this, and did not interfere;
presently he decided to stay awake as long as he could, to watch over
the group while the others slept. He looked about in the brightening
daylight, and saw bare, rocky hills, sand-colored, dun brown, pale violet,
pocked with clumps of vegetation, an occasional gaunt tree festooned
with ragged strips. To the west, more hills against the dark sky; to the
east, there were hills, too, but there was only light behind them, the
morning, running across the long grasslands of Crule The Swale.

In the tumults of the times, many things had been brought to light by
the ministrations of Femisticleo Chugun's Secret Police, but odd as it
might be, much more had remained undiscovered, owing to the organization of the Offworld Watch on Oerlikon, which severely limited
what the lower orders knew. This limitation of essential knowledge,
coupled with the troubles the central government was having to cope
with throughout Lisagor, effectively limited the penetration Chugun's
people were able to effect into the offworld organization, with the immensely practical result that Arunda Palude was able to return to her
concealed communications site and broadcast an emergency recall signal, under which conditions the main support ship was to return and re-
trieve as many as it could, depending on conditions available. This
support ship was not armed, and could not carry out operations in a
hostile environment, nevertheless they would try to pick up as many as

they could. She reported back to Charodei, now with Cesar Kham, the active head of what mission survived. But Charodei did not convey this information to Luto Pternam.

Pternam clearly had his own hands full, and devoted most of his time alternating between hiding in the deepest recesses of The Mask Factory, expecting the return of Tiresio Rael any moment, and working at a manic pace in stints which might carry him across two full days before he collapsed from exhaustion. Despite the heroic measures, however, Lisagor was melting like a cake of ice placed in the hot sunlight: North Tilanque had joined Karshiyaka, as had Severovost and even the extreme easternmost part of Akchil. South Tilanque and Priboy had gone over to the rebels of Zamor, which left Lisagor with only a small strip to the coast in the central parts of the seaboard province, and this was uncertain and full of rival factions contending. In the north, Zefaa and Greyslope were nominally still under control, but this condition clearly existed solely because the inhabitants had nothing better to do, and could change quickly, in a matter of days. The West was long gone: Clisp, the Serpentine, and what passed for population centers in sparsely-inhabited Zolotane had been among the first to break off, and the new borders remained closed. Rumors were widespread that the new rulers of Marisol were assembling an army to invade Zefaa, and there were companion rumors running with those which suggested that the locals there would surrender immediately were such an invasion to take place. In the south, Sertse Solntsa was still holding, but it was clearly by force alone that the province was being held. In fact, so much of the city had been damaged that it was already useless as a port.

So far, Central Lisagor was holding together, partly from fear of change, fear of the surviving cadres of Pallet-Dropped Heavy Troopers, and partly because no one had yet tried to invade it. Oerlikon had no tradition of war, and so when an area rebelled, their chief concern was to be left alone, repulsing attacks and being content with that. Moreover, it did not seem likely that the central government could invade the rebel provinces, either, as they lacked the numbers of Troopers necessary for the task, and the loyalty of their remaining population hinged on an inlanders traditional distaste for the sea-province outlanders. They would not join them, neither would they fight them, and so the one thing that enabled them to hold the inland provinces prevented them from raising an army to recapture any of the outlying provinces.

Charodei was clearly having his own problems as well, chiefly with Pternam, who seemed to be less and less interested in arranging for the

Offworlders to find suitable transceiver equipment, and more interested in holding on to what he already had. Hints and suggestions seemed to have little effect on this eroding situation, and so Charodei called for a meeting on the subject. They met at The Mask Factory, this time in broad daylight. Nobody seemed to mind that Pternam had collected some odd associates lately.

Charodei did not waste words; "You know, Pternam, it's already an open secret that you have allies."

Pternam shivered and said, "So many of you popped out of the woodwork I'm not surprised people talk."

"They don't seem to mind."

"You know us well, and we know nothing of you—nevertheless there is much you miss; no matter your loyalties, there is a bad flavor to this, which we Lisaks try to ignore." He thought a moment, and then added, "We express ourselves in a few selected areas, and elsewhere restrain our plunging lusts—thereby is Change thwarted; by operating openly, more or less, you poison things."

Charodei blinked once, owlishly. "You aver that our assistance is counterproductive to your plans?"

Pternam laughed hollowly, a madman's chuckle at something no one else would find humorous. "Ha-ha! Counterproductive, indeed. Perhaps, were there plan left, but I have given that up long ago!"

"You don't think we can deliver, then."

"Of course you can't deliver. You never could."

"Not so; we could, and can. Of course, there are measures of the quality of appropriateness . . . the time is soon approaching when, in our estimation, the situation will have gone too far to argue for a reorganization of the central provinces under controllable conditions."

"I am well aware that things are still deteriorating. Symbarupol is perilously close to the new Changeist territories; the Tilanque strip is gone, as is most of Puropaigne south of here. There has been talk of moving the Center out of here, to a more protected location out in Crule. Additionally, we do not seem to have the resources to continue at the level we have tried to maintain. Something more is needed, but Crule and Akchil are unwilling to supply it."

"You need troops. . . ."

"Yes." For a moment, a shred of hope arose in Pternam. "We even made some contacts with the Freeholders of Tartary, but to little use; they have come to terms with Change in a way that does not accord with the old way we defend here. Likewise, with loyalists in the rebel areas, who claim to want the old way, but who will send no fighting men to enforce it."

"You can't make up enough Heavy Troopers?"

"It takes time. We never worried about time before. The people, you see, they got used to the troopers, to their transports. Now they ambush them as they land, take their weapons, and turn them on the following waves. That was all we ever needed . . . now it isn't any good anymore. When they move to Crule, The Mask Factory will close; we can't move everything we need to continue."

Charodei could see where things were leading. Pternam was in a funk, burned out, he had already given up. Useless, useless. He had clearly no intention of helping them—he had no idea of how to help himself. "What do you imagine you will do?"

"Survive, that's what. We are already turning out some of the lower orders who were associates here. Some have left, others have run off to the sea provinces. . . ."

After a moment, Charodei said, "Then you are not going to be able to get us access to suitable components to contact the ship?"

Pternam looked away, and then back. He said, "Can you take me with you?"

Charodei felt a surge of anger, and contemptuous mirth with it. The very idea, that this ignorant savage would want to be taken to a world like Heliarcos, which would be incomprehensible to him, even though Charodei knew it in truth to be a backwater world itself. This went through his mind almost instantly, and he let none of it show. He said, instead, ". . . It's never been done. This was supposed to be a no-contact mission, here on Oerlikon, and so no provisions were made for such a contingency. . . ."

"But humans, they move around freely, they travel from world to world, back in the place where you come from?"

"Yes, of course. . . . One has to pay fares, and sometimes there are small restrictions, but in general, that is the nature of things: people more or less move about as they feel the urge."

"You have authority among your group; you could arrange such a novelty."

"Perhaps. Perhaps not. I would have to work with others, who still recall the original doctrine of this operation."

Pternam said, "No contact."

"Exactly."

"But you have violated that principle by contacting me."

"True, we did bend things some."

"Well, I will be brief. My operation is to close down, and there is little else for me to do. Additionally, I have enemies. Here, I have some security against random assassinations, but away . . . Take me with you and you can have The Mask Factory; there are enough components here presumably for your experts to fabricate something that will work."

"Otherwise . . . ?"

"Otherwise, I will have everything destroyed. I can't afford to leave records of what we did. Doubtless there will be those who would like to redress their grievances, even though we have tried to eliminate that negative attitude . . ."

"What could you do for us?"

"I could make you another Morphodite, and all that goes with that; the conscious control of the hormone system." And he thought, deep in his mind, *Yes, I'll make another one for them, and this time I'll loose it early on, and it can savage their worlds like they savaged mine.* He forgot something crucial to reality, that it was he, and not the Offworlders, who had savaged Oerlikon and Lisagor.

Charodei saw the repressed excitement in Pternam, the ratlike hope, and read it correctly: *And when we get him there, he'll turn one loose on us, or so he thinks. Well, we can always jettison him in deep space.* He said, "There might be some use in that, after all—if for nothing else than explaining events here—how they came to be. You'd have to make do with a smaller sample of experimental subjects; we can't drag them off the streets like you could here."

Pternam saw that Charodei did not refuse outright, and therefore still wanted something from him—if nothing else, access within the labyrinthine recesses of The Mask Factory to build a transceiver.

Charodei said, "I cannot promise what will transpire; you understand that I cannot speak for those who may come. At any rate, I will do what I can."

It seemed little, but enough, considering the circumstances. Pternam said, "Very well. I will have Avaria show you where things are; there should be enough left in the Computorium to do the job."

"Excellent! Rest assured that we will leave your equipment in operating condition."

Pternam turned to go. "Oh no. That won't be necessary at all; in fact, I prefer that your people leave it inoperable. And illegible."

"Are things *that* close?"

"Close enough. You can use this building to transmit from. I will give orders that you not be molested."

"I will put Palude on it immediately."

"The sooner the better. . . . Do you think they will come?"

"Depends on what we can put together, where they are, how far. A lot of variables. Remember, we never expected to have to recall the support ship."

Pternam laughed aloud. "What were you planning to do? Stay here forever?"

Charodei felt an odd spasm of irritation, and he suppressed it with difficulty. "A lot of people did; many more supposed that things would remain changeless on the world that lived for changelessness."

"You mean when their duty was over, some elected to stay here?"

Charodei explained. "Why not? Their own world was twenty standard years behind them. Lisagor was all they knew."

"That's amazing! And what would these people do for a living?"

"They would have some funds supplied through suitable covers, but to avoid drawing attention to themselves they would usually take obscure positions . . . it was policy that we did not keep up with those who were retired and had gone native. Needless to say, they were all model citizens . . . by definition. As far as I know, that is."

Pternam laughed, an erratic, plunging chuckle that sounded more than a little out of control. "Sa-ha! So when we were making the Morphodite, we might well have started with one of your retirees."

Charodei felt a chill along his backbone. "Yes, I suppose that would have been possible . . . we would have no way to ascertain if this was the case or not." Charodei suppressed his feelings again. Changelessness had been maintained by many things, but The Mask Factory had played a larger part than they had suspected, performing experiments and transformations outlawed everywhere else, absolutely prohibited. And this Pternam thought it was humorous that he might have made up his weapon out of material that had come from some far world. And if it were true, what a fate to undergo: drugs, shock, electronic stimulation, the artificial attainment of extreme trance states. Yes, as he reflected on it, he could be certain that some of his people had been processed by Pternam. It strengthened his resolve, and he thought, clearly and consciously, *Yes, we'll jettison the son-of-a-bitch; indeed, I'll do it personally. It's a duty, a responsibility. We cannot let this monster walk about on our own worlds, free to hatch more of his plots.*

As if reading his mind, and agreeing with some internal argument, Pternam nodded, and said, "Well, that's a fine set of circumstances, were it true. I agree we'd have no way to know . . . but just imagine: we preyed upon you just as you were preying upon us, and neither of us knew of the symbiosis . . . Well, that chapter is over."

"Yes. Remember whose side we were on."

"Indeed: the side of orthodoxy, of Monclova and Chugun, and Primitive Mercador and Odisio Chang, lifers all. But in the end it did us all no good, eh? Their orthodoxy, your support, my schemes. There were too many plotters, too many throne-upholders, and so we all pushed it over in the press. . . . Well, tell your people they will doubtless be able to come openly after a time. We will probably need the help after these tumults."

"You think they would welcome us again?"

Pternam shrugged. "You would always be welcome in Clisp. You doubtless have the tools to rebuild the Old Port as well."

Charodei said, in a low voice, "I hope you don't assume omnipotence on our part; we, too, have our limits."

Pternam chuckled again, that erratic little laugh: "Ho-ha! Yes, that's always the way it is—you're the miracle workers until we really need you, and then you're only human."

"If I may say, you have an odd perspective."

"You reminded me what you supported; I remind you that this was my world, better or worse, and that it sits unevenly now that we know that one of the things that allowed us to be changeless was the covert support of people we detested and left, back in the beginning days here. We might have done better to accept some change; some of the advice of Clisp and the Serpentine. . . . Nobody likes to be revealed a fool."

"The Morphodite ended our mission here; if you wish revenge, you have already had it."

14

Morning in Zolotane

PHAEDRUS HAD BEEN dreaming; he awoke instantly, and knew he had dreamed, but he could not remember what. And he saw, head clear, that it was already late on in the morning, and that Meliosme was sitting close by, watching him intently, her regard did not change when she saw that he was awake.

He said, "You look as if you knew me."

She nodded, solemnly. "Yes. You remind me of someone I once met, knew for a short time—a short time indeed; I am from the outlands, the wild places, and so to me all townsmen seem alike, weighted by the inertia of their destiny, pressed into a fixed course. Not so you, or the other. You and he share a mannerism, of being live, quick, unweighted. I never knew townsmen before who were like that."

"And others? Not townsmen?"

Meliosme mused for a moment, as if savoring something rather than remembering it, looking off into the distance. "I am a fleischbaum harvester, and I meet little save solitaries like me, and do you know there are few men to it? True, though. You, and the other one—you have no weight behind you, no massiness. You can go as you will."

He listened to her, and looked deeply at the plain, sturdy figure, the face that was not masculine or feminine but human, illuminated from within by a sense of repose and acceptance of the rhythm of the world; outwardly, Meliosme was rough and homely, but interiorly, she was as sleek as some furred and graceful riparian animal, alert, but not tensed. An odd emotion colored his perceptions, a quick shiver, a ripple, something that whispered to him to make bold, to speak openly of himself, of his identity. Well, perhaps not all of it. Some of it, until he could gauge how she would hear it. No one tells all the truth, for if they did, everyone would immediately go up in flames.

He said, "You met Tiresio Rael in a traveler's tavern, and rode on a beamliner with him, to Marula; you went with him to a room, where he bade you leave him for your safety."

Meliosme blinked once, but did not seem otherwise surprised that he would know this. "Yes, it was like that."

Phaedrus continued, "He felt a real emotion for the girl he met, or else he would not have sent her away."

She said, "You know much; then you will know something of what I felt."

"That is so."

She ventured after a long silence, "No spy knows such things, no watcher."

"I was Rael."

"I can see that; I don't know how, but I *see* it. You are him, but also different. You are younger."

"I changed. It was something that was done to me."

"I understand. There were always some like that wandering about; but they were unfinished, un-right, broken. You then were . . . I don't know. You were of two natures, one a spirit of peace, of wisdom; and the other, a destroying angel."

"I had not thought of myself as a sage; yet destroy I have. But I will no more, nor will I change again."

She nodded again, and smiled faintly. "Done. And what will you do?"

"I act only for myself, now. I need a quiet place, where I can perhaps dig out who I am; who I was. When they changed me, they took away that knowledge. I was not always Rael."

"I knew that."

"You could see what I was?"

Meliosme said, "No. That Rael had not always been so. You, too, have that quality of newness."

"But I remember the things I have been; the things I have done."

"You know them, you did them, you were them, but they are not your prison. You will learn from them."

"Where? Here, in this wilderness?"

"Zolotane is not far. I know these hills well, having passed along these trails many times; over the hills are open lands that slope down to the blue salt sea. There are stands of open fleischbaum groves, and sea creatures to catch, and a land of grass, golden under the sun. Few people are there."

Phaedrus glanced at the place where Emerna waited with Janea, still asleep, although the morning was well advanced. "What about them?"

"They must go along their own path; it is not yours, now."

"I was as one dead; she saved me, or I would have been, in the ruin of Marula."

"Marula stands yet." She shrugged. "Such debts . . . one can never repay them, and so one cannot. Let her go—she is weighted, set, bound to something dark, black and red."

"She wants, I think, to go to Clisp."

"We will show them the way. But remain with me or no, you will leave her, now or later. It is better now."

Then Meliosme led him away from the narrow valley, and showed him simple things they could catch or gather; small dried pomes like miniature apples, an evergreen twining vine with leathery leaves and long, stringy pods, both of which were edible. She pointed out a long, snake-like creature with four pairs of legs, and then caught it with a quick motion, killing it instantly.

Phaedrus said, "I would not have guessed there was so much here; it looks like a waste, empty."

She nodded. "It is so. There is abundance if we know how to look, and we take but what we need."

"People do not do that, but grow things of their own and worry if there will be enough."

She said, "There will never be enough to still the fear that there might not be enough. But they do not fear scarcity; they fear fear. Look—we may live on these things, but we will not grow content on them."

He said, "I understand; to become content is to fear that it will end. We are better a little hungry, I think." He gestured with his head toward the east, generally. "*They* feared change so much they made a world that slowed it to nearly zero, but in the end, a pinprick released the years of accumulated pressure, and so it burst."

"You did that."

"Yes."

"Why? Were you their enemy? Was there a revenge to be?"

He waited, and then said, "I knew them not. They were strangers to me. They saw to that in The Mask Factory, that I had no past. They . . . took me apart, and reassembled me, leaving some things out. I did not know it then, but I only knew what they wanted me to do, which was perform a simple, single act that would change the world. The reality of

a world, of its people, rests on a single person, low and unknown, changing, shifting slowly, and if you remove that person, you can change the
world. That was what I knew, and so I did." He sighed, deeply. "And now
it seems like a dream, like some strange vision."

"But you changed . . . And see—the natural world is the same. At a
given moment, it all rests on a single creature which we do not know or
understand. And you could *see* this person!"

"I could . . . calculate who it was—that is the best way to say it."

"You can still do this?"

"Yes . . . They gave me enough so I would believe it, but they thought
the idea nonsense."

Meliosme laughed to herself, a secretive little chuckle. "What fools
they were! To launch a person on the only path he could take, and give
him something to believe. Of course he would do it!"

He said, "So I learned. There are many phases to it . . ."

"You could extend it to the natural world."

He thought for a moment, and said, "Yes, but it would be . . . different. I would have to use other symbols, use different manipulations. But
then after that . . . it would be . . . simpler."

"Then you will use your art, and understand, and you will tell us . . .
and we will listen. They made you for a weapon, but you will be a gentle hand bringing water to a thirsty land." Then she said, "You found the
person, and sent him to the darkness, and the world changed. Then what
happened? Who has it set upon now?"

"When you take the base away, it flickers for instants among others,
but not long enough for stability to be attained. Later, the center slows
and settles on another, as obscure as the first. I have not looked hard
since then, and the only operation I have done suggested that things
were still in flux. It feels that way now to me, but it's trying to find a
place."

"Then you can do it without the symbols, the paper, the figures—in
your head. You can feel it directly."

"I was Rael, I was Damistofia, I am Phaedrus, and through all of those
I wished to forget it."

"But you cannot; you will turn the evil they set upon you to a good—
a worthy thing."

"I fear the use of it again."

"I understand. But you have changed yourself, and you may not return to what you were, but you will have to learn to live with what you
are. I can help."

He wanted then to ask why, but felt the air between them growing delicate, and he did not wish to have the issue resolved just then; it felt right as it was, and so he remained silent, and let it be. She said, "Come along, we'll share with the others, and set them on their way, to Clisp."

Together, they climbed back down into the sheltered little valley, really more a dry wash, to the place where they had been the night before. Then they had done nothing, but coming back from the uplands, he felt an odd sense of immediate past intimacy with Meliosme, as if she had shared something with him; like the sharing of sex, but more intimate in a way that the sweet muscular anodyne of coupling could not reach.

They looked for Emerna and Janea, and found them cowering under a bush with nodding circular leaves, hiding. Not far away stood a solitary bosel, observing, so it appeared, its head crooked comically to the side. This was the first time Phaedrus could remember seeing one, and at first he had to force himself to *see* it, so odd were its outlines, suggestive of parts of animals he could recall, although he did not know where he knew them from. It stood upright on two legs, a bulbous, bird-like body, small, apparently fragile arms, and a gangling long neck supporting a comical head, round at the back, crowned with expandable, flexible ears, two eyes overshadowed not by brows but feathery appendages that looked like rubbery moth antennae. The snout was long and tubular, with one large orifice and two small ones. The upper body was furred, but the legs were bare and fluted with muscle.

He said quietly, "It is dangerous?"

Meliosme walked out into the open, casually, answering over her shoulder. "This one, no. A young buck, only curious." She made a ducking motion and then turned gracefully about, as if dancing, ending by repeatedly crossing her forearms. To Phaedrus's amazement, the bosel responded with a little hop which took it erratically to one side, where it turned its snout to the sky and vented a soft breathy whistling, which suggested amusement, or whimsy. Then, with one last sidelong glance toward the two hiding women, it abruptly turned and loped off up the wash somewhere to the north, vanishing among the rocks.

Meliosme said, "When they're young, they find humans fascinating. They watch them all the time in the wild like this. I don't know what they find so interesting. Later, they become more erratic, unpredictable, although it seems to me that it makes sense to them, somehow, that it is I who don't understand the web here we have trespassed into. That one will wander off, although he will keep us in sight for a while, or within scent."

"There won't be others?"

"They're solitaries—scroungers and scavengers who don't tolerate company very well. They maintain contact at night, when they are active, by sounds which you have doubtless heard. I do not know the import of the sounds, if there is any. They seem to communicate by gesture, and some of the basic motions I have learned."

"You told it something. . . ."

"I told it to go away. It laughed and sent back that it didn't matter."

"That sounds easy."

"It's not. The key motions are short and easy to do wrongly, so that you send a garble, which makes them hostile, or worse, you send something which offends them individually. Even that young one could be dangerous if provoked. They are nowhere near as fragile as they look, or as awkward. They can move fast, and they can . . . anticipate things. It accepted me as its superior immediately, but it also knew I had other interests: you, them. It might have moved on you. Myself I can protect, but I have never tried to defend another—that is an awkward situation."

They walked toward the bush from which Emerna and Janea were now emerging and Phaedrus said, "They sound almost intelligent. Have others tried to contact them?"

"Only such as I, gatherers, and others of the wild places. And I cannot say whether they have minds."

They shared the food they had brought, and rested, saying little among themselves. Phaedrus saw that Emerna had assumed a kind of responsibility for the ragged Janea, and had dismissed him in her mind, and he did not wish to change that. On the other hand, he could see that she saw and resented his easy relationship with Meliosme, who with a night's rest had changed from a haggard prisoner expecting to be tormented and eaten to an alert and confident person at home in the wilds. He thought he caught a reluctance in Emerna to stay at this place, overlaid by a burning desire to get away from it.

They spoke of the bosel, and Emerna admitted that she was terrified of them. Janea claimed that Meliosme could have called bosels to save them had she wished.

Meliosme shook her head and smiled softly. "That's why people have never tried to learn about them; you can't get them to do things for you.

They don't seem to understand doing for something else. Besides, one would have done us no good, even if I could have called one, which I can't—they have never answered my imitations of their calls—they don't do anything together except procreate."

The sun was shining and soon reached the zenith, and the light began to fall in the slanting rays of early afternoon. Janea seemed agitated, eager to be on the way.

Phaedrus said, "You will, then, want to go on to Clisp?"

Emerna answered, "At least the Serpentine." To Meliosme she said, "Do you know the way?"

Meliosme said, "Yes. But I do not wish to go there, so I will tell you how to go. I will stay—" here she gestured westwards—"there in Zolotane."

"What about you?" Emerna directed this at Phaedrus.

"Clisp is too far for me. I have things to unravel for which I need an emptier land."

"There are still empty places in Clisp."

"It needs doing now."

"Very well." Emerna gathered herself and got to her feet with what seemed to Phaedrus to be an attitude of anger, but nothing came of it. She turned and offered her hand to Janea, who took it and got up, too, eager to be on the way. Emerna said, "I suppose the sooner we start . . ." And with no more formality than that, they started out northward again, following the creekbed as it followed the course of the defile it had cut.

As the slanting light changed slowly to twilight, and then evening, they followed the watercourse ever upward and to the northwest. Soon damp patches appeared in the riverbed sand, and then small stretches of standing water, and by evening proper they were walking along the edges of a small creek. The vegetation changed, too; as they went up, the bare ground and vines gave way to a tussocky ground cover, and there began to be trees, with short, barrel-like trunks, supporting gnarled and twisted wide-spreading branches. It was quiet, peaceful country, the aisles in the forest filled with golden light falling on the tussocks that covered the ground between the trees. There was no sign of inhabitants, either native or Oerlikon or alien, a fact which Phaedrus noted and commented on. Meliosme pronounced the open forest a notorious haunt of bosels, and was anxious to be past it before nightfall, for that reason, and Emerna and Janea agreed. As if to underline her words, they began to hear some calls from the east, exhausted, tenuous wailing sounds that seemed to have no great import to them. Phaedrus listened carefully and thought to identify at least four separate callers, but they all seemed far away.

"Not so!" Meliosme asserted with some confidence. "They are great deceivers, standing within arm's-length and pretending to be miles away. But those you hear are of no matter, near or far; if they were interested in us, you would hear calls from all around. Those kinds of sounds soon end—the ones you hear—and no more is seen or heard of them."

What she had said seemed to be borne out a little later on, when the calls, after a rough, rhythmic association, faded out, not suddenly, but as if the callers were finished and had no more to say. But despite Meliosme's arguments to the contrary, Phaedrus thought he had heard distinct repeating patterns among the odd, diverse calls, which had at first seemed alike only in tone and type of utterance.

They were still down in a valley, following the creek north and west, but the sky to the west of them was open and expansive, full of light instead of shadows, and there was a warm lightness to the air that promised a different terrain. Meliosme called them to a halt.

"Here is the place where the paths diverge. Follow the creek north, and you will come to an open hilltop, with a circle worn into it. Bosels use this in midsummer, but none will approach the place now. Follow the rivulet down, on the other side, and you will come to the marshes, which is in Zolotane, but is near to the Serpentine. About a day's walk, I should think, if you're up to moving along smartly. We will turn here and go down into lower Zolotane, where there are few."

Emerna looked north, up the creek, and hesitated. "Could we not follow you to the coast? Then we could go north."

"This part of Zolotane is empty, and the coast is rough." She shrugged. "It is your choice. You saved us from the tramps; who am I to tell you where you can go and not go? I only say that where we go is empty country, and no easy way out of it."

Janea the waif tugged at Emerna's arm. She clearly did not wish to stay in the wilds. For a minute longer, she stood, uncertain, looking at the light fading in the west, and the empty creek bottom north. At last, she said, "So be the throw," and turned up the creek, neither saying farewells nor waiting for any.

After the pair had walked around a bend, Phaedrus said, "An odd and capable creature, that one. I am sorry to see her go, the times being what they are."

Meliosme said, "Surely you could see that she wasn't whole, but was damaged and broken, long before you set the world on edge. And as you were not whole yourself, so she could serve you, but as you grew in knowledge of self, you would threaten her, and in the end, she would be your enemy. She is dangerous. Better we send her back to the world, where the presence of many others may heal her. She needs those others. You know what you need."

He nodded. "Yes. At least for a time. Well, let us go. I think you know the way."

Meliosme smiled, and Phaedrus saw with pleasure that although she was not pretty, when she smiled there was a warmth in her face that was genuine. "Yes, so I do, or at least so much as I remember." She looked shyly at the ground for a moment. "There is an abandoned cabin down there, and a little creek that flows down from the hills and falls into the sea at the cliffs. The land is covered with grassopant, and the sun shines on the land and the water. A nice place. Of course, there is no food, but we can manage. You are, for the time, a gatherer. I will show you."

Phaedrus asked, "Is there more?"

"There is a matter I would take up where it left off, when you were another."

Meliosme led them up a steep path, that wound upward, and farther upward, until at last it emerged on a ridgeline where there was nothing higher to the west. The sun was sinking, near the horizon, which was a ruled line of darkness, straight, upon which there was a golden trail shimmering.

Phaedrus stopped and looked long across the openness that lay before him. At the distant horizon was the sea, and somewhere beyond that, the harsh and bare mountains of southern and eastern Clisp, which faced this bay. But here were rolling hills and ridges slanting down gently to the sea. He turned to Meliosme and asked, "Where shall I go when you have finished?"

To which she said, "I will not be finished." And took his hand. Hers was hardened and tough from years in the wild, but it felt right, and he took what was offered, and together they walked down the first of the slopes that led down to the sea. They had not gone very far when they began to hear bosel calls, liquid, trembling wails, first from behind them, seemingly in the very place they had paused, but also down the slope in front of them, and some more to the north and south. Phaedrus listened carefully, and said that he thought there were six. Meliosme listened and agreed, and also pronounced them not dangerous.

"When they call like that, they're just curious. Actually, it's a good sign that we picked up some like that."

"Why?"

"Because it means that they haven't seen anyone like us for a long time coming this way. We're odd, and new, to them. Or so it seems to me."

"You know them as well as anyone I have known."

"You are kind. But no one knows bosels well, and after we live here for a time, you will know them as well as I—maybe better."

"Why do you say that?"

"The young one we saw before—he is with this group. And it was you he was interested in. They are following you, not me. At least, I have never heard them make that sound while watching me or following."

"Is this group dangerous?"

"I don't think so. Let us go straight ahead, and mind our own affairs; when they can anticipate what we are going to do, they will form a looser group, and move off. If the calls change otherwise . . . well, we will worry about that, then."

15

Final Focus

THERE WAS A small building, far down the long slope, which was
much longer than it seemed when they had seen it from the top of
the ridge that properly divided Zolotane from Crule The Swale. A long
walk, which totally sapped their endurance. And the building; that
wasn't much either. Abandoned for years to the airs of the coast, come
whatever would, one could not tell whether it had been a house, or a
shed, or a small barn, or none of these. And it was the only place in
sight, more, the only one Meliosme had ever known along this part of
the coast.

They had walked all of one night and all of the following day to get
there, and in the later afternoon light, the wind came off the sea and
made a whispering among the grassplants and the old ruins.

Phaedrus asked, after drinking long and deep at the shallow stream
that watered the place, "Do you know who was here, who built, and
why, here?"

"No. I never knew. I never came to this place before. I saw it from
afar. And I heard there was an abandoned place here, the only one down
this far. This is only Zolotane if you make natural borders; actually, it is
no one's. Its style seems to me to be more Crule, but an old Crule not
seen in our lives, mine or yours."

Phaedrus chuckled. "We do not know how long mine is; I was born
only a little ago."

She made a face at him. "Even that much, however long it is. This is
an old place, and the owners long gone. They came for something, and
did not get it, and left, or got so much of it they wanted nothing else
and so became one with it."

Phaedrus looked around for a long time, saying nothing. He took in
the empty sweep of the coast, the expanse of grassplant that tossed to

the coast wind and gave it fleeting suggestion of shape; he saw the open sweep of the sky, the dark water westward of them. He inhaled deeply and tasted the world-ocean. Finally, he said, "Can we live here? Is there enough for us?"

Meliosme had been squatting, looking at the ground as if studying it. Now she stood, and also looked about, slowly. "Yes. A lot of searching and scrabbling, but it will be possible. In time . . ."

He looked at her directly. "I remember you. You have not changed."

She said, "In you there is something which did not change, that I remember."

"Well . . . let us make of this ruin a house of sorts."

She laughed easily. "I do not need one."

"Your wandering days seem to be over."

"For now. But who knows? I may someday wish to take them up again."

"Can you see this time?"

She paused, as if deep in thought. Finally: "No. I cannot. We will rebuild."

"And make some new things."

She added, "Some new things are actually older than humankind on Oerlikon."

"Some are older than humankind itself."

As the light fell, they went into the building and moved a few things around and also searched for whatever they could find. Among their finds were a few plain, worn, and much-rusted tools such as one would have about a home in an empty land. But by then the light was almost gone, and so they did not do more than make a shelter for themselves against the wind, which was still cold, and some protection from bosels, should any approach, although for once the dark seemed curiously free of them. As they became quiet, they could hear short calls, but from very far away, and there was no urgency in those. Phaedrus and Meliosme lay close together for warmth, and presently they became closer, and very warm, and afterward they lay together, wrapped in their collection of odd pieces and scraps, and slept soundly, untroubled by dreams or desires.

The next morning they awoke late and were very hungry. Meliosme led him down to the sea and along the shore, pointing out what was edible, what was not, and what was endurable should the occasion arise. She

said, "We have water, we have the sea, and there is grassplant, and farther back, fleischbaum."

"Everything except clothes."

She laughed, a soft chuckle. "If it will hurry up and get a bit warmer,
we will not need those. There is no flow into the great bay from the
north, and so the water will be warm."

He said, "And then winter again."

She answered, "We will rest here for a while, and then go forth, to get
some things. We can always take a load of fleischbaum with us. I think
people will be hungry, and will trade with ragamuffins, when their values have changed somewhat."

Phaedrus looked out across the water, now more at ease that Meliosme had caught a few things for them. During the night, the wind
had shifted some, and although waves were coming in onto the narrow
beach, on the brown sand, the wind from the land was lifting their crests
back gracefully. He said, "Yes. But I do not want to leave this place any
longer than I have to."

"We won't."

And they returned to the little creek, climbed back up to the golden
plain, and set to rebuilding the house. During the afternoon, Meliosme
set off on an exploring trip, back into the higher country back of them,
for fleischbaum and groundnut which had survived the winter, and returned near evening with her skirts full of things. As she neared the
house, which was even now looking more like a house and less like a
ruin, she saw Phaedrus's slender figure climbing about on the roof he
was rebuilding. Not so far away from the house, south of it, in the slanting, marvelous light of the west, stood quietly three large bosels, of the
appearance of elder bucks of great age and sagacity, who stood and
watched, without comment, without gesture, hoot or grumble. Phaedrus, although she could see by his actions that he was aware of them,
ignored them and went on with his work. When they saw her approaching, they turned and stared solemnly at her, and moved off, a little farther south, but they still stayed and waited for a long time, until
darkness fell. After that, in the night, lying together in their shelter inside the walls, the couple heard the flow of boselcall rippling about
them, intermittently, like distant summer lightning.

Their life now flowed much like the sea winds that flowed over the
golden shoals of grass which covered the flat lands between the seaside

cliffs and the hills in the east. The long days of Oerlikon drifted slowly past them, and with more days, the imperceptible change of the seasons, always subtle and delicate. Phaedrus did not question Meliosme closely about her recent past, but he noticed a change in his own life which was immediate and demonstrable. He could not remember any period save the present when he had not measured events around himself (or herself) by devastating, calamitous events, either things he knew were to come, or those which had passed. Now was different. There was no measure. They slept at dark and arose at light, and in between, without haste, rebuilt the house and made up their stores. It was a simple life of survival thousands of years in tradition, and soon he stopped considering who he had been and worried little over who he might become. It was enough to be as he was at the moment.

In between times when they were working, Meliosme spoke of the things she knew of the world Oerlikon: the texture of sky, the feel and smell of the wind, the quarter it came from. She spoke of the colors of the sky, and the meaning of each; of bosels, and rarer creatures native to the planet. Of plants, harmful, beneficial, medicinal, toxic, and consumable. She added, "It's silly, but this really is a good, easy world. No one need starve, or live badly. But like anything else, you have to understand it. Most of our people who came here brought rigid ideas from elsewhere, and applied them against the wind with great resolve."

He said, "You sound as if you approve of what Rael did."

"It was wrong here, and getting no better. Sometimes cures are not pleasant. Rael, or someone else; it needed doing—something, to break them loose. We who wander knew that the folk inside the cities were all closed in in their minds; they hadn't an enemy on the whole planet, but they were exiles in their minds."

"Do you think they will be any better, now? They could well be worse: doubtless terrible deeds have been done, and back there are the survivors, who are now sharpening their knives and saying under their breath, 'Never forget! Never forgive!' There is no end to revenge."

For a long time, they were alone and untroubled by visitors, but they knew that someday some would come, and after a time which seemed short to them both, wanderers and refugees began to appear, footsore and bedraggled, generally walking northwest out of Serets Solntsa and the torment of Marula, or otherwise out of the southern parts of Crule The Swale. The most of these were dispirited and broken, blown by the wind, and after some kind words, would work a little for some rest and some food, after which they would go on their way. Some of the children stayed, the orphaned ones who knew nothing and who told plain tales in simple language that chilled the soul. Others also came, looking in the confusions of the times to carve out a little place and secure it. Some of these they reasoned with; others they threatened. The most desperate and hostile ones were, in a matter-of-fact manner, either run off or killed, either by Phaedrus, or Meliosme, or, by them all together.

Phaedrus told Meliosme that the changes wrought upon him in the bowels of The Mask Factory had removed his ability to sire children, but she had shrugged, as if it were no matter, and gestured at the collection of children of all sizes who sat at the table with them and said, "We can have as many of these as we want." And that was all was said of the subject.

Phaedrus and Meliosme did not inquire of the world they had left behind, nor of the people in it; nevertheless they heard tales, and from them they could make up a picture of what things were happening across the hills. In general, it could be said that anarchy reigned, with early alliances fissioning down to the village level, save in the area dominated by Clisp, and what was left of Lisagor, which was now effectively limited to a strip along the great river and the northern parts of Marula. Symbarupol had been abandoned, sacked, vandalized, and burned, and no one seemed to have any inclination to re-inhabit the site. It was out of the way.

A year passed. Winter into spring, spring into summer, summer into fall, and winter again. The tales circulating into their small world from the east described the dissolution of what remained of Lisagor by the fanatics of Crule, for lack of doctrinal rigor, and of the recovery of Crule, at least in part. The flow of wanderers from the east over the hills stopped, and that from Marula slowed, but they now sighted crude ships on the sea, always sailing northwest. Some of these wrecked on the foreshore reefs, and sometimes only parts of boats floated in on the waves.

In the meantime, some of those who had stayed wandered off a little and built places of their own, thinking only that this place was half wild and rude, but no warlord wanted it, and so they were left alone. Others came and went between there and Zolotane proper, and there was a small trickle of trade. And of rumor. The trade was simple, things coming down they could not make for themselves, and what went north was mostly food, and people who had been stopped in their fall into despair. And the tale began circulating, first in settled Zolotane, then along the Serpentine, and in Clisp, and in the provinces facing the gray-green northern seas, that in the far south of Zolotane sojourned a wise woman and an enigmatic wise man, who claimed no authority except over what was properly theirs, but who helped those who came to them, in quiet and unassuming ways, and sent them on, ready to rebuild their lives. And some little bit of what really passed there actually reached those settled places, but what little bit it was, it did some little good, and in the west of the continent Karshiyaka, a semblance of order began to come back into shape, and people breathed a little easier.

One day, in the summer, Phaedrus was teaching some children by the edge of the cliffs, when he looked up and saw offshore a sleek and splendid gray ship approaching, moving south down the coast, and now angling closer to the shore. This was, he observed, no refugee sailboat, patched together of packing cases, but a ship of metal, and powered, for a low droning noise came from it as it slowed, and stopped, and anchored, not far offshore. Presently, a small boat was lowered, and people could be seen embarking for the shore. Phaedrus sent the children back inland, more for precaution than anything else, but as the boat approached, he could discern no hostile gesture, and so he waited, watching the people make their way across the water to the shore, and when they drew near, he went down to the beach to meet them.

The men in the longboat, operating some kind of motor, guided the craft to the shore, where they drew it up on the beach a little, so their leader could step out. This was an individual who was dressed neatly and impressively in pants, a stiff gray tunic with a roman collar, and a soft cape which waved in the wind. He alighted on the sand, placing his feet carefully so as not to wet his boots, and observed Phaedrus.

The stranger announced, "I am Casio Salkim, Acting Viceroy of the Southern Expeditionary Flotilla."

A reply seemed proper, so Phaedrus said, "I am Phaedrus. I live here."

Salkim shook his head, as if to clear cobwebs away, and said, "You are the one they call Fedro, or Feydro?"

Phaedrus nodded. "Probably the same." Phaedrus had to admit that the visitor was impressive. A relatively young man, with clean hands and trimmed hair and beard, he set an elegant contrast to Phaedrus, who was clean and healthy, but more than a little ragged. He added, "What hospitality may we offer you?"

Salkim chuckled. "Offer me? No, no, my man, it is I who offer you."

"How so?"

"We are from the principality of Clisp. Marisol, in fact," he added, for emphasis. "In a short and I trust not rude way, let me say that we have come along this empty and barbarous coast looking for you. In Marisol there is little talk of anything else. A place on the south coast in Far Zolotane where people get their heads screwed on right again. Again, to be short about it, Pompeo is and has been prince, and rules and reigns with the common good in mind, and seeks to heal the wounds the land and its people have sustained. To this end, he has done the usual things princes do, but my prince also understands that a peace of swords and guns is not complete without the peace of the heart, and the tales have it that this is only to be reliably found here, and so I was commissioned to come out, seek this 'Fedro' out, and invite him and his family and friends to come to Marisol, in Clisp, and thereby take up employment and assignment as Worthy Advisor to Pompeo IV." It was a long speech, but he added, sagaciously, "It is not a bad thing, especially if you've been living close to the edge."

Phaedrus sat down abruptly on the sand, laughing so hard the tears came to his eyes. After a moment, he came back to his senses, and re-gained his feet, and, chuckling, explained to the mystified Salkim: "Your pardon. In the wild lands we have no manners. We have quite forgotten them. Listen: Here is not the place to make decisions, but here, I say, we here neither fear nor hate Clisp, nor its Prince, and we welcome his rule as an alternative to chaos and warlords and random bandits. A fine idea, that the west recovers. In fact, the sooner the better. But I have had lit-tle to do with it."

Salkim was not visibly moved, and he continued, "No, to the con-trary! There is much you have done here. We do not know what doc-trines or orthodoxies you espouse, but however they are they seem to work."

Phaedrus said, seriously and intently, "You do not know how little I have done that I think you speak of. On the other hand, there has been too much that others know little of indeed. But this is a simple place, and I and my friend, Meliosme, do not rule, nor reign. We maintain a holding where the peaceable are free to come and go, and gather their wits, after having their worlds turned upside down."

Salkim stroked his elegant chain. "I see. Then you claim no lordship."

"None."

"I would imagine that equally you acknowledge none?"

"So far, that is an accurate representation."

"Hm. Well, now consider: This part of the mainland was always one of the worst places; most uncivilized, even in the times before. This area was most stringently watched and guarded against. Not against armies, or sorties, but against bandits and anarchists. And then the tales change. People began coming to the new world with no longer broken spirits, but ready to . . . do things, set things right. This is no mean accomplishment. But it affects the progress of another work—which is the consolidation of the west. We no longer have to watch this area, and so the Prince finds his task easy. He is grateful, but being a prince, he also wonders what sort of person could do this."

Phaedrus interjected, "I make no claim to ambition—least of all to rule."

"You have none?".

"None. I do not wish to affect events. I wish solitude, obscurity, I desire only to . . . uncover who and what I am."

Salkim observed, "Many never answer that riddle, and many more never learn to ask the question, more's the pity."

"You see far; I understand why you represent Pompeo IV."

"Yes. Thank you." Salkim inclined his head, a slight bow, and an acknowledgement. "And so, I am commissioned to find out what is here, in the wilds of Zolotane, and you cannot imagine what kinds of men have passed through my imagination."

"I can. I know that way well. I do not seek it now."

". . . And I find someone who only wants to be left alone. Well, *that* won't be completely possible, as I'm sure you understand, but that does put a different cast on things. We shall not have difficulties after all."

"I have none in mind."

"Nor do I."

"You may remain with us if you wish."

"A little time. All are welcome; so long as they do not rob and murder."

"None of that. The people have come to us for peace and order, and we feel honor-bound to lead them to it, not more of what they have left behind."

Phaedrus said, "I fear you will learn little of use to princes; we are trying to let go of things, not gather them. Also, this is not the city. There are only a few comforts here, and one had to grow accustomed to them."

"No matter! I will endure it. And while I am here, I will try to suade you to come with us, despite your modesty."

Phaedrus looked at the splendid Salkim sidelong. "How much of this 'persuasion' is to be words and discourse, and how much . . . another kind of speech, however politely dressed?"

Salkim waved his arms airily. "All reasoning. Why refer to force when one can use it first and be done with arguments over 'who shot Janno first?' No, and no again. Understand me. I did not come to carry you off: you would then be worthless for the position offered, and also that would remove a valuable source of stability here on the southeast flank of Clisp."

They climbed up the steep bank fronting the now gentle waves of the ocean and laboriously reached the top, where Salkim saw the settlement spread out before him. Not impressive, not even a proper town, but a random collation of shanties, lean-tos, sheds made from scraps of broken ships that had been something else before that. Smoke from cooking fires rose in the air, and in the now-late afternoon, a soft golden light was falling slantwise out of the west. He looked again, and shook his head in disbelief.

Someone volunteered to carry food down to the sailors waiting on the beach, and a few gathered up things, seemingly without instruction or orders, and departed shyly to perform their errand.

Dark fell, a meal was served, and Salkim was made to feel an honored guest. Meliosme observed, as they sat around a fire after eating, "You are the first visitor we have had bearing any sort of order from the civilized world."

Salkim nodded. "I am not surprised. True, there was little conflict in Clisp, but there were hard times, refugees, tense moments along the frontiers." He breathed deeply. "We long chafed under the yoke of the Rectification. Clisp was settled not by the Changeless, but by those who fled from them. And so when things started falling apart on the mainland, we were slow to react. And with good reason, for many of our finest had gone to feed the ranks of the Troopers." He looked bitter for a moment, and then brightened. "But we had no great war, at home. Everyone seemed to feel at one time that the will was gone out of it, and so there was a rising in Marisol, some scuffles, and suddenly it was over. But of course, we are just now starting to reach out."

Phaedrus asked, "Is it the intent of this new-resurgent land to unite ~~per-~~ land again?"

"No. At least, not for the moment. Some say we should, but I think they have not thought of the costs of such a venture. No, we do not fear difference."

Phaedrus said, "You spoke of persuasion . . . but you need to know that we are only holding this together here until those who have come can hold it themselves."

"I saw that. I understood. That is why I have said no more. I see that you are encouraging here what we hoped to save in Clisp—that people would do for themselves, left alone. We prefer a prince, that all can see, but I can see your way too. Fine. But it seems a shame. . . ."

"No shame. I repay a debt, in the part that I can repay."

"Are you done?"

"No . . . Meliosme tells me I will never be done, and so that is so; but I have neared the point where I can let go. We will do so."

"To say I wished you well would be an excess, nevertheless have it so."

"It is well that you say it. Thank you."

Salkim gathered himself to his feet. "Time to return."

Meliosme said, "You will not stay?"

"No. This is tempting, but it is not for me. I have another life to follow. And of course, orders. We have other business along the coasts. . . ." He trailed the words off mysteriously.

Meliosme asked, "Marula?"

"Farther."

She said, "The Pilontaries?"

"So far. We want to make contacts with the outlying new regimes, to find out . . . Crule is an inland place with inland thinking, and they will be slow to realize, although they are trying to hold Marula."

"Can they hold it?"

Salkim said thoughtfully, "They are destroying it in order to save it, if you can make sense out of that. It is already useless as a port. But we will go by there, and lob a few bombs onto them, and see if we can make it more difficult for them. Pompeo wants them kept defensive. Besides, there's a rumor afoot about other things. . . ."

Phaedrus said, "Something from Tartary?"

"By the gods, no. They are still fighting each other out there, and welcome them to it, bust hell loose! No, it's from farther off: there's talk from the innerlands that one of the ships is coming back."

Phaedrus felt an odd feeling, a presentiment. He asked, "Someone has . . . seen?"

"Not so I hear it. No, we've not seen anything, although Pompeo has a crowd of technicians madly working on something that will work. No.

This is from talk we've picked up, from traders, spies, refugees. They say 'The Ship's coming back, to pick up some people it left behind.' "

Phaedrus mused, "To pick them up . . . odd. I thought they'd never risk it."

"Odd to me, too. We heard there were offworlders here, spying and the like."

Phaedrus grimaced. "More than that. But their time is over, and we need not waste words or deeds on them. I would urge Pompeo to let them go."

Salkim agreed. "Such are my thoughts as well. But all the same, we'd like to keep an eye on things, although I don't know what we'd do if they wanted to fight."

"Believe me. That is the last thing they want. Although they will undoubtedly have weapons if some hothead shoots at them."

Salkim chuckled. "Have no fears on that score! We probably don't have anything strong enough to even reach them. Well, good night to you all."

Meliosme said, "We can send someone . . ."

"No matter. I can find the way. And have no fears from us." He strode to the edge of the darkness, near the banks, and waved once at them, and then disappeared into the night. After a time, they heard some small sounds of a boat moving off the beach, strange calls over the water, and after that, a distant throbbing from the ship, and then all was quiet again for a time, until the bosels of the south coast began commenting on the events of the day, their calls echoing back and forth up and down the coast, and also from far inland.

Pternam had been sleeping, and now he was awake. He had to stop for a minute and consider where he was . . . Corytinupol, was it, in the center of Crule The Swale, which was now calling itself Lisagor? Yes. Corytinupol. A dreadful back-country barrack-town, without beauty or flavor, peopled by fanatics, doctrine-quoting idiots and hairsplitters whose existence he had been mercifully shielded from in Symbarupol. Yes. They had been much on the move, first this place, then that one, sometimes uneasy guests who were not entirely sure they were not hostages.

Before they had left Symbarupol, Arunda Palude had gotten contact with the ship that was coming for whomever it could salvage, but they had soon lost that contact, with the abandonment of the city to the barbarians. All over, all dignity lost, thrown away. He understood with an old skill at perception of the situation which had not left him, that his own situation had changed to something new and terrible: he was in fact completely dependent on the mercy or charity of these offworld spies, who either now ignored him (rightly so: Pternam now had no more influence than a sack of meal) or condescended to issue orders to him, none too politely. Avaria had vanished long ago, making his escape, trusting to his own wit rather than to the offworlders, who were now showing their true character, an immiscible blend of professional academic competence and the grimiest sort of treasonous espionage.

Well, give them credit, he thought. They recklessly bartered offworld technology to the stern and unbending fanatics of Crule, to buy time, and this had in fact saved the situation from total disaster. Crule managed to survive, and to hold off further disintegration. In fact, they had even made gains, mostly eastward into Puropaigne, the Innerlands. What was left of Symbarupol they had recovered, but it wasn't worth returning to. Nothing was in this world that he wanted to return to, unless he could personally wring Rael's neck, which was doubtful, even if he could have found him, which the offworlders refused even to bother with.

A squat, totally bald man thrust his head into Pternam's cubicle and glanced about for a moment with a look of icy contempt. He growled, "Pternam? You awake?"

"Yes. I heard some noise outside, I think."

"Right. Get your things. It's time to go."

"We're moving again?"

"The last time. We're the last pickup. We'll have to walk it for a bit, out of town, you know; the elders don't want their people contaminated by seeing a spaceship, even if it's only an exploratory lighter." This was the brutal and effective Cesar Kham, who had gradually taken control of the offworlders from the temporary leadership of Porfirio Charodei.

Kham chuckled to himself. "They would just as soon shoot us as not, but in the final step, they'd rather be rid of us, as if being rid of us could stem what your own people set in motion here."

Pternam got up and began gathering a few things. "I don't imagine I'll need much."

"No."

"You are taking me with you?"

"Are you worried we'd sell you to Crule? No chance. You've seen too much now. You have to go, like it or not. Leaving you here would upset things more than the revolution did. Without you, it's just a bad dream for them. . . . They'll wake up in a year or so and find out the reality's worse, but never mind that. . . ."

"You don't think they can win here?"

"No." That was the way with Kham. Cutting, direct. No. No qualifiers, no modifiers. "No." Kham explained, "I can't fault their theology; they have that down pat; but there's no future in the economics. They can't hold Marula, and without it they have no access to the ocean. They have the center of the continent, but everyone can just sail around them— that's the trouble with living on an island, however big it is. The lords of Tartary are encouraging that, of course."

"You foresee a two-continent world united against Crule?"

"No. Nothing like that. You're in for a long period of contending states and mini-states, but you'll have more world trade. Crule itself isn't worth the trouble. They'll wither in time, and go out."

Pternam rubbed his eyes, and unsteadily walked to the door. The corridor outside was almost empty, now. Pternam mused, aloud, "I often wonder why you stuck with Symbarupol and Crule to the end."

"How so?"

"I am certain from what I know of you that a state such as Clisp would be more to your liking."

"As a place to live and work? Of course! But then you have to understand also that however attractive it may be, it is of course terribly backward. I have a colleague who has made a life's work of studying the principalities of the Renaissance on Old Earth; an expert, one may say, I think the best in his field. But you can bet you wouldn't find him in fourteenth-century Florence, or anything like it. One is always a historian at a distance. Remember that. They would make short work of us in Clisp, you may be sure. In fact, that prince who is running things there openly has posted a reward for any one of us, unharmed. . . . None have taken him up on it. All the people who have decided to go native here have already gone, and you may be certain they'll stay that way."

"I heard some talk. Did you lose many people here?"

"Some." Kham did not elaborate on the single word, which led Pternam to believe that their losses had been severe. He imagined this was so, ironically enough, since the offworlders had not brought down Lisagor, but had supported it, in fact, they had been its strongest pillar. But all of that was gone, now, and hardly mattered.

Kham conducted him outside, where the party was assembling, some afoot, some piling a few things onto draywagons, with the elders of Crule looking on from the sidelines, displaying no emotions. Pternam glanced around the windy darkness and asked, "What wagon do I go on?"

Kham started off on some errand, and looked back, at Pternam's question, and barked, "You walk. Get going." It was rude, especially if one recalled Pternam's former status, but again, now that did not matter greatly either.

Pternam had gradually learned the habit of blanking his mind during the unpleasant parts; of fading out in doing mindlessly, and the dull routines were soon over. This was such an instance. He set out walking into the darkness and concentrated only on keeping up with the rest of the party. He did not look around, or try to see anything of what he was passing through. Only walking, and the dark. Soon the onlookers grew less, and then the lights of the town, and then the buildings, and they were in the open, out in the open and naked grasslands of Crule The Swale, trudging along a pale dirt road that arrowed off into the darkness.

He tried to listen for scraps of what the others might be saying, but they said little that he could hear, although a low and continuous murmur floated above the line of walkers and drays. Nothing in the speech of Lisagor, at any rate. All foreign gibberish. Of course, they would now have no pretense to speak as if they were natives here. He listened to the fragments of the speech: short, clipped, terse, all the words seeming to end on consonants, and all those short and crisp. The vowels were short and rather high in tone. He listened to the whispers and low murmurs about him and he thought that it would be a language he would not speak well, nor would he feel comfortable with such speech, no matter how familiar he became with it. It was not a speech of ceremony and tradition and reassuring identity and place, but a speech of contention, of strife, however well-mannered and controlled, and above all of ceaseless change. But of course that was the way of wherever they had come from.

He often thought of that: Neither Charodei nor Kham had deigned to tell him anything about the world they were going to. When he had asked, the answers had been vague generalities which were completely devoid of informational content. He had not managed to determine if the planet where they were going had a name or not. Or if they were going to a single place; or if they were even going to a planet at all, but perhaps to some unimaginable construction in the void between the worlds, an artificial world. He had heard fleeting allusions to such places, which seemed to have been made for special purposes.

Nor did he know much more about the ship, except that it was too large to land on a planetary surface. Smaller craft, called "lighters" were carried inside it, and served as the landing craft. This was what they were walking out to board, apparently, although again, he was not sure what he was looking for. He belonged to a country of people who had not wanted space flight, and who had rapidly forgotten as fast as they could. Aircraft they had and understood, although their use was severely controlled, and little or no experimental work was done. Somehow, he could not equate spacecraft with aircraft.

Now they were far from the town, and somewhere ahead on the dim, almost-invisible plain ahead, there was a weak light glowing, a pale yellow light that did not waver. The group apparently also saw this light, for the speed and amount of conversation increased, as well as the pace. Pternam noticed that some of the people were now casting things aside as they went, pieces of clothing, odds and ends, mementoes which suddenly seemed less valuable, books and papers they would never need again, as if the actual sight of the lighter reminded them that their time here was over, that they were refugees who would soon be returned to their own. He was one with the group, and yet he felt the alienness of the thought. He was not particularly anxious to leave, and yet in the crowd, he caught the overlay of it from them.

Presently they drew near to something which he assumed was the lighter, a vague structure bulking large in the dark, mysterious, amorphous. He sensed an immense mass, squat and unlovely, resting on a forest of metallic pillars. As they walked under it, he could feel heat from the body poised above him, odd, pungent mechanical odors he did not recognize assaulted his nose. There were sounds of mechanical movements, odd snatches of voices, harsh commands being given and acknowledged.

The group slowed, and Pternam, looking around, saw a rough line forming at the foot of something that looked like a metal stair extending out of the center of the ship. People walked up to a booth alongside the foot of the stair, spoke somewhat, and proceeded up the stairs, most throwing a few more things away as they went. He felt like shouting at them, *Fools! You are throwing away the life-fragments of a whole world!*

The line proceeded at a good pace. No one was excluded or, so it appeared, even questioned much. A short conversation, and then up the stair. Now it bothered him what he might say to whatever was in the booth, whether man, alien, or machine. What speech did it use? He began looking about in concern for someone he knew, and after a moment, caught sight of the bald and shiny cranium of Cesar Kham, who stepped up to the booth smartly, spoke somewhat, and bounded up the steps, taking them two at a time. Pternam looked around in dismay, looking for anyone else he knew, Charodei, Palude, some of the others he had met. None. He was now in the midst of strangers.

Much too soon, he stood at the foot of the stair, which he saw to be indeed metal although it was finished a uniform dull black. The booth contained a single opening whose nature was not apparent, as the opening did not seem to open to anything. Inside, there was simply a formless darkness from which a voice, clipped and peremptory, presently inquired, "Teilisk gak?"

Pternam answered, "I am Luto Pternam, invited guest of men who called themselves here Porfirio Charodei and Cesar Kham. Also Arunda Palude. They brought me here, so I assume to enter."

There was a long pause, during which Pternam could feel the intent stares of those behind him yet in line. He dared not look around, but somehow he felt a prickly sensation along his lower back that he had committed some dreadful breach. After a moment, something inside the darkness of the booth said, "Dilik. Mek Angren." Pause. Then, in his own language, it said, "Wait to the side for the others to pass. Then enter."

It was then, as he stood aside, that he seriously questioned the wisdom of continuing on this course, which he now realized had been as fixed as the course of the stars in the heavens. Now, something shyly whispered to the darkness of his soul. *"You can walk away from here a free man, with no enemies and no obligations."*

The old Pternam asked the new, *"Everything I have burned behind me. Where would I go?"*

The new answered, *"Away, somewhere else. Walk off. No one will stop you. These folk don't care and they don't want you. The elders of Crule think you went in the ship, and so they will say. Get dirty and ragged, and walk into a settled place, and you can get off free."*

Several people passed through the line in rapid succession, and the line of those waiting grew visibly shorter. Pternam answered the questioner inside himself, *"A bargain has been made. They will give me honor; at least they will have a native of this world to speak with. I have value. I was somebody, and I can be so again."*

The voice replied, *"You were a minor functionary with a criminal ambition and your acts loosed Change on this world. Besides, they have had years to bore into Oerlikon like worms. They manifestly do not need you."* The last few people waiting to speak into the booth passed, and Pternam was alone.

He looked around. There were dim lights under the ship, and shadows around the many legs of the craft. Somewhere, something vented off, releasing a soft plume of steam. Overhead, the bulk of the craft was quiet. Waiting.

The booth chirruped to itself, a sound impossible to interpret, and then said plainly, "Enter the ship without delay. We are holding departure for you."

Pternam looked around once more, and all he could see were the landing-legs, the booth, and the metal stairs going up into some dark orifice. Beyond the circle of dim light there was nothing but the endless night of Crule The Swale, a nothingness. He gripped the rail and mounted the stairs.

At the top of the stairs was a dim cubicle, apparently a landing, which he stepped into, and as he did he heard mechanical noises from behind him, motion. The stairs were lifting up, pivoting back into a recess in the hull. A panel slid shut behind him. Ahead was another corridor, ascending ramplike to some other part of the ship. There was a faint metallic odor in the air. He walked up this ramp until he came to another chamber, which he entered without hesitating. Here, too, a panel slid shut behind him. He felt a motion, a small surge of acceleration, and then nothing more.

He wondered what this room was for. Was he being examined by the unknowable medical sciences of the star-folk? Presumably they would not wish him to mingle with the others just yet. He waited for what seemed like a long time. Nothing happened. The air did not seem stale, although he could hear no sound of ventilation. There was another motion, as if of metal sliding on metal, although he could not say exactly how the motion was being done, or in what direction. After a time, this too stopped. Then, for a longer time, again, nothing happened. Finally, he spoke, "Let me speak with Porfirio Charodei! With Cesar Kham! I am Luto Pternam! I made this escape possible!"

There was a sharp grating sound, and instantly Pternam was flung *outside* by a convulsion of the chamber, into naked space. His eyes bulged, a band of iron seized his chest, and his blood boiled, and before him he saw the dark nightside bulk of an immense round object, spattered with points of light. He rotated, and saw, not understanding, a smaller bulk moving away from him, visibly getting smaller. Then the darkness.

The community which had grown around Phaedrus and Meliosme did not have a name. In a sense, it was not a settlement, or a town, or even a camp, considering each of those things just one of many towns, settlements, camps that could be, *were*. This was unique. A single place, the only one for those who had stopped there on their flight from the furies. It was simply home.

But the visit of an emissary from the new world that was growing somehow upset a delicate balance that had existed for them. It was true, and none disputed it, that Salkim's visit had implied no threats; indeed, he had gone out of his way to insure there were none given, and none taken. Yet it made them aware, and awareness was loss of a kind of innocence they all had thought they had regained. And so not long after the visit, there began to be talk about seeing to things, and having a little more of a sense of organization. Factions, weak and tentative, began to emerge. Some desired alliance with Clisp. Others argued for independence, so long as it might last. Still others, just to cover all possibilities, wanted to at least send an emissary to Crule to see what was going on.

Late at night, Phaedrus and Meliosme sat on the packed earthen floor on grass mats and spoke of the change. Meliosme let one of the smaller urchins use her lap for a pillow, and after stroking the child's head and gazing into the fire, she said, "Politics has caught up with us, so I hear."

"Yes, I have heard, too."

"Our original intent was to find a place of solitude and leave all that."

"For a time we had it. But it seems there is little enough of the wild left on this planet."

"The gatherers will not be able yet to wander over the face of the world the way we used to."

"True. I would not wish to go back into the east."

"What do you have in mind to do with this?"

"Little or nothing. I do not wish to rule these people; they manage well enough on their own, once they had a place where they could stop and think."

"But you could still keep this place as it was."

"By rule? Never. Circumstances change, so it seems to me; it can never be the way it was again. They would like it at first—I know that.

But in time that model wouldn't agree with the real world, and there'd be resistance, and then the strife would start."

"Phaedrus, you could pick a line of thinking and stay with it, here. They trust you, and now you trust yourself."

"As I trust myself, so I must trust them to find their own way, whatever it it."

"What would you favor, were you deciding for them?"

"Clisp, of course; they need protection from forays from over the hills. They aren't much of a barrier. It wouldn't work the other way, allying with Crule against Clisp. That goes against everything these people ran from. No—it would be Clisp. Not that I don't have my objections to that, too, but it would have to do."

"Then say so. They will follow you."

"No. Control breeds the need for more control. And in freeing myself from power, I have freed myself from wanting power over others. I would become the slave of the force I used, worse than them. No. I know the way I go. You helped show it to me, and I will keep on that way. Less, not more. Obscurity, not fame. . . ."

She showed no sign of agreement or disagreement, but continued looking at the fire and absentmindedly stroking the child's hair. At last she said, "They are meeting tonight. They want to reward us for what we have done for them."

He nodded. "I know. Well, this place has grown, and it is time we had some sort of leader, isn't it? That is simple enough. Here we have no lord, but we need one. We will tell them, choose one among you who will lead. Not me." He got to his feet wearily. "Even this much I wish I could avoid."

Meliosme said, "I would take it, but I want it no more than you. . . . I miss the old freedoms."

"They are gone in the new world, but we still have a few left within ourselves."

"You say we could be so anywhere."

"More or less."

"And what then?"

"I think that we have done something here; but whatever it was, our part in it has faded, and now it's time to go further. I've rested, and been healed of some madness; and so I'd go on to find the rest of it."

"Where? You yourself said there was no wild left."

"Clisp. Would you walk with me there?"

She did not hesitate. "I have walked with you since then, a long time ago. I would not change now. What would we do there?"

"Just be, that's all. Struggle, suffer. Do what we could."

Meliosme smiled, an expression that always illuminated her plain face with a warm glow. She said, "Well, I was not destined to be a great lady anyway . . . I will go with you. What about the children?"

"They are all our children, and then none. Let those who would come, come. And those who would stay, stay."

She gently disengaged herself from the child, and stood up to join him. "Very well. So it will be. And now we will tell them."

"Yes."

"You know that will be a novel idea to them. Me, too. Choosing—there's an idea."

"It won't cure the flaw we all have in us, but it cools it down a lot. It's hard to imagine yourself a savior when everybody knows you're a bosel's arse, and in fact you know it, too."

They stepped outside, into the night, which was filled up with the sound of the sea and the gentle winds in the grass, and from far off they could also hear distant calls of bosels, uninterested, remote.

They went together to the place among the huts and sheds where the others had assembled, and when Phaedrus came, they all stood up, remembering some of their manners from the older days, and already having decided in their minds that he was to be their lord, since he was here before them; but he asked that they but hear him once, and when they sat and listened, he told them what they should do. At first, they resisted the idea, but after a little time had passed, some of them understood enough of it to see what they should do, and presently, those who were so minded stood up and spoke of what they should do, and sometime later, a rough agreement was reached that a certain Olenzo, formerly of Near Priboy, seemed to have the best head for that sort of thing, and so was chosen leader, subject to recall.

But before that, Phaedrus and Meliosme had slipped away, and made their way back, through the dark, to their house, where they gathered a few simple things, as if they were leaving then, not waiting for the dawn.

She said, "You'd not wait for the morning?"

"No. Even that. I can do the most for these people by leaving now. In the morning, they will have regrets, questions, referrals."

Two of the orphans wanted to leave with them, and so they took some extra things for them, too, so that in the end they wound up carrying more than they had planned, but their burdens were not heavy.

Phaedrus stepped out into the night again, and looked out over the water, to the west. He sighed, deeply. And turned and said, "Yes. This is the right way."

Something moving in the sky caught at the edge of his awareness, and he looked up. In the sky was a falling star, a meteor, but not the quick little flicker of the usual meteor; this one was slow, tumbling and burning, red and orange, and at last it went out, drifting off toward the east. He continued looking at the night sky, at the few stars he could see, the unremarkable stars of the sky of Oerlikon. And he thought he saw, a little to the east, a point of light moving, dimming as it went.

Meliosme was watching, too. After a time, she said, "There was something up there."

Phaedrus nodded. "Yes. Ever seen anything moving in the night sky before?"

"A long time ago, once. Like that. I didn't know then what it was. Now I think I know."

"Lights in the sky. Ships. Something fell out of that one."

"Or something was dumped that wouldn't fit. They must have been crowded. We would never find it."

He agreed. "No. Useless to look. I suppose we won't see any more of those for a while . . . and when we do, they'll come openly. Come on."

And so they walked quietly down to the beach, and began walking northward, and after a long time, they found some shelter in the rocks back from the water and rested for the night.

In easy stages, then, Phaedrus and Meliosme made their way northward along the coast of Zolotane, and after many days they came to a shallow river, in a flat land where the hill country had receded back over the horizons. But ahead, across the river, were more rugged mountains, trailing off to the southwest. The Serpentine. There they joined a group of other pilgrims, as ragged and undistinguished as they were, and with them, they went across the river on a causeway which had been built, so Meliosme informed him, since the Troubles.

Their way down the length of the Serpentine was even slower. They would stop. Work for a while, and drift on, slowing down as they went. And at last they reached the outskirts of the great city Marisol, that stood on a high plain with the sea to the north and mountains to the south, a place of sun and light and people rushing everywhere, and after a time Phaedrus found a place as a gardener in one of the immense public parks that they were fond of in Clisp, and they found a modest place to live, and to their surprise, no one troubled them, and their lives settled into a routine.

Marisol, being exposed to the northern winds off the ocean, had more obvious seasons that Phaedrus could remember, and he lived through two more of the rainy winters. One night, late, as the wind blustered and fussed around the corners of the stone house where they lived, and the rain runoff was brawling in the downspouts and street gutters, Meliosme asked him, quite out of nowhere, "Do you ever have regrets that you gave up the power you had?"

He looked up and at her for a long time, still surprised that for all her plain looks and wandering origins, she was still perceptive enough to awaken him to his deepest thoughts. He said, "Yes, sometimes. You can't forget, and you'd love to tamper. But you dare not. Just once, and it would start all over again. No. There has been enough suffering."

"You told me how you could find the one person, who, obscure and unknown, was the support of the world."

"Yes. I could do that. I have not done it for years. I have not wanted to know."

"Would it be safe to look now?"

Phaedrus sat back and looked at her attentively. "I suppose I could, if I can remember all the routines, the formulae, the operations. Remember it used a system of logic that doesn't agree with the usual one people steer their lives by."

"Do it. See if you can get an answer now."

There was an impish smile on her face, as if she knew something. Phaedrus got up from his chair and went looking about for a piece of paper, and a pen. After a time, he found one, and began, slowly and uncertainly at first, but with growing assurance, as the routines came back to him from their long disuse. He began building the logical framework, and then the inputs, using the symbolism they had forcefed him in another age, so it seemed, and then it began working easily, and he asked for more paper, feeling the flow smoothing, and at last he was forming the symbols in the system for the conclusion of the operation, and it was clear what the Answer was, as he filled in the last line that completed the whole. The pivotal person of this new world was himself. He looked up at Meliosme. He said, unsteadily, "It's me."

Meliosme, smiling still, nodded, and gave him a quick hug, and said, "Knew it."

Transformer

For Don and Elsie, for put up with my erratic schedule and surprise packages with great good humor.
And for Betsy, with whom I proposed bizarre covers for this story at the '78 Worldon, Phoenix.

1

"Civilization is not technology, as those who rely too heavily on technology find out. This is an error of both perception and judgment, which normally leads to conclusions which are dire, if not fatal."

—H.C., Atropine

CESAR KHAM WAITED for the arrival of the Regents, occupying the time by reminding himself who he was now and where he was. To mistake one mutable identity for another, here, now, could have unpleasant consequences, not only for himself, but for many others. He began by denying the name, and the identity that went with it, an identity cultivated for almost two decades of standard years on Oerlikon. *I am not, here, Cesar Kham. If these people know that name at all, it is only as an obscure footnote to a datascan. That means nothing here. Here, on Heliarcos, I am Czermak Pentrel'k, which is who I was a long time ago.* The name was strange, seemed not to fit. He had come to think of himself as Cesar Kham, as had most of the long-timers in the Oerlikon Project. That was why so many of them retired there, still in the possession of their clandestine secrets. As many had been the flaws of Oerlikon, one got used to it, to its verities that changed, if at all, so slowly that the rate was imperceptible.

Some things remained the same, here as well. But one had to be observant, cautious. He forced himself to *observe* the chamber in which he waited, not just receive impressions: bare, sparse, functional. There were some plain desks, for administrative aides, behind him, now empty. There was a podium at the place where he would stand, surrounded by a simple wooden rail on three sides. Before him, a long table covered by a metallic cloth. There were backless chairs, stools, behind that table. The ceiling was high and illuminated from the sides; the walls were hung with heavy draperies. As far as he could determine from where he stood, a point precisely located at the spot which divided the length of the room into the Golden Ratio, the room was a perfect cube.

Pentrel'k had chosen to wear the clothing of a service technician. This was a simple tunic top with a Roman collar, and pants of plain cut, both a uniform gray. In this clothing, he made a statement to those who would come here—that he considered himself a simple workman, of no pretensions. He had only done the duty that had been required of him by extraordinary circumstances. He had, formally, the right to wear the academic gown and the badges of excellence he had earned long ago, but he had left them behind. Arunda Palude would be doing the same, by common consent. Arunda? No longer. Here, she was Morelat Eickarinst.

They would see here not a professed member of their own exclusive circles, but a technician, a workman, a fixer. Pentrel'k was of less than average height, stocky of build, bald, with a slightly sallow complexion. His face was notable for a heavy, lumpy nose, deep-set brown eyes, a mouth which was harsh and sensual at the same time. His beard, shaven (even here) and not depilated, showed as a faint steel-blue sheen along the lines of his jaw.

Behind him, he heard the door open, and a rustling began, unbroken by conversation. He did not look around. Presently the Regents filed to the front of the hearing room and in line took their places, remaining standing until all were in place, whereupon they all sat, like a single organism. There were seven, and in this room, in this conclave, they held something more than the power of Life and Death.

They all wore dark gowns which concealed their bodies, and hoods. The gowns were ornamented only with small colored diamonds on the sleeves, right, left, or both. The one in the center wore two such diamonds, white, on the left. This one opened a bound document, without rattling it, and began immediately, without ceremony, "You are Czermak Pentrel'k."

"That is correct."

The central member continued, "You maintained on the world Oerlikon the identity Cesar Kham." The remarks were not intoned as questions, but as statements.

"I was so assigned."

"What were your duties there?"

Kham-Pentrel'k began, "I was Senior Field Evaluator."

"Explain in some detail, please."

"My function was to maintain security of the mission, and to evaluate all expressions of change, such as revolutionary movements, as well as activities on the part of the local government authorities. I spent the majority of my time in the city Marula, in the province Clisp, and in selected locations from which government power was exercised."

A Regent, second left from center asked, "Did you act independently or with permission?"

"Normally, with coordination and direction from Mission Central. There were circumstances when I could act voluntarily, but this was not required until the last events."

The central Regent now asked, "What did you do then, and why?"

Pentrel'k began slowly, as if trying to recall with exactitude, "I was in Clisp, evaluating an odd incident, and making normal reports through our mnemonicist, Arunda Palude. I came to understand that I was, for unknown reasons, suddenly cut off from Central. Simultaneously, seemingly out of the ground, a series of rapid changes began happening. The situation in Clisp rapidly changed, and the locals there took control of their own affairs, seeing that the government was preoccupied. They were not challenged. I made my way back to Central, to report in person, and by the time I got there, disintegration of the central authority, that is, for the locals, was well advanced, and a low-grade civil war was on. Also the Head of Mission was absent, reportedly mad, and wandering somewhere. The Second Head of Mission was acting in an incompetent manner. Palude and I took command of the mission and salvaged what we could. Those who wished to leave Oerlikon were given a fair chance at it, and most made it. I turned Porfirio Charodei over to the authorties here when we arrived."

"We have discussed events on Oerlikon with Charodei. You need not inquire his real identity."

Pentrel'k made no comment.

The central Regent continued, "Charodei has made some statements about events on Oerlikon which are difficult to credit."

"I have heard some of these. At first, I did not believe them, but later I met the Lisak who claimed to have set the events off, and his story matched exactly with Charodei's. I worked with this individual for some time, and grew to distrust him greatly. He most urgently wished to come here. I suspected a devious plot on his part, revenge, whatnot, and had him ejected into space."

The second on the left said, "We understand the pressure of events was demanding; on the whole you did extremely well. Yet, one can question the judgment involved in the execution of Luto Pternam. His organization had succeeded in an area of research we have not mastered to that degree yet, and his knowledge would have been invaluable."

Pentrel'k said, "I accept the criticism; yet also I say that I had the weight of decision; and Pternam had created a force that was out of control, and was wrecking his . . ."

"Yes?"

"I was going to say 'country,' but it was rather more than that. He held us responsible for the ruin of his world, and I felt certain his eagerness to come here was to unleash another such creature on us, and see us in the same ruin as his people."

"That is most irrational. We did not ruin his country. He did."

Pentrel'k paused, and said, "I had the testimony of Pternam, and also that of Charodei. There were others whom we were able to interrogate. Given the equipment and time, he could probably do it again. On Oerlikon, whatever the creature did was limited to that world. I did not feel secure in bringing him here, but to secure his cooperation, I agreed to allow him to board the lighter."

The Second said, "You assumed we would let him operate unsupervised?"

"He found a way to do it there, which I would not have thought possible. We had evaluated Lisagor as being impermeable to ambitious plots. Yet Pternam made such an attempt. He failed only because his creation was *too* successful."

"You believe that Pternam actually made up some sort of . . . assassin?"

"More than that! Some kind of changeling, and reportedly possessed of an ability to see into the heart of a society and bring it down."

"We know. We heard it all, of Charodei. And something else we heard of Charodei: immortal."

"I heard that and discounted it."

"Charodei didn't. Given what we have on the changeling, it may be possible. That is why we have such high regrets that you left both Pternam and his creature behind."

Pentrel'k did not flinch. He said, "I remind you I had my hands full with recovering our people out of there. It could have turned against us and there'd have been one hell of a massacre. We lived minute by minute. As it was, we got out clean, and those who stayed were not endangered. As for Pternam, you have my reasons. I was there: I saw what happened to Lisagor."

"We cannot fault the empiricism of your knowledge, nor the accomplishments you performed under stress. So now we wish to know what happened to the creature—what you know of it."

"I know little, and that through Charodei and others. They thought they had it trapped after it changed, and then it vanished. There was a report that a woman Azart vanished during a raid in Marula, where she was. It was widely assumed by those who knew about the changeling that it was killed then, by accident."

The Regents looked at one another, up and down the line. At last the one in the center spoke, "But this was not confirmed."

"No. If I may add, I can say that Pternam had access to these reports and doubted them. He was obsessed with the idea that the creature would come after him and would live through anything to do so. I saw no evidence to support this objectively and devoted the time to the primary mission."

"Charodei claimed that this creature was trained in survival attitudes and methodology in addition to its . . . other talents. And he also said that when acting in his role as member of the revolutionaries, he had operatives in contact with the creature, and that Pternam insisted on killing it."

"I heard that, of Pternam. I did not hear that they were successful."

"Indeed. We have a report from another informant that the operative assigned to the creature was found dead."

"In the raid on Marula. . . ."

"No. Not in the raid. An accident. Witnesses said he had been playing in a game, and was injured. There had been a woman with him. She disappeared."

Pentrel'k said nothing.

The central member said, "The prime computation is that the creature Pternam made changed identity and survived."

Again, Pentrel'k said nothing.

"Let me explore this a little for you. . . . What we have, at large on Oerlikon, is a human who can initiate severe and extreme bodily changes, major structural modifications, without burning itself up in metabolic stress. This bespeaks fine control of an area we can't control ourselves. Plus its apparent immortality. For these reasons alone we would wish to examine it. But there is something more."

Pentrel'k ventured, "What more could you want of it."

"Not what we want of it, but that we defend ourselves from it?"

Pentrel'k said, hesitating, "Ah . . . what I heard of it was that it was highly oriented to its own world; I could see no reason then, on Oerlikon, to worry about its having an offworld target. I still see none."

The outermost member on the right said, "Did you hear in your contacts who this creature was originally?"

"I heard that it originally had been an elderly woman, a person of no consequence who was picked up by Pternam's goons."

"Does the name Jedily Tulilly mean anything to you?"

"No. That was, I believe, the name of the subject Pternam started with. The name has no significance to me."

The Regents now stopped and glanced at each other, all up and down the line, with a slow, measured cadence, the stuff of nightmares. Now Pentrel'k knew for certain that they were playing with him. Now they would reel the line in closer.

The central member said, "Charodei also knew nothing about that name, even though he has so reported it. We know that in the initial training and changes Pternam caused the creature to undergo, it forgot much; who could blame it? It knows the name, and that's an Oerlikon name, at that, but as far as we know, that is all it has of the identity. Yet if it survived, would it not come to want to know who it had been? Wouldn't you, had such an event happened to you?"

"I would want to know, yes. Sooner or later."

"This must not happen."

"Your pardon, Regent?"

"Pternam did not know what he had taken, the woman who called herself Jedily Tulilly in Lisagor on Oerlikon. You do not know. Charodei did not know. Palude did not know. We know. She was not a native of that world, and . . ."

"Yes?"

". . . if that creature, assumed alive and well-hidden, starts looking for who he was, and finds anything, that would not be desirable."

"Continue."

"If it unravels who Jedily Tulilly was and why she was on Oerlikon in the condition she was in, we can expect a visitor . . . here, on Heliarcos, perhaps other places. An immortal assassin who can change identity."

Pentrel'k interrupted, "Surely you don't think that that creature can get off Oerlikon, with no more connection than that place has with the rest of the worlds, and find its way successfully here, or anywhere else. . . ."

"If it remembers, or if it can deduce it out, it will have the necessary motivation. And we don't know who we are looking for. Do you see some of the problem?"

"Quarantine Oerlikon. That's simple enough."

"It's already broken. We cannot impose embargo without revealing the reason why we wish it imposed."

Pentrel'k suddenly felt more confidence. He was still in piercing danger, but they still had use for him. He said, "Somebody did something to Tulilly . . . something secret."

The central Regent said, "It is not important that you know what that was; or who Tulilly was in reality, or what she did. A heinous punishment for a heinous crime, that's the word. You also need not know who pronounced the sentence. You do very much need to comprehend the magnitude of this problem."

"Knowing no more than I do, it is difficult, but I do see that you do not wish to have this creature perambulating about."

"Exactly! We would like to have it here, for study, since we have lost Pternam and his files; but under control. Under iron control, and from Charodei's testimony, we are not sure we can control it. He reported Pternam feared it and took extraordinary security precautions. Failing that, we want it eradicated."

Pentrel'k said, "I see your desires clearly; but as the former Cesar Kham, a field operative, I would doubt the wisdom of trying to do both."

"Not both. One or the other. Known and demonstrable security, or elimination."

"Who will accomplish this mission?" he asked, but he already knew most of the answer.

"As you say, Cesar Kham is a field operative, a specialist in security."

"Cesar Kham is no specialist in murder and kidnapping."

"You secured the net; you took actions, where required."

"Cesar Kham made decisions; technicians, specialists, carried those decisions out."

Again, the mutual glancing back and forth. At last, the central Regent said, reflectively, "This may not be germane. Yet you and Palude are the ranking survivors of the mission on Oerlikon, and you are certainly more knowledgeable about conditions there than anyone else. You yourself we know to be a sensitive investigator."

"All else aside, I appreciate your confidence. But if you have followed my career as closely as I assume you have, you also know that I did not unravel the last events in Clisp in time. Had I done so, perhaps I could have averted . . ."

The central Regent said, "No. You couldn't have. You wouldn't have suspected this kind of penetration. But now of course you can."

Pentrel'k nodded. "Yes. I suppose so. Damned difficult, though. You understand the difficulties?"

"We have some measure of it. You will have to be extremely cautious, and not alert it, because if it thinks you are hunting it, it has, apparently, ways to perceive your approach. So you won't get but one chance. And . . ."

"And? Yes?"

"Don't miss. We can't send backup to Oerlikon, and once it gets loose in space, we cannot predict what it will do."

"I think I understand what you have in mind. I assume all the necessary arrangements have been made."

"Correct. We knew you would not refuse."

"What choices do I have?"

"None."

"May I speak with Charodei? He knows things about this I didn't have time to cover in more than cursory detail. . . ."

"Denied. A full report text will be made available to you. Many more than Charodei were interrogated, and the results have been synthesized. Charodei . . . is unavailable."

"I see. When do I get to consult with Palude?"

"Immediately. She is waiting outside. She has the report. She also has the names you must contact there. That is all."

It was dismissal. Yet he waited, before turning from the examination dock. "What fault will you have against me if I kill it?"

"None. Assess proper risk and do what you must. There will be no censure. You have that under seal."

"At the risk of the charge of impertinence, may I ask if I will be enlightened as to the ultimate causes of your concern?"

The central Regent smiled a most unpleasant smile. "In the normal course of events, after your return from the field, permanently, you might well reach the Board of Regents; possession of this data pertaining to the Tulilly case is an integral part of the process of acceptance of the responsibility of office. Possession and acquiescence with, in full."

"Then there is something I would have to agree to."

"You might say that."

"Are there those who refuse to . . . acquiesce?"

"There have been some."

"What happens in these cases?"

"They share Tulilly's portion. Are there any further questions? Then you have leave to depart. Palude waits outside, and has the details." The Regents stood, abruptly, folding their hands in their voluminous sleeves, in the formal manner of their tradition. The interview was over.

2

"Individuals attain the power, the Mana, to create something merely by asking for it; Institutions, at vast and great labor, obtain finally the power to obstruct."

—H.C., Atropine

THIS TIME, THEY would wait for him to leave the hearing room, after which the Regents would leave in their own good time. Pentrel'k stepped out of the auditor's podium, and walked briskly across the room to the tall, narrow doors, which opened as he reached them. He passed through without looking back, or to either side. Once outside the hearing room, he turned right and walked down a long corridor, his footfalls echoing. On either side were closed doors at regular intervals: examination rooms, similar to the one he had just left. The only lighting came from translucent skylights high overhead, and suspended from the distant peaked roof, long, severe chandeliers dimly illuminated from within. At the end of the building was an immense stained-glass window stretching from floor to ceiling.

As he walked, he reflected that in his long years on Oerlikon, he had forgotten how different Heliarcos was: on Oerlikon, in Lisagor, the buildings were large, firmly founded, plain, enduring. The crowds flowed among them like children, most of them content to let the higher-ups worry about things, amusing themselves with the anarchy of Dragon, their only game. The streets were level, more or less, gently curving, filled with the constant hum of the soft tyres of the velocipedes. But on Heliarcos . . .

There was considerable use of stone on Heliarcos, mostly granite, and since the inhabited lands were hilly, or mountainous, there were abrupt changes of level. The streets were dark cobblestones, the buildings gray granite, built in a spiky, abrupt style the archaicists called neo-gothic. Most of the traffic was on foot, mixed with three-wheeled teardrop-shaped metal cars on the broader ways, that went by silently, their windows opaqued. Here, you could hear the wind in the groves of conifers, the spatter of runoff from the downspouts . . . little else. Passing footsteps.

Pentrel'k stopped only when he reached the foyer of the examination building, and from a dim little cloakroom off the entrance, retrieved one of the basic garments of this part of Heliarcos: a long raincoat with a hood, which he put on hurriedly, and pulled the hood up. Then he stepped outside.

The front of the examination building was a broad plaza, joined to the streets by long stairs, which were flanked with enormous granite pots, each housing ornamental junipers of ancient aspect, oversize bonsai. Palude was waiting beside the first of these, in the rain. At the sight of the trees and Palude, Pentrel'k glanced at the leaden sky, now beginning to darken into a pale blue dusk of a rainy day. It was late.

He walked directly to the woman, and said, "Well, I am here, as you can see."

Palude nodded. "So I see. And so you also agreed to go back?"

"Yes. I assume they offered you the same choices they offered me . . . none."

She said, "Yes. You understand we are fortunate in that regard. Very few of the returnees got anything. They might conceivably have been better off to have stayed on Oerlikon."

Pentrel'k said, softly, "They thought along the same lines I did, as you did: that we'd all have some reward for getting as much out as we did." He daydreamed, aloud, "We'd all come back here, go back into the Instructional Branches, do research . . . I would have taught a series of courses on Tactical Theory . . . I suppose we were all a bit naïve."

Palude nodded again, "Yes. I don't know what happened to most. The ones I do know of . . . well, it's not so good. A lot of those got the stoneworks."

"And Charodei?"

She shrugged. "To interrogation. Wise not to ask too closely beyond that."

"I quite agree; it was close in there. They said nothing, mind you—it was what they didn't say. There was no need for them to. And so here we are, standing in the rain like a couple of bedraggled bosels! Shall we wind on down the hill and find a dry place in which to compare notes and plan strategies?"

"Yes." Palude glanced up at the rapidly darkening clouds. "We can go down in the lower city. The student taverns will be enough for us. No one will notice us there. And we should do so without delay: I have booked passage already."

"How did you know I would come?"

"I didn't. They told me it would be me and one other. Presumably they had a replacement if you failed to meet their expectations."

Pentrel'k snorted as he started off down the stairs, "Hmff! They couldn't replace us and they knew it."

Palude joined him. "Not both. But either one they could have replaced."

"When do we leave?"

"Tomorrow."

Heliarcos was a small planet at the outer section of its primary's life zone; its warmest climatic zone was decidedly cool by human standards. Both poles were under permanent ice caps. With considerable axial tilt, and a fast rotation, it had changeable, stormy weather. Its parent star was a relatively young F8 type of an odd color between oyster and the palest of yellows, and when it did shine through the clouds, it seemed both brighter and larger than the sun of Earth, despite the greater distance.

The surface was highly mineralized with heavy elements, and the life forms few in type and rather unspecialized. Its discoverers had pronounced it "a mountainous Permian," and rated it for the mineral concessions. The habitable land surface was simply too small, and the climate too severe, for large-scale human habitation.

One well-known account described it: "Fogs and mists, and when none of those, rain, snow, hail, at any season, often mixed in the same storm, or all at once. The vegetation is all dull green, and no flowers break the monotony. The animal life either placidly munches conifers, or else, almost as placidly, munches other animals. The animals are silent—they issue forth no challenges, mating calls, or expressions of well-being. One might wait years to hear even a serious grunt of exertion. Their reproductive methodology is efficient and uninspiring, their forms generalized and lumplike, a committee's-eye view of an evolutionary scheme. They stalk or repulse attacks with stolid persistence." In the end, the explorer had begged to be relieved of his post, resorting to the final damnation in French: *"J'ai le Cafard!"* This was boredom, L'Ennui, beyond hope.

Heliarcos had one advantage, however: it had a priceless location close by busy and populous systems, and because of its mineral deposits, rapidly became self-supporting. Several academic groups, seeing its possibilities for a convenient retreat, early established institutions of higher learning. Certain religious groups also moved onto the planet to make retreats and monastic communities. These, with the mining concessions, became the dominant form of human inhabitation there, and in a relatively short time, the three types of organization grew to resemble one another, and finally became indistinguishable. In this last phase, offplanet governments and industrial concerns set up research groups, which fit in without a ripple. The process had been completed.

The history of Heliarcos was utterly unlike any other planet's; there were no kings, presidents, statesmen, conquerors or revolutionaries—likewise there had been no countries, empires, states, principalities or interregnums. The larger habitable continent was parcelled out more or less equitably to the various groups, and the smaller one, by common consent, left wild and uninhabited by humans. Supported by offplanet organizations and the specialty mineral trade, there had never been an opportunity for nationalism to develop. And in effect, the planet had no central government, nor even its own currency. It became a place devoted exclusively to the cultivation of the mind, whose predominant cultural form was an institute of learning surrounded by the support activities necessary to a functioning human community.

Heliarcos, then, became a place whose unique product was the distillation of human learning: a university whose scale and diversity had never been attempted before in a single location. To this harsh little world came the best of all the worlds, to undergo courses of instruction, to receive professional finishing and polish, and to sharpen the muscles of the mind. Through its contacts with the other worlds, it carried an influence far greater than could have been obtained through armies or political power, and was agreed by all to be neutral ground—whatever the factional issue. It became, in its own way, immensely powerful, and men and women who were high in the society of Heliarcos had few equals elsewhere and were indebted to fewer. The governments who ruled unruly men had their locations elsewhere, but the influence of the Regents and Proctors of Heliarcos reached out through an intricate network onto all worlds, even some that knew of Heliarcos only by the dimmest of rumors.

*　　*　　*

The organization to which Cesar Kham and Arunda Palude belonged had originally been founded as a study institute whose purpose was to examine the ways humans adapted to new environments, or invented new cultural forms for newly opened planets. This had rapidly grown into several specialized areas, which had in turn given birth to even more specializations. Major areas included language, sociology, anthropology, political science, history, literature, as well as what were politely known as "support disciplines," such as computer science, mathematics, and physics, although these latter were not pursued with the single-minded devotion they knew at institutes where they were studied as the primary arts.

The Oerlikon Project, as it had been known, had been a joint field project supported by several major departments, and coordinated by its own semi-independent operations staff, which had of course grown in time and gradually assumed its own inertia. This situation could have endured indefinitely, until either the Opstaff changed, or until a revolution occurred on Oerlikon. Neither had been considered likely. Now, of course, all had been changed. The flow of students and field operatives onto Oerlikon had stopped, and those people who had escaped from Oerlikon had to be placed somewhere, as well as the now-unnecessary Opstaff members. It had been a trying time, a demanding time, and in a changing situation, it was natural that many expectations could not be fulfilled, which was a delicate way of putting it.

This particular inhabited area was called Pompitus Hall, from a once-prominent building which housed, originally, a small mathematics faculty. The Oerlikon operations staff had taken up two rooms of the original hall. But as the complexity of the operation had grown, it had gradually taken over the whole building, spread into several annexes, which had been consolidated back into newer buildings and rebuildings, and in turn sprouted further annexes. The Upper town was devoted to the faculty buildings proper, while lower down the slopes the Lower town filled a narrow river valley.

Kham and Palude made their way through the rapidly falling darkness and rain down the hill, through the housing areas into the town proper. The streets were still narrow and paved with granite cobblestones, but the buildings became smaller and somewhat more erratic in design. Here the streets were busy, and windows were lighted. Crowds passed along the streets in easy confusion, and commercial places, hardly noticed during the day, now came to life. After some searching, they settled on a modest place calling itself The Armonela Inn, which had a large lower public room fronting on the river and warmed by several fireplaces. This was quiet, and frequented by students who appeared to wish to finish some studying away from the faculty buildings; the room was modestly lit, and free of heavy drinking and noise. Despite the quiet, however, it was well-filled, and they had to wait for one of the more secluded booths.

Pentrel'k and Morelat Eickarinst ordered a simple meal of braised fowl and dumplings, assigning the cost to the accounts of the Bursar of the Faculty, a procedure that was accepted without question. After a short delay, the meal was served and they set to it without ceremony or talk; for both of them the day had been both long and trying, and in fact they had both gone without lunch. They had serious matters to settle, and it could not be covered well by small talk between bites, for they were neither on a party nor an evening's pleasant games; this was serious business.

After dinner, however, over steaming mugs of the astringent tea which was the specialty of the house, flavored heavily with resin and some other acidic flavor which neither of them could identify, they began exploring the subject at hand. By this time the crowd had thinned a little, and they would be left alone.

Pentrel'k opened the discussion. "Well, as of tomorrow we will assume our identities of old. I will be Cesar Kham, and you Arunda Palude. We may as well resume tonight."

Palude raised her mug in a slight salute. "Indeed. Of course, being a mnemonicist, I never forgot Morelat, but I did put it off a bit. I never knew you, anyway, as Czermak."

"Of course not. We were of different classes. I had been on Oerlikon for some time when you came."

"I know. You did not matriculate here, did you?"

"No. Calomark. In the south. But enough of that, I suppose; we will have time to fill this in as we go." Here Kham betrayed a facet of his character that few ever saw. Secretive and careful to the point of willful paranoia within the guise of his assignment, he was abrupt and tactless with relationships in reality. He continued, "I assume you have had some access to the debriefings they have worked up."

"Yes—indeed, they let me see all of it, as soon as it was set in that I would be going back."

"Conclusions that they saw?"

"None. I read, I studied, I reflected. I made no report. But it would be less than accurate to say that I saw in the reports what they did."

Kham observed, "I should think they would see more. I mean, they are here, supervising, while we in the field . . ."

"Not necessarily so! In fact, I early on came to understand that the people in the field were much more . . . What's that old student slang word we used to use? *Dapt.* That's what we used to say. Meaning adept, able. And besides, Mnemonicism-Integration is a difficult discipline, one you have to work at. I am sure that none of these I've seen here can match my level without artificial aids."

"Well, whatever else we may say and do, I like your cynical candor. You kept it veiled on Oerlikon."

"Womancraft, Cesar. It is a part of discretion that a woman never reveals her true self casually, be that selfness ability of mind, strength of desire to achieve, or sexual desire. It's a legacy of old oppressions that are not yet entirely vanished. All subordinate peoples learn to dissemble, to walk clothed."

"Aha! Then what is it you show me?"

"One layer down. Not necessarily the reality."

"Well said!"

"You did rather well at this, yourself . . . Glist, on the other hand, always let down too easily."

"Glist was not, in my opinion, a good choice for coordinator."

"One gets what one gets."

"Just so." He sighed. "What kind of particulars have you managed to build?"

She looked down at her mug, which was empty, now. Palude raised it on high, for a moment, and presently a waiter appeared, with a fresh pot. She shook her head. "I now know things I missed there in the heat of the fray. Things I overlooked, or didn't see at all. It is considerably more difficult than they make it out to be."

"I had an instinct for this and felt the same, although I could not justify it."

"That's the tactician talking. It feels wrong. And you know the old tactical motto: 'If it feels good, do it. Until it feels bad. Then quit.' This feels bad now, and won't get any better; still, what choices do we have?"

"None. Well, go on. What are we to face?"

"First: We will have to determine if the subject is alive. Positive identification and hard evidence. We do not in fact know now if it survived the tumults of Marula. If it died or was killed, then the task is simple. We return an report."

"We'll have to see if Pternam left any records, notes, bring those—or what survives of them."

"Or destroy them there."

"How so?"

"You saw yourself what that creature, that thing could do. There, in that time, it was limited in scope. It carried out its maker's instruction, and then pursued its own survival. But Oerlikon was then a severely limited environment—virtually encapsulated. It is not now. Also this: suppose we bring back enough textual material to enable them to reach for the Morphodite again, here? This world is not isolated, but interwoven with the whole human community. If it goes rogue, we are not talking about one continent on one world, but thousands."

"You believe, then, that such a creature could do it?"

"Absolutely. Now then—let's follow the other track. It lives. Very well. It will have to now be a male, because no trace of the woman Damistofia Azart has ever been found. Up to a point they trace her to a specific date and time. Then nothing. No corpse, and no further movement."

"Some held that it died."

"The evidence I have suggests that it changed successfully and escaped, and went somewhere to hide. It probably intended to do that anyway, because it knew that too many people knew it as Damistofia, for her to follow any kind of normal life."

"Well, hellation and damnanimity! It could have made more than one change!"

"No. Only one. If it lived. The process is a horror to endure. It's like experiencing death, directly. No. It won't change for casual reasons."

"That still doesn't help us. All we have done is eliminated half the population!"

"More than half—51.89 percent, to be exact. And we know something else about it."

"What?"

"That it's young. Probable mid-twenties, standard. And such a person won't have any past. Also we know where to start looking. Clisp. Because Damistofia was in Marula, and she had no contacts except what she could make on her own, so she wouldn't be likely to leave Lisagor proper. And she wouldn't walk back into Crule—that's where his/her enemies were. The only place she could go and vanish would be a large city, like Marisol, in Clisp. It's the only logical place."

"Aha! I see your drift. . . ."

"And you know Clisp and Marisol. . . ."

"Indeed I do. But it has some kind of ability to see what's going on around it."

"Yes. But that has limitations."

"It's nice to know that."

"No need to be sarcastic. The creature has profound gifts, some given it by Pternam, some of those inadvertently, and a lot of what it developed of its own accord. But remember this: its weakness is that its system isn't passive, and . . ."

"Explain."

"It has a method of seeing conditions around it; but it has to 'ask,' as it were. It has to *look*, and the process isn't easy. So it doesn't spend all its time searching. . . ."

"So we have to move without alarming it, or becoming visible to its powers . . . but . . ." He stopped, puzzling over an impossible contradiction. Then he continued, "I understand that the creature has the ability to see distant events and circumstances that bear on it. If it looks, now, it can see that we are coming!"

"Now, let me explain what I think I know about what it does. This will help. It isn't all-powerful. It has limits. I will describe what I believe to be its limits, and you, the tactician, with an understanding of the territory, can then conceive an attack."

"You say that with some finality."

"I don't want it brought here under any circumstances. *Any*."

"Well, they don't either, unless it can be controlled."

"It can't be controlled. Once alerted, it can find the place and time when it can escape, or make a move that will bring the house down around us. They underestimate it. I don't."

"Proceed."

"Its ability to find the pivot of a society and change that is a by-product of the system it uses to perceive events around it. Embedded in that theory, a pseudotheory as Pternam thought it; but the way it really is, is that the creature developed the perceptive system first, in secret. Or it saw in Pternam's idea a germ of a greater truth."

"All right. How does it do it?"

"Are you familiar with the *I Ching?*"

"The *Book of Changes?* Somewhat. I never studied it deeply."

"Basically, it is a binary code of two-to-the-sixth-power states, with selected elements being changeable according to specific rules. Sixty-four 'states' cover all human events."

"Go on."

"What is your opinion of that?"

"Mysticism, farrago, nonsense, occultism, fortune-telling. All other objections aside, I believe in the influences of the application of Will and Desire, and of course, it would seem that sixty-four conditions are much too shallow a reading."

"Well. The *I Ching,* in the hands of an adept, has some remarkable powers that defy rational explanation, as we define rationality. It is outside the bounds of what we understand as causality. But throughout human history, it has never been given up. Even now, we could go out to the street of the booksellers and buy a copy. I would almost recommend it." Arunda Palude smiled at this, as if the idea were too much to bear. "But however that is . . . have you heard of the Tarot?"

"Distantly. More fortune-telling."

"Instead of sixty-four basic states, it has twenty-two."

"That's less. So I would say it lacks subtlety."

"But in the use of either system, the states interact. In an *I Ching* consultation, if all lines are changeable, then you double the possibilities to one hundred and twenty-eight. With Tarot, it's larger, because you consider twenty-two values in a sequence of ten. Not twwenty-two to the tenth power, but twenty-two partial factorial: still an enormous number. And so *that* is very subtle indeed. And both of those two systems are founded on a base of some very shrewd observations. Nevertheless all of the bases are arbitrary value judgments, however well they approximate. You follow this?"

"Yes, I think so. It's a good guess, but not scientific, so so speak."

"So. Imagine a system with a base larger than Tarot, but worked out in practice rather like the *I Ching,* with some 'lines' changeable. We didn't recover his bases, or what he calls them, but we do know that there are fifty-five values in the base sequence, and that the 'word' length is variable. And now imagine that the values in the base sequence are not developed empirically, but by ruthless scientific experimentation."

"I can imagine such a concept, but it would be hard to remember it in practice."

"It consults by knowing the base values, and then performing specific operations. There is some peculiar mathematics involved, as well. At any rate, that is what it does. And the system is, as far as we can determine, and for all practical purposes, absolute."

"You have this data as factual?"

"Observations melded for commonality, from observers, remarks, things people heard it say, or heard repeated."

"You have done a remarkable job of getting that much."

"That's about all I have. That's how it perceives. Now consider it received the most intense training in the use of weapons, and of martial arts. Reputedly, it can kill with bare hands, or build a nuclear weapon from scratch, or set up total conversion objects. Whatever it needs to do the job."

"Then this is much worse than I thought."

"Agreed. Much, much worse. Our only chance will be in surprise."

Kham asked, "Then you don't think we could capture it."

"No. I don't think so."

"We have a third choice."

"Which is?"

"We could help it escape."

"Why ever would you say that?"

"If we could contact it and persuade it to go away, somewhere. . . ."

"You heard the Regents: it must not know who Jedily Tulilly was. It can, theoretically, determine that from any place, if it becomes motivated to. Then we have no idea what might happen."

"Then it would seem that a surprise attack from space, total sterilization of Oerlikon, might work."

"Conceivably. If we knew it was on Oerlikon. And besides that, that option has been ruled out." Palude stopped now and considered Cesar Kham across the table from her. Bald, stocky, a powerful man who emitted absolute confidence in himself, but with limits. And these limits were easy to seek, easy to find. A superb tactician who thrived on emergencies, he totally lacked the long view, the powerful sense of consequences, of *karma*, which the mnemonicist could never escape. It was useless to try to provoke something out of him which did not exist.

Kham said, "I understand that: it would show the hand that guides."

Palude nodded. "That would bring much out into the open. You see, in a way, the Regents who set all this in motion. . . ."

Kham interrupted her. ". . . The ones who set this in motion are long since removed from retribution."

"True. But the ones who inherited, they feel limited, boxed in by these circumstances. If they act, they reveal. If they don't act, they get Jedily Tulilly back, but they don't know when. So they try to find the middle."

"Hmf. A difficult path, this. You understand we could die of this?"

"Cesar, I understand that; and that there are worse things than personal extinction."

"Oh, yes, there I agree. I know that sense well. Many times. Now you speak my language. So in that language, I ask you: why does this creature, who has demonstrable powers, not attack immediately?"

Palude looked off into the crowd. No one seemed to be observing them. If they had been taken for anything, it would be as members of the faculty, out on an evening's slumming, among the students. She leaned forward and said quietly, "We have grown so used to illusory pseudopower, in human history, that we read the real thing wrongly. One who *thinks* he has power—there's the one who attacks, but the one who has the real thing, that one lies low, seeks the unwatched space, the quiet time. It is the truthful confirmation, that we have this strong suspicion that the creature yet lives, and yet it does nothing."

"Then, if I follow you aright, the Morphodite does not seek to apply his powers, to rule, to revenge."

Palude said, emphatically, "That is my analysis."

Kham continued. "Then, paradoxically, there is little to fear from it, even if it uncovers Jedily."

Palude smiled. "Exactly."

"Did you make this point?"

"I made it. It wasn't accepted."

Kham pressed, "Then they don't want it known, even if nothing happens. . . ."

"Correct."

"Did they suggest anything to you?"

"About Tulilly? No. They guard it well. I can follow the thread myself up to a point, and then blank. There's a logic to it. She was dumped, so to speak, on Oerlikon, for some reason. I've tried conjecture: nothing fits."

Kham now nodded, slowly. "Yes, I see. So . . . we get to go and fix things up. Very well. I vote for murder. No reason to mince words."

"As odious as it is, that seems to be the only course. I could not in good conscience consider allying myself with that creature, when I have no idea of his aims. This is devil's work. I know it clear-eyed, but all the same, it's out of devils I know well enough."

Kham smiled, a rictus Palude had not seen in his face before. It was an expression of vast, calculating cynicism. He said, "Aye, you and I know them, don't we, but we don't know why they dumped Tulilly, or even where she came from, and there's devils of another Aleph ordinal, as we used to say."

Palude changed the subject. "There were dependable operatives left behind when we left Oerlikon?"

"Yes. I imagine a good many of them can be rounded up for a little quiet work. In addition we had sleepers controlling natives in a number of places, and these can be activated as well, although I don't think we'll rouse all of them, that follows. But we designed considerable redundancy into our systems there, so I am sure a few days' work will suffice to open something up."

"Good. You think we can determine something, then?"

"From here, a guess? Probable. I can say more when we get back. How do we re-enter Lisagor, or whatever it's called now?"

"We're going by courier *Frigate*. There's an inbound freighter we'll match with and transfer to, to actually land. The landing will be in Tartary, but reports have it there's trade now and we can get a place. The plan is that we try to get a ship for a Tilanque port, rather than Karshiyaka. This is supposed to be feasible, according to the sources they still have active."

"They are still reporting?"

"Sporadically, from Lisagor. Tartary station never went down."

Kham mused, "Tartary station wasn't under us, as I'm sure you recall."

"True. But they weren't hostile to offworlders there, either. Just indifferent. But it will be early, so I suggest we retire without revel or carouse."

Now Kham looked closely at Arunda Palude. By all accounts, a distant, cool woman, who, although no longer young, still maintained handsome good looks. Kham had heard no tales about her, as he had heard about the others posted to Lisagor, who took advantage of the native concern with footloose sex to have a good time on the sly. Palude was tall, with a modest, but well-shaped figure. She had a strong, clear face, formed by the intense concentration of her profession, and loose, flowing hair the color of walnut wood. Kham made an internal adjustment, evaluating Arunda as probably not one prone to dalliance. But sharp, and direct. And if on Oerlikon before, she had followed his lead in organizing the chaos, it did not bother him now to accept her lead in setting the long-range goals. That kind of flexibility also fitted with the dancer's poise of the tactician. He thought: *A shame we can't do more, but we'll probably work well together. That will have to do.* He said, "Yes. Where are you staying, and where do I meet you?"

"At the Ozalide Inn. Come there at the fifth hour."

"Very well. Good evening." He arose and made a courteous gesture. Then added, "You understand that a lot will be different this time."

Palude nodded. "Yes. Very different."

"We may have to move about quickly, alone, without the support network. You'll need to move with me."

"Why . . . ? I thought you would . . ."

"You have a weapon to help us. You mentioned the *I Ching;* you know about it, yes? Get a copy of the book. You're going to use it. Ours may not be as subtle as his, but a map's a map, no matter how crudely drawn, and Lisagor only has one shape. And so I will pull the trigger, but you will be doing some aiming." And with that request Cesar Kham turned away and departed for his own lodgings.

3

"Even paranoids sometimes have real enemies."
　　　　　　　　—Remark attributed to Spiro T. Agnew

"Paranoia is most definitely a survival trait."
　　　　　　　　　　　　—H.C., Atropine

THE SOUTHERN AND western parts of Clisp were, geologically, a continuation of the ranges that made up the rugged spine of the isthmus which the inhabitants of Lisagor called the Serpentine, the narrow neck joining Lisagor with its subcontinent. But the peaks that marched across the southern horizon from east to west did more than provide the inhabitants of Marisol with a spectacular skyline; they blocked Clisp off from the influences of the southwestern ocean airs, and let the cool winds in from the northwest. Clisp was cool and somewhat arid, with frequent fogs along the northern seaboard, sometimes creeping as far inland as Marisol.

The northern part of Clisp was a low plain descending gently to the sea, traced and eroded by small ravines. Rain fell often in the mountains, and this runoff kept the water level up. Several of these streams had been diverted into feeder canals and shifted to the site of Marisol, where, through an easy descent of locks, the open sea could be contacted through a canal.

Marisol, then, partook of several natures at once, none dominating: it was the administrative seat of government for a large and frequently turbulent province; inland commercial center for the province, which outside Marisol was largely agricultural; and it was a seaport, with canals linking many parts of the city. Lastly, it was the last place on Oerlikon where rebels against the stultifying sameness of Lisagor might gather and have a moment's respite, if not their way. Consequently, Marisol was a large city of mostly low buildings, without monumental edifices, but equally lacking slums and squatter camps. The air, save during the fogs, was clear and transparent, and the wind made merry, sliding across the plains out of the northwest. And in the south, under the slow passages of the primary of Oerlikon, Gysa, the bold mountains marched across the face of the world, and played with towers of cloud and lightning. It was a place in which one had to strive to retain a bad feeling. There was always something in the wind.

Phaedrus and Meliosme had come to Marisol for the bottomless obscurity he sought, and she accepted, knowing peace within herself from her long days in the wild. And for a long time their lives settled into routine and stability; known things, not hard decisions. Phaedrus worked as a landscaper and Meliosme took on the weight of making the lives of the urchins and orphans they had collected along the way whole again. There were more of these than they had planned for; they had gained some on the long road up from Zolotane, along the edge, the sea on one side, and chaos on the other, people fleeing, order disturbed. Phaedrus took them in without question. He remembered, he knew. He had wrought this. He accepted the terrified children without rancor, bearing them as a light burden he knew he owed and could never fill.

He told Meliosme that because of the changes wrought in him, he could sire no children, so the runaways and strays became their own children. They, in turn, brought more in, and in time the family of Phaedrus and Meliosme grew large. Since they needed help in meeting the expense of feeding them, Phaedrus had gone to the public audiences which the heriditary ruler of Clisp was wont to give from time to time, and plainly asked for aid. Pressed for details by Pompeo's clerks, he had revealed his connection with events in Zolotane, and Pompeo had made the necessary connection. The prince, a middle-aged man with a balding head and a visible paunch, who stood on little ceremony, asked Phaedrus to attend him in his private chambers.

There, Pompeo sat in a plain armchair and had spoken directly, "You are the fellow we heard about some time ago. I had reports. One of my men met you. Salkim."

"Yes. I remember him. He is well?"

Pompeo shook his head. "Dead. Led a raiding party ashore in the Far Pilontaries. Good man. Bit of a dandy, but nonetheless true. Better than most. But his command won the day and returned. I read their reports."

"You do not fault me that I did not take up his offer?"

"No. I wish you had, but no matter. And so you come to Clisp anyway."

"Yes. Almost directly. As a fact, I got here rather sooner than if I'd left with Salkim."

"That's so . . . Well, you haven't been invisible here, either. We keep an eye on things here, just like other places, but with an eye to helping the good instead of punishing the evil. Why bother? The evil will harm themselves."

"You knew it was me . . . ?"

"Not necessarily. We knew someone was taking in orphans and strays and runaways and setting them straight. Rest easy. We can help you do that easily enough. See Patroclo, the Bursar. Use discretion, which I know you will."

"I will do my best."

Pompeo stroked his jowls with his middle finger and thumb, looking downward, thoughtful. Then he had said, gruffly and directly, "But all things are, in Clisp, desirous of balance."

Phaedrus had said, "Yes, m'lord."

"You are held in regard as being clearheaded, now a rarity. It pleases me to help you in your work. I request that you help me in mine."

"How so?"

"Attend me here. About once every four weeks, or as I call on you. Then we will speak of values, ethics, the right choices. I have many advisers, out to succeed at Court. I have not seen your application, nor do you bow and scrape."

Phaedrus breathed in relief, silently. "I will do so with pleasure, if it pleases you."

"I do not know how you order your life, or those whose lives touch yours. But I have heard well of you. We try to reward excellence here . . . but these have been difficult times, more so than for most of my predecessors. There is the sense of great Change in the air; a new age for Oerlikon. I have my successor, a son, Amadeo, but I wish to set things on a certain course . . ."

"I understand. I am, however, neither a sage, nor a thaumaturge; I do not heal the sick, raise the dead, nor make the little girls talk out of their head."

Pompeo smiled, in great good humor. "Of course not." And the prince stood, indicating that Phaedrus should leave. "About four weeks. Come as you will; I will see they come and get me."

And with no more formality than that, Phaedrus undertook to fill the part of one of Pompeo's many advisers and confidants. The meetings occurred as scheduled, but while Phaedrus was relieved that his secret was safe, there was a curious disjointed air to the talks he had with Pompeo. They never seemed to broach a subject openly, indeed, if there was any subject at all. Pompeo clearly wanted something from him, but at the same time seemed satisfied with the little he got.

Finally, Phaedrus asked him what he was gaining out of their meetings. Pompeo looked off through the careful landscaping of the palace grounds, to the far mountains, and said, reflectively, "I am trying to learn your sense of effortless composure. It would seem that virtually everyone would wish to be more than he is. You do not. True, I am prince here, and should I wish to exercise it, have in fact considerable power to order things. I use it seldom. But because you do not seek more, I have little hold on you."

Phaedrus said cautiously, "There were times before Zolotane, before Clisp. I once chased the illusions as well. At least, let us condense it to that. I saw once that we have all the scope we can handle immediately before us—we do not need to look far afield."

"You do not seek esteem, regard, repute."

"There is never enough of that. No matter how much you get, it always needs more. I must step out of that cycle and *act*, here, now, in front of me. There is always much to be done."

"And what more would a prince want?"

"To be free of the weight of his obligations; one could not remain a prince and be unconscious of them."

"Exactly so! Do you read minds?"

"Not at all."

"And so you do what needs to be done. How do you know it?"

"Everyone knows it. They just don't want to do it. They keep putting it off, for one more try, one more chance. It was in knowing the waste of the old way that I looked and asked, 'is there value in the other way—obscurity, nobodyness?' "

"Are you succeeding?"

"It is difficult at times. But I remind myself of what I know of the other way, and then dig a little deeper."

"You know we tried to trace you, but the trail fades out in the hills between Crule The Swale and Zolotane. You were something before."

"Many things."

"You have no vendettas, no revenges?"

"None. Those things will never be that way again. We have *now*."

"You would not reveal them."

"I would prefer not to."

"Is there anything you would ask, now, for yourself?"

"Meliosme misses the hoots and calls of bosels. You have none in Clisp. We would go back to the east when things are settled down and folk can move about freely again."

"The one thing I can't grant. The breakup left many areas cut off, forced to operate as smaller units. Things are quieter, now, much more so, yet the old days of unity, however bad it might have been, are gone. Movements are restricted. No longer can one wander the length and breadth of Karshiyaka. Here in the West, we have gathered in as much as we can comfortably handle: Zefaa, the Serpentine, Zolotane. That is as far as Greater Clisp goes. There are other countries back there, now. Foreign lands, as hard to reach as Tartary."

For a moment, Pompeo looked off again, and then said, off-handedly, "If you were to speak your mind to me, advising me plainly, what would you have me do? A great time came upon my days, and I know I have not altogether done what I could have. The work of repacification is far from finished."

Phaedrus breathed deeply. Then, "You have done much. You let Clisp expand to its natural limits, when it was time for it to. Now let it go."

"Let go?"

"You have your successor; turn it over to him."

"And then what should I do? All my life I lived in secret, waiting for a restoration we were sure would never come. Then the great changes; and so here we are. But it's unfinished. . . ."

"It will never be finished. You have done well. You were there, but do not stay to mar it. Be content with your acts."

"Exactly as I have thought. You know, only a few more years and this would have missed me. Amadeo . . . He's capable enough for these times, but I often wonder how it would have gone if this change had come in his time."

"You will never know that. Leave it now, while you can still smile about it."

"Very well, but what should I do, then?"

"We always have room for another guide . . ."

Pompeo laughed aloud and stood up. He said, expansively, "It will be as you recommend! But in my own time. In my own time." And with that note they parted.

* * *

For some time, Phaedrus heard no more from Pompeo. Once or twice he stopped by, but did not find the prince in either time. And shortly after that, there was a brief public announcement to the effect that Pompeo had retired in favor of the new prince, Amadeo II, who would now assume the proper executive functions. There was no great ceremony, no parades, nor did anyone think them necessary. Continuity had been assured. Things continued with no visible interruption. More significantly, the financial assistance he and Meliosme received, as well as certain administrative favors, continued without interruption.

The change of seasons in Clisp was more notable than the parts of old Lisagor Phaedrus could remember. The autumn was marked by a notable increase in night fogs, swept away by storms that blew in from the northwest. In these days, few ventured out at night. One such night, while the outside was muffled and supernaturally quiet, Phaedrus and Meliosme were preparing for bed, when they heard outside the faint noise of a motorcar, one of the rare electrics Clispish dignitaries favored. Presently there was a soft knock at the door. Phaedrus went to the door, and opening it, met a silent, elderly gentleman wearing the very plain clothing preferred by the inside servitors of the Ruling House. He said, "I am Phaedrus."

The chauffeur nodded, and said, "Pompeo requires a service of you, in accordance with your agreement."

"Now?"

"Now."

Phaedrus looked about uncertainly at Meliosme. Then back at the unsmiling chauffeur. "In Marisol?"

The chauffeur shook his head. "At the family estates. Cape Forever."

"That's in the farthest west of Clisp. And it's dense fog out there."

The man was undisturbed. He said, in his undertaker's voice, "No matter. I know the way well. We will be there by morning. You will be back tomorrow evening."

Phaedrus, still hesitating, asked, "Is there haste?"

"Not if you leave now," was all that was said.

Phaedrus gathered up his old night-cloak and threw it over his shoulders, glancing at Meliosme. She made a small gesture to him with her hand. "It's all right. Go on." He nodded, and stepped out into the night. The chauffeur followed, closing the door behind him, and opening the door to the passenger compartment for Phaedrus.

Inside was another man, almost invisible in the shadows, save for soft highlights reflected from the dimmed streetlamps. This person was tall, rangy, bald and carried a weapon, some sort of gun which Phaedrus could not identify. The chauffeur got in after him, settling himself in his own compartment, and spoke through a mesh connecting the two cabins. "This is Olin, a trusted retainer and man-at-arms. Trust him as you trust me. We are the personal staff of the Prince Emeritus. You do not walk in harm's way while under our guidance."

Phaedrus asked, "Is the prince well? Why do we need such secrecy?"

The chauffeur turned to his motorcar and started it off through the damp, foggy, leaf-spattered streets, shiny with moisture. Olin answered, "The prince is not well. He will explain everything. It will go as Bautisto has said: you should be back tomorrow evening."

Olin settled back, and Phaedrus, uneasy, nevertheless made an attempt to find a comfortable position among the overstuffed seats. The car whirred off into the fog.

Bautisto indeed seemed to know where he was going with supernatural accuracy. Although the fog was dense, thicker than usual for the season, he navigated through the silent and nearly empty streets of Marisol without any hesitation, and at a considerable speed. Phaedrus, who knew little of the city except the main streets and boulevards and the immediate area of his own house, was soon lost, but as near as he could tell, they were proceeding west in the night, and after a time, the few lights of Marisol grew even less, then rare, and at last there were no lights, save the running lights of the car, and an occasional isolated post along the road. Neither Bautisto nor Olin seemed to relax, but maintained an almost palpable sense of animal awareness which Phaedrus found profoundly disturbing, for all that they had said.

Notwithstanding his sense of foreboding, after a time the motion of the car and the sense of confidence Bautisto expressed in his driving over the empty roads of Clisp relaxed Phaedrus, and he dozed off. Once or twice, he awoke briefly, as they stopped to have the power cells recharged, at bare little stations where a single overhead lamp made a bright, furry cone out of the darkness that began just beyond the windows.

Phaedrus felt the road change, from the smooth gritty friction of the public roads to something more uneven. He opened his eyes to fog-shrouded daylight, broken by darker patches when they passed under enormous trees, of which he could see no detail except shredded, fibrous bark. He said, "Where are we?"

Olin grunted, "Cape Forever Plantation."

"I felt the road change."

"Um. Still a little ways."

Phaedrus settled back, and Bautisto drove on, following a double path seemingly going nowhere through the forest. He could feel in the wheels the changing surface they rolled upon; sometimes sandy, sometimes silent, as if they were rolling on fine leaf-dust. Other times, rocky spurs. The estate road was passable, but not well kept up. And although the road went mostly level, there were now a lot of gentle curves, and there was the sense of having left level ground long ago.

Finally, with almost no warning, they passed through an enormous stucco gate with a circular entrance, and only a low wall dividing the inside from the forest. The inside looked no different. They Founded a sharp curve and stopped before what looked like a rough stone wall, irregular, higher than a man. Bautisto nodded, turning to speak through the mesh, "Toward the direction the car is pointing, you will find an entry. The door is unlocked. Go in. You are expected."

"Just walk in?"

"That is correct. This is not Court, but the house of one who wishes you well. Accept it. They pick their friends with care."

Phaedrus opened the door and hesitantly stepped out into the damp air. As soon as he closed the door, the car started rolling, and in a moment it was gone, vanishing into the morning fog almost as if it had never been there. For a moment, Phaedrus stood, trying to sense the place, capture something of its suchness. He smelled a dry, resinous odor from the forest, and a sharp overtone from something else. He listened. No wind, but a soft, burry muttering as from far off, or perhaps the other side of the wall. Something familiar in that; the sea? He began walking along the wall. Presently he came to a rather plain doorway, well-done, intentionally rustic, but by no means grand. Not exactly the front door of a prince. He turned the iron handle, worn almost to a shapeless lump, and went in.

He was in a long foyer, which led directly ahead, the walls similar to the outside. Phaedrus walked along the hall until he came to a raised porchlike area, opening onto a large, but comfortable room, the far wall of which was glass, still opening onto the silvery blankness of the fog. The light was gray and weak. Inside, lamos and chandeliers banished some of the gloom. The floor was flagstones, covered by carpets in intricate and subtle patterns. At the far end, off to his right, there was a fireplace with a fire going, and several couches. And Pompeo, sitting in a chair by the fire, wrapped in a dark shawl and looking much older. Frail, thin, not at all the robust man of mature years Phaedrus remembered. Phaedrus walked across the flagstones without hesitation until he was standing before the fireplace, which gave off a dull warmth. Only then did Pompeo look up.

He pursed his mouth, as if collecting his words. After a moment, the prince began, hesitantly, "Forgive me if I stumble. Drugs, medicines."

"You are ill." It was a statement, not a question.

"Yes. Man's last enemy, save himself. Cancer. Sometimes it seems almost gone, but it always comes back."

"Is there anything I can do?"

"You always seemed supernaturally wise, but always veiled, something you did not choose to show, or exploit. Tell me something."

Phaedrus understood, he thought. *Make this worthwhile.* He said, "I imagine the Moral Guides have counseled you."

Pompeo nodded. "Just so. But they do not *know.* I sense it. They repeat credo, verse and line, but there is no certainty. I am, in a word, dissatisfied."

"Each one of us endures initiations through life, which become steadily more challenging, more difficult. Free childhood, when innocence first reaches out into the imagination. Puberty, the learning and mastery of desire. Adulthood. Birth. Courtship. The family. Setting the children free. All these are tests. But they are all training, nothing more, for the final test of a person's innermost selfness, when he faces the eternity that is within each of us. Review what you have done, and see this as the final test for excellence."

Pompeo listened, nodding a bit, and when Phaedrus had finished, he said softly, "You cite no authorities, no verse and line, but you *know.*"

Phaedrus shook his head. "I can't even claim that. Say that I have suspicions."

"You speak like a man who has looked death in the eye."

"I have."

"I will not ask. Keep your secret."

"More than once I have come within a hair's-breadth of telling you."

"No. Keep it."

"That is why I almost did. That you do not ask."

"Excellent! As always, you can manage, with a few simple words, to energize me. Would I could have persuaded you earlier. Were it not for other matters, I would urge you to stand by me now, but the little is sufficient, at least for the while. I may falter later. But I did not summon you here in secrecy for selfish reasons. You have only said what was in my heart anyway, which is wisdom enough, is it not?"

"There is another matter, m'lord?"

"Yes. To the point: late in my reign, we uncovered some odd traces of trafficking between persons high up in my regime and parties elsewhere. At first, we thought of the usual sort of spies, such as we read of in the old tales, and some that we know direct from the days of the Rectification. It was exquisitely done, subtle, but we followed it out, tracing every loop and line, stitch and draw. In essense we found a careful line between Patroclo, the Bursar, to parties in such places as Tartary. More recently, to different locations in Old Lisagor. The subject was not state secrets, but you."

Phaedrus stood very still, and he felt an emotion he had never known and for which he had no name. *But it was an icy certainty that this was an absolutely unique moment.* He selected a sofa and sat down, saying nothing.

After a pause, Pompeo continued, "The nature of the thing was as if a passive unit were activated, at first with a vague and general search pattern, later, which focused on you." Pompeo sighed. "That was curious, you know? I thought spies would be interested in the disposition of soldiers, of ships. Of orders-of-battle. Perhaps on the vices of Amadeo, who is fond to excess of pretty women. But no. Of all Clisp could divulge to foreign devils, they were most interested in you, and they pursued you with incredible subtlety and secrecy."

"Do you know who *they* are?"

"No. We have conjectures, but no confirmations."

"Patroclo. May I speak with him?"

"I fear it is no longer possible. He took poison when we confronted him. He had associates, but they also elected to step into the darkness. A few may have escaped us, but it does not appear so."

"Who do you think it is?"

"Olin thinks offworlders."

Phaedrus thought, *The bastards! Why bring it all back? They would know I would have stayed here forever. I had no mission in the stars. Or did I?* A suspicion struck him, but for now, he dismissed it. He said, "You thought I was in danger."

"We let it go on too long, trying to understand it. Time grew valuable. You needed to be told this, so you can take whatever measures you are able to. They seemed to regard you as capable of anything, indeed, they seem to fear you more than they do Clisp."

"They are more correct than you know, in that."

"What can you do?"

"I have . . . certain defenses. Ways of perception. Techniques."

"But you need to be out in the open, and aware."

"Yes."

"You need mobility, to move if need be, beyond the borders of Clisp. . . ."

"Maybe farther."

"Beyond Old Lisagor. Tartary. Perhaps even off Oerlikon."

"How can I do that? The offworlders have gone."

"They still maintain contact in Tartary, openly, as traders."

"Then there is some traffic yet?"

"Yes. And so I know you have little. You could survive in the wild, and presumably you have means to conceal yourself . . . we gathered that information. But you would find it hard to get offworld without funds." Here, Pompeo made an almost-invisible gesture, to which a servant responded, entering the vast room, bearing a small tray. Pompeo continued, "I have put something modest at your disposal. I valued what you gave me, and I would not have a quiet person hunted like a bosel by foreign devils, no matter what he was in past life."

Phaedrus said, "I fear they do not come for my past, but to prevent a future I do not even know, now."

"Then that is even more reason." Pompeo took a small object from the tray, a small medallion on a chain. The medallion was shaped like an ancient Egyptian cartouche, and bore stylized emblems on its surface. It was metal, similar to a dull stainless steel, but when Pompeo handed it to him, it was uncharacteristically heavy. He said, "Platinum. This is an authenticator seal. They have been on Oerlikon since my ancestors first came here."

"What do the symbols mean?"

"We do not know. There are theories, conjectures, but no knowledge. Remember, in a land that pursues the sameness of the eternal present, historians are in no great demand, nor are students of ancient languages. But from the beginning, the Family has used them as authentications for the most secret matters. Including offworld. Use it. Where you need to go, identify yourself as an agent of Clisp and have the charges invoiced to the palace. It will be accepted without question—or knowledge of who has it. Apparently it cannot be counterfeited. Trace elements."

"This is a powerful amulet; surely you do not give such a teasure away?"

"Do what you must. Then return, and serve Clisp as you will, doing your best to insure that we are not overrun by evil and fear and ignorance."

"You did not mention greed and lust."

"They are self-limiting. But the others partake of the endless dark I will soon meet."

"I am moved, and will do as you ask."

"Even though I will not be here to see it, I believe you will." Pompeo made another gesture, and other servants entered, bringing trays of food. "Breakfast. I assume Bautisto did not stop along the way?"

"He did not. He and Olin seemed iron men."

"We had to move when you were not watched. We knew that at that particular time you were not."

"That suggests something I do not care for."

"So we thought. So, let us eat. Enjoy the view. Stay as long as you will. Leave as you must."

Pompeo and Phaedrus breakfasted alone, uninterrupted by even the silent and subtle servants of the retired prince. Both men elected, for the moment, to keep their silences to themselves. After breakfast, Pompeo indicated that it was time for one of his treatments, and he excused himself, indicating that Phaedrus should consider himself free to wander about, or rest, as he felt. The light falling through the window-wall was much brighter now, and the fog was gone, so he could see across an old-fashioned walled garden.

After a moment's search, Phaedrus found the door leading out into the garden and went out. He did not feel like resting at the moment; the information Pompeo had imparted to him was disturbing.

For a time he wandered aimlessly about the garden, admiring the sense of restraint the landscapers had held in mind when they had done the planting, and in maintaining it through the years, for it was obviously not a new garden. After a time, he found a narrow gate, almost hidden away in an acute corner. He made his way to it, and stepped through. Before him was the blue expanse of the northern ocean.

Immediately before him was a rocky shingle beach which curved off into misty distances far to the right, to the east, fading into the horizon and the line of sea-spray. To the left, the land became rockier, then mostly outcrops of brown stone, and at last a headland jutting into the ocean, crowned by a thin group of wind-contorted trees, their limbs distorted by the sea-wind into strange, histrionic shapes. Beneath the trees, a lone fisherman was casting a circular net into the blue water, pausing, withdrawing it, timeless motions that had passed unchanged since the dawn of history.

Phaedrus walked slowly out to the point, savoring the ripe sense of suchness of this scene: the clear northern sky, the open sea, a limitless deep indigo color. He felt a sudden urge to sail off into those distances, although he knew very well that for all practical purposes there was nothing out there, all the way around the world, except Tartary on the other side.

Drawing near to the fisherman, he saw it to be Olin, who was not catching much. This seemed to have no perceptible effect on the man, who continued casting his net, pausing, and withdrawing it; his catch was scanty, small fishes and strange creatures Phaedrus did not know, living things combining features of mollusk and insect in equal measures.

At one of the pauses, he ventured, "I see they are not cooperating this morning."

Olin withdrew the net, nodding. He said, "True."

Phaedrus said, "I am not a fisherman, but I would imagine you do not do this entirely with the catch alone in mind."

Olin folded the net up, carefully. "No. One could use a huge dragline and scoop it all up, or plant blurt along the bottom and blow them to the top. But what then?"

"There would be no more."

Olin sorted through his catch, placed perhaps a dozen in his basket, and threw the rest back into the cold water. "Exactly."

For a time, neither said anything, then Olin said, "Now you know. What are your plans?"

"I thought to return to Marisol, but that seems unwise. At the least, I should arrange some way to get Meliosme out of there."

"Your woman."

"Yes."

"I agree."

"Are you aware of the situation?"

"That someone was having you watched? Of course."

"Who interrogated Patroclo?"

"Bautisto. And few escape the old bustard, too. But that one got away, he did."

"The prince told me; but what is your own evaluation?" Phaedrus felt an instant trust, an instinctive regard, for the redoubtable Olin, whom Pompeo apparently trusted without question.

Olin looked off at the sea distances for a moment, and then said, as if musing to himself, "I would have said something out of Old Crule. You know, all the diehards and lifers ran there after Symbarupol fell to the rebels. But their reporting nets didn't fit that pattern. There was contact with Tilanque, Karshiyaka, and Tartary. A lot of moving about on the far end. Decision was made to collect you because the usual spy networks stopped abruptly. We assumed they were close enough to use more ordinary methods. All the signs pointed to that."

"You mean the people they were reporting to . . . were in Clisp."

"Perhaps not that close. But close enough to get here in a day."

Phaedrus didn't say anything. Olin added, "Rumor has it you did something vile in Lisagor."

"Yes, one might say that."

"Well, it's none of my affair. You've done well here, and Pompeo is satisfied with that. So are we. But I've orders to assist you, and so I will. What would you do? Pull out and go into the wild? There isn't much of it left, you know."

"If they found me in Clisp . . ."

"Yah. They can probably follow you anywhere on Oerlikon. Do you know who and what they are? Perhaps we can eliminate some of them. . . ."

"If this is truly offworld, then there are more behind this than we can reach . . ." He let it trail off, thinking, *But I can reach into places Olin can't see.* Still, he would have to move, and he would have to have some data. He doubted he could derive an accurate answer with the limited amount and values he had. Assumptions. They could be oracles, better than gods, and they could be fools, worse than charlatans. . . . "But at any rate, I should get Meliosme out. Some of the hardier kids."

"No worry there. We would take over what was left. Your place was well-known, and needs keeping. We have people we can put to that."

"Have you rested?"

"Enough. Bautisto went home, so I'd have to round up a couple of worthy lads. No matter, that. We have plenty about."

"We should leave, and go to a place near Marisol, where we can arrange to have Meliosme contacted."

Olin picked up his catch, and the net, and set off, as if glad to have something decided. "I'll go get the car. It's charged up now and ready to go. We'll get the lads along the way. Go back through the house, tell the factotum. I'll meet you in front."

Phaedrus nodded, and set off toward the garden wall, but before he stepped through it, he looked back, once, at the limitless blue horizon, the darkness of the sea, the depths of the sky. He thought to himself, *I was shown paradise, but only to demonstrate that I can't have it. Someday. . . .* And he thought that it would be a good idea, after they had picked up Meliosme, for them to go off into the wild lands of Southern Clisp, among the mountains, for a while.

The fog had cleared inland as well as along the coast when they set out, leaving the estate behind, and Cape Forever. Phaedrus had come up this same road before, but it had been at night, in dense fog, and he remembered no landmarks. Now, with the sun in the south near noon, he saw a smooth road made of compacted yellow gravel, very fine and even-surfaced, that ran straight between cultivated fields. In the far distances on both sides could be seen the low, spreading turf roofs and sturdy stucco walls of houses and outbuildings, and in the south, farther still, the mountains of Clisp rose up, tier on tier, layer on layer, each level becoming lighter in tone until the last one, flecked and spotted with snow, nearly matched the pearlescent color of the southern horizon.

The car moved along the road eastward now, easily, silently. No one took notice of them as they passed. The road, although dry, left no dust trail behind them. Olin sat in the back, as before, with Phaedrus, apparently catnapping, but remaining wary as an animal. The two "boys" Olin had brought with him looked like hardened veterans of border wars.

Olin noted, out of the corner of his eye, that Phaedrus was watching the two in front closely. He said, quietly, "Not by tradition alone, nor by good manners, was the House of Clisp maintained during the cycle of darkness. We were quiet, we kept our own counsels, but now and again muscle was needed. These are representative of that class."

Phaedrus nodded. "They appear capable and loyal."

"Whatever comes, you are among friends and comrades. His word suffices." Olin nodded back over his shoulder toward the west, a curt, chopped motion. "I don't doubt we're dealing with planted agents and buried sleepers in the government, back in Marisol. You simply can't be sure of that many people. But these are our own."

Phaedrus saw the one on the passenger side bend over and work with the communicator, speaking at length. He could not make out what was being discussed. The man used a single earphone, and spoke so quietly nothing could be made of it. After a few moments, he replaced the earphone and turned, gesturing to Olin. Olin leaned forward in his seat, and carried on a close, whispered conversation, none of which, judging by the grim expressions on their faces, bore anything good. At last, Olin, finished, hesitated and turned to Phaedrus.

Phaedrus said, "Something not good. . . ."

Olin said, in a careful monotone, "Early this morning, unknown parties attacked your place. We were out of range until we passed that last milepost, and so, could not be informed. There were other problems as well. They delayed until now to attempt contact. They would have to insure they had no plants, as well."

Phaedrus sat back, his face very still. "Go on."

"It was hit and run, very fast job. Apparently they wanted to catch you by surprise, so they did not waste time identifying victims. They came in shooting, scattered incendiaries all over, fired the place and left. By the time the police and guards responded, it was too late. The number of dead is very high. Some got out, helped the youngest ones, but Meliosme was not one of them. They haven't finished counting and finding the bodies yet, and the identifications. . . . They will have to figure backwards from the survivors."

The car rolled on, an almost inaudible hum coming from the electric motors. The two in front looked stolidly ahead, more alertly than before. Phaedrus nodded, reflectively, very still, seeing only the clear air, the mountains, with an impossible clarity. Finally, he said, "I see."

Olin sat back for a long moment, and said, "None of them were caught, and there were few witnesses, and what they report will have to be carefully sifted. It's a long chase, friend. We will do what we can."

Phaedrus said, dully, "They will have at least a day headstart on us."

Olin nodded, vigorously. "Exactly. Not that we can't pick up the trail, but by the time we do get on it, several more days will have gone."

Phaedrus mused, out loud, "I owe your organization a debt. Those who wished me harm came thinking I was there. Sure of it. So sure they didn't stop to even see who they were shooting. I owe you, not you me. Your group was proof against their penetration."

"Luck, in a way, Phaedrus. We moved fast, according to orders. But another day and you'd have been in there, too."

"Yes."

"You seemed to know something. Do you know where we should start?"

Phaedrus said, slowly, "I don't doubt what I can see of this. The ones who came on the raid, they were tools, they were order-takers, not originators. The orders came from somewhere else."

Olin agreed. "Exactly."

"I think offworld. But I don't know who, or why. Or from where. 'Offworld' is just a word, a symbol, but it takes in more than we know here, in Clisp, on Oerlikon. The people turned their backs on the places they came from, and so we really don't know what is out there."

Olin said, "True. A long way for Clisp to reach."

Phaedrus rubbed his chin thoughtfully. He thought, *Revenge, of course. But I've been caught by surprise, and blind reactions will accomplish nothing. In fact, if I rushed blind into that, they might be waiting for something like that. No. It will have to be measured, considered, planned, read out.* He turned to Olin, and asked, "Do you carry any rations in the car?"

"Rations? Like survival gear? Yes. Two packs, in the luggage compartment. We used to have to have them. We went the long way through the lower mountains."

"They have food?"

"Food, simple hand weapons, a shelter. Not much."

"Do you need them?"

"No."

"Could we combine the food from both into one?"

"Hm. Would be hard, but I think we could. Could throw some of the other stuff out. What have you in mind?"

"I have to disappear. That is all I can say to you, even in trust. You will never see me again."

"There is something you can do alone that we can't?" His tone was practical and faintly scornful, but not hostile.

"There is something I must do alone. . . . How isolated are the mountains?"

"Scattered steads along the lower hills facing north. Nothing, in the high mountains. On the south slope, wild folk and isolated fishermen. Are you going south? There are no roads and no passes to the south side of Clisp; in fact, but for the name, it's another country. . . ."

"Where can you let me off?"

"You are serious?"

"Yes."

Olin leaned forward and spoke briefly to the driver, then leaned back. "Not far, there's a side road. We can cut across to the old foothill track. Does it matter where?"

"Where? Ah, no. No matter. I could start from right here. There are the mountains." He gestured to the south. "I would proceed until I got there."

"No need. We'll take you to a suitable place. As a fact, back in the old days, I made a couple of stops there myself. Are you sure you don't want someone along? All of us, while fat and content now, were not always so. Once, we slunk in the dark through those empty mountains, while lobotomized cretins marched in ranks up and down the roads of the plain."

"You, yourself?"

"Myself, or Bucephalo, or Pandolfo. If you have desperate and evil deeds in mind, there are none better. As a fact, we'd do so without obligation. Peace, and the rule restored, now they're good things, but all the same, it is a clarity to the mind to have an outright enemy—no subtle stuff, no justice and mercy, just simple revenge. Our enemies are fallen of their own plots. Let, let us . . . borrow yours."

Phaedrus managed a weak smile on a face that had become separated from the soul that animated it. "You say it truly. But all the same, let me go alone. Now will come a part of cunning and stealth—much later the night of the knives, or worse. Later will come in a far place—I know it not, now—and you would be far from your best loyalties, your own nature. I thank you, but I must go alone. I am stranger than you or the prince imagines."

Olin sat back, as the car proceeded now south, with the mountains ahead of them, already looming higher than the windscreen. Neither Olin nor Phaedrus said more.

The land soon began to roll and pitch, forming swells and rises, and the road sometimes dipped down into narrow little draws shaded by low, wide-spreading trees. The farmhouses and outbuildings did not increase in number, but they did draw closer to the road, sleepy places in the waning afternoon light, seemingly untenanted except for an indefinable air about them, an order one could sense without being aware of it. *Someone lived there, even if you couldn't see them in front of you.*

The road narrowed, became rougher, and Pandolfo, who was driving, turned the car into a narrow lane heading back to the west. He made the turn, and drove along the farm track, with the easy assurance of one who had driven along that very road many times before. This road did not run straight for long, but turned up into the foothills, now beginning to be in shadow; it passed through cuts, ran across sudden flats covered with erect, spiky trees, switched back and forth, and forded shallow, rocky streams tumbling down from the heights. At last, in a dense grove of the low, spreading trees he had seen earlier, the car stopped.

Phaedrus got out, and stood very still, listening, looking, trying to absorb the place and time. There was no wind, and the forest was silent, save for the mutter of a nearby creek, over the rocks. Olin and the other two busied themselves making up the one pack as Phaedrus had asked. Finally Olin came around the corner of the car, carrying the pack, looking a bit fuller than it had been designed to be.

He said, "Here it is. We had to leave a lot of the stuff out, but there're rations in plenty, if you can stand them. All stuff you add water to. Don't stint on their use. Eat as much as you can stand; it's high-protein concentrate. If you pace yourself, you can go far. I suppose it's useless to ask . . ."

Phaedrus took the pack, and shouldered it. It was surprisingly heavy, but he would manage it. "If I told you, you wouldn't believe me, and if you did, I could not be sure of your loyalty. No, I can't say where I'm going. But I have one last request."

"Say it. By the prince and his House, we'll do it."

"Have them announce to the public that I was killed in the raid. And make sure that no one else ever learns that I wasn't."

"To the first, consider it done. We will have that set this night. From then on, you are deceased. As for the rest, I see no problem . . . but we will be as sure as possible. Very few saw you, and we know them all."

"Then good-bye. Tell the prince I will never forget his generosity, and that in days to come, one whom his House does not know will come here and repay the debt he conferred on me. And that where I walk, I will conduct myself to bring credit to Clisp, as if I were a native."

"That I will also do. Phaedrus . . . ?"

"Yes?"

"We'll see to the remaining children. And that there will be a place for others."

"Good." And he turned away, and started walking. It didn't matter really which direction he set off in, just to be moving.

He had walked on for a good ways, out of sight of the car, when he heard it start up, just barely, and then heard the noise of its passage back the way they had come, fading rapidly, and then nothing. The road ahead of him dipped down sharply and forded a shallow stream, which had worked its way down from the mountains. When he reached it, he stopped and drank deeply, and looked up. He couldn't see much, because of the forest growth, but he knew the stream came down from the snows far above. *As good a place as any.* It was only after he had gotten well into the climb that he stopped and allowed the grief and anger and regret to flow through him. He let it run free, let it possess him; and when he could think clearly again, the light of day was gone and the forest and the stream were dark and still. Only far overhead was there light, a luminous blue sky, traced with a lacy fretwork of cirrus clouds, tinted pink by the setting sun.

4

"The wise man anticipates; the fool grapples with what happened; the shaman determines events by deciding, defining the environment in which things 'happen.' "

—H.C., Atropine

PHAEDRUS DID NOT stop for the night, but kept on walking, using the weight of the pack as a goad, a whip. He followed dim trails that led up, or south, or both, paths that narrowed rapidly down to hardly more than animal passages, or were perhaps only random arrangements of the way things grew. Tier by tier, ridge by ridge, he trudged steadily ahead, walking through the long night of Oerlikon. Now and again, he would look up, to the highest ridge above him, to see if it seemed any lower. It didn't, so after a time he ignored it, and watched the ground, only looking about to gauge the best way forward.

In Clisp, the mountains were left mostly alone. Phaedrus met no wayfarers, saw no signs of habitation. The land was dark and empty, and there was nothing but the night sky overhead, with its random and meaningless assembly of faint stars.

He stopped to catch his breath, looked up, and thought, *There. One of those points, or better, one I can't even see. One of those points has a world circling it, and on that world, men gave orders. They spent much, they came back, to track me down and put a cruel and drastic plan into operation. Strike quick, without warning, almost randomly. Only something like that would get me. But for the concern of Pompeo and his men, there would I have been, too.*

But for what reason? Revenge I want, now, and revenge I will have, but if I do not unravel why this occurred, I will be striking at gaseous bubbles while the real enemy stalks again unseen.

He saw without effort that punishment for what he had done to Lisagor would not explain the viciousness of the attack. Indeed, it would be foolish to punish him at all—he was the tool of a deeper conspiracy, and one does not govern a complex civilization spread across many planets by punishing tools, or performing other absurdities of like nature. *Punishment is not their aim.*

Those star-folk; they came here, stayed here, manipulated Lisagor to their liking, cleverly. And when it started to fall, coordinated with marvelous swiftness and decisiveness, and pulled out. These are not people who do foolish things. They plan, they think, and they act. They undertook a seemingly reckless act, one of potential high cost, to get me. The answer stood before him as obvious as the darkness of the night sky: *They attack, to prevent me from doing something.*

He reflected that it wouldn't be hard to understand how they knew of him. Several knew about the plan, back in Symbarupol. If they had been captured, or gone over voluntarily, then they would have known. But surely it was obvious he had no aims beyond his original task—and that once that was done, he would try only to regain some sort of normal life. He tried, as Damistofiya, but the old group tried to kill her. Again, as Phaedrus, he had tried, been as low as water, learned ambitiouslessness. No matter. Still they came. But this last attack—that had been the work of offworlders, not renegade Lisaks, however it looked. But there was the curious part, the part that wouldn't fit, no matter how he tried to move it about: if they knew what he was, then it followed that they knew he had no interest whatsoever in the offworlders. He could be no threat to them . . . unless they knew something about him that he didn't know himself. Phaedrus arrived at that point, and decided to walk on for a bit, and concentrate on the pack: that thought opened up more speculations than he wanted to explore right at the moment.

Crossing a watershed line whose gentle slope concealed its height, Phaedrus stopped and looked back along the way he had come; behind and below was darkness absolute, but beyond that, far off toward the horizon, he could make out the open lands of the plains in the dim starlight—a lighter tone of purple darkness, dotted with an occasional light. Ahead of him were a few more ridges, interrupted with startling lone peaks, rather more to the east than near him. Another group far off in the west. The night was clear, and far to the northeast a soft glow suggested the probable location of Marisol. And south, beyond the ridges, only the sky, dim and dark near the horizon. He couldn't see the ocean yet.

Differing emotions strove within him, each one wanting the mastery, each one clamoring for the decisive position. In one set, he berated himself for failing to protect the people who depended upon him—Meliosme, the children they had taken in. In this mode, he accused, *Fool! You scamped your responsibilities! You should have been sharpening your knife!* But the answer was clearer than the accusation. *But we went the rightest way. And for me to have given over to paranoid fantasies of self-importance would have set the crucial tone of the world wrong. Had he leered and plied his whetstone and blade, while the keystone, so would it have been throughout. And who knows how far that could have reached.* And he wondered if he was still in the position. He had only looked once.

Another voice clamored, *Revenge, that's the stuff! Get even! You have the power to see to the uttermost point, and fling bolts of doom like Zeus!* That much was true, he ruefully admitted, although he doubted he had enough data to get anything but a very dim picture of the offworlders, and his aim would be correspondingly bad—and bad aim demands high Circular Error Probable strikes—the main reason for the existence of nuclear weapons in the far past. But there was a more important counter to this. Revenge in any measurable degree of equality would involve suffering of innocents far beyond any compensation for what had been done to him. And even after that, Meliosme wouldn't be back. *No. Pure revenge is idiotic, nonproductive, and entropic. A reaction. No, at best we need to look at this as an exercise in solving a problem. But formulating the problem, that's the rub! What was the problem here?* It could not be defined as crime, nor even as terrorism, but the area it lay within was vague and ill-defined.

But a third voice, sliding up like a sleazy solicitor, offered something that, despite it's tone, seemed the most promising of all. This one said, *Ask yourself why often enough and maybe it'll dawn on you. Go ahead, do it!* And the answer was not hidden at all, but rather something that he'd hoped he'd not have to go into. *It's something to do with Jedily. . . . What she was. How Pternam got her as his subject for the one successful try to attain the Morphodite.* Phaedrus walked on, now briefly downhill, and looked at that one plainly. *That's either a circular answer, leading me back where I started—or else it's a rug to sweep everything under.* He couldn't remember Jedily, so she was a blank tablet—he could write all sorts of virtues and vices there—but writing them was no proof they had ever been there in reality. And this was reality—people don't spend large amounts of money and travel immense distances between the stars to murder for trivial reasons. But he could see a third possibility, *if Jedily*

*had once been, not an Oerlikonian Lisak native, but an offworlder
herself . . . perhaps one of the manipulators herself, once. But something
changed, if this was true, and . . .*

IF. A big dependant to hang a future on, and he could feel the shakiness of that branch. And he could not read and get an answer clean. But
there was a test he would have to make before he could go further. Yes.
But what was the right question? Who was Jedily Tulilly? If she was
what he had been told—an indigent scrubwoman turned over to The
Mask Factory, very well. But if she had been something else. . . . They
would possibly not wish him to find out who she was, had been, did, or
said, or claimed, or could do. . . . Yes. Possible. Phaedrus felt his head
clear a little. He increased his pace, driving deeper and deeper into the
mountains of Clisp, into the deepest recess of the night. *Yes. We'll need
to start at Symbarupol, take up the trail there. They think I'll track agents
of fortune, but what I'll do is track myself—back into the past, and I'll bet
the paths intersect. They'll think they got away clean, and as they think it,
I'll step from behind a tree and say, "Ahem. Good Evening!"*

And with that he settled a little better into place, and he increased
his speed. It was not that he had to hurry to get where he was going,
but that he could go there and meet what was coming with more confidence, instead of fear and loathing. Yes. Phaedrus had to meet someone, a woman by night. And Phaedrus wouldn't be, anymore. He
glanced at the sky. *But not tonight. No. We have to find a place where we
won't be seen, and also where we can do some, uh, calculations. This time
we're going to try to control it a bit. What of it we can control.*

By the slow light of dawn he found a high place that looked isolated
enough, with a good view all around down along the slants of the ridges
falling away. Far off, on the very horizon, was the line of the ocean,
south.

It was a mossy alpine meadow, slanting gently down from a small
scree flaking off a rock face. There were no thornbushes or large rocks.
Nor were there steep slopes he could roll down. Not so far away a tiny
stream bubbled in the rocks. Water. He'd need a lot of water.

The day he spent sleeping, arranging the packs, and eating on one of
the packages of concentrate. And trying to empty his mind; all thoughts,
all striving, were to be laid aside. Phaedrus sat up and stared long into
the blue distances, and watched the star Gysa wheel across the sky in its
measured pace.

* * *

When the sun got close enough to the horizon not to cast shadows anymore, he sat up, and began to focus on the task at hand. All day, he had thought of nothing but the methods of his unique art of *seeing*, of *reading*. Now he assembled those rules of the game and laid out the lines of it the way he knew how. First he cast for the identity of who he would be after Change.

He knew it would be female. As the exercise progressed, the lineaments began filling in, one by one, in odd, fragmented groups that seemed to occur deliberately so as to prevent anticipation. That was the way of it: recursive. You had to play out every step: no shortcuts. When the image began to come in, it was not precisely seeing, but feeling who you yourself were. A kind of self-image. This one did not sit well.

A long body and longer limbs, probably taller at full adult size than Rael had been, but now hopelessly oversized and uncoordinated. That was the age-regression of Change, too. He wondered if he could slow that. What he had to do would be hard on a girl just past childhood.

Large eyes, a large, full mouth. He shook his head. He had never been one to complain about appearances. Rael had been no prize, with his morose and saturnine countenance. Still, this didn't feel right at all. He erased his marks on the flat rock he had made and started over from the beginning, taking extra verification steps.

If anything changed, it was the clarity of the image. It was clearer. She would be attractive, would catch eyes. He examined that more closely. Could that conceal as well? Could he become that role? Could he slow the reversal process? This was a separate question.

The answer was hard, and took up most of the faint daylight that was left. Yes, but there were limits. He saw them clearly. The girl would have to make do with the end of adolescence. He couldn't tamper with the process Pternam had ingrained into him beyond certain limits. If everything went right, he might be able to get her up to twenty standard years, and he had no time to do the computation for another look at what she'd be *then*. Hopefully she'd have outgrown the worst of the childishness still in the image he had of her.

Phaedrus looked around himself. *One last time, I'll see this scene as me-now. It'll be different, then. Probably daylight by the time I come around.* He lay back and began relaxing, one muscle at a time, floating backward, away from consciousness, seeking the internal state of balance and self-awareness by which he could initiate the process of Change. He did not consider the pain and terror at all. Of what use was worrying about it? This had to be. Phaedrus had done what was proper for Phaedrus to do. Now it was another's turn. He drifted further within, reflecting with some wry humor that he hadn't even bothered to name this one. The outrageous awkward limbs suggested something preposterous: Beumadine. Hephzibah. Euwayla. No. Maybe it wouldn't be like that, at all. Let it go. He was sinking fast. He had to steer this, or else now fall into a sleep from which he would be too far in to awaken. Already outside sensation was gone. And deeper, he could begin to sense the glow of that center he was seeking, the core, where bright threads crawled and writhed in an impossible dance that never ended. Now they were clear, moving at blurred speeds, enlarging, multiplying, filling the universe, immense. In danger of being lost in that, he pushed back, almost losing the state. *Now, maintain orientation and slow them down.* This was the hardest one yet. But by great effort of will, the bright threads slowed, became visible, slowed still more, moving closer. Now. Dead stop. *This one.* He changed it. *And this one* for the control of age regression, and he saw with sad resignation why there were limits on this, but he could not have explained it in words. There weren't any. *And what else are these?* All his pasts were in there, encoded, reduced to a single set of rules which would set a recursive sequence in motion and expand to the whole: there was Phaedrus. Inside himself, he saw the reduction of what he had been. And there: Damistofiya. And Rael. That one was odd, not like the others. There were gaps in it. And one more . . . That one, that would have to be Jedily. And it was badly damaged. Shorter than the others, as if hacked off, but there were parts of it intact. He looked further, feeling once again the pressure of Time; he could not hold this stasis indefinitely. How could he recover that part, the only thing left of the original. *Yes.* There, make that one change and splice that Jedily section onto the template now ready to form for her who was to be. A name came into his mind from nowhere: Nazarine. He made the final change, and let go, and saw the core whirl away angrily, as if he had tampered too much. He felt a great fear, rising back up through the levels of consciousness and finally opening his eyes.

There was nothing but the night. In fact, there was still a glow on the far horizon. He sat up. He shook his head, expecting some symptom, some feeling. Nausea, lightheadedness. That one had been rough. This Change might well be a real ride. But there was nothing. He smelled clean air, the smell of moss and grasses, his own scent, more than a little tired and sweaty. He laughed, aloud. *No worry now about cleanliness!*

In an hour I'll have layers of every sort of nastiness. He heard the wind, far off, moving lazily around the peaks and defiles. He tried to organize what he had seen into some pattern of order; what part of Jedily had he recovered. Now he could consider it. It was not any of her substance, or of her continuous memory. That was gone forever. Pternam had burned that out. *No. Wait.* He struggled to remember it as it had been. There were two levels of damage to the Jedily segment. One was clearly done by Pternam, reaching for the Morphodite. Jedily had forgotten all that under the stress she had somehow endured. Mindless in the end, personalityless. But there was an earlier set of damages to the "tape" and those were clear and methodical, not at all like the accidental erasures and smears of the last damages. That part had been done to Jedily before Pternam ever got her.

Phaedrus felt the ground move under him, a faint, seesaw motion, a jelly like trembling on the edge of perception. Earthquake? It went on a bit, and then subsided. *Of course!* He wanted to go back within, and examine it again, but he knew he couldn't; inside him a time bomb was running, and Change would start any moment. *Besides,* he thought, *I spliced the Jedily section onto Nazarine, because these isn't any structure or memory per se on it. Whatever's on that section will add onto Nazarine. It's fragments of some kind of knowledge, and she'll know it, without knowing how. And Jedily will be truly gone, then. It will transfer and vanish. If I ever go within again, there will be no Jedily tape there.* In the end, he himself had been the last assassin who struck the final blow. Whatever Jedily was, he would have to learn by conventional methods. That part of him was gone.

He felt the ground motion again, start up, shaking, growing stronger. *Oh, shit, I have to change in the middle of an earthquake!* He lay back flat on the moss, and watched a small stone sitting atop another. The motion became more violent, but the rocks didn't move. Nor did grassstems wave. But they had to move. The ground was shuddering like an animal in pain! He sat up and looked around, at everything he could see, the moss, the talus pile, rocks around him. Nothing was moving, falling over. He started to stand up, but the shaking was so intense he couldn't, and instead got on his knees, as if he were going to crawl. There was a loud buzzing in his ear, a piercing high tone, growing louder, painful, and he looked in desperation to the ocean horizon, the black line forty kilometers away, south. Steady, but then yellow glowing lava crawled down his forehead and slid over his eyes, and he was buried, covered, still in the crawling position. *Roasting! Some geologist will find me and*

wonder how the hell . . . And then Phaedrus didn't have any more
thoughts to think.

In the uninhabited wilds of the mountains of Clisp, a creature underwent terrible changes. It grovelled, made tentative crawling motions, fell
back, moved its limbs uncertainly. From time to time, sudden and drastic alterations would take place: fluids erupted from every orifice in
shuddering heaves and convulsions. Pungent and sickening odors vented
off it, and patches of its body produced copious flows of loathsome substances. It made sounds, but they resembled nothing intelligible. Parts of
its body steamed and smoked in the cool night air, and the rocky ground
on which it lay was stained with secretions that left phosphorescent
runnels for a time. For a long time it continued its random movements,
but as the night progressed, these slowed and by daylight the thing was
still, although clearly some reactions were still taking place.

Daylight revealed what to a casual observer might resemble a plague
victim who had been burned badly and extensively. All the hair of the
head and limbs was gone; the head and face were a shapeless lump. It
did not move, and appeared dead, but there was a pulse, and if one
could have looked very close, there was breathing, although almost imperceptible. The clothing it had worn was stained and soaked, unrecognizable now. And there was a very curious thing about the clothing: it
was singularly ill-fitting. The hands, bony claws, protruded from the
sleeves, and the feet, similarly, stuck out awkwardly from the bottoms
of its pants, and the general appearance was that of a person tall and
bony, with swollen, enlarged joints.

During the long Oerlikonian day, the creature did not move, or if it
did, it was so slowly that the motion was unobservable. The starlight of
Gysa shone down on it indifferently, and the shadows around it moved,
following the sun. Dusk came, and then the night. In the first darkness,
some of the stains around it on the rocks glowed faintly, a pale yellowish light like cave fungi, but after a time, this faded.

It was dark when consciousness returned to him, and he thought it was
the same night. He remembered almost nothing; all he could experience
was pain unrelenting. Skin like roasting meat, bones and joints like dis-
locations on the rack, muscles tearing, over and over again. He could
move a little; his shoes hurt and cramped, and somehow he managed to

kick them off, although the effort was almost beyond him, both from lack of strength and lack of coordination. Patches of flesh went with the shoes. He also managed to loosen some of the clothing, but could not get any of it off, and after a time faded out again, but this time, he was prey to numerous hallucinations, which he encouraged as an interested observer. Within themselves, they were perfectly coherent, but they did not connect with anything, or make any sense; he could not interpret them.

He awoke later, sometime; the stars were different, although it was yet dark, without a hint of dawn in the east. The pain was still with him, and he felt the delirious giddyness of high fever, but this at least seemed orderly. He could barely move. Now he remembered some things, and could begin to place some order on his perceptions. Odd fragments of scenes drifted before his eyes, sometimes obscuring what his senses reported, but at least he could understand that these were temporary lapses, not realities. He lay on the rocks for a long time, until a soft rosy glow begin to appear in parts of the east, and then he slept. But this time, it was sleep, not unconsciousness.

He awoke again, and his head was clearer. He remembered that he was Phaedrus, and that he had initiated Change, and that something had happened. The sun was far in the west, and shadows were long, but it was yet daylight. His body sent him conflicting messages: an incredible thirst and hunger, an emptiness such as he could not ever recall knowing, and simultaneously a nausea so powerful he dared not move for fear of making it worse. He reasoned carefully, like a drunk, that part of the reason for the nausea was the incredible stench that assaulted his sense of smell. With halting motions, he dragged himself to the little rivulet bubbling over the rocks. He remembered it had been nearby. Now it seemed as far away as the planets of the offworlders. He spent the rest of the daylight crawling to that water; and much of the dusk he spent arguing with himself whether to drink first or start washing. Thirst won. At the first, he could not keep the water down, but after several tries, he managed to retain some. He shivered violently with bone-chilling cold, and understood that the sensation was part of a fever that yet raged within his body. Still, slowly, interspersed with short flights of sleep, or fever hallucinations, he struggled out of his clothing, and began washing the worst off, feeling the sting of the cold water ten times over. And by the dawn of the next day, he understood that he wasn't Phaedrus any longer. By the light of dawn, he laboriously crept to the place where he had cached his survival pack, and dug out some thin blankets. Among the oddments of gear in the bag he found a signaling mirror, and looked in it curiously, seeing in the image distorted by the shaking of his hand a person he did not know, a clown's face with only a dark shadow where the hair would be, puffy eyes, a pulpy mouth of no recognizable shape, rubbery lips. He shook his head. He examined the body tentatively. Female. But she wasn't very much to look at. The frame was wasted and cadaverous, with bones showing everywhere. It did not resemble the image he had procured within of Nazarine, but whatever she was, she was long of limb, as long as Rael had been, maybe longer, and where the skin had settled down to just being skin, it was a sallow olive color. She put the mirror back in the bottom of the pack. Now to begin trying to eat something, and put some shape on this body. And she thought, *That Change was the worst I can remember. Is this the way of it? Does it get worse each time? Is this worth it?* For now, she admitted the answer was probably no, but she also knew that as her strength returned, it would assume more worth. Even so, she knew that it would be a long time before she could face Change again. Decades, perhaps. And that put limitations on her, what she would have to do. She had shed Phaedrus and become Nazarine, but Nazarine would have to be careful. Starting here. Now.

She had difficulty keeping solid food down, and was weak, for a long time unable to stand. It was ten days before she was able to walk any distance, and was still thin as a labor camp inmate. Nevertheless, Nazarine decided that it was time to start the long slopes back toward Marisol. She would have to build herself up as she went. There was a problem: the food concentrate in the survival packs was almost gone.

As she walked, she worked her arms, trying to loosen up. All her limbs felt stiff, overstrained. And she thought, *And until I can make use of the amulet Pompeo gave Phaedrus, I am going to look a sight.* She looked down at the long body she now possessed. Her feet stuck out of Phaedrus's old, serviceable pants, and already her chest filled his old shirt. She laughed, even though it hurt terribly around the ribs: *I look like a tramp!* The shoes had proven impossible to adapt, so she went barefooted, which made progress slow.

Two days later, the last of the food gave out. But she had come a long way down from the high mountains, and at night could see outlying settlements below her on the plains. She had also stopped one day at noon, and *read* for the pivot of the World. It was no longer herself. Who it was, she didn't *read*. Only that it wasn't her. She was free.

She walked on, concentrating on one step at a time, finally reaching the flat alluvial plains of Clisp. It was cool, but she still had the survival blanket, and wrapped it around herself. She walked along a dusty road for a day and a night, stopping only short periods to rest, and then going on. But finally her strength, none too sure to start with, began giving out, and the rests became longer. At dusk, she stopped under a huge spreading tree and leaned against its trunk wearily. She would just close her eyes for a moment. . . .

. . . She woke up and it was late afternoon: the sun was far off over the western peaks, and shadows were long. It was disorienting—waking up before one went to sleep. Impossible. Her stomach growled. How long had she been here? *A whole day.*

She felt a small motion at her neck, and brushed, as if pushing an insect away. It came back. She brushed again. Nothing. Then something touched her hair. She grasped at it, and her fingers closed on a hand, which was quickly snatched out of her grip, accompanied by a grunting giggle: "Hunh-hunh-hunh-hunh." She turned painfully to look, and saw an enormous cretin, grinning and reaching for her. She tried to get up, but sprawled out on the side of the road. Weak. She looked again. The creature was an overgrown boy with an expression of constant beaming mirth on his face, but larger than most men. Easily twice her weight, and in her present condition, much stronger. She doubted she had the ordination of those long, thin limbs. He shook his head, reprovingly, and came forward, kneeling down beside her. "Woman," he breathed. Then he reached, as if reaching for an overripe fruit, and grasped her left breast. It was still filling out and was sore and tender. She pulled away, freeing her legs, and shaking her head. The cretin nodded. He said, "Uh-huh. Woman." He leaned forward, clumsily, to touch her again.

Nazarine rolled a little back and kicked hard at the cretin's solar plexus, and to her surprise, it connected. It felt like she had kicked a tree trunk. What with normal strength would have disabled him, and left him gasping for breath in the middle of the road, now only rolled him off balance and made him mad. "Uh." He grunted. "Hurt." He surged to his feet like a tiger and stood over her with an altogether unearthly expression on his now red face. Nazarine tried to recall everything she could, desperately. He reached, suddenly, before she could counter it, picked her up and pummeled her viciously. It was like being dismembered by a whirlwind. Clumsy, he succeeded from sheer strength. She found herself lying in the road on her back with the cretin sitting on her stomach, pinning her arms with his tremendous knees, her head swimming. She heard something off to the side somewhere, to which the cretin responded, looking up suddenly. He shouted, sidelong, not speaking directly, "Colly find, Colly keep. This one not run away."

The voice hardened a bit, and said, now a lot closer, "No, Colly. Get up and let her be. Or we'll put the sparker on you."

Colly shook his head. "No sparker."

The unseen voice, thin and with an edge in it, repeated, "No, Colly. Not yours. Off!" She sensed motion, and there was a vicious crackling, like electricity, and with a sudden thrust in his knees, Colly abruptly stood up, moving to the side, making odd, tentative motions with his hands, held low, and shaking his head like an angry and baffled animal.

There was someone standing in the road, in the shadows of the tree, holding a thick metal tube longer than his arm, which had four stubby projections at the end of it. This he waved, back and forth in measured time. He said, "Get gone and don't come back—or I'll hot-wire your fundament to the house generator." This was not said in heat, but coolly, matter-of-factly, almost as if an idle comment. But Colly apparently understood the rod and the words well, for he turned and loped off, heading toward the west.

Nazarine slowly sat up, rolling over on her knees first, and tried to stand. Her legs felt like water. The figure stepped out of the shadows and offered her his hand. She took it, a little uncertain, but it was firm and she stood, shakily, but on her own feet.

She could see more clearly now. In the road stood a man of indeterminate age, rather thin, with sharp, crisp features, and the evidence of a hard life on the lines of his face. His eyes, however, were large, deep set, and alert. He looked at her carefully.

He said, "Sorry you had to find Colly. Or he find you. He's only dangerous if you let him slip up on you."

"What is he?"

"Colly is Colly. He's always been like that. Not all there." He shrugged, and made a motion with his forefinger to his temple as if he were screwing a bolt into place. Then he tapped it. "Like that. He does odd and heavy jobs around the farms, sleeps in odd corners of barns. . . . He's always looking for a woman, but of course no one would have him. He doesn't really know what to do, should he find one. The local topers once took him to a happy-house and threw a lot of money in the door after him. Thought it would calm him down."

"Did it?" She asked coolly.

"No. He's quite incompetent. The trouble is, he's strong enough to give someone a bad lick, if by nothing else than accident, and if you tried to fight him . . ." He shook his head. "Bad move, that."

"If things were normal, I could have handled him."

He nodded. "I see they are not. You appear to have had an adventure."

She said, "It is a longish story I would as soon leave. I walked over the mountains from the South Coast."

He shifted position, relaxing a little. "From the coast. Ah, now. You are not Clispish; I heard it in your speech."

"That is so. However, I was and am in the employ of the prince."

"Present?"

"Not Amadeo. Pompeo."

"Well, good. We thought well of him, even though he was no hero. Things come to one in their own time, do they not? And so for Pompeo the great days came at the end of his reign, most of which was illegal, as you know. Still and all he wore them well. But of course Amadeo now holds the purse strings. Will you work for him as well?" There was a subtle undertone in his question, a subtle probing.

"I did not work for the government, but for the prince himself. One of his servants. A courier."

"He still uses some?"

"A few. There are things he wishes to know, to do."

"Good, there. You will find Amadeo very different."

"So I have heard."

"Well. You were on your way from the South Coast to somewhere; would you return to Cape Forever?"

"No. I am for Marisol. But I need to stop for a while. I don't think I can make it as I am."

"Your mission continues, then?"

"My mission has just started."

"Allow me to further the work of the old prince, then. I see you need some clothing, rest, food. These I can share, although they are plain enough. Come along." He turned and started off along the road, soon ducking under a low branch, and following a faint path across the side ditch into the fields. He looked back. "Are you coming?"

She nodded weakly, and started after him, slowly.

5

"The virtue of the Tarot, the I Ching, and the Sabean Symbols, and acts of divination using these schemata, is not that they reveal a future which was hidden from us, but that they remind us of the understandings we already possessed, but did not openly acknowledge."

—H.C., Atropine

WHILE THE PEOPLE of Old Lisagor were in appearance an undistinguished group that could have walked anywhere among the civilized worlds without notice, the inhabitants of the other continent of Oerlikon, Tartary, would have been noticeable in almost any crowd. Tall and gaunt, with horselike faces and flapping black robes, each one lived essentially alone in a rude stone castle, preferably reared by their own hands, and each one was a law unto themselves. There was no government and no law in Tartary, save the complicated etiquette by which the Makhaks lubricated those rare occasions of social intercourse they tolerated.

With indifference they allowed the offworlders to establish an enclave on a small embayment in the south, which was hardly less harsh a climate than the north. Those foreigners who could cope with the incessant winds, the complicated, arcane manners which all were expected to master without instruction, were welcome to visit; most stayed only long enough to transact a piece of business, and then left, eager to be away from the gaunt natives who asked no quarter and gave none. Nevertheless, among a few of the holds near the Enclave, offworlders were tolerated for somewhat longer periods and cynically pumped for everything they knew.

Master Amew Madraz maintained a freehold on Dankmoss Moor, an open, and to offworld eyes, curiously undefined patch of land a daywalk* north of the Enclave. Master Madraz seemed uncommonly well-off for a Makhak, having half a dozen men-at-arms and retainers quartered within his hold, bound to him by the stiff and blood-curdling formulae by which Makhaks defined relationships involving personal services. And for some time, Madraz had kept as guests an offworld man and woman, an unheard of thing, who had chosen to rent a section of one of the eccentric towers reared by a previous tenant. To these at various times came other visitors, as well as an occasional Lisak. They claimed that they had business which would not bear airing within the close confines of the Enclave, where everyone knew everyone else, and any-one's business was soon the property of all.

The visitors were a curious lot: they had come on one arrival of the offworlders' scheduled liner, missed another arrival, and were now ap-parently awaiting the next, their business finished. They were more self-contained than most, and evidenced no curiosity at all toward the makhak custom, or the land itself. Intense and disciplined, those were the words! Moreover, they acted as much like Makhaks as their own custom allowed, a fact which left Madraz considerably at ease; they did not interact much with himself, or with his bondsmen. Curious. Yet they would shortly be gone, a minor incident of little importance.

Cesar Kham and Arunda Palude occupied a tower which had been part of an earlier part of Schloss Madraz, and which they had repaired with their own hands, correcting the worst of its drafty and cold habitats. Still, it was cold and drafty enough. They wore extra clothing, and ex-ercised when it became too much to bear. The stony, flat expanses of Tartary, grim and hopeless under its virtually perpetual overcast, offered little in the way of trees for firewood, and there were no grazing animals to provide inflammable dung chips, either. There were peat bogs, but their use was carefully guarded, and no makhak would have thought twice about using fuel merely for personal comfort. The very concept was impossible to frame in their language without a circuitous series of euphemisms, typical of such a grim folk.

Their sole heat source came from candles, made, it was said, by cer-tain Makhaks of the north coasts who meticulously wove gossamer nets and strained from the frigid northern seas tiny crustaceans whose bod-ies were filled with wax. The candles emitted a dense, oily yellow light

* All distances within Tartary were spoken of relatively, rather than ab-solutely.

and left behind them a distinct marine odor. They spent much of their considerable idle time playing intricate games, complicated and over-complicated to serve the purpose of passing time. Now and again, they would have a visit from one or another of their agents, and then spend days considering every aspect of the agent's report.

Their last visitor had left before dark, and now, over the thin gruel and swampberry hash the makhaks subsisted on, they considered his findings.

Kham ventured, "We'll have a few more reports before we leave, of course, but from all indications it seems that the job has been done successfully. There are no traces of that creature whatsoever."

Palude, her face pinched and prematurely aging from the constant cold, sniffled contemptuously and answered, "Yes, they are all certain, aren't they?"

"You don't think so?" He raised his almost invisible eyebrows, and, grimacing at the dank, smoky flavor, swallowed another spoonful of crushed swampberries.

"Well, you know they won't have to live with the consequences if they made a mistake. From what we know of that thing, it will probably be able to figure out where such an attack came from. If it didn't have any motivation before, it certainly will now."

"You've heard the same data I have."

"Yes, and I'm an integrator by trade. And there are some things missing. No positive identification, for one thing. And for lack of anything else, it just doesn't feel right. We did similar things back in the old days, and I tell you there is something slipshod—is that the proper word?—about all this."

"You have been practicing with those fortune-telling systems; what sort of answers do they give?"

"Ambiguous and haunting. Or openly disastrous."

Kham made a peculiar grimace in which he pressed his thin lips together so that his mouth became an almost-invisible line. "For example?"

Palude reached into her traveling bag and produced a small metal tube, shaking it. A dry rattling came from within. "Here are the yarrow stalks. They cost me even more than the book did—the *I Ching*. I have been studying it closely, learning its ways, which are somewhat opposed to the way we look at things. We believe in causality; it explains coincidence and change. It is disturbing."

"Go on."

"When they sent the message that the attack had been done, I threw the stalks, asking the question, 'Did it succeed?' I got this answer: #44, Kou, 'Coming to Meet.' The maiden is powerful; one should not marry. There were changeable lines in positions one, two, four and six, leading to #63, Chi Chi, 'After Completion.' That one says, 'At the beginning, good fortune; at the end, disorder.' There is a lot more to it, and of course in some cases such a reading could imply a favorable course, but I found it not so good, considering what we were dealing with. So disturbing was this that I then asked, 'Specify the outcome of this event.' I got #49, Ko, 'Molting or Revolution,' changing lines one, three, four, five and six to become #23, Po, 'Splitting Apart.' "

Kham chuckled. "I thought one did not question oracles."

Palude shook her head. "One does not doubt. But it is permitted to ask for further explanation."

"Your interpretation?"

"We assumed that the Morphodite would be a young man, if it had survived; most likely in Clisp, hiding. We found, after, what we believed to be such a person, who seemed to have no origin, and who was leading a quiet and a charitable life. If he survived the attack, the elimination operation, he would change as an act of self-preservation, becoming a woman again. 'The maiden is powerful.' Then, 'At the end, disorder.' That appears to be his unique power, to institute Change at a fundamental level, a stage of disorder leading to another stable configuration."

"And the rest?"

"I should say it needs little reading-into. Assuming we read it specifically from our point of view, that reading means that change is due, will be caused, and that people opposed to our way of thinking will come to predominate."

Kham hunched forward in his seat, more attentive and not smiling. "If you believe that, than we have done worse than simple failure. We have stirred up something dire and evil."

"Cesar, you left out the best part of this."

"Eh? What's that?"

"We don't know who we're looking for, now."

"Hm. That's so, just so. *If* it's as you say, there. How about the rest? Let me hear an integrator speak."

"We got a body count. No identities, save that of his woman. There were four more adult-sized bodies in there; any one could have been him, or might not have. There is no confirmation."

"What report from the agents?"

"Official mourning. Righteous anger, and the dispatch of Clispish agents to various parts to see what they can turn up. The actions look proper, but there's a shakiness to them that doesn't quite look right . . . There is too much attention to it. It looks like a stage-act, with very few people knowing the truth, but this course does not reveal motives."

"Then he had help we didn't know about!"

"Not necessarily. The reports indicate no knowledge of his true abilities. That would have surfaced if it had been known. But he may have had some help without this knowledge. High up."

"Can we look into this? We have time to confirm something of this, surely, before the next ship departs."

Palude said, "I have already set that in motion, and we should soon be getting reports. I have instructed our plants to concentrate in two areas—accidental case, and help from very high. I expect nothing from the first, but we might get something from the second."

Kham nodded. "You were emphatic?"

"Rather. I told them, in fact, to take some chances and not be overly concerned about having to bolt and run. We need confirmation of success or failure before we go back."

Kham mused, "Well, if success, contrary to your oracle, we should have no worry."

Palude sat still in the dimness of the stone tower room, and then said, softly, "And if failure, there isn't anything we can do about it."

Nazarine had little reserve left after the long walk, and the exertion with the cretinous Colly, and when she finally arrived at the house, she did little for the next several days except sleep. Sometimes she woke for a time, and ate. Someone was there; at least, someone seemed to know when she'd need food. The meals were uniform, bland, and to her surprise, nourishing. She still retained a tremendous desire to sleep, and stayed awake only long enough to take minimal care of her body, but after an uncertain passage of time she noticed that she felt better, and her sleep was lighter. More significantly, her body was filling out.

She learned a little, but not much, about her host, who apparently was called Marcian. There was also a ghostly-quiet small girl-child, Cerulara, who came and went, saying nothing, and vanishing immediately. Both were quiet, busy with their own affairs. They gave her a place to recover, and left her alone.

Recovering more of her strength, Nazarine began to explore the house, and some of the grounds around it. It seemed to be nothing more than a farm, although it was very neatly kept. Marcian spent much of the day either out in the fields, or working silently and intently in one of the small outbuildings, repairing some piece of machinery, while the little girl seemed to keep the household chores at bay. Nazarine estimated the girl's age at no more than ten no matter what, but she suspected younger.

They were so strange and silent. She could have easily read the answer, but she sensed something private about their ghostly movements, about their grim silences, and she left it alone. Whatever it was, it did not concern her. It was curiously like the routines people adopt to put grief off, except that the original object had long since withered away, leaving them with a routine which they still adhered to. And what was their relationship? Father and daughter? She thought so, and yet there was something missing there as well. And if so, then where was the mother? Dead? She probed their movements and habits, sensing rather than doing a reading; there were none of the essential markers of a death in the family.

She approached Cerulara about repairing and refitting her clothing, which the child acknowledged with the fewest words possible, but also as if Nazarine had asked her an impossible question. The girl hurried off to find Marcian, for whatever he could add. Nazarine shook her head in confusion. But later that day, in the afternoon, late, when the shadows were falling down from the mountains into the glades of the dooryard, Cerulara came out into the yard, where Nazarine was sitting, with an armload of clothing, all of which seemed to have been stored away. Together, they went through it, piece by piece, selecting the suitable, returning the obviously unsuitable. Nazarine picked things that were serviceable and plain, and left aside the rest. She wanted now merely something to wear besides the ancient bathrobe Marcian had given her. Cerulara made several trips in and out of the old wooden house.

Cerulara fixed supper as the sun, Gysa, was sinking behind the ranges far off in the southwest, layers of blue and violet lightening as they approached the sky to a color not greatly different from the pale blue wash of the sky itself. Marcian always washed outside, in a homemade shower room he had built behind one of the outbuildings. Nazarine met him, wearing some of the things: a pair of loose brown pants, a soft beige blouse, and a vest over that. The nights were cool now, as fall deepened.

She said, "I am well enough to walk about."

"I know. You have done very well. You recover fast."

She added, "Carulara brought me some old clothes . . ."

"I see. Well, they seem to fit you well enough."

"I only need to borrow them for a while. . . ." He nodded, absent-mindedly, going on into the house. Nazarine turned and asked, "Can I take my meals with you two now? I am well enough? Certainly not an invalid."

"Certainly. Although you may find it hard to make breakfast with us. We arise early."

"Get me up. And if you wish, I can help. I would like to repay some of your kindness."

"I know. We saw you had nothing but that cartouche. That's a powerful talisman. You don't need anything else. But of course you have to be somewhere where they can credit it back. At the moment, you're as poor as the rest of us." He seemed to be making some calculation back in his mind, weighing her. "You don't look much like a field hand, and that's what I need. No offense, but you've got a city woman's body."

"Perhaps. I am only what I am. However, I need exercise and motion."

He nodded assent, slowly. "Very well. You'll be leaving soon, then?"

Nazarine looked at Marcian closely. There was no barb in his question, but under it, there was a curious tone of sad resignation. "No. I'm in no hurry. I owe you something . . . for pulling me in off the road; and of course Colly."

"I hope you weren't planning to walk to Marisol in the condition you were in."

"I had nowhere else to go."

"You can stay as long as you want, and go when you want." It was incredibly generous, and yet there was an icy aloofness in it, too. She saw something else in him, too: a deep, intense appreciation of her body, but one he kept under strong control. *How did she know that?* Damistofia had hardly interacted with normal men, and Nazarine now recalled her responses as clumsy and rude approximations at best. *But now she knew, instinctively.* How? Then she remembered *Change,* and those torn fragments of the Jedily section. Jedily had lived a woman all her life, from youth to age, and apparently knew men well. There was no memory of anything. *That* was as blank as before. But there was something else present in her now. An established pattern of identity. And she appreciated Marcian seeing her that way, even if nothing ever came of it. All this went through her mind in a flash, and when the thought was gone, she looked back, returning at least the gesture-acknowledgment of his attention, from which he looked away abruptly. He said, "Ruli will set supper out."

Supper was an occasion which was no more animated than the rest of the routines they lived through. Cerulara cooked and set supper out, but at the end, everyone set to cleaning things up, and as soon as Cerulara saw that things were proceeding as they should, vanished into whatever part of the house was hers, presumably to bed. Marcian puttered about for a moment, and then found what he was looking for, a jar of some herb, with which Nazarine's nose wasn't familiar, from which he steeped up a fragrant herb tea. He offered Nazarine some. "It's the only luxury I allow myself."

"What is it?"

"Wintergall. Muscle relaxant." After a moment, he added, "You sleep without dreams you remember."

She took the cup and sat down. "The clothes are very nice. Thank you."

"No need. There's no one else to wear them, and they'd probably dry-rot before Ruli grows enough to fill them out. Take what you need."

"Is Cerulara your daughter?"

"Yes."

"Is the lady of the house dead?"

"Not as far as I know."

"But she's not coming back?"

"No. Have no fears on that score. She won't be back." And he tossed off the cup of tea and began making ready to leave the room. He started to turn the light off, but saw that she wasn't finished, and so left it on. For a time, Nazarine sat in the silent kitchen and thought aimless things, hearing Marcian make small noises elsewhere in the house, until they, too, stopped. She finished the tea, turned out the lights, and returned to her own small room behind the kitchen.

And so it became that Nazarine entered into yet another routine of nothing more complicated than Basic Life, with all its attendant compromises and nagging problems whose solutions were never final. Weeding, harvesting, cleaning and repairing machinery. And as before, when she had been Phaedrus, seemingly in another geologic era, she found something deep and satisfying in it. And at the time, terrifying: all these people confronted nothingness daily, insignificance, nobodyhood, oblivion. Wherever they had originally come from, now they were stranded on a piece of star-stuff—and the starry stuff was no different from a clot of earth. But their every action expressed their basic drive to attain some kind of meaning to their lives.

She was particularly sensitive to this, having started her present consciousness from Rael, who had been placed at the very center of significance and, through her serial personality, had been running from that ever since. Yes. All people wanted to defy time, have power, make changes, leave something permanent, but to have such a power was worse: one walked with warlocks and evil wizards, perverse gods and terrifying demons. When people attained that power, they invariably went bad as they grasped at it.

And she felt the pressure now to re-enter that stream again, for many reasons, and yet she also sensed a deep-seated repugnance and disgust. Once back on that path, it would never end. There would never be an end to the uses she could put Rael's system to, and with potential immortality, there was no end-check on it. Yes. Phaedrus had been right to leave that.

But as she worked, she also knew that somewhere, something was hunting her, with a will that did not flag; some malevolent aim that was passed on from hand to hand. They would suspect, eventually, that they had missed Phaedrus, and then the apparatus would be activated again. She could hide here, certainly, in the back-country of Clisp, but who could say what further crimes could be done against, say, Marcian, or even Cerulara, should she remain here. She glanced across the rows to where Marcian was untangling some tangleweed from the tines of a harvester, and thought, *This cannot be again.*

At first, they tolerated her, as a well-meaning, but hopelessly inexperienced city-bred idiot who had no feel for the unending drudgery of keeping a farm up—or appreciating its rare moments when everything, for a moment, was done, and one could laze the day away. Rare, rare. But gradually, she kept at it, and the toleration slowly mutated into acceptance. But one thing did not change: the grim silence and the locked emotions that both Marcian and Cerulara kept. And yet they both responded more openly to her. More than once she had caught a small shred of affection from Cerulara, and also more than once, she had caught hints of Marcian's appreciation of her body, and unlike the boyish and subtle Damistofia, as Nazarine she had developed a full, ripe figure, distributed on a tall, loose frame. There was no leer in his glance, but simple desire, and something, probably from Jedily, also caught herself wondering how it would be to have love with such a one. For the moment, she let the question go unanswered, even in speculation.

As the autumn wore on into the gates of winter, the cooler air began to bite a little at night, and the work, at the same time, slowed, and they all had considerably more leisure time. She went on several trips with Marcian and Cerulara, to visit brokers, or to buy supplies for the house, and Nazarine found herself becoming attached to the simple life she had fallen into, the open air, the direct experience, the sunburned hands. To be sure, she remembered vividly the composite pasts of her former selves, the intrigue, and its brother, fear. Constantly. And she also remembered a thirsty enemy and the riddle she had not yet tried to answer—who had Jedily been. She was sitting in the open power-wagon Marcian used for all his errands, looking at the brightly dressed crowds milling about among the benches and stalls, with Cerulara behind her. She caught sight of Marcian making his way through the crowd, and when he saw her, his stern, angular face brightened. Fractionally, but enough. It was time to go.

That night, back at the farm, after supper there was more animation than she had seen since coming there, and as they were clearing everything away afterward, once Marcian briefly put his hand on her shoulder, affectionately.

Late, very late, after the house had long become quiet, Nazarine made up a packet of the most serviceable clothing, and after a quick, silent tour of the house, slipped out into the soft anonymous night of Oerlikon, with its random weak stars. She drew a deep breath of the cold night air, sighed, and set off down the road, away from the mountains behind her, and toward the northeast, where dimly one could barely make out the lights of something, perhaps a city, glowing faintly in the haze above the city proper. More than once she stopped and looked back. Twice, she stopped, hesitated, and then went on. Once she turned back, but she only went a few steps before resuming her old course.

She had left a short note, explaining why she had left, and promising to send some money from Marisol to help pay for her upkeep while she had been with them. She knew it wouldn't be sufficient. But it was better for them, and sometimes, she knew, one had to leave the things one wanted. (An image in her mind of Marcian, walking across the evening light in the yard, half-dressed, the muscles visible along his taut, slim frame. The harsh planes of his face, and the softness behind them. She hoped he would find someone to replace the woman who had left him, and the girl.)

The farm had receded out of sight, and the mountains seemed lower, smaller, less significant, and she was walking at a steady pace, which would cover a good part of the way to Marisol before tomorrow sunset. She felt confident, right, on the way at last, to whatever her search might bring. She did not feel any fatigue.

It was then that she noticed that she was being followed by someone along the dim, pale road behind her. Someone who did not bother to conceal himself, a large figure with a lumpy, heavy, rolling motion to his walk. Colly, no doubt, out prowling in the night. Nazarine stepped up the pace, thinking that he'd tire of it and leave off. But when she looked back, he was still there, puffing and blowing, but making an effort to catch up. She looked back toward the farm. It was gone into the darkness under the mountains in the starlight. Colly was a long way from his own area, and if he'd followed her this far, he'd follow her all the way to Marisol.

She stopped, and when he came puffing up, she looked about the empty fields and called out, "Go home! Leave me alone!"

Colly didn't even slow down, but he said, between breaths, "No sparker, no Marcian. Just pretty woman."

"I don't want to hurt you," she warned, calling up images in her mind from Rael, from Damistofia, and she felt her limbs settle into a posture someone in her knew well, deceptively relaxed in appearance. Colly stepped inside her circle, and reached for her, and grasping his wrist, falling back, she threw him across the road, and he landed tumbling, fetching up smartly against a fencepost. Rubbing his head, he lumbered to his feet and came at her with arms wide, to catch her if she tried to duck off either way. That was far from her mind: instead, she stepped inside the wide-flung arms, and making a flattened fist with her right hand, she drove a deep stroke into the man's solar plexus. He stopped with a surprised, driven exhalation, but his mass pushed him forward, as if stumbling. She chopped his ear with the other forearm and he went down like a felled tree, grunting as he hit the hard dirt of the road. For a second, he seemed stunned, but he bounded to his feet with terrifying speed for his bulk, reaching instinctively sideways. His arm brushed her leg, and it nearly threw her. Now she released the full sequence that she knew.

According to the training Rael had been put through, the martial arts blows and throws she now used without restraint were designed to maim and kill, but Colly, through some innate lack of ability to feel pain, or some deep force within him, kept coming, although he was accepting terrible injuries. She couldn't seem to hit a spot that would stop him. This rapidly became a nightmare. Even after she had broken both kneecaps, several ribs, he continued to come on, crawling when he could no longer walk, and finally she had to kill him with a blow to the temple, followed by pressure on the carotid arteries. He finally stopped moving, and the night became quiet; Nazarine listened closely. There was no breathing. She stood up, getting off the bulky body, lightheaded, dizzy, and walked a short distance away. She looked back at the still bulk, lying in the road in the starlight, and suddenly she turned and was violently sick in the ditch by the side of the road, her stomach heaving and knotting.

After a time, the cramps ceased, and she regained her senses, filled with disgust and a sense of waste. And after a long time, she gathered up her things that had fallen, and started off along the road again. There was no one there to see it, but as she walked, for a long time tears dribbled out of the corners of her eyes, streaking her face.

6

"Time: the infinite past, the infinite future, and between them the infinitely small zero-dimensional present, which moreover moves constantly, changing one into the other, a veritable nothingness. But all of the future and all of the past is contained within the present."

—H.C., Atropine

IT IS A commendable thing to require work of subordinates, but a fully functioning spy net is one thing, and a remnant tattered by revolution and restoration, and ripped to shreds by desperate actions, is another matter entirely. In Tartary, Cesar Kham and Arunda Palude shortly found that their line of command into Clisp was both precarious and tenuous. What reports they did receive shed no more light on the subject, and Palude's early apparent successes with the oracles apparently failed her, and the answers became contradictory gibberish.

She had told Kham, "In Tarot, you can often feel the flow in it, the internal consistency. But the readings I am getting make no sense whatsoever!"

Kham and Palude had been walking outside in the bitter Tartarean airs. He had shrugged, and said, "Maybe you're not asking the right questions; that seems to have a lot to do with it. Or the card you use to identify the problem. That book you have puts a great deal of stress on choosing that symbol carefully."

"Perhaps. At any rate, the flow is gone."

Kham asked, half-jokingly, "Can one exhaust the oracle?"

"Supposedly not. I have never heard of that. But . . ."

"What have you been asking?"

"The usual sort. Success of our venture, allegiance of subjects; that sort of thing."

"Ask it if the Morphodite lives."

"I . . . I don't really know what symbol I'd use. I tried that once, using *The Devil* as significator, but I got gibberish."

"Try it with another card. Now."

And so they returned to the tower, and after some reflection, Palude shuffled the cards carefully, three times as prescribed by rote, using #1, *The Magus*. The result was inconclusive. Kham picked up the pack and looked through the strange, enigmatic emblems of the deck. This one was so done to show ancient medieval scenes, most of which were only barely comprehensible in themselves. He snorted in derision a couple of times, and then pulled a card out of the deck, handing it to Palude. "Use this one."

Palude took the card. It was #14, *Temperance, or An*. The figure depicted upon its face was that of an androgyne, hard at work in the laboratory of an alchemist. Kham added, "Ask if it's alive; what it intends."

Palude shuffled again, and then laid out an eleven-card reading. The cards read:

1. Self/Definition: *The High Priestess*.
2. Opposes: *Page of Swords*, reversed.
3. Ideal, or best expected: *Justice or Balance*.
4. Foundation: *Death*.
5. Behind: *Knight of Wands*.
6. Before: *Strength*.
7. Self, moving: *The Magus*.
8. Environment: *Nine of Wands*.
9. Hope or fears: *Ace of Wands*.
10. Summation to come: *The Hanged Man*.
11. Explanation: *The Star*.

Palude sat and stared at the layout for a long time, and then began writing in a commonplace notebook of crude paper, a local product. After a moment, she said, "Seven of the cards are Trumps Major, an arrangement you seldom see. That in itself is indicative of great forces moving. . . ."

Kham observed, "I see you drew a Death card."

"It's in the wrong place, and there's no card of violence associated with it. Note that it moves *from* Death, not toward it. Hmm, and here, of the four lesser cards, they are all Wands except one, a Sword. That one means espionage, surveillance. The first card is fairly obvious, as is the third. No mystery there. Behind it is Flight, Departure. Before it, Strength. It is a formidable antagonist; And its hopes are for a starting point, a beginning. To come are trials and sacrifice, because of . . . Truth. That's a strong ending."

"Sum it up."

"It's alive. It's a woman. It's not moving yet toward us. But it will. But this doesn't suggest what it is going to actually do. There's no real suggestion of violence, which I would expect to see. . . ."

"Do you believe *that?*"

"It has the internal consistency."

"Can we get any more juice out of the agents there?"

"I doubt it."

"Then one of us is going to have to go to Clisp. You don't know the area. I do."

"I agree."

"I hope this isn't a wild-goose chase?"

"I hope you can find what you're looking for. There are probably a lot of young women in Clisp."

"Doubtless. But this one won't have any roots. And . . ."

"Yes?"

"That suggests it's still in Clisp."

"Yes. So it does."

And so Cesar Kham took the long journey back into Lisagor, across the ocean; Tilanque; across the broad valley of Puropaigne, through Symbarupol, now only a back-country junction town for the beamline, half wrecked by war, half abandoned, with only parts of it coming back to life. A melancholy place, filled with the ghosts of the past, victories and defeats. Then across the northern reaches of Crule The Swale, the silvery-buff grass flowing in the wind, and dour, silent locals watching the beamliner pass with intolerance in their rigid erect postures. Then the barren, rocky mountains of the Serpentine, harrowing suspensions across dry gulches that fell abruptly to the sea, never far away in this narrow land. And at last into Clisp.

Marisol was a city which managed to retain a decently cosmopolitan air without the overwhelming presence of vice and depravity which usually went hand in glove with such cities. Even in the old days, Marisol had always been substantially freer than the other cities of the Changeless Land. Kham felt somewhat at sea now, in Marisol. Except for the plain wood-and-stucco facades, it almost seemed like a mainstream city, anywhere else in the universe. An overgrown college town, perhaps, or some pleasant backwater. Something was gone. He grimaced with the pungent irony of his reflection; that Marisol, which had never gone to the full rigor of Changelessness, but had always tolerated more than other places in Lisagor, now had suffered the least change from the revolution, while Symbarupol, a pharaonic bastion of stability and eternity, had vanished as an entity. The junction would remain; but in time, that city would be forgotten. Marula had simply collapsed into itself and had been abandoned. It would come back, but not as it had been.

He had little difficulty unearthing his prime agents in Marisol. They were safely burrowed into the woodwork like little mice. But after several days of following blind leads, they were unable to unearth anything. If the Morphodite lived, they had lost him. Or her. Or whatever the damned thing was. No trace. It was both frustrating and thankless work, for the surviving members of the net in Clisp remained certain that the person known as Phaedrus had vanished without a trace, and no one had evidenced any further interest in it. The terrorists responsible for the deed had vanished back into the wilder country eastward; the prevailing rumors seemed to place them somewhere in Crule. At any rate, out of reach. None had remained behind.

Reluctantly, Kham disengaged himself from the net and began his journey back. If Phaedrus had survived and now walked this earth as a woman, she had left no traces, and possibly had not even come to Marisol. Doubts gnawed at him like termites in a rotten log, but there was nothing he could grasp. Silence.

The trip back across Lisagor was distressingly the same as the way he had come. Few got on, or off, the beamliner, which was allowed to pass the frontier between Clispish lands and Crule without any more than glares from the border guards, while other traffic was held up for hours, sometimes days. In fact, the only notable point on the whole journey back occurred in Symbarupol, where an attractive young woman boarded the beamliner coach he was riding in. Unlike the locals, who now invariably wore clothing that was simultaneously old, dark, and rather in ill repair, this woman (or girl; Kham could not make a precise definition—she looked young, but she carried herself with the confidence of someone much more adult) was tall and graceful, long-legged, with a ripe figure. She had a rather round face, accented by brown hair which seemed to fall naturally into soft, loose curls, and wore clothing that seemed almost modern: loose, flowing pants, soft but serviceable shoes of plain design, a tunic of the same gray color as the pants, and a darker cloak.

Packing her small luggage away, she turned once, catching his attention out of the corner of her eye, and directed toward him one of those enigmatic glances women always directed toward strangers: as if asking, "Well, what is it you want?" She turned her back and settled in the wooden seat, but not before something flickered in her eyes, in an instant, something Kham could not identify, but which chilled any ardor her appearance might have incited. He looked away as well, out the window across the sad ruins of Symbarupol, softening in the long twilight of early winter. He shook his head. *Not that one, this time. But curious, all the same. What was she, with that much poise, dressed that well, in this ruinous city?* He gave it up, thinking that he would not be able to derive that answer any better than he had been able to find the Morphodite. As night drew on after the slow passage of time on Oerlikon, the coach dimmed, and the lighting system, never completely trustworthy, refused to work at all. The coach grew dark. Kham nodded, settled into a better position, and slept, knowing he would reach the shores of the ocean tomorrow morning.

When the coach lurched, passing under an uneven switch point, Kham awoke, stiff from sleeping sitting up on a wooden bench seat all night. It was daylight, and his land journey was almost over. He was now moving into Thurso's Landing, the small port that served the scant commerce that still trickled across from Tartary. He stood up to stretch. And noticed that the attractive girl was gone. Gone? Not in the coach. Where had she gotten off? And for what? There was essentially nothing between Symbarupol and the coast except farms. If she had been an enigma boarding the beamliner in Symbarupol, getting off in the middle of nowhere was even more mystifying. He moved to the place where she had sat. No luggage, no trace. She had vanished into the night. But this occupied his attention only for a moment, and presently, engaged in getting off the beamliner, and making his way to the shipping offices where he spent the day booking passage for Tartary, he soon forgot about the tall, slender girl he had seen on the beamliner. It was no matter. Kham had seen a lot of pretty girls pass, and they had vanished as easily as they had appeared. The only troubling thing was that as he aged, there seemed to be more of them as time went on.

*   *   *

Nazarine had reached Marisol without further incident, and now using the cartouche of Pompeo, secured lodgings temporarily in a small pension located rather far from the center of the city on the banks of the Grand Canal. Here she rested, made short forays into town for new clothing, a few pieces of modern, durable things for travel, and during the late hours of night began slowly casting her oracular net.

The problem with oracles is that the questions have to be maddeningly specific. The looser the questions, the looser the answer. If one asked any oracle if one was in danger, the answer would certainly be affirmative, for danger was an inherent condition of life, but some events had a higher probability than others; and in the loose casting, the calculation, as she preferred to call it, there was no discrimination. So she had to take one piece at the time, and unravel that one strand.

She quickly disposed of the question of Marcian. Totally uninvolved with any plot, by intent or accident, the only thing she could pick up about him was that he had been falling in love with her, and she already knew that. As a fact, she had begun to find the idea interesting herself. She had liked his grim reserve, his taut slimness, the intense, focused personality, the lean, hard body. And curiously, also the fact that he had obviously been emotionally injured sometime in the past. This was as visceral as the sexual urgings she had begun to feel, probably something from Jedily. It didn't make sense. She wanted to say to herself that a woman wouldn't normally want a man who had been badly hurt emotionally, but nevertheless there was something appealing about the idea of . . . what? Nurturing him? Healing an otherwise attractive man, guiding him . . . ? Perhaps. She wondered about that. She remembered Damistofia well enough, especially the memories of Cliofino, which she enjoyed. Cliofino had been a rat, but as a lover he gave a lot more than he knew himself. What a dilemma! The men who were good lovers invariably either had severe character defects or obstacles to coming to one, or else they were good fellows and dull lovers. Women liked fireworks, too! *Damn!* She thought, suddenly, shaking all over. These intrusions of Jedily's were like possession's, a déjà vu experience, where it was not remembering, but feeling your whole mind slip into a well-worn groove. Whatever Jedily had been, she apparently had led an active life, with plenty of men. Yes. She had thought the thing herself . . . but the pattern had been Jedily's. Patterns but no memory. And with Damistofia, she had memory, but no patterns.

She also used the calculation to carefully sift Marisol and Clisp for any indication of plot or organized efforts to find her. Curiously, there was none, but in all the scans she ran, there was the hint of something . . . but not here. Something malevolent, full of evil will . . . but very far off. Now ineffective, unable to see *her*. Good. She had time. The prince, Amadeo, she also found to be uninvolved. But he was weak, undisciplined, subject to considerable pressure through the number of women he entertained himself with. *Them*. Sooner or later they'd find him out. Probably already knew. And they'd . . . what? She erased the *Map*, and cast another. *Aha*, she thought as the counters fell into place on the paper, aligning into a pattern. Yes . . . they would not use him. That day had passed, but they could derive intelligence through him, without his awareness of it. They would know what he knew. Therefore he must not know. This was indeed useful information. She had room to breathe and plan, now, but not much. And it was clear that the answers she sought were not to be found in Marisol, or in all of Clisp. Clisp, for all its contemporary resurgence as a nation-state, was an incident on the periphery of the larger problem . . . which had started in Symbarupol.

As she turned her thoughts to Symbarupol, she felt a flash of momentary horror, something unimaginable, pass through her. More. Disgust, loathing, incredible horror. But not the emotion itself, or the memories that would cause such an emotion, but simply the pattern of reactions left behind by them. She, Nazarine, followed them out without understanding why. The moment passed. She shivered, shook her head, and got up from the small table and went to the window over the canal, opening it wide, breathing deeply of the midnight air alongside the canal. She inhaled the clean air, the canal scents. When she had put her thoughts directly on Symbarupol, thought of it, directed her attention to it, that was when it had occurred, probably because she had sensitized herself to Jedily's old reactions earlier by the thought-pattern about men. And Symbarupol keyed something unspeakable in the pattern Jedily had left behind. Not something . . . that happened to her. It didn't have that flavor, but happening to someone else.

Nazarine felt faint from the strength of that pattern, and that was just a fragment. Horror, disgust, outrage, they were all there. But not done to Jedily. Nazarine knew well enough what had been done to Jedily, and no one remembered that. Of that—whatever they had done to induce her to *Change* into Rael, there was absolutely no trace. She didn't need the aid of the calculation to help her see that Jedily had once known something. In Symbarupol. But what?

She sighed. There was no avoiding it. She now realized that that pattern had been so strong she had actually avoided thinking about Symbarupol, and had been avoiding the inevitable trip she would have to make there. And she would have to go. To do a reading, she would have to have an idea of where to start, how to aim the question, and at present she had none. She breathed deeply. But it would start there.

She closed the window, leaving it open at the bottom, and sat on the edge of the bed, starting to undress for bed. She was down to her underpants when it occurred to her to ask one more question of her system: *Was there need for haste?* Still half-naked, she went to the table and ran one more scan, asking the deceptively simple question, making sure to include the extra computation at the end, the line item that gave the reason why.

The answer was a clear "yes," the clearest affirmative she had ever seen. But the reason line read *"mu." No answer.* No reason. It was the blank line. Data insufficient. Fill in whatever you wanted. It was the first time she could remember the oracle failing her, or anyone she had been. She turned out the light and lay down, weary. *The beamliner leaves in the morning.* She did not sleep particularly well, waking often. But she made it to the station on time, and left Clisp behind, with an odd sadness she did not entirely understand. But she felt a distinct premonition, a certainty, that she would never see Clisp again.

The entire journey back to Symbarupol had been a horror for her and she endured it as best she could, relishing each moment of the journey falling away in time. The journey back: that was one thing she would never have to do again.

Once there, she found a place to stay, one of the few surviving hostels left over and functioning from the old days, and then went straight to work. She found there was a little trouble in using the cartouche, but not much—rather less than she had expected. It seemed that whatever doctrinal differences existed between Clisp and Crule, which Symbarupol was nominally a part of, these mutual detestations did not extend to money. Pompeo's cartouche was good, and it was honored, if grudgingly. No one seemed to be put off that she would be poking about the ruins, either. This was adequate commentary on the fall of Symbarupol. The action had shifted somewhere else.

Much was ruinous in the city, evidence of revolution and turmoil. The Mask Factory complex, somewhat on the edges of the city, showed some damage; someone had tried to burn it, and there was considerable evidence of vandalism, but in the main, it had remained mostly whole, if deserted.

Posing as a researcher, Nazarine had gotten permission to investigate The Mask Factory, although she had been required to sign a series of hair-raising oaths and testimonials certifying that she would make no claim in case of injury, maiming, fright, impotence, or disease, any of the above being related to her voluntary entry into a prohibited ruin.

Coming up the walk to the building, she felt a curious emotional state, of at least three components: the excitement of anticipation of what she might find here; the curious abstract emotions of Rael, which did not correspond with any normal human emotion directly; and the pattern from Jedily. No doubt about it. Jedily had been deeply involved with this place, in more than one way, none of those ways positive. She looked up at the soft-cube shape, which had been preferred in mainland Lisagor for government buildings, now with cannon-fire pock-marks spotted randomly on it, and the main doors blown open and not repaired or even boarded, and recalled wryly that even with Rael's memories, she had no idea of where to begin. There was a patch of rubble off to one side. She assumed that it was what was left of the Residence. Total destruction, there. Besides, it was unlikely they would have kept records there. That was what she was looking for. Records. The Changeless State had believed in voluminous records of the most trivial events, and recorded *everything*, believing that somehow, as in faith in magic, that the simple act of perpetuation would keep Change away. *Perhaps it had helped.*

There was a guard just inside the door, but he was bored and disinterested, and made no comment at her pass. She asked, "Where did they keep the records?"

The guard glanced along the lines of her body, once, and then decided she was unreachable for any number of reasons, and said, "I don't know, except somewhere toward the back of the building, so I'm told. Not much left back there. What wasn't looted out during the troubles was hauled off by salvagers. They came from nowhere, everywhere, wanting to buy everything left."

"What, the furniture?"

"Everything. The building's just a shell. Some idiot even hauled off all the old paperwork."

"What about the computers? They had some. . . ."

"First thing to go. Some of that was still operable. Down and dead, of course. But they had that stuff in a separate building, out back of this one."

Nazarine stepped back toward the entrance a little, and made an uncertain motion. "They had records and computers both?"

The guard shook his head as if disbelieving. "They used the computers in the lab. Computations only. The records section was all hand work. Most of the back part was storage. They tried to burn it, but there was a lot left."

"You ever hear who bought them?"

"A Makhak trader living in Karshiyaka. It's his hobby. I've seen him myself since they put me on this post. He finished clearing out the last of it not all that long ago."

"Whatever in the world would a Makhak want with old records?"

"You got me short, miss. You know Makhaks, or what we hear of them; every one of them has some odd thing they spend their lives on. This one wanted old records, and he didn't much care what kind, as long as there were plenty of them. He was pleased with what he got! He can spend the rest of his life on them."

"You said you saw him. Did you speak with him?"

"Once; asked him what he wanted all that junk for, and he rolled his eyes and exclaimed, 'Statistics.' Then he left. Who knows?"

"You don't recall his name?"

"No."

"Well . . ."

"There's almost nothing left in there. Go look."

"Thanks. I will." And working her way through the piles of rubble and some broken walls, she found the place where the records had been kept, but it was as the guard had said. It had been cleaned out. You could even see scars in the floor and walls where the metal racks and cabinets had been torn out. A few scraps of paper left on the floor. Nothing. She returned to the main entry and spoke with the guard. "You were right. They even dug the screws out of the walls in there. Nothing left."

"Didn't think there would be, say, ah . . ."

Nazarine made a polite, if cool parting, and set back out for the main city. There was nothing in Symbarupol for her, at least nothing of note in The Mask Factory. Some Makhak trader living in Karshiyaka took them for his hobby. There was perhaps one other place she might look while she was here—the old registration section. If their records were still intact, she could find out what Jedily had been before she went in The Mask Factory. If the records still existed.

They had. The same day, in the afternoon, Nazarine found the Hall of Records, and posing as a long-lost relative trying to trace her Guardian after losing her during the Troubles, soon gained access to the records. But not directly. These records and files were still active, and it took a small army of clerks to keep up with them, even in these dimished days. So the clerk she spoke with averred. But after much muttering and pacing back and forth, the clerk returned from the stacks and presented Nazarine a dossier with the name Jedily Tulilly written plain along the file designation strip. The strip also had an extra notation opposite the name: RESETTLED. (File Inactive.)

Nazarine asked the clerk what this notation meant. And the clerk, a small, pale girl who gave the impression of having been sold into slavery as a child and never having known any happiness whatsoever, answered, in a peculiar, off-center manner musing off into some neutral space, "Well, it's supposed to mean that those personnel so designated were sent off somewhere else, but since those days are gone, I would venture my own private opinion that this was how they indicated invoices into the Medical Research Facility."

"In short, she was so listed as a conscript to The Mask Factory."

"Yes."

"You have been in Records a long time?"

"All my life."

"You saw a lot of this?"

"Some . . . some more. A bit. I couldn't say 'a lot.' Maybe it was. I shipped no one off. I kept records."

"You have done well . . . you survived. But did you ever see any indication of how such people were selected?" And here Nazarine felt the urge to embroider things a little: "I mean, I lived here, but I never saw anyone carted off, and no one I know saw this, either. How did they do it, never mind whether it was right or wrong?"

The clerk brightened a little. Here she could tell her story. "Oh, that's easy enough! They picked up the loners, the self-destructive, the dissatisfied, you know, the kind of people who . . . move around a lot, play with other people, then leave them. People who had fallen to vices. Sick people with no friends. *People who had already disappeared!* Nobody missed them!"

"That doesn't sound like the Jedily Tullily I remember, or that I've heard friends speak of."

The clerk retrieved the dossier. "Let me see, perhaps there's a clue in here. . . ." She opened the folder and began scanning through the entries, the forms, the singular traces left behind of a woman's life in a community.

As she looked, Nazarine watched her face begin to register some emotions: first, puzzlement, then a kind of shock, and as she leafed further, finally a kind of anger.

The clerk pursed her lips, and said, in an undertone, "There is a lot wrong with this file, and as far as I'm concerned, whoever posted it last did it badly!"

"How so?"

"Well, to begin with, they show here that she was a dischargee from a rehab center, and was employed as a sanitary technician fourth class at the Bureau of Public Roads. But there's no entry form, or when. Then there's a huge gap between her early entries, which show educational level and so forth, and this last thing. They show several associations and registered liaisons*, and there are several children shown, three, spaced out at rather large intervals, but that's all of the middle part of her life. There should be much more! I shouldn't say this, but my guess is that somebody . . . changed this file. And did a poor job of it." The clerk glanced back over another form, which was still in the file. "Yes, this is odd, indeed. According to this profile, such a person would expect to lead a life of stability and considerable progress, and the few mid-life entries left bear that out, and yet, there she comes out of rehab and winds up a scrubwoman. Then selected for The Mask Factory." The pale girl had gotten so agitated over the condition of the file that she had forgotten her official phraseology, and dropped into the argot of the street, the alley, and the Dragon gamefield.

"Well, that's curious. I left when I was young; I was not one of her natural children." Here, the clerk nodded knowingly. "But I recall her as being very stable, very . . . how should I say, forward-moving. She enjoyed things greatly, you know." Here, Nazarine favored the pale girl with a lewd wink, which the clerk acknowledged and understood, but also gave a look which suggested a degree of prim disapproval. Nazarine added, "I saw nothing which would have caused anyone to remand her to a rehab center."

The clerk nodded sagely. "There is certainly nothing in here to indicate any reason. But there is something else missing."

"What's that?"

---

* Lisagor had no social equivalent to marriage. An "association," resembling an article of incorporation more than a marriage, was the nearest thing to a permanent bond. A "registered liaison" was nothing more than an affair which had been registered at City Hall.

"Her employment. I look here and there's no way you could tell where she worked, or what she did. I know she wasn't a scrubwoman."

"How do you know this?"

"The children's indicators. Jedily paid for the maternity services. All three times. Not her lover, and she didn't use the public facilities. No, no. She took the best, *and paid for it out of her own pocket!* Whatever she was, she was well-set."

Nazarine said, to hide her emotions more than anything else, "Well we never wanted for anything we really needed, I recall that."

"Right! Then you know what she did for a living?"

"Of course . . . but it doesn't matter now. And I'd imagine you couldn't correct your file without something more than recollection. Documentation."

The clerk shook her head, but with sympathy. "I am glad you understand. So few do. It is a thankless job."

"Just so. So, then, there's no more to be had in this. . . ."

"I'm afraid not."

"Well, then, I will be on my way." Nazarine turned away from the counter, and then turned back. The pale girl clerk was already headed into the stacks. Nazarine asked, "Would The Mask Factory have had any control over people going into rehab?"

The clerk turned and said, quite without thinking, "Generally not, as I recall, although they always had a representative in here who scanned the rehab rosters."

"Really? Do you recall if it was anyone you knew?"

The girl blurted out, "Who could forget that repulsive little slug, always creeping around the stacks, grabbing a feel here, a feel there, always groping. That flunky over at The Mask Factory, the errand-boy. Avaria was his name. Elegro Avaria. I can say that because he vanished in the Troubles and hasn't been seen in these parts since."

Nazarine made a motion with her hand, indicating that she wished the clerk farewell, and turned away to go, but her real reason in turning away was to hide her face from the girl, because when she heard Avaria's name, the alarm bells in her head must have been nearly audible to passersby. Oh, yes, Nazarine as Rael-memory recalled Avaria well enough. Well enough indeed. And there was something worth finding out. She could hardly wait to get off in solitude, where she could add this datum into the oracle. On the surface, it wasn't much. But of necessity, the entering edge of the wedge is narrow and sharp. But it can widen enough to crack open the thing it's applied against.

7

"At the impassable and irreducible core of every meaningful and deeply real thing there lies irrationality pure and undisguised: Transcendental Numbers, irreducible fractions, even,—gasp!— imaginary numbers. And that is how you tell the Real from the unreal. And those things that can be reduced to rational, fixed ends? Trash, illusion, nonsense, Maya, ghosts, the demonic. They only have power over us to the extent that we waste time worrying about them."

—H.C., Atropine

NAZARINE RETURNED TO her tiny rooms at the Symbarupol Traveller's hostel and stretched her long body out on the simple cot that served as a bed, watching the mellow, diffused light of the afternoon sun evolve across the wall on which it slanted. Evolve, not move. Sunlights and shadows alike moved too slowly to perceive on Oerlikon, but move they did, whether one watched them or not. Now she reviewed the facts and suggestions she possessed, reaching for the right question.

She now knew, with reasonable validity, that Jedily had been selected for The Mask Factory, by no less a person than Elegro Avaria. Pternam didn't pick his victims. They were brought to him. Also that Jedily had once, most of her life, been somebody of some success. The records had been badly stripped. Whoever did it hadn't cared if his work was noticed. Only that her former life vanish from records. Why? At the first approximation, for the simple reason that the record of her life would not justify "rehabilitation." Also that she wasn't well-known. A success, but quiet about it. But why rehab a quiet success? Jedily didn't fit the pattern. There was definitely something here that didn't fit. In one sense, the question went nowhere. But these unknowings were the life blood to the original Rael, and Nazarine had not forgotten how to work with these "unknowns." One solved equations for them!

She sat up for a moment, watching the sky beyond the window, and then went to the crude little table under the window. There was a blank pad of paper there, which she had left. Now she bent over it and began laying out the lines of Rael's oracle, concentrating on the question of what had Jedily been. One by one the outlines began filling in, an indecipherable hieroglyph to the uninitiated, barely comprehensible even to her until the very last step. But at last she had it: *Jedily Tulilly was a spy.*

Nazarine pushed the chair back and leaned back even farther. *A spy. Then she had been caught.* But that made no more sense than before. *A spy for whom? Doing what?* Nazarine knew that because of the majestic indifference of the Makhaks, and the monolithic Lisak society, there were in fact few real spies and those that were, were in a local resistance. Or were . . . offworlders, of which the Lisaks knew nothing. What had the Answer said? A spy. If she had been of the Lisak Underground, there would have been no rehab, but outright execution, summary justice on the spot. And if for the offworlders, there would have been more hue and cry. She went through rehab. They knew everything. And yet they did nothing, and in fact she knew very well as Rael that they didn't know about the offworlders. Dead end either way. Another unknown. Now how to address it: in what direction should she approach this still-unknown? She bent to the pad again, and began concentrating. A spy for whom? And who caught her?

The sunlight faded, became more golden, and moved imperceptibly diagonally across the wall a bit before she had this answer: *Jedily was an offworlder. She was caught by the offworlders.*

Nazarine ran her slender fingers through the brown, loose curls of her hair, and pursed her full mouth in perplexity. There, too, was ambiguity. She was an offworlder, then, working for the offworld group which was actually maintaining an artificial stability on Oerlikon, for their own purposes. Presumably Jedily had also worked to those ends. Quietly, but in such a way as to lead a quiet and prosperous life, with plenty of time for three children at wide intervals, presumably with different lovers, that being the custom of Lisagor. She reached for the memory knowing it wouldn't be there, but she felt a framework it had left behind. A sense of completion, satisfaction. There had been no bitterness in it.

Very well. Then I am an offworlder myself. I am not child of Jedily, but a replication of her, in a different body, derived from the potentials latent in the orginal Jedily DNA. For a moment, the knowledge made her a bit lightheaded, dizzy. But caught by the same group she belonged to . . . ? How so? Would she have gone too far native and turned against her masters? Nazarine did not think so. That didn't feel right. The off-worlders were the most conservative group on the planet, and if one had turned on them, surely such an event would have left traces. No. There were no ripples of that anywhere. But somehow she opposed them, and they "caught her." Nazarine did not wish to ask another scan. She felt the presence of too many unknowns. She needed to try to find those records from The Mask Factory, and she'd have to catch the beamliner late tonight, to start for Karshiyaka. She removed the used pages from the pad and shredded them into tiny pieces in the wastebag. Satisfied that the room looked secure, she glanced at the fading light, and nodded, leaving the room for supper at one of the few remaining operable communal dining halls.

After supper, alone in the midst of multitudes, absorbed in her own thoughts, she returned to the hostel and retrieved her few belongings, and checked out, walking slowly through the deserted streets, still guarded by the improbable monolithic government buildings, now untenanted save for a handful of squatters.

Using the cartouche, she went to the beamliner station and purchased a ticket for the end of the line, Thurso's Landing, and when the liner came in, swaying on its suspended track of I-beams, she boarded it, without looking back. But she was still wrestling with the unanswered questions and an incomplete oracle. There was something here that escaped her powers. And that could only happen in such a case that the answer could be derived by the ordinary progress of everyday reasoning. But it was maddening: she couldn't find where the discrepancy was. She was still worrying herself like a dog with a bone when she found an empty seat, and in arranging her bag, she looked up, sensing that she was the object of someone's attentions. A few seats back was a bald man of no determinable age, watching her with interest, and perhaps appreciation. She returned the look, with a slight internal grimace: *No. Not that one.* But as she started to sit, some subliminal alarm system planted long ago by Rael went off. She didn't dare look back to find out what it was, but something he'd done wasn't right, wasn't Lisak. A thrill slid upward from the small of her back, and lodged high up between her shoulder blades. Offworlder! On the liner, from parts west, perhaps Clisp. Looking for a trace of Phaedrus? She shivered. *I'm getting paranoid.* A second inner voice suggested, *Maybe not paranoid enough?* The voice of reason answered, *Maybe not looking, but he can at least find one who does.* So she sat very still for a long time, until she felt it worth risking a glance back to where the bald man sat, and to her immense relief, he was asleep, his mouth slightly open. With almost no movement, save a series of graceful flows from one position to another, she carefully gathered her bag up, and slid out of the seat, and then out of the coach. At the next stop, she got off, and it wasn't until she caught a fleeting glimpse of the bald man passing in the departing coach that she felt some measure of reassurance. The pressure had been intense. And suddenly letting down, the answer she had been looking for crystallized and emerged fully developed, complete. *Of course! It couldn't be any other way! Jedily hadn't been sent to a Lisak rehab at all: her own people, the offworlders, did their own version first. They didn't care what rehab got out of her then—she'd already been cleaned out like a gourd. She knew or did something, and they—* she hesitated at the word—*erased her, and dumped her back into the process by which The Mask Factory obtained its recruits.* And now she had a real problem for the oracle: what was Avaria's connection? How could they be so sure she would vanish into that hole? But as Nazarine walked tiredly through the unpaved streets of a very minor little town, looking for a place to stay, she thought that she would hold those questions until she had tried to find the missing Mask Factory records. She needed one more piece of Jedily, if possible, before *asking* again. And of course it was also true that you couldn't push it too hard, and depend on the answers. So for now she would let it be.

She never found a place open, but returned to the station, where she made do on one of the wooden benches. And in the morning, red-eyed and stiff, she wandered all over the town until she finally located a dray-wagon headed north for Karshiyaka, the end of the world, whose driver reluctantly agreed to take her aboard as a passenger. She rode in the back of the wagon with the load, apparently large burlap bags full of legumes, and watched the rolling, empty lands pass under the indigo skies of the north.

Karshiyaka was the place where the northern tier of hills across Lisagor turned to the northeast, diminished to a series of hogback hills and low rises, and vanished into the gray-green waters of the Cold Ocean. There were no trees; the land was covered by a low, brushy plant which gave off a bitter, aromatic odor. The climate was damp and misty, and the houses and towns were half-sunken into the rocky ground. The monotony of the landscape was broken only occasionally by squat, low towers with conical roofs, apparently the residences of hermits, for to Nazarine's eye they seemed to have little relationship to any activity near to them or far away. Going by what little she could see, it was cold, and she had burrowed deep into the harsh bags for warmth. This was the northeast, far from the sunny, light-swept distances of Clisp, plain and mountains, or from Marula, far away in the south. And the season, however mild, was indeed winter. She burrowed deeper into the lumpy bags and tried to ignore hunger and cold some more.

After the passage of several days, which had stretched into a uniform dull blur, the power-wagon and its trailer rolled onto hard, stony streets, closed in tightly by the lowering, half-submerged houses and shops. The streets curved and intersected with a sense of willful perversity, all eventually winding down slippery cobblestones to the harbor, which surprisingly looked full and busy. The wind off the water had a bite to it, and the few people she saw about went about their business without wasted motions or socializing. The wagon reached a section of warehouses along the docks, and Nazarine got off there, and went looking for an inn or hostel. She did not know what she would find here, in this land's-end corner of Lisagor: already it had a foreign air to it.

The town was called, unimaginatively, Karshiyaka. But whatever went on here apparently called for a lot of transients, for there were a lot of inns and taverns, not to mention the traditional Lisak hostels. Nazarine, feeling more secure now in this impossible corner of the country, and feeling acutely both hunger and fatigue, decided on one of the better inns, which included a warm tavern, and to her relief they accepted the credit of the cartouche that Pompeo had given Phaedrus without question. In fact, they accepted it willingly. She selected a large room with heavy half-timber walls, small round windows, and which had a plain but well-furnished bath attached. And the water was hot. She glanced at the blue, overcast twilight, through the windows, and ordered supper sent up to her. After supper, a bowl of herbal sea stew, accompanied by a hard-crust bread and hot beer, she filled the old iron tub full of water, and after bolting the doors, removed her clothes and settled gently into the steaming water, where she scrubbed madly, and then lay back to soak. She woke up a bit later, feeling guilty, surrounded by now-cool water. The room was cool, too, but she found enough blankets to pile on the bed, and lay down wearily and slept deeply, untroubled by dreams or problems that she could remember.

*   *   *

She slept through the day and the next night as well, waking only enough to roll over. But by the next morning she finally woke, and set about the things she had come to Karshiyaka to do. First came some heavier clothing, and then she went about the town making discreet inquiries about an eccentric Makhak supposed to have settled in the area. Eventually she derived directions to one of the towers on the southern side of the projecting finger of land, and set out for it, walking.

It was a bit farther than she had thought, and she could feel the cold through the heavy clothing by the time she approached it, but there was no mistaking it. The Makhak immigrant lived in an eccentric stone castle built out on the end of a low headland, an irregular structure of no particular shape, with three towers of different heights, none especially tall.

The building was enigmatic and blank-faced; Nazarine walked around it three times before she found what appeared to be an entrance, and the day, already well-gone toward evening, was nearer night before someone within finally opened the door for her. This was, apparently, a servant or bondsman. Or bondswoman; she could not tell. The person was tall and gaunt and curiously indeterminate of gender. It met her without a single word at the door, and conveyed her through a series of empty stone corridors to a large, drafty room, where another tall and cadaverous person, not a great deal different from the servant, sat before a peat fire and brooded. The servant left.

Presently the one by the fire turned and stood up. This one, at least, seemed to be male, and well-advanced in years as well. He was thin and sticklike in build, moving with an odd reserve which suggested fragility—but great strength as well. He spoke first, in a low, muttering tone, almost a whisper. He held his hands stuffed into voluminous sleeves.

"I am Yakhin Pakhad."

She said, "Nazarine Alea."

"Lisak?"

"Yes and no."

"Ah, the followers of the old ways; always ambiguity, duality."

Nazarine smiled a tremulous little half-smile to herself. "Indeed, sir, duality . . . and the half has not yet been told."

Pakhad nodded, recognizing something of a private humor he had keyed in her. He said, after a moment, "We are private people, you know, we Makhaks. And you being young and graceful and with an entire continent of stalwarts at your back, I must conjecture, I must assume . . ."

Nazarine knew of the Makhak distaste for superfluous conversation. She interrupted, "I have heard of the Makhak ways, of how each of you follows an 'excellence.' "

"Just so; we are great scholars."

"It was described to me how a certain scholar of Tartary resided in this neighborhood, one whose excellence was the study of statistics."

"I am such a person."

"I am in the service of Clisp. . . ."

"We do not require reasons."

"You obtained the records of the old Mask Factory, of Symbarupol? This was reported to me there."

He made a slight nod of agreement, leaving his face turned down.

"I am no statistician. But in those records there may be mention of a person I am trying to trace. Therefore I ask your assistance." She hoped it was short enough. One never knew with Makhaks exactly where the line was between essential speech and rudeness.

"Curious."

"Why so?"

"I would have imagined them valuable—the records. But they sold cheaply, and no one has come asking anything. A poor investment, but a treasure-trove for me. I will never finish unraveling them. And of course it will be difficult to find one person in all that. Is there haste?"

"I don't know. If I must say yes or no, I will say yes, but it is no emergency . . . yet."

Pakhad made a subtle signal with a hand, which he removed from its sleeve, to which responded the servant. Pakhad made a few more signs, and then made an easy waving motion to Nazarine. "All is arranged. Food and rest. Sleep well, rise early. Tomorrow we will see. Do you require entertainment tonight?"

"Entertainment?"

"Young men? Girls?"

Nazarine smiled openly, at last able to give something back. "Neither. I have an excellence of my own to pursue. Food and rest will suffice."

"Curious, curious. Have you considered emigration to the Free Land?"

"No, but I think I will wind up there, whether I would or not."

Pakhad raised his bushy eyebrows at that, but turned away to his peat fire and private thoughts, signifying that for the moment, conversation was over. Presently the servant reappeared with a bowl of some crushed fruit and a loaf of crusty bread, and a flagon of cold water, which had something of the flavor of the outside to it. Nazarine suspected it was rainwater. She accepted it without comment, and ate stolidly, not entirely certain when her next meal might be. And after that, the servant appeared again, and in total silence led her through the odd and disjointed corridors of the old castle to one of the towers, so she surmised from the stairs she ascended, and to a cold room with a rude cot, which thankfully was furnished with a number of coarse homespun blankets. In the darkness, she climbed into the cot, piled blankets around herself, and listened for any sounds she might hear. She only heard a distant, soft murmuring, of an easy surf on a narrow sandy beach.

Pakhad was as good as his word, and sent the servant for her at dawn, or something near to it. She could see little difference from night itself. Breakfast was half a loaf and more rainwater. And then another passage through the dusty, random corridors, apparently to another one of the towers, where she was conducted to a large room filled from floor to ceiling with stacks of paper. Pakhad waited for her.

"And now we begin."

She looked at the untidy stacks of paper, seemingly in no order whatsoever, and for a moment almost gave in to total despair. *This bookworm couldn't find his own name in that mess!* She drew a deep, slow breath of the cold air, and let it out in a long, uninterrupted sigh. "I am looking for one each Jedily Tulilly."

Pakhad looked about thoughtfully and asked, "Give me some categories, some references. A woman, yes? That alone will not help us."

"I know very little of exact facts; what I have is approximate, relative. Age elderly, past maturity. I know she was in The Mask Factory, but I do not know how long, or when she went in."

"Did she come out?"

"No. She ended there."

"More?"

"Before she went in, she was apparently well off, but I don't know the occupation, or residence. Presumably Symbarupol, although there I am guessing."

"But definitely in The Mask Factory?"

"Yes. Immediately before that, she was a rehabilitee, working in the Bureau of Public Roads. I think she was in The Mask Factory for a long time. What they did to her there couldn't have been done fast." Nazarine suddenly felt a hot flash of embarrassment, at herself. For all her powers and all she knew, what she had on Jedily was still almost nothing.

Pakhad glanced about the random stacks of paper, scratched his chin, paced back and forth, adjusted the lamps, and muttered to himself, inaudibly. Finally he selected a stack of papers, and went through it, searching. Then he put the stack back in its place. He said, "I haven't yet succeeded in setting up the kind of order I want, so one has to try things out. There is no index. I was not, of course, interested in individual cases, so I have little on that. Only as one of a category will we find anything."

"Can I help?"

He shook his head. And went on searching. Pakhad tried another stack, with the same results. And another. Presently, he came to a stack which he first started going through rapidly, and then slowed down. Leafing through, he finally stopped on a single bound sheaf, which he extracted, and handed to Nazarine. "This is it. Do you want it, or will you study it here?"

"Here will do. I travel light. There may be something there, maybe not. But what I need from there . . . I don't need a copy."

"I have work here. Use the main room."

Nazarine took the papers and threaded her way through the structure, back to the sitting room, where she settled in a chair before the smoldering fire and began to read through the forgotten documents. Hesitantly at first, but with growing absorption. The nameless servant brought her some herb tea in an earthenware pot, with a matching cup, but it cooled before she thought to drink it.

Nazarine walked slowly back up the coast road, if one could call it that, back toward Karshiyaka Town, her head full of unassimilated facts. Much of the file had dealt with the regimen of treatments which Jedily had been put through, at which Nazarine alternated between outrage and astonishment. Those things had been done to her herself. True, she had no memory of them, or at best, mercifully obscured horrors which even Rael had avoided and forgot as much as he could. But what was the most amazing thing of all was that the procedure they were using on Jedily was one that had been used many times before, an exercise that took place in territory which was very familiar to the people performing the . . . exercises. They had had plenty of failures, but they were working within the bounds of a known system. Something that had collected its own idioms and cross-references. *They had been trying for the Morphodite for a long time.*

They had expected more of Jedily than the usual subject that fell into their nets. There were notes jotted down along the margins of some of the sheets, to indicate that someone knew she was less than their usual prey. More than one marginal note made reference to "twice-rehab." So they had not been grabbing at random. Perhaps at first. Not with Jedily. They knew what they were getting. That could only mean that there was someone within The Mask Factory who had contact with the off-worlders—the group covered by the Oerlikon Mission.

As for Pternam, who had seemingly set the process in motion, he was revealed to be a relative latecomer, only brought into things late in the game, when they began to think that they would succeed. There was their error, she thought wryly. Pternam had been ever more unprincipled than they had been, and quickly took over the whole project to his own ends. And that raised its own question, which she dared not ask, knowing that there are evils in the world and time that one would rather not know: what would they have done with Rael without Pternam? They had been reaching for the deadliest weapon in the universe, and surely somewhere someone knew what that weapon's target was to have been. It was Pternam who had turned Rael loose upon Lisagor.

The file had contained numerous reproductions of Jedily at various parts of her life. Nazarine had looked at these with disbelief, and some amusement. An odd sensation of vertigo. *After all, this was me!* Jedily had been a rounded, soft woman, with a ready smile and alert, flashing eyes, slightly taller than average. There was no resemblance at all to the thin and saturnine Rael, who resembled a half-civilized Makhak, or the petite Damistofia. Jedily had had a slight double chin which, someone had noted, suggested a sensual disposition.

They were thorough, and covered their tracks only superficially. There were two types of visual reproductions easily distinguishable: One set covered Jedily's life in Lisagor, which apparently commenced when she had been in her late twenties, standard. There was another set covering her younger days. No mention was made of where those came from, but they were equally obviously not Lisagor: spiky stone buildings and odd vegetation with needlelike foliage in the backgrounds. Within that group, there were a few of Jedily as a child. There the backgrounds were innocuous, but there was something alien about them. Not Lisagor. Not Oerlikon.

Jedily's profession had been interesting, too. She had been a physician.

Although few women practiced medicine on Oerlikon, apparently no one had questioned her, once she was established. She had worked within one of the larger clinics in Symbarupol, and specialized in the treatment of degenerative ailments of the aged. Her certifications had been managed as a case of self-education and success as passing the myriad tests of Lisak society. Once established, she promptly buried herself in one of the enormous civil service hierarchies as a supervisor of some obscure program. This was traced out with meticulous care. They seemed to think it important, as if somehow these facts were justification for something. There was one line which had been particularly interesting: it had read:

"*Last assignment:* Certification Section, Symbarupol. Oversees induction of indigents and defectives into rehabilitation processes. Approves quotas set by Medical Experimental Station."

Indeed it was! Jedily had been the monitor of the input into The Mask Factory! The conclusion was unavoidable: she had been promoted routinely into a routine position, but there was something she saw in that for which . . . the offworlders silenced her by erasing her and dumping her into the very program she was monitoring.

Nazarine walked on, shivering in the cold wind; perhaps more than from the wind blowing off the gray-green sea, under the damp cloud cover. She felt emotions for which she had no name, but which gnawed at her vitals, at the foundations of her precarious existence. She had drained the cup of revenge upon Lisagor and The Mask Factory, but had not yet tasted that which was of the killing of Meliosme and the children. And now another draught was set, as it were, by an unseen hand, on the counter before her: she wondered if there was any bottom to this evil at all, and she was reminded of the Tale of the Chagrined Optimist, a folk tale widely circulated throughout Lisagor: The Optimist said, as disaster befell him, "Cheer up! Things could be worse!" And as he cheered up, so indeed things got worse. And for the first time, she began to wonder if the way Phaedrus had chosen hadn't been the right way, after all. *Disengage.* It was beginning to seem as if there were wrongs whose scope visibly exceeded her formidable powers as the Morphodite to right. But just when the gloom of hopelessness closed in on her, she looked around herself at the bleak shores of Karshiyaka, and she thought, *Disengage, is it? Go back to the warmer parts of Lisagor and find an obscure place for myself, with a bit of fun with men to liven up the times . . . Yes, and no matter who I found, no matter how much it would mean, there would never be an escape for me, or those I might love, like Phaedrus. They killed Jedily, and they hunted Phaedrus, and they'll come for me, too. And whatever powers Rael developed, nursing his own plots, none of us expressions of the immortal is a god. We've got a blind side, and they'll waste enough agents to find it. No. And I've painted myself into a corner with the identity changes. The next one's to be early childhood. I could die of nothing more willfully evil than simple overexposure after Change, lying in the open and feverish. No. This has got to be seen to the end, and the definitive action carried out.* Some of the chill left her then and, rounding a headland, she saw ahead in the evening gloom the lights of Karshiyaka Town, riding lights on the ships in the harbor.

8

"When the situation has become impossible, incomprehensible, the meaning invisible, then we are wont to cry out: 'Give us the Truth! We must have it, come what may!' But it is in these very situations that the truth is in fact a horror that we could not bear to see, something far more awful than we could have imagined in our darkest hours. And then we do not change it, but it changes us. No, I think we don't want Truth, whatever we say. Facts, maybe, and not so very many of them, either."

—H.C., Atropine

IT WAS EVENING, in Tartary. Cesar Kham imagined that he had been walking for hours, with that same rude castle bulking on the horizon like some unlovely animal, that he had ceased to move and that it was the castle drifting, enlarging, obscuring the western sky, where a tattered yellow fragment, like burnt cloth, peeked under the masses of gray and streaked clouds that covered the sky. Did they never see blue sky in this land?

He shook his head, annoyed with himself. First failure in Clisp, and then this, brought on by having to operate out of this impossible location. Two failures, not one! Failure to accomplish the mission with confirmed results, and failure to turn anything up, a trip undertaken at great risk. And now he would have to spend more time in this bleak country, arguing endlessly with Palude over what they could do next. He came into the darkness of the castle, close, now, and thought, *"Well, absence of proof is not proof of absence. Perhaps that raid did the job, anyway. Perhaps if it didn't actually get The Morphodite it scared it off. Might well be skulking along the south coast of Clisp, hiding out in that empty land. What the hell—a person neutralized by fear was the same as dead, anyway."*

When he came to the door, it was opened by Arunda Palude, at which he expressed surprise, stepping quickly over the threshold to keep the cold, windy, dry air out of the chill castle.

"Waiting up for me?"

She said, pulling a cloak closer around her, "We knew you were coming; besides, out here on the plain you can see someone coming for hours. There's not much else worth doing, you know."

"I know. You must be bored to death."

"I am."

They made their way through the castle to their own quarters and sat down before the fire. Kham said, "Well, vile as it is, I'm glad to be back."

Palude sat before the fire, trying to wheedle a bit more warmth out of it, the light casting harsh shadows along the planes and lines of her face. She looked drawn and pinched. She said nothing for a long time, but then asked, "Find anything?"

"Not a trace. Nothing. Zero. I'm almost convinced that the job got done, or else it scared it off."

"None of the agents you contacted had anything?"

"Nothing. No trace of it. I'm sure that fortune-telling must be wrong. After all, if you asked for a reading on a dead man, you'd get a present answer, which is nonsense."

"There's a convention to these things: one doesn't predict death, and one doesn't ask nonsense questions of the oracle to test it—of course, the answer would be nonsense. But however that is . . . I imagine it was after you left Clisp, but one of our agents in the palace managed to get a report out by radio. It was relayed into the port, and a messenger carried it to me."

She had said the last with some difficulty, not looking directly at Kham. Now she looked at him. "It was the custom of the old days of Clisp to allow certain agents of the House to carry a sort of medallion, something they had had from the old days. There were very few of them, all under strict controls. Amadeo doesn't believe in handing them out, and so has recalled them all, and so they reside now in the State Museum. Except one."

Kham shrugged. "Could have been lost. Agents get killed, or accidents happen, otherwise."

"Somebody is using one. It's like a credit card. The user can buy anything he wants, and bill it to Clisp. They are honored all over Oerlikon."

"Why didn't we know about them?"

"The danger has been so great their use had been rare. But they are good everywhere on the planet and, so I am told, in more civilized places off it. And somebody is using one now. The royal Bursar has invoices from Marisol, and from Symbarupol. Somebody has one of the originals, and is currently using it."

Kham looked across the room, small as it was, as if seeing a great distance. "What sort of purchases?"

"Women's clothing. Food, lodging, all temporary."

"Did anybody get a description?"

"No. The agent sent what he had. Fortunately the invoice for the clothing was highly detailed, as would befit a billing to the Royal House of Clisp. Sizes were included. The agent was able to derive some generalities therefrom: a rather tall woman, slender in build, rather full-breasted. She also picked up some cash, but small amounts at any one place. The second report was on a billing from Symbarupol."

Something began stirring in Kham's mind. A coincidence? He began sweating. "What kind of clothing—nice stuff or workmen's coveralls?"

"Serviceable stuff, but rather nice in cut. She didn't stint on the quality, or so he said. It was also all stuff which could be adapted to different climates by using less of it. Why?"

"How long ago the report?"

"At least a tenday. You were probably still in Lisagor."

"Fits."

"What do you mean?"

"I think I saw her. She boarded the beamliner at Symbarupol. Something caught my eye. She looked out of place, taking the night train, and economy class, but dressed well."

"You saw her!"

"Yes. Same as the description. Young and good-looking, tall, with curly brown hair. I was going to keep an eye on her just in case, but I dozed off and she was gone. Some intermediate stop in the eastern mountains. Of course, it could be just coincidence, but I did see a woman that fits that description, who had no good reason in these times of poverty to be traveling at night, dressed that well."

"Did she see you?"

"Looked right at me, but turned away. She didn't look interested, if you know what I mean."

"How old? According to the information I have from back there, when that thing does *Change*, it regresses in age."

"Definitely not adolescent, but young adult. Twenty to twenty-five standard. I wasn't close enough to see better."

The expression on Palude's face softened somewhat. "Then it

couldn't be the one we're looking for. The one you saw is too old. We're looking for an adolescent, and one nearer childhood. From the predictions I have, I don't see how there could be any confusion. No matter how well built."

Kham leaned back and rubbed his bald head thoughtfully. "Maybe. It was an odd incident, though."

"Would you recognize her again if you saw her?"

"Oh, yes. No doubt. The one I saw isn't bland or plain. Very aristocratic, good-looking, sure of herself . . . only one thing: she doesn't look like any woman I ever saw in Lisagor."

"How do you mean?"

"I can't put it into words, exactly. I don't know if it was the appearance or the mannerisms, but there was something very un-Lisak about the one I saw. More like someone back where we are from. A more sophisticated society, a different gene-pool. Not Clispish, either."

"Could be nothing more alarming than one of ours."

"They aren't bringing any more in to my knowledge, and all those from the old days had full training in Lisak mannerisms—you, for example, fit perfectly."

"A Makhak?"

"Doubtful. This one looked too soft for that."

Palude sat quietly for a long time, and then said, "All my past experience suggests strongly that this one has a high probability of being the one we look for. But it's too old. I can't figure that. The process of change is supposed to be invariable in the rate of regression. If that one we found in Clisp was the Morphodite, then his successor would have to be no older than about, say, fourteen standard."

"No way this one was fourteen. This was an adult."

"Blocked."

"Maybe we are overreacting."

Palude considered, and then said, "We can't take the chance, as I see it. The last ship in sent a message to that effect. They want results. We can't stall them much longer."

"Hellfire and brimstone! We don't even have proof it's alive! And if worse comes to worst, I'll bite the bullet, report failure, and have the planet quarantined. We can stand it here if we can't do anything else."

"We need to find that girl you saw."

"Difficult. Trail's old by now. All I have is a description."

"Possible use of a medallion. That would be sure."

"*If* she's the one using it. We don't know that. Besides, I am not going back to Lisagor, ransacking the countryside, on a lead that small."

Palude nodded, and said, "I see. Very well, you are basically right. The tactics are impossible. But if that movement we saw reported is that thing, it's coming this way, and it will have to get here, in Tartary, to get offworld. And if a young woman like you saw showed up in the port, with a medallion, and tried to buy passage offworld . . . we'd know it."

"I can circulate the description down there."

"Do so immediately . . . have you eaten?"

"In the port. Not since."

"Let it wait. I'll have them bring food, and some hot water for a bath. Rest, relax. Go tomorrow morning." She stopped, and looked at the fire again, an unfathomable expression on her face.

Kham thought he understood. He hadn't thought she'd be made of nothing but mission dedication and logic. He said, "I'd imagine it was no fun here, either, waiting."

"Impossible. We . . ."

"Never mind. Don't speak of it. I understand. I, too. Leave it at what it is."

Arunda looked up at Kham from the fire, and said, "I fit in Lisagor, you said."

"So do I. We all did."

"Just so. And there are customs of that country."

"I know them well. Most of my life. No one will judge it amiss if two Lisaks spend the night together to console one another's loneliness. Certainly not two Lisaks, rather more native than the originals."

She nodded, and her face softened, and her eyes took on more life in the firelight. "I'll send for the food and the tub."

Kham thought that his appearance always convinced the women he met that he would be violent, stormy, tempestuous. For some, who seemed to expect this most, he allowed himself to be. But with others, who would allow him to be himself, he was softer, gentler, more feminine. He let Arunda create the situation, let her manifest what was deepest in her. They had both been without for a long time, they both had needs. This was no deep striking of the thunderbolt, but a truce, a sharing, a treaty. It was not really what they wanted, either of them, but it was good for a while.

Now they lay side by side in the cold dark, wrapped up in the rough homespun blankets of Tartary, hearing the wind moan and fret outside, angry at finding this stony obstruction in the midst of this empty land of boundless air and spaces.

She said softly, "In the old days, I never saw much of you; when I did, you never looked at me the way you did at others."

He: "You were too important. Not Glist, or whoever had been before him. Just a figurehead. You did the summations, the real work. No disrespect—to the contrary."

"I know. I always spent the nights with real Lisaks. None of the mission people."

"That's why they always thought you cold-blooded."

"There were many of us who did it that way. It was dangerous for associates to have affairs. Aril, who was always carrying on with our own people, she was the first one pulled in when the trouble started, and her links with others . . . we knew it would come that way. And you?"

"Much the same. I was terrified of it, though. I always feared that I'd become entangled with some Lisak girl . . . and I'd want to give her everything. Take her offworld, the whole thing. Doubtless she'd have thought it worse than leprosy: 'I gave you diamonds, you gave me disease.' Returning to a universe of flux and change, inbred for generations to hate it."

She: "They were less like that in Clisp, in Marula."

"True about Clisp, although not as much as you might think. Remember that province is the one that retained a royal family more or less covertly—the very epitome of conservatism. As for Marula, that was only surface. They were deeply even more extreme than the rest. You could never trust anyone in Marula, and one never forgot it, either."

Arunda sighed. "That wasn't such a bad world."

"True. I miss it already. Things seem less clear, now. I don't like this business at all. I've done my duty, very well, but it's not like before. The lightness is gone out of it."

"I, too. Well-said. The lightness is gone. But what can we do?"

"I considered vanishing back into Lisagor. The Morphodite may be worth all that trouble, but I'm not. I could disappear. So could you."

"Is this a proposal?"

"No. An alternative. We can run."

She: "Not very far. And you only saw *them* at the end, when they had already made up their minds. I saw more of it. I could not avoid the idea that this problem with the Morphodite was more important than the whole project . . . and had been for a long time."

"Did you try to extract data from these impressions? I recall in the old days you were pretty good at that."

"No. I did not want to ask. I did not want to know. I always had somebody to report to, when I knew something, someone to hand over the dirty work to, and with this, there was nowhere to turn—had I found it out. I turned away."

"No escape there. Now we're back here, worrying."

"Yes. And I feel that we'll find out, too, in the end."

He: "Perhaps."

"Did you know anything about how they made the creature?"

"No. Nothing. I knew that some funny things went on in The Mask Factory, but not making anything like that."

"I have the same lack of knowledge, and that bothers me."

"Why?"

"Because we penetrated every facet of life within Lisagor. In effect, we really were Lisagor. It couldn't have lasted without us. You know that. But I never picked up anything about them trying to make a mutable human in The Mask Factory. Nothing. And don't you think that's odd? I mean, they couldn't just jump up and do it, could they? There would have to be some preparatory time, research, experiments, trials, failures. There is no reasonable path from point A to B. This implies. . . ." Arunda left it dangling. She did not wish to say it.

Cesar said it for her. "That was closed to us."

"How? We penetrated everywhere else!"

Kham: "Our own people!"

"It's the only conclusion. But I don't understand why."

"Right now I don't even want to think about that."

"Exactly. All the possible implications are ill."

He: "If we follow that out, as they may well imagine that we may do, then our lives are worthless. If they would send us here, back, to kill the Morphodite, then if we returned we'd be walking into a trap."

She: "Possible. I'll run a computation on it tomorrow. Not tonight."

"What do we do about *it?*"

"Report it dead, depart, run away from Heliarcos."

Kham was shocked at the candor, and more at the boundless mistake that would be: "Foolish. We don't know the old worlds well. We've been here, on this backwater planet."

"We may have to. I want to think about this. Weigh alternatives." At the last, her voice had sounded weightless, drifting. Kham listened for her to ask something else, but instead he heard the deep and regular movements of the breathing of sleep. He readjusted his position slightly, feeling the warmth of the woman next to him, and fell asleep effortlessly, like a child. But he had some disturbing dreams of running from a formless thing that materialized wherever he turned. And another one, about a sworn enemy protecting him. He remembered these dreams, because he had few that he could remember.

In the morning, they slept late, and woke up looking guiltily at each other; not for finding a fellow-body in bed with one, but for becoming so lazy. Palude chided Cesar Kham: "One night with a woman, and already you've gone to hell in a handbasket."

Kham sighed and put his hands behind his head. "Worthless, I admit it. Absolutely worthless. And you know, there's something to that, too."

Arunda sat up, wrapping the blanket around her, and untangling the strands of her hair. Some of the strands were gray. She yawned lazily and asked, "What?"

"I was thinking of a way to make sure that you would have a society that would be proof against change, against responsibility, against all forces. Make sure it's acceptable for everyone to have as many affairs as possible, and all the rest of the decisions will be made for them by the higher-ups. And of course cover food, housing, and a little money. Not much. None of that happened by mistake, I think."

"You mean by accident."

"Yes. By accident. I think it was designed in from the beginning. And the Changeless weren't anywhere smart enough to do that. They just wanted a place to get to where they could stop Time. They didn't have any idea why it moves."

"You mean the Regents were on this planet . . . from the beginning?"

"A long way back. Maybe before the Changeless came. But they saw the opportunity . . . and that with all those different cultures and racial types coming together, they would never, never fuse together into the monolithic whole they wanted unless one built in the sexual connection from the beginning."

Arunda leaned back, and said, "But they always said that they wanted to study this society, that it was unique in its resistance to change. . . ."

"Then how is it we had no warning about what was going on in The Mask Factory? That place should have been crawling with our people, reporting through you at Glist."

"No reports, no people."

Arunda looked at Cesar. "I never questioned that. That was just the way it was when I came to Oerlikon. I assumed that we had enough control to ignore it."

"Uh-huh," he grunted. "Just right. Me, too. We were all told we were there to . . . study it, and add a little bit of stability; but how many of us were there, really? Do you know?"

"I only knew the actives. And when we did pull out, even of those we only took the key people. There were many others. . . ."

"How many? Assume all this had been going on from the beginning. . . ."

She looked up at the dim ceiling, sooty beams, and thought. Finally she said, hushed, "Cesar, that's almost sixteen hundred years—Oerlikon years, according to that insane calendar."

"A lot of continuity, a lot of people shunted onto Oerlikon over that period."

Arunda looked away, and then back. "Why? If it went on that long, there would have to be an iron will behind it, maintained with more severity than the Lisaks used. Transferred from generation to generation. That's hard to believe."

"You were deeper into the administration than I. How far back do you know it goes?"

She: "Well, I don't *know*. I mean, I ran into the Oerlikon project when I was in the University, on Heliarcos. It was in existence *then*. They described it as a long-term project. I never saw how long. I assumed it went back a few generations, but never how many." She stopped. "This is unreal! What could possibly be the purpose for such a long-term project?"

Kham looked off, straight ahead, eyes unfocused as if viewing some personal demonland. "Consider the possibility: if true, then the population of Lisagor would come to consist of a majority of offworlders, trained to a specific social identity, sworn to secrecy, and retiring on the planet. *There were no Lisaks!*" He stopped, and then went on, "I exaggerate. But a situation was created in which the stabilizing faction came to become a majority. And who would question it? Most of the project people either retired with a stipend on Lisagor or went back to Heliarcos to teach, or enter the Regents. We were never on Lisagor to observe. We were there to control!"

"Why?"

"To make sure that there was one place where somebody would have a long time to do something, long-term effects of hormone and endocrine controls. And what did The Mask Factory do? And why was there no entry into it for our people?"

"For God's sake, Cesar! Next you'll tell me the Regents were the ones making the Morphodite."

"Well?"

"Why?"

"Who knows that? But here, they would have time, and they would also have a place where the people wouldn't ask questions. Those who did would wind up finding out first hand what went on in The Mask Factory. The planet was out of the way, and of no great interest to anyone, everyone there tied up with his own pet interests. And if they were trying to create a creature like the Morphodite, and it got loose, they would have it isolated here. Let it ravage Oerlikon! They could keep it here!"

"But your argument fails in the present. They don't want quarantine."

"Of course not! They'd have to say why. Doubtless the reason they would give would be untrue, but there's still great risk there. It contaminates the experiment."

"Then that is why they sent us back."

"Exactly."

"When did you . . . understand this?"

"This morning. I just thought of it. It came together in my head. Remember? They want us to use these priorities: first, to capture it and secure it; second, to kill it. Losing Pternam was a real blow to them, but they could work from a specimen backwards. They *want* it."

"What about Pternam? Was he one?"

"Of them? Oh, no. They'd have their controls there, but it wouldn't be the visible key people. No, Pternam was working his own game. He was a real Lisak, and now that I think of it, probably a very sick one, too. I mean, he had no relationships with anyone, and he was pathetically eager to sell out to the offworlders. I detested him after we cut Charodei out of influence, and had him thrown overboard with a great deal of pleasure."

Palude reached out of the rough bed to the cold floor, trying to find her robe where she had thrown it out from under the covers the night before. Finding it, she slipped into it, and stood up, wrapping herself in it against the cold. She said, turned away from Kham, "I didn't feel at all good about coming back here on this mission. Here, I felt more uneasy. There was something profoundly unright about it, some concealed purpose I could sense but couldn't define. But if half of your conjecture is true . . ."

"Oh, I'm sure the idea I have seen isn't all of it. It may be yet worse. But so much is enough, anyway."

"Too much! And this of course makes the problem a personal one, now. And if we haven't scared it off, but awakened it, it certainly has reason to come looking for you and me."

"It might well pursue you to the ends of the universe."

"Perhaps. But it may also see a more pertinent target and not spend so much time on us."

"Cesar, we set off a series of events that killed its closest relations!"

"If not us, they would have sent someone else. Oh, we are guilty enough—I do not scamp that. But the impetus comes from back *there*," and he gestured with his head at the invisible sky beyond the ceiling. "*There.* And if that thing is as dangerous and perceptive as they seem to think, it probably isn't going to waste a lot of time on tools. One doesn't execute guns for murder, nor does one maim hands. One goes back to the will, the heart of the matter. At least, that."

"Will you alert the port authorities?"

"I think not. But we should move down there. If it's that girl I saw, I'll recognize her again. I want to . . . make the decision then. Anyway, we won't have another opportunity."

9

"A stable and a worthy world, a quality world in the sense the Sophists used the term, a Tao world, is built, line by line, not of brilliance and technique, but simply a matter of timing, as in music. And after John Cage, sometimes the right note is silence. One measures the beat by the emptiness between. Figure and ground. This is neither old-knowledge nor that which is yet to be seen, but a transcendental that each must reaffirm."

—H.C., Atropine

AFTER SHE HAD returned to Karshiyaka, Nazarine had spent several days integrating the facts from Pakhad's files into what she already knew, and building a new base for a reading of conditions as they were. The results, in one part, did not surprise her: the impetus for the sustained work on creating the Morphodite, which they referred to as the Transformer, was wholly offworld, as had come the decision to dismind Jedily and dump her into The Mask Factory. Wholly. The minds behind those decisions were not on Oerlikon, had never been. For her there was even less reason to pursue the remnants of that group than there was to disengage. They were scattered to the four winds. When she ran a scan through the oracle for the location of Avaria, the reading was "not available." Not "died," or "in a particular place," but "not available." Unreachable. When she had tried to amplify the scan, push it a bit, it gave out the symbol for insignificance. Wherever Avaria had gone, he was both powerless and inconsequential.

And if the Change in Lisagor had caught the main body of offworlders by surprise, it had devastated the creators of the Transformer. They were not only unprepared, they could not even conceive of such a thing happening. Nazarine did not know how far back the work went. But it was far back, and in the tumults she had set off by Rael's single act, she had managed to negate the laborious plodding and secrecies of generations. If for no other reason, they would punish the creature they had suffered so much from, that its freedom and escape not go un-avenged. She could not run, she could not hide, and she could not interpose a defense between her and them. Therefore the only course remaining open was to attack. And to attack meant that she had to go offworld, back into whatever kind of society had sent them all out in the first place.

She reasoned that since there was no direct contact with Lisagor, that the contact would have to have been done from Tartary. Somewhere in Tartary. And careful listening in taverns and along the docks soon revealed that there was only one port of significance in Tartary, and that strange folk walked there yet, people neither Lisak mariners, Makhaks, nor any other Oerlikonian race. The oracle confirmed it.

Passage across the ocean to Tartary was not easy to arrange. Most of the ships and crew tied up in Karshiyaka harbor were strictly local traders who worked across the north coasts in the easy seasons, and southwards to the Pilontaries in the winter. A few venturesome souls rounded the point of Zamor to go on to Marula (where there was much destruction of porting facilities yet). A trip around the continent to Clisp seemed to evoke astonishment, and a voyage to Tartary elicited gasps of awe.

Nevertheless, she eventually turned up one, the *Rondinello*, loading fleischbaum pod, and its captain and owner-aboard sailed whenever he had a full cargo, fair sea or foul, and he rarely asked questions. He and his scanty crew made a living working the margins where others dared not go. The *Rondinello* was a rounded, ungraceful sailing ship with a central hold for cargo, a forecastle for the crew, one cabin for the captain and the mate, and two small cabins, hardly more than closets, for whatever passengers might wish to risk the vast unknown seas of Oerlikon. She had contacted the captain, paid her debts off with the cartouche, and carried her small baggage aboard.

Nazarine noticed the crew paid little attention to her; they were so inured to the stark ways of the *Rondinello* that even a woman aboard did not seem to wake them up. They glanced at her once, dismissing her as totally out of reach, and then went stolidly back to work.

The navigator was a dour little man, pot-bellied and bandylegged, and when asked about departure, growled, "Evening, night, maybe dawn. The cargo's loaded, the ship's stowed. We're waiting for the captain now. Stay aboard. He's looking for another passenger. Bad luck to go with an odd number of them." At that, the mate vented off a muffled little chuckle, turning his mouth down to one side, as if finding another passenger in this season were the most impossible task imaginable. Nazarine went inside her tiny cabin, in the chill harbor-damp air, and wrapped herself up in blankets from a wall-cupboard, and waited. After a time, the afternoon, already late, slowly faded into evening, and lights began to come on in the ships anchored out in the harbor, and across the docks in town. She made herself comfortable, and drifted off into a dreamless light sleep, soothed by the quiet motions the *Rondinello* made at her moorings.

She awoke in darkness. She looked through the porthole and saw nothing. No lights, no ships. There were no stars. The ship was moving with a gentle, but deep rolling motion, and Nazarine understood that they were underway. The wood and cordage made quiet flexing noises, and the water made soft noises against the hull. The rest of the ship was quiet. She arranged things as best she could, made a light supper of some bread and hardcurd she had thought to bring with her, and went back to sleep.

The morning came under leaden skies, a bitter wind out of the northwest, and a loping, rolling motion of the ship. Nazarine came out onto the deck and glanced at the steersman's binnacle. Their course was northeast, edged off toward the north. Into the dim daylight of the high latitudes, regions of wind and wave that circled the watery poles of Oerlikon forever.

Tied up alongside the dock in Karshiyaka, half hidden by bales and boxes, the sails shipped, the *Rondinello* had been nothing more than a thing, an artifact, a member of a class. But now, out on the open ocean, it became individual, realized, something powerful real and unique. Nazarine, who had never seen any sort of ship except in pictures, the act of seeing, perceiving the *Rondinello*, was a luminous experience. She went to the rail over the bulwarks and steadied herself against the powerful roll and pitch, cloaked and hooded against the cold wind, surrendering to becoming part of the flow of real time, now, eternity.

Like all the ships of Oerlikon, save the powered vessels used only by Clisp, the *Rondinello* carried lateen sails on the main and mizzenmast, the mizzen considerably smaller. In addition, a stubby bowsprit protruded from under the forecastle, supporting a small artemon to steady the head. Three pieces of canvas against the immense gray ocean, the overcast sky, the wind that never stopped. The ship itself was all of wood, cloth, and cord, round and tubby at bow and stern, broad-bellied in the tradition of millennia of merchantmen on the seas of a thousand planets, about thirty meters in length, ten broad at the widest part aft of the mainmast.

The wind was steady, and few of the small crew were visible. Nazarine, while experiencing this moment as something pristine, nevertheless felt herself unconsciously adjusting to the ship. It came so easily that she forced herself to ask herself: *How do I know how to walk, to stand without motion sickness?* Jedily again, the template left behind: not a memory, but the set of actions left behind by the imprint of a memory. Jedily had sailed on this very ocean, sometime, somewhen. Long ago. Perhaps she had made this very journey to Tartary, for reporting to her superiors. There and back. And certainly she would have made the first trip, from Tartary. Maybe more than once. She shook her head, trying to banish the ghosts of ancient movements, to return to the present and the *Rondinello*. She thought, *I am now only what I am and I have a job to do.* And that worked, but as all real acts do, it raised further questions. *And what in truth is that job? To release the Apocalypse? To punish the guilty? Bullshit. The guilty punish themselves to the end of time, and the misery they cause is only a by-product of their self-torment. A billion deaths would not bring Meliosme back for a microsecond, nor would they restore the center feeling that Phaedrus once, for a little while, attained.* Then, out of nowhere, the connection invisible, came the thought, the realization, *I was created an instrument of a hostility and a rage so deep it could not be plumbed. Down the ten thousand stairs! But I have to learn to love, to give. That is all that prevents us from falling upon one another like vermin and rending one another. I have the Power to destroy; but how would I configure this Power, to create? I was Rael, the Angel of Death, I was Phaedrus, centered, desireless, at rest, neutral.* She sighed deeply, inhaling the cold air. *And now I must learn the most difficult of all the arts. And stay alive while I'm doing it.*

Returning to the present, into existential time, she saw that the other passenger had come up from the cabins and was standing by the mizzenmast, steadying himself with one hand, and looking out over the endless ocean as if he found it difficult to believe.

The outline of the passenger was hooded and cloaked against the wind and cold, and little identifiable showed. The pearly, shadowless light further obscured the figure of the passenger, flattening the relief of the shape beneath. It could be anyone, any age, any sex. The figure turned slightly, an alert, defined movement, without hesitation. Not old.

Some of the face showed, but only hints. Nazarine stepped back from the rail and joined the passenger at the mizzenmast.

The passenger proved to be a young man of slightly shorter height than Nazarine, pale of skin and dark of eye and hair. He had a delicate, almost girlish face, but the finely drawn features were utterly without the harshness of Marcian or the perverse willfulness of Cliofino. It was, refreshingly, a face whose innocence was still written plain on it. She said, "You're the passenger we were waiting for?"

"Yes." He spoke hesitantly, and then added, "They found me. I had just about given up getting a passage."

She looked off at the sea, and said, "It's a strange thing that people should now pay to sail to Tartary, when not long ago they would avoid even speaking of it much."

"True. All sorts of things now happen. Why would you be going?"

She thought before answering. *Is this one they have sent? Impossible!* She looked closely at him and decided to step off blind, trusting to reflexes. "I'm going to go offworld. I hear one can do that from Tartary."

Now he looked out over the moving, tumbling waves. "I also." He shifted his position, as if uneasy, or thinking something over. Then he said, "Returning."

She leaned closer to the mast, feeling guided by something inside herself that was less than a memory and more than an instinct. "I have heard tales. . . . You were one of our visitors?"

"Yes. They say we can speak of it openly in Tartary. No one bothers with keeping it secret anymore, but all the same they don't advertise it, either. I came in the last group, just before everything fell apart."

"Were you in danger?"

"No, not really. I was in Symbarupol for a time, acclimating, but they sent me on to Severevost. There was little action there, and what we heard was always yesterday's news. When we heard they were trying to get some people off in Crule, it was too late."

"You take considerable chance telling me this."

For an instant, something flickered across his eyes. Fear? Calculation? She did not know. He said nervously, "You are not a Lisak, whatever you are."

Nazarine smiled now, looking directly at him. "True. I am Nazarine Alea, an agent of Clisp. Tell me your name."

"Lisak or real?"

"Lisagor is gone forever and Change is upon us. We have to be ourselves, for better or worse. How do you want it?"

"Cinoe Dzholin is as it was, and will be again. On Oerlikon, I was for a time Aristido Bandirma."

"Your name is strange and foreign, but it sounds more fitting to you, even though I do not know its meaning or significance." She glanced toward the forecastle, and added, "We will still have to be discreet until we get off the ship."

"I agree. But it's also true that they don't seem to care very much, now. At first there were some incidents, but it quieted down, faster than anyone expected."

Nazarine nodded. "It's true, that. But people were used to the idea of stability, of . . . channeling energy into private pursuits, and of seeing without perceiving. That was the way of life, here. They'll learn another way, but it'll come slow. I'd imagine there aren't so many of you going back, now, are there?"

"After the pickup, most of the older ones elected to stay. They'd grown used to it. A lot of the younger ones, too."

"But you didn't."

"No."

"Could you have?"

"Yes. But there really wasn't anything here for me. In the initial tumults, I lost some close friends."

"I'm sorry. I apologize for the circumstances." She thought, *You don't know how sincere I am in that. You were clearly not one of those who ran The Mask Factory in secret, but one of the gullible supporters. And whatever, whoever you lost, it wasn't because of the random mishaps of the planet, but was caused by me. These people suffered cruelty, too.* She said, "Only tell me what you will. I do not pry. I lost much, too."

"What interest has Clisp in us?"

"In the sense of absolutes, I do not know. I have imagined that they wish to find out what really was going on, here, and why; those are reasonable questions an alert and perceptive native might ask. At any rate, so I ventured aloud, and no one corrected me. At any rate, there is little enough Clisp could do about it . . . or prevent a recurrence, since by no means does Clisp control Oerlikon."

"Could it?"

"I doubt it. If you know Oerlikon well, you know we only had one war, and Clisp lost that one; we are not, by nature, grandiose people. Events like that are far off. No, revenge is not, as far as I know, what they have in mind." She thought, *It's easier to cite a government reason than a private one, as if that alone conveys legitimacy.* She added, "Besides, the

events allowed things to fall our way. And I imagine that we will rejoin
the community of those peoples whom we can reach. We have forgotten much here—we know little about the stars we came from. And so
here we are." She laughed a little. "You were a harmless spy, and I am
about to become one."

Cinoe laughed, too, a shy little chuckle with a hint of a sly reserve,
too. "Yes, I was harmless. We had all sorts of ideas about cloaks and dag-
gers, but when we got here, it was not that way. . . ."

"Never forget that Lisagor had real powers, and did not hesitate to
use them in the end. I don't know how you people live back where you
came from, but Femisticleo Chugun was as evil and ruthless as anything
you'd have elsewhere."

"Yes, yes, but we didn't worry about that. It was as if we were somehow more *Lisaschi* than the real Lisaks."

She answered, "And when we get back there, among all the strangers,
perhaps we will be even more strange, after the same manner: poetic
justice, would it not be?"

She half-thought he might take offense, but he didn't. He said, "You
have a wicked wit."

"I learned it at Court. That's one thing at least such governments are
good for."

"We lost them long ago, in the idea we could do better. What we got
in place of kings and princes were even more ambitious, and less
principled."

Nazarine said, "I believe you are a covert royalist at heart. First a spy,
and then royalist sympathies. That is two. Are there more?" Nazarine
felt control of events slipping away from her, felt herself saying things
she herself did not wish to say, necessarily. Of course, Cinoe was attractive enough, and maybe under other circumstances, she might have
taken time to explore this part of herself. But inside her deepest memory there was a pattern of a woman who had taken the Lisak way of life
to heart and wrung it dry. Jedily. Presumably she had responded so to
men she wished to meet. She wanted to take some control back, but at
the same time she also wanted to trust the Jedily-perception inside, too.

Cinoe said, as if relaying her own mind, "Are we going too fast, or are
we just disoriented travelers seeking company?"

She looked out to sea. "Both." She gestured at the forecastle. "These
are worthy men, hard-working, brave . . . but they are not mine. And I
see no other women. Circumstances . . . The Lisak way is to make do
with what opportunity and fortune present, for these alignments will

never happen again. They are unique. I admit, it's a lazy way, an irresponsible way, but we both know it."

"As strangers who learned it."

"Yes. There is more stress on legitimacy in Clisp, an obligation and mutual owing. How are things where you come from?"

Cinoe shrugged. "The young people have some adventures more or less, according to temperament; later, they become settled and make more permanent arrangements. Being in Lisagor was like . . . never growing up, and yet never being a child either. But I learned something there."

"What was that?"

"That it is important to share, to reach; everyone brings something of value."

"If the other can but find it."

He came back, "If the one that has it can find it to give."

"Well met! Well met, indeed! And now, let us go back toward the captain's cabin and find out if there is something aboard the *Rondinello* we can eat. I am starved already, and I'm sure we have many days yet ahead of us."

There was a cook, who lived and worked somewhere below the poop, in a part of the aft hold walled off for his purposes. Moreover, there was some heat in the officers' cabins, conveyed through the bulkheads by an ingenious system of flues and pipes from the cooking fires below. Some mild complaining by Cinoe and Nazarine uncovered the fact that some of the hot air could also be diverted by the two passenger cabins, although it didn't do very much good. Nevertheless, the mate said he would try to adjust the system so they could have some heat as well. Presently he went off to see if the adjustments could be made.

They also met the cook and discovered the hours of service: four meals a day were served on the *Rondinello*, dawn, noon, dusk, and midnight. They were early for noon meal, but the cook made allowances and set up something for them. On precisely the stroke of the noon hour, the captain came in, said nothing, and ate standing up. He left immediately. The mate returned, bearing the information that only one of the cabins was heatable, ate, and then he also left, muttering something about changing course more around to the north, so they could pick up a stronger wind. Cinoe and Nazarine were left alone.

She looked around the small cabin. After a moment, she said, "I don't want to pry through his things; I'm sure he would resent it, even if he's said little or nothing about what we can or can't do."

"True. I'd feel uneasy. This is no luxury cruise. We could go and see which cabin has heat."

"Yes." She made a face. "Probably yours. I always get the bad luck."

"Maybe not."

As it turned out, it was Nazarine's cabin that had the heat, and although by no means warm, at least in that small space the warm walls took some of the edge off the sea cold. They sat side by side on the edge of the bunk. Cinoe pulled his hood back, revealing shoulder-length thick dark hair. He said, "I became accustomed to the cold in Severovost. But you, in Clisp, you had no cold there."

She said, "No. Although Clisp is never hot, neither is it very cold. I have to admit I was thinking of desperate acts."

He looked at her sidelong, from under his eyebrows. "Such as?"

"I thought that if we were agreeable to each other, we might have to agree to share what warmth we could find."

"I had thought of that. But . . ."

She leaned back against the wall, feeling the warmth at her back. "Your cabin is still icy. And according to the mate, the captain is taking us farther north still. It will be colder. However hardy you became in Severevost, I'll bet you had heat in the houses."

"We did." He placed his hand over hers, lightly. She did not withdraw hers. Cinoe seemed to lack the brash self-assurance of Cliofino; he hesitated, as if waiting for a clearer sign from her.

She said, "You should stay here, then."

He leaned back against the wall beside her, letting their shoulders touch. "I would like that very much."

Nazarine knew what was happening, and something in her wanted it to. She moved closer, to feel the body-warmth forming between them. The part of her that was continuous shouted *No, no, not this way.* But the template of Jedily reactions said, softly, *Lie back and enjoy this. There's little enough joy in the world: Anyone's world. Take your share, too.* She avoided Rael, Phaedrus; she remembered Damistofia, how she felt. She could smell his scent: sea-air, cordage, smoke, something pungent, faint, underneath, that communicated directly to her body. *It* knew what to do. She leaned her face over toward his, and he turned his face to hers, too, and kissed her, softly, barely touching. Their lips were dry.

She relaxed, and then drew back a little. "Go lock the door. Something's happening to us." He got up, and fastened the narrow cabin door, and came back, settling closer to her, touching her arm to arm, flank to flank, hip and thigh against hip and thigh. Nazarine felt unworldly, not of the world, and yet focused at its very center, softening, melting, flowing; her legs felt weak at the knees, disjointed. Cinoe started to say something, but before he could voice it, she shook her head. "Don't talk, now." They turned to face each other, now kissing again, mouths opening, relaxing, exploring each other. Sliding over in the narrow bunk, clumsy with the motions of the ship, the newness of this; he whispered, "Better than the words." And she whispered back, "Let them speak as they will," pulling his body close to hers, and they lay down, touching face-to-face along the length of their bodies. His mouth was soft, light, gentle nibbles, and the body was wiry and strong beneath the heavy clothing, which they now began to remove without losing contact; a difficult maneuvering, full of elbows and knees, a tender, patient clumsiness with which they tangled themselves together, lower bodies bare, warm flesh behind cool air. She hardly felt his weight. There was a soft, insistent pressure between her legs, and then he was inside her and they were one, and for a little time, time stopped, except for the motions they made, together. Like climbing a long hill, steepening toward the top, and there a bright plateau where her breath caught in her throat and she felt a sudden surge of heat from him, deep inside her, then, at that moment, at her center. And very slowly, then they kissed each other's faces like children as they fell back into the present, the world, ordinary time. They felt the chill air, the sea damp, the motions of the ship; the rough covers of the bunk. They could hear the water against the hull, the voices of waves, the wind, the tramp of the mate on the deck, odd and random calls to and from the crew, as if from far away. The light from the tiny porthole was bluer, dimmer, later. They shifted a little so they could lie side by side, her leg curled over him, but they did not disengage for a long time, and they did not say anything; what was there to say that was of greater truth than that which they had just told each other?

Cinoe curled close to her, his face between her breasts, and Nazarine enfolded him, twining around him, feeling both their breathing lengthening, evening out. She felt, all at once, invaded, possessed, captured, and also an emptiness filled, and something long denied now completed. She felt very good, for the first time she could remember. She thought, *There is a rightness here and now, a flow I could surrender to.* A flower was unfolding at the center of her chest, and she wanted to sing, to shout, to whisper in a hoarse voice unspeakable things. It felt so good.

10

"Constantly, over and over again, one discovers that the people who made the greatest virtuoso use of a discipline, an Art, really discovered something within it (instead of exploiting it), were most often those who cast about courseless for years, usually gaining reputations as hopeless ne'er-do-wells. Then, one day, they saw the light. Chance meetings, coincidences, accidents. All this is undeniably true; equally true is the question, what becomes of those for whom the door never opens, the light never shines?"

—H.C., Atropine

NAZARINE UNDERSTOOD WITH the wisdom of several pasts inside her, that to love, to experience the unblended pleasure of it, one had to lay down defenses and become vulnerable, exposed. The nudity with which one made love was more than exposure of skin, it was an analogue of a deeper emotional nudity. But more, it was irrational and impractical, an utter refusal to consider consequences, where things might lead, or what could be in this for her. Or him. They felt timelessness. They filled the endless shipdays with each other.

The difficulties they transcended or ignored. That was the way it had always been. Nor did they, either one, ask why, except now and then, as a rhetorical question that expected no answer.

But deep down, she knew that this love affair that filled her with light *was* illusory, that the endless ocean, gray and wrinkled and heaving with its own passions, was not endless. Somewhere ahead was Tartary, and beyond that, another voyage across a deeper ocean. Here, Cinoe was just another wanderer in the no-time of Oerlikon. That was, too, illusion. He had come from somewhere else, another life, another time. He was returning to his own past. And she was about to leave hers forever. They were both passing through unstable zones of transition. She thought again. Perhaps it was so good for that very reason.

Now she stood on deck by the rail and looked out over the waters. The sea was always the same, and never the same. The waves and the patterns and motions they made changed hourly, and sometimes by the minute, and above the waves, the sky changed equally fast. She had lost count of the days, down below. She had lived in a different world. This one had become a little strange. Now the sky was more broken up, streaks and patches of open sky alternating with multiple layers of clouds. The worst of the bone-chilling cold was gone. Nevertheless she felt a chill pass through her. She knew she was, in some tormented and torturous way, Jedily, who had come *here* from *there*, but that was neat, logical, reasoned out. She only could remember back to Rael. Oerlikon was all she knew. She had been a weapon tailored to this particular world with a precision never before attempted, or attained. Her sense of the arts she knew told her that the art would work anywhere, and yet there were so many unknowns there beyond the sky. So many!

Cinoe appeared from the passageway leading down to the cook's cubby, looked about for a moment uncertainly, and then brightened when he saw her. He crossed the deck and stood beside her at the rail, content now just to stand close. "Watching the sea again?"

"Yes. It is the same, but it always changes and is never the same. Both, at once." She shrugged. "There is little else to do." She laughed warmly, "When we are together . . ."

"I know. Plenty there to do. I haven't done all, yet."

"Nor I."

"I was talking with the navigator. Ran him down in the galley. He says we look for landfall sometime tomorrow. We have made a record passage."

"How would he know? They have no idea of time here."

Cinoe chuckled to himself, showing laughlines at the corners of his eyes. "Oh, yes, on land. But navigators compute things differently. They use sidereal time. And their dayclocks, on land as well as sea, are quite accurate."

"Landfall, then. And then?"

"They'll have to see, where on the west coast of Tartary we actually are. Then we follow the coast around to the south. Might be a day or so more."

"So the voyage is ending?"

"Yes."

"And us?"

"We're both leaving Oerlikon. . . . At least for a time, we can stay together."

"True. We never spoke of that, did we?"

He said, "No. I didn't want to. It would have spoiled the magic."

"Just so."

"I don't know where you are going."

"I don't know myself. I always assumed that you would be returning to Heliarcos."

He said, "Yes. At least there, first. Then, I don't know. We have passage back there. But I don't know how things are there, what with all those who went back earlier. There may be nothing there for me to do. So I would have to find another place." He shrugged. "You are being sent out to see and observe. Certainly we could be together for a time. I don't want this to end."

"You are inviting me to Heliarcos, with you?"

"Of course."

"I will come with you. I don't want this to end, either. It has been good, what we've made between us."

He went on, "You've not been offworld. It's different, out there. The same, other ways. Humans don't change that much, but there are a lot of things you'll need to know. I'll show you."

"I won't embarrass you?"

"Definitely not!"

She mused, "You give me so much. I wish I could give you as much . . ."

"You already have. Yourself."

"Humbug. I gave you me, you gave me you; I mean something else."

"Well, maybe you'll find something. Or not. It doesn't matter."

She said, "I'll look." And for a moment, she was tempted, as she had never been tempted before, to give him at least part of the terrible secret she bore within her. The many deaths of immortality. Think of it. Forever. What every lover dreamed of. But here, a warning, a sourness, that came from the echoes of Jedily. If she tried, she could put it into words: *Never give everything. Love is sweet, but it fades. It's a moment. And it changes. Remember that. It changes. It's the best thing in the world, never forget that, but second only to that is knowing when to leave. Love was given us to console our loneliness. But to loneliness we always return. The contrast is what makes both worthwhile.* She said, "What kinds of things do I need to expect, where we're going?"

Cinoe looked off over the sea for a moment. "I don't know you well enough to tell you what would be hard or easy for you; there are places, little enclaves, that are more primitive technologically compared with the whole than Oerlikon, and those people don't seem to have great difficulties adjusting. In fact, they often become themselves the foremost modernists in the use of things that are really wonders in their own right, but most people just take for granted."

She ventured, "I think I understand; standing in a line is much the same wherever it occurs. You do have lines to stand in?"

"Oh, yes. Lines to get a place in other lines."

"I can manage that."

"Some of the . . . devices you'll run into may require you to learn new forms of dexterity, coordination. A different language. But that's all basic stuff. What will be hard is something I am not sure I can describe."

"Try. I am from Clisp, remember?"

"Compared with here, the way people relate to each other is more casual and more selfish at the same time. It is easier for strangers to meet and make love; harder to feel any lasting loyalty. It has to be that way: people move around a lot. There's little sense of permanence."

Nazarine heard this and thought, herself, *Here is a key I need to understand what happened! This was why they could be so cruel and ruthless and casual, about matters of life, death, revenge.* She said, "People who love don't necessarily stay together."

"No." He stopped there.

"What else?"

"You have to be alert, clear-headed, to find your own way among diversions that can trap you, prevent you from accomplishing; people are more casual about sex. You can't afford to become obsessed with it. Mind, it's not restrictive or possessive. But you won't find much like you had here, except in certain lower-order areas, ah, people there who have given up the idea of personal development."

"You sound as if you're hinting at something."

"That was one way they kept Change from happening here. It was set up that way and kept that way from the beginning. The energy spent on affairs would leave little energy left for more serious pursuits. There were some subtle methods involved."

Nazarine felt as if she were being pulled, firmly, in two different directions. On the one hand, the loss of something that had been very good. Cinoe was telling her plainly that once they crossed that line that demarcated Oerlikon with its artificial environment from *there*, they'd go their own ways, sooner or later. On the other hand, lovely as he was, and as good a lover as he was, he really wasn't very alert to the power she had to extract meaningful data out of very little original material. He had already dropped two pieces, casually, completely misunderstanding the value of those bits to her. She sighed. "I think I understand what you are trying to say kindly. Well, that's not so different as you might think from here. And of course I have things to do on my own."

"I hoped you'd feel that way. I thought you might. There's something about you I can't see, but that makes me think you would understand and adjust. And of course, for now . . ." He took her hand and held it.

She returned the pressure. "Can the cook heat us some water for a bath?"

"Salt water."

"Enough. We should make tonight last."

He said, "I thought so. Tomorrow everything will get busy."

She turned from the rail, taking him with her.

When she woke up, she was conscious of two things immediately: the small bunk she shared with Cinoe was empty, save herself. The second thing was that the motion of the ship was different: all the way across the ocean it had been mostly a pitching. She had gotten so accustomed to it she had forgotten about it. She wryly smiled to herself, and stretched her legs out into the cold parts at the foot of the bunk. *Got used to it already, did you?* It was time to start waking up, to become alert, to use the *art*.

The motion of the ship was now more a roll, with a shorter and more choppy motion. Nerving herself for the chill air, she threw back the covers and stood up quickly, feeling her bare skin prickle with the sudden cold. The deck underfoot felt odd, unlike the surface she had been walking on for so many uncounted days. She washed quickly, shivering from the cold water, to wake herself up. She looked down along the lines of her body, which apparently had stabilized: her nipples were pinched and wrinkled. This body had high, full breasts that filled the space across her pectorals rather than out. The belly, flat, carried a hint of an opulent curve to it. She thought, *Watch that: this body will run to fat if I'm not careful.* The thighs were long and lean, the legs graceful, but filled out and solid. She smiled again, despite the cold: *I like this body.*

Nazarine dressed and went up on deck. The sky was clear, for a change, a flat, opalescent blue streaked with pearl: high ice clouds. The sea was deep blue, almost black, broken with white-caps. And to her left, a long, low brown smudge along the horizon, seemingly as flat as the ocean, but slightly higher: a brown line that faded away over the horizon to the north. She looked about uncertainly for Cinoe, and found him up on the quarterdeck, speaking with the helmsman and looking about. He saw her, and came down to meet her. Together they went to the port rail and looked long at the loom of Tartary.

She said, "Tartary, of course."

He nodded. "Tartary. They raised Cape Malheur at dawn. Or so the watch announced. I cannot make any details out of that line on the horizon. At any rate, the landfall was somewhat farther to the south than they expected, and so the coasting will be shorter. They expect to make port sometime tonight."

She felt a sudden odd discordant emotion; as if it were one part fear and one part anticipation. The real adventure was about to begin. And perhaps another adventure was beginning to end.

She said, "We might well be here for some time, waiting for a ship out."

"Perhaps. And one might be in now. One never knows."

"Are you anxious to return?"

The wind ruffled his dark hair, stray black loose strands escaping from under his weather-hood. He looked off at the distant continent for a long time, and then said, "I was before. There was nothing for me here, in Severovost. Now? For a dare, I'd turn around and go back to Severovost, fish processing and all, if you'd go back with me."

She looked at her lover closely now, trying to see him as he was, not as she had let herself see him. The two images were only slightly different. He was a slender young man, graceful and strong, delicate and almost pretty around the face. For a minute she was tempted more strongly than she could ever remember being before. It took a terrible effort to refuse, to say no, to herself. She said, taking his hand and squeezing it, "I, too, have been tempted to just that. You will not know how much. But you know the world has no patience with people in love. We have things to do. I am to go out and see this fabulous yonder we abhorred so strongly, to see what place has Clisp in this new universe we've inherited."

He said, turning to look at her, "That's odd, you know? Usually it's the man who has to move on, for duty."

"I'm not leaving you; we're going together." She shrugged. "Besides, it's not as if we had been together for years. We really just met not so many days ago, even though it seems like longer. . . . Or maybe you do not fear me leaving, but what you'll do once you get, ah, back."

Cinoe leaned on the rail and looked down at the water. "We will both change, when we go back, that is true, Nazarine. One mask will come off. Another will take its place. But the past doesn't haunt me, anywhere there." He glanced up at the sky. "I brought my past here with me when I came, and that vanished without a trace. But it was long gone before that."

"You did not leave a girl behind; you came here with her."

"Yes, that is the way it was. No matter now. I say that to show you that in the way of lovers I am as free as you. There's nothing back there."

"Tell me. I have also known happiness and disappointments before."

He looked sidelong at her, curiously. "You are passionate and gallant. Yes, that's the word. But it was long ago."

"Say rather that it was in a different time. It seems long ago. I ended it, but it hurt as if it had been done to me. Tell me of yours." For a moment she caught an echo of Rael, and she tried to project this young man in the arms of another woman, a girl. What would she have looked like?

"I don't suppose her name matters. What it was back there isn't important. Here she was to be Aril Procand, and that was mostly how I knew her. We assumed our identities some time before we came to Oerlikon. It was all very ordinary—we were students together, and we sort of drifted into it. On the way here, she became interested in someone else. When we arrived, we found out we would be posted to different locations. Or perhaps she had gotten her new friend to arrange it. She went to Symbarupol and I went to Severovost."

Nazarine's skin prickled, and she felt a violent chill.

Cinoe asked, "You shivered. Are you cold?"

"Just a moment. It's fresh out here. I had to awake alone this morning, you remember." But something was opening up in her memory, a configuration of reality which she had once, as Rael, manipulated. Aril Procand! She asked, "Who did she have an affair with? I know some of that group—from Clisp." It was a hasty lie, but she needed confirmation.

Cinoe said, "His name, here, was Enthone Sheptun. He had somehow gotten connections with Central Coordination, and was playing an influence game. Aril fell for it."

Nazarine nodded, absorbed. Sheptun! What incredible fortune! She said, "You know, of course, that he was killed. There was a great outcry."

"Yes. They say Aril died during interrogation. Rumor. I don't know. She was never seen again. She didn't ship either. I asked."

"I'm sorry." But it wasn't the tale of love and betrayal that interested her but the information that, even after the complete disruption of the operation, this very green spy had still managed to get some kind of contact with the outsiders, and probably still had enough of that contact to arrange his passage out. She wouldn't need to cast about all over the universe looking for her answer; Cinoe would take her directly to it.

He asked, "And yours?"

"Cliofino. Let it go. I put that behind me, and now I want us to go as far as we can."

He chuckled. "We've tried a little of that."

"Not enough. And now let us raid the galley once more. I haven't had anything to eat yet today, remember. I'll bet you've already been at the ship biscuit."

Amew Madraz entered the common room that served Kham and Palude as workroom, dining room, and rarely as a gathering place for various sorts of conspirators, all of whom had negative reports to tender. Madraz restrained his contempt for these gabbling offworlders who spent their entire lives worrying over time in the conditional tense. Like most Makhaks, he was tall and gaunt to the point of emaciation, but in addition to the usual traits of the race, he possessed an extra quantity of a prized trait the Makhaks called *indzhosti*, a word which did not readily translate into any single concept. Aloofness, reserve, effortless calculation and mastery of realities, great personal force released only under steely, precision control. All of his movements occurred with a measured, inevitable cadence, the effortless grace of a dance whose rules and music could only be guessed at, for the uninitiated.

Madraz looked down at his guests from under overhanging brows and said, in the same low, uninflected voice he always spoke in, "Word comes from the port that we have a visitor from space."

Kham and Palude had been laying out alternating series of probability tracks, and they were surrounded by an untidy mass of papers and curious diagrams which somewhat resembled logic flow-charts. Now Kham looked up at the austere Madraz and asked, with some surprise, "How so? According to what we heard during the last communications cycle, transport isn't due here for months yet. Should be summer, or what passes for summer here, before we hear from them."

Palude looked up also, adding, "The *St. Regis* isn't anywhere near Cerlikon, now. Did they turn and come back?"

Madraz intoned, "Not your support ship. That one still runs on schedule as far as I know. This is another. Before, such ships passed through this section without stopping, when they came at all. Now perhaps their captain hears that Oerlikon is open to visitors. This one, according to tale, is called *Kalmia*. The lighter is down now, its agents going all up and down looking for fares, cargo, trade. Our factors engage them now."

Kham looked at Palude, and she looked back. He said, "Accident. The astrogator stopped reading comic books long enough to notice where they were, and they stopped on a whim. What luck!" To Madraz he asked, "And those passengers who were waiting for the *St Regis* to come back?"

"The ones who can pay or have it billed are boarding."

Kham asked of Palude, "What now?"

"At the least, we have to go down there and see who has gotten on."

"What had your last reading of the oracle suggested?"

" 'Journey by water,' from Tarot. *I Ching* said #64, 'Almost There.' "

Kham asked Madraz, "Are there any waterships in the port?"

"Two. One yesterday morning from the Pilontaries, so they say, loaded with refugees. Another from Karshiyaka, a trader with a load of fleischbaum, last night."

"Judas!" Kham exclaimed. "Chance sets us all astray, while we wait and ponder! Arunda, get your things. We'll have to go, and maybe keep on going."

Palude got up, hesitantly, but stood quietly. At last she asked, "Are you not going to report? Shouldn't we wait . . . ?"

"Wait for what? If that thing gets loose back there, we'll probably find out about it when the ships stop coming here at all. Come on. We've got to see if there's a young woman loose down there. Before the lighter rejoins the main ship. Once she gets on one of those things it'll be worse than trying to find it here."

"How do you mean? It's just a ship. It's got limited space; we can run it to Earth there, surely. And it's a long way to the next port of call from here."

"It's a long way between calls, yes, but if you've never spaced out commercial, you don't know. Those commercial liners are enormous, the size of cities. Cargo and people, both. That ship up there in orbit is probably larger than Marula. And we won't get any cooperation from the crew, either."

"Then if you think it's gotten aboard, you'll follow it and try to kill it."

"Find it and follow it if I can. Kill it? Not on a commercial liner. Captain's his own law aboard one of those. Traditional penalty for murder is ejection into space, *in transit*."

"Then what could you do?"

"Identify it and follow. Are you coming?"

"I . . . yes, I will come."

"Good!" Kham set about gathering his few possessions, and said, over his shoulder, "Settle accounts with Master Madraz, in case we don't come back. I'm going ahead."

Kham disappeared into one of the back rooms, reappearing after some noisy efforts with his things crammed into a bulging travel bag. Madraz was still there, unmoved and unmoving. He seemed to view the activity with the mild disdain of a small boy who had just poked an anthill with a stick. He withdrew his hands from the folds of his robe and proffered a small package to Palude and Kham. "Our commercial representative sent this along with the word of the arrival. Well he listened to your words, and well he complied. This, he said, was for you."

Kham stopped, came across the room and took the package. It was wrapped in brown paper, the sort used in wrapping breakable goods, but it seemed unwontedly heavy for its size. Kham unwrapped it carefully. What was inside appeared to be a small metallic tablet, about the size of a small woman's hand, rectangular, with rounded corners. It bore curious pictographic signs, some line figures of animals, others heraldic symbols whose pictographic aspect had been lost. The metal was silvery, untarnished, utterly without color of its own. It was very heavy in his hand. Kham looked at it for a long time in utter silence, and then handed it to Palude without a word. She took it, and asked, "What is it?"

"Bad news. That's the missing Clispish credit card."

"Then it's aboard the lighter."

"Exactly. And that thing can buy a lot of privacy. Yes, settle things here. We're going traveling."

else bare mud and rock. The mud was brown and apparently sticky, the rocks gray or dull black. The port had a hasty, ramshackle look to it, and also a foreign look, as if it did not belong here. There were native Makhaks in evidence, but only as the lowest sorts of laborers—she could sense that they were outcasts, and that the real Tartary lay elsewhere, somewhere off over the northern horizon.

Tartary was enigmatic, hidden, subtle. Nazarine looked out the window, sensing a powerful secret doctrine locked in the tawdry and ordinary scene she was looking at, if she could but find it. There was the weakness of her skill, carried forward from Rael, Damistofia, Phaedrus, and now herself: *She had to know what questions to ask.* Without that, she was as blind as the rest of the confused and terrified people around her, each seeking their tiny shred of the future surety, even if one of foreboding and dread. Tartary was like a bosel. They, too, were fascinating, enigmatic, full of arcane secrets, arrangements of life stranger than anything she could imagine. But bosels did not send forgotten people to The Mask Factory to become obedient lobos . . . nor did Makhaks invade one another's holds with the fire and steel of the Pallet-Dropped Heavy Troopers. Interesting, yes, but not important. Bosels were distractions; so was Tartary, however ordinary this part of it seemed—mud, stone quays, winding paths down the bluffs, sweating undermen, ramshackle taverns. Yes, that was it. One was surrounded by a million things that cried for attention, but only a precious few mattered, in some cases, only one thing. One could die of nothing more serious than simple fascination. She looked from the window to Cinoe, seeing his girl-delicate face in profile. She felt a reflex constriction in her loins, a desire-reflex that she did not deny. She had given herself over to it utterly, and felt no regret or condemnation. *It was beautiful. It is so yet. But it, too, is a distraction no less deadly than the rest of the things I have seen.* Phaedrus had tried to reach for oblivion, for utter ordinarily, complete submersion, and it had failed, and in pain and terror for those he loved most, a gentle, lustless love. She thought, somberly, *I did not ask for it, nor did I wish it, but I was created to a deadly purpose, and I must use that in order to . . . what? They created more than they could imagine when they made me. I could create a universe in which such evil could not exist, could not be imagined, could not even be denounced as a vice. Yes. I have that power.* And even as the strange joy of that realization flooded through her mind, like an echo there followed on it the converse, inseparable: *without the freedom to commit evil unimaginable, what little good managed to get done by accident would be meaningless!* Even more clearly, she saw this simultaneously: an image of herself and Cinoe joined in love, climaxing together, (how different his face was then from now. Her own, too, she supposed), knowing that sex was not an end in itself but a way to reach for a deeper sweetness that was ultimately unreachable, that essence of loneliness one could never share. All that, a meaningless procreative rite, conducted in boredom, without those other losses, those other never-was, never-could-be's. Figure and background. Signal and noise. *And I'm in terrible danger of being swamped by noise.*

She stood up and laid her hand on his shoulder affectionately. When he looked up, away from those others with whom he shared something she would never know, she said, "I'm going to the cabin and wait. I feel too exposed here."

In that instant, she glimpsed something flicker across his face, a slight annoyance. When they stepped across the threshold of the bursar's office down below, she had become a burden, someone who would have to be shown everything. He nodded. "You're still worried about being followed?"

"You get an instinct for these things."

"I'm not one to disagree; I've known that feeling myself. Well, then— go ahead. Tell you what you could do, while you're waiting; there's a self-paced language-assimilation set in there. Drugs, RNA, hypnotic learning programs. If you strap yourself into that, you should have the basics down by the time we join the main ship. They have them because you never know where one of these ships is going to stop. It will make things a lot easier for you, on the ship and back in the real world, so to speak. You can pick up the fine points as you go."

"I wondered how I was going to get through that."

"It won't change you at all—just give you the means to communicate."

"Do they really have the language of Oerlikon stored in there?"

"Oerlikonian? I doubt it. No, you'll talk to the machine, and it will learn from you, enough to start you off. I'll stay here—don't worry about being in the way."

"You're sure it's all right?"

"Certainly. I'm just catching up on things, swapping horror stories. I'll stay here, and meet you upside when we link up. And then you can begin to experience the real world."

"You're sure it's safe."

"Absolutely. Just lock the doorseal and engage the wall set. No one can hear you. Let it do its program on you—it won't change you, so don't fight it."

"When do we leave here?"

"According to what I hear, it will probably be night, and then at least a couple of hours getting docked with the mother ship."

"How will you get in?"

"Once you lock it, I can't. Come and get me when you're finished." He glanced at the others. "We'll be here, just telling yarns. No worry, we won't run out of them before takeoff. Go on and do it and get it over with, and come speak to me in my own speech."

She turned, saying, "Just so." Then Nazarine made her way through the eddying crowds in the lounges and passageways back to the small cabin they had taken. She opened the door, entered without looking back, and turned and locked it. Then she looked around. The bed was high up and partly enclosed. The cabin was spare and functional. Some pop-out seats along the wall, a bath cubicle in the rear. No windows. She nodded to herself, and began methodically taking her clothes off. *First, a hot bath. Then, the machine.* She only had one concern, and that was about possible side effects of the accelerated learning she was going to take. She remembered that the particular arts she practiced as the Morphodite could not be expressed in the language of Oerlikon—that whole system was both illogical and impossible in that language. What effect would Cinoe's language have on the oracular powers of the Morphodite? She tried to reason it out by analogy, but lacking any knowledge about how the offworlders' speech was structured, she could only guess. While showering, she tried to run a short-scan mentally, without using the hand symbols she had developed, and she actually did get a very blurred and indistinct reading. The question she formulated was: *Will learning another language degrade my abilities to compute in the oracular system?* The answer seemed to be negative, but it was a curious negative, with all sorts of side-features and eddies growing out of it. Still, it was a negative. She reluctantly rinsed off, dried in a warm air blast, and climbed into the bed, still naked. There, in the wall, she found a pull-out fixture whose operation seemed to be self-evident and failsafe even for one like herself. She feared this more than anything she had done yet, but after one deep breath, she activated the device, catching herself thinking that it was, after all, a shame that Cinoe would not be here with her. She smiled wryly at that. *This place was the first thing we had done together, in concert. Ours. And not really ours at all. Well.* And as the operating light illuminated on the viewscreen of the device, she said to it, in her own speech, "Very well, bucket of bolts. Do your worst!"

* * *

At the foot of the entryway to the lighter, Kham and Arunda Palude found a temporary office which had been erected for the convenience of the bursar. The lighter was itself a large construction of curiously irregular shape, as if it had been constructed with no aim for dynamic flow whatsoever. It stood on the flats before the water on many metal legs, a flattish, angular thing like a small city, casting a cold and windy shadow underneath.

The "office" was made of timbers lashed together, scraps, pieces of plastic sheeting that bowed and fluttered in the wind. Inside was a very modern communicator, presumably linked with the mainship *Kalmia* topside, and perhaps through it to other places. The bursar had thoughtfully brought down a portable heater which labored mightily to fill the tent with heat, but much of its output leaked out through flaps and rents in the plastic. Still, the outside noises faded. Kham felt an odd prickling about his ears and thought he could sense a sonic deadener. Speaking, he confirmed it. Their voices had, in this place, a flatness, a loss of timbre.

They had no difficulty identifying themselves and booking passage. But there seemed to be some problem about finding the person they were looking for, whom they identified as an associate long lost in the tumults of the revolution in Lisagor.

The bursar rubbed his chin, scratched his temples, and ruminated, "Well, yes, in fact, er, ah, I was the one who handled the transaction with that metallic slab. Well, myself and the local factor, who vouched for its authenticity. That was no problem. We've had some of these Clispians before and knew where to set up the billing to. But it very definitely was not a woman who traded it in, but a young man. Odd, that. He knew our procedures fairly well, but seemed, ah, a bit unsure of himself about the tablet itself. But no matter. It's a bearer-security, and the account has been an honorable one. They pay their bills."

Kham asked, "You are sure it was a young man? After all, identities can be disguised."

"The person who came to me . . . Wait, I'll describe him to you. Then you can see if this is your friend. He was not tall, but slender, a little nervous. A straight nose, large eyes, a well-formed mouth. Delicate, like a girl in a way, but he didn't move like a woman, if you understand my meaning. No beard or mustache; as a fact, I couldn't see any trace of one. Didn't look depilated. Rather long hair, shoulder length, loose and wavy, very dark, almost black. He had no special mannerisms, except for a slight nervousness."

Palude asked, "What language did he speak?"

"Same one we speak now: Universal Semantic Reference System. Spoke it like a native, too."

Kham: "Voice?"

"Definitely male, although I thought rather young, or someone from a late-maturing stock. That seemed to fit the beardlessness. Oh, yes, he looked green and inexperienced, but he also had something of the air of a small-time bravo with a woman stashed somewhere."

Kham sat back, puzzled. He glanced over at Arunda, and in her eyes he read the same perplexity. He had given her a full description of the woman he had seen on the beamliner, and in the descriptive system they used, she would have almost as good an image in her mind as his, which was memory, and a trained one at that. He remembered the girl well. And in no way did this person the bursar was describing resemble that girl. Especially the nervousness. Kham remembered that particularly vividly. The girl on the train had possessed an almost supernatural, reptilian calm. And from what they knew about the Morphodite, there was no possible way it could have *Changed* and retained its age. Unless: unless the girl he had seen was just an ordinary person. Possible? Still, what had happened to the one living in Clisp? He felt a powerful surge of indecision, of the sense of an impending mistake of judgment so vast that it could never be corrected from. He fought a panicky urge to throw his passage vouchers down on the desk and bolt from the tent. They had been wrong from the beginning! Then he went back over the ground he and Arunda had covered and recovered a thousand times, waiting up in that castle, speaking with furtive men who came by night, and spoke in whispers. He said, to the bursar, "Well, it seems like we've missed something somewhere, but we're reasonably certain that our friend is aboard."

"Could be. This one bought an open-group ticket. You know, like a family plan. He could have had friends with him. We were encouraging that procedure to make the workload lighter."

"Yes, of course. Well, we will go on and board, and see if we can find our friend."

"I wish you good fortune."

Kham motioned to Palude to follow him, and left the tent. Outside, in the windy, dusty open spaces under the bulk of the lighter, he said,

"The only thing I can figure is that our target *is* here. But somehow she's managed to pick up a decoy."

Palude sniffed, "Hm. Fine piece of work, to catch someone and then trust him enough to handle that financial transaction. The value of that cartouche is immense! It's pure platinum as well as I can tell, and in itself worth a fortune."

"Maybe he didn't understand that. Whoever he is, he seems to be a bit young."

"It's possible. I have the image you painted for me, and I admit she must be rather attractive, tall and good-looking, sure of herself, enough not to skulk. She could do it."

Kham gestured upward with his head, motioning to the metal bulk above them. "She's up there, sure as the sea's salt. And I don't think we can hope to find her before this thing lifts off and docks with the main ship. That will hold a lot of people."

Arunda nodded. "True. We've got less than a day to go through the lighter, and it doesn't look feasible with just the two of us. But remember that the voyage back to more settled space is a long one, even in a liner like *Kalmia*. Not impossible. Just hard."

"You know what bothers me?"

"No. Speak of it."

"That thing has an uncanny ability to move unnoticed right out in the open."

Arunda: "Yes, that especially. A sneak I could deal with. But this open invisibility . . . that's scary. You know, if she's as attractive as you say, that in itself could be a screen, too. And then of course she's got the *Art*."

"True. But we don't know how much she's using it. I think it's difficult and time-consuming for her to perform one of those divinations, and she's using it very little. I think that *was* her on the beamliner, and I think further that I surprised her."

"But you said she disappeared."

"That can be explained by nothing more than a little fashionable paranoia, or extra care, however you want it. From what we have managed to put together of that thing's abilities, I feel reasonably certain that if she had known what I was, I would never have seen her, and never returned from Lisagor on that last trip, and . . ."

"And?"

"And we have one advantage."

"Tell me."

"She doesn't know you. And I don't think she's sure of me, yet. But we know what she looks like."

Arunda reminded him, "We know what the one we *think* it is looks like."

"Very well."

"But your argument has weight. I think she's in there, too."

"Has to be. Her mission has been long done here. And because the assassination squad failed, she knows Oerlikon's not safe. She may just be moving for those reasons alone."

Arunda said, reflectively, "I follow it well enough. But mark, Cesar; she's got time now to start asking questions and use her *Art*. We have to be more careful now than we ever were before. And we won't have the freedom of movement we had here."

"Oh yes, a fine merry mess. But never you fear. We've still got a chance, and it may be the best thing yet, having that thing locked up in a ship with us. At least that narrows the range of the hunt."

"How are you going to handle it? You know you can't kill it aboard and get away clean."

"We'll identify it, and then transmit ahead for help. Sooner or later we can surround it in a space small enough to control it." And as he said that, something flickered through his mind about not killing the Morphodite, but capturing it and harnessing its vast incomprehensible powers. That was very tempting. And, as Cesar Kham saw it, within the realm of possibility. Only they had to be careful; they walked on eggshells and razors, and below that lay the descent into hell unimaginable. He shook his head. Yes, tempting, but the price of failure. *Consider the price of failure.*

Nazarine had not slept, but she awakened. She could remember every moment, every hour, every motion of the lighter, but distantly, as if the reality had been the dream. The instruction program was completed. She now possessed a foreigner's grammar, rudiments of rhetoric, and a basic vocabulary from which she could build. She sat up in the bed, conscious suddenly of a backwash of fatigue. And of other things, too; the passage of time.

She knew more than language; she knew certain basic machine skills, how to speak to machines. She reached, stroked a touchplate, absentmindedly, as if she had done it all her life. She thought, *And so I did, once, in another age, another life.* The questions she asked were simple:

how much time has elapsed, and, where are we now? The machine voice answered. She translated the unfamiliar time system into Oerlikon divisions of the day, and was surprised at the length of time she had been under. And the lighter had been late taking off, and was having to chase the main ship around the planet, instead of going directly there. But they were in initial approach already—the lighter pilot had mainship in sight. She commanded, "Show surface of planet."

The screen flickered, jumped, and then steadied as the proper sensor was selected. The screen showed a watery, deep-blue world slowly turning beneath, a land mass visible, curious and spiky in shape, the main body illuminated in soft morning slants, and a spine of mountains cast in sharp relief far to the west. *Dawn among the peaks of the Serpentine.* Clisp was yet in darkness. Swirls of cloud shrouded the north country, and fish scales and curdled masses covered the southeastern extension of the land, Zamor and the Pilontary Islands. Simultaneous thoughts and emotions collided in her mind, making her eyes burn: *I am leaving a place where I was tormented and mutated into a thing, and . . . I am leaving the only home I can remember. In any event, never to return. Never.* She commanded the image to terminate. The screen went blank.

Nazarine climbed down out of the bed and went to her luggage to find some better clothing than the traveling clothes she had been living in aboard the *Rondinello.* She selected a light knit gown, boots; the gown was a soft gray and followed the lines of her body, moving with her. The bottom of it was loose and fell to mid-calf. Over it she put on a darker gray felt half-tunic, very loose, a sleeveless strip almost as long as the gown. She moved about, experimentally. It had been an extravagance, hopelessly exotic for Oerlikon, but here, among all these strange people . . . She leaned over the bed and touched the commplate again, commanding the screen to show her typical female clothing of the times: the screen illuminated and displayed a series of images of women, of all ages, shapes, races, and occupations. The variety bewildered her, but also reassured her. There was here a variegated pattern she could hide within. She asked the machine what was the suitability of what she wore. The machine flashed STAND BY FOR HUMAN OPERATOR. And the scene shifted to an unidentified space. A woman was there, older, thin, intense. Bushy gray hair, coveralls and a loose jacket. Crew? The woman said brusquely, "Passenger. You need assistance?"

Nazarine said, "I'm a stranger to your ways. What is my clothing suitable for?"

The woman looked hard, offscreen, as if at another monitor, and said, after a moment, "Tasteful day clothes for a rich man's mistress going on a long cruise. Are you?"

Nazarine laughed. "No, to the first; maybe, to the second."

The woman made a wry face. "Whatever. What do you want to do?"

"Feel comfortable and not be particularly noticed."

"That does it, although with your body you'll have a time being invisible. But a nice choice. Nice stuff. Get it downworld?"

"Yes."

"Local?"

"Oh, yes. They don't have full trade yet."

"Hmf. Go on and wear it. It'll be all right." For a moment, the woman stopped, as if she were finished. But hesitated, and then added, "You're a local, from downworld?"

"Yes."

"On your own?"

"More or less."

"I understand; stop there. Look me up after we secure, I'm on the crew roster: Faren Kiricky, Structeering Section. I'll show you. Clothing is messages and meaning. Going to stay with us?".

"I think so."

"To find a place? Fine. Look me up. I can at least keep you from making statements about yourself that you may not want to be true.'"

"I'll do it. I need that."

"Super. Call me then." And the screen blanked. And Nazarine stood back on the floor feeling very risky and foolishly pleased with herself. What were the woman's motives for offering her help? Charity? Simple? Complex? It didn't matter. She had dealt directly with an offworld stranger, someone with no connection at all with the hidden manipulators of her world. That one, Kiricky, was not hunting her. The encounter had been totally ordinary. It was such a relief she laughed out loud.

She climbed down out of the bed and stood for a moment, uncertainly. Something was incomplete, but what was it? There was something she was supposed to do. What? She shook her head, sending her hair flying. Something was wrong. She stopped herself dead, centering. Where was she? On the lighter, moving to docking with the starship *Kalmia*. She had spoken with a woman of the crew, Faren Kiricky. There was where the wrongness was. But what about it was wrong? She cocked her head, disturbed. *Gods, I'm slow!* She had spoken with Faren, in Faren's language. That was what was wrong. She had felt the idea and spoke it. Simple basic everyday language, but it had come without thinking. She was thinking in it now. She could see the holes in its continuum where there were words and concepts she didn't know.

Nazarine pulled down one of the little foldout seats and sat wearily on it, putting her head in her hands. A fit of dread and fear washed over her, icy cold along her back, which was suddenly damp with sweat. Her hands were wet, too. She suppressed a sudden nervous urge to urinate. She looked up, at the blank and silent walls of the machine she was riding, to an unknown destination. She remembered Oerlikon.

What did that goddam machine do to me?! She felt tears of anger flush her eyes. *I gave myself to that incredible unknown mechanism, and the damn thing even gave me words to curse with. What else did it give me, and what has it taken away? Yes, gave myself, guessing, just like I gave myself to Cinoe. Unknowns there, too.*

She got up and went to her baggage, from which she extracted a common paper tablet and a pen, and she began working furiously, sketching in the outlines of a reading of the oracle, finding that it somehow went differently. Harder some ways, easier, others. It was subtle, but the way she handled it was different. She was doing a general reading of the environment around herself, with herself and two knowns, Cinoe and Faren, and an unqualified unknown who was the one, or group, who had sent terrorists against Phaedrus. Some of the operations she had to stop and reach for, hard, wincing at the memory that in some ways this was harder than when she had first tried *reading* as Damistofia. But it came to her. She remembered, and the operations began to flow smoothly, building to their conclusion. Nazarine sat back and looked at the diagram she had made, which she understood now resembled an ideogram of an ancient language, Chinese, only fantastically more detailed. Where in the Chinese, there had been a single line, in this there were scores of finger lines. It was as if the Chinese characters were blurred-out and overprinted blotches of her oracular answers. And of course, her ideograms were complete sequences, not just single word units.

This oracle said: *Protective coloration. Change guides; your old one has lost the way. You will have to lead him. Danger is present, but ineffective, as long as you move in shadow. Remain firm in course. On the way. Attempt no attack—this line is now too fragile. You cannot change it without affecting yourself.*

She looked up and sighed deeply. She had been completely oblivious of time, and wondered how much time had elapsed while she had been *reading.* But she knew one thing about her system that this exercise had taught her: it was a great deal more sensitive to subtleties. The finer focusing came a lot easier. She could still sense the upper range of it, but now she saw that as just the beginnings of the whole system. She could now ask for and do a lot more finely focused things. She breathed deeply, relieved. Her hands were dry.

Nazarine looked up at the bed, absently, and felt a short, small, sharp motion in the lighter. There was a distant, muffled, mechanical bumping, which did not alarm her. The lighter was docked. She was a part of the world of *Kalmia* now.

12

"Power is always relative—appropriate. In the conventional sense, one who is a power in one environment loses that power in changing to a different surround. Few change willingly; they are usually changed by others who arrange shifts to make this lessening possible. Is it any wonder change is a fearsome thing?"
—H.C., Atropine

DURING THE WAIT after boarding, and during the trip up world From Oerlikon to *Kalmia*, Kham and Palude had separated and circulated quietly among the passengers and open spaces of the lighter, hoping to catch a glimpse of a tall girl-woman whose image they both carried in their heads. Kham himself saw a couple who might have been, but on discreet closer inspection proved to be different from the one sighting he had had of the girl on the train. One in particular had her height and general bearing, color hair, and smoothness of face, but when he saw her from the front, any resemblance vanished; this girl had a long, equine face and a nose that was distinctive in that there was no indention of the brow line. His target had a rounder face, and a rather small nose. The other lacked the body, although she was graceful and willowy. Too slender.

As agreed, he met Arunda Palude by the exit ramp as they were nearing docking. He said, without gesture, "I had no luck. You?"

"Nothing. Although there's no shortage of smallish men with delicate features, girlish."

"Spacers of the commercial variety. Travelers. Bad fortune, that we never saw him and only had a fragmentary description to go on. Could be anyone."

"Why so many like that?"

"Agility, precision, fine-detail work. That's the sort you see in this kind of travel. Not like what we're used to."

"She couldn't possibly know what she was doing when she picked him."

"Couldn't she? What if she's recovered Jedily Tulilly? What if she's used her *Art* to see beyond Oerlikon?"

Arunda looked off at the wall for a moment. "You're assuming the worst, which is good tactical thinking, but which may not be true. I have another explanation, which will do almost as well: the attack that failed alerted it enough so that it knows it has to get offworld. It's moving blind. Cautious, sighted in part through its oracle, but nothing more. And some luck on its side. That won't run forever, and it's in our world now, not us in its world. Sooner or later it will have to move, and it will become visible. Then we can deal with it."

"Possible. Either way. But we'll get one more shot here in the lighter, here, by the exit ramp. After that, we've got a larger environment to search."

Palude did not seem worried. "And more time to look for it in. Here, it could hide somewhere, but there it will have to move eventually."

"It's seen me. If it sees me again . . ."

"I know. That means I do most of the looking."

"Not the way you think. You'll do the close work. But I'll be working, too."

"We don't have people on *Kalmia?*"

"Doubt it. Almost surely not."

There was a small movement of the lighter, followed by a short vibration, and then silence. Far off down the corridor they could hear announcements being made through the PA system, and while they were waiting, a crewmember, wearing a plain gray coverall marked only by a horizontal color strip above the left breast, approached them. He looked them over, and then made a visual inspection of the telltales, before unsealing. Apparently everything was in order, for he reached into a recessed panel and operated the switches that would activate the door. Behind him, the corridor was filling with people, none walking hurriedly, more drifting along in the general direction, most of them carrying bundles, some larger, some smaller.

For a time, they were able to wait by the door, but eventually the movement of the people created a small bottleneck, and one of the crew asked them politely but firmly to move along, and at a glance from Kham, Arunda complied. They entered the *Kalmia*, which at least by the entry seemed not greatly different from the lighter that serviced it. A long, dim corridor, unbroken and gently curving, unrelieved by side openings, windows, vents, or wickets.

They walked slowly along the corridor, and Kham said, "We only had one shot at it back there. Best to move on. We don't want to attract any attention. Not until I've had a chance to feel out the security officer."

"Where do you think it is?"

Kham gestured over his shoulder. "Back there. It'll be one of the last out. If this runway was straight and we could stop and look, we could probably see it now."

"Why don't we wait here?"

"Under observation."

"Then we've got the whole ship to go through."

"Right."

"Then we'd better get settled and get on with it."

Kham nodded, dolefully. He had an idea how difficult it was going to be, aboard a ship the size of *Kalmia*. "Right. Soon as we do get settled, I want you to relax, concentrate, and do a reading, see what you get."

Nazarine knew they were docked, but she composed herself and waited. She knew Cinoe had to come back here before he went on to the main ship, and she thought it would be better to wait for him, although she knew very well now, from her session with the teaching machine, that she could very well go on alone. *No. Let this develop as it will.*

It seemed a long time after they docked, but eventually he knocked at the door, and then tried it. He said, "I thought you might have gone on."

Now he spoke in the language of the offworlders, which to Nazarine's ear, although sensible and comprehensible, sounded harsh and clipped, congested with consonants. She answered him in the same speech, "No. I waited."

"Do you still want to share a room?"

"I don't know. I realized from the machine how little I know. I will have to have a lot more. I suppose they have such devices aboard."

"Yes. That one, like on this lighter, is just the rudiments. You can tie into the mainship's computer to get the rest of it."

"I feel like a fleischbaum gatherer in the city for the first time."

Cinoe stood back and looked at Nazarine carefully. "You certainly don't look like one."

She almost told him of her conversation with the crewmember, but she didn't. She said, "What do I seem like to you? I bought some clothes to travel in, but I don't know how these people present themselves."

Cinoe laughed, but there was a slight uneasiness in it. "What you have is fine. Very good taste."

"We are by no means bumpkins in Clisp."

"Yes, just so. Well, you will have to excuse me; the way I must go involves no frills. I get three meals a day and a place to sleep, and the good fortune to have a ride back to civilization. Otherwise, it's much the same as on the *Rondinello*. Except, of course, the heat. We won't be cold again."

She smiled. "Yes, the heat. I thought I would never get warm again."

"Nor I. But we seem to recover fast."

"Yes."

He hesitated, and then ventured, "You understand that if you remain with me, we'll go into the steerage dormitory, with the rest of us refugees."

She said, thoughtfully, "I'm not a refugee. I'm a spy, remember?"

"Yes. With an unlimited expense account underwritten by the Prince of Clisp. Well, down there it's pretty plain and not a lot of privacy. . . ."

"You could come with me. . . ."

For a long moment, she saw indecision reflected in Cinoe's face, in his body movements. Then she saw the change in him: he decided. "Might be better for us both if I didn't. Of course, we're not prisoners down there—we have the run of the ship. There's a lot here; has to be. This kind of ship does some pretty long runs. Months, sometimes years. So everything is here. . . ."

She sensed that he was looking for a graceful way to leave her. Why? She said, "I suppose you'll want to spend a lot of time with people you haven't seen in years."

"I've already met several I knew before. All have amazing tales to tell. There were some events in Marula!"

"Yes. I have heard some, from our side."

"And you will need to move around, learn, study. And do whatever things you must do."

"Yes. But we could still meet."

"I'd like that."

"I would also." She picked up her bags. "Come on. They'll lock us out here in the lighter."

Cinoe laughed, "Already you're learning to be civilized and be in a hurry."

Nazarine flashed him a quick, sharp glance, and let it go. It angered her that he would toss that off so easily. Uncivilized, was she? She had felt a dull pain in her chest at the thought of losing someone with whom she had been in love, with whom she had made love, yielded up everything, held nothing back, but that revelation from him blunted it a great deal, and restored some of the simmering anger she had almost forgotten. Of course, it didn't make up all the difference, but she thought she could live with what she had to live with. And she caught herself smiling, and thinking with some of the corrosive cynicism of Rael, from long ago, *You aren't here to rub bellies with prettymens, you're here to visit some of these people with fire and sword and worse. Like microsurgery.* She tossed her head, sending the gold-brown curls flying. "Come on." And she set off out of the room, into the corridor toward the gate, walking with a confidence she did not really feel, but she knew that would come in its own time. Cinoe followed, not saying anything, as if he knew he had already said too much.

When they had traversed the long corridor into the ship proper, they came at last to a long counter where accommodations were assigned. Cinoe went first, identified himself, and was assigned a place in steerage with a minimum of comment. The officer handling the assignments motioned him toward a group waiting toward the end of the counter. When Nazarine's turn came, she presented her credit voucher and asked what was available. It turned out that the *Kalmia* was somewhat crowded, more so than usual, but some places were still left, and so she settled eventually for a single room, with its own entertainment connection and a separate recreation room. The cost of it caused her to swallow hard, but she signed the voucher and the officer handed her a packet containing a chart of the ship and where she could find various things, including her rooms.

She approached the group Cinoe had joined. They were all silent now, not chattering as they had on the lighter. She said, "I will tell you my room number."

He shrugged. "No need. You can query through the shipmind. It'll tell you, unless you pay extra for unlisted registry."

She shook her head. "Too much already. No, I am listed as myself. Nazarine Florissante Alea, native of Oerlikon."

"I am listed as Cinoe Dzholin, as you know."

"I'll call you."

"Please do. I'll wait."

At that moment, a porter appeared from a side passage, and picked up her bags. This one wore a crew uniform, and asked her what her number was. The porter was a girl, stocky and solid, but graceful and smoothly economical of movement. She didn't even acknowledge the presence of the group of refugees. "What apartment, Serra?"

Nazarine hesitated a moment, looking uncertainly at Cinoe, who had turned his attention to a girl in the group and was talking with her. "Four-Q-two."

The portress nodded. "Right along. Up the lift and along the slide. Good choice. Come along. Won't be but a minute." She hefted the bags and set off down an adjoining passageway, not looking back. Nazarine looked back once, and then followed the girl, who strode along purposefully, looking neither left nor right.

Up to this point, everything she had seen had been more or less like things on Oerlikon. Now was when she began to feel the strangeness of the environment she had launched herself into. The portress went a short way along the passageway, and turned at a set of double doors in the wall. The girl said, to the doors, "Open," and they did. On nothing. A shaft, full of a curdled milky radiance. The girl waited for Nazarine to catch up with her, and then stepped off into the nothingness of the shaft, calling out, "Q." She fell upward. Nazarine followed her, stepping off into the lights. Nothing happened. She hung in space, supported somehow although she didn't feel that she was standing on anything. After a moment, she said, "Q," with a resolve she didn't feel at that moment. Then she began moving upward. Eventually she stopped at an open door, where the girl was waiting for her with a bored expression on her face.

She stepped out of the lift, not aware of having traversed any great distance. The girl said, "A short walk now, and we'll transition to section four. That's a slideway, but it's a fast one."

"Do I need to pay attention to how we are going?"

The girl looked around, and said, over her shoulder, "Good question, Serra, for a newcomer."

"Do I look it?"

She shrugged. "They all do. Look scared to death. Never worry. Ship doesn't bite."

"How do you find your way?"

"Oh, that. These are service runs. You'll never see these again, likely. They gave you a map?"

"Yes."

"Spend the next day shiptime studying it. If you get lost, in the passenger section there are commpoints all along the walls. Just use one. Say, 'Where in the bloody hell am I?' and it'll tell you straight off, it will.

Then venture out as much as you can, get a feel for it. It's a long run to next halt."

"Is this that isolated?"

"You wouldn't believe. . . . The Jefe-Maximo heard there'd been trouble here and diverted for it. Plenty of money in those rescue billings, he says. Otherwise we'd have transited straight across. Stop in the middle like this and the time's quadrupled. Passengers don't care— they don't pay by the light, but by mapcoords."

"Explain."

"The space the ship moves in is like a diagram of realspace, except that the distances in transspace don't always match. What's a light in real might be a cent, trans. And vice versa. This place is in the middle of a hole. Nothing there. Long in real, long in trans, both. Funny place, that way."

The girl now shifted through an oval opening onto a tubular passage whose floor seemed unstable, not there. She stepped onto the "floor" and was whisked off. Nazarine followed.

After several more arcane routes and traverses along floors that weren't floors, and passageways that seemed to go nowhere, they emerged through an ordinary push-door onto a balcony, overlooking an enormous open space which Nazarine first failed to grasp. She had to stop and get her bearings.

She was on a balcony or walkway, floored with ceramic tile in subtle geometric patterns, with a rail, which overlooked an immense atrium or park or vivarium. She couldn't tell. Down there, somewhere far below, was a forest, or a park, or a city. She couldn't tell. She saw what looked like trees, interspersed with low buildings and parklands. She could tell there was another side, somewhere far off, but she couldn't make out details. It was dim. All she could make out were strings of lights.

They passed one door, stopped at the second. The girl said, "Put your hand flat, palm down on the plate." Nazarine did so. The door opened, swinging inward silently.

The room was modest, quiet, low-ceilinged. There was a single large bed, a sunken area with a lot of cushions, and another door leading off to the side. The girl followed her eyes, and said, "Bath there." She went in, and saw another door on the other side. "Study cubicle." The portress set the bags down, and paused.

Nazarine handed the girl some of the money she'd changed down below, with Cinoe's help. The girl looked at it for a moment, and then fished in a pocket and handed Nazarine some change back, "Too much the first time. I'm honest."

"May I ask your name? I may have to ask for you again. I don't know many people here, and there are some things I need to do. . . ."

"Esme Szilishch. But you probably won't see me anymore."

"But could I ask, if I need to ask something? This is my first trip."

"Um. You grow up down there?"

"Yes."

"Call if you like. Got someone?"

Nazarine stopped, unsure of herself, and of offworld manners. She said, uncertainly, "I had. Not sure so much now."

Esme nodded, as if thinking to herself. She looked up, spoke with an odd directness. "Plenty of time to find someone. But I'll help if you like." She made a short little curtsey, which caught Nazarine a little off guard, and left. Now she was alone, in her own place. *First, I need to sleep*, she thought, and began pulling clothes off, all the time looking at the large bed, which looked more inviting by the second.

Sometime much later, she woke up, and for the first time in what seemed like months, her mind was clear. She turned on the lights and began looking. She didn't move from the bed. The room was surprisingly large, larger than the rooms of most houses she had seen, and larger than some of the rooms in the palace she had seen when she had been Phaedrus. But low-ceilinged. She guessed she could stand and stretch and touch the ceiling with palms flattened. There were no windows, real or imitation, nor were there any sort of decorations on the walls. Bath *there*, on her left, Study cubicle *there*, on her right. She nodded. All seemed correct. Now to explore.

After dressing in the same clothes she had worn before, she went through the information packet carefully. Her fare included room service, which was handled by an automatic dumbwaiter, and so she ordered breakfast. All of it was slightly odd, but there were fruits and cereals and something like meat, and so she ate it. They had no hagdrupe, which she recalled Rael being fond of, but they had coffee, which was a bit better, and she ordered a pot of it. Then she began reading in earnest, puzzling over odd phrases which made no sense to her. That was the most curious, puzzling aspect of the robolearning she had taken: when she came to a word she didn't know, her mind refused to recognize it. It looked meaningless. She had to stare at it a long time. But time she had, and she worked at it until most of them did make sense. She found out this class of room also had a complement of clothing for the convenience of travelers, who might have to spend months aboard. Already sized from holograms taken of her during entry. Standard stuff in basic cuts, but it would certainly do. She thought back to the price of the fare and smiled to herself. Perhaps it would be worth it after all.

Then she began unraveling the map of the ship, which was rendered in a highly abstract manner that revealed nothing of the shape of the ship or its size. But it made considerable sense, once she began to understand it, and was able to locate her own quarters, which she felt was a real accomplishment. The one thing that puzzled her was that she couldn't find the access ways Esme had taken her through. Well, natural enough. They wouldn't want mere passengers wandering around, but she bet that the ship was riddled with them, and she made herself a promise to look further into that. She might have to use them.

She also found out how to use the comm facilities in the room, and with some anticipation she touched the commpoint, querying the ship.

A short buzz from the speaker beside the bed, and a neutral male voice said, "Ready."

She said, "Reference Passenger Cinoe Dzholin, location and call-code."

The speaker produced a time marker, a soft repeating bass pulse, and then said, "Passenger Cinoe Dzholin ten Sub D barracks five bay sixteen zero delta zero five one six." Then the tone ended. She punched this number through a small touch keyboard and waited for someone to answer. It seemed a long time, but finally someone did answer.

"Sixteen."

"Cinoe Dzholin, please."

"Wait . . . not here."

"Did he leave a message?"

"No."

"Thank you." She wrote the number down, but sat back now, pondering. *Well. I couldn't expect that he'd always be there. It must be a dreary place, down there, with the whole ship to wander around in.* She touched the query button again.

Buzz, then, "Ready."

"Contact reference, Crew Faren Kiricky."

"Crew freetime now, two alpha delta five one six."

Nazarine coded in the number, and presently a woman's voice answered, "Kiricky." The voice was neutral, efficient. No more.

She said, "Nazarine Alea. I'm the girl who got contact with you on the lighter."

"I remember." It was short, but the voice warmed, became more personable.

"Are you free? If it's not a bother, I'd like to ask to meet you."

"Free? Yes, a couple of shipdays, and after that a tenday of standbys, where I'm free, but on call, you know?"

"I'd like to ask some . . . ah, guidance, if I may."

"Are you afraid of somebody?"

"Is this line secure?"

"Reasonably."

"I think somebody followed me aboard. I need to learn to fade."

"I understand. Yes, I think so. Where are you?"

"Four-Q-two."

"Well! Who's paying the rent?"

"My employers, so to speak."

"Well, I don't suppose they have any other way to learn. Very well. Go to your left, to the lift, and then to level A. That will put you on the section-four concourse. Follow the walk straight out into the concourse from the lift, until you come to a diamond-shaped intersection. There's a small park there, and I'll see you."

"When?"

"Start now. I'll be along." She broke the connection from the other end.

From above, it had seemed vague and blurred, but from what Nazarine kept thinking was the ground level, the concourse resembled nothing in her experience. It was in part a public park, and in part a commercial district of small shops, some offering everyday things, others extremely exclusive. There were restaurants, bars, every sort of entertainment. She had to admit she was impressed.

She had waited for some time, and was thinking of giving up when Kiricky approached the bench she was sitting on. Nazarine got up and greeted the woman. Faren Kiricky in person looked different from the image on the screen. For one thing, her hair was not gray, but a tightly curled mass of mixed black and silver. She was slight in build, shorter than Nazarine, but not petite or small. The face was sharp-featured, crisp and a little foxy, and there were laugh lines at the corners of her eyes and fainter ones at the corners of her mouth. She wore pants which were tight at the hip and loose and flowing at the bottoms, tan, and a black turtleneck sweater.

They touched hands briefly, and Nazarine said, "You don't look like I expected."

"What did you expect?"

"Crew."

"And so I am, when I'm on duty. Now I'm off, and I can be as much me as the rest of the idle passengers."

The voice was slightly roughened. Kiricky was not a young woman, but Nazarine could not accurately guess her age. She said, "You've been in space some time."

Kiricky nodded. "Most of my life, so it seems sometimes. Backwater planet, ran away from home, stowed away, got caught, choice of prison or navy, much the same. Took navy. Then the merchant service, and finally liners, like this. This isn't the best pay, but it's probably the closest most of us will get to the good life. All in all not bad. And I get to meet people sometimes who have interesting stories to tell."

Nazarine admired the brevity of the story. This woman had compressed her life into a few scant sentences, and yet she sensed no hint of failure or regret. It sounded rough, and she said so.

Faren agreed, without resentment. "Truth there. I've seen some hard times, and some scary ones, too. But some good ones, and those I enjoyed when I had them."

"I had some scary times, too."

"We heard you had some kind of revolution downworld."

"Something of that sort. I took employment with one of the surviving states, and so was sent here. Now I find that I'm more at sea than I thought. I need to know what kind of world I've walked into."

"You mentioned someone following you."

"That, too. I don't know who, but I'm sure someone is."

"Where from? Downworld?"

"No. Offworld."

"They were there? What was going on down there?"

"Rightly, I don't know. Something was going on, and it went all to pieces. I've been shadowed since Clisp—the place I came from. I don't know where they come from."

Kiricky thought for a moment and then said, "Since you ask, I'll do what I can. You were not as I expected, either. You look younger in person. But at least you have enough sense to ask. Yes. I love a little intrigue."

"I need to know values." This was not curiosity about manners, solely. From the data she could get from the value system of these people, she could work that into her system. Nazarine *knew* that the same idea that built and staffed this spaceship and filled it with passengers also produced the sequence of events that led to Oerlikon and the Morphodite.

Faren said, "Come along. I'll show you some sights. We can talk along the way. I'll tell you some things, and you can tell me a few as well. And if you've got an enemy, maybe we can lose him or her." Faren glanced around and her face shifted into an expression of sly but triumphant wickedness. Her eyes flashed and she smiled easily, "When I was a bit more reckless than I am now, I did a bit of smuggling, and if I may say so, did rather well at it. But I knew then when to quit; I enjoyed the chase as much as I did the money. That's time to quit."

Nazarine raised her eyebrows in mock surprise, glancing upward and rolling her eyes as if it had been more than she could stand, but she set off with Faren in the direction the woman had indicated.

Faren asked, "You're not offended?"

"Why should I be?"

"I just admitted a criminal habit, and a most demanding vice."

"I saw some things down there, where I'm from, that make what you call vices seem to be almost admirable virtures. Offended? I'm relieved."

Kiricky nodded. "Just so. So now I'll risk offense one more time and tell you something: you look young and empty-headed, but I sense something behind you with depth. No, not a disguise. You're who you seem to be, all right, a scared and mostly proper young lady with looks that would be stunning in the right clothing. . . ."

Nazarine interrupted Faren, "Or lack?"

"Strategic lack," Faren corrected. "And a wit, too. But you're hiding something."

For a second, Nazarine's heart stopped dead. A wave of fear washed over her, falling down from her shoulders through her legs. She actually felt faint. *What had Kiricky seen? How far?*

Faren took her arm gently, and continued on, walking through the concourse as if nothing had happened. She leaned slightly toward Nazarine, and whispered conspiratorially, "I don't see it, and I won't ask. Tell me what you will. But you're not one of us yet, and you don't look like one of us, and if you really want to fade, then there's some things we need to do. It's like swimming. You jumped, fell, or were thrown in, and don't swim well or at all. I'll show you how. Simple."

Nazarine recovered, and said, "That would be fine. Why would you do that?"

"Curiosity. Boredom is the ever-present enemy. But more important, a sense of relaxation and being able to be myself without watching too closely. I *know* you mean me no harm. No one, no matter how polished, would have been so direct. And so here we are, a couple of girls idling our break away, strolling around the gardens, just as if we were looking for a couple of pleasant and assertive fellows to have an adventure with." Her eyes flashed and sparkled, and the mischievous enthusiasm was so convincing that Nazarine actually thought Faren might do just that. But Faren looked suddenly thoughtful, and said, in a lower tone, "But we aren't, are we?"

Nazarine shook her head. She said, "No. And we aren't really looking for those assertive fellows, either, are we?"

Faren looked off into the green distances, and said, barely audibly, "No. Not that now. Maybe later. Maybe not. We'll gamble with the cards we have dealt to us."

13

"People fear war; people fear violence and threat and economic ruin and disease. Also loss of status. They fear change, and lack of change. But most of all, they fear each other. All our loneliness is self made."

—H.C., Atropine

CESAR KHAM SAT in the side street of a cafe, watching people passing by. This one was in the lower decks, a concourse much like others placed throughout the ship. He imagined that the others would be more tastefully arranged, larger, cleaner. But this one was acceptable. He had seen much worse in Marula, although he had to admit that public places in Clisp had more style. But they served their purpose—to give people something to do while passing the long voyage times.

Kham was too experienced to go rushing off to the upper decks, checking passing faces. Brute force. Number crunching. Mass. He had a better idea than his quarry how big this ship was. If he tried to look at random, with the procedures he could use he could easily spend the whole voyage to the next port of call and never once see her. He could easily move about; passengers were not generally restricted. But for the present, he waited, felt out his environment, and waited. Now, he had a little time. He wanted to think it through very carefully.

The girl's name. That was key. If she used her own, or the one she traveled with. He couldn't have asked the bursar for it, down below, because he wouldn't have given it anyway. And besides, they'd have had him thrown out of the office. Ship Security Sections were notorious for keeping incidents from happening. They could deny passage to anyone they didn't want, and above all, they didn't want trouble. More than one starship had been overrun by crazed passengers whose hysteria had been ignited by a vendetta, or even an overzealous Enforcement member. The large ships recognized no sovereignty save what their captain and his troops could enforce at gunpoint: a legacy of the Times of Trouble. He smiled faintly to himself. It was a notable problem.

Palude was working another area, like this one a few decks up, casting a loose net to catch rumors, just like him. He finished the coffee, left a charge chit on the table, and got up to leave. He had already decided that contacting Ship Security was not a feasible course. They'd laugh, whatever he thought up, and say, "Your sectarian differences have no bearing on a Captain's Bond—to ship passengers in safety." And if he told them the truth, they'd lock him up in the brig and put him off at first port of call. He understood this was delicate and probably foolish, but it was, after all, their last chance.

As he walked along, through the crowds and the massed hum of conversations, he thought, *There's got to be a way. Aside from his/her abilities, she's had incredible luck and coincidence all along the line, from Clisp on.* Cesar Kham did not believe in luck, and he never relied on it. *More likely extreme caution on her part. And even more so, now. She's vulnerable to identification, now, because she's too young to run another identity/sex switch. But we know one valuable piece about her: somewhere along the way she picked up a young buck, and he's here, too. And the probability is high he doesn't know enough to keep silent. And so we cast a net of ears. Only two pair, but might be enough.* Kham was looking for a young man with fine features, in with the refugees, hence, somewhere here or nearby, who might recount something of what happened to him. Kham smiled wickedly to himself. *She trusted him with incredible value, to do a transaction for her, knowing he would do it. She had had a hold on him. What?* He thought he could guess. And he wondered at that, how it would be to see the most ancient human problem from either pole, both. And according to their information, it had been sexually active: testimony on Rael, testimony on Damistofia, and their own conclusions about Phaedrus. An irreverent thought crossed his mind and he chuckled almost out loud over it: *She must be an incredible lay. Make a man call out for God.* Trouble was, they had no direct testimony, no witnesses. He added ruefully, *Or else we made sure with our bumbling that there weren't any.*

There was an open space nearby, a kind of park, in which some kind of entertainment was taking place, and Kham allowed his walk to drift over that way. He couldn't quite see what it was because a fair crowd had collected. Moving subtly through the crowd, he managed to see what was happening; a troupe of tumblers was performing. Presumably something put on by the ship, a diversion. Such things were known on the larger ships that made the really long runs between major terminal areas. This was a small group, three men and three woman, slender and agile, working through graceful routines without music; they didn't seem to need it. Kham admired their agility and timing, and in particular the supple grace of the women, who moved effortlessly, sometimes seeming almost to float in the air. A gravity grid? Possible, but he didn't think so. all wore pastel skintights that concealed very little, but at the same time did not reveal anything. As he watched the act, he also listened about him, to the noises of the watchers, and to their random conversations. Most of it was about the tumblers or related topics, or perhaps the attractiveness of the members of the troupe. Kham agreed; they were all singularly attractive, if a bit exotic for his tastes, although with their faces heavily made up in mime makeup, it was nearly impossible to determine what stock they were.

The act concluded, and after a discreet pause, those watching began applauding, restrained in good taste, but with genuine enthusiasm. The members of the troupe performed a little bow, repeated several times to different sides, and then the group broke up, like little birds scattering, and they ran into the audience, to mingle with the people who had been watching. Kham thought he understood. Ship's whores, every one of them. For some who had watched, there would now come an unforgettable experience—perhaps nothing more serious than an innocent thrill of meeting one of these exotic creatures, and for others, as dictated by circumstances, there would be something more serious, but equally entrancing. He still listened carefully; the crowd was beginning to drift now, the center of attention gone, except now for seeing who would meet whom.

". . . Heard of this before, but never saw it."

". . . Tumas came down to Marula with us, but he didn't show up one day and we never heard any more."

". . . I heard they come from a place called Pintang; put on these shows all the time. Every community has at least one troupe . . ."

". . . Girl in blue . . ."

". . . Bunch of crap, stopping off at that planet. No damn good—take forever . . ."

". . . Bring any locals out with you?"

"Not in our bunch."

"Ours neither. Some tried, but we couldn't get any to leave."

"I guess they heard about the awful offworlders, poor devils."

"Guy in my cubicle had one, but she went off on her own. I never saw her, but Franko saw them down below, said she was really nice."

Kham had almost missed it, but now he listened more closely, straining with every ounce of skill he knew to be invisible, just another unknown part of a random crowd.

The conversation continued:

". . . had her own income, and went to a better section. He wanted to get loose of her anyway, didn't want to be a tour guide to the known universe."

"That rascal. He was like that, though."

"Right. Get the sugar off before the bloom fades."

"Good old Cinoe. Never changed. I guess he liked it down there."

"I would have thought so, but he told me that they put too much into it for his taste, got too involved. But you know it was the national pastime—having affairs. Nothing like a light little one-nighter, you know, recreational sex, something to make you sleep better."

"Better than sleeping pills!"

"And as habit-forming!"

"What's that fellow doing? I haven't seen him since school."

"Didn't you see him? He was across the way. Girl in dusty-orange was headed that way."

Number two looked about. "I don't see him now."

"Oh, Mona. Did you know him then?"

"Oh, yah. Never forget Cinoe Dzholin. I always wanted to have his skill at catching them, but I guess I always wanted to keep them too long. Maybe it shows, or something."

"Well, if he's that way, he's right on top of it, you know. You heard that old song, 'Ya gotta get out before you get got out on.' "

Number two laughed. "Hadn't heard that one in a long time. 'Good old days' says it all. Wonder how things have changed back there."

"Not much, judging by the crew. Going back to Heliarcos?"

"Not me. I'm going home and find a quiet place. I signed on for adventure, and I had one. Shit, a revolution! Who'd have thought it!"

Then the two who had been talking drifted on their separate ways, making small waves. Kham allowed his steps to continue, but he really wasn't paying much attention to where he was going at the moment. He tried to evaluate what he had overheard. A false lead? He had heard a tale of a young man who brought a local girl on with him, a girl with money of her own, and none of the others had managed to bring locals with them from Oerlikon. The girl was allegedly attractive, and this bunch was from Marula. And he had a name. Cinoe Dzholin. Across the park with a harlequin. For a moment he hesitated, as if to strike out over there. Find a slim girl in dusty-orange, and there he would be. But he thought better of it. *No. Not now.* He could find out where Cinoe resided, and catch him there, and then he'd find out what name the Morphodite was using, and then find her through the ship's computer. *If that was the one.* Well, he still had to follow it up, either way.

But before he left the area entirely, he did turn back and circled back across the park, slowly, inconspicuously, just to see if he could perhaps catch sight of something. Nothing appeared to be out of order, nor did he catch sight of a girl in dusty-orange. So Kham continued along that way, heading for an eventual meeting with Arunda at one of their agreed-to places. He was early, but that didn't matter.

Kham stopped off at a kiosk and purchased a small brochure which told about the tumblers. He read the text and looked at the pictures, confirming his suspicions. He smiled to himself. It was part of the local religion, an honored role in that society. In fact, so popular was the practice that they had too many of them and many went to space, where they were welcomed on the ships. Dance and pick up strangers; who knew why they did it? Who knew why anyone did anything? Kham chuckled at that cynical reference to anthropology, and caught sight of one of the tumblers walking alone by herself. In dusty-orange. She looked downcast, disappointed and walked slowly.

On an impulse, Kham got up and approached the girl. When he neared her she noticed him and smiled, but weakly, and said, "Thank you, but of course it's too late now. It has to be the one whose eyes catch yours during the exercises."

Kham nodded politely. "Let me extend my appreciation anyway. Your people put on a fascinating display."

The girl bowed slightly. "I understand."

He said, "Perhaps we might meet again."

"Or others. It is to be hoped."

"Indeed. Forgive a stranger to your customs, but how do you know who to go to?"

"It is part of the rite, a long process. We know what to look for, but of course these things are not exact, and so you can't always judge. I made a wrong choice just now. I understand and obey the will of 'Rizheong in this. By being refused I know I have fault, and must correct myself. I go now to purify my thoughts."

"You were refused? A girl as lovely as you are, as graceful as a dancer?"

She looked down submissively. "To value the self too much, that is a great error. But it must be true, because when I went to him, his thoughts were not of me, but of a girl he had left on her own. I sensed it, because we are trained in these things, and the aim of desire. I asked him, because I must, and he told me. And now I must go, and become corrected. The person of Cinoe Dzholin was surely motivated by 'Rizheong in this."

Kham asked, masking his excitement, "May I ask for you?"

She looked thoughtful, and then shook her head. "I think not. That would go against the rite. We seek to eradicate the idea, that one human can possess another, and if you asked for me, or I hoped to see you . . . I'm sure you understand."

Kham nodded and made a little bow. "I wish you the success of your rite, then. Perhaps someday."

"Or another. May the magic visit you, Ser."

Kham watched her walk away. And went back to the bench, to await Palude. But he felt an irrational sense of fortune riding with him now, of a thread growing into a rope, a cable, a hawser, that would lead him straight to the Morphodite. *Now, now,* he thought, hoping that his excitement didn't show.

But the time came and went for Arunda to show up, and there was no sign of her. Kham reasoned that she had gotten farther afield than she thought to, and was late. In a way, that suited him well enough. Now was as good a time as any to check things out. He got up, and began looking for a public comm terminal.

Nazarine and Faren walked through the concourse aimlessly for a time, saying little of substance, watching each other covertly, making small talk, mostly Faren pointing out the real value of some of the things offered for sale in the little shops worked tastefully into the landscaping of the parklike interior space. Large as it was, it was carefully arranged to seem larger than it was; the distant enclosing walls of the ship were kept in dim light, while the concourse itself seemed bright and sunny; looking up or toward the horizon one expected, one only saw a dim suggestion of shape. Or, during the nocturnal periods, banks of lights that seemed to shimmer like distant city lights. The illusion was very strong that one was not *inside* anything, but *outside,* under the stars or in ordinary daylight.

They stopped beside a wooded glade, which had an upper level of gracefully contorted trees with smooth, gray fluted trunks and small, delicate leaves. There was an intermediate level of smaller trees or shrubs with broad, glossy leaves and brown, fibrous trunks, slender and twisted, almost like vines. The ground was covered with several different kinds of mosslike plants. It was fenced off by what looked like an ornamental iron fence, but along which were the telltale probes of a repellent field.

Nazarine asked, "What's in here?"

"An enclosure for Lenosz. The landscaping, I am told, is Old Earth Authentic; those are real trees and moss."

Nazarine peered into the shade, the denser parts. For the moment, she saw nothing. "What's Lenosz?"

Faren smiled archly. "It's just an animal. I don't know where they came from originally."

"Dangerous?"

"Yes and no. Mostly not. At least, in the conventional sense that we understand danger from animals—nature red in tooth and claw, as it were. No, they are quite gentle. Omnivores most of the time, not at all aggressive."

Something gray moved in the forest and Nazarine looked that way, certain that nothing had been there before. It moved again, tentatively and stood out more in the open, and she saw it clearly: a Lenosz. It had four legs and a tail and gray fur, and looked ordinary at first glance. Something doglike, perhaps. Everyone learned the animals of early man. Except this was subtly different.

There are, it had been said, certain outlines and shapes of things which terrify, or disgust. These are ancient archetypes of ideas that never reach the verbal level—childhood engrams shaped into resonance by thousands of generations, of subtle reactions shared. Were that true, then the other pole would be true also, that there would be shapes and outlines that stimulated other emotions, longing, desire, admiration, affection. This was such a creature. On the second look, it ceased to look doglike at all, but became something supernatural. It ambled over toward the fence, approaching, until it wrinkled its nose in distaste at the sensations the field transmitted, and there it sat back on its haunches, looking elegant and idle, glancing first at Nazarine and Faren, and then out of its cage into the concourse.

The Lenosz had a long, tapered muzzle, delicate flap ears that drooped like a hound's, a rather long neck. It was furred, the fur being so short and dense and soft it looked like a second layer of skin. It was a living embodiment of the idea of dogness raised to the tenth power of aesthetics and form. It made an ordinary dog seem like a child's drawing by comparison, honest in form and function but crude in execution. Nazarine said, "It's beautiful."

Faren nodded. "That's the problem. They are very affectionate, and also either intelligent or gifted mimics. And of course they are indeed beautiful. That's the danger. They seem to form a symbiotic attachment with sapient life forms, and eventually become parasitic. In short, people become too attached to them."

"You mean pets."

"The practice was outlawed, and severe penalties were set out for possessing one. The ones that were pets were gathered up, one by one, and put in enclosures like this one. No one had the heart to kill any of them."

"Why?"

"You own one, you fall in love with it. Unlike other animals, it doesn't grow fat or ugly on pampering, but becomes even more beautiful."

Nazarine looked at the gray-furred creature across the fence, and it seemed to respond to her attention. It looked back at her out of fathomless liquid brown eyes. The soft fur seemed to be made expressly for touching. Sleek, gray, streamlined. Nazarine looked away from the animal with an effort.

Faren said, "On the planet where they were discovered, they found evidence of a high sentient culture: houses, roads, some remains of machines, writing. Not much, but enough to know something had been there. Native to that planet. All gone. No war, no craters, no nothing. Just gone. And these creatures."

"Their descendants."

She shook her head. "No. These didn't originate on that planet. Their chemistry is different, their DNA is different. Not that planet. Close enough so that they can eat our food, and presumably their food, on that planet. They have a special chemistry that enables them to ingest and use many different substances. The explorers . . . the Lenosz were glad to see them, when they came. It was much later that they understood what they had done on that world. Somewhere a spacefaring people found them, and took them in, and they became part of that people, and so much so that these people dwindled and died out. Keeping Lenosz. Or so they think. There are all sorts of dangers."

"You showed me this for a reason."

Faren looked down at the ground for a moment, and then directly at Nazarine. "Yes. The message is obvious enough, I think."

Nazarine shook her head. "I don't need reminding."

"You need learning that there are things out here you haven't even dreamed of, and that some things can only be enjoyed at a distance, and then you must go on about the things you must do. *Those* are our values. We'll start from that. That thing's not dangerous: there's no record anywhere of one ever attacking a human without extreme provocation, without clear and obvious reason. You get one of those and take it home. It's clean, it learns and adapts easily, it needs nothing of its own, and it responds to you. It's even a comfortable size—about that of an adult human of small stature. You feed it, breed it, take care of it."

"What happens if you mistreat one?"

"They make fast animals look like slow-motion. And it will protect you, too. But now tell me of your danger."

"Someone, I am sure, followed me on the ship."

"No great problem. You simply lose yourself. Does it know your name?"

"No, I don't think so, yet. But I became involved with someone on the way here." And in much abbreviated form, Nazarine sketched in an outline of her adventure, and the present curious limbo it had gone into once on the ship. Faren did not seem to be surprised.

After a moment, she asked, "He never tried to call you?"

"No. I tried to call him, but he wasn't there. Still no answer."

"So. Wait here." Faren left the Lenosz enclosure and walked away a short distance to a small, inconspicuous post set into the ground near some shrubbery. She opened the upper part, and removed a device which expanded into a headset, through which she spoke with someone or something. Then she put it back, and returned to Nazarine. "That does that."

"What?"

"Now you are carried on the ship's roll as an unlisted number. I hope it's not too late. That will slow them down."

"What about him?"

"Were he going to come to you, he would have done so directly, or called you immediately after boarding. You can follow that up, if you wish."

"I know—never mind how—that he is not part of any operation against me."

"Doesn't matter. You've got to cut the possible others off."

She gave Faren the number she had for Cinoe's area. "Could he be in trouble?"

Faren said, "If someone saw you with him, or tied you to him, they can get to you through him. May be doing so now."

"How do we know they haven't already?"

"Ship's registry says no calls to your place, no queries logged. Are you certain they are real?"

"They tried to kill me once. They missed and I went into hiding. They will keep trying."

"Why are you such an important item?"

Nazarine shook her head. "I know something . . . or they think I know something. It doesn't matter which way it really is."

Faren leaned closer. "What do you know?"

The intensity of her eyes was terrific. Nazarine could see nothing else. Faren's eyes were a pale blue-green, almost gray. She came to a dead stop inside, and then said, "Not all of it. I'm still working on it." She felt control coming back. And she added, "What would you do if you knew? Sell me to them?"

Faren laughed, exposing even, perfect teeth. And the expression on her face softened noticeably. "No, no. I might use it for myself, but I won't sell you to anyone. That I promise. We are thieves and deceivers one and all, but we still have some honor, we star-folk, whatever you think of us."

Nazarine looked back directly at Faren, and said, "You may but these people don't. They kill children even when they miss."

Faren thought a moment, and then said, "All right. Come along. We need to collect your friend and get him out of the way for a while."

"How? What are you going to do?"

"We'll get him in a part of the ship where he isn't so easy to find. Won't hurt him at all. And we'll also find out if he's been contacted. Then we'll know more what to do."

"We're going in the open?"

"Why not? Don't worry, I know a few tricks of my own. But one way or the other, we've got to get him out. And the way we're going will be just as fast. And fast we need." She stopped a moment, and looked back at Nazarine. "You're getting more complicated all the time."

She smiled in spite of herself. "You don't seem to mind."

Faren raised her eyebrows and glanced at the invisible ceiling. Flick. Nazarine sensed it was a standard gesture. Faren said, "Not yet, anyway."

Between the concourses of the ship, the public areas, ran narrower public areas which were something more than access tubes and something less than actual concourses. Illuminated signs hung from the ceiling indicating routes to various areas, and various diversions alternated with blank passages to make passage through them diversions in themselves. In the first part of a flight, the new passengers walked around a lot, finding various areas of interest, so now the number of passersby was steady. By no means crowded, the ways were still reasonably full, and Arunda Palude had spent a very tiring morning searching out faces. To no good result. She hadn't even had the exercise of making a close match.

She stopped for a time at a health-foods shop and purchased a sack of salted nuts and a flask of mineral water which had a faint sulfurous odor and left a metallic aftertaste of iron. She winced at the taste, and thought, *Why is it that everything good for you tastes so bad, and the stuff that tastes good is bad for you or actually harmful? Now there's a mystery.* She took the flask outside into the hallway and settled on a bench, glancing idly up and down, seeing a few people, none of any particular interest. She had looked over the shipmaps carefully and picked this area out as the goal of her first line of search; it was near a junction of several other cross-lines, and one might expect to see more here than just any place picked at random. But this hadn't seemed to work, either. The density of people was not a great deal greater here than anywhere else. But she was persevering and long-suffering, and so decided to stay for a bit and watch before turning back. Rest in the afternoon, and then try again in the night-cycle.

To pass the time, she tried to fit professions to the people she watched passing; this was all the harder because some were wearing the pastel shades and neutral styling of shipwear, which conferred a certain anonymity to the wearer. These she watched closely. Others wore what Arunda imagined to be approved local costume appropriate to their station. Still others strode along with a jaunty familiarity and an arrogance that suggested crew, some in various uniforms, others in their own clothing. Yes. Far down the corridor she saw two women walking along, not in a hurry, but not idling either. They were crew, for sure. She looked away. She felt the hair on the nape of her neck prickle, a hot flash across the shoulders, and a tingling along her back. She looked again. The pair were much closer now and she could see them better. One was average height, rather slender in build, and although attractive, bore some evidence of aging and a hardened disposition on her face. *That one's been rode hard and put up wet.* The other was taller and walked with a looser striding motion. The taller one was barely a woman, more a girl. *But God, she's tall.* Arunda looked very close at the tall girl. Long in the legs, well-filled-out at bust and hip, but also trim. The face: small straight nose, large eyes, pale tan coloration, loose curly brown hair. She walked along with the smaller woman, holding back her natural stride to match her companion's. She wore a knit gray dress, a darker gray vestlike overgarment, and soft gray boots. *I see how I almost missed her. An older crew and a younger, out on an adventure, that's precisely what they look like.* The older woman wore smooth tan pants and a black turtleneck sweater, but despite the difference in type, they both cast the same impression. *How does she, it, do it? She can't have known that woman more than a day, and yet they look part of the same environment, and knew each other well. That thing's got abilities we don't know anything about.* She found the thought chilling; they knew from briefings and various reports some of the abilities of the Morphodite, and as they were, they were bad enough. But to have a chameleon's gift of background mimicry, that bothered her more. *That thing's damn near invisible.* She had guessed about clothing and come up right.

Palude did not rise and follow them, but watched them carefully out of the corner of her eye as they passed her, and turned off onto an access ramp leading downward to Concourse Area One. She evaluated what she could see of the two and decided she did not want to risk identification. Even though the Morphodite was reported to be rare to use violence, it certainly had the abilities, and the other woman, the crew, looked capable enough on her own. They could be formidable if confronted. She reasoned correctly that at least she needed to inform Cesar and get confirmation of identity before going farther. Yes. That tall girl matched the ID coordinates Cesar had given her.

Palude noted that they had gone into the express access tube, and she knew there was no faster way she could use, but she got up and set off purposefully, getting into full stride and pushing it, going back the way she had come. She thought, *The girl doesn't know Cesar yet. She's only seen him once, and knew nothing then. But if she sees him again, she'll know. And then it'll hit the fan for sure. I know they're not looking for him or me, yet. Yet.* She repeated that word to herself. She had already decided, she realized, that she did not want to have the Morphodite looking for her. Oh, no. No way at all. And then she thought, *But they're going down there for some purpose. What?* She increased her pace until it began to hurt very slightly in her thighs.

14

"A crisis is the definition of a situation in which you know what you have to do, but you hesitated to do it and so lost control of events. One takes sensible and reasonable precautions, but if action is needed to head off negative patterns, that's the best cure for it. Because no matter how much talk you hear about good intentions and positive attitudes, some still do cruel evils, and nowhere, in no law or philosophy, does it state that one is required to be a victim."

—H.C., Atropine

KHAM GOT THE listing for Cinoe Dzholin easily enough. As a fact, it was close by his own, and easy enough to check. He didn't expect to find the fellow in, but he could wait for him. He didn't have a clear idea of who he was looking for, just a general and vague description, but he trusted enough in his reflexes to pull it off. *Trust to proven tactics!* First, meet him, then attain temporary confidence, and then, in a quiet place, some discreet questions, with persuasion as required. Here, Kham felt back in an environment, a situation, in which he could trust his own reflexes. His quarry now was no changeling Morphodite, with the ability to see him coming, or suggested skills in defense. Oh, no. Lisak or operative, Kham felt certain of himself. He flexed his fingers as he walked, moving swiftly and covering distance without seeming to do so.

It didn't take Kham long to arrive in the section he wanted. This section had what they called bays, which housed ten men or women each, all connected by a staggered hallway, strung along like peas on a pod. Ahead, he saw a young man using one of the public comm terminals, or more correctly, finishing using one. The young man turned away from the commpoint and started toward the room Kham was headed for. This one matched the description from downside. On an impulse, Kham approached, cutting him off before he went in. He said, "Cinoe Dzholin?"

The young man answered, "Yes." Guarded, but not suspicious. Kham felt good. This one knew little.

Kham said, "I am Cesar Kham. Does that name mean anything to you?"

He hesitated. Then, "Yes. Oerlikon. I've heard of you."

He looked now both impressed and a little apprehensive. Yes, it was certain he'd heard of Cesar Kham. After a moment, the young man added, "I thought you had gone back."

"I did. But there was some unfinished business on Oerlikon, and so I had to come back. And now there is another matter I must follow up, and I ask to speak with you for a bit."

"Go ahead."

"Not here. A more private place."

Cinoe looked around, as if getting his bearings, "There's a cohab lounge down the hall. Place where strangers can meet and . . . you know. We find an empty one, lock it, and it's pretty private, so the ship's brochure claims."

"Lead the way, then." They went onward along the passageway, plain gray, unrelieved by decoration or suggestion of functional shipform. At the end of the passage were several doors, all closed, with a red and a green light over each. One showed green. The remainder were red. Cinoe laughed a little nervously. "I didn't expect they'd be so full this time of day." He pushed open the green-marked doorway, and went in, Kham following. Inside, there was a spartan little room, with some soft chairs, a severely efficient bath, and a fold-down bed, still in its wall cubby. Cinoe locked the door. He turned around. "Very well. Private. Ask on."

Before speaking, Kham observed the young man closely. Dark, loose hair, almost black, worn long. A thin, straight nose, small mouth, a little slack and sensual. Deepset eyes. He looked girlishly delicate, slender in build. Kham decided to come to the point. "You came on board with a woman. I need to know her name. We need to ask her some questions."

A shadow passed over Dzholin's face, something too short to be an expression. Just the shadow of one. He said, "What for? She's not one of us."

Kham thought, *Aha, he wants to fence a little. Very well.* "Then you acknowledge my allegation?"

"Yes . . . To my knowledge, she is not one of us, but a native. I tested her."

"How?"

"Speech. She didn't react at all to our speech."

"Well, that's true enough. She's definitely not one of us."

For a time, there was silence, which Cinoe felt as a pressure to say something. "What do you want her for?"

"You don't need to know, but I'll tell you part of it. She possesses some very dangerous knowledge, and we need to find out how she got it."

"She said she was a spy for Clisp."

"We know that she is that, in part. She is something much more. Her name!"

"Oerlikon is finished. The project is over. I don't see what use this is."

"Let me tell you something. I came back here for the sole purpose of tracking her down, and you are the only thing that stands between me and her now. But excuse my manners. Let me advise you that you protect something dangerous to a degree you cannot imagine."

Kham knew as soon as he'd said it that it had been the wrong move. Cinoe's face registered disbelief, confidence. *Amazing! The fool actually thought he could talk his way out of this. He might even take a poke at me.*

Cinoe said, after a moment, "She's not dangerous. She's just a woman, no, a girl. You've got the wrong one."

"How do you know that?"

He said, defiantly, "I slept with her, that's what."

Kham barked out, derisively, "Are you fool enough to think you can understand a woman from between her legs?"

"It's not like that. She's not the one you're looking for. This girl is green as grass. I know the difference."

Kham shook his head. "There's a lot more I could tell you, but it's just not the best thing. Let me contact her. I'll decide. I know what I'm looking for."

"What are you looking for, Ser Kham?"

"A destroyer of worlds who is on the way right now to turn loose the apocalypse in our own system of worlds."

Cinoe turned a little, tense, but he shrugged. "Wouldn't do you any good to know it. I tried to contact her. She's unlisted herself."

Boseldung!, Kham thought. *Already alerted somehow! How does the bitch do it?* He said patiently, "I can take care of that problem. But I need a name."

Cinoe said, "I know the law and custom. Your authority doesn't pass between worlds. Only back there, and that's finished. Go Captain's-Mast with me, and I'll tell you."

More delays, and even now she's somehow gotten alerted. Dammit! And this moonstruck smartass wants to play legal games. He said, "I don't have time anymore for games. Give me her name and let's put an end to this. What passed between you and her, that's your business. This is mine."

Kham saw him tense and began his motion countering by reflex, before the blow actually started. Cinoe aimed a quick, hard jab at Kham's head, but it never connected. Kham was already moving backwards, thinking, *Fool again! Punching to hurt or warn off!* He hadn't been in position to disable or kill, and that was, to Kham's mind, the only possible motivation for violence. He fell back, grasping the fist that had come at him and pulling toward him. A simplistic maneuver, but it worked like a textbook exercise. Cinoe, off-balance from throwing the blow, fell forward onto Kham and before he could grasp the older man, Kham threw him neatly into the corner, where he landed with the sound of meat against something solid. Kham recovered his balance and faced Cinoe, partly crouching, arms wide, hands loose, betraying no identifiable skill save readiness.

But the stance was unnecessary, for Cinoe wasn't moving very well. His face was twisted with pain, gray, perspiring, mouth working. The boy's arm was at an odd angle, and his shoulder looked lumpy, distorted. Kham looked incredulously. *Dislocated shoulder, maybe a compound fracture with it.* Kham shook his head at what he must do now.

He approached Cinoe slowly, measuring his steps. When he was at the proper distance and angle, he reached forward in a blur of motion and, grasped Cinoe before he could resist, and made a series of curious motions about the shoulder. He felt the ball reset in its socket, but the boy had fainted. Kham revived him. "Now, the name!"

The boy reached with his good arm and began throttling Kham, a move so unexpected that Kham actually was taken off guard and felt the hot surge of panic. But only for a split second. Then he broke the choke, and straddled Cinoe, performing certain motions in a careful, quick sequence. He worked on certain nerve systems, junctions, ganglia. His operations made no sound, and Cinoe made only throaty, gargling noises of no great volume, and after a time, even those stopped. At last, himself perspiring from the effort, Kham leaned back and looked at the boy. The face was almost unrecognizable. Blank, utterly vacant. Kham leaned close again and whispered, "The name. You want more of that?"

Cinoe muttered, in a low monotone, uninflected, "Nazarine Alea."

Kham got up off the boy. He said, "There's no fixing what's been done here. It's irreversible. I didn't want this, but it can't be helped. And

I can't wait through explanations. So I'll leave, and after I release this hold, you'll sink and go to sleep. No more pain. And I'll lock the door going out, so you'll be left alone for a long time."

Cinoe said nothing. He looked off at some noplace, eyes unfocused. Kham thoughtfully added, "You shouldn't have tried to resist. She isn't worth it. And she left you anyway. No nothing all around." He shook his head regretfully. Then he released the last hold. Cinoe seemed to shrink and fold into himself, although his actual position only shifted a little. The change was more in attitude than anything else. Kham turned away.

Then he made a quick inspection of the room, looking around, making sure he hadn't touched anything. At the door, he set it to lock, and left, pulling it shut behind him. There was no one in the corridor, and the other cohab lounge door lights were all still red. He nodded to himself, and set off back down the corridor, headed for the level concourse again. He moved with decisive speed, because he had to get clear of this area as fast as possible. Now for two reasons. One, to run the girl to earth, and the other to escape association with this area. He was well out in the concourse, sitting on a bench, sorting out things in his mind, when he realized the situation he might have precipitated. He thought, edging carefully around the idea, as if he didn't want to touch it, *Now I've got two enemies, her, and Shipsecurity.* He understood. Cesar Kham knew how to hide, and how to move invisibly. Had he not done so for years on Oerlikon? Had he not been the chief field operative of Lisagor? The exertion had left him a little lightheaded, and he let it flow, moving with it. He set priorities in his mind, and identified Shipsecurity as a distant nuisance. The real problem was Nazarine Alea. Unlisted callnumber. *Well. There are ways around that, too.*

Nazarine noticed that Faren picked up the pace after she turned off to enter the express passage, but did not stop or say anything until they were secured in the small *pneumatique* and moving. She said then, "Just before the turnoff, as we came down the openway, there was a woman sitting on a bench. Seen her before?"

"No. I noticed her then, but never before."

"She had a backwater-planet look to her, but also something else: a spotter."

"You're sure?"

"Yes. We'll not see her again. She's gone to report, and bring up a field operative who will doubtless try to get in closer. That'll be a man."

Nazarine asked, "How do you know that?" She was astounded at the quick responses of Faren. To spot things that fast she must have done some things in which observation and responses had to be honed to a fine degree of perception and unquestioning reaction.

"When they use a woman as a no-contact spotter, it's always a man who does the dirty work. Sometimes you'll find a man spotter in some tricky, sneaky situations, and then expect a woman, and a bad one at that, to close in." She shivered. "Brr. Worst scapes I ever had were reverses. But pay attention: she noted me, but spotted on you. That means description. What do you make of that?"

"They couldn't have a description of me, I . . ."

"You what?"

"Never mind. I've been careful." But she thought about the facts as Faren presented them, and it had to be that way. The woman knew who to look for. How? Suddenly she felt very foolish. She had moved openly, trusting to her new identity to protect her. But she had been in the open, and used the cartouche of Pompeo. Bought clothing. But that would give such a general description that you couldn't react on it. That she didn't believe. No, it was something else. Who? When? Not Cinoe, surely. She said as much to Faren.

Faren nodded. "No, not Cinoe. I agree with that. He had his chance on the ship coming across the ocean, as you told me. This is not young-man work. But somewhere, somebody saw enough of you to derive a transmittable image. Wasn't that woman. Her reactions were too obvious, and *slow.*"

Nazarine thought, hard, trying to remember the past months, looking for something. The guard at Symbarupol? The Makhak in the castle? The one had been too ordinary, the other too Makhak in his detachment. They wouldn't even chase a Lisak for pay.

She remembered there had been one occasion, on the beamliner from Symbarupol, when she had felt uncomfortable about a man, and changed, just to be sure. The bald one. Him?

"A man watched me too closely on . . . a train, something like that. I thought it would be prudent to lose him, and so I did. But he didn't follow me. There was only a moment."

"If he was trained well, and experienced, that would be enough. There exists a standard set of descriptive tags so that he could transmit a passable image of you to one similarly trained. What did that one look like?"

Nazarine recalled what she could. "Bald, stocky, heavy torso, like a wrestler. An intense, disturbing stare."

"Can you fight?"

"Yes."

"You don't look it."

"Trust me. Call it one of my secrets."

Faren did not look convinced, but she assented reluctantly. "All right. A bald, stocky man. It will be sneaky, so we had better stick close for a while. Two pair of eyes is better. And seeing me with you, they've got an item on me, too, and will assume partnership. So I have to depend on you."

Nazarine said, "I can contribute something to this, but I have to have some time to do it. Quiet."

"What?"

"Get me five minutes, maybe ten. I'll show you."

"Now we get Cinoe out if we can find him. Stash him somewhere and you forget him; we can cure that."

"What about the woman? Are we walking into a trap?"

"Not likely. Possible, but probably not so. We'll get to Cinoe's area before she can: we are on the fastest route to that area."

The express *Pneumatique* ran level for a short space and then slanted down sharply, sounding into the belly of the ship *Kalmia*. Then it stopped, and they emerged into another accessway similar to the one they had left. This one, however, showed less care than the upper: there were faint smudges on the walls, marks left unfinished from patching. Faren commented, "These are the haunts of the sloggers, the proles, and the riffraff. Traditionally it is called steerage." She spoke in an even, conversational tone, but her eyes betrayed her anxiety: they shifted in a regular pattern from side to side, sweeping, calculating. She added, "Come along smartly, now, and be alert, if you know how. We want to be bold marauders, coming boldly and leaving silently as ghosts."

Shortly they came to another of the vast, cavernous concourses, this one being much more plain and functional than the upper one. They skirted around the edge of it, avoiding the more densely populated center. Each person they passed they watched carefully, but neither one observed anything suspicious, and they traversed it without incident. As they entered the residence areas, Faren turned and said, "We won't come back this way. Wouldn't have done it this way from the beginning if I had known." She stopped, and then went on, rather more thoughtfully, "If I had known, might not have come at all."

Nazarine said, "Regrets?"

"No. I'm being cynical—another of our vices, which you must learn."

Faren knew the quarters number she was looking for and led them directly to it, walking along the passageways with an easy familiarity which Nazarine followed closely and soon fell into. When they came to the door, it was open, and three young men, ostensible Lisaks by their clothing and shoulder-length curls, invited them in, speaking in the language of Oerlikon. Faren shook her head and insisted, in her own speech, inquiring after one Cinoe Dzholin, and eventually, one of the young men said, stumbling a little, that Dzholin had gone out much earlier and not returned.

Refusing invitations to come in and party, Faren and Nazarine stepped back into the hall. Faren said shortly, "Not impossible, of course, but it's a fine mess having to go look for him. I could have him paged, but that would attract a great deal of attention, the kind we don't want. And things being as they are, I don't favor the idea of milling around out in that concourse, either. It's not a trap, but it's too easy for us to be seen. Do you have any ideas?"

Nazarine looked at the room, the hall, and the light of the concourse beyond, flooding down the passage behind them. Reluctantly, she guessed, and concluded she would have to expose something. "I have another way. I do not display it before observers, but it seems there is no other way." She hesitated. Then, "Is there a place where we can go where we can get privacy for a time? This takes time, and I can't be interrupted."

Faren put her hand up alongside her nose and rubbed the side of her nose, looking off and thinking. "Yes. For each one of these sections they have an adjoining suite of cohabs—rooms where people can go and be alone. The usual reasons. We can use one of those, if we can find one unlocked. Randy lot down here."

"Show me," Nazarine said, and Faren nodded and set off, going deeper into the section, following the passageway as it began to turn and twist. At last, the passageway narrowed down into a corridor, which terminated in a cluster of small doors, each with a red and green lamp above it. All the lit lamps were red.

Faren looked disgusted and said, "Just our luck. Everybody decides in this section they all want love in the afternoon at the same time." She looked disgustedly at the closed doors, and then looked again. One of them wasn't quite closed.

She indicated this to Nazarine. Then she knocked at the door, and

stood back, listening. She whispered, "Could be just carelessness, haste."
But no sound came forth from the room. She said, "Come on. We'll see."
Faren pushed the door open, looking into the room, seeing no one, and
stepped up and inside. "Nothing here. Hm. Wonder why they left the
red light on. It looks like nobody's been here."

Nazarine followed her, but just inside, Faren, slightly ahead of her,
motioned her to stop. She said, very quietly, "Nazarine, close and lock
the door."

"Why?"

"Do it." Nazarine complied. When she turned around, she saw Faren
move stealthily across the room, around the corner, to where a body lay,
sprawled in an odd and grotesque contortion. Faren muttered, "No wonder it was left like that. Good-looking kid, too. Was. Doesn't cut much
of a figure now." Nazarine came forward and looked more closely. She
said, "We're too late."

She looked at the curious still figure in the corner. Unquestionably
dead. She felt nothing, oddly. This did not resemble the Cinoe in life
that she knew. The feeling of it would come later. She knew now they
had little time, and she had to act fast. She did not need Jedily, or
Damistofia, or Nazarine, now. She needed Rael, and from deep in the
most buried part of her memory, she summoned Tiresio Rael, the callous, the merciless. She felt Rael's lanky, awkward figure fit uncom-
formably into her own supple limbs. She felt odd, ill-fitted, in her own
body, that she'd spent so much of herself to really become. When she
spoke, it was in a harsher, colder voice. "That was Cinoe. The conclusion
is that the one hunting me killed him, either to prevent him from getting to me, or to derive information from him. Probably my name, so he
can trace me through the ship. If so, now he knows how I call myself,
and he knows what I look like."

Faren looked back at Nazarine sharply, sensing some change in the
girl. After a moment, she said softly, "You take the death of your lover
lightly."

Nazarine did not look at her, but said, "I take it as I must. I will feel
later. But know that this is not the first. They tried for me once before,
and missed. And before that, they sent an assassin against me. I killed
him."

Faren observed, "It seems I place myself in immediate peril by associating with you."

Nazarine nodded. "Just so. You may leave if you wish. I am grateful
for the help you have given me. Go. I understand. I do not ask you to

stay. I will do what I have to do. I can find him on my own. We will end this forever."

"You actually think you can find the person who did this, on this ship, and punish him?"

"I will hunt this swine to the end of the universe." It came unbidden. Cliofino, Krikorio, Emerna, Meliosme, Cinoe, persons in her past came flooding into her mind. And with them came an emotion for which she had no name: it was icy, cold, calculating, implacable. It made hatred seem like mild displeasure by comparison. She added, "I can. I will. But first I have to do something."

Faren turned to her and held her shoulders. "Listen. I believe you. I believe that you believe you can do this thing. But alone? No, that's not the way. I will stay. I do not know why they hunt you like this," here she glanced over her shoulder at the still figure in the corner, "but you must have allies, and I will have them for you. This is an evil thing, and I think if we look closer at him, we will see something else."

Nazarine relaxed a little. "Show me. I know something of these things. We may call them different things, but if a pattern is there, it should show to both of us."

They approached the body carefully, not touching it. Faren squatted down on her haunches and examined the body, searching it completely. Nazarine, beside her, got down on her knees and also examined it, in time touching it, feeling certain parts. After some time they both finished and looked at each other.

Nazarine said, "This work was done by someone very knowledgeable of the uses of pain. Slow. There are almost no impact marks."

Faren nodded. Her voice was now cold also. "The shoulder was dislocated, and then reset. The other things . . . There are several forms of this kind of art, and I will not bore you with terminology. I know some things, but of this, I know only enough to recognize the marks of a master craftsman. This man hunting you is dangerous. If he would do this just for a name . . ."

Nazarine stood up. "We have seen enough here. Are we still secure?"

"Yes. No one will pass the door."

"Should we report it?"

"I think it would be a good idea. It will distract him."

Nazarine said, "Do it discreetly. I want no outcry, no hounds-and-hunt. This one I reserve for myself."

Faren assented, "There's such a way. I have friends, and some of them will help me. They owe me, so to speak. I will call on those obligations."

"Press the case, but let him run loose. I want him alive."

"We'll do as much as we can. But mind, if he stands and fights, it'll go as it must."

She agreed, reluctantly. But agreed. "If it comes, then. Now I need some paper."

"Paper?"

"Paper and something to write with. And some time."

Faren looked around uncertainly. "May be something here, but . . . can it wait?"

Nazarine's face was set in grim determination. "This has to go before we leave this room, and I will let no one see it save you. And ask me no questions."

Faren said, "Very well. I will see." And she began looking through the room for something to write on. Eventually, she did find some note-paper and an electric pen, which she handed to Nazarine without comment. And she felt curious about the other girl, too. When they had met, Faren had assumed a certain position of superiority. It had to be. She was older, more sophisticated, experienced, and Nazarine had been . . . over her head. Now she wasn't so sure about those identifications. She neither feared nor disliked the girl; but she felt almost as if it was she who was the inferior, and it was more than a little uncomfortable. Still she asked herself: who was Nazarine Alea? More importantly, what was Nazarine Alea? She watched Nazarine sit in a chair and begin writing, as if drawing something, and she shrugged. *Well*, she thought. *I did ask for an adventure.*

Nazarine took up the pad and pen and sat on the bed, for a moment looking off into space, eyes unfocused and not tracking, and then she looked down at the pad, and, hesitantly at first, began sketching in what seemed to Faren to be an odd, abstract diagram. She would work like that for a time, and then tear a sheet off, and transfer part of the figure, leaving much of it behind, and seemingly start the process over again. On the discarded sheets she did something that looked like math—it was symbols and simple operational signs—but in no known number system, and what Faren could see of it followed no logical system which she could recall. The results of these computations would affect the developing figure.

After a time, Faren could not sit still any longer, and she asked, "What are you doing?" Nazarine did not answer, but cast her a glance of such intense malignity that she turned away.

The girl became oblivious to her surroundings, and made small sub-vocal noises under her breath. Some seemed to express a grim satisfaction, or exultation, such as at the fall of an especially hated enemy. Other times, they approximated groans of woe, or gasps of horror. Gradually, the noises slowed and stopped, and it seemed that Nazarine reviewed the steps she had progressed through, nodding at some places, glaring at others as if *they* were her enemy. Then she put the papers aside, and hung her head down, wearily. After a moment, she began speaking softly, in a breathy, low voice that was barely audible, even in the silences of the cohab suite.

She said, "His name is Cesar Kham. At least, such is how it was on Oerlikon. I knew of him, very distantly, almost solely by rumor. He did this, he also sent terrorists against me in Clisp. These things are not important to him. And yet this is not decided by him, but by someone behind him. The same people that fixed events on Oerlikon to their own purpose. I can get echoes of them, but I can't locate them—either my system is too ill-defined to work well in space or they are well-concealed. I see here that he was sent to kill me, but now he leans more toward capture—hah. His motives are unclear; sometimes he wants to use me to his own benefit, other times, he would take me somewhere."

Faren interrupted, "Do you fear that?"

She answered, "I fear nothing. They have me to fear." Then she went on: "That much is clear. What is difficult to see into is what we can do about it. We can run and conceal ourselves, but for a period of time—less than the voyage time of this ship, but not much less—we cannot attack him."

Faren said, "When attacked, you can move, screen or counterattack."

Nazarine nodded. "Exactly. Also do nothing: that's also an option. But access to all the lines going to him directly is blocked, and even if you can get through them, the consequences are all of negative value. I have done this before, but I have never seen a snarl like this. We will have to wait. There's a place where it clears, I can see that, but I can't see through it now. It must have been learning your speech that changes it this way—I see now in much greater detail."

"What were you doing? Are you a . . . what? I don't have the words. A Witch?"

She shook her head. "Nothing like that." She looked down at the floor. "What I do looks miraculous to you, but to me it's ordinary, every-day. It is difficult to do, certainly, but still ordinary. To me."

"Could I learn it?"

"Not as you are. You could not remain Faren Kiricky and do this. You have to start with a clean slate, a blank. . . . You know, it is the everyday world that looks peculiar to me. I have spent all the life I can remember trying to become a part of it, to be free of what I am. Yes. Really. There is much, much more to it than that." She sighed deeply and looked up, directly into Faren's eyes. "I want you to understand something. Everyone in your world works for power of some kind. The exchange varies, the payoff, but all the same: power. Cratotropic. And I, who have it, want nothing in the world so much as to throw what I do have away. And I can't. Somebody is hunting me, something that does not stop no matter what I do or where I go." Her eyes now were very bright. "And this was why Cinoe . . . I almost thought that I could do it through him. I sensed the failure of it even as we did it, the impossibility, but that never matters, when we reach so hard—it is the reaching that distinguishes us, not our failures. He was selfish and shallow, but he did not know what he gave me, which was greater than anything he took. And now this. I know this does not make sense to you."

Faren said, "I understand better than you think about wanting, and seeing those dreams fail. That much I know well. And fighting back as you can against . . . the smug, the self-satisfied, the idiots who get a little edge and step on everybody else's fingers."

"Do you fear me?"

"No. I think I should, but I don't. I am not one for causes. I mind my own affairs. But I think you need someone to help you, and I will offer it. With some misgivings, but nonetheless. . . ."

"Why? You know little enough of me."

"Because I think that you can do the things I cannot but always wanted to. You are driven by your own . . . oracle, but it's mine too. Don't misunderstand me, but it's like falling in love—you know it, when to reach, very soon. Not instantly, but very shortly. Will work, won't work."

Nazarine nodded, agreeing. "Yes, like that."

"So I've seen some things, done others, liked some, and feared some. So, you looked clumsy, worse than a tourist, but you had a light in you. In fact, what I want you to do is learn to conceal that, to become a little more like us, adept at concealing, able to rationalize away our own best interests in favor of trash. . . . Then you can really be invisible. Those are not all my motives, be so advised. And now we have some practical things to attend to. I have a friend in Shipsecurity who can handle this with no fuss."

Nazarine looked blankly at the still figure lying in the corner. "Yes, I understand. Can you keep this discreet?"

"How discreet? There'll be questions. Never mind us being suspects—neither you nor I could do this kind of work. But still they will want to know something. Anyone can see it's no accident."

"Can we say we don't know who did this?"

"We could. . . ."

"It's important that Kham run loose. I can't see why yet, but it must be, for anyone to have an open course to him later. I mean, if anyone catches or stops him now, I lose my only link to what I came here to do, and also, I lose the ability to do anything about it. Things are balanced on razors right now."

"All right. If you think so. Is that from the oracle?"

Nazarine looked up sharply. "Not an oracle, not fortune-telling. Not occult. *Science.* A method of organizing, objectively, what you know, but more importantly, what you don't realize you know, and projecting from it. And what I have to do is let Kham lead me to the people he comes from. Once I have that, then I can set a balance with him."

"In other words, we follow this maniac, as he hunts us."

Nazarine laughed, shakily, but a laugh despite everything. "Essentially, yes."

Faren stepped close to Nazarine, and placed an arm lightly on her shoulders. "I am sincerely sorry about this. No one earns deeds of this sort. What of it that was good—remember that. Believe someone older and wiser—there'll be others."

She answered, "Being what I have been, you lose faith that a final answer exists, for this."

Now Faren laughed out loud. "You don't have to be you to understand that. I gave up long ago. Now. Let's get out of here—another way. I'll see to the reporting."

15

"Not seldom, passersby glance my way and marvel, smiling: 'Who is that village idiot, that fool, that wild man?' What they miss is a deeper truth that madcap antics, appreciation of irony, and zany remarks bordering perilously close to bad taste are all, considered together, the best defense possible against cruelties and disappointments. I never heard a blues song with these words but one might well be written: 'Laugh or cry, there ain't no in-between.' "

—H.C., Atropine

ARUNDA PALUDE RETURNED to the section she and Kham had been assigned to, and she carefully checked places that they had previously agreed would be good sighting-places, but he was not in evidence. A quick run by the room he had been in also revealed nothing. She returned to the center concourse for their level and sat on a park bench, disconsolately. That was just like the way everything had gone since they had been on this terrible mission. Everything went wrong, constantly. Now she had valuable information, and she couldn't find Kham.

Someone stepped from behind the bench; she hadn't heard him approach, and say, passing, "Follow me at a distance." She glanced up and saw it was Kham, who seemed to stroll along no differently from the rest of the passengers, now wandering off through the aimlessly milling crowds. She got up from the bench and started out, and then fell back, barely keeping him in sight. Something was wrong, something had gone badly wrong for him to drop into a defensive mode of behavior like that.

Kham led her along roundabout, wandering courses that seemed to have no destination or purpose, but after a very long and tiring walk she saw him duck into a darkened drinking place. She waited for a time, but he did not come out, so she followed, as if she had had the greatest

difficulty making up her mind. Inside the bar, which bore a softly illuminated wall plaque calling itself the "Nile Green Potationary," complete with illustrative pyramids, camels, palm trees and other equally
improbable flourishes, the dimness and dark furnishings made it impossible to make anything out clearly, but after some uncertain motions,
she finally saw Kham and joined him in a booth. He had already ordered
a drink for her, something in a plain glass. She picked the drink up and
looked at it skeptically. "What is it?"

Kham said, "House specialty: Lillie Mae's Reliable Vermifuge. It's
supposed to cure warts, etc. It's also rather strong, so don't bolt it
down."

Palude sipped at the drink, made a face, and then sat back with a foolish grin on her face. "Tastes awful going in, but the aftertaste is spectacular! A few of those and you'd bay at the moon, even if there wasn't
one."

Kham glanced at one of the florid, arabesqued decorations arranged
along the walls. It would have been a crime to call them paintings. He
indicated she should also look and reflect. "True; the management has
thoughtfully provided one for those who require such an orbital object
to bay at." The moon bore, in subtle shadings, the suggestion of a the-
atrically overdone princess in the headdress of the ancient Egyptians.

She said, "You have the oddest tastes in meeting places."

"This is a good one. It's never crowded. It's done up so low-class people will think it high-class. Naturally, only serious drinkers visit."

"I have information for you."

"I likewise. Perhaps you should say yours first."

"Very well. I saw the girl, according to the coordinates you gave me.
She has a helper, or comrade, or something I don't know." Here she gave
Kham a set of coordinates for the recognition of the older woman she
had seen with the girl. Kham nodded when he had a fair grasp of the
image in his mind's eye. She continued, "I did not follow; they seemed
alert and poised. The older woman looks street-wise and partly reformed. They were headed this way, and probably got into this area
ahead of me—took the express passage down here."

"I've seen neither. But we now have another problem . . ." And here
he related, in sparse, tactical language, the events encompassing the
death of Cinoe Dzholin." He finished, "The girl's name is Nazarine Alea.
I tried the listings. She's unlisted."

Palude placed both hands on the glass and held it, on the table, but
at arm's length, for a long time, saying nothing. Finally, she ventured,

carefully, "I have no specific comments on that, of course. You already understand the error."

Kham nodded.

"No need for me to add to what you already know. This could put some serious complications into things."

Kham said, "There were no witnesses. It is possible nothing might happen at all."

Pahide looked directly at Kham. "Yes, maybe. *Maybe*. And *maybe* we might wind up being the hunted instead of the hunter. Somebody's going to find that body, eventually, and then the fun and games starts. How good is Shipsecurity?"

"Thorough and professional. Slow and steady, and bound by few or no laws. It won't take them long to link him with her."

"And so she'll know, and she also will have an alibi."

"Presumably. You are sure the girl you saw matched the coordinates I gave you."

"Yes. A Class-one match. No doubt. The girl you saw in Symbarupol, on the beamliner, is on this ship."

"Your evaluation?"

"Her appearance works against her, and she seems . . . what's the right word? Clumsy isn't it, maybe inept. And yet there's an order back of her, too. If she was inept as she seems she couldn't have made contact so fast. And I have a suspicion the older woman made me. Maybe not. But she looked directly at me. Not casually. For strategy, assume she did, and warned the girl."

Kham reflected, "So what they warned us of has occurred?"

"What? Oh, yes, that it would be alerted. Well, certainly that, by now."

Kham said, with wry fatalism, "Then we may expect the worst."

"I don't know . . . There is something very strange about all this, if you think about it. I keep having this suspicion about all this case that she's not really looking for you or me. That with the ability that thing has to read the present and determine courses of action, if she were after you she would have come long before. Or she could have set something in motion."

"Yes, I have thought that, too. Odd, that. By any ordinary standard, she would certainly have reason to bear a grudge."

"Exactly. But against whom? There's the question. Face it this way: assume she knows you are the root of the events that have happened to her. Two attacks. And assume she's still using the original system, the one whose parameters I was briefed on: and yet she doesn't attack."

Kham added sardonically, "Not yet."

"You are the field tactician. Isn't there a circumstance in which you would allow a lesser figure to run loose, even though you had a clear case against that person?"

"Oh, yes. Common practice."

"In such a circumstance, you'd wait, and go for the higher-ups . . ."

"Where you had the feel of reasonable expectation you could get at them through your obvious target."

"Yes."

"Then there's your answer. She's going to let us lead her to her real enemies."

"In a way, that's worse than being the target. Do you have any clear idea of her range?"

"I don't even believe in what they say about it. Range doesn't seem to enter into it at all. Spatial distance . . . Using that system she's got, apparently she ignores it."

Kham looked into the darkness, focusing on nothing. "Then it becomes vital we get to her before she gets the range of her target. To our knowledge, she hasn't done it yet. This means she either can't see it yet, or she can't act yet. Either way, her powers are neutralized, and we've got time and opportunity. There is sense in what you suggest."

"We have comm through the ship. The committee should be notified."

"I suppose so, although we will pay a price for that, you know. Have you considered it? They'll say, 'You let that animal *loose!*' No matter what we do, it's no-win if we call them."

Palude stopped and reflected for a long time. Then, "So you'll try again."

"Have to. Hold your report for a bit. This is, after all, a closed environment. That thing can't breathe space, or transit-continuum. It's here, on a very small, closed world. And listen."

"Yes?"

"This world it doesn't know. We do."

Palude looked back at the mad Egyptian moon on the bar mirror. It seemed to communicate moonly wisdom, impalpable and subverbal, but something wise nonetheless. She said, "Maybe. But don't be too sure." She added, after a moment, "I'm sure you've heard the phrase, 'Crisis management is a contradiction of terms.' Remember it. What do you have in mind now?"

Kham was ready. "We should stop off at those rooms and see if the work has been discovered. I was unseen. We can of course pose as a cou-

ple seeking privacy. If necessary, we can report the heinous crime ourselves. It might be a good touch."

She asked, "Why not from here, now?"

"Would be a bad move if it's already been reported. Things would get
warm fast."

Palude slid out of the slick leather seats and stood, now somewhat
uncertainly. "Very well . . . my!"

Kham smiled. "Yes, indeed. Strong, isn't it?"

"One would never know."

"Come along, then. Then we'll know something. And know things we
must, now, all of it."

On the ship, the illusion of day and night alternation was maintained as
rigorously as that of gravity. When Kham and Palude emerged from the
dim interior of the bar, the faraway overhead illumination seemed
softer, dimmer than when they had entered. It now seemed like early
twilight, under a high overcast. Kham glanced instinctively upwards, as
if to judge the impending weather by the sky. Arunda chuckled when
she noted this gesture. "Ha! Looking for the sky, are you?"

Kham shook his head ruefully. "The illusion is strong, true enough.
One spends a lifetime outside, one looks at the sky, whatever the
world."

Arunda took Kham's elbow and said, "No fault there. But it's not a
world, this ship, and it doesn't have weather."

Kham nodded. "I understand your meaning. Very perceptive. Our
usual reactions, even good ones, won't be good enough." He made a grimace. "They weren't good enough, on Oerlikon."

Palude pursed her lips thoughtfully, and suggested, "I have spent
many long nights thinking about that. If it were just one thing, one incident, perhaps it would be meaningless. But it begins to form a pattern.
It does not emanate from us—you are not making mistakes. You are
going about it with uncommon skill. And yet at the crucial instant, the
actions don't work, or misfire. Do you know what I think?"

"That the Morphodite has luck? If so, I would agree."

"No, something like that, but stated differently, and the difference is
crucial. I begin to think that that thing . . . disrupts probabilities. There
is an expected range of coincidence operant in the universe. For some
reason, that thing, by existing, somehow de-coincidizes space around it,
or trains of probabilities that lead to it. I don't think it's conscious, or

even an ability, but a condition its existence imposes on the fabric of the universe. I'm not sure, of course, but there is a funny pattern to all the events leading up to now."

Kham walked along, silently, thinking. He said, "Perhaps. That would explain much. And yet it raises questions, too."

"Yes. Exactly what I thought. They told me, back on Heliarcos, that it changed the world, at least Lisagor, to a different configuration, a different idea-world. Things shifted. Kham, that thing created a world somewhere along the line, knowingly or unknowingly, that protects it, somehow. Shields it."

Kham was skeptical. "Lisagor, maybe. But here?"

"I don't think it knows it; how far it reaches, at least yet."

They had now left the lower-class concourse and were passing along one of the dim hallways leading to the residence areas. Kham said, "That would be in our favor."

"But think! Every time we have moved with violence against it, it has become more . . . enhanced, so to speak. We may have to rethink our options on what we must do with it."

"I think I see. The more we attack, the stronger it gets. And where before its effective range was limited to a single continent, now it can reach farther."

"Much farther. I say again, I believe it doesn't understand how far it can reach, or how far into the basic fabric its effects go. I do not want the basic probabilities of the universe tampered with. They're in a certain range, that makes things possible."

Kham walked along, turning into a side-corridor. "Perhaps. And yet what are our options? No matter what the cause, it's moving now, and it's in our world, motivated by our own acts. We don't know what it knows, what it doesn't know, of what it wasn't supposed to see. Do you imagine we should try to negotiate with it? Can you imagine the price? Even if we could find it and deal directly, there's no assurance it would stop with us. Its actions suggest it knows there is something behind you and me; so it would take us and just keep on going."

"I want to suggest we try to make some kind of contact with it."

"It's difficult to even see. I only saw her once, and you once. So far it's evaded every snare we've set for it."

"You agree we would have to find it on the ship before we take any further action?"

"Oh, yes, without doubt."

Now they had arrived at the section given over to cohabs for this residence area. The corridor light was dim, dimmer than the normal corridor lighting. Ahead, the rooms were closed, with the small witchlights above them indicating occupancy. Three were open, one of which was the room in which Kham had dispatched Cinoe into the darkness. "Last house on the left." Kham said, "Come on."

They stepped up to the doorsill and pushed the door open. Arunda held her breath. This was a crucial instant of time. Also, she found, looking at herself, that she really did not wish to be in this room with a dead man. There was a sense of profound wrongness about it. But inside, she looked around, forced herself to look, and there was nothing in the room. It was as if nothing had happened. The covers were neatly arranged on the bed, the lights were turned down low, everything was in order. She turned to Kham, who was looking around uncertainly. "Are you sure this is the right cohab?"

Kham nodded. "Assuredly. Indeed, this is the very room. No mistake."

"There's no body."

"Just so. I verified the room. So it's been discovered. Lock the door. We'll stay about half an hour, and then leave. We should return to our own quarters. I'll meet you tomorrow, on the concourse. It should be safe."

Arunda observed, "We should go somewhere and eat. I'm starved and I can't recall the last meal I had. That drink just set it off. And on the way out, we ought to nose around a little, to see if anybody around here knows anything."

Kham agreed. "Aye, that. Both. To hell with the half-hour—we'll go now."

With a last glance around the undisturbed room, they turned and left it, pulling the door shut behind them. Inside, its sensors picked up the door closing, and turned the lights out. And high up on the wall, in a dim corner, something infinitesimally small glittered for a second, and then also became as dark as the rest of the room.

Cesar Kham and Arunda walked back along the corridor, Kham looking along the plain gray walls for the room number he had derived for Cinoe Dzholin. He found it, and was on the verge of knocking, when a group, apparently bound for the furtive nighttime activity of the lower concourse, opened the door and came out. Kham started back for a moment, and then recovered, and like the good tactician he was, asked, of the group in general, "Excuse me, is this the room where a Cinoe Dzholin is billeted?"

One of the party turned back momentarily and said, "He's signed here, sure enough, but nobody's seen him all day. Popular fellow, that Dzholin!"

Kham asked, "How so?"

The other said, "Two women came looking for him awhile back."

Arunda, sensing the flow of things, asked, "What did they look like? They may have come from the party we came to fetch him to."

The other fellow pondered for a moment, and then said, "Young girl and an older woman. They didn't say who they were. The younger one was tall, very nice." The others agreed, smirking. He added, "The other one was average size, a little hard-looking. Looked like, the pair of them, one from the upper decks and a crew on off-time. Must be some party."

Arunda nodded and said to Kham, "They already came for him, and they didn't tell us."

Kham made a polite gesture to the party, who responded and started off. Kham added, so they would hear, "Probably dragged him off for awhile first. Hmf." He thought his voice carried just enough disapproval, tinged with a bit of envy. They remained by the door, as if uncertain what to do next, and as they waited, the others passed up the corridor and turned a corner.

Kham said, "All right. Now we know."

Arunda said, "They came down here to get him, probably, and found him. Doubtless we may assume it was reported, and the body removed."

Kham nodded.

"What do you have in mind now?"

Kham rubbed his bald cranium thoughtfully. "I don't think they have anything yet. You are clearly not in danger—they have no way to connect you. So what I recommend is that you move to better quarters, a room of your own. But stay on this level."

Palude shook her head. "They aren't on this level. And they probably won't come back, unless it's on the hunt. And we should not be separated, now."

Kham was insistent. "If they came soon enough, they will have picked up traces of whoever was in that room, and they could possibly make me. You don't know. There is a possibility I could be captured. In that eventuality, you must carry on, and do what you must. But however it would have to be, someone would have to stay behind, here, to see if they have started. How else would you know? So you see it's all clear."

She nodded. "Now, for some food. I see your argument, but I am not convinced yet. Let us talk it over, over a meal."

"Agreed! Most assuredly agreed!"

*   *   *

They returned to the concourse, now darkened into its night cycle. Kham had not been conscious of the place being crowded before, during day-cycle, but now it seemed busy, full of people, all strolling along, looking for something to see, something to do. He and Palude selected a place without ceremony, an open-air restaurant serving plain and simple fare, and sat down to eat. Both of them were hungry, and so they spoke little for some time, nor did they pay much attention to what was going on around them. He was surprised when Arunda pushed at his leg under the table with her foot. He glanced up, caught her expression, and suddenly became alert, without visibly seeming to do so.

He listened. At first, there was only a confused blur of sound from the nearby diners, and the nearer members of the passing crowds. Then a pattern began to emerge:

". . . told Corlean that she could take it and shove . . ."

". . . and after that, let me tell you, we . . ."

". . . not any new ones out tonight. Same stuff . . ."

". . . haven't seen them once this trip, and now out in force."

"When did you ever see two, and in uniform?"

"Carrying Tracker-Lenosz, too."

"Never mind, they're probably looking for a purse-snatcher."

Kham let his eyes wander, as if aimlessly looking over the crowd. For a second, he saw nothing significant, but then he registered the image. Two men, rather thin, wearing one-piece gray coveralls, walking now away from the restaurant, accompanied by two sleek, gray animals who loped along beside them without visible connection, but who also moved as if they were part of the two men. Their passage seemed aimless, but the agent part of Cesar Kham noted the subtle movements of their heads, men and animals, which indicated a careful scanning pattern, even though he could not see their faces from this angle. Ship-security agents, patrolling, of course. But looking for what? They had passed, certainly, within hailing distance of himself and Arunda, and yet passed on. He breathed deeply, and turned again to his meal, as if he had seen nothing. The murmur of voices around them continued, against a background susurrus from which it was impossible to extract anything.

". . . saw them carry a body-bag out of . . ."

". . . go upstairs and harass the swells in . . ."

". . . wouldn't mess with . . ."

". . . and when we got to Havaerque, we ran slap out . . ."

". . . Nedro is nothing but a hoage. . . ."

". . . onliest way I know to . . ."

". . . and she was so fat that if you told her to haul-arse, she'd have to make two trips. . . ."

". . . routine patrol, likely. On the *Banastre Tarleton* they patrolled steerage almost hourly. And we were glad to have it, I can tell you, all those crazy religious colonists . . ."

". . . on the *Pedro Francisco,* they'd turn Lenosz loose in a heartbeat."

Kham looked up at Arunda. "Shipsecurity. Seems to be a routine patrol. Somewhat out of ordinary, but within tolerance. Why worry? Had they been coming for us, they'd have had us now."

"All the same, it gave me a fright. When did they start using Lenosz?"

"I wasn't aware they were being used. It's news to me. Still, we've been out of touch. Heliarcos, then Oerlikon, Heliarcos, and back here. Who knows?"

Arunda ruffled her fingers through her hair, shaking her head slowly. "There is much we don't seem to know, ourselves. I have to vote for us staying close together."

Kham leaned forward, massaged his eyebrows. "Yes, of course. Tonight. But here's the way we arrange it: you get yourself shifted to one level up, a double. Then I'll follow."

"Why not come with me?"

"I've got to find out how much of an alarm is out. Some fine work. I can't do it with a partner. We have to know some of this—how bad it is. Then we can decide what we need to do."

"Very well. How long will it take?"

"About a day, should be. Stay put."

"How will you know where to find me?"

"Re-register openly. I'll call."

Arunda nodded. "Tonight."

"Oh, yes. Tonight, for a fact."

"And what about the girl? Are you going to press on with that, too?"

"For the moment, the girl will have to wait." Kham picked up the bill, studied it for a moment, critically, and then signed it, citing a particular alphanumeric code group. Then he said to Arunda, who had already gotten up to leave, "Do what you can to try to trace the girl. We'll take that up again directly."

16

"For the hard choices that define you there are no preset priorities, no magic answer; you place value and choose. But the proof lies in the obverse—when we start explaining away things by saying 'it just happened,' or some such similar nonsense, we admit that we did not choose anything, save to drift away into oblivion on a current of vagrant passions and miscellaneous lusts. No one can deny the beauty and ecstasy, but those moments were also balanced by equivalent amounts of terror, heartbreak, self-doubts of truly industrial strength. And in the end, surrounded by ruins, we ask why, and blame a cruel god."

— H.C., Atropine

A SOFT, ALMOST-INAUDIBLE chime of exquisite high pitch sounded, having no perceptible source. Nazarine had been lying back across the bed, not asleep, nor yet awake, but when she heard the chime she looked across the room immediately, to where Faren had been dozing in a soft chair. Faren left the chair and stood by the bed, touching the commset. "Who calls?"

"Ngellathy here."

Faren said, to Nazarine, "My contact in Shipsecurity. That one is safe."

"Let him in."

Faren released the door, and into the dimmed room stepped a slender man in one of the ubiquitous shipgray uniform coveralls. Slipped into the room might be better. Or even better, flowed. He locked the door behind him and joined the two by the bed. To Nazarine's sharpened senses, it seemed something brief passed between Faren and the man, who seemed a curious blend of irreconcilable opposites: tense, yet also internally totally relaxed.

Faren glanced at him once more, and then to Nazarine. "Here we have Dorje Ngellathy, a Securityman who most of the time is a hopeless

attitude case, but who, in a tight spot, is the only one I can depend on."
And to Ngellathy she added, "This is Nazarine Alea, lately of Oerlikon,
our unscheduled stop."

Ngellathy nodded, impatiently, curtly. Satisfied at last that the preliminaries were done with, he sat in the chair Faren had just vacated. He
said, "Here is how things stand now. The body has been picked up.
Faren, you were right in your suspicion of the pattern of trauma. Medical is going over it before ejection to see if they can derive a pattern.
Some of these hand-assassins follow discrete schools. As for the killer,
we used Alea's description of the probable, and presently he reappeared
at the room. We had a viscoder installed. Had a woman with him,
matches your description. They came aboard at Oerlikon, but are not,
apparently, using Oerlikonian names. He lists as Czermak Pentrel'k, she
as Morelat Eikarinst."

Nazarine said, "You haven't done anything!"

"No. We are holding, partly on your request, partly because we want
to find out exactly what we are dealing with. Sec/Chief doesn't care for
that pattern of injuries and wants to know."

"How?"

"We have an intermediate stop on Teragon. It's not in the route, and
you can't buy a ticket for it, but *Kalmia* always drops in for a while."

Nazarine looked across the space between them. Ngellathy was difficult to see, to realize, to describe. Shadowy, subtle, even sneaky, there
was strangeness writ hard all over him, but even so, she could see no
particular evil in him. At the least, he was no more disreputable than
Faren. She said, "What's Teragon?"

"Once was a small planet on a small system. That was long ago.
Turned out it's near the center of our planetary communications system, so there they built a city. And more city. The whole planet is now
city. They even figured out a way to make their own food. You can read
about it. But there, we can tie in and get the proper patches to link up
and dig deep before we move. And never fear—Pentrel'k isn't getting
off this ship alive."

Faren asked, "Dorje, you don't know where they come from?"

"No. They claim to be from that planet we stopped at, but we have
eliminated that right away. No, we've got him where we want him, and
he'll stay there."

Nazarine said, in a low voice, almost a mutter, "I need him alive."

Ngellathy turned now directly toward her, and said, "I hear, but I
can't understand why."

"He has been hunting me, and I need to find out where he comes from. Not where he was born."

He laughed, softly. "Why not ask him?"

Nazarine folded her arms under her breasts. "Perhaps. But consider: the woman with him—would she not be from the same place?"

"High probability."

"Are you watching her?"

"Certainly."

Nazarine looked away from Ngellathy, lest he read what was in her face. He saw the motion, and added, "Shipmatter now, of course. I know you understand how that must be. No vendettas, revanches, loitering with intent to suborn mayhem, and so forth. I'm no stickler for forms for their own sake—there are more people involved in this than just you, now."

"No, nothing like that. I was thinking that it might be possible for your people to separate them, and we would . . . have a short chat with her. All under supervision, naturally."

Again, that small, assured chuckle. "Naturally."

"What do you think?"

He looked off into the shadows of the darker parts of the room. Then back, abruptly fixing her with a strong gaze. "It could be arranged. And what afterward? Confinement?"

"I was thinking you could simply turn her loose. She'll tell her partner what I asked, and what I said. . . ." She let it hang.

"Maybe not so good. We don't want him too highly motivated to excellence."

"Could you just put her off, say, at the planet we'll stop over at? Teragon?"

"Hmf. Now there's a rich one. You're full of them. They have cross-world comms there, and doubtless she'd report back to their bosses. Might stir up forty kinds of hellation. We don't know yet who they work for. Some of the more obvious things we have already eliminated, but that doesn't mean they don't have connections, in fact, that they are not obvious argues for excellent connections. We don't want to arrive at the first scheduled port of call and have *Kalmia* impounded."

"I see." Nazarine stood up. "Take me to her. No recordings, nobody but me. And arrest me if she's harmed."

Faren now interjected, "Are you sure you want to do this?"

"Yes."

Faren now stood up and said, to Ngellathy, "Take her."

He shook his head, but stood anyway, still shaking his head. "Come on. We'll cook something up on the way. I will probably have her confined afterward."

Nazarine added emphatically, "I don't want them dead or harmed. They're worth nothing to me dead."

"Let's go," said Ngellathy, and the three of them stepped out of Nazarine's room, into the balcony-passage high over the middle-level concourse. It was night cycle now out in the immense inside space, and the overheads that illuminated it and lent the appearance of daylight were now out and the space was dark. But far below, there were piercingly bright lights under the trees and awnings, and across the concourse, watchlights by another wall of rooms and suites glimmered like distant city lights. Nazarine walked with energy and anticipation, but looking out over that space, and understanding that she was riding, a passive passenger inside an enormous artifact, she caught herself holding a fugitive memory from Phaedrus, of the open, empty spaces and starry nights of Zolotane.

Down on the floor of the concourse, it was now the ship's analogue of night, and nighttime gaiety was well advanced: well-behaved crowds sat to their tipple in taverns, while in other places, the throb and wail of music wafted out into the illuminated squares and plazas, and in the dim interiors they sensed rather than saw directly the pulse and motion of dancers. Outside, small groups and solitary individuals strolled, leered, followed one another, or gathered in small groups to watch troupes of acrobats, or musicians, or wonderworking prestidigitators who plucked flowers from ears, removed gold rings from pockets, or perhaps colored handkerchiefs would be made to appear from the most unlikely, and slightly vulgar places.

As they walked through the plazas, Nazarine covertly watched Faren and Dorje Ngellathy out of the corner of her eyes. They both seemed perfectly in their element, not so much as participants in the merrymaking, but more, perhaps, as lifeguards on a beach, who might take a short stroll from time to time. She also saw that they seemed to lose concern, and concentrate more on each other, at least in short, fleeting fragments of time. For a time they held hands lightly, almost absentmindedly, and by some change in inner state Nazarine saw an expression of innocent girlishness flicker into life on Faren's face. Dorje, who was more visible in the plain light of the concourse streetlights, now became something less mysterious and more human. The face was basically that of some hardened mercenary, or veteran of obscure border actions: high, prominent cheekbones, a hawk nose, a wide slash mouth whose upper lip was fuller than the lower, and epicanthic folds at the corners of long, drooping eyelids. He wore his hair cropped off unfashionably short. In build, he was slender, but wide at the shoulders, as tall as Nazarine herself. He moved easily, loosely, but wary. And he, too, changed in short little instants, managing in those times to shed the hardness and seem something from another time, another place. A young hunter; a successful candidate from the tribe's Rite of Passage, one who had undertaken the long quest and who had seen the Holy Man.

They stopped briefly at one of the communications-points, and Ngellathy spoke for a time. When he had finished, he said, "She's taken a couple of rooms down here on the floor, in a small pension above a jeweler's shop. Now she is alone. It's not far from here."

Nazarine asked, "How will we do it?"

"We'll go in and talk with her a bit, and then you can go in."

Nazarine nodded assent, and they continued. Their walk now took them into a part of the concourse arranged to appear as if it were some small shopping quarter of a fashionable resort: small buildings of light-colored stone or soapstone tiles alternated with discreet little shops of stucco and stained wood. In between were carefully arranged plots that seemed like vacant lots until one noted the careful, almost over-tidy landscaping, the fussy attention to details.

They arrived at the shop, which had an upper floor devoted to apartments, as seemed common in this district. It was situated on an alley, with more of the same sort of structures behind it, most connected to the street level by a series of rambling staircases of old-fashioned and quaint construction.

The second floor of the jeweler's shop was reached by one of these stairs, and they went up the narrow way in a line, Nazarine last. At the landing at the top, Dorje and Faren knocked on the door. After a time, it was opened cautiously, and a brief conversation ensued, after which the door opened farther and they went in. The door closed. Nazarine held her place on the stairs, waiting, occasionally glancing around. A few people passed by out on the main thoroughfare, but none seemed to look up or notice her; they were preoccupied with their own concerns. And while she waited, she slowly let herself move into a greater awareness, listening, sensing everything she could. As she did so, the illusion of a city on a surface faded, and the concourse seemed shadowy, insubstantial. She could hear a very soft but persistent ultrabass vibration, which was of course the ship. Sounds also had an echoing ring to them, unnatural in a true open space. The smells were too clean, too mechanical, technological. Somewhere, someone should have been frying onions. There was no woodsmoke, no sweat, no pungent scent of some domesticated animal.

Above, on the landing, the door opened, and Faren came out, followed by Dorje, who motioned to her. She mounted the remaining stairs and turned at the top, while Dorje said, in passing, "Remember. No action."

She nodded, and went through the door Dorje held open for her. Inside was a small room, rather like a parlor, connected with others on the far side. There was a simple sofa, facing wooden chairs. On the sofa sat a woman who stood when Nazarine came in. The woman was well-proportioned with no fat, but she was clearly past her prime, retaining as her most striking feature a long cascade of rich, dark brown hair. Her features were regular and clear, unremarkable save for a mouth that was slightly too large for the face, which gave her a slightly childish look. But one other thing distinguished the woman's features as Nazarine saw them: the woman was holding herself under rigid control, and was clearly terrified.

Nazarine did not know how to begin. The woman was so tense, almost anything could happen. She decided to keep it simple, and retain the advantage of fear that she held. She reached for Rael, and found that selfness waiting. As that came into her awareness, her perception of the woman shifted slightly, subtly: she seemed less vulnerable, and more contemptible, rather like a child caught doing something dangerous about which it has been repeatedly warned. She said, softly, "You recognize me." Statement, not question.

The woman hesitated, then said, "Yes, I know you from ID Mindset."

"My name is now Nazarine Alea. You also know what I am and who else I have been."

"Yes."

"Please sit down. I arranged this, not to attack you, but to try to understand some things. As you know, a Securityman waits outside on the stoop; had it been my method to use violence, I would not have asked him to announce me, or to wait."

She sat gingerly, watching Nazarine all the time. Nazarine sat on one of the wooden chairs. After a few uneasy moments, the woman said, "You seem to have thought of everything."

Nazarine said, "Neither you nor your partner have any meaning for me dead."

The woman said, "I fear you, but what I fear worse than that is knowing the probable consequences of your remaining alive, and finding your way back. We seem to have lost initiative in the latter case, and so await the former with the usual dread. What else?"

Nazarine observed tautly, "When I was Phaedrus, you sent commandos against unarmed children to get me. Your agents killed what little family I had. I lived with a plain woman who could see forever and was one with the earth; she was one in that house who died. And in my present embodiment, your partner killed my lover. True, I understand he was selfish and had his faults, but such as he was, he was mine. Someone sent a man to seduce me and then kill me when I was Damistofia Azart. Who are you to inflict such terror, and in whose name?"

Palude said, "I will tell you nothing."

Nazarine said, "How would you prefer it? I can do what I need to do from where I stand with what I know, or can determine without you. But the focus is ill-defined, smeared-out. It will be like on Oerlikon, in Lisagor. Or you can cooperate, and what I have to do will then be clean, surgical. No innocent need feel the blow."

"But you'd do something, all the same."

"I'd do something. I'm not sure yet exactly what. But I know that when I'm finished, you'll make no more Morphodites. And there won't be any more Oerlikons."

Palude shook her head. "There will always be Oerlikons. Fools hide from the inevitable, and exploiters come and ransack them, without their ever knowing it."

Nazarine digested the cynical remark, which Palude had said easily, as if the thought had been an integral part of her selfness. She thought, *That's a widespread view in her world, and interesting for that reason.* She formulated that in the peculiar symbology of reading she used. A statement of belief. She said, "Don't you understand that when victims come easy, anyone can become one—even you. Whoever your bosses are, they exploit you as callously as they exploited Oerlikon, and to no better purpose. Is this the meaning of your life, that you travel unimaginable light-years to suborn the killing of children?"

Palude looked down, unwilling to meet Nazarine's eyes. But she said, "You're no better than they are; you would end up destroying our whole way of life, an honorable mode that has existed for thousands of years. And you don't know as much as you think you do; if you knew where we came from, you wouldn't be here talking to me."

Nazarine again let the remarks settle. A picture was forming in her mind, but it wasn't yet clear exactly what it was. She thought a moment, and then said, "Have it your way. But you've failed in your mission: you haven't gotten me."

"Yet."

"Knowing where your enemy is, that's the best defense there is. We have Cesar Kham bottled up in this ship. We have you. This ship will stop at Teragon. They have proper facilities there. What I need to know, I'll find out. Security is checking the account number you billed your passage to."

Palude said, "The transit isn't over yet."

Nazarine shrugged. "It's as long for you as it is for me. Maybe longer."

"What are you going to do with me?"

"You? Nothing. You're free to wander as you will. I imagine you'll tell Kham I spoke to you. That's exactly what I want you to do. It will stimulate him to take certain actions."

"You've seen the consequences of this?"

"Of course." Nazarine lied, deliberately now, relying on the woman's resistance and fear of losing something for this failure. Not her life. Not drugs. But they had some kind of hold on her, and it was long-term and powerful. She added, "And of course there's the option of doing nothing at all. I really want to be free of you people—that's what I want. I could disappear again."

Palude smiled now, an eerie expression in the context. She said, "Oh, we know enough about you to know you can't do that again. You lose age in Change, we know that. And you should be a lot younger than you are, so we know that you've found a way to slow that—but not eliminate it. So you're stuck now as Nazarine, for a while, at least. And as long as you're one person, you can be traced, no matter what."

"You've been briefed very well. That information could only come from The Mask Factory, from Pternam, or three of the leaders of the Heraclitan Society. So now I know that there's a connection between you-now and them-then. And it's reasonable to assume that you were sent back because you knew Oerlikon well, hence were there before."

"I'll say no more to you."

"Think about what I've said." Nazarine stood up and turned to go. She looked back, over her shoulder, and added, "Since you know so much about me, consider what you must know about how far Rael can see. I am still Rael, you know. Tulilly, too. I want the ones who gave the orders."

Palude said, "The ones who gave the original orders are long dead. They have escaped you."

Nazarine reached for the door. "The ones who gave you *your* orders are alive and prosperous somewhere: I will change both circumstances. Have a pleasant evening." And she went out, to where Faren and Dorje awaited her on the landing. Dorje looked inside to assure himself that Palude was unharmed, and then rejoined them.

He said, "Did you accomplish anything?"

Nazarine shook her head. "No. Or very little. She is defiant and uncooperative." They went down the stairs to the street, where they let their footsteps guide them back into the main open areas of the concourse. After a long time, Nazarine said, "She fears her own people more than she fears me, or Shipsecurity."

Dorje looked off, and said, "That might tell you something about what kind of organization she comes from. But let me ask you, what are you that they would hunt you so thoroughly?"

She answered, "I am someone who escaped something no one was supposed to escape from. They fear what I know. What they don't know is that I don't know what they think I do. If they had left it alone, I would never have come this far."

He said, "You should move to a more secure room."

She shook her head. "No. That one is not an operative. I could see that. And you have Kham under surveillance. He will doubtless become aware of that. No, I can protect myself adequately."

Out in the concourse, they passed one of the small uprights containing a communications terminal, and Dorje checked in on the net now covering the movements of Cesar Kham. After a moment, he told Faren and Nazarine, "He doesn't seem to be aware he's being covered, but nonetheless he seems to have retired for the night. Curious, that: it's early yet. But in essence they have him covered. I think we can relax for a little bit. I would like to stop working for a bit and sit down to a fine dinner—or at the least a glass of cold beer. Yes?"

Faren immediately agreed. Nazarine first demurred, but as she did so she became conscious of the undeniable fact that she couldn't recall when she had eaten last. Then she agreed.

Dorje said, "There's a fine place not very far from here that serves an excellent braised fowl, accompanied by pilaf and green peppers, ranging from interesting to excruciating. And they serve cold beer," he added, raising one finger vertically, demonstratively. "I believe it's called The Bel Canto." And suiting action to intent, he set off across a wooded glade of drooping shaggybark trees to emerge on the far side almost in front of the very place he was seeking.

Nazarine looked at the place and exclaimed, "It looks like a water-front tavern, and disreputable at that!" She laughed, and added, "Do they include drunken sailors as part of the decor?"

Dorje pretended to look aloof, and said, in a mock-haughty tone, "No aspect of the illusion of reality is too good for our guests. We even furnish brawls for a fee."

Nazarine nodded. "I'm sure." The establishment bore the façade of stucco arches, washed a stained pink, with globular lanterns hanging from metal rods bridging them. Through this arcade crowds eddied and flowed, around flimsy metal tables at which customers sat, reading newspapers, books, or drinking various beverages: espresso, clear ouzo which turned milky when one added water to it, slender, crude glasses filled with an oily green liquid—absinth—and crocks of brew. Inside, as they passed through the foyer, was even more detailed: here people were eating, drinking, conversing, devouring various grilled, spitted, and smoked foods, gesticulating with their hands to emphasize various points. The din of their voices and the rattle of crockery was deafening.

They found a winding path through the chaos, ducked down a low hallway, and emerged, after a short, cramped stairwell, back into the night, and the matchless quiet of an arbor covered with grapevines growing along rustic rough-hewn poles. This part was almost empty, and they could choose their table, rude planks covered by a checkered table-cloth. A girl came to take their order, wearing a linen peasant blouse, a loose cotton skirt, and barefooted.

Dorje ordered, including a round of beer for each of them, and sat back in his chair. "And now, for a small carouse."

Nazarine looked off across the arbor, under the grapevines, and said, "It will have to be small. The events of the day are catching up with me."

He said, "To be sure. We have a cure for that, too. You are our guest."

Faren added, "Whether they have a handle on Kham or not, I would hold your room to be less than safe. We should watch over you for a time."

The girl returned, bringing a tray of frosted mugs and a pitcher of beer. Nazarine said, taking a mug for herself, "I don't refuse, but I need to be alone for a bit."

Faren answered, "No, it's the other way. You shouldn't be. Now is when you need company, forgetfulness. And," she added, "there is still much you should learn about us. The best way is to experience it."

Nazarine sensed a subtle pressure behind the statements, almost an invitation, but she wasn't sure yet to what. She shrugged the feeling off.

What of it? No matter what they have in mind, it certainly won't be hunting me as I have been. I could almost welcome that.

After what seemed a short time, the barefoot peasant girl returned with a larger tray, containing, as Dorje had claimed, platters of braised fowl, pilaf, and a plate of several sorts of peppers, some of which looked suspicious indeed. Dorje stirred from his reclining posture and indicated a round, pale pepper which seemed inoffensive. "Appearances are deceiving with these if you have no experience with them. This one, for example, is not for the unprepared, while this deadly looking little purple number has nothing but fine taste to recommend it." He rolled his eyes, popped the round pepper in his mouth, and immediately followed it with a bite of fowl, an expression of alarm growing across his face.

After the meal, which all three attacked with singleminded determination with little conversation in between, the serving girl brought another round of the icy beer, pungent with hops, and they settled back. Nazarine had, more than once, caught herself smiling at Dorje's adventures with the peppers, which had been heroic, epic, and wildly comical all at once. Now, his face perspiring from his exertions, he sat back and sipped guiltily at the beer, looking around from time to time to see if anyone had noticed them. Faren had been more restrained, less volatile, but she also had attacked the peppers and beer. Now her eyes were alight, dancing, alert. She thought, *How could I have ever thought her dull and businesslike?*

But there was an element common to both of them, presumably both members of this strange transtellar civilization, which she could not recall seeing on Oerlikon: an ability to let go, to become a magnified version of themselves, to express a unique strangeness which lay at the heart of every individual. This was part of the whole she was seeking, too.

She ventured, "I am now full, also of beer, and wonder, why of all you could choose to ask, why you have not asked why these people follow me with such dedicated persistence, causing so much ruin along the way."

Faren volunteered, "You were clearly being harried by tramps and thieves! It didn't take me long to understand that! And since you were as green as you were, it would engage me to oppose whatever was going on."

Dorje's answer was more complex, and much of the merriment left him gradually while he composed it. "Inhabited space is large, larger than one person can encompass in a lifetime. Crime and vice exist, never doubt it! Enforcement remains limited. One cannot correct all evils. Therefore we try, as an ideal, to attain an overlapping consensus on agreeable points. We agree to differ, so to speak. Also consider that some things remain relatively stable. This ship, for example. Many factors shape this vessel, and only a minority are within the realm of science and technology. Some forces are economic, others are human constants, others still constants of other sapient creatures with which we have traffic through a series of mutual accommodations. You can't enforce ways of thinking—only behavior. So here, for me, this: your pursuers, for one reason or another, do not choose to invite us to help capture you. Either that pursuit is clearly criminal in itself, or else we have a spillover from one sphere into another. This life Faren and I inhabit is one sphere, with clear limits. Suppose you were a religious refugee, fleeing the grim derogators of infallible doctrine. So long as you behave reasonably *here*, your differences *there* must not enter into it. You came to us, asked us what *our* rules were; they set to work breaking them without stint, and they show signs of knowing them better than you, perhaps better than I."

"Surely you have curiosity."

"Of course! And yet we are each in part dreams and fluff and projections of what we would wish to be. This is how we come to terms with all the interesting things we will never have a chance to be. In order that I have the ability to project, I must allow you that same latitude. I see before me someone who is driven by purpose—whatever that is—and I also see an attractive girl who wishes very much to be accepted as what she seems to be. What you were before—therefore—must be your own. I will not spoil your illusion. Besides, you did not ask us what we were beforetimes, or why we spend our lives in this cargo-pallet between worlds, why I reside in the Securityman barracks and Faren keeps to the Technicians' cubicles. It is in part a germ of truth in what the Acrobats of Pintang suggest in their rites, that the magic is accidental, aleatory, and we must take it as we may. Let the higher-ups scheme and plot: we will take what is ours, the fleeting luminous moment."

Faren said, "Well said! I had not heard you declaim so before. But true! Antinomy lies everywhere, therefore we do not inquire into ultimates too closely. It would fracture what little coherence we have. We

accept you as you are, yes. Be what you wish to be. Conduct no inqui-
sitions, attack no innocents, and . . ."

Dorje added, nonsensically, "Rotate your tires." He had become
slightly tipsy.

Faren stood up and stretched, catlike, and suggested, "We will fall into
terrible habits if we stay here."

Dorje agreed, and also stood. "Exactly! There are more sights to be
seen, things we will show you. You fear forgetting what was good and
will be no more. We do not ask you to forget, but to understand. It all
has its place."

Nazarine smiled despite herself. "Where to now?"

Dorje said, "First a longer stroll, to clear the fumes away, and then, I
think, to the baths."

"The baths?"

"You are new to us, but you will become us. We will initiate you. You
must become."

"Become what?"

"Yourself."

Arunda Palude sat where she had been for a long time after Nazarine
had left, thinking, reflecting, considering. She could not, try as she
would, find an alternative to the situation as it appeared to her. She
thought she had done well enough in meeting with the girl. She
thought, *It's impossible, but that thing actually is a complete, genuine
woman. No imitation! And sure of herself, too.* Yes, she had done well
enough, but of course it wasn't good enough; merely a sop to the little
sense of honor she had left, the old loyalties. Their efforts and long mission had come to nothing, outmaneuvered at every turn and juncture
by this creature, who seemed to distort the very laws of probability.
She had cut them apart like a surgeon, isolated them with an instinct
which was terrifying, like a magic, or some fantastic superability. *We
have failed. Moreover, our acts may have, probably did, activate it against
the very thing we feared.* It seemed to her in one way that this arrangement of things had just happened, but another way, she could see a
thread of causality stretching back and back, past herself and Kham,
into a time she could not imagine. She caught herself almost, but not
quite, asking the fatal question—what had the regents been doing on
Oerlikon, anyway?

But she rejected that line of thinking. *That way leads me into impossible, totally untenable paths.* She thought of the long years on Oer-likon, a lifetime committed to a specific sense of identity, purpose, goals. *I cannot throw it away.* But the conclusions of this evening's work could not be escaped, either: *we have failed. What was to have been mine cannot now be. We cannot return, we cannot go forward. For a time Kham may proceed, but his progress is an illusion. Zeno's paradox! The closer he comes, the slower he goes. He will never catch her while she dismembers Heliarcos like a witless cretin dismembering some insect.* And Kham, she saw, would dredge up every skill he knew, long after it had become hopeless. It was already past that point. And he would blunder onward like a berserk machine out of control, steadily increasing the casualty rate of by-standers, innocents. She saw it!

For a second, the possibility flickered before her of going the other way, of giving Nazarine the pieces of the puzzle she needed. That would be a relief. Perhaps the girl was correct, right, and their pattern wrong. Tempting, but unthinkable. She could not go against every decision she had participated in. It was a sorry pass to be in.

The awful sense of depression deepened as she thought of one more horror: they could not communicate with Heliarcos, either. Not until they stopped at some place which had planetary mass. The old way, when the project had been on, they had relays good to a certain dis-tance. But here, now, they were bound to the routines of the everyday universe. *We can't even tell them that the thunderbolt is loosed, and falling on them, through the negation of transitspace.*

She arose, and went to the windows, to look out on the street below the apartment over the jeweler's. It was late, and passersby were few, or else congregating in the parks and plazas of the concourse proper, not in this isolated little byway. The shops were all closed now, anyway.

She turned away from the window, and walked slowly, carefully blanking her mind, into the small bedroom. There it was dark, the shades drawn against the streetlights outside. She felt the edge of the bed, and lay out full-length on it, feeling a sense of purpose coming back to her. She thought clearly, *I do not wish to witness any more of this.* And, *There is one way left.*

She felt back in her mouth for a false tooth, implanted against the ne-cessity that one day she might have had to face the redoubtable Femisti-cleo Chugun in the interrogation rooms of Lisagor. Arunda clamped her jaw down hard, feeling the material give a little, and then snap. A sud-den flavor, as if of cardamom, or oil of eucalyptus, filled her mouth and nostrils. She swallowed, nervously, and waited, fearing, and yet relieved.

17

"Looking at a collection of old photographs, it came to me that those events, now so quaint and meaningless to me/now, once meant something terribly important to them/then; now all for the most part vanished back into the earth they sprung from, leaving only these small artifacts behind no one understands the significance of today. But for them the sky displayed its infinite permutations, the seasons changed, wheel in the sky. For them, the men were handsome, stalwart, full of visions, and the women lovely, immediate, supple. . . the vine-covered sun-drenched summer afternoons of a thousand watermelon yesterdays. That/then was as real as is this/now, to us: terribly significant, filled with meaning and mystery, by turns warm and comforting, or else dire and full of unspeakable menace. Each of us would like to think that our own view is the brightest, but it was always bright to each of us, bittersweet and fading even as we reached for it. Perhaps a commonplace, still it needs resaying, maybe several times over, that we don't denigrate them, and that we don't enlarge ourselves too much."

—H.C., Atropine

IN HIS LONG career as an agent, fixer of mistakes, instiller of renewed zeal, and supervisor of various clandestine operations, actions, and deeds by night and day, Cesar Kham had always operated well within the bounds of the elementary tactical theory he had learned when he had been selected to enter the Oerlikon project. He had grown used to that theory, at home in it, sensitive to degrees of concepts within it. He knew, sometimes to fine detail, exactly to what degree he was being followed, if indeed he was. The problem was that on Oerlikon, within Lisagor, one only saw a certain range of these activities, and for the rest of possible techniques, one either forgot them from disuse or came in time to ignore them. He understood now, aboard *Kalmia*, that this was a failing that could be fatal, and so he spent his first few hours away from Palude recalling his lessons, some of them rusty indeed, trying once again to bring up the skills that had enabled him—and others—to move about Lisagor undetected and unsuspected.

Back in the multiple-occupant quarters he had been assigned to, too big to be called a room, and too small to be called a barracks or dormitory, Kham lay back on his bunk and meditated on what he had seen so far, and what inferences he could possibly draw from it. *This kind of accommodation they called a "bay,"* he thought irrelevantly. But he recalled in full clarity and high contrast the fact that he had sighted another group of strolling, apparently aimless Securitymen, near the entrance to his bay section. *They've got a random grid on me.*

This was a refined pattern designed to keep a loose tether on a subject, and to narrow the search range should they wish to move in. So soon! But a glaring anomaly persisted. That they reacted so swiftly, that argued for the solution of a crime; but that in turn brought with it the idea that apprehension would shortly follow. And it hadn't. Instead, this zone-defense operation. Kham had carefully pruned his psyche of paranoid tendencies, but even with that, he knew with virtual certainty that the net he had seen was clearly aimed at him. And he could reasonably assume that they'd know within minutes if he tried to escape the confines of this bay, for some other part of the ship. Openly. There had to be a way. One could evade a zone defense of men. There were simple exercises to accomplish that. And that was why the Securitymen were accompanied by Lenosz. You could make a play on the human nervous system by sleight of hand, but the olfactory sense of the Lenosz would render the usual range of disguises useless. The conclusion was not difficult: he had to find some point of access into the ship's own internal passageway system. Use of the public corridors and areas would alert them immediately. Thus invisible, he could accomplish many things, before they could locate him again. Kham had no doubts what the conclusion of this would be, no illusions. He knew that if he could reach the peak of his powers, he could probably survive for some time aboard *Kalmia*—he had heard tales of that very thing. But he'd never get off it anywhere or within any time that would do him any good.

Ironic, that: the name of the ship was the name of a lovely, delicate flower, quite scentless, which grew on a quaint, gnarled, fibrous-barked tree of Earth. Whose sap and foliage were deadly poisonous. Yes. One moved warily among the evergreen shiny leaves of Kalmia Latifolia.

Kham tried to recall what he knew about the interior arrangement of the large, deep-space liners. They were irregular, bulky structures, utterly unstreamlined. Inside, they were chains of open areas, the concourses, which were joined by trunk corridors, often deliberately designed to be rambling, indirect, partly to give the passengers something to do, and partly to discourage mass movements from one area to another. Between areas there were more direct routes, not really restricted, but plain and intended primarily for crew use. Besides these accessible volumes, there were the crew areas, generally insulated from the passenger areas by blind pockets and mazes. But there was also a maintenance access system, a way technicians could follow and repair the miles of piping, HVAC ductwork from Environmental, electropneumatic lines. There were also waveguides and optical channels for inship communications and cybernetic systems. Kham reasoned that access into the maintways would have to be simple and available at many points. But of course the entries would be hidden, or locked, or subtly disguised. After all, it wouldn't do to make it easy. A person could hide in one of these ships, assuming he had food and water, for years.

He knew from the orientation of the corridor outside, that the bays were separated from their neighbors only by a simple bulkhead. He doubted if the maintways ran as far as between rooms and bays. But there was the floor, the ceiling, and the back wall opposite the door. He was alone, so his task was a bit easier: he carefully went over the floor, looking for almost invisible seam lines, recessed DZUS fasteners, slight mismatches of tilings that would betray an access point. There were none. The floor was tiled in a curious irregular pentagonal tiling that was difficult to follow with the eye, which suggested camouflage, but there was no break in it. The ceiling was featureless and seamless. The light fixtures were clearly only that, and besides, were far too small. That left the back wall.

There was a row of small vents along the juncture with the ceiling, small, unobtrusive. He looked along the floor line; another set of the small vents there. Inlet below, outlet above. He looked harder at the wall. It was divided into vertical bands, broken at odd intervals by horizontal mouldings. Yes. It had to be somewhere on that wall. The vertical bands were separated by different widths of paneling; some narrow, some broad. He went to one side and began testing the wider ones.

Kham finished at the far end of the back wall. None of the panels seemed to have any give, either way. Moreover, they sounded solid when rapped.

Part of the wall was interrupted by a small table or shelf, partly built-in, part supported by struts from the floor. He looked under the table. There was a single square panel there, not quite the same color as the rest of the room. As if it had been replaced. Yes. He felt along the edge, pushed, at first to no purpose, but by pushing in and up in the center, the panel gave first inward, and then swung up. Kham crawled into the space without hesitation, reached back, and swung the panel shut, taking one last look back into the room as he did so. There was no one there. The panel clicked faintly.

He breathed deeply, looked around. This was a different universe. There was lighting here but it was very dim, just enough to make out general outlines. This was at the end of the maintways, and was close. Piping, cable trays, ductwork joining into larger assemblies. He recognized a microwave waveguide. He was in a small pocket, joined to a corridor, a little wider, in which he could stand. He looked carefully. To the left, that was the way to the cohab rooms. The sound down there was flat, deadened. The ductwork got smaller down that way as it passed bay junctions. That had to be dead-ended. The other way, then, to the right. He stepped onto a metal grating, roughened for sure tread and set off along the corridor. At first, his footsteps sounded on the grating, but he forced himself to step lightly, almost glide along, using an irregular rhythm; there were faint sounds in the maintway, clicks, hollow, distant thuds, fragments of sounds, logoi of an unknown language. At intervals small lights illuminated the dark tangle, which grew more dense to the sides as he went farther. The corridor turned and twisted, running in short, straight jogs. Finally he reached stairs going down through several turns. There was slightly more light down there, but no sense of presence. Kham carefully negotiated the stairs, guessing that he had made it out to the main trunk corridor leading out onto the lower concourse.

At the bottom, he was disappointed for a moment. This was a small junction with no frills, no hint of going anywhere. But as he looked around, he felt a surge of anticipation. There was a map. It was mounted on a board, behind scarred and dented plastic, difficult to see in the weak light, but it was a map. Kham forced himself to relax, and then began making a series of stretching motions to limber himself up. A map. Now he could move. He had known that there would have to be one, somewhere.

* * *

The orthography of the system map was simple and direct, and presented the ship, as seen from the point of view of its functioning systems; to the end of simplifying the system aspect, some distortion could not be avoided, and the particular distortion was in the area of scale. What was a straight line on the map might not be, and usually was not, a straight line upon which a human being could walk. But Cesar Kham was not daunted by these difficulties: he plotted the courses he would have to take, and began following them out, doggedly and persistently, passing along the dim catwalks and runs, sometimes in near-darkness. In many ways, it was a strange and surrealistic journey he was making, a passage through the underworld. Sometimes he could catch faint echoes of voices, or of distant work going on, a dropped wrench, a profane or scatological exclamation. Then he stopped, and became very silent, and listened. More often than not, he heard nothing. Had he heard anything? He could not be sure.

Apparently the maintways were not popular places. It was easy to understand that: they were ill-lit, where lit at all, and their routes seemed convenient to no passage. This was the slow way. A labyrinth. But when he came to relatively broad thoroughfares, straight bores running directly through the bowels of the ship, he fairly raced along, exulting that if it was troublesome to him, it would be doubly so to anyone interested in following him. They would have to take the ship apart a section at a time.

For a time, he caught himself almost enjoying the experience, the thrill, the subterranean ecstasy of slinking unseen through the hidden ways. They even thoughtfully provided ration stations at certain points along the way, presumably for the workers who might be engaged in these passages for extended times. The food wasn't fancy: basic nutriment cakes and distilled water. Kham thought more than once that if worse came to worst, he could just remain here. Become a ghost, living from moment to moment, while outside the years passed, and uncounted parsecs between stars, sectors, crossings run over and over again.

In no way could the shape of the ship be discerned from the arrangement of the maintway access lines. Neither the outside nor the open, public interior parts. Indeed, from what he could see of it, he could not recognize any part; he might have been near a concourse or far away from one. All he knew were the piping, the ductwork, the careful geometry of waveguides, the odd angularity of water and reclamation lines.

Once he caught sight of a party of people. They didn't see him, he thought. At first, he thought they might be a maintenance crew, but as he watched, they seemed to accomplish no activity, nor did they seem prepared to work. Far off, across a tangle of piping, the group sat in an unused open section with a cleated floor. They spoke to one another in low, whispery voices that seemed to float, disembodied, in the damp and the cool darkness. Stowaways, escapees? He did not know; he could not discern their conversation, which seemed to go on interminably. And if they were hiding down here, then what would they talk about? The world they left behind, now virtually imaginary, legendary, the "real world," where people succeeded, built bright, shining cities, walked proudly among the shining towers with their healthy, prosperous families. Here they were safe, more or less, at least as safe as the crew and passengers, fed. Somehow they found a way to make some sort of order among themselves. But they were prisoners, too. Safe here, in the guts and nerve linkages, they could never reenter the other world.

The journey went on, interminably. He reached an area, which according to the diagrams and schematics, was close by concourse level four, where he was going. He knew he had to start looking for a way out. In this section, there were a lot of water lines, and underneath, holding tanks, heaters, all sorts of accessory equipment. Overhead there was a tremendous flat construction, condensation dripping randomly from the bottom. From the main section, which seemed to have no visible end from his viewpoint, smaller lines seemed to connect to satellite enclosures which had both power and air connections, as well as the extensive water lines, pumps, and filtration associated with the larger mass. A hydroponic unit? Possible. But why the side tanks? And, more significantly, there seemed to be no entry from the maintway system, which he would have thought would have been a necessity. Also, there was heavy structural bracing and supporting structure associated with this area, much more than usual.

Kham consulted the chart, at the next major junction. Deciphering the small print and symbols in the dim light, he discovered he was under an area called The Baths, which was in fact an enormous swimming pool. Presumably the satellite tanks were smaller cubicles which could only be reached underwater, by swimming. He looked upward again, tracing out the outlines. Yes. There were different levels, and the thing was mostly flat-bottomed. He went back to the schematic, now tracing out the water lines, the conventions of architectural symbols. Circulation, heating, and here (tracing the pathways out with his finger), he could follow the main fill lines, as well as an emergency dump system, with simply huge pipes, which seemed to lead to a sealed reservoir. How did they keep the people from going down the drains when they dumped? Sirens, early warnings, waterphones? That they would have such a construction aboard a ship argued an ability to anticipate emergencies in time to act on them which amazed him.

And a pool, too. That implied something about the long-term stability of the ship, too. One would never think twice about a pool on the surface of a planet, but in a spaceship? The idea gave him a subtle sense of distortion, a nightmarish world-gone-negative quality. He was crawling about on the wrong side, of an interface between two unrealities. The real universe had ceased to matter, and of course, once that, had ceased to exist. What moved? Ship or passing universe? He shook his head violently and muttered a Clispish oath under his breath, an incestuous obscenity.

Kham looked back at the map. Here would certainly be a number of access-points into the other world of the passengers' ship. He oriented himself according to the chart, and, glancing upward from time to time, studied the configuration of the massive tanks overhead. Finally, he saw there was an access point, not too far away, up an elevated catwalk, into a warm-air ductwork system, and out through a grille. Looking about once more to get his bearings fixed, he started off, away from the chart junction.

He found the catwalk, which rapidly ascended into the maze of lines either serving the baths or detouring around it. It was just like the chart symbolized, easy to follow from memory; Kham climbed ascending ramps, ladders, short traverses, presently finding himself passing directly beside the bulging flank of the main tank. He felt the material, gently, so as not to make any noise. It was not metal, but a composite material, covered with a layer of a softer mass, perhaps insulation. Here and there the covering had been disturbed—torn or abraded, and the inner material showed through. It seemed glassy, transparent.

Ahead was one of the side-tanks. His pathway passed over the tube that connected it with the main tank, over a short ladder. At the top something caught his eye in the darkness, a streak of light from the satellite tank. He looked closer. Here a patch of the insulating material had been carefully peeled back. Kham stopped and looked. The material on the tanks was semi-transparent, and here one could see through it, somewhat indistinctly, but nevertheless one could see. He suppressed an inane chuckle. Was that entertainment for the maintcrews? To climb up in here and peer into a side chamber? He looked into the tank.

Whatever the material was, it did not transmit sound well, or at all, and it only transmitted light along a narrow path. You could not see the far edges of the chamber.

In this one there were three people, a man and two women, sitting on a ledge built into the tank. All three were nude, but at the moment seemed to be doing nothing of particular interest. The view was slightly blurred, but he tried to make them out. The man was slim, wiry, well-muscled. One woman was pale, with a rather long body and short legs, slightly built, not particularly young. The other was . . . hard to see, because of the angle. Something familiar, something just beyond perception. Yes. Long legs, full breasts. Younger than the other two, more smoothly curved. She sat, clasping her knees. The other woman moved out of the field of view momentarily, and returned, and began rubbing the girl's back. She lifted her face up from her knees, and almost looked directly at him. However, she was not looking at anything. Her eyes were unfocused. But he recognized the face immediately. It was Nazarine. The slender woman moved closer, on her knees, and began working the girl's shoulders, the back of her neck. He could see movement of their faces; they were talking. The man gestured to her with a hand, and extended it to her, and she reached, hesitantly, and took it.

Kham looked away, back into the underways, the dimness, the half-light. The piping, the ductwork. He put the insulating material back the way he had found it, and violently rubbed his face to massage the tension out of it.

Right there! Not three meters away! Playing threesomes while I crawl through the sewers for my very life. And there's no way to get through that stuff, we don't even know how thick it is. And even if I can actually get out, up farther, there's no way I could find that particular chamber before they left it. Crap and diarrhea!

He thought of what he was actually doing, trying to reach Palude secretly, and the thought sobered him. Kham looked about him, regrouped his bearings, and climbed down, to the next catwalk. After a passage through a narrowing series of rising accesses, Kham found his way blocked by a large, smooth tube, with an oval airlock protruding from it. The way ended here. This was the ductwork. He looked back along the way he had come: the view was no different than what he had been looking at before: pipes, tubes, grids of narrow walkways, bulkheads. Dim, distant lights. A maze, a labyrinth. He opened the outer door and crawled into a mini-airlock, pulling the door shut behind him before opening the other door, immediately in front of him. Not to have a pressure leak—that would set alarms off all over this ship.

Opening the inner lock, he found himself in a tubular passage, the air moving slowly, warm and humid. This would be the exit air line from the baths, and to his left, facing the airflow, there would be a removable grille. Kham stooped over, half-crouched, and began walking forward, feeling his muscles protest at the unnatural posture, grimacing in the dark. Not quite completely dark. Light was leaking into the air duct from somewhere ahead.

The line ended at a locker room, which seemed to be empty. There was no motion, no sound. Far off, he could hear splashing, voices, but it was far away. *Now.* He pressed at the grille, and for a moment felt a cold wash of pure panic when it didn't give. He sat back, trying to think it out. He reached, caught the grille, and pulled, felt it move, and release, and then it swung up, back into the locker room. Kham stepped out, and replaced the grille.

He wasn't certain which way to go from here, but toward the sounds seemed the only way; he set off and traversed the room, finding that it ended at a blind passage that led one way, left, to the baths, and right, apparently, to the concourse. Kham went right, and began walking in what he imagined was an ordinary manner after the stooping and ducking under pipes he had been doing. This passageway joined others, flowed into a lobby, and into a courtyard of ornamental paving, overhung by the graceful shapes of Benjamin Figs, here grown to unheard-of sizes. The courtyard apparently was down. One had to go up. The lights of the concourse seemed far away, across enormous spaces. Here, small footlights followed the pathways. But there was a sense of open space, and darkness far, far overhead. Much more so than the area he had left behind. Other folk passed, parties of several men and women, couples, some family groups, all busy, chattering, oblivious. Kham wanted to run but could think of no reasonable excuse to do so.

At the top, where the sunken courtyard merged with the general level of the concourse, he located a bank of public communicators, and used one to call for the location of one passenger Morelat Eikarinst. The operator read out the address, and on the accompanying vid display, caused a simple map to be traced, showing him where it was in relation to where he was. He broke the connection and set off. At another commpoint, he called the number that went with the rooms, but there was no answer. Now Kham looked about him carefully, eyes scanning the crowds, now thinning as night became very late indeed. He sensed no pattern. He thought that curious, inasmuch as he had almost given them his position, if they were covering him closely as he thought they might. He thought about that as he walked, and of all of it, that made the least sense. Or perhaps he had truly done something unexpected, and actually gotten away from the watch on him, momentarily. They would still be looking, back down in steerage, area-covering, waiting for him to move. If so, he had to make the most of it. He couldn't keep on going up, into higher classes; even here, he would be out of place, but higher—he'd stand out like a polecat at a picnic.

Kham found the area, rather sooner than he imagined it would be, and located the store easily. The rooms above were dark. He went up the stairs, and knocked at the door. No one answered. He hesitated, listening, feeling. There was no presence, no sense of tension. He tried the door, and it was unlocked. Inside, light came from the streetlights outside, and the faraway concourse lights. It was a simple arrangement: a sitting room, with a small kitchen unit toward the rear. A hallway with doors—there would be closets and the bathroom. And double doors beyond. Two bedrooms.

There was a peculiar air to the place, a suspense he couldn't quite identify. Someone had been here, he could tell that. Small things were out of place. A glass by the sink. Palude's wrap was laid across the sofa. She had been here. He went quickly to one of the rooms, pushed open the door. Nothing. The room was empty. He pushed the other door, and saw Palude asleep on the bed, completely relaxed, mouth open slightly. But it bothered him that she would lie down to sleep and leave the door unlocked, or that she would sleep with her clothes on. And then it dawned on him that she was very still, and that her chest did not move with breathing. He approached the bed slowly, reached to Palude hesitantly, and touched her forearm. Cold. It was cold. Arunda was dead.

Kham's first thought was, *Dead, and not a mark on her! Now Nazarine repays me for the things I have inflicted on her.* He turned away, and stepped back out into the hallway. There was still no sound, no sign of pursuit, or of a trap closing. Then he thought, *There is nothing I can do here. Best I leave quickly. I've got things to do yet before they close the net on me.* Kham looked back, once, and then turned back to the apartment. He left, closing the door behind him, and walked down the stairs to the alley and the street, not thinking anything. He let his steps guide him aimlessly back into the concourse, now noticeably thinning out and almost empty, save for a few night owls and small groups of tipsy revelers, who ignored him. It seemed that he thought nothing as he walked, but when he reached a secluded spot and sat on a bench to think it over, he understood that in some strange subterranean manner, he had already made up his mind. Oh, yes, it was all clear now. He knew what he had to do with a clarity he had seldom known in his life. And from here on it would be for himself, not for Oerlikon, not for Heliarcos. He assayed the difficulties, the odds, the forces now arraying against him. It would be difficult, yes. But it could be done.

18

"The real evil in the world (never never never doubt for an instant that it exists) does not reside in the dark towers of sorcerers nor in the black hearts of thaumaturges, nor yet in the schemes of dictators, kings, or chairmen, but simply in the petty crimes, evasions, petit-betrayals, arrogances and insults we all take on the hubris to practice on one another, imagining that each of us is the center of the universe, that it was created expressly for us. Ha! Don't expect you can cure this by law or logic; the counter simply doesn't exist in those quarters."

—H.C., Atropine

NAZARINE WOKE UP in a strange room, to the sounds of someone apparently pottering around in a kitchen. These quarters were not passenger spaces, she could see that; a long, narrow room, with an oddly high ceiling. A cubicle behind the head of the bed, and across the room, the other wall was taken up with bookshelves, electronic devices, a desk, whose sole ornament was an abstract sculpture in some lustrous gray metal, all flowing curves. Everything was done in apparently industrial fabrics, in soft, muted colors, neutral gray, dove-blue, accents in rust and plum. It conveyed a subtle sense of ownership, and of opposites carefully balanced: discipline, countered by slight luxuries: the bed was soft to the touch, but firm in support. She called out, "Where did I wind up?"

Faren Kiricky looked around the corner, the black and silver curls making a contrast with the hard gray lines of the room. "It seems I entertained guests last night in my modest suite." She vanished back into the kitchen unit, an alcove off to the right. Presently she reappeared, wearing a loose caftan of a soft, flowing charcoal-colored stuff. "After the baths, we went to Harry's for a nightcap. You were much taken with the potations, and, Dorje and I, thinking you would be better off with us, brought you here and tucked you in. Simple."

"True, I was very relaxed. We . . ."

"A little magic, that's all. May not have the chance again. Not to worry."

"I felt good."

"Of course. So did I. They are rare occasions: something extra."

"I feel as if I'd stolen something from you."

"Wouldn't be here if you had."

"What is your relationship with Dorje?"

"We are something more than simple friends, and something less than owning each other. We do not seek to imprison the other by reaching for what permanently can't be had."

"Is this unusual?"

"Not in the circumstances, no. People like us, living as we do . . . it couldn't be much of any other way. We form loose groups because no one can take them away from us, and yet we also leave the door open for chance encounters, a little magic. You are new to this, I can see, so have a care. Take it and learn and go free."

"Where is Dorje, back at work?"

"In part. He is out looking into the whereabouts of our friend. As a fact, he's overdue, now. He was supposed to come back here for something to eat."

Nazarine sat up and slid out of the bed gingerly, expecting a sudden headache, but there wasn't one. The cubicle behind the bed proved to be a bath cabinet, which she used after some hesitation over the controls. And after she had gotten it started, she hadn't wanted to come out. But eventually she did. Her clothes were folded neatly on the bed, freshly cleaned. As she dressed, Faren told her, "We didn't want to go all the way back to your room to get fresh clothes, so . . ."

"You went to no trouble."

"No. It's automatic. A processor in the closet."

There was a soft rapping at the door. Faren opened it from the kitchen, and Dorje entered Faren's room, with his usual loose alertness and dancer's grace overlaid with some tension. Nazarine saw it immediately. She said, "Something's wrong?"

He nodded. "Very wrong. Two wrongs. The woman, who is listed as Morelat Eikarinst, killed herself last night after we left her. Had a false tooth, complete with poison."

Faren came out of the kitchen unit and asked, "Do they know what kind? Different groups have their preferences. . . ."

"Ship's surgeon says the main ingredient was a buffered andrometoxin.

It primarily lowers blood pressure. The buffering apparently is to mask its intense bitter flavor and subdue the side effects. Interesting stuff: $C_{31}H_{50}O_{10}$."

Faren asked, "Why interesting?"

"It's not common at all. As a fact, it comes from plants originally found on Earth, the laurel group."

"Then she was from Earth?"

"Definitely not. Body chemistry indicates two places, neither on Earth. One is recent, the other traces. Where she lived and where she came from. Where she lived, they can't identify."

Nazarine said, "That would be Oerlikon. She was there."

Dorje nodded. "Reasonable enough. Then you'd show the same trace elements, as would Pentrel'k, or Kham. But the other part, that's a rich one. Heliarcos." He looked at Faren, meaningfully.

Nazarine asked, "What's Heliarcos?"

Dorje answered, "A strange sort of place. It's in part a university, in part a research center, maybe some other things. But it happens to be a place where the early settlers brought the laurel group, and they apparently thrived. It's fairly well known for that; most Earth plants don't do well on other planets. But andrometoxin's associated with a history of, shall we say, very odd incidents."

Nazarine asked, "What sort?"

"Different places. . . . The deaths are always suicides, and the victims are always ultimately associated with Heliarcos. But beyond that, they don't follow it up: the circumstances don't seem to threaten anyone."

"What are the circumstances?"

"People working in medical research areas."

Nazarine could almost see the answer coming. But she asked anyway, "Do you know what kind of medical research?"

"Odd that you'd ask. The surgeon knew and told me. Hormone system work. Anything from the way the body makes specific message units up from a cholesterol precursor, to organ responses. I mean, it's open scientific work, so why have a spy in it in the first place. But he said it's odd enough to have been cited in the literature."

"Why do they elect to kill themselves?"

"No one has ever found that out. Oh, there are suspicions, but nothing that can be confirmed. And remember, it's not very common. There are a lot of worlds, and people die every day. Andrometoxin's had its day, and now it's something else in the poisoner's handbook. Yesterday, Andrometoxins; tomorrow, Phalloidins."

"How so, 'had its day'?"

"Most of the cases noted are several generations back, in fact, some are far enough to be called, properly, history."

Faren interrupted, "You said two wrongs. What's the other one?"

"Survey lost Kham-Pentrel'k."

"Lost him?"

"He was in a cul-de-sac, couldn't get out without being tracked. But he vanished."

Faren nodded, and said, "Then he's gone into the maintways."

"That seems to be the case. Comm reports a call was made for the woman, data given, and not much later, someone tried to call her. Both calls were from the level four concourse. It's a fair bet it was him. So what we think is that he used the maintways to go to level four, emerged briefly, and then went back underground. Lenosz confirmed he was in her rooms, but they lost the scent."

Nazarine asked, "Can they catch him there?"

Dorje shook his head slowly, indicating not a negative, but that he didn't know the answer. "Hard to say. Down there, it would take years to go through every part of the system. We already know we have stowaways down in there—some of them have been there for years."

"Could he do any damage to the ship? He might do so, thinking he could get me that way and be sure."

Faren said, "He could make a nuisance in specific areas. But the ship-critical areas are sealed off. There's no way he could get into those. No, I'm not worried about that. But I am worried about you; he shows unusual persistence."

Nazarine looked at them thoughtfully. "Yes. I see what I will have to do."

Dorje said, "Ah, never worry. We can handle the likes of that, or at least keep him on the move. When you leave us, he'll remain behind. I mean, whatever he might have been working to save, that's useless to him now. He's truly trapped down there."

Nazarine said, "No offense, but I need more than defense, however good it might be."

Dorje looked at her sidelong. "You can't take action against him. That would endanger you. Then you would have to hide, or Shipsec would come after you. We don't want that. As you are, you are worth holding on to."

Nazarine said, "No, I don't want to attack him. But I do want to find him and ask him some things. I need to know why he pursued me so far and with such force."

Dorje took her arm gently. "All right. Assuming this is true, understand that you would be dealing with a skilled and alert killer, who has risked everything and now apparently has nothing to lose. He would be hard to find, harder to attack, because of possible side effects. We'd have to subdue him mano-a-mano, so to speak. Hand to hand. He won't do much talking."

"I can handle that part. Just help me find him."

"I can't. We don't have enough surveillance systems to close off areas and eliminate them, the way we could in the public parts of the ship. There's food and water down there, and as long as he keeps moving and disturbs nothing, then he could avoid us indefinitely. We know there are some down there, already. And he can't locate you by using shiprecords. You were already on limited-access. Now we've isolated you completely. Whatever he wanted to do, that's over now. He's got a defense, but the price of that is his goal. So we'll keep you until we make planetfall by Teragon, and there you can transship. Think about it. Carefully."

Faren interrupted, "While you think, eat. Breakfast is ready."

Kham now sat back in the comfortable darkness, or more precisely, dim semi-darkness, of the maintways, munching on meal-cake, washing the dry stuff down with a flask of distilled water. He congratulated himself on having acted with such boldness and verve. True, he was back underground, as he chose to think of it, although to the best of his sense of spatial orientation he was not actually "under" but somewhere over the section-four concourse. They hadn't expected him to suspect the interface which allowed him to escape into the maintways, and they were certainly laggards with regards to responding to his call. Curious, that, indeed. He reflected that their response seemed lax, even uncaring. He finished the meal-cake and the last of the water, and looked about himself observantly. From where he sat, on an enormous section of ductwork, he could see only more of the same: ducts of various sizes and shapes in cross-section, some plain and covered only with a protective anticorrosive, others painted in bright primary colors and further identified with cubist tiles of color patches, which doubtless revealed more information. There were also cable trays, catwalks, inspection ladders, piping of a hundred sorts, waveguides, all coded or lettered. The letters, of an obscure blocky style, conveyed no more information to him than the color patches, although he assumed he could eventually locate a manual which would render the system intelligible.

So far, in his inspections, he had found very few places where he could have attempted any control of the channels he saw all about him. At some junctions there were various switch cabinets, circuit-breaker boxes, monitor units. Some enigmatic blank units, marked only with a pattern of colored lights, he suspected of being slave computer monitors. All these devices were carefully secured, not with the primitive locks and plates and chains of Oerlikon, but with more sophisticated modern methods. Many of the cabinets were monolithic, to fission and open only under a careful sequence of magnetic commands. Some, he did not doubt, could only be opened with the cooperation of a remote unit, complete with passwords and authentications. These he did not have, and could not reasonably expect to get. Commpoints were fairly common, but of course he would have to be extremely careful in using them. He would plan lines of retreat, make his tests of the system, very small tests, one at a time, always leaving the area immediately. In that manner he could eventually build up the requisite knowledge, and finish the Morphodite off.

This area was clearly an area of no great significance. He stood up, forgetting to duck, and bumped his head against a cable tray, causing him to make an exclamation. He stopped, rubbing his head gingerly, and listened carefully. No sound. Good. He had to be careful. With all the metallic and hard surfaces around, sound seemed to carry in unexpected fashions; many times already he had thought to hear sounds of movement, or work, or conversation, only to find that the source was either very far away, or invisible, hidden behind the tangles of piping. Yes, quiet. He climbed back onto the catwalk he had been moving on and set off the same way he had been going. There was nothing in this immediate area he could use.

The expanded-metal walk went forward a few meters, and then made a remarkable detour around a mass of junctions. Beyond the junctions, the way ended in a metal spiral with cleated metal steps, leading down. There was a nearby light, dim, of course, but in this light, the steps seemed to be worn with much traffic, and the way suggested somewhere important, down below. Kham set out without delay.

He had a picture in his mind's eye of his approximate location, relative to the level-four concourse. But as he went down, flexing his knees at the steepness of the spiral, he noted only an occasional landing or access-point, and his legs began to tire. Still, he followed the spiral down. Sooner or later it had to terminate at the ceiling of the concourse. He tried to estimate how far he had come, but found that he could not with any accuracy. In addition, the spiral did not run straight, but shifted orientation every so often, so that one could not look up or down and see any great distance along its length. Impossible to estimate. He stopped, and paused, and then set forth again, still down. No point in going back up: he already knew there was nothing up there. Apparently the environment was controlled at various points, too, in here as well as out there in the main part of the ship. But now he began counting the steps he took down. The scenery, as it were, seemed not to change appreciably. Still pipes, waveguides, cable trays, ducts of various cross-section.

When he had counted a thousand steps, he got off the spiral at the first landing, his legs aching. And the spiral continued, after a slight radial jog, even farther down! Here there was a certain dankness to the air, and some odors seemed magnified. He touched a pipe passing overhead. It was cool, and his hand came away wet. He looked again: beads of condensation covered the pipe. It bore no legend save an arrow indicating direction of flow. And the landing was even more enigmatic: The only object here was a small fuse-panel, an adjoining panel of switches, with indicator lights, all a dull green now, and a commpoint transceiver.

Kham looked about uncertainly. He was sure he had started his descent from a point over the concourse, and that being true, long before now he should have reached the ceiling. He looked into the dim confusions of the piping, ending in darkness only a score of feet away. Nowhere did he sense a wall or border. Just the darkness, and the piping. He listened. There were faint sounds of things moving in the pipes, distant drippings, a soft hum of an induction pump running somewhere. Another sound, even softer, more percussive. And something else. Like singing, or chanting, in time with the pump:

> "Ai mft- tu Jai-nmf dum,
> dumdum duh eh fumdum,
> Wuh bah n o hun kun,
> N duh u hunh dusung:
> Tai-samóhkambú dai-yéi!
> Tai-samóh Kambú!"

Kham could hear the repetitive choruses, but the verses were muffled and distorted, and the words made no sense in any language he knew or had heard of. Some sort of folk chant by the nearly invisible denizens of the maintways, stowaways and renegades? He did not know, and at the moment did not wish to find out. It sounded vaguely menacing, in an alien way that made his skin crawl. He decided to go, for a time, along a catwalk, very narrow, that seemed to lead away from the chanting.

Kham followed the catwalk for a time, not paying much attention to whether it went right or left, up or down, or in what order. The catwalk, assisted by metal stairs and short ladders, made all four changes in vector, and after a time, Kham could no longer hear the chanting. He tried to see through the piping to determine where the spiral was, but he could not locate it. He stopped for a moment and looked around himself, suddenly realizing that he was hungry. And that he was quite lost. He had no idea where he was in relation to anywhere. And this section seemed to be narrowing, closing in. He looked again. The ways were narrow here, very close, but he could not make out a wall or termination to any of the lines. He thought back, and all he could recall clearly was that he had come a long way down from where he had started. Now there was something more important to attend to. Finding another junction, with a map, and a food-store cabinet. The Morphodite could wait. At least for a while. It wouldn't do to starve down here.

After she had finished breakfasting with Dorje and Faren, Nazarine told them that she wanted to return to her own room for a time, in part to sort things out, and to make some queries of the ship's computer.

She was halfway out the door when she realized she didn't know where she was. "Hey!"

Faren looked up. "Did you forget something?"

"I don't remember how we got here from section four."

Faren looked curiously at nothing for a second, and then said, "That's right. You start off down the passage until it forks to the right, and then you take the first lift to the left . . . Wait a minute. Let me get dressed, and I'll show you."

"Where are we?"

Faren's voice was muffled by the closet, which she was halfway into, pulling clothing out. "Section one: Crew. Besides, we took some shortcuts, you know, crew only, last night. Would be better if I went along, at least until you get back into public space." She pulled out several things, but in the end settled on a crew coverall, not greatly different from what Dorje was wearing. As she stepped into it, and then pulled it up the rest of the way over her shoulders, she added, "I'm on standby anyway, and if they called me, I'd have to come back here and change. Party's over, at least until next break."

Faren finished zipping the coverall up and hung a communicator on a loop by her waist. "Can't go anywhere without my trusty bitch-box." And to Dorje she said, hurriedly, over her shoulder, "Lock it up when you leave, will you?"

"Right." Dorje was still in the kitchen, drinking coffee, smoking a cigar, and stuffing dishes in the cleaner. He called out, as they went out the door, "Don't worry about Pentrel'k-Kham. Ship's computer is set now to alarm whenever he tries to use any comm device. We register voiceprints on boarding. And major access points are also keyed. He may be loose, but he can't do anything."

As they walked, for a long time they said nothing, save directions, and some small talk about places they passed. But as they neared section four, a silence fell between them which did not end until they were actually in it, and Faren had shown Nazarine the correct corridor.

"This one. Just follow it straight on, and wind up at the base of your block of suites."

"Do you have anything else to do?"

"No. Not really. I've got the box, if they want me. Why?"

"I've got an idea that you know those maintways better than you'd like to talk about openly."

Faren blinked, and then smiled, a wicked, knowing smile. A delinquent smile, perhaps even a peccant smile. "I thought you'd never ask; yes, I know my way around down there. But have a caution: only *somewhat*. Nobody knows everything there is in the maintways. Not even the ship's computer. We've had maintechs get lost there, too."

"Is that why Dorje doesn't want to press it in there?"

"In part. He knows how difficult it is. And he puts limits on things— he has to. As far as he goes, the problem with this Kham is solved: if he shows or tries to communicate, they'll have him, and then it'll be Captain's-Mast, and doubtless, *outside* with him. Or else he'll dig in deeper and stay there."

"But they're strict about ship security! What about the maintways?"

"No-man's land. A jungle. Weapons are damn near useless: you'd hit or cut something that didn't need cutting. As far as that goes, there is considerable risk in going into the system. Not for crew—they leave us alone. But it's said they prey on each other." '

Nazarine looked at Faren sharply. "For what?"

"Not money; they don't use it. Nor basic foodstuff—there are ration boxes throughout. But one gets tired of meal-cake and distilled water, so they combine the thrill of the hunt with a bit of fresh meat."

"So that's why Dorje's not concerned about Kham."

"More or less, that. He stands a good chance of being caught and eaten. Dorje didn't want you going in there after Kham, for that reason, and he thought you might have that in mind. I thought so, too . . . so I thought I'd go along a little bit. We're maybe more casual than you're used to, but we care, too."

Nazarine looked away momentarily, and then said, "I wasn't sure I'd do it. There's some things I have to do first."

"Another reading?"

"Yes. But also I need more facts to put in it. I'm still missing pieces; I can't reach for the answer I need yet. And I'm glad you came; I will push it harder this time. And to know what I must do, Kham is essential. I don't want to kill him; I only want to talk to him."

"The woman gave you nothing."

"That's true, in a sense . . . but she also added a valuable piece. I'm waiting to use it. Come on."

When Nazarine pressed her palm to the door latch, and it opened for her, she half-expected to see the room in disorder, totally ransacked. It wasn't; the lights came on, and everything was in place. It looked exactly like the first time she had seen it. First she went to the closet and quickly flipped the clothing through, selecting a loose pullover of a soft, deep-brown velour, and a pair of pants. While she changed, she explained, "What I had on, that's fine for protective camouflage, strolling along the concourses, and being inconspicuous in a genteel atmosphere, but we will be climbing around, and may need to be freer in movement."

"Those will do fine."

She went to the study cubicle, slid the port aside, and motioned to Faren. "Please show me how to work this thing."

Faren joined Nazarine in the cubicle and touched a small green rectangle. "You're on. What do you want to know?"

"Dorje said the poison she used was associated with a place called Heliarcos. We have to start with some assumption; I will assume they came from there."

Faren nodded, saying, "I would suspect as much . . . here, we'll insert the code for Gazeteer, yes, and here, Heliarcos, and initiate scan, and go. Read."

On the screen of the console, writing began flowing into view, beginning at the bottom of the screen and moving upward as more lines filled in below:

HELIARCOS (Orig. "HEMIARCTOS"), Second planet of Theta Palinuri system, which consists of . . .

Faren pressed in PASS. The screen cleared, and started printing again:

History: Discovered 1366 Lerone Tuzjuoglu, it was rated marginal-habitable and initially surveyed by mining interests who located suitable grounds of Lanthanide-series rare earths, (assays which see), and exploited under charter of Hector-Grovius Metals Ltd. . . .

Faren pressed PASS again, but this time only for a little. She said, "Doubt mine poobahs would go to so much trouble. They are a direct sort, dispensing with poisons and plots at the first. Prospectors, likewise. Let's see who else is there. We can always come back."

The St. Aristides Society established a scholarly retreat, soon followed by other bodies. Their successes soon encouraged other groups to do likewise, and several faculties were founded, these bodies gradually asserting greater degrees of autonomy from their parent bodies, and eventaully becoming independent *de facto* if not, in all cases, *de jure*. Notable among contemporary institutions are (see under separate cover, Higher Education) Hudson-Bruhner Institute, Hubbard College, Velikovsky Foundation, Hammer School of the Arts, Graham Theological Seminary, Wu Wang Society, Zed Aleph Tav Group (Setzer Memorial Division), as well as numerous smaller units treating with restricted technological areas, such as . . .

Faren pressed in PAUSE. She said, "This looks awfully dry. What are we looking for?"

Nazarine leaned back for a moment, thinking. Then, "Hormone research. Also something in the psychology-sociology-anthropology area."

"Why those?"

"The people I am looking for work in those areas, and have been for a long time. Find an organization that does both, in some depth."

"Hmm . . . let's see. We will want to list them all, according to known specialties, which would show up in notable publications. Also . . . Wait a moment, this will be a little tricky, and will take up a lot of print space. I'll have it print a hard copy. So . . ." She rapidly pressed in a series of commands, and shortly, a strip of paper began unrolling from the printer slot.

It seemed that the researchers and students of Heliarcos had been both numerous and busy. Some of the institutions which produced the most intense efforts were hardly notable as major institutions, while others seemed to scatter area studies all over the academic subject list. Most of the major ones had active psychology and anthropology departments, with sociology running a poor third. One medical school, The Reich School, was especially strong in endocrinology and related topics but seemed to have no other areas of interest.

The list that confronted them was both long and highly detailed, and they had to read through it, noting likely candidates. But in the end, they found one. Pompitus Hall. Faren went back to the console and requested a detailed description, to be printed on hard copy. The printer began rolling.

19

"There is no such creature as a realist: that is only another pose, another fantasy, for all are dreamers and fantasists. We do not opt to dream or not to dream, but rather select from a catalogue of fictions. Some of these are more worthy than others, doubtless, in the sense of being productive or the opposite, to be destructive to self or others, but this utilitarianism has no bearing on the reality of the projection. This one pursues Business—that one, political action and social goals; this one seeks sensual gratification and strews broken hearts behind like fallen leaves, that one cultivates a voice that would worm a dog; this one tinkers with automobiles and that one writes novels—it doesn't matter which, Fords or Chevrolets, or romances or science fiction. We are all on the endless sea and the only thing that matters is the skill of our sailing. Therefore identify the dream and you have identified the person and their aims. Outer reflects inner, as electrons match the number of protons in the nucleus. Ionizations are special exceptions. Some people live in very strange worlds indeed, and often the most bizarre of them all are those who seem the most ordinary at first glance. Or as the mad poet avers, 'secure behind the masks of their automobiles, I have seen their mad faces gleaming in the twilight, the spittle flying in the throes of their rage.' "

FAREN FINISHED READING the print the terminal had provided and handed it back to Nazarine. "That would seem to be the one you are looking for. Hormones, biochemistry, and related disciplines, and then, oddly, an extremely heavy social sciences concentration."

"It's the only one that displays that particular mix."

"Well, yes, that; but the clincher was 'Conducts unspecified field research under Beneficial Grant 377Y.' And when we ran that one down, turns out to be a charitable grant of The Alytra Foundation, which in turn is owned wholly by Bogatyr Mining, whose stockholders are the Regents of Pompitus Hall. I should say a nice setup, if one wished to do questionable things."

"Questionable things indeed."

"What was going on, back there on that world you came from? And what are you, that they should single you out?"

"They were conducting some of that unspecified field research on that world. All on the quiet, hidden by a very clever double-blind system that gave them a place to work on something without anyone asking questions. I don't doubt they stumbled on Oerlikon by accident, in the beginning. But they took it over, and used it both as a place to obtain raw human material for their experiments, and as an overflow point for their own personnel, who wished to retire, or who were relieved of duty."

Faren looked at the print again. "What were they working for?"

Nazarine shook her head. "I don't know for certain. I have had some suspicions, but ultimately, none seems to fit. What I think they were originally trying to do was find a way to fuse the nervous system and the hormone system under one conscious mind. But they were caught by a revolution, which wasn't even directed at them, and even after the old order had been overturned, they were more or less ignored. How ironic. Where I fit in this is a longer story than I can tell you, because there are some missing pieces I don't have yet. I think I have the basic outline of it, but I'm still working on the details. Suffice it to say that I was originally one of them. Who found out what the real purpose of the Oerlikon Operation was, and made some waves about it. And was disposed of into their research station, there. They called it 'The Mask Factory,' on the streets, because inside it one underwent changes."

Faren said, softly, "You were changed. . . ."

"To a degree you may not be able to manage to believe. But yes; so indeed I was. I was not supposed to have survived, and I was not supposed to have remembered. I did both. And so they sent those two after me, to finish the job. Apparently, in my original identity, I knew a lot about their procedures, and could have damaged their program."

"You haven't recovered it; I know people. You have a strangeness about you, a fey quality, but not that kind of purpose."

"I recovered *that* it was; not *what* it was the original knew. That is gone forever, lost. All I have left of that is sometimes a rightness about the way things feel—or a wrongness. The barest shreds of the echoes of a personality. What you see and feel is me, not some stranger."

Faren straightened, standing away from the console. "Well, so be it.

You are fine, as you are. Nor do I blame you for being desirous of a revenge: indeed an excellent idea! But also consider: these are people who, whatever their origins, stepped over the line, saying then, 'the rules don't apply to us.' That's not an idle pleasure-seeker or fun-seeker speaking at that point, but a criminal, and they are not reticent about using criminal methods—spies and assassins. They have a certain measure of power and will not happily suffer threats. How much damage can you do them, one person, against, in essence, a University, a sophisticated Financial Management Company, and a mining Trust?"

Nazarine said calmly, "For now, you must take it on faith, but I have the ability to end them. All. My problem is that I do not wish the blow to fall on innocents, too."

"Most wouldn't care one way or the other."

"I know what happens when you don't. I have used it before, without worrying overmuch about the consequences to the innocent."

"All right. What if you can't get a clear shot at them?"

"I suppose I'll have to give it up."

"Are you serious?"

"Yes. Absolute limits. We have to have them."

"What would you do—I mean, for a living?"

"File reports to Clisp, I suppose, about the strangeness of the rest of the universe. I don't have an income, but they pay my expenses—at least for now. That was my last arrangement with the only home I can remember."

"You mentioned a little of that in passing a couple of times. But what are you going to do now?"

Nazarine looked upward at the blank walls and thought for a moment. Eventually she sighed and said, "I want to try to make some kind of contact with Kham. And I want to do a reading before we try it. A hard one, a deep one."

"You want me to leave you alone for a while?"

"A little while. But come back. Please."

Faren nodded. "I understand—leave it to me. I can run an errand while you are working on it."

"What sort of errand?"

"I'll go collect a small assistant."

"What sort of assistant?"

"A surprise. Leave a few of them for me, will you? And don't push it too hard while I'm gone—where you are going next, you are going to need all the alertness you can manage."

Faren turned and left. For a moment, Nazarine sat very still at the console and stared at the keyboard. She thought, *I could use this thing to do some of the routine steps in the reading I am about to do. But that is the deadly way, isn't it? I can always shut it off, but once you create this kind of logic in a machine, there's no way to turn it off. That's the analogue of what they ran into when they created me—Rael. The Monster's out of control.* Nazarine managed a wintry smile, which she could see a little of in the reflections on the console screen. But no. *This monster's under deeper controls than they ever imagined.* There was some blank paper by the machine. Nazarine took the sheaf of it and began carefully laying out the questions she wanted to ask of it, this time the full divination, if one could call it that. She knew she wouldn't be finished by the time Kiricky got back, but hopefully, she would have the hardest parts of it done with by then, with just the routine fill-ins left. It was a shame, having to force it this way, without the data she wanted to put in it, but she felt the subterranean pressure of time passing working on her. Even without actually doing the exercise, she could sense that Kham was fading, fading. She could sense it directly without going through the formal procedure. Yes, that, and she was beginning to sense how she affected events around her, too. *It's not a gift*, she thought. *It's an unbearable weight. I will work harder to suppress it than an ordinary person would labor to attain it.*

She settled on the first question, and even as she began to assemble it within the symbolic formulae she used, she could see that the three questions she was to ask were in reality phases of the same question. In their parts, they asked: What is the method to reach Pompitus Hall? What is to be done with Kham? And what am I to do with myself? She changed a line here, adjusted a symbol there. Yes. All one unity, one question.

Nazarine finished the final strokes of the ideogram, this one intricate beyond anything she had ever done before, but for all its baroque richness of detail, there was no partitioning of it: it was One Answer. She drew back a little and looked at it as a whole. She shook her head, slowly, and then released her breath slowly. She had been holding it for so long she couldn't remember when she had last drawn a breath. Yes. The way was clear, absolute, no doubt, and there could be no hesitation. It followed the outlines Rael had discovered and put into such ruthless practice: all the time since Rael, and even with him, even then, she had looked for a way to negate the limits and demands required by this form of . . . what? Knowing? Divination? Operation on living societies, a form of vivisection? Here, knowing and doing were one, and the observer intruded upon the observed, and affected it, powerfully. She could do it. She had enough to act on. The moment was now. The focus was soft, but not especially blurred. Another shot at it wouldn't come for a long time . . . maybe never. Yes, it would work, and yes, there would be minimal effect on bystanders. It worked just as it had in Lisagor. But of course there was a price. She took another deep breath. *Very well.*

The door chimed, and Nazarine reached around and touched the release switch inside the console cubicle. Faren Kiricky came into the room, followed by one of the lithe gray shapes of the doglike Lenosz.

She stood and said, "This was your surprise."

Faren smiled. "Yes. I borrowed one from the patrol that was out in a pattern for Kham. This one has the scent."

"You know how to handle one?"

"Of course. Don't worry—they are not naturally vicious, but they are extremely good trackers, and we do use them now and then for that. We have made formal agreement, after the manner of Lenosz."

Nazarine looked closely at the sleek, limber animal, now resting on its hindquarters and looking up at Faren with its soft chocolate eyes. This one was large, despite its sleekness and svelte lines, which made it seem smaller. On closer inspection it seemed less doglike. That shape and the recollection it suggested in the human mind was an accident and an illusion. The paws were more handlike than any dog's could have been, and instead of a dewclaw there was a small, but fully opposable thumb, and although it did walk digitigrade, the paws, or hands, more properly, seemed deft enough to grasp and to handle.

Faren followed her eyes, and said, "Yes, it can climb. Will you need a weapon?"

"No. I have what I need."

"Ready?"

"Yes."

"Did you find what you were looking for?"

"Yes."

"You will do it."

"Yes. Everything is clear."

"Well . . . let's go."

*   *   *

Sometimes he thought he was in immense spaces which were almost filled with the systems that kept the ship a living and moving object. There was no solid wall ending this interior support system labyrinth at all. It was all support. The world the passengers thought they moved through was nothing but a carefully prepared illusion, miniature living environments controlled and ministered to by miles of feed lines, rec sumps, HVAC flow lines and ducts, breeder vats for bacteria which had in turn viral controls. He could not remember seeing a ship from the outside, nor could he remember seeing a diagram of one. Sometimes he laughed to himself, and whispered that the reality was that the whole universe was in fact a support network, in which were imbedded small and limited little spaces in which people (and possibly other sorts of creatures) moved and imagined that what they saw was all there was.

And sometimes, in his travels, the surrounding free space compressed into tiny crawl ways so narrow one had to slip through them sideways, or else so low one had to get down on one's belly and crawl like a reptile. There was something on the other sides of the bulkheads, but he could not determine what those somethings were.

And alternately, sometimes he came close to the passenger spaces of one class or another, or perhaps portions of the crew space. A long gray corridor, which he observed through a floor level vent grille. He had watched for a long time, but no one had passed along that corridor. Nor had there been any sound. (He had thought himself safe, and allowed himself a short catnap.) A large, communal dining room, more like a mess hall than anything else. Rows of plain metal tables, casual diners coming and going, a loose camaraderie in effect. Crew? Something even lower than steerage? Higher than the highest he could imagine? An arcade, where people stood in tight ranks and pitted their skill against electronic and mechanical games, but the most popular of all the games was a simple mechanical one in which one fired a ball-bearing to the top of an obstacle course of little pins and wheels. Vertical. The cascading balls made a bright and tinkly sound and the patrons stood enraptured, putting their all into the release of the spring, hoping for the correct collection pocket at the bottom, exulting when they won, groaning when they lost.

Walking onto the ship from the lighter, he believed that it had been arranged in actual levels, one atop the other, or maybe one in front of the other, like soldiers in a line ('Tighten that line up, soldier, until the man in front of you *smiles!*'). Yes, levels. That was the word. Levels. But seen from this side, air, warmth, coolness, water, sewage, power, communications, structure, there seemed to be no order whatsoever: the levels were all mixed together, and the differences were actually only in the minds of the passengers.

For some time, he had followed the route indicators which he sometimes found at major junctions, but these proved not to be uniformly dependable. And as he had burrowed deeper and deeper into the real workings of the ship, he had gradually lost his conception of reference. Kham could neither remember meaningfully where he had been, nor conceive meaningfully where he wished to go. Therefore the schematics and route designations were totally meaningless. The ship was a sphere, including within its volume an unspecified number of smaller spheres or ovoidal areas. Once, he had found a dim and scratched transparent panel, of some sort of polycarbonate material which did not give when he pressed on it. Inside, poorly visible, had been people working at some kind of controls, a large console completely filled with meters, readouts, graphics, switches, keyboards, touchplates. They all seemed at ease, but also intent on their work, engaged in it, not just passing time. Something to do with the ship, he thought, but he also thought that the actions didn't look terribly different from those people playing games in the arcade. Maybe the rules were different.

But those were secondary problems now. He had, in his travels, noted a major junction, and threaded his way to a catwalk leading to it. Approaching, he had seen a number of people, and had gone forward with anticipation, knowing that here, at least, he would be able to find something out. But the light had been poor, and as he had drawn nearer, he had seen that they were dressed either in rags or borrowed things which fit them poorly, when at all. There had been six of them. They ignored his emergence into the junction, which Kham thought curious until it dawned on him that they probably had heard him coming a long time. He had gone to the food locker, but it was empty. They moved aside to let him go to it. And closed behind him.

Kham had tried to speak, his voice strangely loud and raspy after long disuse. They had not answered, but made quick, flickering and lambent glances at each other, and rarely at him. He remembered their words, which made no sense whatsoever:

—*Pisha boot?*

—*Da-la dum-li totchel 'orosha.*

—*Da pisha, Seich' Zakwat im!*

And the six of them had all stepped forward, and their attitudes had not been those of friends, but of animals closing on prey. Kham remembered his training, and slipped into a relaxed slump, from which he could move easily, by relaxing. He had a wall behind him, man's best friend. The first one to come forward had been kicked in the crotch, the body rebounding to lay on the grating, where it emitted an odd series of multilingual cries, a strange, borrowed half-language, half jargon, half animal sub vocalizations. "O *ti malalacula! Bolezin! Bomogi, beysti!*" it had cried.

The others had drawn back a little, eyes glittering like those of feral insects. They were impressed, but not daunted. Two others had moved as one, from opposite sides. Kham pulled them to him and cracked their heads together. Both fell. One lay on the grating, making swimming motions and twitching his feet, while the other one lay still with blood oozing from his ears. The rest stepped back, eyes alive, darting, their bodies moving slowly, deliberately, the stuff of nightmares. And gradually they moved back, out of the light of the single dim bulb and a few illuminated panels.

Since then, he had moved quietly, making certain he made as little noise as possible, but he never lost the crawling sensation that somewhere off in the jungle of pipes and ducts someone—or someones—was watching him, following him, at a distance.

Now he approached groups he saw warily. He would catch glimpses of people, ghostly shadows by a lighted junction point, but when he got there, they would all be gone. Vanished, as if they had never been. He allowed himself short little catnaps, after finding places he felt more secure in than along the open catwalks where one could be seen from above, below, and also from the sides. But never long. He would catch himself nodding, and set his head upright with a jerk. He sometimes saw lights when there were none. Odd clusters of moving lights. They were waiting for him, out there in the well-lighted open spaces through which the passengers and crew moved so easily, so unconsciously. And in here, they were waiting for him, too. There was not too much difference, subjectively, in the final result in either case, save that one would transpire with solemn ceremony and judicial pronouncements, while the other would be with grunts and howls and the smacking of unclean lips.

But Kham reasoned that if he could survive long enough, down here, he might in time come to gain a measure of security. For one thing seemed certain: those above did not pursue those who went below, nor did they seem to harass those few who stayed below. There, it was surrender. Here, he had a chance. But then he remembered to ask himself: why didn't they follow people below?

*   *   *

Faren led Nazarine and the Lenosz, first along some passageways which seemed innocuous enough, although they seemed to lead nowhere; these soon became both narrow and empty, and after a short walk, terminated in a heavy metal door which operated from a single handwheel set in its center.

"Here we are. Can you read the graffito scratched in above the door, on the lintel, as it were?"

Nazarine moved closer, stretched, stood on tiptoe. She read, " 'Abandon all hope, ye who enter here.' "

Faren chuckled. "A wit among the crew at some time. That was supposed to be the inscription over the gates of hell. This is one of the legitimate entrances. Work the wheel and go. But from the other side—now that's different. It's a procedure even for someone with a pass, like me. No pass—ah, well, one creates a problem. All the legitimate accesses have traps built into them; you have to walk into the trap to operate the identification system. Blow it, and they come and collect you. So we don't have unwanted visitors."

"There are other places they could come out, I'm sure."

"They don't. There are very few of them in there, and the ones who survive don't want to come back. That's probably a crucial reason why they survive."

"How many are in there, do you think?"

"No more than thirty, probably less than twenty. Somewhere in that range. Might be as high as fifty—but I doubt that."

"How do you know?"

"Rate of ration turnover. There are drop points throughout the system where ration packets are dropped off—the system refills itself automatically. Shipcomputer estimates how many are probably alive based on the rate of turnover."

"What's the food for?"

"For us, when we get in a job we can't stop. You get a problem down in the system, you don't stop until it's fixed."

"So you've been in here before."

"Several times too many."

"And you know it reasonably well?"

"There are some that know it better but they wouldn't take you in."

Faren turned the wheel and the door swung open. Inside was a bare little chamber, lit by a single panel, which gave off a dim light compared with the corridor lights. They went inside, and the outer door closed behind them, latched itself, and locked. "Now we're in." She turned to a panel, laid her hand on it, and spoke rapidly into a small dull spot on the wall, a string of numbers and letters. On the other side, a panel simply swung open, and there was a deeper darkness beyond. They stepped out onto a metal grating platform. Stairs led down in two directions.

Faren looked around and then indicated the left stairwell. "We'll start this way. There's a connection down below where we can move along fairly rapidly, and farther on, we'll see if this overfed pooch can pick up a scent. A long way."

Nazarine said nothing. Faren led the way, and the Lenosz followed behind, several paces back, at first moving along easily, as if on some errand of its own, but gradually it became wary, its nostrils flared delicately, and its ears swivelled and turned, searching for sounds. As they descended into the guts of the ship, the open space closed in and began to fill with piping and machinery. Most of the machinery was incomprehensible to Nazarine, but it appeared as if this particular area was a sort of node where the different support flows were collected and rerouted. Some of the larger devices made noises. Others made none. They passed many indicator panels, covered with readouts, meters, generated graphs on CRTs, and simple colored lights; amber, green, red, violet, blue, orange, yellow. Then they were at the bottom, at least as far down as they were going now. There was a ladder off to the side descending still farther.

This was a broad walkway, solid underfoot, with a cleated surface, wider than Nazarine could reach. Here they set out at a hard walk. The lighting was very poor, consisting of single glow-tubes set inside thick covers, about every fifty meters. On the left was a wall of welded metal, almost covered by layers of piping and the square-section shapes of waveguides. It looked to Nazarine like a wall of the outside world of a surface, overgrown by a dense mosaic of vines, but set into a rigid, surrealistic pattern. To the right was open space, but mostly filled with larger ducting, or platforms on which sat junction boxes, machines of enigmatic function, pumps, repeaters. Then she concentrated on walking, and they walked hard for a very long time. The scenery, if one could call it that, did not change.

It seemed to Nazarine they had been walking for about an hour, more or less, some of which had been through relatively long, straight sections, similar to that which they had passed through after entering. Other sections had been ramps, elevators, drop-shafts and spirals descending, ascending. Faren strode along with the quiet authority of one who knew her way well, and along the way she had made little or no comment. Nazarine had no idea where they were in relation to any other part of the ship, and said so.

Faren stopped, and said quietly, "We've been descending along the main tracks. Sooner or later the fugitives always do this. It's easier. The various passenger areas are near the outside layer, crew deeper, control still deeper. As you go deeper, there are more control zones, more security. That is why we don't worry so much about stowaways roaming about. We are now beneath the economy section where Kham first operated from."

"Why here?"

"Good a place as any to pick up a trail. Hst! Note the Lenosz!"

Nazarine looked about, but in the subterranean gloom she failed to catch sight of the creature, which had sidled around them and now quested and ranged nervously back and forth, nostrils flared and held high. Faren nodded, approvingly. "Got a scent, it did." She made a peculiar motion with her left arm and hand, and the Lenosz came to her, making undulating motions with its slender body, as if trying to swim, nodding its head abruptly upward. Faren said, "Not old, not fresh. Passed along here, crossing. He has fear, now." She made another motion, pressing her palms together and counter-rotating them, briskly. "I told it to follow. Slow, so we can be close. Come on, and be alert, now."

The Lenosz loped off, following an air-scent for the most part, only occasionally inspecting the side walls or the deck, almost as if it felt such a crude method of scent-following was distasteful. Presently it paused at a landing, which led to a metal openwork stairs leading down into a deeper darkness. Faren made a short, sweeping motion with her hand, and the Lenosz stepped out on the openwork gingerly, placing its delicate feet gently and purposefully, so as to avoid stepping through the open spaces. Faren and Nazarine followed.

For the next stage of their journey, Nazarine opened her own senses to the strange environment listening, watching, smelling. The odors were mostly slightly stale, suggestive of damp, and overlaid by an oily reek suggestive of machinery. They passed by several landings with hardly a pause; but at one, where there was one of the ration-cabinets, they stopped, while the Lenosz carefully investigated the landing and junction with meticulous attention to every point along the walls and floor. Faren commented, in a quiet, breathy voice barely above a whisper, "Stopped here, rested, then left in a hurry. Recently."

The Lenosz continued quartering about, but Nazarine caught a shred of movement out of the corner of her eye. She looked at the place, and then away, remembering peripheral vision was better at catching motion in such uncertain half-light. She kept her eyes slightly averted, and said, in a whisper, "We have company. There, to the right, beyond that row of orange pipes."

Faren looked. When she did, the visitors, understanding that they had been sighted, made no further attempt to conceal themselves, and stood out in the open. They could see four clearly, and to Nazarine, it seemed as if they made small, betraying motions that suggested more, somewhere beyond, out of sight.

Faren seemed not to notice. She said, "They'll come to us, to parley. I see four. We can handle that." The four made their way soundlessly toward them, climbing, sometimes walking normally, sometimes clambering over and through obstructions, as if they had had long practice. And though soundless, they moved so as to remain in view constantly. Faren watched them closely, as did the Lenosz, but Nazarine felt a wrongness, a pressure. It was too obvious, too open. She turned her face toward the newcomers, but continued to scan all around, above, below, listening behind, letting an animal sort of fear drive her, but not master her. The four finally emerged from behind a massive vertical girder and stood in a group.

They were clothed in rags and scraps that might once have been clothing. A woman and three men, judging by the shaggy beards on three of them. They were wary as animals. Faren, continuing to observe them, said, "These are long-timers. Be wary." She removed a slim baton from her coverall, where she had concealed it. Flexible and limber, it became rigid when she grasped the handle. She then spoke rapidly, using an argot Nazarine could not follow. It was no language she could remember or recall, but whatever it was, it was full of hesitations, pauses, odd reduplications of certain sound-groups. It suggested a pidgin form of a speech that had once had a full and an elegant repertoire, now reduced to a minimal set.

The members of the group replied, in an offhand, disorganized manner, as if time had no meaning for them. Languid, affected, although speaking the same, oddly broken speech. She also saw extremely brief eye-flickers darting back and forth among them, independent of the words they uttered, and she tuned herself to an even higher pitch. *There,* she thought, feeling habits she associated with Rael come back easily. *Above, in the piping. Very well. Let it be.* She looked hard at the group.

Nazarine sensed a soft, barely audible motion from above, and felt a puff of air, and then pressure about her arms, pinning her. She was ready, had inhaled deeply and held her arms rigid. Now she exhaled, pulled her arms tight, and fell out of the grasp. She grasped the arms with her hands and pulled, hard, and the attacker, already off-balance began toppling forward, trying to regain balance and break their arms free. Nazarine slammed its face down onto the metal floor, levered it aside, gained her feet and stamped its windpipe flat. There was no time to see further to it, for two had grappled Faren, one turning toward her, as if in slow motion. Baring a long knife, obviously ground down from some scrap. With a motion she stepped close, almost dancing, brushing the knife-arm aside and striking with the heel of her free hand, directly onto its sternum, which shattered under the impact. The other, struggling with Faren, swung around, and Nazarine leaped up, reaching for the pipes she knew were there, finding them, getting leverage, and kicking while pivoting her hips. The other one's neck broke with an audible snap.

Still thinking as Rael, she took a quick inventory of those left. The four they had first seen had stepped closer, to be in on the spoil, but now they turned, were turning to vanish off into the night, the darkness. Nazarine swung, hand over hand, and dropped in the midst of them, felling two with simultaneous forearm blows. In one, she felt a collarbone snap, and in the other, the tendons holding the head up tore. She seized the woman of the group by her long, greasy hair and pulled her off her feet, feeling about half the hair give way. This one she swung to the deck and she quickly performed a series of manipulations to vital nerve centers, during which the woman emitted a series of surprised subvocalized grunts and sudden plangent cries of agony. At last, she lay on the floor, eyes vacant and glassy, but still breathing. Nazarine said, in a harsh voice, "Ask her what you will!" She drew a deep breath, held it, and cleared her lungs. Seven had become two, and one of those was a captive.

Faren shook her head, and bent over the woman. She looked at Nazarine. "What did you do to her?"

"Made her more cooperative. Now speak with her. She won't live long!"

Faren bent over the woman, looked at the glassy eyes, and whispered something in the strange, broken pidgin speech. The woman replied, like an automaton, tonelessly, at some length, and then expired, rolling her eyes back into their sockets in a ghastly fashion. Faren breathed deeply, and said, "They were hunting Kham, or so I think one who fits his eidolon. Down and not far ahead. They herd them with a small advance group, and the main party closes in. This was the main group. They thought we would make a small diversion before they took Kham. They feared him—he was held to be a great fighter, having already bested Aquarius Beasley the Bandit."

She stood up and added, "And this was an old band, one of the oldest and most adept. And you destroyed them within seconds. What in Hellviter are you?"

Nazarine shook her head, wiped her hands on her pants. "Less than successful. One got away. I have allowed myself to go slack; of old, I could have had them all and caught at least three for conversation."

The two she had injured were still where they had fallen. The one with a broken collarbone was trying to crawl away, but the other one was dead. Apparently she had also broken its neck. They turned to the single survivor. When it sensed that they were coming for him, it squirmed to the edge of the walkway, and rolled over the side without hesitating. In silence it fell, and they heard it strike objects on the way down, a series of hard, ringing, metallic blows, accompanied only by grunts, at first, and then by only silence, as it continued falling. At last, the sodden sounds stopped, far below. The echoes died away.

Nazarine said, "You see? Not that one either."

Faren stepped back a little, and asked her again, "What are you, that you could do that?"

Nazarine looked away, and said reluctantly, "Long ago, I was made to bring misery into the world. I did not desire it, but I had no other way to be free of those who held me. I did my one crime, and I have been trying to escape them since, and trying to become an ordinary person who might live her life out in peace, to know the direct pleasures and pains. Kham was somehow related to those who set me on this path. . . ." She allowed the sentence to trail off, with no definite ending.

"You're not telling everything."

"No, but I will. Soon. But first, we have to find Kham before they do. We may be reduced to the disgusting expedient of saving him from these cannibals."

"What will you do when you've talked to him?"

"Let him go."

"I don't understand."

"I said I knew what I had to do. I *read* what must be, for the pattern I want to fulfill itself. In that, for everything to work, I must permit Kham to follow his own destiny out to the end. You understand? For what I want to come true, I have to let him go. And there is one other thing I have to do."

"What is that?"

"Not yet, Faren. You and I will do one more thing, and you, who have given me so much, will give me one more thing."

20

"If you stop planting trees because you think you won't be around to see them grow up, then you are already dead."
—H.C., Atropine

THEY FOUND KHAM without too much difficulty, letting the Lenosz lead them by scent: along a narrow way off the junction, down a ramp, along a slanted catwalk, and down a spiral to another junction, this one a plain one on a grating deck without food or water. Here the advance party of the stowaway tribe had closed in on Kham and pinned him down. They had all the exits covered, save one, and along that one they had expected to see their own people coming along that way. Perhaps it had become too easy. This one they had cornered at last had seemed to give up wanting to go on farther. Still, it was dangerous. It half-stood, half-slumped against a circuit box, with heavy eyes that did not look directly up, but glanced off sideways, downwards. And so they waited. Patiently. This one knew what was coming, and had chosen this place—as good as any other—to meet his last engagement. No point in rushing things; they had seen this condition before. They would all come, and wait for the moment.

Nazarine and Faren and the Lenosz walked openly, no longer muffling their footsteps, and came down the final slant into the junction unhesitatingly. Faren glanced around, into the shadows, away from this chamber, and spoke quickly in the pidgin language of the underworld. For a long moment, there was no sound or movement, so she repeated some of what she had said. And one by one, silently, eerily as ghosts, the shadows became empty. The band departed.

Kham looked at them dully, almost as if he did not recognize them, although certainly he did. Faren and the Lenosz made a careful circuit of the chamber, and then retired to the entrance to one of the walkways. She said, "Here he is: cornered like a rat. Do as you must."

Kham looked up, now, and focused his eyes directly on Nazarine.

She said, "I am the one you have been working so hard to find."

Kham nodded, slowly. He said, after a moment, in a soft voice full of resignation, "You differ somewhat from how I imagined you, even though I saw you on the beamliner. You are something that does not confine within an identity-imago."

Nazarine stepped closer. "That's what multiple personalities in sequence does to one. Different people animate my face, make motions with my body. I imagine you know about that well enough."

"Rael we had reports on; Damistofia less. Phaedrus hardly at all—he was difficult to track down. You have proven impossible. You distort probabilities just by existing."

"I know."

"How much control have you been using?"

"I have been trying to escape it. That started way back, in Marula. I would have disengaged, then. You people wouldn't let me. The early ones I came to understand. But you people wouldn't stop. There was only one answer for it—it did not really require *the art* to find it. But I still don't have it confirmed why."

Kham sighed deeply, and ended it with a chuckle, which turned into a sudden racking cough. Then, "You know who you were?"

"Yes. I tracked it down. Jedily Tulilly, one of your own people."

He said, shrewdly, "You haven't recovered all of it, or you wouldn't risk the pits to ask me."

"I have recovered enough; I know where you come from, and I know their real product. I can guess easily enough—Jedily saw the true purpose of Oerlikon and Lisagor, and tried to report it—to whoever she thought might stop it. But that world your people had victimized, exploited, parasitized for untold cycles, you had become as dependent on it as it on you. So Jedily was erased, and dumped in The Mask Factory for Pternam to dispose of, or wear out. I suppose I could say I owed you for that one, too, but it wouldn't change anything I would now do."

Kham agreed. "I wasn't there, but you have me here, handy enough."

"Do you know what happened to Jedily?"

"In truth, no. I was told that if we succeeded, we would find out in the course of time, by the time we became regents of the faculty."

"So you went forth, solely on orders from those who did know?"

"I suppose that would cover it. You realize, there never was anything personal in it—it was just part of the job."

Nazarine nodded. "I understand. That is what makes this whole thing so vile—that it was just a job. To get personal—that's where realities are—love and hate alike. When you get personal, you limit. It's when you say, 'It's just a job,' that the real devil enters into it. So you understand that it's personal with me, not just a job."

"So you'll go on and do it, then?"

"Do what?"

"Take your revenge on me and go on to turn the furies loose on Heliarcos."

"As for you, I intend doing nothing. When I leave this place, you are free. And as for them, I have already set that in motion. I don't need to go *there* to end their criminal tenure. I didn't need to leave Oerlikon to do that; I can reach as far as I need. I left Oerlikon to make sure I could get away from you people. And others like you."

Kham said coldly, "You will never escape people like me; we are everywhere—we make things run. And there are others dispatched, as well, I am sure. And we know something of how you make it work."

"You say there'll be others, other efforts."

"Of course."

"Well, you won't die, so you can go back and tell them you failed."

Kham smiled, but the facial configuration he made was a rictus that had absolutely nothing to do with humor in any ordinary sense. "All so well for you to say. Charity: Caritas, to speak the ancient word. Generous, doubtless. All you do is leave me down here. Up there, they are waiting for me. A fine freedom."

Nazarine looked slightly to the side, as if bemused. "No, it won't be like that. You will go back topside, and by the time you get there, you'll be free. To report, to return to Heliarcos, or to run to the end of the universe—whatever suits you."

"How will you arrange that?"

"You don't need to worry about that. Or you can stay down here, if you like."

"Not much choice there. Hobson would be ecstatic."

"The ones you forced on me were no better."

"Going back . . . now there's a real barbed gift. But you know that."

"Of course. I've put you, alive and fully cognizant, into a place you can't escape from, and you'll know it every moment. This is a lot more satisfactory. And understand this, Kham: any way you move—any way whatsoever, including the choice of not to move at all, will set in motion the chain of events I need to validate Jedily. But only if I leave you this way. And so I bid you good-bye. Enjoy your freedom." And then,

without pausing, she turned and left the junction point, motioning to
Faren to follow her.

Nazarine set out at a hard walk, going back the way they had come,
and she did not look back. Faren remained in place for a moment, and
then turned and followed Nazarine. It was some time before she caught
up with her, and when she did, Nazarine put a finger to her lips, indicating silence. She whispered, "Show me a way away from here, as far as
possible, someplace where he can't follow."

Faren nodded, and motioned to her, saying, "Follow me."

Faren led them, as she had indicated, along a series of paths through the
maintways, using pass-doors, which she knew Kham would not follow,
not returning to the upper parts of the ship, but moving across, and
slightly downward, even deeper into the bowels of the ship. At length,
they arrived at a security door, which Faren opened without difficulty,
and they passed through, into a small, spartan cubicle.

Faren let the Lenosz in, and closed the door. She gestured with her
hand about the small room, a complete habitation in miniature. "Is this
secure enough?"

"This is secure?"

"It's a refuge-point—where we can go to escape harassment. There's
a direct line back. Now you tell me: what was all that you told him? He
can't go back. There's a warrant out for him, and it won't be cancelled
until he's out."

Nazarine smiled. "But if you had it solved, and reported a confession,
then Kham would be free."

"Maybe. But I have no such confession."

"We can make one up."

"Would you please explain what you are trying to do? I thought you
wanted to hunt him down!"

"He's an arrow that I'll launch into flight—an arrow that will strike
precisely at the point where it's needed most. But for that to work,
there has to be a . . . giving-up. You understand? The kinds of things I
can do require a life to energize them. That is why I kept seeing in my
readings that I couldn't touch Kham; he was to be my weapon. And I
was to be the energy. I couldn't face that, and so I wrote it off as an unknown I couldn't understand. But it was there all along. It is true that I
have a power to change things, an absolute power such as no one has
ever wielded before. But by using it to achieve ends, I cannot continue

as I am and realize those ends. I can create a new universe, but the act of creation locks me-as-I-am out of it."

Faren shook her head, and sat on the edge of one of the plain bunks in the refuge-room. She said, "I would have claimed you were deranged, had you said this earlier. But I have seen you read, and I saw you fight, and I never saw anything like that before. So you may be as you say. But what do you require of me?"

"You will clear Kham of charges by reporting that I confessed to a crime of passion and then exited the ship into transitspace."

"What is going to happen to you?"

"That's the rest of it. In one sense, I will vanish; in another sense, you will have me longer than you've had anyone else in your life. And that is what I have to ask you if you'll do, and to do that, I have to tell you the truth about who and what I am."

Faren nodded thoughtfully. "Go on. I'm listening."

"It's like this: Kham spoke of other names, you heard him. Jedily, Rael, Damistofia, Phaedrus. I was all those people."

"You wore a disguise. . . ."

"No disguise. I *was* them, in every way. And who I am now, this was the best of all and I give it up with great pain. But here is how it happened, and why you must do this . . ." And she began at the beginning, retelling the story, not as it had grudgingly revealed itself, but as she had reconstructed it, in sequence, beginning far back, before Jedily Tulilly, even, explaining, clarifying. Faren leaned back on the bunk and closed her eyes, to better visualize the things Nazarine told her, and the Lenosz curled up on the floor and placed its head on its paws.

". . . and that's how it fits together. I've told you all of it."

Faren opened her eyes, shook her head slightly, and said, "All right. Let's say I accept this tale, and everything that will result from this. Let's say it. So, then—why me?"

"In part, it's something I have read you would do. It's there, in the fabric, for anyone who has the skill or the curse I do to see; you never told me, but what you did tell me of your life, along the ways we have gone, weaves a fabric whose pattern extends into that area. You know the truth of that even as I say it—see this in your face by the most ordinary means."

Faren accepted this with neither surprise nor refusal. She nodded coolly, and said, "So, then: why else?"

Nazarine pressed her lips together until all the color went out of them, collecting her thoughts. "It's like this: this is what we would do—an essentially irrational act. By the standards this universe operates by. Irrational. I will entrust my life and the powers they buried in me to a stranger. But consider this—that by following this course, completing the sequence I started with following and confronting Kham and letting him go free, I have engaged in an act of faith alone."

"Ha! I should say so, even for openers!"

"But balance that against Oerlikon and Heliarcos—reason extended without hindrance, and measure the strength of it against what I did to Lisagor. This is the theorem of Operation extended much further. To kill the lowest changes the whole—and on to this. If you choose to look at what I do as a kind of magic—it isn't, but it helps to see it that way—then I tell you this is the most complicated operation I ever attempted, and its resultants will change the entire human community. There will be no more Mask Factories, no more Morphodites, no more Pompitus Halls."

"First you. And then me."

"And then Dorje. You will tell him the truth, come one day, and him, too."

"But you'll be gone!"

"I won't. You'll always have me—all your life."

"But you won't be you anymore, just like you're not Rael, or Damistofia. I liked those things we all did together—it had a lightness, for once—all of it."

"You know what was right about it—then pass that on. I give you a vehicle to do that to, to continue it, to spread it. You'll never see it take root—that's centuries away. So you walk into a faith as great as mine."

Faren looked down, hiding her eyes beneath her eyebrows. She muttered, "I don't have enough of what you want."

"Yes, you do. You answered me when I called on you, and you gave more than I asked."

Faren looked up, her eyes bright. "You argue all too well. But you knew it would be this way . . ."

"I don't know any more about the next instant, the very next microsecond, than you do. I read NOWS. The Present is forever, a wave. What we do changes the wave if we so wish it. Just by wishing, by believing, by dreams. To seek only the rational to the exclusion of all else makes us prisoner of the underlying patterns that lie accidentally about and so scatter the wave into entropic fragments. Life itself stores energy against the grain; life-continuity reverses the entropy gradient. But through will and idea, faith and dream."

Faren shifted her position. "Well, all else aside, you have certainly changed me."

Nazarine said, "You changed me; I could not have found this course without you. And Dorje."

"What would you have done, elsewise?"

"Tracked Kham's source down to its roots, and destroyed it, utterly, with misery on a much vaster scale than was done in Lisagor. But this is better."

"I can understand that. Revenge is a poor source of inspiration for artists, so they say, and even more so to others."

"We are all artists—it's just that we don't understand that yet."

"You understand you are going to cause me all sorts of problems with the personnel section. . . . They may even offer me the option of paying off my profit-sharing, my lays, and putting me off at next port of call, which is Teragon."

"I understand that. But you are skilled, in metallurgy and structures, joining and separating constructions, welding and cutting—those are the prime operations of alchemy—*solve et coagula*, or so the ship's computer tells me."

"Yes."

"They have need of you there. And Dorje . . . what would he miss there, and what more could he do?"

"No matter; we can survive well enough on Teragon. Probably better than aboard ship."

"You never landed anywhere."

"There was nothing to land for."

"Now there is. Take it."

"I will. What must we do?"

"Call in and isolate yourself for several days. Notify Dorje, but tell him nothing. This can't be sent over any comm link. Then be quiet and let me concentrate. After that, we'll have a few minutes, and then it's up to you. You know what's going to happen to me. The sequence will keep me alive while it's running, while I'm changing, but afterward I'll be helpless. I distorted it badly to get Nazarine, but dammit, I needed an adult body, not a subteen's. Now I've got to pay that debt back. I read I'll finish up slightly premature. Keep me warm, and get me to an infant life-support system."

"How will I know?"

"I'll cry normally."

"And you'll forget everything. . . ."

"According to what I know about the process, yes. And if you don't tell me about it, I'll never look for it. It will all be there, of course; as a fact, going through Change makes it stronger, but I'll lose conscious continuity with how to do it. The terrible secret ends in this chamber. And in a sense, those who wished me terminated gained their wish. Their enemy will have ended. And they will ruin themselves, thinking that they succeeded in protecting their secret, but they'll overstep, and by their own arrogance be ground to a powder. And you'll have a child, and I'll have my innocence back."

"You never lost it. That was why . . ."

"I know. Now quiet."

Nazarine had long thought about this moment, for a long time thinking it would come after many long years and adventures, or else dreading what she would have to do. And in either case, she imagined that it would be difficult to reach for that particular trance state of consciousness necessary to set Change off. But it wasn't. She felt no fear and sank easily down through the layers of imagination, of dream, of hallucination, of atavistic visions, to the central ground of the inner vision.

To Faren, who hadn't known what to expect, it looked like nothing: the girl seemed to relax, sink into herself, breathing deeply but quietly, almost as if she were sleeping, and then she looked up, with a face that was suddenly clear of all doubts that had colored it before. Whatever she might have seen in the lines and planes of that face before, coquetry or innocence, or open concern, that was nothing to what she saw now.

Nazarine said, "It's done, and coming fast. Are you ready?"

"I can handle it; I helped clean up after the Onswud riots in '83 on Kopal."

"There's not enough time to say the words I want to, to imagine all the things that might have been."

"Never mind. I know them, too. We'd just be repeating each other. I saw the possibilities, too."

"Teach me, next time aro . . ." She stopped in mid-word, and her eyes glazed over, losing their lucid translucency and becoming blank as china eyes painted on a doll. Faren got up and reached for Nazarine, touching her face. It was burning hot, damp, feverish, and beneath the skin she could feel the muscles of her face rigid, working against each other. She moved the girl's body, carefully, like a bomb preparing to go off, and gently slid her off the bunk onto the floor, where she laid her down on her side. She bent close and looked at those terrible blind eyes. "Nazarine? Can you hear me?" The girl made no sign she had heard, but continued to stare sightlessly ahead of herself onto an imaginary point under the other bunk.

Faren straightened, kneeling on the floor beside Nazarine, and pulled the pocket communicator out of her coveralls. She made two calls in rapid succession, one to Central Maintenance Scheduling, and one to Dorje, and then she replaced the unit, and bent forward once more. She brushed the loose brown curls back from Nazarine's forehead, and kissed the girl's hot cheek, gently, as one might kiss a child goodnight. And she said, in a soft voice no one heard save herself, "Go without fear. You knew us rightly and we'll do it right. You're safe." Then she sat back on her haunches and waited for the transformations Nazarine had told her would come, a series of controlled destructive changes that would reduce her to an infant. It would be several days, possibly as long as a week. She did not worry; there was food in the emergency locker. Not without fear, but with a sense of engagement she had never known before, Faren Kiricky sat back, still gently stroking the soft curls, and waited.

> *"Some say the evil of our days is love of machines over people, or of money; others speak of drugs, or of debauchery, but I disagree: it is nothing more than love of authority without responsibility. There is a remedy, but few choose it even for themselves, and fewer still for all."*
>
> —H.C., Atropine

Preserver

For Maurice J. Foster, 1903–1970

1

The only interesting part of a drama is the underlying skeleton of the morality play. The issue is not that the good guys versus the bad guys is shallow, banal and juvenile. That it undeniably is. But rather that, without the morality play, there simply is no way to distinguish good guy from bad guy. Whatsoever.
— H.C., Atropine 1984

DEMSING KNEW THAT he was being followed and had made careful allowances. His shadow was skilled and made remarkably few betrayals; of that he could be certain, having tested the situation to make sure. What remained to trouble him was that, even now, he could not determine the purpose of the surveillance, nor could he assign a probable originator to it. However, he knew this spoke of a degree of risk to himself he could not afford to misunderstand. He did not reason this out, but perceived it virtually immediately, instinctively; survivors of Teragon did no less and lived long.

Although it was night, the glow from the city meant no particular advantage. In fact, for some operations, so-called daylight was equally good or better: the white dwarf which was Teragon's primary was small in the sky, and Teragon's thin atmosphere did not scatter much light, so shadows were both sharp and deep.

He was working his way higher into one of the older areas which had been built up into a gently rounded hill, long overgrown and encrusted with minor holdings along the slopes. He used walks, wheelways, and foot-alleys when convenient, but he also took shortcuts across courts, atriums, walls, swung on exposed reclamation lines and cable-ways, and even some roofs. Around him as he worked his way, the city surrounded him as far as he could see. The entire landscape was city, but not a city of soaring towers and intimidating giant structures; rather an erratic, softly rounded, coral-like organic growth which would have soon smothered abrupt forms. The individual units were simple blocky shapes with the edges rounded off and most roofs domed. The material was invariably *kamen*, the universal recyclable residue of the planet's interior, its colors pale pastels or off-whites, streaked and stained with organic residues. Blocks piled haphazardly, stacked in groups, and forming little hillocks separated by gulfs, which were not accidents of topography but only places which hadn't yet been filled in. It looked like preserved photographs from old Earth depicting a type of city called a *Casbah*, and from the outside it was secretive and reassuring at the same time. Inside those structures was where the fear lay. About a third of the units were lit within, which gave a magic quality to the still landscape.

Demsing knew that from any point on the planet, the view was more or less the same. *Which saves us travel money*, he added to himself. The city covered the entire planet all the way to the poles, which, owing to Teragon's rapid rotation and severe tilt as well as the recycling of the planet's internal energy, were not especially different from other points.

He hoped that his shadow, skilled as it might be, could not yet draw conclusions about where he was leading it. He thought that his path had been suitably random, deliberately giving the impression, in accordance with the suspected skill level of the tracker, of a simple attempt to shake a pursuer. He did not worry about being anticipated and run to earth, because, strictly speaking, he had no earth to run to. *That, too, was the code of Teragon.*

Now he was nearing the top of one of the hills, half-trotting easily in a relaxed, ground-covering lope along a deserted alley-way which was used to demarcate the upper-class places, higher up the slope, from the proles below. At the point he was looking for, he scaled up a drain line onto the low privacy wall and began sprinting across wall-lines and roofs, carefully skirting walled little gardens where increasingly deadly traps awaited the unwary; some were mechanical, some electronic, and the deadliest were the living forms. And as he neared the top of Ararry Rise, the traps would become still more deadly. He counted on that.

Now he was almost at the summit, and as he passed along a low wall separating sectors, he caught a faint trace of a scent he had been waiting to find. It had a harsh aromatic pungency overlain with a sweetness so intense it was cloying: Carrionflower in predative phase, close enough to be dangerous and cleverly concealed, as was its habit. Demsing knew that whoever was behind him could also pick up this peculiar scent and understand its meaning. And so now the game became deadly.

As far as he knew, no one knew where Carrionflowers had originated, or precisely what they were. They combined attributes of plant, animal, and fungus with a sophisticated ease that spoke of a long evolution somewhere where things were radically different from the way humans usually found them. Essentially, a Carrionflower was a semi-mobile preying plantlike organism which preferred flesh for its main diet and actively sought it out. It captured by luring its prey within reach with psychosexual pheromones and hallucinogens of enormous power, and then tapping into the captured organism with ropy tendrils. The victim would be stung, paralyzed, and kept alive by intravenous feeding of glucose while the plant replenished its store of required chemical compounds, and seeded offspring from a store of previously fertilized gametes. It was said that the plant provided its unwilling hosts with psychedelic hallucinations of unsurpassed detail and clarity. Sometimes distraught souls would seek one out, imagining that the plant would provide a vision of paradise while feeding on it. In fact, it created and amplified chemically whatever might be the leaning of the mood of the victim, and so for one deeply depressed, giving oneself to a Carrionflower was in truth an invitation to hell unplumbed.

Demsing breathed deeply, to take in as much of the scent as he could before subtle trace compounds concealed within its brew shut off his perception of his own sense of smell. For a moment, he felt nothing; then came a heightened sense of clarity, a lift, a confidence. But yet no images, nothing concrete. The concealed plant was, somewhere in its tissues, registering the presence of prey that was not yet close enough to identify so it could attune its chemistry. He knew this one; the Llai Tong kept one near their training halls, and this particular plant was old and wise and very sly.

Contact! Demsing's sense of smell vanished as if it had been switched off, and simultaneously he felt an unexpected, unexplained sexual desire in his loins—unfocussed and unpersonalized, but very sudden and very strong, like a panicky urge to defecate. He ignored it as much as he could, suppressed it, and continued carefully, extra-consciously, along the way he had previously chosen. He thought he knew where this plant usually kept its main body, and he wanted to come as close as he could.

And now he began to catch hints of flickering images, almost-memories of females he had known, evanescent shifting pictures that vanished as fast as they appeared. Nearer to the heart's desire, that was the word; Carrionflower found out what your resonance was by chemistry and tuned you up to the point of madness. Even as he made himself remember this, it also occurred to him out of nowhere that he had indeed come to this place at this time to meet Sherith, and so indeed was she here, waiting for him, melting, ardent, in this garden, all he had to do was step into it, she waited in the shadows for him.

The urge was intense and irresistible. But he knew and could not forget that the real Sherith was dead, and so while the powerful chemical illusion haunted him, his own mind generated images to match the chemistry. *Sherith is dead*, he repeated, opening himself and allowing the response to that death to grasp him, as he never allowed it to in ordinary life. It was enough; the hold of the Carrionflower was broken, and once again his present reality returned to focus. He continued over a low wall, up a short drainpipe, across a roof with a low dome bulging its center. He glanced back across the landscape of the starlit city, spreading to the horizon. A flashback caught him, entangling his mind momentarily with a nonsense verse he totally misconstrued: *Oh little town of Bethlehem*, followed by an image of a much smaller version of the same city, with groves of peculiar trees with feathery, drooping tops. But the sensation of desire slackened a little, leaving him shaken and weak with the effort of denial. *Yes, but that was a lifesaving denial!*

He still had no perception of a sense of smell, and was still getting images and flickers of memories or pseudomemories, but the effects were now noticeably weaker. He stopped in a patch of deep shadow, and concealed himself beside an exhalator vent from somewhere deeper inside, which helped dilute the chemical barrage which the damned plant was emitting.

But unexpectedly, suddenly, the surge of desire came again, rose alarmingly and Demsing began moving, haltingly, exerting all his will to hold himself back, and it was not enough! It was close! And it could move, if it had to, itself. He groped in one of the shallow pockets of his coverall for an ampule of Atropine, but before he could administer it, he hallucinated a powerful image: a young man or perhaps late-adolescent. Demsing, bemused, did not object to that per se, but what puzzled him was that the image was, however clear, of no one he had ever known, that he could remember. The image, however attractive, was of a stranger. But, tantalizingly, he could almost put a name to the boy. He experienced a momentary confusion, because some still-conscious part of his mind knew that this was one of the limitations of the system of perception which the Carrionflower exploited: the mind of the intended victim *always* keyed the attractant to an image in memory, specifically a memory of a real person, not a projection.

The boy was slim and intensely vital, with clear and well-defined features, and a most peculiar mustache, soft and close to the skin, trimmed out (or not growing) in the center of his lip, drooping lazily at the corners of his mouth. Demsing almost reached for it, but he also insisted, even as he reached with an impossible lust for that face, that he had never known such a person, and for an instant his mind divided into two warring parts, and that conflict broke the hold of the plant. It tried to compensate by making the image even sharper, but the details were becoming blurry and Demsing was able to shake it off. Soon, it faded out entirely, and was replaced by a nearly uncontrollable urge to run as fast as possible from this place, in any direction. The fear was palpable.

Demsing smiled to himself, knowing that the trap he had set had indeed worked. The plant had picked up another prey, shifted to it, locked on, and had accomplished a successful catch. It always put out a warn-off chemical. He put the remembered ampule of Atropine away, and reached for another ampule of somewhat more specific effects, which he used, grimacing at the sting of it where he drove the point in.

Presently his senses returned to him. He waited, unmoving, measuring out the time it would take the Carrionflower to complete its connections with its new host. But while he waited, the image which the plant had caused him to hallucinate came clearly back to him. That, too, was unusual. A boy, or young man, with an odd mustache, distinctive and memorable. In the background, he could sense somehow that a city was burning, and there was an oppressive sense of dread, of onrushing, slowly magnificent doom, which had only been lightened by the sensual encounter he had had with . . . him. The name still eluded him. Still the image did not match any conscious memory, and there was now something else he had not seen before: in the image, he was perceiving the unknown nameless young man from a woman's point of view. He was *her* lover, not his. Right. It had been difficult seeing this at first, but once one caught on, it was obvious. He shook his head, hard, as if to clear away the cobwebs of a too-vivid nightmare, and thought, cynically, *Nice kid, that one, yeah, but I've never been a woman. Too bad!*

Back in the present, he reflected that, after all, the trap had worked, and about now, it would be time to slip down there and see what had fallen into the Carrionflower's embrace. Perhaps that might tell him something. But without delay: the Llai Tong certainly possessed chemoreceptors in their compound which would now be telling some unsleeping guard that their pet had caught someone. They would be interested, too. Maybe more than he.

The garden of the Tong appeared to be the typical rooftop garden of this sort of level, appreciably larger than most, but not greatly different from other places this high up on the rise. The predominant vegetation was of the hardy stock which everyone presumed to be native: sturdy, twisted fibrous trunks and small, fleshy leaves. Many of these were sensitive and semi-mobile and followed the rapid path of Primary across the dark sky of the painfully short day of Teragon.

He dropped soundlessly down onto the patio floor and examined each part of the garden closely. After a careful search, he found it in a dark corner, more or less where he had expected it to be. The main body of the plant looked to be an ancient, short tree-trunk, sinuous and twisted as if it had been out in hostile climes for centuries. It appeared rigid, and wooden; neither was true. All parts of the organism were slowly mobile, and it seemed to capture its prey by simply anticipating it, as a human might capture much-swifter flies in its hand by anticipating where the fly *would be*, not where it was, or had been. Then all one had to do was *be there*. But it was easy to understand how a human could do that, with a brain thousands of times the size of the fly's entire body; more difficult to comprehend how a hundred-kilo thing which looked like a cross between a bristlecone pine and a strangler fig, and which seemed to have nothing in its structure resembling either brain or nerves, could anticipate a human, or indeed any animal. *There was always the last category: OTHER,* he thought. *No system ever maps the universe 100 percent. It is a deadly arrogance to imagine that one could.*

Speed itself was of no ultimate advantage to the anticipated fly: neither in some cases did the maneuvering of a human avail against the uncanny powers of the Carrionflower. This one had clasped its prey to itself near the base of the trunk by rootlike branches which looked as if they had grown that way. It was already attached, and so that was that. Nothing, or very little, one could do about it, once it was attached and feeding. At any event, nothing absolute you could do in haste. It would kill the victim and defend itself. Once in a great while, an inexperienced Carrionflower might be persuaded to release a catch, but the process required a surrogate catch, and an excessively long time. They *were* treelike in their patience. At this moment, Demsing had little time, no prey, and very little patience. He stepped closer to examine the catch, repressing a crawling sensation of horror which was not completely caused by emanations from the plant.

This one had been a girl. Branches clasped her limbs and body in a parody of an embrace, and vine-like tendrils touched her at several places he could see. Her clothing was disarrayed, but not removed: the plant never removed clothing, but simply grew through it. Her face was distorted, her head thrown back, and her mouth was opened in a grimace of mingled ecstasy and horror. While he watched, he could see her breathing shallowly and rapidly, and he could also see her abdomen contracting as if in the throes of the sexual act. A pale trumpetlike flower hovered directly above her uplifted face, a tiny bladder in its base working insistently, like a pulse, drenching her nervous system in hallucinogens which it synthesized on the spot, tuned by chemical feedback to the exact requirements of control of her body.

Demsing saw enough to identify the girl as a *Kobith* of the Wa'an* School of Assassins, an organization of impressive and admirable techniques, composed primarily but not exclusively of women. This girl was the nearest available example, in this universe and time, to a ninja, one of the legendary assassins from the far side of the past. She wore a loose, pajamalike garment of dull black. Her face had been carefully blackened out.

Demsing started to draw away, motivated by the waves of .fear-substance the thing was emitting at him. All the data he could get from this event, directly, had registered. There was no more to be done. It was a shame, he thought; the girl was slender and childlike, with a face which under other circumstances might be described as elfin and lovely. The lines of her face betrayed the soft blurred features of youth.

Her training at the School would have involved, as a matter of course, not only the mastery of martial arts, dance, and gymnastics, but techniques of seduction and sexual performances. Taken at birth, selectees were taught to swim while still suckling babes. She would be skilled in the use of internal muscles, and now that skill and control would, under the stresses induced by the plant, start tearing her internal organs loose within a matter of hours. It was doubtful she would live more than a standard day, even with the plant helping to keep her alive.

He also knew he would have to leave this place quickly, before he could be discovered by the flunkies of the Tong. Demsing stepped back, leaving, when he heard an almost inaudible sound from the girl, an inhuman sound that made the back of his neck prickle and his bladder weak. He turned back to the girl, moved close to her.

---

* An apostrophe indicates use of the glottal stop ('Alif/Arabic) which is used in the local dialect of Teragon.

She had, with incredible effort, brought her head forward; her mouth was still open, slack, and saliva ran from one corner. Sweat stained her clothing and ran down her forehead into her eyes. Her eyes were still glassy, focused upon some internal hellish panorama only she could imagine, a *she'ol* of unendurable pleasure indefinitely prolonged. But somehow she had called on all of her resources and was using them now. It seemed that she could see him, dimly, part of the time. She seemed to flicker in and out of consciousness.

The lovely, blurred mouth worked, tried to shape words, and at last forced out, in a faint hoarse whisper broken by involuntary whimpers and catches, ". . . can't stand it. Give me . . ."

Demsing drew his knife. "Who are you? Why follow me?"

". . . ah! Can't die. . . ." Her head fell back and her body moved in the throes of some deep inner convulsion. Her eyes focused on him again. ". . . years . . . inside here. Torn inside . . . die . . . can't . . . you won . . . kill me . . ."

He felt beside her left breast for the heart, which was now beating rapidly. He readied himself for the thrust. "Why?"

She groaned out, infinitely slowly, ". . . Vollbrecht . . . do it now. . . ."

Her eyes rolled back into her head alarmingly until only the whites showed, and her voice made a low throbbing sound, an animal noise Demsing could not interpret. When her head came back to near-normal, and her eyes returned, the eyes faced in different directions and moved independently. She repeated, ". . . Vollbrecht . . . please . . . now . . ."

Demsing began to hear sounds from the far side of the Garden: he had just enough time. He thrust in the knife, and felt her heart jump violently on it. Her body made one last powerful contraction, releasing her bladder and bowels in the reaction of death.

The Carrionflower seemed hardly to notice. After the initial relaxation, the contractions began again, although at a much-reduced strength and rate. The plant was now maintaining her body systems independently, and could prolong her as a chemical factory for its needs for several more hours. Left alone, it would eventually consume the entire body.

Demsing did not wait, but faded to the wall and slid up it like a shadow, only seconds ahead of the Tong flunkies.

On Teragon, as everywhere else, whether its inhabitants knew it or not, information did not merely represent power, it *was* power. Therefore after leaving the neighborhood of the Tong, Demsing carefully thought over what he had just seen, because in this there was the unmistakable flow of the powerful currents of real and hard information. So who knew it, and how soon? And information was even more perishable than food.

To be followed, briefly, occasionally, or even habitually, was neither unusual nor alarming for most of the inhabitants of Teragon. But in this case, because of who had been following, and because of the unusual persistence she had displayed, even to the point of becoming captured by a Carrionflower, the act was exceptional and definitely worth examination. The surveillance had been paid for, and it had not been cheap, which implied the attention of real powers on Teragon which Demsing did not wish aroused or alerted.

His mission this night had been in his view of negligible importance, or at least so he had calculated it: a minor arrangement of negotiation between an obscure neighborhood sovyet and the Metallists' Syndic. The matter had been so routine that he had considered it worthy of lesser diplos, and had almost not taken it. So now he reconsidered the task in the new light.

And arrived at no new conclusions. The job had been minor-league, and remained so on second and third examinations. Therefore the shadow had been on him, and not on the job. And so who had paid, and for what purpose? The neighborhood sovyet couldn't afford a *kobith*, and the Metallists were too tight to pay.

Then he considered the girl. For a moment, Demsing felt regrets at having killed her. But she had begged for it. And besides, victims of Carrionflowers needed considerable care; her own people wouldn't have provided it, because *kobith* were sent out absolutely on their own. That was their code. And he had no place to keep such a girl. And of course the beauty was a carefully selected illusion. No more dangerous or independent an adversary could be found. It would be equivalent to attempting to heal a wild animal. And that, too, was part of Teragon: no one took in strays, and need was the most bottomless pit of all.

She had walked into a Carrionflower trap. Obviously, she could be expected to know about such things, and to be thoroughly trained to resist them, so why she did so required some thinking out. He had not recognized her for what she was until after she was caught; before that, the only impression he had had of her was that she was good at her work, definitely in the upper orders. He thought wryly that had he known she was a *Kobith*, he would not have tried the Carrionflower stunt; he would have expected her to walk right past it. This was a piece with a loose end he couldn't tie down. She should not have failed.

A long shot was the possibility that she had intended to fail, which fit in with himself being the target. But that, in turn, suggested an accuracy of assessment of his own capabilities which he seriously doubted anyone competent to make: Demsing had learned early to keep his mouth shut and had not survived as a free agent into his middle thirties standard by opening it—or, equally important, allowing any assessments of his ability to be revealed. Still, that was a possibility and it needed evaluating in its turn. And if she had been the target, then there was a reason for that, too. But that didn't concern him. It could have been a thousand things—one of their arcane and ironic punishments for some imaginary transgression. Still, it made him uncomfortable, and for that, he needed to make some tests over the next few days.

And of course, the only data she had given him: Vollbrecht. She knew like everyone else on this world that no one got anything for nothing, not even death, and so, with the superhuman reserves of her class, she had broken all her vows and given him something in exchange for the service of releasing her from the plant. "Vollbrecht." He rolled the word over in his mind. A who or a what? And as he expected, it was a loaded gift: asking questions carelessly about "Vollbrecht" could be the most foolhardy thing he'd ever done. Still, he had subtle ways of teasing information out of his planet.

Lastly, there was the problem of the "scene" the plant's hallucinogens had evoked; not an image from memory, but something alien and strange. A memory not his own. This was not the first time such a flashback had occurred to him, but it was the first in which the gender crossover had been so clear and well-defined. Perhaps the presence of the girl had confused the plant's feedback chemistry, and that had manufactured a response out of nothing. And the plant, sensing it had two, had stepped up the concentration to compensate. Certainly that blast at the end had been overwhelming. But something remained, even after that careful hypothesis: it was part of the known rules of the game that Carrionflower hallucinations always involved memory.

Unlike the other questions he had, this last one gave him no access to Teragon's plots within plots, the games within games, *indeed some played for their own sake and no other goal.* This last question could be the most dangerous question of all that had emerged from the events of this incident. Whom could he ask, except himself? And if that self answered, what would it say—or do?

Demsing filed this all away in his mind, in a system of priorities which he would return to until he had dug it all out, and then proceeded with his original mission, satisfied again that this time, there was no shadow on him. He checked his watch just before he entered the zone of the particular neighborhood sovyet, and smiled at himself and the night; even considering the delays, the Carrionflower incident, and the incidental time he had used up, he was only running about an hour behind the original schedule, which was well within the tolerances of his contract.

2

We say of Fire that it's a good servant but a bad master, and that seems agreeable enough, and so everyone smiles at the "folksy" expression. But what we don't see quite so easily is how that perception applies to all of the unique inventions of humanity, and most especially to Language. Language is so marvelous a tool that it seduces us into believing that something can exist merely because we may, at our pleasure, assign a name to an imaginary something, and then perform grammatical operations on that noun, just as if it were a symbol for an iron ball. Consider the word "levity," which used to describe a force opposing gravity, or "Coriolis Force," which isn't a force at all. Now consider "talent." This is a word which is heard daily. But there is no such thing as talent: it is as fraudulent as Piltdown Man, as erroneous as the Ether, and as dangerous as Lysenko's genetics, because it leads us to look for and anticipate a phantom belief. What does exist is a will to succeed through self-discipline, which is, as they say, a horse of an entirely different color.

H.C., Atropine 1984

SA'ANDRO PREFERRED TO refer to himself as a futures broker, but the futures which he served were, for the most part, illicit, even according to the habitual practices of Teragon. Occasionally, his activities bordered on conceptual regions for which there was no word denoting degree of criminality. These degrees were certainly as real and measurable as wavelengths of ultraviolet light, but as yet humans had not learned to assign color names to different parts of the spectrum. For these reasons, then, and because even at an advanced age and devoted to well-developed epicurean appetites, he was accorded great respect, and the confidentiality of his house was a byword. Sometimes coins, never highly valued on Teragon, were lent legitimacy by the redeemer claiming, "Sa'andro spit on this very coin!"*

It was for these very qualities that Demsing occasionally sought out the Fat Man. Sa'andro was also a reputable broker of hard information, especially on the subject of who wanted what for how much. He maintained his own network of informers and watchers, and made up the difference for using second-raters by enfolding them within a subtle and powerful organization.

The Fat Man himself kept mostly to the Meroe District, where he did not have to stir far, nor wait long, for his tidbits. He operated an old-fashioned teahouse as a front, displaying to idle passersby an outdoor patio, an inner public room, a serving-bar, and an alcove where sometimes musicians played for the subtle approvals of their dour audience. The Fat Man himself presided in a room upstairs, enthroned on or within an ancient sofa reputed to have come from Earth itself with the original discoverers of Teragon, surrounded by paper and junk which transcended all of the ordinary uses of the words.

It was here, then, that Demsing would begin his search for the answers which fit subtle and dangerous questions; he wandered past the teahouse like a casual passerby, and hesitated before he went in, as if the thought had just occurred to him. Once inside, he drifted over to a booth near the musicians' alcove, requested a mug of the local brew, which he knew was not "tea" proper, but the leaves of the Yaupon, which grew well in the hydroponic gardens underground.

He waited; that was the way it normally worked. No one seemed to be watching overtly, but invariably whoever came in was duly noted and reported. Demsing frankly did not know exactly how it was done; presumably by a sophisticated gesture language of secret signs, the practice of which was a high art form. According to whom the visitor might be, various things might happen: a summons to the upper room, or, equally probable, an invitation to leave.

The musicians were filing in for their performance. Their *evening* performance, as it were, even though one could, with one's very eyes, look

---

* "Money" on Teragon consisted of essentially private promissory notes issued by various organizations with wildly varying degrees of confidence and redeemability.

out the window and see Primary gliding across the dark indigo sky of Teragon.*

It happened that it was the bassist who carried the summons. As he passed, carrying his cumbersome but expressive instrument, he leaned over, as if to pass a pleasantry, and said, in a low voice, "The Fat Man knows you know the way."

Demsing said nothing, and stood up as if nothing had happened. There was no gratuity; it was an unwritten code that the sender of a message bore the cost of compensation. He tossed off the remainder of his tea, which was indeed bitter, but which lent a particular clarity to the senses, and strolled away from the booth, as leisurely as he had come in, and just as leisurely, turned at the bar, passed through a frayed flower-print curtain, and started up the narrow stairs to the upper room. He wondered how the Fat Man negotiated these stairs: they were damnably narrow, and the riser tread was burglar-steep, these stairs an effort even for the best. Demsing smiled faintly at the message this perception conveyed: *the stairs are obviously too easy to defend or block entirely. Therefore the Fat Man never uses this passage. This is only for permitted approaches, not interceptions.* Demsing constantly read the environment around him, noting placements, patterns, obvious statements and some not so obvious.

At the top of the stair, the upper room was much as he had seen it before: piles of paper everywhere, in untidy stacks which overflowed onto the floor. The Fat Man sat on his sofa as if he'd grown into it, sweating with the sustained effort of holding his bulk up in a sitting position. With him, sitting on a hard chair in the corner, was a sharp-faced little rat of a fellow Demsing guessed might be sixty standard years old, thin,

---

* Time on Teragon is synchronized with Interplanetary Standard Time, and ignores the local "day" of the planet as much as possible. Teragon, slightly smaller than Venus, orbits an FO white dwarf of about one solar mass at a distance of 17 million miles. The resultant "year" is 29 days long. However, Teragon itself rotates once in 13 Standard Hours, retrograde, and its axis of rotation intersects the plane of the orbit at an angle of 22 degrees, which gives an erratic "daylight" to the surface. In fact, the daylight is rather dim, barely strong enough to read by. Primary shows a small disk, larger than a planet, smaller than a moon, an intense off-white, chalky glare, dangerous to stare at, which casts razor-sharp shadows.

The planet does not receive enough heat from Primary to sustain life or habitable temperature, so the contribution of Primary is negligible. The planet's heat comes from careful and sophisticated controls of the energy waste of its civilization.

Teragon, although deep in a steep gravity well, does not exhibit noticeable tidal phenomena.

short, intense. That one bore the look of having been abused often, from an early date. He constantly glanced around, all over the room, as if at any moment he expected to see an army of centipedes erupting out of one of the cracks in the ancient masonry. Meroe was an old section.

Sa'andro spoke in a soft basso rumble which had the peculiar property of projecting with virtually no sensible volume, nor could a hearer determine from where he spoke; it seemed to emanate from the very walls. He said, "I am very happy to see you, Demsing." (He breathed hard in pauses between words and phrases.) "The Metallists' Syndic was most pleased with the arrangements you helped them firm up. I told Horga, their rep, that those kinds of things followed naturally when one took the time to hire the services of the best."

Demsing flinched inwardly; he knew that a conversation which began with compliments could not but lead to more requests for even more services, some of them probably exotic, indeed. Perhaps he had allowed himself to become slack by stopping by here as much as he did, which in the abstract wasn't all that often. There were others besides Sa'andro.

As if divining part of his thought, Sa'andro panted and mused, "Certainly, there was a time when we saw more of you than we do now."

Demsing said, plainly, but respectfully, "One thing leads to another; some of the contacts I make with your aid sometimes ask for additional services." He paused a moment, and then added, "I always mention royalties and the courtesies of the trade."

"Of course, my friend! And would you believe that they also ratify their sentiments with definite quid-pro-quos! Absolutely marvelous in the context of an age in which one has to send out a small army to collect debits which, in my day, were paid out of pocket receipts. No, indeed, not a word of odious reproof; by far, you have the best repute of all my independents. More than once I have speculated, I have daydreamed, what it might be like to have the better of my bondsmen study under you, learn your methodology . . . but I also suspect that this is a hopeless, unrequited situation in which I might ever be the wishful suitor."*

* The speech of Teragon is full of allusions and elliptical constructions because it is carefully attempting to obtain information without giving any away, or at best, to maintain the best ratio between the two functions. It is the habit of natives to extract information from a questioner by careful analysis of the questions; therefore, persons who have legitimate questions or exploratory probes will cloak them in extremely tactful constructions or else cast misleading or muddying implied sources. In this particular case, Sa'andro represented himself as a romantic suitor, as if admiring a beauty from a distance, which is without question a case of false flattery.

Demsing thought through his own answer carefully before committing it to words. After a moment, he said, "It is true that I used to take some in, sporadically, and that I do not, currently. The reason is that not enough of them work out. There is some waste in the process. I found I could not in truth offer the genuine article to group operators, without a severe price in manpower which none of them would wish to pay. Such a course would in time become highly counterproductive."

"Would there not be a cure for this? Could one be found?"

Demsing said, "Possibly. It would be beyond the scope of my operations, and probably beyond that of most group operators to search it out and perfect it. Realistically, your own operators seem to do well enough for the goals you set them to."

"That is true, but one has to watch them so closely. . . . In your opinion, do other group operators have the same problem?"

"All groups share this to lesser or greater extent. It is a function of group operations. For some, it is a severe problem; for others, it's a minor irritant. One has to have a good structure, and one also has to match the agents and their capabilities against realistic goals. Such systems seem to work well enough. I would, candidly, rate your organization as one of the better ones. But of course it exhibits the features I mentioned."

"Stroke for stroke, dear Demsing, that is why I ask for your company! But the price I have to pay for that . . . you would not imagine! But you have given me useful information and I will trade for that."

Demsing shifted the subject. "You have heard of peculiar events in conjunction with my most recent stunt?"

Sa'andro made pursing motions with his enormous lips which moved masses of gristle over the sweating face. For a long time, the Fat Man said nothing, but eventually, words rumbled out: "I have heard a persistent rumor to the effect that the Order of Sisters of Our Lady of Mercy would be very interested in ascertaining how one of their best novices came to reside in the embrace of a Carrionflower."

Demsing answered, agreeably, smiling, "Sometimes hard and dependable answers are very costly."

"Oh, they are aware of the cost, you may be certain."

Demsing said nothing, implying that he thought the Fat Man hadn't completed his thought, which would help him say more. He thought Sa'andro could see through that, but if the other did, he gave no sign of it, which was damn good control. After a pause, he continued speaking.

"There was something of an issue over it. The Sisters are currently embroiled in controversy with the Llai Tong as a result. Other than that and the fancy footwork on both parts, we have been able to recover nothing—not concrete, not hints."

"Then they aren't talking."

"My boy, they don't even talk about routine things: that is precisely why they are who they are. They start with the basics: I *expect* it of them."

Demsing mused, "One might speculate on the subject of revenge."

"Who among us has no enemies? But there seems to be no reflection of that whatsoever. That might itself tell a lot."

"It might tell me . . . that my shadow was paid for so highly in advance that the loss was negligible by comparison, or that the mission was so trivial that the loss was, from my position, equally negligible. I should disqualify the latter."

"I had similar thoughts."

"Well, one can't live in a hole, can one?"

Sa'andro agreed, "No. And now allow me to introduce my friend, who has been here all along. I am a poor host." He nodded toward the small, thin man. "This will be Urst, who is my Archive. Not many have met him, but his reach is far and we have been friends and comrades in adventure for a long time, as time goes on this world."

Demsing nodded to the thin man, Urst, acknowledging him. He understood immediately the importance of what he was being shown. The descriptive terms for such a person as Urst were almost as numerous as their personal names, but they all meant the same thing in function: one who collected facts and connected them, and made that up into a map, and made sense of that map for their masters. Where did such types come from? He thought that perhaps they arose in the streets as sharpers who watched intently from the sidelines, but who lacked the will and nerve to engage themselves directly. Such men and women became gossips and idle tale-bearers on worlds of less-essential realities; here, they made themselves useful to emerging leaders who didn't know much but who possessed an excess of nerve. Once that connection had been made and proven with demonstrable success, they would withdraw into the shadows they loved, fed with selected tasks and provided information from the streets. And if they survived, they would become something more than slaves—and something less than fully formed individuals. It might be proper to describe them as extensions of their masters; so much so that few of them survived the loss of a master. They were hated and feared, with justification.

They were also kept away from the direct dealings of their masters, under the doctrine that "excessive exposure of Minds to direct operational matters clouded their insights." And empirical history, such as was generally known, tended to bear this view out.

So for Sa'andro to show Urst to him certainly carried meaning far beyond what was immediately apparent. *The truth was that Sa'andro was showing Demsing to Urst, not vice-versa. And that in turn meant that the Archive's assessment in situ was crucial for something which Sa'andro or Urst had in mind.*

Like the compliment with which Sa'andro had opened the meeting, this was also a most loaded gift. And he saw that neither of them cared if he saw this, as he certainly did. In fact, they wanted him to see it: that was the piece they were waiting for.

Demsing asked, "Do I fit the projections?"

Urst answered, speaking to Sa'andro, "Use him."

Sa'andro sighed deeply, quivering his pendulous jowls, and extracted a scented handkerchief to mop his brow. Demsing wondered at that: it was a bit chilly now, really too cool for sweating, so something was indeed balanced precariously here.

The Fat Man began, "In the past, I have acted as a broker for a small and select group of independent operators, and for my own . . . ah, personal ventures, I used my own people."

Demsing agreed, "Yes, that is true."

"I have a matter to advance which is most confidential. In fact, not to be rude, but I would have to have your service guaranteed before I could bring such a thing up. There would be penalty clauses, of course."

"Of course."

"How would you feel about such a proposal?"

Demsing appeared to stop and think deeply for a moment, which was solely for effect. The moment was now. He ruminated, "You know that to the independent agent, his or her independence of operation is the single thing that enables him to operate in some of the areas he might have to visit. So, if I, for example, were to enter a restricted service agreement with a given operator, I would lose that part of myself which is most for sale."

"For a time!"

"You probably know better than I, how these things work. In this case, 'for a time' means forever. Others use mindsmen; they hear, they see, they expand and project data. So others would know. As an independent, I can serve operators who would become the untouchable enemy within someone's specific service. Understand, I am not one to shy away from hard work—what's needed; but these things breed vendettas and that's bad for all of us."

Sa'andro leaned forward, puffing, "Such things do not go unknown— nor uncompensated. I am aware of the independent's stock in trade and how much I would be taking." He added, peevishly, "Everyone knows I pay too much!"

Demsing thought, *Whatever it is, it's big and that's certain.* The Fat Man never haggled, and yet here he was, suggesting he would, and then some more. Demsing said, "How much?"

"You do the stunt, and then it's semi-retired protected immunity. You train my troops."

The offer was substantial. It meant, in effect, guaranteed income for life, and within reason, anything you wanted. And Demsing knew how much "anything" meant on Teragon. And protection, too! This had to be something so big and so radical that Sa'andro wouldn't dare try it with his own people, and he wouldn't put it out for contract for fear of having it get out. But there was the price—you had to pay to hear what it was.

He said, "That's a lot. But remember, I'd be giving up a life I'd worked long to build—and giving up the chance to start my own operation up someday." This was standard independent idle talk, something every agent claimed to want. And few attained.

Sa'andro said nothing.

Demsing added, "Based on what I know at this moment, I would have to rate this as a risk greater than I'd care to take, as presented. It's not that I want to know more; just that without something concrete in advance . . ."

Sa'andro squinted hard at him, his eyes becoming porcine and dangerously feral. The Fat Man glanced swiftly at Urst, and then rumbled in a sub-basso even deeper than the tones he'd used before, "All right, I'll give you three wishes of Urst: ask him anything! Then you serve!"

Demsing countered, "One question, not pertaining to this operation under discussion, bonded confidentiality both sides, and the freedom to say yes or no. I have a question, and I'll risk that. According to the answer I get."

"According to the answer?" Sa'andro sat back, making small blowing motions with his lips. "That puts me out in the cold, blind and naked with a target painted on my arse."

Demsing: "If his answer isn't enough, then you can't protect me no matter what you think your organization can do." This was hard bargaining, the hardest he'd ever attempted with the Fat Man. And win, lose, or draw, something permanent was changing right now in this room whether he liked it or not. There were some transactions that changed things, to where there was no return to *status quo ante bellum*. No return. A lot of transactions were that way, but some were subtle. No one could miss this. He thought, *Well—one adapts. I have survived sometimes because I assigned changer status to what others thought were trivial events.*

Sa'andro hesitated just long enough for Demsing to see easily and clearly that the pause was entirely theatrical. Then, he breathed, wearily, "Done. Ask it!"

Demsing turned to the mindsman, Urst. "Tell me about Vollbrecht." Then he added, "Free association."

Urst registered neither surprise nor recognition, which was the expected response. Mindsmen learned poker-faces early on. What was unexpected was the reply: "I have nothing on a Vollbrecht of any sort. Give me a key: what is it? A person, an organization, what?"

"You know *nothing*?"

"I have never heard the name in any context."

Sa'andro settled his unruly bulk back into the recesses of the smelly sofa, and Demsing realized how tense the Fat Man had been. And the gambit had failed for both of them. Dead end. But there was one datum here: Whatever it was, the Fat Man was not in on it. He asked, "Restricted data?"

Sa'andro said, "Tell the truth. It's blown, anyway."

Urst said, quietly, "Truth: nothing."

Demsing shrugged, and sighed, "You can't protect me better than I can myself. So whatever your project is, I am better off to pass. But I understand what a resource I used, and so in trade I offer you one contract stunt for another operator at no charge to you. I can at least show some gratitude."

The Fat Man asked, softly, "Is Vollbrecht your enemy?"

Demsing started to say yes, but something stopped him. Not necessarily what that might reveal to this dangerous broker of arrangements, but in truth, something deep in his mind told him that he really did not know the answer to that question. He said, "I don't know that at this point. It is something I am working on, and before I proceed along that line of development any further, I should determine what Vollbrecht is."

"But it could be your enemy?"

"That is certainly possible."

Sa'andro nodded and rumbled, " 'Probable' for the cautious man. Very well: I will consider the stunt offer. As for the present, I have nothing immediately suitable."

And Demsing understood that, too. It meant, clearly enough, that he was being cut off because of his asking price. But all things considered, it was probably better that he left Sa'andro for a time. Certainly he did not want to be involved in a radical operation that failed. Such things left a lot of wreckage behind and not infrequently sucked in good agents as well.

Sa'andro had revealed a lot. But Demsing had revealed a name of interest, too. Yes. It was time to fade out of this sector of Teragon. Bond or not, Sa'andro would be looking for a buyer for that piece of data before Demsing had cleared the teahouse. The relationship had become uncomfortable.

In fact, the relationship had become dangerous. And as if the very walls had read the minds within the room, a fourth man entered the room behind Sa'andro, from a concealed passage. Demsing recognized the type instantly, and understood how fast things had decayed here. The fourth man was young, of graceful, lean build, muscular but not excessively so. Here was no independent agent, to take on any assignment and expect to average out ahead on one's wits, but rather a narrow-specialist who was uncontestably superior in one thing and useless in all others. This would be a bodyguard who was highly specialized and tuned to small, enclosed spaces, and close combat. Demsing had confidence in his own abilities, but prudence was part of his repertory as well, and he did not as a rule take on specialists in their own proper environments.

They knew he would see that. The bodyguard wasn't so much an open threat, as the cover of an avenue of action. They were telling him he'd have to leave with the risks as they were, intact. On both sides.

Demsing nodded politely to the newcomer, and stood, very relaxed, turning to go. He said, "I should leave. I have another contact I had scheduled. . . ."

Sa'andro rumbled, pleasantly, "You would not stay for dinner? One of my clients owes me a dinner as a debt, and as it happens, he has obtained a fine cook in his employ who makes a fine and authentic cous-cous. . . ."

"Perhaps another time, if the invitation is a standing one."

The Fat Man wobbled his head in agreement. "Yes, just so. Ahem, but our times have become so hasty. Yes, that is the word: hasty. I wish there were more time for the little amenities."

"You would probably be surprised to hear that many of my colleagues also feel that way, even as events press them into courses which might be considered 'hasty.' Still, what is one to do?"

Sa'andro waved his hand, as if shooing away an insect, fastidiously. "Certainly, certainly. But come again! Often, in fact: my house is yours!"

"Great regrets."

"Indeed, regrets. But good hunting to you!"

With that ending to their conversation, Demsing left the cluttered upper room and returned to the public room of the teahouse by the narrow stairs. When he reached the main room, the musicians were still playing, and Demsing took a mug from the counter and paused to listen to their progress through the complexities of an interminable song. The music of Teragon was based upon a system of improvisation within a broad harmonic and rhythmic framework which seemingly allowed almost anything, so long as it was done well and with style. This lent the music a strange, haunting quality, one always full of surprises.

He had also stopped to listen because it was unexpected. Upstairs now, they would expect him to hit the street running. But he knew he couldn't outrun street rumor, nor a comcircuit connection. So he waited, and smiled to himself at the thought of how much consternation and confusion this pause would be causing, and how many estimations and predictions were being re-evaluated.

The Bassist was playing an acoustic bass guitar, five-stringed and fretless, of course; now in the song, he took up his solo part, taking the implied melody and the rhythmic pattern and moving with them in the ways in which a windsailor might use the wind, steering a varied course only he knew, but in constant reference to the unseen wind. He did not land on each note, so much as he sidled into each one, sliding the notes from above and below and bending the heavy strings as well, and damping the notes with the palm of his right hand. The solo went smooth, like warm oil.

Demsing put down the mug. Now it was time to go, time to lose the inevitable shadow Sa'andro would put on him, at least for a while. He knew very well that the Fat Man wouldn't expect his own people to keep up with him for very long, but it was worth doing for as long as they could. Perhaps they thought they would derive something from the reports.

He stepped outside now, into the street, narrow and winding, with low buildings decorated with eccentric cupolas and bays hanging out over the street. It was T-night, now: Primary had sailed off somewhere behind the planet. Demsing set off easily and openly down the street, generally in the direction of the Fa'am District, walking easily as if he had all the time in the universe.

So much the watchers reported as well. They continued their reports for a considerable time, until one of them reported back that the target had vanished somewhere in the neighborhood of Aume's brothel, and was nowhere to be found. Sa'andro waved his hands in the air in dismay, Urst shrugged noncommitally. Aume was their own man, on their own street. One wouldn't think an outsider could find a way; but with Demsing, one had to expect the unexpected. Surprises.

As routine, they had all their field men check their territories, but of course, there was no report. Demsing had simply vanished.

Sa'andro finished his meal, wiped his face and told Urst, "Find out what this Vollbrecht is, and his connection with it."

Urst nodded, and excused himself. After a time he reported back, and his report was negative.

3

The attraction of the SF story is that it essentially happens some-
where else or somewhen else. We do not read it to find out what
the Joneses are doing in Peoria or why things are the way they are
in China. And that's fine: to read for adventure and visits to
imaginary places is, for the most part, good for the soul. But you
must always keep in mind that the very strangeness that you the
reader enjoy so much is almost never perceived by the characters
of the story itself. For them, to the contrary, the environment of the
story is Home—familiar, everyday, ordinary, accepted without
question, boring, exhilarating or terrifying to the same degrees
and for the same reasons that our world is all those things to us
in our turn. It is also good to recall that all fiction is elaboration
of selected simplifications; this is why truth is stranger than fic-
tion. Read the paper. So keep that borderline in mind; for if they,
the characters, could see across it the way we see into their world,
they'd think they were looking into an interplanetary zoo.

H. C., Atropine 1984

NOW DEMSING MOVED across the face of Teragon on one of its two
long-range systems. Sometimes he was deep underground, but it
was under only in the sense of being under the apparent roots of the
buildings above. Teragon was like a tropical forest that way. There was
no real surface—just deeper and deeper roots, becoming more tangled
and intertwined the farther one went down. Sometimes he passed
among places near or on the surface, riding in a singles compartment,
watching the districts move past him in the artificially lit days and
nights of the planet. Sometimes where the track went deep between
areas, the shadows cast by the floodlights overhead were sharper than
the shadows cast by Primary. *But Primary's shadows moved.* Constantly.
Never still. And sometimes the track ran along elevated runways

supported on pylons far above areas, the endless city passing beneath, a magic soft lumpy organic growth in the starlight fading to the black horizon.

Most people hated and avoided travel on Teragon, because it was disturbing in ways they had few defenses against. No effort had been made to make it pleasurable or entertaining: bodies were *freight*, and so the idea of travel was a functional and severely ascetic experience, designed so to discourage idle wandering. Idle wanderers saw things they did not understand, and began to ask questions.

The two main long-distance lines were neither speedy nor direct, but were labyrinthine and vine-like fractal entanglements which spread over the planet like roots, like tentacles, narrow little roadways powered by a linear induction system which drove coupled strings of soft-tired drays.

There were no ships: no open water. There were no aircraft: the atmosphere thinned too abruptly, and there was no open land upon which to build runways. Orbital vehicles were considered irrelevant. Nothing but the Linduc Roadways, with their strings of rounded, clumsy drays trundling along them at a steady speed of fifty kilometers an hour, headless trains of sausages bumping along in the twilight.

Demsing had come a great distance around the planet, far enough to put Sa'andro out of reach. Moving on was nothing new to him; he moved frequently, often shifting operating areas completely around the planet for no reasons at all, or else expressing rationalizations which he knew were nonsense even as he voiced them. The real reason was that he perceived more clearly as a stranger; events and patterns were not clouded by the fog of associations. And that he used the long and arduous journeys to clear his mind of a sort of dust, cobwebs and general untidiness which it seemed to collect from remaining in a smaller area for too long. It was a way of not simply becoming nobody, but of reaching beyond that for nothingness.

Long ago, he had understood, directly, without climbing an abstraction ladder to reach it, that thinking and dreaming were similar states of mind, closely related, both equally distant from the true state of the universe. It followed easily that if you could wake up from dreaming, you could also wake up from thinking, reaching a state of mind which somehow eluded Time, an Aorist kind of tense, unbounded, unlimited. *To think was to step out of the flow, and to lodge against dead monuments to the past.* To think was equivalent to attempting to retain a dream. It didn't help: it made things worse and more muddied.

He had often tried to pass this Aorist state on to others. Aorist Subjunctive. *What if?* But so far, he had not found one who could reach it. This disturbed one of his most basic assumptions, that everyone was basically similar and had similar abilities, if they would only reach for them, call on them. But they never did—or could. It eluded him, slid away. He saw creation as unfinished, that all were still immersed in Creation itself, that it was not some mysterious event in the unreachable past, but still here, now. You could write it as you went, write in what you wanted; the only thing was that one had to perform odd little acts, in themselves often unimportant and meaningless, but which seemed to energize the intended written state-to-be.

Sometimes it involved doing odd things to people he didn't know and had no interest in. Sometimes these acts were, of themselves, cruelties; equally probable, they could also be inexplicable kindnesses. *The moral valence of the acts seemed to have no relationship whatsoever with the valence of the completed state.*

But he couldn't pass it on. There was a wrongness there, but he couldn't quite see it, even in the Aorist. Something was in the way. And the flashbacks, too. They were related in some way to this, but again, he could not get a clear sight on it. For a long time, this had been in the back of his mind. He had seen it long ago, but put it away, for there were more important things to do. But it had never gone away, and in fact, he had become more conscious of it as time had passed. Certain things came easy to him without reason; and yet other actions came normally, as if he were learning them just like everyone else. Those things did not add up. He had begun to consider that perhaps it might be time to explore that anomaly.

Demsing got off the Linduc six days later at a place with a small port called Desimetre. The port area was like many others scattered across the face of Teragon, a closely woven series of Linduc roadways, terminating in a warehouse quarter on the left and an insignificant junction climbing off to the right up a narrow cleft which divided what was called Desimetre.

Desimetre occupied the south slope, where it tumbled steeply down to the deepest part, where the Linduc line ran. North of the line was another district, Petroniu, which held an altogether different ambiance. He had remarked that fact often, but not questioned it: it seemed perfectly correct that the division between areas should be both insignificant and subtle, for that was indeed the way of things. Petroniu was impoverished, dark, dangerous, and dirty. Desimetre was none of those things. It was sometimes almost as if a sunlight which Teragon had never known illuminated Desimetre, despite the undeniable fact that the poor light of Primary fell on all alike, the rich and educated, the ignorant and the poor. And on vice and virtue, which assumed different meanings according to where you were.

The streets and lanes among the compounds and shops of Desimetre were subtly wider, the compounds a little more finished, and the shops were more open. More people were on the street, and their business seemed less furtive. Nobody *scuttled* here. It was considerably quieter than most districts and was viewed as somewhat of a retirement resort and an entry point for offworlders, infrequent though they were, who were of course totally unfamiliar with the protocols of Teragon.

It was also a place where he had the most contacts; most, and most trustworthy, for it was his own home district. Here was where he had started from. Not that Desimetre was easy: far from it. Demsing continually assessed the District as one of the hardest to work in, not because of the relaxation, but because powerful and subtle groups operated from there, and they saw to it that the atmosphere remained unchained. To Demsing, lower-class districts like Petroniu were much easier to work, because they were invariably controlled by more sophisticated forces outside them, and so their inhabitants never initiated, but simply reacted to stimuli delivered according to someone else's plans and designs.

His first contact, after some routine exercises to ensure he was not being observed by anyone, was with a woman called Klippisch, who operated a small group similar to the Fat Man's, but of much higher quality and of greatly reduced scope. Unlike the Fat Man, in far off Meroe, she operated without a front, which still impressed Demsing: and to continue to do so was proof positive of diplomacy raised to the level of a performing art. Also, unlike many operators, she maintained a positive apprenticeship program which spotted many excellent youngsters coming along and provided them with good and basic standards for their later lives. And thanks to Klippisch, most of them had later lives to benefit from.

When he walked into the old office she was still using, she was having an intricate discussion with two men, apparently her own people, concerning the training of a new group which had just come in; they were so involved in this matter that none of them paid any attention to him. They knew someone was there, but who was unimportant. Then Klippisch recognized him.

She made fists of both hands, arms akimbo, and leaned back in her chair, grinning broadly. She was a compact woman of middle years whose active life had left her as supple and sleek as an otter, and solid as a brick. Her hair was clipped off short, except in the very back, where a short queue hung down, and was iron-gray in color. Her face showed an intricate network of wrinkles, frown lines as well as laugh lines. She had powerful, muscular hands and forearms, and still participated in stunts personally, which not many chiefs did.

Klippish exclaimed, from her leaned-back position, "Well, well! A stranger in these parts!"

"A stranger's stranger! But greetings to you all."

"Wonderful to see you again, Demsing. You are well?"

"Fed and profitable."

"Do you remember Dossifey?" She indicated the younger of the two men. "Maybe not. He was coming in about the time you were leaving. And Galitzyn?" She indicated the other. "We had to replace old Betancourt, who unfortunately died, just like the old beezer." Betancourt had been her Mind in the old days.

Demsing nodded to the two. Dossifey volunteered, "I remember you, but you've changed some. Of course, so have we all!" He chuckled to himself.

Klippisch cocked her left eye and asked, "Are you looking for work? I always have room."

"I wasn't especially looking, but if you need help, I'll do my part."

She nodded. "Need a place?"

"Wouldn't be a bad idea, actually."

She pursed her lips and said, "Dossifey can show you. Want to help out with some of the youngsters?"

"Fine. I've not worked with the kids for a long time."

"Well, well, what a find! We were just trying to figure out how we were going to get this bunch through, and in the door you stroll! What a day! Dossifey, go over to the safe house and check out a place for Demsing, will you?"

Dossifey touched his forehead with his right knuckles, smiled, and departed. Galitzyn nodded, and also left. Then she stopped, as if collecting her wits and her usual calmness, and asked, "You visiting openly, or you want it quiet?"

"Quite, please, as always. I'm invisible most of the time, now."

"I thought you'd go that way. Good. No problem." She put both hands on the desk in front of her, interlocked her fingers, and cracked her knuckles with a powerful rippling motion. "I'll lay it out, what I know: I haven't heard a thing about you since that Chukchai business."

Demsing smiled, faintly. "That was a while back."

"I thought you'd been offworld."

"Why?"

"A ship came in a while back, and after a discreet interval, here you are. Convenient. It was the *Vitus Bering*, out of Novosantiago. They parked out in the trailing trojan and sent a lighter over full of people. Some went back, some stayed. We are tracking a couple of them, on contract. Some, we are using for tow-targets for the kids. The rest . . . God only knows."

"You only had contract on some of them?"

"Right. No one can keep track of everyone. These were the usual sorts we get every now and then: traders, old relatives back for a visit. A couple of unexplaineds, I think. . . . And you, you fox, you could have sleazed right in there with them."

Demsing took a chair and slid into it. "Might have."

"Tell me nothing! I wish no knowledge of the beastly offworlds! Such a thing would distort my concentration."

"I also wish to know nothing."

"Then we shall make a fine pair . . ." She let it trail off.

Demsing asked, "Does my mother still live in Desimetre?"

"Faren? Indeed she does! Want to see her? I know she'd like to see you."

"What's she doing now?"

"Pipe inspection and repair for the Water Cabal, checking for sneaks and tappers and the like, and good at it, too. She's not in tip-top shape, of course, but considering her age, doing well enough. Age . . . you know, the one thing we don't have here is geriatrics, so we're all back to square one with the old three-score and ten business. Still, I wouldn't have it any other way. I can tell her . . ."

"Tell her I'm around. Presently, I'll stop by."

"You heard about Dorje?"

"Yes."

"Condolences. You're not here about that, are you?"

"No. I heard sometime back he'd been killed, before . . . Just before. I had some of my contacts look into it. There was nothing I could have done, and nothing I should do now. You know I wasn't born of them, but adopted offworld. We all came from somewhere else. I learned. . . ."

"Indeed you did. Abnormally fast, I should say!"

". . . Faren learned. She'd been a smuggler. Dorje . . . he did well enough, but there was always something in him that wouldn't change. He was in Enforcement before, and I think that he never adapted to the concept here of private enforcement and negotiated settlements."

"Yes," Klippisch said, slowly. "Out there, they think we are totally lawless, wild animals living in the ruins like rats."

Demsing smiled. "Pretty civilized, when you think about it."

"Wouldn't have it any other way. When I think about all those poor slogs out there in the dark beyond poor Primary, busting their arses for a gold chronograph with fourteen time zones of fifteen planets on it, a pat on the back, a kick in the toufass . . . no way!"

Demsing chuckled, "You should take a vacation out there, just to look at the natives!"

"Not me! Imagine having a sun that gave out real light and heat! Imagine! There you'd be, out in the open, with that goddamn bright *thing* glaring over your shoulder all day long . . . I hear some of those places have longer daylights than one of our whole days. Awful!"

"How are things, otherwise?"

"If the truth be told, a little quiet for my taste. It's been that way for a while, and of course nobody really wants to upset it. We have plenty to do, mind, in other districts. But it's quiet, here."

Demsing reflected, "I could stand a little quiet."

Klippisch agreed, "Everyone should slack off now and then. If you stayed up and alert all the time, you'd go fraggo, and if you slacked constantly, you'd be bored and starve. No solution but to mix them in proper order."

"I think I'll stay around for a time. But mind who knows I'm here, in Desimetre."

"Oh, for a certainty! We're as silent as the Sphinx, here."

"Did you really not know I had come?"

Klippisch looked at him sharply. "No, as a fact. Slipped by me again. And as far as I know, you very well could have stepped off the *Vitus Bering*. Whatever it was, I don't want to know."

"I may have some questions for the net, if I may. I'll trade some current from the other parts for it."

"Are you working on some private thing?"

"Just a little insurance, so to speak."

*   *   *

Demsing spent the next few standard days relearning Klippisch's routines and meeting her key people. The routines were as intricate and cautious as he remembered them, and the people, as he expected, were, to a man and woman, long on performance and short on ego. They seemed to work together easily and noiselessly without the need for excessive reflections of themselves in the eyes of others.

The main characters he saw the most of were Dossifey, who looked intense, with a hard, muscular frame and craggy good looks, but who wasn't, but was instead relaxed and placid, almost lazy, except for an uncanny skill he seemed to have cultivated to be in the right place in the right position at the right time. He made it look effortless, like all good artists, but the reality of it was that it was a lifelong discipline and he simply had never had time for anything else.

There was also a young woman, Thelledy, who looked like an attractive bit of fluff, but who certainly could not be, and who seemed to specialize in disappearing while one wasn't looking. Demsing caught glimpses of her, met her in short, chance meetings, and understood that without directed intent, he was not likely to see much more of her than that. As far as what she actually did in the organization, he could not quite see it, without devoting considerable effort to it.

The Mind, Galitzyn, was considerably more accessible than most of the cases he had seen, and certainly not evasive or apparently fuddled, as Demsing remembered the old Mind, Betancourt. Like many Minds, however, he was thin and underdeveloped, a middle-aged nonentity who scarcely bothered to conceal addictive vices which they all seemed to have in one form or another.

He spent his time divided between working with the youngsters in conjunction with Dossifey, who seemed to be in charge of that part of the operation, and with Galitzyn, who responded to patient questioning provided he was fed information in turn, and who brought Demsing gradually up to date on the general state of affairs in and around Desimetre, and what, in very general terms, the Klippisch Group was working on currently.

One of the items he traded Galitzyn concerned the increasing usage of computers in some of the Groups he had had contact with, a fact which seemed to rouse the old man out of his vulturine absorption.

"*Computers*, now, is it?"

"Paper Fan Group was further into that than anyone I saw, but I heard some talk there were others even further in. Even to the point of allowing Minds to erode themselves out of existence."

"Where you were, how do the others react to that?"

"Some fear it, that it gives the users an edge; others want the same thing because they think it's the thing to do. A minority are ignoring the whole thing."

Galitzyn growled, "The ones who ignore it will be the operations still in existence for the next generation."

"Why so?"

"Don't you think that's been done before? A thousand times on a thousand worlds! It's a failure of nerve, that's all." He stopped, as if the subject were one he did not dare give full expression to. He said, after a moment in which he had tried to sum up the essentially unsummable, "The problem isn't with the machines, but with the abuse of usage that the people fall into. Basically, this is a variation of the weapons argument, from the most ancient days of which we can have record. What things like this do is expand the reach of idiots and cretins, which allows a clumsiness and a lack of foresight and goals to swamp the efforts of better-trained people. Eventually, the contest slips over into a contest of firepower, or horsepower, or some other-power which fools can buy instead of building the capability into themselves. And what restores the balance? A sort of self-perception and will which has to be managed very carefully so that it itself does not become berserker-destructive. Initially, in a cycle like this, it seems to go all to the machine-users, but when a certain density is reached, then raiders chip it all away. People who are enraged beyond the controls of reason don't need guns, if it comes to it, nor knives. They have hands and teeth, if need be. I am sorry to hear of this, though; I thought we had all pretty well painted that corner over."

Demsing volunteered, "You see that trait in the apprentices: to take the short cuts, which in the end gloss over the key things you need to see yourself and handle."

"Exactly. Handle. That's the word."

"Can you use that information here?"

"Oh, yes. Indeed we can. Klip will want to start exploiting that weakness immediately. As I said, it's not the machine, but the use. We have methods of identifying that sort of abuse once we have reason to believe it exists. Very useful. So, now: you have given one, so you can take one."

"I have two, but one is more confirmation than anything else."

"One, two, what are numbers among associates? Honor among thieves, so to speak."

And by this, Demsing knew that the information he had carried was extremely valuable. That meant, with high probability, that one of their rival organizations had been displaying those, or similar traits. He asked, "The small one is about Carrionflower poisoning."

"Go on."

"When they receive the chemical tracers of one's body chemistry, they emit a tuned scent to key into the recognition areas of the brain. My question is, do they evoke random images, or images stored in memory?"

"Easy enough: memory only. Gollehon did experiments with chained volunteers, in 3035 Standard, which demonstrated beyond doubt that a specific area of the brain was activated—a section which deals specifically with the recognition and meaningfulness of remembered faces and bodies. Sometimes it seems otherwise subjectively, but in every case, there was a memory linkage, however weak. No cases of the contrary have been cited. In this case, the official version resembles the popular one."

"What happens with multiple potential victims?"

"If the plant perceives the two as equal in strength, two or more, it selects a sex randomly, one or the other, and emits accordingly. If the multiple persons are predisposed toward one sex, it increases the dosage to increase the possibility one will approach close enough for capture. In the latter case, for the comparatively weaker individuals, the increased emission can be expected to overwhelm any defenses such a person might have. In this pattern, it operates, if that is the proper word, almost exactly like the classical predator: it takes the weakest, and it acts to heighten probabilities."

"Does anyone know where they originated?"

"Unknown. According to my information, Carrionflowers are found on several planets, evenly dispersed throughout the volume of the part of the Galaxy we know directly. In no case can they be demonstrated to be products of the native ecosystem."

"Someone should pursue this."

"Doubtless they should. There are, however, more questions at present than there are savants to answer them. Certainly there are more questions than answers, which is as it should be. The situation is basically unsolvable."

"That is number one. This will be two: Vollbrecht."

"That's all you have?"

"That's all. I don't know what it refers to."

"On the *Vitus Bering*'s passenger list, there was an entry for a person Pitalny Vollbrecht. That is all I have."

"Restricted?"

"No. We held no commission to track such a person, and did not. I can tell you that several untracked persons debarked here, and I can also tell you that the number who left was the same as those who came. I cannot tell you if those were precisely the same. Again, we held no such commission."

Demsing thought, wide awake, *But they did hold a commission to check the passenger list. Why? For whom? Somebody reported that information, and Galitzyn memorized it. Curious, indeed.* He observed Galitzyn closely, and detected signs of the beginning of agitation. Perhaps it would be best not to press him further, at least for now.

And what he had wasn't much. But it was something. He asked, "What sort of ship was the *Bering?*"

"Express packet." *A small ship.* "Outbound for the 47 Tucanae Cluster."

"That's a *long* way off!"

"Obviously someone wants to go there, or send something." Galitzyn was becoming impatient.

Demsing and Galitzyn parted, and Demsing was certain that the Mind would report to Klippisch what questions he had asked. There was no cure for that, either. But he had something.

4

The trees of the forest front make an excellent screen for activity or states of being behind them, and let this be understood metaphorically as well as actually, for there are many kinds of screens and camouflage. However, one may see through this screen by standing still and observing motion beyond the screen, or else moving, and observing what stands still beyond. In both cases, there is a difference of perspective-perceived motion, real or illusory, which enables the master of this art to see through the screen as if it had never been there. It may also be noted in this context that the use of screening practices for cover approaches identity as it approaches perfection of concealment. Or, an enemy who is perfectly concealed may be unable to extricate himself from the structure of concealment.

H. C., Atropine Extracts

THERE WAS SOMETHING to Galitzyn's answers which rang out of tune; not enough to alarm, but noticeable. At first, Demsing could not quite perceive the wrong, even though he could sense its presence, so he let it go for the moment, but he did not forget it in the days that followed, as he integrated himself into the routines and functions of Klippisch's organization. Quite naturally, the small group of apprentices he took over represented the ones Thelledy and Dossifey wanted to get rid of; he accepted this without complaint. Demsing had ways of making them bloom, and he began bringing them out as soon as he could be sure he had decent security within his group.

There were four of them, as random a collection of street urchins as one could hope to pick up off the streets of the districts of Teragon: Weenix and Slezer were underfed, sallow emigrants from Petroniu, precociously streetwise and perilously unsubtle, boys of mid-adolescence. Fintry was an even younger lad from Desimetre who seemed to have no apparent virtues save an eagerness to please. The last was Chalmour, a hoydenish ragamuffin who claimed to be from the far side of The Palterie, the district immediately to the south. Chalmour was agile and adept, of indeterminate age, and although definitely female, somewhat uncertain of role.

She was clearly the oldest, but all of them were full of observations, rumors, tales and legends which Demsing sifted through patiently, never correcting errors, indeed, he acted convincingly as if he had never noticed them.

One fact emerged which was very interesting to Demsing. The Mind, Galitzyn, was of recent vintage; very recent, and none of them knew where he had come from, or how Klippisch had come to take him in. There was no contradiction among the four of them, who all predated the arrival of Galitzyn.

Dossifey, Demsing remembered, dimly, as an undefined young boy coming in as he had been leaving. He had had little contact with him, but it was enough to place him. And on this the tales of the four agreed as well. It was Thelledy where the stories broke down.

Weenix and Slezer credited her with supernatural powers without question. Fintry was the most recent, and knew her least well, however, he had once seen her in a secret conversation with Galitzyn, which had awed him to silence. Chalmour provided another interesting item, that Thelledy had been knowledgeable of certain sexual techniques and had attempted to teach her some of them, but had presently given up.

Demsing had, as a matter of course, seduced Chalmour early, or allowed himself to be seduced. The distinction was neither clear nor especially important. It was expected, and pleasant, and no one made any serious objection to it. Chalmour was enthusiastic and cooperative, but displayed no unusual skills or practices. How Demsing had learned about Thelledy was through a peculiar movement Chalmour had attempted to perform, which had not seemed one of her own instinctive responses. She had explained, "Thelledy tried to show me how to do that, but I could never quite get the feel of it. You must grade me for trying."

"Oh, yes! An 'A' for effort! At least!"

She lay with him in the small room in the safe house, stretched across his chest, wrapped up in the rough blanket to keep the chill away.

Demsing asked, "Did Thelledy prefer girls?"

"Oh, no, at least not so you could tell. The boys in her group she whipped into line and the girls she terrorized."

"I can imagine."

"Weenix and Slezer were with Dossifey's group, but Fintry and I were in hers."

"Why did she give me you and Fintry?"

"Fintry, I think, was too young. He's new. We all help with him. As for me, I always came off well in all the exercises and techniques, but she wanted me to try certain things. . . . I never seemed to respond to her satisfaction."

"What kinds of things?"

"Well, sex things, all of them, close or far. Sometimes it was a way to look, or walk, or smile. I couldn't remember to do it right. Other things were closer to the bone, you know, but doing them always seemed to get in the way, and . . . ha, ha, I'd forget! I thought it was a big joke, extra stuff, something she was culty on, because she was a bit fanny about it."

"Fanatic?"

"She covered it well, but it was something deep, all right. She really believed in it. And she could do it, too, all of it. Her boys . . . I don't think they were normal anymore. They took chances for her, and she always lost more than anyone else."

"Accidents in action."

"Yes. But she was new, and so we all figured Klip was trying her out. You have to expect some losses."

"I don't like losing students. Afterwards, that's different."

"Klip was pleased with what she turned out. And they were pretty good!"

And nobody knew where she had come from, either.

And most interesting was the information, courtesy Chalmour, that Thelledy had gone out to meet the *Vitus Bering*, with two assistants, Boncle and Poulwart, who were both lost on operations shortly afterwards in Petroniu.

Presently, after she had talked on about everything under Primary and then some, Demsing had felt her muscles relax, her slender body settle closer, warm and girl-fragrant, and her breathing become deep and regular, and he was alone with a head ringing with sudden suspicions. It was the kind of thing he recognized with an inward smile: just out of reach logically, but also close enough to be suspicious. And he had one of his own methods of dealing with that level. He relaxed. Now was not the time. He settled more loosely around the young girl, and cradled her more than a little protectively; if what he suspected was even close to being true—verifiable and predictive—she was extremely fortunate to have escaped Thelledy with her life. And she was too good to waste.

*   *   *

Desimetre was bounded on the north by the Linduc line, its marshalling yards, the cleft in which it ran, and beyond that, the dreary purlieus of Petroniu. Southwards, the district climbed an apparent ridge which always seemed too steep for Teragon, for it had, as far as anyone had discovered to date, no natural topography whatsoever. Southwards, beyond the top of the rise, the tops of buildings descended slightly and faded off to the horizon without distinguishing feature. This area was called The Palterie, allegedly owing to its lack of desirable targets.

Eastwards, the rise dipped into a spoon-shaped depression called Shehir, a small and self-conscious enclave which had gone over almost entirely to a defensivist attitude and was currently suffering from an excess of security mercenaries, which had the end result of making the district even more vulnerable.

Westwards, there were two small districts, the one nearest to the Linduc line being a surface manifestation of the Water Cabal called Gueldres; and on the south side, shading off into The Palterie, was an even smaller district called Ctameron, whose distinguishing feature seemed to be modest towers surfaced with a particularly smooth glaze.

These areas Demsing knew well, as well as he knew any part of Teragon; but even here, there was always change and one had to figure for it. Gueldres was considered a truce zone and little, if anything, went on there. Shehir had broken off from a section of Desimetre, and had gone severely downhill since. Ctameron seemed to be creeping slowly into The Palterie. Petroniu and The Palterie remained as they always had been, the one meaninglessly dark and malevolent, and the other equally meaninglessly light and threatless, although such terms were of course modified by the peculiar relativities of Teragon, where light and dark were sometimes hard to distinguish.

Now Demsing was alone, in his own place, a bare little room. They had sent the apprentices off on a short vacation, Klippisch advising them, "Enjoy the time. Soon, there will only be such Time as is stealable." Practicing their new skills, Demsing's group had appeared to hang around uncertainly, but when Klippisch looked for one of them to run a short errand, thinking perhaps that they were useless underfoot, she discovered to her surprise that all of them were gone, vanished without a trace, and that Thelledy's group were the ones still milling around. Klippisch looked sharply at Demsing, who met her eyes and pointedly turned away. But he watched Thelledy with his peripheral vision, never leaving her unobserved, and for an instant, something alien and hostile glared out of her eyes, something more emphatic than an outclassed group leader.

Yes. He remembered that. And other things, too, things he had been told, and things he had observed himself.

At times, he could call on something deeper within himself which he didn't entirely understand, a state of being he had no description for, and something which in truth he feared. It was never easy: he had to work at it, harder than anything he knew, and a specific kind of stress helped trigger it. It was a strange, contradictory path: he would sink deeper within his consciousness, but at the same time maintaining a tension, calling on himself to "wake up from thinking," to let go. And if he entered the state correctly, carefully, he could extrapolate predictable certainties from amazingly small fragmentary artifacts of reality, as he thought of them. Another thing happened to him: his perception of Time shifted radically.

Now Primary was slowing in its mad careen across the sky and hung in space, spinning deliberately, its enormous degenerate mass dangerously approaching absolute limits of Time and Space. Spinning. *Spinning!* He almost lost it when he saw that. Primary had enormous spin, left over, like its worthless heat, from the time when it had been a real star, fueled, running.

In this state he was a transit point for data, a junction on an intersection of infinite lines of communications. He saw everything, and everything could not be contained in the perception of a finite being, nor formed within the limits of linear language. He had to abandon Will, but he had to exercise it to select. Primary obsessed him, dominated him, and he blocked it out just as he blocked out the ramifications of the definition of a city, a junction point among lines of communications at which flows were shifted from one line to others. Teragon was such a place; so was he.

The vision, the realization did not unfold, but came through like some unimaginable hyperideogram which conveyed not a word, a unit of meaning, but entire developed monographs. Then, to untangle it and spread it out linearly, he had to *think*. Pass.

Thelledy was the subject. Galitzyn was the subject. In his inner vision, it moved internally, rotated, and assembled itself, the known, into an abstract structure in five dimensions which, could it be projected coherently onto the Plane, would look something like an ideogram manifested in repeating detail. All Demsing did was to nudge it into an "assembly" state, and release, and of itself, it fell into a completed state, and then he could retreat back into *thinking* to untangle it within the plodding pace of Linear Time.

Item: Thelledy was a long-term mole who had been trained very well somewhere else on Teragon and planted in this group for long-term goals.

Item: Thelledy was of near certainty a *Kobith* of the Wa'an Assassins, and now he saw the difference between Thelledy and the girl whom the Carrionflower had caught. Of virtual certainty was the fact that she had checked the passenger list of the *Vitus Bering,* looking for someone specific, and those who might have deduced that were conveniently lost not long after.

Item: There was a long-term operation, partly offworld, maybe its major part offworld, targeted on him, Demsing, and contracted through the best-run operation on the planet.

Item: Pitalny Vollbrecht was certainly on Teragon, now. And where was the best possible place to hide an offworlder? In the one place where he didn't have to *do* anything: the Group Mind. He could be trained offworld in the basics and, once in place, updated by the worldwide Wa'an network. He would be impressive, and accurate. And Galitzyn had appeared after the *Bering* had come. This had other ramifications which were alarming indeed.

Item: There would be no revenge for the girl who had been caught by the Carrionflower in Meroe, not within an operation of this scale. She had been expendable—and there was a strong possibility that she had been sent to fail, as some sort of punishment.

Item: The worst thing about answers was that they posed more questions, world without end. What was it he had or used that made him an object of an elaborate plot? He reviewed the chain of circumstances, and found it still standing. He was neither jumping at shadows nor reading into things. The surveillance of the girl in Meroe was fact, Vollbrecht was fact, and the connection of Wa'an to Thelledy to Galtizyn was fact, and all of the latter part could be easily verified by tests he could perform without their being aware of it. Subtle and some trouble, yes, but worth it, now, because he could not move further without determining what he faced, and then performing the proper maneuver to neutralize it. But that was a separate operation, and one of his limits seemed to be that it was, itself, a demanding process which cost a lot in terms of energy.

5

We tend to reach only for those things whose ends may be seen clearly, and then wonder why their promise evaporates even as we grasp them most tightly. To get close to an answer is to suggest that we do not see clearly, no matter what we say. But closer still is the realization that the real things that matter, that ultimately define our lives, what we are and who we are, are invariably and precisely those things whose ends we cannot see, or will not see.

H. C., Atropine Extracts

THE ARCHIVE, OR Mind, of an organization was a valuable quantity and protected at all times, from himself or herself, or others, as required. In the case of Klippisch's small organization, this duty was exchanged between Dossifey and Thelledy, when Galitzyn was not working directly with Klippisch herself. Dossifey took most of the shifts, mainly because he had been with the organization longest. Thelledy took fewer, because she had been with them a lesser time, but it was a measure of the trust that Klippisch held her in that she got them at all, and she had earned that trust by a demonstrated unswerving loyalty to the things Klippisch directed, a quality she held to be rare in "these degenerate times."

The watch duties were not demanding; keep the Mind safe, and make sure he got rest. Thelledy always did this by moving the location around in a random manner and keeping Galitzyn in places only she seemed to know, and frequently contacting Klippisch or whoever was acting with her at that time.

It also provided an opportunity for Thelledy to make contact with Galitzyn. She had chosen this place with care, even more than her usual standard, which was always high by the standards of Teragon: a small, bare apartment which at some time in the past had been added on after the fashion of the planet to a large exhalor, an air shaft connecting with the deep interior levels. Here, the oxygen level was noticeably high and the temperature was more comfortable than the Teragon norm. It also had a good view on all sides and was difficult to approach, concealed.

Galitzyn had, in his own past, thought himself a fairly competent field operative. He was alert, he noticed things many others, themselves considered proficient, missed. Here, in this place, he sometimes doubted the wisdom of coming here. This district, Desimetre, was widely considered to be relatively safe for offworlders, according to Teragon practices, but it had required every resource he possessed to maintain his cover here, and from what he had heard, he doubted seriously if he could survive more than a few standard days anywhere else on this planet.

He thought of it as the Feral Planet, where humans had, in the course of time, turned into something quite unimaginable. The natives here seemed to be immune to all the accepted forms of manipulation practiced elsewhere, and had taken on values which were difficult to describe, if at all. Definitions had a way of dissolving here. And despite the fact that the surface was completely covered with what might be called a vast and poorly organized city, it was, to all evidence, severely underpopulated. The humans who lived there seemed like scattered survivors inhabiting ruins built to house a population much higher.

Thelledy always raised these questions. On the surface, she seemed to be a young woman, more than normally pleasant in appearance, with an oval, soft face, loose thick, black hair which was cut short, and a sturdy, muscular figure. But other things about her terrified him. She appeared to have no possessions whatsoever and formed no attachments he was aware of. He had no idea where she lived, if that was the word for what she did on her own time. And she moved in Time with an awareness he could barely imagine. And by her own estimation, she rated herself "above average, but not completely excellent." Galitzyn often found himself wishing he would never meet someone she looked up to.

She had such an estimation of Demsing. As she had put it to him once, "Demsing at full awareness cannot be countered by any one operative I know of, which is why he keeps himself as secretive as he does; if he were to become widely known, he would cease to have value, because of that. We check ourselves and each other, and simply put, one-on-one, he can't be covered."

"Then your group would not hire him, having formed that estimation?"

"No. We wouldn't anyway, for other reasons, but even if we did outside contracting, we wouldn't hire him. He is totally independent."

"How many people know that, here?"

"We know it. Now you do. We won't sell that to anybody, and you can't, so he's safe."

"Why wouldn't you sell that information?"

"He voluntarily does not oppose our goals directly, and does not contest with us in any area."

That had sounded curious, but no more so than the usual responses he got, here.

Galitzyn knew very little about Thelledy; she was his contact here, and an apparently junior member of an organization which was composed predominantly of women, deadly women. He himself had not established the working relationship, so he had no idea how it had been arranged, or who they were. They were being paid to track Demsing, and they would lose him often, and they were accounted the best of the groups that operated planetwide.

From her side, all she knew was that offworlders wanted Demsing tracked, and if possible, brought to an area where they could observe him directly. She never allowed her contempt to show openly, but Galitzyn could read it there, all the same.

According to the chronometers which everyone wore, it was standard night. Outside, through the single window, he could see Primary moving across the dark sky, casting razor shadows that looked sharp enough to cut the careless.

Thelledy slipped into the room with a graceful minimum of motion that for a moment beguiled him. She said, without preliminaries, "Well, he's here, now. What are you going to do with him?"

"What's he doing currently?"

"Ostensibly training the kids he's been given. I spotted him a girl, and he took the bait."

"That's not usual for him, is it?"

"Not usual at all. We estimate it doesn't make any difference to him, however, so don't expect any leverage. He does that every so often."

"What? Picks up a girl?"

Thelledy favored Galitzyn with a glance one might see in a housekeeper looking at a roach. "No. He forms relationships, with people who have no apparent value, and trains them. Somehow he can see a value in them others can't; at any rate, he manages to turn them into extraordinary people. Useless to us, I might add. This girl, Chalmour, I rated as subnormal and bumbling, not really trainable even for this group, so for me, she was a throwaway. He scooped her up like he'd found gold. We know from past observation that he's seen something valuable in her and will bring it out. What it is we can't determine. Why don't you ask him?"

For some reason, this frightened Galitzyn more than anything she could have said, and he knew she knew it.

"The report I'm sending back at next contact will suggest that there may not be a way to contact him for what we have in mind. We thought putting an operator in place here might clarify this problem, which we have had for some time, but I don't see any way clear to make contact without a level of hazard we can't risk."

"What do you people want him for? I mean, he's certainly one of the best, but if you can hire us, you can pay for what you want, and with a good, tight operation, surely a combination could be found that could do it."

"That's the problem. He's operating, the best we can determine, at about 10 percent of capacity. Teragon isn't even a challenge to him. He acts as if he doesn't know what he can do. So we would have to tell him that, and that's the dangerous part."

"Your people rate him as dangerous?"

She had asked this before, but continued to ask it from time to time, as if she did not believe his answers.

"More dangerous than you can imagine, if he's contacted wrong."

"Well, the only way we deal with him is, by and large, with candor. We have found out that you can't hide much from him, once he gets on the scent. That was how we got him here, you know, and that was iffy. And by the way, when do you people compensate us for the loss of Asztali?"

Galitzyn bridled a little, "I thought that was covered from your end. She was supposed to fail, wasn't she?"

"You know the contract as well as I do: you pay for losses. At no time were we to engage him openly. Nor would we, and that's from the top. They rate him even higher than I do. She was to fail, that is true, but the method was more drastic than required. She was not supposed to fall into a Carrionflower, and normally wouldn't have. We are investigating why that happened."

"You don't know?"

Thelledy left it unanswered. After a time, Galitzyn said, "I'll see to it. Goes out next report. The usual rates?"

"The usual."

"Do you know where he is at this moment? I saw that he left for a while."

"Went home with Chalmour, over in The Palterie somewhere. Now *that's* unusual, I can tell you that. Girls, yes. Boys, even, occasionally. But taking them home? Definitely out of character!"

"What do you have on this Chalmour?"

"To us, she's ordinary." She shrugged, as if the girl weren't worth discussing.

"Why would he go to her parents' home with her?"

"We can't predict his actions. He must have reasons even more opaque. I can think of several possibilities, some of which are relatively innocent . . . some aren't." Again, she shrugged. "You see, we know from his actions we've tracked that whatever he does with her won't affect us."

"Why is that?"

"Because he doesn't build organizations. He destroys them."

Galitzyn seemed to shrink. He said, softly, "We know that."

Demsing had done something slightly more intricate than Thelledy's report might have it; he had, it was true, "gone home with Chalmour." But that wasn't all of it. What he actually had done was take his entire crew of apprentices off on an extended field trip into the apparently boundless suburbs of The Palterie, where they supported themselves by doing a wide range of small tasks, some of which were simple and ordinary odd jobs by any planet's estimation, and some of which were beginner's exercises in the kind of subtle sophistication Demsing preferred. All of the apprentices enjoyed this and performed at their best.

What he had learned from Chalmour had motivated him to follow this course. She was the youngest member of what had been a large family for Teragon, and her parents still had the room to house them all, provided they could contribute to the ongoing operations of the house. Klippisch knew about it and approved.

More importantly, Chalmour's parents approved. They had managed to place six children without failure, none of them expert but all competent survivors, and they had thought Chalmour a little slow, and were delighted with Demsing, despite the apparent age difference between himself and the girl. True, he was an unknown stranger, and bore the marks of a fearsome competence, but he treated her well, and took time with her. Their relationship was obviously still new, but already they could see changes in her which seemed well, for her future. She still retained her flighty sense of humor, but moved about the things she did with a new sense of precision and confidence, and if Demsing gave her this out of a sense of potential he saw in her, that was all to the good. That was why they had sent her to Klippisch in the first place.

While the apprentices were all out on one of Demsing's exercises, Demsing brought this subject and others out in the open with the girl's parents, Elsonek and Lelkempre.

Elsonek began, "We have to make excuses in this day and this place for feelings of overprotection."

"Don't apologize; far too many send them out without a word of encouragement."

Lelkempre added, "Too often, you have to look another way . . ."

Demsing said, "We do have a lot of this here; I have often wondered about that. Undoubtedly that attitude certainly produces survivors, but its cost is high in the . . . development of things that sometimes lie hidden."

Elsonek asked, "Then you see something special in Chalmour, something you can enhance?"

"Not really. She is mostly what she seems. The difference in her is that she is open enough to allow me to bring it out of her, what seems to lie quietly hidden in most of us. From that standpoint, she is very special, but not in any abstract sense, but in the particular case of her and me."

"Why should you do this thing?"

Demsing understood the question. Elsonek and Lelkempre were astute enough to recognize part of what Demsing was within the context of Teragon—a confident and powerful self-supported individual who operated without outside backing. He worked for himself. And so why should such a person, who could obviously have the symbols of competence with little effort, choose a girl like Chalmour, who was pleasant enough, but who did not seem to be remarkable in any way?

He answered, "There are those who would see this as an indulgence; after all, most people indulge if they can. This is not the case. There is something real there, rare enough for me to feel I should follow it. She is good for me, and apparently I do the same for her. I am not a justifier, nor a signifier, one to prevent unique events because of sets of abstract principles. Too long I have lived for myself."

"Then there is no concealed purpose in this."

"If there is anything concealed, it is what Chalmour can become after I have taught her to bring it out and protect herself while she's doing it."

Lelkempre exclaimed, "You don't know what you're going to get!"

"Exactly that!"

Elsonek suggested, "You might get something you wouldn't like so much."

"To endure difference is to grow; most people are fixated children because once they obtain power, they strive to make everything in their own image."

"Then your intent is long range. That would include, of necessity, children."

"In the usual case. I, however, do not reproduce. I do not know the reason. Nothing appears to malfunction. There are more than enough strays on Teragon—we can make do adequately with those." As Demsing said that, he felt an odd and immensely strong sense of déjà vu, as if either the words, or the image underlying them, were a life he'd lived before. It was so strong it forced him off the track of the present, in this house, now, and he had to exert considerable effort to return to it. The sensation of recapitulating something within himself was overpowering, but he could not identify it, and as he thought to search for it in memory, it faded and vanished even as he reached for it. "Fertile, ah, that is correct: I am sterile."

"You have spoken with her about these things?"

"Yes."

"Why would you bring them to us? Chalmour is, after all, on her own in these things and has been for some time."

"I cannot explain further than it seemed the proper thing to do. I normally do not question such suggestions of perception. Chalmour is as unique to me as I am to her, and something out of the ordinary practice seemed . . . well, correct. That was another unique event in itself, our conversation on this, but it echoes the uniqueness of the relationship in a resonant manner. The two reinforce each other. You might say legitimize."

Elsonek laughed, "Nothing is legitimate on Teragon!"

"Perhaps it should be, and perhaps this might be the place to start."

Elsonek glanced at Lelkempre. He said, "Some sort of response seems to be necessary at this point . . . I will permit it." Lelkempre nodded her agreement. "I do ask that you train her properly before you turn her loose; she is a bit scatterbrained."

Demsing nodded in return, as if the ritual whose outlines he could only guess had been fulfilled. "If such comes to be, she may leave of her own will. I, however, have no such intent."

Lelkempre said, "Nor does she. She has spoken with us about this. And so I tell you that same I told her: you have opened up something rare and valuable—something people search for all their lives and do not find. But beware its power, too. It is dangerous. We all know that instinctively."

"I would like to create a world in which such dangers, as you call them, were not dangers, but were seen for what they really were, prized gifts."

Elsonek turned sharply at this and said, "And what about the rest?"

"There are corrosive evils we have learned to ignore, and whose consequences we accept as if they were natural, if unhappy, accidents. These elements and the consequential world they form as they unfold are generated by an ancient fear which I should like to remove."

Elsonek said, "Most do not ask such questions."

Demsing responded, "They do not ask because they fear the potential of the answers; as if one could always ask, 'could I live independently, on my own?' But they almost never ask it out of the fear of possible negative. More, they build a conceptual universe in which such questions cannot even be framed, and one more step, too, that of building a logical system within whose bounds clear evidence is arrayed into distorted patterns called straight. There is a lot of learning and a lot of Time behind such habits, and it is neither easy nor casual to unstructure such artifacts."

"I might agree that such an artifact exists, but what was the reason for its construction?"

"The best I can tell you now is that it appears that it exists to prevent perception of, and implementation thereof, the obvious, to favor specific attitudes of those who found they could control groups by obstructing that flow."

Elsonek looked away. "You have said a lot."

"I have said more than I intended, and more than I have dared say to anyone before. It is difficult to frame it in speech which has been deliberately designed to blur and obscure it. This did not originate here on Teragon, but has deep roots in Time. It was brought here, and found a fertile soil which allows it to express itself here with particular clarity. But if that amplification makes it, the idea, particularly powerful over us, it also makes it particularly perceptible, and hence, vulnerable."

"That is a heavy load for, as you say, an ordinary girl."

"It is no load at all, and its resolution is within the grasp of all of us; only the way to say it, so to speak, is hard."

Lelkempre said, "Make enough money to leave, and buy your way offplanet, to a better world, the two of you."

"I could do so, but I know the answer is here, strange as that sounds."

Demsing set the apprentices on some more exercises, with Chalmour set up as a loose control, and then left them behind while he made a quick trip back to Desimetre, under the tightest level of covered movement he could manage. Should anyone have been following him or keeping him under surveillance, they would have seen him do simple, ordinary things, and fade from view, and then vanish.

Faren Kiricky lived in a modest but comfortable house in the part of Desimetre closest to Gueldres, a plain masonry structure of one main room and two smaller ones added on the sides, topped with the low dome characteristic of the houses of Desimetre. There was a wall around the front part, enclosing a small patio on which a Suntracker plant was displayed in a large pot.

The Suntracker was another of the odd plants found on Teragon whose origin could not be explained. Growing from a thick, sturdy trunk, it expanded its form in a series of random and assymetric tiers of flat structures assumed to be leaves, which moved constantly so as to maintain a constant angle on Primary. Here its resemblance to a plant ended, for the trunk and branches were a bright metallic blue, reticulated and scaled like the hide of some ophidian creature, and the "leaves" were delicate, fleshy structures colored in iridescent patterns of changing colors. During the short "day" of Teragon, the leaves tracked the course of Primary with unerring accuracy, and during the night, it reset itself to that point on its horizon where Primary would reappear.

The Suntracker was a luxury, because it required considerable care to maintain it in its best condition, and the treatment suggested an origin whose environmental conditions were odd in the extreme. It required watering with a precise solution of 1 percent hydrogen peroxide, and trace amounts of a peculiar compound, arsenous selenide applied at rare intervals. After such treatment, the plant would give off a faint odor of mustard, which had been found to be infinitesimal amounts of arsine gas.

Demsing found Faren at home, as it were, giving the Suntracker one of its periodic treatments. He let himself in the gate, just as he had when he had lived there. She did not seem surprised to see him, but stood and held out her hands to him, which he took.

Demsing saw that Faren had aged, as he had expected, but Time had been surprisingly kind to her. She was still trim of figure, active and precise in her movements, although her hair had turned white and her face was thinner and traced by a fine network of lines.

He said, "You look well; you always do."

"Nonsense. I am falling apart. It is all I can do now to crawl out of bed; but you look fit. Have you been busy?"

"Well enough. I have not been bored, that's a fact."

"Klippisch had them tell me you were about."

"Yes. I wanted to wait awhile before I came to see you; it seemed the right way to do it."

Faren did not question this. Demsing had always seemed to move according to some subtle internal timer, and it had always seemed to work out best to let things happen according to it. She said, "Are you living with anyone?"

"A girl, from here now, but originally from The Palterie."

"Good, I approve. It is not good to live alone."

"I'm looking for a way to put some permanence in it."

"That would also be to the good. Doubtless you'll have to change your ways."

"That's what I'm looking for. Difficult to find, though."

"I quite understand, now. At first I didn't, here, but . . . There is a way, if you can find it. You will, eventually."

"Yes."

"Have you time to come in?"

"Yes. I had wanted to ask you some things."

"Come in, then." Faren finished the few remaining tasks with the Suntracker, and motioned Demsing to follow her into the house. The large part, under the main dome, contained a few simple things, much as he remembered it: a narrow bed on one side, a table and two chairs on the other. It also had a window facing the patio, arched across the top, framing the view of the Suntracker. The smaller sections contained a kitchen and a bathroom, respectively. The floor was covered by a woven rug of geometric patterns. On one wall was a contrastgraph image of Dorje, a severe black and white representation which expressed an image of a face solely by the highlights of it, in themselves random patterns of no specific shape which the mind assembled into a face. On the other was a similar contrastgraph of himself as a young boy. By the door was another, depicting the face of a young woman which, by its full and rounded contours, seemed to suggest a full-figured body.

All was as it had always been, including the contrastgraphs. Demsing had never known who the woman was. He had always been told, "It was someone we wanted to remember," and that had been all there was to it. He had not followed it out; Teragon, he had learned at an early age, did not permit the luxury of nostalgia or reminiscences.

The house was cool and quiet, with an imperceptible scent of familiar things used and kept up for a long time. How long?

Faren prepared them a simple meal of noodles, an oil or sauce which was a disturbing carmine color but which had a bland and inoffensive taste, some greens, and a bowl of chickpeas, served with a honey-colored near-beer. During the meal, they did not talk, but savored the rarity of the time and the silence. He remembered it well: it always had been a quiet house, a refuge, and she had kept it that way.

Finishing, Faren ventured, "How does it seem?"

"Like always. Things never change here. That is difficult to do."

"I would let it change, or move away, sometimes, but then I don't. We have only one life—why live it in an uproar? I moved around a lot as a girl, and Dorje had also. When we came here, it wasn't at all like we expected, and so we worked to make this place something . . . special." It was, to Demsing, the simple statement of someone who had learned to live within her limits without resentment or envy, and he admired Faren for attaining it, and expressing it thus as well.

He thought a moment, and then said, "You could have gone back to space. For that matter, you could have stayed there."

She shrugged. "Possibly."

Demsing began, "I have a problem, which I haven't taken to anyone else, and I am uncertain how to approach it."

"Is it the same as you had before? The visions of places you'd never been?"

"Yes, that. Only now there are more of them, more often, than there used to be, and they are clearer. To one, they feel like memories."

Faren busied herself in the kitchen with the dishes and avoided Demsing's eyes. It was a problem she had, within her limits, tried to ignore in the hope that it would go away. But of course, it hadn't. Demsing was Nazarine, and she knew him as both, and by implication, all the other lives Nazarine had told her she had been, as the Morphodite: Nazarine Alea, Phaedrus, Damistofia Azart, Rael, Jedily Tulilly. Nazarine was the face in the third contrastgraph.

The Morphodite had the ability to *change*, to undergo a terrifying metamorphosis into another person, of different gender and about twenty years lower age, sometimes more, sometimes less. Nazarine had been her friend, but she had herself seen Nazarine's powers of perception work, and also her power to *change* . . . the last time, the change had produced an infant with premature characteristics, which she and Dorje Ngellathy had taken and accepted responsibility for.

Faren did not entirely understand the process, which seemed to generate its own peculiar rules as it went, rules which seemed, as anything unknown, to be arbitrary and capricious. But one thing which was constant seemed to be the retention of memory. There was a slippage from one persona to another, as if the process of change did not carry over the entire memory, but edited it down into some condensed form. It had been Nazarine's opinion that having to pass through infancy would limit severely the memory of the past and that the resultant persona would forget or never remember being the Morphodite, live out a normal life, and vanish from the stage.

It had been her hope, too. But it had not been long before the child, Demsing, had begun to display unusual abilities, and to have "visions," as he had put it. She and Dorje, while Dorje had lived, had neither suppressed such things in the growing boy, nor had they encouraged them. They had cautioned him about revealing his unusual abilities and perceptions to anyone, and so he had grown up with it.

As Demsing had matured, the unknown abilities had not lessened, but instead had grown, and had enabled him to become, with envied ease, an adept and ruthless operative in the endless personal conflict which passed for society on Teragon. Demsing drew on the capabilities of the Morphodite without knowing their source. In a sense, then, Demsing was innocent of the full extent of his powers, and more dangerously, innocent entirely of the uses to which such powers could be put.

Faren knew some of it from Nazarine, but she suspected she was only a witness of a part of it, and at that, a part Nazarine had held back. And now the problem had not gone away, indeed, but had come back, rather more oppressive than before. It was, after all, a question of how Demsing realized what he could do, that would determine how he used it, or if he used it.

She and Dorje had worked on that assumption, and tried to build a strong and secure character in Demsing. And to their credit, a considerable part of it had taken; Demsing had no traces of sadism, cruelty, perversity, or bizarre urges, and did not, to her knowledge, exploit others because of their weaknesses, as many did. But the other side of the

Demsing coin was that he represented a peak in the type of ideal citizen of Teragon, competent and ruthless where such behavior was called for. Demsing, in short, had turned out well, according to the ideals, if one could call them that, of Teragon. But no one could foresee what he was capable of, if he regained his full powers and memory of his pasts.

She said, "Medicine here has remained rudimentary, simple survival medicine, almost like combat medicine. So they never developed much in psychiatrics. I don't even know whom we could ask to help you with that. In fact, there may not be anyone on Teragon who could. How much of a problem is it?"

She watched him closely. Demsing had always been something of a mystery to her. He was of average height, but something about his movements seemed to make him appear shorter, and similarly, although he had a slight build, he seemed stocky. His face bore virtually no distinguishing marks, but people always remembered him as seeming "hard" and "determined." Perhaps. She did not know the girl he had met, and she wondered what *she* saw in that face.

Demsing put his hands behind his head and leaned back. "I can handle it if I have to. I just thought you might have heard something, somebody who worked with these things. I have looked along such lines as I can, and I can't find anyone, nor can I find anyone with this condition. Do you have any idea why this might be?"

"No. We saw it in you at an early age and had no explanation for it. It never seemed like a sickness, just something extra we never could explain. And conditions here, then, were the same as now. We had no experts to turn to."

"In Pontossaget District, there's a place where they keep lunatics; I even looked into their visions, or what they would reveal of them, and there's no comparison. But I think I may be on the verge of solving part of it."

"You are?"

"Yes. It's just a suspicion right now, but . . . this is really hard to explain. But basically, I have had a suspicion for some time that I can build these fragments back into something like their original shape. I can't explain how it works, because there simply aren't words for it. Up to now, one thing or another has prevented it, but . . . It takes time, you understand, and that I've had little of, and few enough to cover me while I experiment with it. I don't question now that the fragments are real. I've tested some of them, and they meet every validity test, which dreams and hallucinations do not."

Faren said, carefully, "I would be frightened to experiment with my own mind, if that is what you're doing."

Demsing looked blandly at her across the room. "It's not, if you anchor the reference system in reality, the outside, and everybody's always said I was good at reality."

"Yes, that's true. Still . . ."

"Well, I'd like to get to the bottom of it, you know. I think it's dangerous to me to be walking around with something in my head whose nature I don't know. After all, it could be something more strange than we could imagine—it could be some kind of projection from another person. I want to isolate all the alternative explanations."

"I don't know what to say, except that you must be careful, and remember who you are at all times."

"Yes! Odd that you said it that way: that's just what it feels like: remembering who I am."

6

Certainly, we perceivers, recorders, revealers of phenomena need most earnestly to learn to stalk and attack live prey—by that I mean current, contemporary superstitions, shibboleths, and fetishes which arise of our own world now, and not waste our time and that of our audience by beating, however vigorously, the dead horses of a past generation.

H. C., Atropine

DEMSING COLLECTED THE four apprentices and returned to Desimetre, and set up a local routine again. Klippisch was so pleased with the changes she could see for herself that she put Demsing on the duty of guarding Galitzyn, relieving Dossifey of some of the work.

Although he had not influenced this action, he could see the value of it instantly, and made the most of it on the first shift he took.

He started by rambling on at some length about the progress he had made with the four apprentices he'd been given, and with special emphasis on Chalmour.

Galitzyn rose to the bait like a novice of less skill than the apprentices, waiting until the conversation in the safe house hit a soft spot, and asked, "You've taken an interest in Chalmour."

Demsing did not look at Galitzyn, fearing the leer of triumph on his face would be obvious even to this offworlder. "Well, in fact it did work out that way."

"Are you looking further than tomorrow?"

He answered, shyly, as if wishing to conceal it, "We have talked about it. You know how these things go; one never knows, that's all. One day . . . there you are. You understand things you missed when you didn't know they were lacking before. Would, do you think, Klippisch be interested in making this more permanent?"

"Possibly. More than that, actually. She is well pleased with you."

"Um. I'll bring it up with her in a bit. I've got something else to work on, in the meantime—a little private project, so to speak, Research, you might call it."

Galitzyn looked oddly at Demsing. "What sort of 'research'?"

"A thing I'd like to settle before I make hard commitments involving others. Basically, what I need for this part of it is to have a long conversation with a specialist in psychiatric healing . . . there doesn't seem to be such a person in easy reach."

Demsing could hear the confusion in Galitzyn's voice. "There's always Pontossaget."

"They don't know anything. They just lock them up."

Galitzyn was silent a long time, weighing something. Finally he offered, "There's supposed to be a certain lady down in the lower levels, Tudomany by name, who has a varying success in that area. Be advised I personally rate her as something between a witch and a faith healer, but one always hears things."

"Tudomany . . . I've heard that name."

"Way down. Near the Lysine section, below Gueldras."*

"I thought I heard she was old. Does this Tudomany still live?"

"Far as I know. She tells fortunes too."

Demsing allowed a low laugh to slide around and sang, off key, "She made a fortune sellin' voodoo, and interpret the dream!"**

"You'll never make a singer! Where did you hear *that*?"

"Don't know. Some song I heard once, I guess. Well, that will work really well—I can combine a field trip with that."

"Chalmour . . . ?"

"Yes. She's ready for that phase."

"What do you plan to do with her?"

"Teach her. She trusts me." And that was the truth.

If Galitzyn had based his estimates of the under-population of Teragon on what he had seen on the surface, underground the discrepancy was even more marked. Groups and individuals who could not cope with

* Food on Teragon was manufactured, not grown. Some was cultured in hydroponic vats underground, other components were synthesized, either directly (chemically) or else as the product of fermentation vats. Certain compounds were easily made, others were more difficult. Some were rare and valuable. Lysine, an amino acid, was one of them.
** "Marie Laveau, Part I," Oscar "Papa" Celestin.

the surface often went underground, if for no other reason than there was more room, indeed, so it seemed, endless amounts of it. The problem for them all was that the underground was an endless labyrinth with many dead ends, closed passages, and areas which were being rebuilt to support some new surface artifact.

And if it had been Demsing's aim to stir the net watching him into a series of actions which would bring them into a more open and vulnerable position, he could not have selected a better tale, nor one to tell it to. He had reasoned that if whoever Galitzyn represented had had a watch on him for as long as he thought they had, the report of two apparently irrational breaks with the past pattern might move them to move unwisely. The one was Chalmour, and what made it work with particular validity was the fact that it was true. The second part was more subtle, an attempt to see if he could find out what they really wanted of him.

He also had little doubt who would actually cover his trip underground: Thelledy or one of her associates from nearby. As to recognizing who the shadow might be, he didn't worry about that at all. Long ago he had developed the habit of learning what they were before he unraveled who they were, picking up fragments from the background and putting them together, knowing that the more the operator relied on an external system of training and discipline, the more obvious they became.

He stopped by the safe house and picked up Chalmour. As they set out into the twilight day of Teragon, she asked, "Aren't we going to take any food packs with us, any weapons?"

"No, and no. If they are covering us to the degree I think they are, they would see that immediately as preparations for a long trip, or perhaps a siege somewhere. Preparations for a siege invites besiegers. As for the weapons . . . we have what we can easily conceal on us. You brought yours?"

"Yes. All the ones I can handle easily, not the new ones I don't do so well on yet."

"Good." He reached to her and touched her face, and she moved close beside him, brushing her shoulder against his and looking up at him expectantly. It was at these moments that Demsing felt most tempted to abandon the whole thing, vanish and elude them somehow, and just run away. Today she was wearing her favorite clothing, loose pants, a sweater with a hood, soft low boots all faded with age into an indescribable gray-tan color that would blend well underground. And it was moments like these when it was most difficult to perceive her. Demsing was well aware of the classical lover's problem, of not being able to form a clear image of your lover's face in one's mind, except with great effort; he knew it went further than that, to all the senses. You never identified the lover with any particular scent, either, or taste. She tasted like pure water, and smelled like pure air. He believed that this sensory blindless had a purpose—to establish a deeper perception which almost entirely ignored the body and any specific feature of it. If the deeper perception was there, the body would become the perfect object of desire, knowing that the real desire was something much deeper. They had walked into that and had been caught in it before either one of them had realized what was happening.

She was slender and wiry, more angular and boyish than most girls, but she moved with a smooth grace and a fluidity which no male could hope to match. Her face was the most arresting thing about her, although Demsing knew very well that any face was not beautiful in itself, but in what it expressed and what the expectations of the seer were. An interaction. Chalmour's face was delicate toward the chin, and given an interesting accent by a longish nose which lay close to the planes of her face and had been given an additional emphasis by having been broken in a fall. Her eyes were deepset and dark-brown, her mouth thin and concise. It was a wry and agile face that expressed emotions well.

At first they walked along openly, almost idly strolling, looking into passing shops and commenting on certain buildings of Desimetre which had an odd or erratic air about them. This part of the City was relatively well-lit, with some overheads, lights and beacons on many of the buildings, and watchlights at curbs and low walls. The effect was pleasant, relaxed, and an impression of security. Here, as elsewhere on Teragon, the buildings were low, one, two or three stories, made of the inevitable *kamen* masonry, with rounded corners and many low domes. Demsing had once seen a travel poster of Old Earth, depicting a Greek island in the Aegean sea, and that was what Desimetre most closely resembled, except that it was always illuminated in its day by a light that resembled extremely strong moonlight more than the "sunlight" of a more normal world.

Primary was rising ahead of them in the northwest behind Gueldres, a hot, cream-colored or pearly spot with a visible disk which moved as one watched it, a BB shot at arm's-length, while around them the magic sharp shadows moved and flowed along the streets.* Demsing knew that he had probably instigated something drastic, possibly final, but despite that, or because of it, he felt a spring come into his step.

Chalmour said, "We should begin evading; even I can feel the pressure."

"You notice it?"

"Yes. It is clear sometimes, sometimes fading out, but always there. What did you tell them?"

Demsing shrugged and grinned at her. "The Truth."

"Well, you know how dangerous *that* is."

"Sometimes you have to risk that, that way, to get the kind of reaction you want. I want to draw them out into the open a little, so they can make a mistake."

"You have actually told me very little about this."

"I don't know very much. Somebody's following me, but they don't seem to want to close for action, and they hold back from coming closer. I tried to figure out what they want from me, but I don't have enough data . . . yet."

"The way they expose themselves will give you that?"

"It could. It may. You learn to see patterns of organization, rhythms, it's like that, nothing more."

"You make it sound simple. I rather have a time trying even the simple tricks you tried to show me."

"You do mine better than you do Thelledy's . . ."

"Oh, *those*, ha ha!" She pressed his arm quickly. "I think I do well enough for me on my own, thank you.

"Well, as far as evading them, now is not the time. We want them to

---

* Even at the close orbital radius of 17 million miles, Primary, although possessing one solar mass, was in fact a body only 8200 miles in diameter and at that distance, it did not appear to be a very large object; it did not appear to be a *sun* at all, but an intensely bright star which displayed a small disk. It may be added that with an F spectrum from the light-emitting surface, it was also cool for such objects, implying greater age than the far more common A-spectrum white dwarfs. It may also be added here that the region about the Primary/Teragon System was thin in gases and dust and that there were no other orbiting bodies in the system, so that Primary was exceptionally stable and did not exhibit detectable fluctuations. No companion body to this system, i.e., another star, gravitationally bound, has ever been discovered.

see beyond a shadow of a doubt where we're going. That will confuse them even more, because they expect me to deceive them."

"Have you an option for no reaction from them?"

"Yes. Vanish."

"You will vanish with me?"

"Without a doubt."

"Then we might not ever come back from this walk?"

"That's right. Might never come back. But that's nothing different from living every day here. Most people, even here, fear that profoundly and though they may preach it, they don't practice it by a long shot. When every moment might be your last, you live out each one to its full potential. And of course you have to be ready to move instantly and take off across the world to a district you've never seen, and not only survive, but prosper."

Chalmour said nothing for a long time. Finally she said, "That's like that old nonsense joke about the boy and girl walking underground in this endless tunnel, and she says, 'Olvaso, where are we going?' and he replies, 'Just keep walking.' But before you tell me to keep walking, what I want to know is how you could evade them there?"

"I know they're looking, now. That makes a difference. Before, I didn't know."

By now, they had come a good distance west along one of the streets of Desimetre which followed an imaginary contour and mostly kept to an equivalent elevation. Ahead, however, all ways dipped slightly and went down, to the left into Ctameron with its squat sleek towers, and right, to the district of Gueldres, which had an old-time air of respectability and probity to it, an atmosphere of business affairs of long tradition carried on at a slow and relaxed pace designed to bring out and enhance every nuance, simply for style.

Entering Gueldres, crossing a line that was no less definitive for all that it was, in the most obvious sense, invisible, Demsing and Chalmour continued along the street, which now seemed deeper between the buildings, although the buildings were not especially higher, nor the street deeper. The effect seemed to be a reflection of nothing more substantial than a subtle change of style, certain lines emphasized while others were concealed, so that the street *seemed* narrower.

There were also many more gratings covering lower passages, and there was less an illusion of being on a hard surface. Demsing went along these ways openly and directly, but not hurriedly, and seemed to know exactly where he was going. And when a kiosk indicated the opening to a set of steep metal stairs leading downwards, they entered without pausing and followed the stairs down into the lower parts of Gueldres.

The stairs, which were broad enough for six abreast, continued downwards in sections interrupted by a landing in the middle, doubling back at each level they passed. At first, on the upper levels, there were rather more people about their affairs than in the streets of the surface, which was true of Gueldres, that it was developed vertically more than horizontally. But even lower, the numbers rapidly dropped off and by the time they were ten levels down, there were hardly any people at all. Their steps on the metal rang into eerie echoes.

Here, there were few shops, if any. Occasionally they saw open areas where pumping operations were carried out, mostly by automatic machinery with a mechanic on duty, or else offices, or, more rarely, large open areas where it seemed some sort of chemical refining operations were being carried out.

The nature of the corridors changed as well; on the upper levels, the corridors were similar to the street in width and seemed to follow the general patterns of the streets, only they did not extend very far in any straight direction. But lower, this sense of replicating patterns faded and the corridors narrowed until the cross section became square, and the side walls began to take on an unmistakable look of solidity. At each landing, what seemed to be the main corridor might lead off in any direction. Some seemed to end at the landings and go off a short distance before turning a corner, or appearing to end.

Chalmour said, quietly, just slightly above a whisper, "I can't say I like this very much."

Demsing agreed mildly. "True. You can't move around as well, here. Of course, it also limits how well followers can work, too."

"I picked up some of them, topside."

"You did better than I expected; I could see you make them. But you only saw a third or so."

"How do they commmunicate?"

"Hand signs or body gestures. In a good team that has trained together, such methods actually are faster, within a certain area, than electronics, because there's no interpretation step going through a machine. Let's get off, here."

"And you don't see them carrying equipment."

"No. They have none. Down here, of course, they'll have to rely more on machine transmission systems, sampling, and reports into some central point. We won't see so many people, but the percentage of watchers will actually go up. There will be places we pass where all of the people we see are watchers, or certainly, no less than eight out of every ten."

"What's down here?"

"More stations, plant operations, pumps, generators, that kind of thing. There are people. I've not ever been so far down I saw none at all. And of course you get some more predatory types down here, who try to live on the leavings that filter down from above. They are normally extremely cautious and one has little to fear, but it is wise to remain alert."

The landing at this level seemed to be in a kind of dead end, but the walls around them had metal doors which seemed to have no locks. One way, the corridor narrowed to a hallway and turned, but there were slot lights alternating along the floor and ceiling lines, so there was plenty of light, and, so it seemed, a blurred muttering which seemed to indicate people and machinery, but some distance away. Demsing set off and said, "I don't know exactly where this Tudomany stays, but we're far enough down that we should pick up some trace of her."

"You're going to just step up to some innocent bystander and *ask* where she is?"

"Sure. We want to get there, and we want them to know we're going. Sure, we're bait, then, but it's the only way to find out. And besides, I have heard tales of this Tudomany . . . it may well be worth the trip. I should warn you that if I have misjudged this, they may try to take you as a hostage to hold over me."

Chalmour started to speak as they walked toward the muttering sounds, the hum and buzz, but Demsing placed two fingers over her mouth. "No, no heroics! Absolutely none! Here, if you have been slack all your life, you must do exactly as I say, on faith. On this world, hostages are indeed kept, but they are almost never harmed, because dead or maimed, they have no value except revenge, and very few people want that turned loose."

Chalmour displayed an understanding of what Demsing was implying. "I see. All motives have natural limits, but revenge has none."

"And it ignites more in turn. So the possibility exists. A sharp operation could do it. I, like everyone else, have limits, and if they were willing to pay the price, they could do it. If that happens, behave yourself and wait patiently. I will not, no matter what, abandon you."

"Yes, I see that." She grasped Demsing's arm and pulled herself close to him. "But then you would compromise yourself, for me, and you must not do that. They want you, for whatever reasons. I have no value save as a coin to buy you."

"I have the distinct feeling that they don't want that . . . but there are always people of bad judgment everywhere who coast up to higher levels than they deserve, and you have to estimate for them. They make it hard for the rest of us."

Chalmour added, with a knife-edged cynicism that marked her for a true child of Teragon, "Right, just like all these *mouthy* people who talk honor, honor, more honor, and it turns out *they* have none themselves, and steer others by their calls to it."

Demsing nodded. "That's one of those catchwords that lead you to reach for your gun. There are a lot of them. I am glad you have learned that; some never do."

The corridor continued on, making several shallow turns, and finally opened up into a much larger space, almost a hall, which had echoes and an enormous high ceiling lost somewhere up in the shadows. Apparently at one time it had housed some sort of machinery, for marks were still on the *kamen* floor of metal foundations and the sheared-off bolts were still in the floor as well. At odd intervals, there were windows up in the walls, some frosted and translucent, others clear, some lighted, some not. Now it was used for a marketplace, everything from food and obviously new finished objects to the worst leavings of the thieves' markets. There seemed to be no order, no arrangement, just wherever the vendors could find space. Some had a lot, some had hardly any, and there was still a lot of space left, and the market was nowhere near working at capacity. There were few customers.

Demsing approached the first vendor they would pass, an old man displaying bolts of cloth. Demsing showed the man a coin, but the vendor shook his head. They moved on to the next one, where Demsing showed the same coin to a group of urchins of about the same size and age as Fintry, but a lot less well-kept. They took the coin and began arguing over whose it was. Demsing made a complicated gesture, flamboyant, with his hand and seemed to pluck several more of the same sort of coin out of the air, which he held up for inspection.

"Tudomany the fortune teller." He waved the coins suggestively.

Two of them turned away and pretended to be interested in a set of enormous rusty stains on the near wall. The rest stared at him blankly. One finally said, "Elemezve the courtesan. On the farside, there." He pointed. "Give me the coins; I will see to a just distribution."

"We don't need courtesans."

"Ah, now, and who knows what they need? But if they needs Tudo-many the Witch, Our Lady of the Sewers, they gots to aks Elemezve, they do, 'cos Tudy don't tell just anyone where she lies. That's the way it runs downhill."

Demsing handed over the coins, which immediately started an argument, all unintelligible, then, with Chalmour, set off across the hall in the direction the urchin had indicated.

Chalmour asked, "Is it all like this underground?"

Demsing glanced upwards, and said, "It gets worse. And, of course, there are a lot of empty areas, and other spaces where organized activity is carried out. There's plenty of room, but the view's not all that great."

Where the urchin had indicated, there was a large packing case laid on its side, and beyond it, another corridor, which was very dimly lit. They looked into the corridor, seeing nothing and suspecting that they had been swindled, but at that moment the end of the packing case creaked open, and a face peered out of it. A woman's face. Demsing thought that some faces showed evil, some showed goodness, some showed anger or lust. But this face showed none of these, only fatigue, endless years of it. It made him tired to look at her.

The face was followed by a heavyset body wreathed in swirling gauze veils whose color had faded. It announced, "I am Elemezve. What are your needs? Aha, a pair of them! They need novelty, education, instruction, entertainment! I can provide them all! All positions, all permutations, including those known only to trained religious atheletes." She pushed the crate-end open all the way, to reveal a blowsy den full of antique lamps, print curtains, and astrological mandalas juxtaposed with sexual instructional diagrams, illustrated by photographs of somber models engaged in the utmost degree of seriousness. A sign on the wall proclaimed, with true sporting intent, "I no come forth, you must pay; I come forth, you no pay; I come forth twice, I pay you."

Demsing smiled, "You are a true gambler! I salute you!"

Elemezve observed where his attention was and agreed, expansively, "It is the motto of my business! One may not live by avarice alone: it stifles the loins and clabbers the bowels. In addition to the usual performances, I also offer the Wall Job, the Knot Job, the Pearl Trick, the Birdcage . . ."

Chalmour interrupted, "I beg your pardon, but do you have a menu?"

Elemezve pulled her head back in astonishment. "Oh, now! If you could have heard just what I've seen."

Demsing glanced back over his shoulder, where the urchins had vanished, and others were starting to pick through their flea-market offerings, and then back to Elemezve. "I am a student of the Holy Tantra and will pass on further instruction for the moment; however I do need to find a lady called Tudomany, or Tudy."

The aged courtesan smiled knowingly. "I see, I know. But it is unfair to use magic on a girl who has aleady surrendered without it."

Chalmour's face darkened visibly, even in the uncertain and indirect light of the hall. Demsing continued, "The boys over there suggested you might exchange some directions."

Elemezve seemed to reflect for a time, as if pondering the theory of Quantum Gravitation, but this also had the air of a worn-out stage gesture. Finally she said, as if into the air, "Tudomany is retired and does not, to my knowledge, take on new accounts."

He said quietly, "I have heard much the same tale topside; but I also bring the news that Tudomany may be able to resolve peculiar questions which no one up there is interested in."

Elemezve performed an odd little dance-in-place. "Just so! Just so! None of them is interested in the least in the vital issues of life, where one's very foundations lie! They sail along and thrust the unfortunate below, but what they need, they come along. Tudomany could very well be dead. Long ago! Then what should they do for the so-called irrationals they don't wish to bother with, I ask you!"

Demsing said, "The problem is mine, and there is no one up there I trust to answer it."

"I quite understand. I am Tudomany. Come in." And instantly, as if she had been making her evaluation, a mask fell away and a persona rather different from the blown rose of the old courtesan appeared. She added, "Those boys do not know."

Demsing said back, "They will soon enough. We don't have much time."

The old woman responded, "I know that, too, as I saw what was between you two. Come. Sit. Speak of these things. Tell me your tale."

7

In the parlance of the Intelligence Community, a city is a place where Lines of Communication intersect in a manner that enables quanta from one line to shift to another, or others. A Line of Communication can be anything along which something flows: electronic impulses, ideas, bulk substances, finished goods, money, food. The City is an artifact of these processes, not the creator of them, and derives its reason for existence from this meaningful interaction. We have worked with diligence to reach this point, but it is a beginning, not a summation, and a tool, not a result.

H. C., The Illusions of Form

THE PLACE WAS one of the infrequent dance halls where people could find some transitory release from the unending and unrelenting pressure of Teragon. Not that the pressure was intense, by any absolute measurement—it wasn't in actual fact. In truth, at its upper measure, the density of pressure on Teragon was about a third of what it could be on certain planets and certain societies. The problem on Teragon was that the maximum and the minimum were the same. There was no variation, no release, no letup and, in essence, no slack.

The basic beat of the dance was provided by a Drum Machine and a Bass Tone Sequencer pumping out a very basic progression in 5/4 time, to which live musicians provided words, basic chants, squeals, grunts, and short but poignant solo runs and breaks, and the dancers provided the motions, more grunts, and considerable sweat, even in the decidedly cool air of Teragon. To the untrained ear it sounded very mechanical at first, but after a time one could begin to perceive the subtle *ritards* and anticipations, the syncopation behind the beat, and the excursions into backbeat and prebeat provided by a live Bass player, who played circles around the Sequencer with contemptuous ease. In addition, the basic rhythm would shift from 5/4 to a combination of 4/4 mixed with 6/4, which produced an odd pattern of cadences and kept the dancers alert.

It was also a place where the ancient codes of body language flowed and rippled over the dancers, the musicians, and idlers who stopped by to watch, with an unending panorama of sexual messages whose content ranged from the near side of innocent exaltations of healthy young bodies all the way to unspeakable, incomprehensible corruptions. It was also the most perfectly camouflaged location on Teragon for the open transmission of information by subtle modifications of body motion.

Thelledy viewed her own life as one of monastic discipline and the intense exertion of will to the limits of human ability. Whatever the appearance was to the outside world, within the discipline of the Wa'an School life was a hard and grim reality without much release. The Dance halls provided what release there was, and an excellent opportunity for communication between field operatives and key decision-makers within the Wa'an structure, and that was exactly what she was doing now. In the actual flow of information, the effect was that of a high-speed conversation among several participants, some of whom were not even on the floor. It was, for Thelledy, both the most demanding activity she could imagine, and an incredible release at the same time.

Her major partner was a wiry young man she knew as Ilyen, who moved like a serpent, but there were others in the net: a nearby couple known to her as Cellila and Meldogast—both stocky and powerful in their movements—and a watcher off the dance floor, a woman of mature appearance called Telny.

Their motions, rhythms, and convolutions made up, a form of communication which flowed like speech among them, and provided an information environment considerably quieter and more noise-free than the normal range of human speech. The motions of the others, dancing their hearts out, created, within this system, random noise of low volume which was reduced by the discipline to a distant dull muttering, like a light surf on a beach.

THELLEDY: As I outlined in my request for this meeting, the subject Demsing continues to follow what is for him an irrational course.

MELDOGAST: Current location?

THELLEDY: He and the girl have made contact with Tudomany.

CELLILA: They made no concealment?

TELNY: Demsing has never performed a direct action since we have had him under observation.

MELDOGAST: This action then is concealment for something else.

ILYEN: Or is irrational, or else may be a direct action for other undetermined purposes.

THELLEDY: No evasive action. They went directly there.

MELDOGAST: The girl Chalmour is also uncharacteristic.

THELLEDY: That was the reason for my initial alert.

TELNY: Galitzyn is aware of these events?

ILYEN: Affirmative. He has been kept informed.

TELNY: His reactions?

THELLEDY: Fear.

TELNY: Demsing is aware of his surveillance, and of our contact with Galitzyn. This has been demonstrated.

CELLILA: In that light, then, this action is an open provocation.

THELLEDY: Exactly. But to what end?

TELNY: Obvious. He wants to see someone make a more obvious move.

MELDOGAST: Then we should not respond.

TELNY: That does not necessarily follow. The evaluation by the Advisory Board is that if no one makes a move, he will take the girl and vanish.

THELLEDY: Galitzyn also has fear of that. He and his people have made repeated references to "untimely activation."

CELLILA: We have seen several references to that. Activate what?

THELLEDY: Demsing has something he himself is currently unaware of. We have not been able to recover the nature of this possession.

TELNY: It is not a physical object of macroscopic dimension. Therefore it is abstract: knowledge or an ability.

MELDOGAST: He has put us all in a nice quandary.

TELNY: He has very neatly taken the initiative.

CELLILA: This contingency was considered as a possible outcome of the Asztali operation.

TELNY: The Board assigned a lower probability to that. The conclusion must be that Demsing is potentially more dangerous than our estimates, though for everyone else our predictions appear to remain accurate.

ILYEN: We must not be used in this manner.

TELNY: We have lost many choices we might have preferred.

THELLEDY: Is Demsing a potential threat to us?

TELNY: He has the potential. To date, he has not revealed any such intent.

CELLILA: This unknown possession of his remains an unevaluated threat.

MELDOGAST: The fears of others are often instructive.

THELLEDY: Galitzyn is a poor operative, despite what he thinks he knows.

CELLILA: The fears of a wimp lead to no answers.

MELDOGAST: Can we derive information from this Galitzyn?

THELLEDY: He has the signs of Deathreflex protection.

MELDOGAST: What, then, of Chalmour?

TELNY: Chalmour is a complication.

ILYEN: We have no charter nor reason to press Demsing.

MELDOGAST: He killed Asztali.

CELLILA: Demsing terminated a mistake we all share in.

TELNY: Demsing released Asztali from her obligations in an honorable manner.

MELDOGAST: I understand well enough that if we do nothing, Demsing will vanish and attempt to recover this possession on his own.

CELLILA: Assuming he suspects.

THELLEDY: He suspects. He has left an obvious trail.

MELDOGAST: What about Faren Kiricky?

ILYEN: Protected by arrangement with the Water Cabal.

MELDOGAST: But she knows.

TELNY: She knows. But she has spent her life concealing it from Demsing.

THELLEDY: What she knows is less than Galitzyn. We know that.

CELLILA: Does she fear Demsing?

ILYEN: No. She fears for him.

MELDOGAST: That is extremely interesting.

THELLEDY: He is trailing Chalmour plainly as a target.

ILYEN: That is why we must not reach for her. We can expect a trap.

TELNY: Chalmour is our only key. His actions state that clearly. Direct your operatives to pick her up before we completely lose control of this.

THELLEDY: Galitzyn will not like this.

CELLILA: The tasking says we are not to . . .

TELNY: Galitzyn is relatively unimportant now.

THELLEDY: That may be difficult.

TELNY: Pick up the girl unharmed. Absolutely. No experiments. And no interrogation. She is to be our envoy. And see that he sees that.

THELLEDY: He already knows that. This will cost a lot of people.

TELNY: Then use expendables.

THELLEDY: What about Tudomany?

TELNY: Taken alive. Interrogated.

ILYEN: What about her role underground?

TELNY: Cellila will replace her as wisewoman. Use workname Jollensie.

CELLILA: I hear.

ILYEN: Why are we taking this action?

TELNY: Demsing is generating too many unknowns. We have to know, so we may deal with this in an appropriate manner.

THELLEDY: What about Galitzyn?

TELNY: You know nothing. Demsing has ordinary enemies.

THELLEDY: I hear.

TELNY: Central is in contact with me. The order is do it now.

MELDOGAST: Demsing must be kept from Galitzyn at all cost.

TELNY: I concur.

Suddenly Telny dropped out of the net, and in response, the entire net fell silent. They all remained, though, waiting. Thelledy hesitated a fraction of a second, considering possibilities, and not finding much comfort in them, but she did as she had been instructed, nevertheless, and dropping out of the net, she made a series of gestures to a relay-man off on another part of the floor who was blind to the net motional language they had used, but highly tuned to her specific operations. The message was simple and direct, and took less than thirty standard seconds to transmit. It took another sixty to retransmit those instructions to another relay-man, who picked up a telephone, waited for the other end to pick up, and spoke one word into the mouthpiece.

It was at that point that the series of events assumed a momentum of its own.

What Demsing told Tudomany was a strange tale of a lifetime of inexplicable hallucinations which felt like memories but logically could not be. He also told of learning how to perform certain actions much easier than he thought he could, and learning to conceal this at an early age. And more, of a growing ability to perceive the true structure of events around him on what he himself considered to be too few clues.

Tudomany settled back in a pile of ornamental cushions and asked, "Why would you question such a gift?"

"Because I don't know its source, and what else of it there might be. But I would not have questioned it, if it had not come to my attention that I was being followed by the Wa'an School, in conjunction with a planted offworlder posing as an Archivist. Until then, I had just accepted it and used as much of it as I could. But after that, I wondered. . . . I mean, until then, I could explain it away as any number of things, but the conclusion is unavoidable that there is something there, and others know about it, and seem to be trying to reach something."

"You don't see purpose behind this?"

"Not yet."

"Wa'an School . . . Those are not so good to have as shadows. What do you think they know?"

"Their actions suggest a pattern within which they are working under a very tight contract, going on very little factual information. I have not tested this theory, but it rings true."

Tudomany looked off, and then at one of the illustrated positions tacked on the faded walls. She said, musing into space, "Other than what you call operational necessity, you have not tried to explore this thing in yourself?"

"No. In a sense, I have not believed in it. I have been living under the arbitrary assumption . . ."

"So do we all."

". . . that this was not real, and an attempt to explore it would endanger me needlessly."

"I can understand that. Well . . . you can do several things. You could always arrange to confront your suspect Archivist with a simple direct question—'who am I and why do you want me, and what will you pay for it?' Something like that."

"They don't want negotiation, and they don't want to buy it: they want a certain level of control."

Chalmour, who had been quiet, now hissed, "They want to give orders and have the flunkies jump, but they don't want to be responsible for what happens!"

Demsing agreed, "Yes, that, too. I think that they fear whatever it is and want to have some control over how it emerges."

Tudomany snorted, "That's nothing new! The bastards fear everything they don't understand, even simple things ordinary people learn to do. Well, I suggest that, but I don't think you'll get very far. So the alternative is to go within and go exploring until you find the key, and then unlock it. If you dare."

"Oh, if I have it, I'll use it. It's looking for it that's the daring part."

Chalmour said, guardedly, "Is that . . . ?"

Demsing said, "No. It was not calculated. It was only after I learned how much we trusted each other that it became possible to consider it." Here he stopped. "But . . . I don't know what I'll be, and there are things I don't want changed, now."

Chalmour looked at him long and hard, and said, "Do it. I will take my chances, after hearing that. You'll remember. You have to believe in something, and you have to test that faith."

Tudomany said, "There you have it. What more could you ask?"

"Nothing."

"But not here. No, not here, not now. Get somewhere where you can take the time to do it right, and where you can be helped if you fail. In fact, you are in danger here, I . . ."

Demsing stopped her as well as Chalmour with a raised finger, and then indicated they were to be silent.

Tudomany asked, softly, "What?"

Demsing said, even more softly, "There was a constant noise out in the hall as we came to it, and when we came here. It stopped just a moment ago."

Chalmour sat up suddenly. "It's now!"

He asked, "How do we get out of this box?"

Tudomany smiled at this and struggled to her feet, reaching for a large picture-book. She did something to the title, touching the ornamental letters in a certain sequence, and then laid the book down. Then she scuffed a rug aside and pointed to a trapdoor. Demsing lifted it and saw a square access plate, which he lifted also.

Tudomany whispered, "Quick, now!"

Demsing motioned Chalmour into the black hole below, a shaft leading somewhere unknown. After a moment, she stepped onto the rungs and began climbing down with surprising agility. Demsing followed her, and after him, with unexpected agility, came the bulk of Tudomany, who arranged the hatches.

In the total darkness, she hissed down the shaft, "That won't hold them up long—they'll see the hatch. But I left them a surprise."

"The book?"

"Exactly." She stopped, hearing a grating noise from above, and a sudden commotion, as of many persons suddenly rushing into the box. There was silence while the intruders obviously looked about the empty packing-case with consternation, and then another hubbub as someone noticed the trapdoor. Tudomany called down to them, "Fast, now! They found it!"

There came another sliding noise, and a metallic sound, and at the top of the shaft, a bright square light, yellowish like Tudomany's lamps, illuminated the shaft, and then there was a sharp, stabbing blue flash, and the metal panel slammed shut with a painful ringing clang, which was completely covered over even as it rang in their ears by the unmistakable roar of a demolition grenade. Flakes and particles rained down on them in the shaft.

Tudomany called down, "That will give us a little time, now, so downwards, my children, waste no time. This goes a long way down and there aren't many exits, and we won't use them. All the way to the bottom, and keep it quiet."

The climb down the shaft was in darkness and silence; padding on the rungs reduced any sound they might have made. In addition, the unusual position of the descent, and the use of muscle groups not normally used, made the extended downward climb tiring and demanding; there was no conversation, not even about which way to go, since Tudomany had plainly said "All the way to the bottom," and that was that.

There were some unidentifiable noises, mostly faint and far away, sometimes emanating from side-tubes which they passed occasionally, or from deeper down. The message of the noises was clear to Demsing; that however deep they were, there was more farther down.

As they descended, Chalmour's supple, agile body suffered least from the strain of the climb and she lengthened her lead on Demsing, while Tudomany, not at all suited to this kind of exercise, quickly fell behind, with the result that Demsing found himself mostly alone, with only an occasional scrape or rattle identifying the girl below him or the woman above. Soon, the motions of climbing became almost automatic, and he had time to think about where he was and what they were doing.

They had certainly taken the bait. The response had been faster than he had expected, and considerably stronger. That was powerful information, because it told him definitely that whatever it was he concealed, they didn't want him finding it on his own. Demsing chuckled silently to himself on that one: that was nothing new, just a slightly more powerful version of a much older idea. People who surrendered to organizations tended to suppress self-discovery of any kind, even trivial manifestations of it.

Demsing had some question as to who it might have been, but he felt fairly certain that the attack had come from Thelledy's group. How much they were acting on behalf of their client, Galitzyn and whomever he represented, remained questionable. Indeed, as he thought about it, it seemed less Galitzyn and more Thelledy. That was not a considered estimate, or even what he would have called a perception, but a characteristic feel of the way it had gone. He made a mental note to explore that in detail, later, when they had reached wherever Tudomany was leading them.

And where would that be? Below a certain level, Demsing's knowledge of the underworld of Teragon fell off rapidly. For the most part, the inhabitants of Teragon favored the surface, accepting its dim daylight and impossible local time as minor inconveniences, as opposed to delving deeply into the lower regions. No one Demsing knew had systematically explored the underside. Certain parts of it were known, and used, more or less regularly; many of the industrial processes were underground, and all of the necessary functional industries, such as the food production plants, fermenteries, and hydroponic tanks, where the atmosphere of Teragon was presumably recycled, and the water extracted.

Those things were known, more or less, according to who used such information. But no one knew the full extent of the underworld. In general, the deeper one went, the more localized became the transportation systems, so people who went under for their own reasons were far more local in their movements than the surface-dwellers.

One thing was known about it, which seemed to be true all over the planet. The Oxygen content of the atmosphere decreased slightly as one went down, and the Carbon Dioxide content went up. And since the main component of the atmosphere was known to be Argon* in the deeper levels the pressure increased and the temperature did also.

These were generalities, which were useless in specific situations. All he knew was that they were going down an unspecified distance, where, presumably they would be free of pursuit, and able to gain some time.

At rare intervals, he would come to a small landing, which seemed to be nothing more than a shelf and a junction with other shafts, some of which were larger, some smaller. Down, she had said, and so he contin-

* The atmosphere of Teragon at the surface displayed the following constituent percentages: 51% Argon, 25% Oxygen (in the form O_2. A shallow layer above the surface of O_3, Ozone, accounted for another 1% of total Oxygen volume), 1% Ozone, Nitrogen 12%, 3% Carbon Dioxide, 7% Neon, 1% Water Vapor and other trace elements and compounds. The nominal standard pressure at the surface is 610 Millibars, which is equivalent to Earth-standard altitudes of approximately 11,000 to 12,000 feet.

ued, reassured by occasional calls from above and below, as Chalmour, ahead, and Tudomany, behind, passed through the same points. Demsing continued down.

At last, after what had seemed like an eternity of climbing, his arms and the backs of his thighs starting to burn and sting, he stepped down for a rung and felt solid *kamen* underfoot.

Wherever he was, there had been no sense of transition from the shaft to the space. He had been climbing down, and then the shaft ended. The air was, to his senses, dense and still, but not dead air. This chamber opened onto other areas. And, though he did not notice it immediately, he could tell there was no one in it except him. Furthermore, there was obviously no one in the shaft above him. Somewhere in the shaft, both Tudomany and Chalmour had been taken without a sound.

8

*In the seventies, a famous experiment was conducted in which
researchers, disguised as psychopaths who had been committed
to that institution, penetrated a certain psychiatric institution.
These sane people were never discovered by the staff, even when
they acted normally. (One of the favorite diagnoses was "Flight
into Normality.") And of course that was the whole purpose of
the experiment. What was totally unexpected was the serendipi-
tous discovery that the inmates, the real psychopaths, knew the
difference immediately without aids or clues, and identified the
false psychopaths without visible logical deductive processes.*

    *There are available a large number of conclusions which one
might draw from this, or jump to as the case might be; but being
suspicious and cynical of expressed motivations as I am, I cannot avoid concluding that the victims always perceive that they
are being jerked around by callous manipulators, and that even
psychopaths can see through a line of buzzword shuck and jive.
Perhaps we might even suspect that is why they are as they are.
And if we suspect that sanity is the perception, comprehension,
and functional integration of reality, then we may ask, indeed,
who are the sane, and who are the basket cases?*

                                  —H. C. Attitude Papers

CHALMOUR PLAINLY DID not know where she was, and hadn't since
she had been taken in the shaft. There had been no time to call out:
at a cross-shaft junction, she had been snatched to one side as another
had soundlessly slipped into her place. She had been held in an odd
hold, with pressure applied at certain points, which had made it impossible to speak. She had tried. Nothing worked.

    They had let Demsing pass before they moved on, somewhere un-
known, reached through a maze of tunnels and shafts they had traversed

in silence and almost total darkness, with a lot of turns and climbs seemingly thrown in for added confusion. She had understood then that it was useless to try to navigate in her head, and had concentrated on keeping her mind carefully blank and receptive, ready to untangle what would finally be presented to it.

It was pleasing to her to see Demsing's prediction come true with such ease: They neither harmed her nor molested her during the long journey, and when they reached wherever they were, they had shut her up in—not a cell—but a decent room with facilities. The facilities—running water and a toilet—were decoration. The room was impregnable, as best as she could determine.

Initially, they shut her in and left her alone, all in total silence, and in darkness as well. She thought she had heard a faint, dry, sliding sound, like short sequences of raspy chattering nearby, and supposed that they communicated with each other by means of a touch-code: fingers met in a pattern of pressures, taps, and slides. But although she knew such things existed, she didn't know any herself, and couldn't read *theirs*.

For a while, they left her in the dark. Chalmour explored the room with her fingers and soon had an accurate representation of it in her mind. It was small and plain and there were no traps or movable walls. It was just a room with a door which locked from the outside. The ceiling was out of reach for her, standing, but she could jump and touch it, and it was as solid as the rest. That kept her busy for a long time, because she was not adept, but they appeared to give her plenty of time, and she used it as best she could.

Also, she listened, and felt for vibrations in the walls and floor. At first she felt and heard nothing, but she expected that. As the time wore on, her senses became more sensitive, and she began to pick up faint sounds and weak vibrations. Demsing had talked to her about this, but had only shown her certain basic exercises. Now she learned as she went, and learned to perceive through the noise her own body made, creaks and snaps of joints, low rumbles of muscles, her heartbeat and breathing, swallowing, and the rumbles of her digestive tract. It was that quiet. But she waited, and presently some things began to appear. Not so near, she heard a soft, thudding vibration, fairly frequent, but at odd intervals in a rhythm and pattern she could not quite identify. As her senses sharpened, she detected a suggestion of movement to this vibration, and tentatively identified it as of the Linduc line. They had not crossed it on the surface, and it seemed off to the side, very slightly higher than the horizontal.

She learned to feel people walking. That one was very dull and blurred-out and impossible to follow, but she could tell there were several by the way they overlapped. And there were faint sounds, too: conversations too weak and far-off to resolve, but perceptible enough for her to guess at how many there were, and where. The footfalls were connected with her, and so was one set of the muttering conversations. Another set, somewhat fainter, seemed to have no relation to her, nor did any other noises. That one, she adjudged to be a living area or work area a little farther off. She was near the surface, and gravity told her which way was up.

Demsing had told her: *Use the time! Never sit idle. Listen, feel, walk around. Work on making a picture. And don't worry or anticipate. They want you bored and sensory-deprived. Keep busy! Make up an imaginary language and conjugate verbs in it! Invent a non-decimal number system and hunt for Prime Numbers. Memorize the results. And pace yourself. Sleep if you feel like it, and know the difference between sleep and waking. Stimulate yourself sexually—it's fun and it breaks a tension they damn sure want you to have. Explore chord progressions in music. And learn the basic routine pattern of where you are and who is there. And then watch for the breaks in the flow. Learn to use that and it will tell you a lot more than they want you to know. If you see a break, go for it. Nine times out of ten it's a real opportunity. The odds actually favor you. Prisoners are their own best guards, repeating to themselves, "I can't."*

Chalmour also knew about the old trick of wetting your hands, cooling them by blowing on them, and feeling about for Infra-red emitters. As far as she could tell, there were none, although the room was warmer than the usual Teragon chill, but the warmth seemed to come solely from a hot water pipe to the washbasin.

And he had said, And if they ask about me, tell them whatever you know. Because you don't know what they want to know; I don't know it, either, so you couldn't know it.

She smirked to herself in the dark. *This could wind up being less of a bother than a trip to the dentist.* There was, of course, another way it could go, equally probable, but that she only considered long enough to make herself know that it existed. That was sufficient.

She knew that her perception of Time would be distorted and magnified, so for a long stretch she ignored the seemingly endless passage of hours. Eventually, however, she felt hunger pangs, which she put off by drinking water, which she smelled carefully before drinking it. As far as she could tell, it was just plain tap water, put there to drink. The toilet worked, flushing with a deafening industrial-strength roar which she found extremely funny. She even thought of telling them, when they eventually arrived, that they should be careful what they put in it: it charged when wounded. But she later decided not to, because that remark would reveal the nature of her defenses—and that Thelledy thought that she had been clumsy. She'd show her, and in such a way that Thelledy would know it only after she had gone.

And so Thelledy: Chalmour never questioned who was behind this, and expected to confront Thelledy herself whenever her captors appeared. Therefore she was a little disappointed when footfalls outside stopped at her door. A small lamp lit in a wall alcove, and a panel slid open, revealing dim light outside. A man, rather young by the sound of his voice, said, "Dinnertime," and slid a tray in with hot food. She mumbled a muffled gratitude, surprised at her creaky voice, and the unseen young man slid in a package through the opening. "Here's some fresh clothes, too. It may be a little warm in there for what you have." He sounded pleasant enough, and seemed to be going to some trouble to avoid a threatening appearance. But she only thanked him and said nothing else, though her mind was boiling with questions. She thought it an extraordinary piece of self-discipline: Demsing had told her: *Never, never ask anything! Questions reveal more than answers!*

The food was better than average, and tasted good. She had no ill effects from it. After she ate, she washed the tray and the spoon they had provided, and then looked at the clothing. The light remained on; although rather dim, it was a vast improvement over total darkness. In the light, the clothing appeared to be a loose caftan made of soft cloth. It was a dull neutral brown in color, and was of no specific size, although she could wear it without doing too much to it. Without hesitating, she stripped, put it on, washed her old clothing out, and draped it over the end of the bunk to dry. Then, pleased with herself, she lay down on the bunk to relax, and took a nap with her arms propped behind her head.

"Psht! But you're a cool one!"

It woke Chalmour up, and her head cleared instantly. She had been asleep, but not very deep, not dreaming; now someone was in the room with her, and the time had come.

She opened her eyes, but made no move. The voice was familiar, the same one who had brought the tray earlier. This resolved into a slender young man slightly taller than herself, so she estimated, wearing a loose caftan similar to the one she had on, the one they had given her. His was a very dark blue, almost black. *What does that tell you? That wherever you are, there's a distinctive dress worn internally, that they can spot you instantly, and that if you escape, they can pick you out of a crowd. Thank you, Demsing.* Chalmour risked a quick glance around the room, at nothing in particular, but including the foot of the bunk in its sweep: her clothes were gone, sure enough.

She sat up, rubbing her eyes, and swung her feet over the side. "Would you run that by me again?"

"I said, you were cool and collected for one who was just pulled out of an air shaft on her way somewhere."

She shrugged. "I was tired; I took a nap."

It seemed to put him off, as if he had been prepared for another response. He waited a moment, and then said, "I am Ilyen. Mainly why I am here is to reassure you that you are not in any danger. You might consider this protective custody, temporary in nature."

"I see."

"Is there anything I can get you? Books, handicrafts?"

"Out."

For a moment, he stepped back, as if her ambiguous reply had confused him. "What do you want?"

"I want out, in the simplest possible way of saying it. If you can't do that, then get out."

For a fraction of a second, something utterly dark and maleficent flickered across his face, a narrowing of the eyes, a tightening of the mouth, but it was gone almost before she could see it, and the bland expression returned. He said, quite evenly, and Chalmour admired his control, "Well, actually, I'm as much compelled by circumstance as you find yourself, so that is quite beyond me at the moment. But I will bring you such items as you would like to have. Also I will take the tray back. And later, when I bring the things you want back, we might converse for a little."

Chalmour stared fixedly at the toilet, and said, in a monotone, "You have the key; come and go as you will. If you insist on bringing something, then bring a folio copy of *Malinoski's Contrapunctus Semidecimus;* I should like to review my exercises."

He picked up the tray and gave a slight, stiff bow. "I am not familiar with the work you mention, but I will see if I can obtain a copy; we have an excellent library." For a moment, he stopped, uncertainly. Then he asked, sheepishly, "To what does this volume refer?"

"Musical theory and chord progression." And as Ilyen reached for the door to leave, she added, "And when you come back, knock first, will you?"

The door closed behind him and locked automatically, a fact Chalmour did not miss; she smirked, suppressing a giggle. She had improvised on one of Demsing's principles: the work she had asked for was imaginary, and she thought that it might give them some difficulty. She had no idea how much difficulty this actually did cause.

As she measured time, it wasn't very long until Ilyen returned, and to her surprise, he did knock before he unlocked the door. Needless to say, he had no book with him. He was dressed as before, and carried about him an air composed of subtle wariness, which had not been there before, and a curious shy wistfulness which made him rather more attractive.

He opened the conversation, apologetically, "I was unable to obtain it. Are you certain such a volume exists?"

"Oh, it exists, all right. It is as real as your reasons for holding me."

"It must be uncommon. We could find no reference to it."

"I worked with a private copy. It is a very old work. Possibly your index is incomplete."

Ilyen nodded, agreeably, "It is certainly possible. Never fear! We are unrelenting and will get to the bottom of it, eventually."

Chalmour understood the remark perfectly, and the threat it represented. She decided it was time to be more bland with them. "What would you like to discuss? Here, sit on the edge of the bed; if you have to be here, you might as well be comfortable."

"Some of us have expressed a certain curiosity about a person called Demsing, who sometimes uses the surname Ngellathy; we have a certain interest in your relationship with him, and some general things you might know about him."

"That seems a large list."

Ilyen sat on the end of the bed. "You do have a certain association with him?"

Chalmour was quite impatient with this pussyfooting, but she answered, "I could hardly avoid such association. He was given duty as chief of apprentices over the group of apprentices to which I belong."

"Who made the assignment?"

"Klippisch assigned Demsing to that duty; Thelledy volunteered myself out of her group. Myself, and Fintry, that is."

Ilyen stretched; she caught the nagged motion out of the corner of her eye. He seemed to relax a little more, and asked, "But there is more to it than that."

Chalmour wondered about this line of questioning; surely they already knew this. Or perhaps it was more an exercise to allow her to babble on. It didn't matter, because she didn't, she thought, know anything, and perhaps by talking she could occupy their attention. And waste their time. She said, pensively, "Yes, there was more."

"What?" *Was this idiot a total cretin?*

"I found him attractive and went to bed with him. He made no resistance and seemed to enjoy himself. We continued the relationship because it became pleasant. It's really simple."

"I understand that simplicity." Ilyen leaned back so that he displayed his slender grace to advantage. It caught her attention, however much she disliked the situation she was in, which he represented. It was as if she had two minds. He added, "Did this cause any problem in the job to which Demsing was assigned?"

"No. He seemed to evaluate each of us according to what he thought we could do, and then suited the exercises he gave us to that. He was all work, and that's the way it was; I understood that and practiced no public displays. What we did, he and I, we did in free time." She felt oddly relieved as she said this.

"Would you continue this, if free to do so?"

"We have made arrangements to make it permanent."

"Yes, of course." He stretched again, a subtle and slight motion, and looked at her intently. She saw that the questions didn't really matter. They already knew all this.

Ilyen turned on his side, facing her, and said, "You have had other lovers?"

Oddly, she didn't find this offensive. "Yes."

"How were they?"

"Some were good, some not so good, some very good. None were bad." She felt lazy, relaxed, and sensual. A lassitude was creeping into her limbs. She saw it happening, as if from outside. She thought, *I don't want to do this, but I don't seem to be able to stop it. What the hell is he doing to me and how is he doing it?* Ilyen had only a small distance to reach across to touch her knee, did so, casually, and she did not move her leg. Perhaps she could have; she didn't know. She didn't try. Nor did she raise any objection to what followed, seemingly naturally and easily enough, and very slowly, too. She remembered that. And the part of her that didn't object enjoyed it very much. It lasted a long time, that wiry, agile body joined to hers, and, to the part of her that did object, incredibly, she asked him to stay. He reassured her he would return often.

After he left, she allowed herself to become very angry. But even that took a long time. And with the anger came fear, too. *If he can do that to me so easily, and he does come back, how long can I hold up against that.* And she added, *Those bastards know I don't know anything, so what Ilyen's doing is just playing with me. I'm nothing to them but bait: they'll keep me alive, fed, and well-laid, and it's some trick he's learned how to do, like Thelledy. And if I throw him out, they'll send one even better, or worse, depending on how you look at it.* Now she understood Demsing's lessons, some of which she had taken rather lightly. *The real enemy was the despair you felt yourself when you realized how much power those people had. What did he have to resist them?*

Ilyen opened the door to a small room similar to the one he had just left, but this one held no toilet, there was no lock on the door, and there were two people inside waiting for his analysis: Thelledy and Telny.

Thelledy said, "You took long enough."

Telny glanced at the younger woman, but said nothing.

Ilyen answered, carefully, "Chalmour has no defenses whatsoever against skills we take for granted." He shook his head. "She rather enjoyed herself, and wanted more."

Telny observed, "That's very interesting. You mean Demsing has taught her nothing about projection and control?"

"Apparently not. She seems to have no defenses. Additionally, she knows little or nothing. He seems to have revealed nothing to her that we don't already know; that he's extraordinarily adept and perceptive. We are not going to get an answer from her as to why they want him."

Telny said, "Nor out of that Tudomany, either. She didn't know Demsing from *reclama**. Told him to seek answers inside himself, that's what she did. We tried to dig deeper, but she was obviously working for somebody, because she activated a very crude deathlock which beat us very neatly. Dead end there, and no pun. Lost her."

---

* *Reclama* is the combined slurry which is recycled and fractionated into basic chemical components. In effect, sewage, although reclama is considerably more complicated than that.

Ilyen breathed deeply, and said, "It occurs to me that we could wind up with a problem, holding Chalmour."

Telny questioned this. "How so?"

"Demsing is considered a formidable individual with informal skills which approach the levels of the best of formal systems, and, from our file material on him, he has a wider range than do members of formalistic disciplines. He can be a dangerous and destructive adversary, as he stands. Now, from other sources, we come to understand that there may be some unknown quantity related to him, which has unknown consequences. And we elect to challenge him directly . . . and hold a girl as a hostage, so to speak, whom he has selected. . . ."

Thelledy interrupted, "Ilyen, I cannot find fault with your summary, except in this very soft area of Demsing and Chalmour. That is a soft area because we cannot comprehend the reasons behind it. That is what is disturbing, so we continue to search. Chalmour must be the leading edge of that probe."

Ilyen responded, with a faint aura of anger well-hidden, "That is what I am trying to tell you: we may be looking for something which may not exist. While we manufacture imaginary mythology, Demsing erects a system in reality which we don't anticipate because we can't imagine it. I have tested Chalmour and my evaluation is that there is nothing hidden in her. Nothing. I suspect very strongly that that is precisely the reason Demsing has responded to her, and . . ."

Thelledy interrupted again, "If you open that door . . ."

Telny made a slight hand motion which stopped Thelledy. She said, pointedly, to Ilyen, "Your line of thinking interests me."

Thelledy countered, "He is not being paid to think, but to act. All he does is serve as a challenge target* for field agents such as myself . . ."

Telny turned, slowly, until she was facing Thelledy directly, and paused for emphasis, allowing all of them to recognize the taut physique, the short, closely trimmed gray hair, and the controlled bearing that characterized Telny and her rank within the Wa'an School. She said nothing for a long time. Finally she said, slowly, "Good ideas are not intrinsically coupled to a given source. Intelligence and stupidity are

* A challenge target was a person who served, by analogy, as a sort of sparring partner, by which an operative might practice skills, techniques, and routines. It was assumed that the target would be of high skill level, but of necessity slightly lower than the main operatives. In the context of the Wa'an School, such a person might be assigned to "service" as many as five to ten field agents such as Thelledy.

equal in that: they may occur anywhere. Ilyen, continue your exposition."

"As I may have implied, Chalmour was easy because she has no defensive procedures to protect her against advanced psychosexual manipulations carried out by someone trained in their use, at whatever level. Very well. *Because* of this, there is a very great danger that continued application of the techniques can and probably will cause psychological damage to her which may not be treatable in the context of Teragon. Yes, it was easy. But only because during such manipulation, her mind divides into two parts and she fights herself without knowing what the true source of the conflict is. Under the manipulation, she is deeply oriented toward Demsing and from what I could detect of the far side of *that*, he appears to be oriented toward her in similar fashion."

Telny looked up, into space, thoughtfully. "You can *feel* Demsing?"

"Yes. Weak, but definite. I used Alcinoë's Perceptor, in the third mode, and all confirmations fit the receptor sites."

Telny mused, "Then you understand the consequences of that? No? I shall explain: If she is that transparent to him, then he is also transparent to her. They have removed all defenses and blocks. This is significant and important, and we must follow it out. It is a rare condition."

Whatever train of thought Telny was following was interrupted by a soft knock at the door, followed by a messenger, a slight girl with close-cropped curly hair. The girl said, "I have information for Lodgemaster Telny."

"Speak."

"A follow-up search was conducted and the whereabouts of the subject, one each Demsing Ngellathy, are not known."

Telny responded instantly, "Instruct the field agents to increase their efforts. Have the agent in charge of operations to request negotiation with Demsing on contact. Send this message: 'Chalmour to be returned to you as soon as we know your location, no questions asked, request consultation. Urgent.' Repeat it back to me."

The girl did as instructed. Telny told her, "Go now."

The girl left, and Telny turned her attention again to Ilyen. "Who directed you to seduce Chalmour?"

Ilyen did not hesitate. "Thelledy."

Telny nodded. "Too late to undo that. See that it does not occur again, under my personal seal, no excuses, your sole responsibility direct to me. Understood?"

"Yes."

She turned to Thelledy. "You will make contact with Galitzyn and derive what we are looking for from him. Use standard contract Clause Five: Suspect danger, will void contract unless information is provided."

Thelledy asked, "Will you take an active part in this?"

"I will contact Faren Kiricky, and try to obtain by honest diplomacy what we have failed to get by force."

"And then?"

"And then we will attempt to deal with Demsing."

9

In the broadest sense of the word, technology and technique have the potential for becoming exercises in the studied avoidance of action and perception. That they do not is testimony to the strength of Will and Idea.

H. C., Atropine

IN THE DARKNESS at the bottom of the shaft, Demsing wasted no time on extravagant emotions, although he was aware of those emotions, as it were, existing in a vague continuum in reserve. Now he concentrated on action, sitting perfectly still in the darkness.

He had underestimated two things: the strength of their response, and the skill that had gone into it. Probably Tudomany had pulled that box-over-the-shaft trick before, and somebody remembered it, and that was all there was to it. The gang who had invaded the box? Slugs, some local hoodlums, who had been given no information and who had been expected to be sacrificed whether necessary or not. How many had that book bomb killed? He had no way of knowing. He breathed deeply, slowly, savoring the rancid taste of damp air. And again. *It's time we ended this.*

But first things first. This was not a place of safety, a place to rest, or explore within, as Tudomany had suggested. If they could plan that well, then they should also be able to know he was waiting at the bottom of the shaft. And they would come, in the dark, in soft black clothing, moving in the silent ballet of sudden death. *It's time we ended this.*

Tudomany was no claim on him. Demsing knew the underworld as well as any surface person could expect to, and it was expected that she had old scores hidden away, old enemies. They knew that, too, and nothing would inhibit them with her, as it might with Chalmour. And what about Chalmour? *It's time we ended this.*

They would expect him to move laterally as he could, rising all the time, reaching, reacting. Demsing had made his life work doing the unexpected, the irrational, the unpredictable. He would go *down*, into the unexplored bowels of Teragon, as far down as down was, even out the other side if it could be done. He had been squatting on his haunches, but now he stood up to his full height and flexed his hands in the darkness. *I will go inside, whatever lies there: and for myself, the same, inside and negotiate with demons. And if I meet the Angel of Death, I will turn him loose to walk the surface with feet of fire.*

And there was something about that, too, which resonated like a tuning fork with something lost, just out of reach.

To advance, one first takes a step back. Then, forward. To descend, one first goes up, because the little square pit at the bottom of the shaft was a dead end, and even if it had possessed the finest door on Teragon he would not have gone through it. He climbed up, quick and flowing like a cat, moving against time, missing the first cross-shaft, the second, the third, even the fourth and fifth. But the sixth, that was the one, and it was a long way up. Why the sixth? It had to be the sixth, the number rang in his head, six, six, six, six. Something he knew, but did not know why he knew. And they didn't. Six.

Six it was.

And sixth up was a good choice, because it opened up a little, good enough to be fast as a roach in, and then it began slanting down, down, down, in long swoops and runs, joining with others, intersecting, dropping, not a straight section in it. He used his nose, his ears, his proximity sense, touch, and only sometimes eyes, because sometimes there were small lights, enough to see a little by. He was terrified, truly terrified, more so than at any time he could ever remember, not of them who followed him but of what awaited him at the farthermost corner of the dark: himself, the concealed one, the one who remembered things which could not be, never had been. Down.

In a rare moment of lucidity when he stopped to catch his breath, Demsing noticed that there were lights. Not many. Most of them were burned out. But there were some. More, in fact, as he went down.

He thought about it, and understood that he was lost. He welcomed it. He got to his feet, and began descending again. And as he went, he muttered to himself, to the dark, to the air that had begun to throb with the unseen and unknown hand of deep machinery, *Chalmour, Chalmour, hang on, I'm coming back . . . Something will come back.* And the way turned steeper. Now ramps and tunnels wouldn't do; the way became stairs and slides, and the slides were always lit at the bottom, dirty and dim fixtures, some of them out, but always some burning behind translucent windows. Who changed them in the upper levels?

There was one long slide, longer than all the others, and when he slid out into the chamber at the bottom of it, he saw before him, at the opposite end of the chamber, an open doorway into an open shaft, and there were no other exits. Two other slide-shafts, just like the one he had come down, entered the chamber. The slides down, an open hall, and an ogive-arch doorway into nothing.

Demsing walked slowly, approaching the portal with vertigo before he got to it, properly. Something in him knew what he was going to see. He looked over the edge, holding on to the side, which was not *Kamen*, but an inlaid design in various metals, their colors shifting in the uncertain light. Above, it was simple: a few meters up, the shaft ended in a dome, from whose underside protruded an odd decoration of multicolored metals like the inlay design of the portal. Some small spotlights shone, dim and red; others were burned out. Down, there was no end. There seemed to be a slight haze in the shaft, which was cylindrical in cross-section, which distorted the far distances. No matter. As far as he could see, the shaft had no end. And down there, the air was heavy. It was heavy here, and warm.

The soft thrumming of machinery was almost gone, and it was all above him. Down there, it was quiet. He looked around the receiving-chamber, looking for signs of passage. He found his way from the middle slide. Marks. There wasn't much dust. None elsewhere disturbed. Nobody came here. Nobody had ever been here. This was the place, then.

One place was as good as another, and he settled down near the portal, resting his back against the wall. It felt reassuringly solid, although he could feel a faint vibration in it, several frequencies overlapping, at the very limit of perception. He settled into himself, relaxing with that peculiar sense of duality of falling, drifting into sleep and waking up from thinking. Now. He waited, letting it come at its own pace, and as it did, he saw how he had always controlled it, pushing a little *here*, holding back *there*, stopping *here*. Not this time. There was something beyond, just as there was a bottom to the shaft behind him, and so he let it go as it would. It apparently had its own pace, too. Sometimes it almost stopped, and he remembered the image of a slow and looping river, worming across the flat surface of a delta, pouring out the suck and glut of a continent into a sea. There were no seas on Teragon, never had been, never could be. Not Teragon. No, not Teragon. At the sharper turns of his drift, he caught flickers of abrupt, broken mountains rising from the tumult of the sea in the dawn, a rich brown color, a black ocean, an impossible neon-indigo sky, time slower than you could measure, a sun drifting up impossibly slowly out of the distant ranges farther east. Gone. Yes. That was the right way, where it was deep down, where the images came fast and thick, too fast to identify individual segments. Here. Now.

There are things hidden within all of us which we write over because they do not fit the piece we have chosen. But we can only paper over them, not erase them. They live beyond us, they form our clothing, our sexual preferences, our speech (O traitorous instrument!) which conceals ideas thousands of years old, invented by leering filthy barbarians squatting by the greasy campfire, whose names we never knew, whose names we could never know, but whose horrid personas are resurrected in us, that flit from body to body, which are to *them* like shadows within which they may conceal themselves, and one fine day, at the crisis, all *our* fine talk goes out the window, thrown out the window and forgotten, *over-forgotten*, never remembered, like the foil cover of a prophylactic in a moment of blind lust. Yes, lust. And at our finest hour, Zabbakak the Barbarian materializes in our hearts and extracts a few seconds from our lives.

The evil and the good and the neutral, also. The abilities and gifts we paper over because they cause sight we'd rather not have, inconveniences to the present. All those things. Demsing was no different there and he knew it. He had all those demons, and knew them by name. But there was more in him, and his names for *those* things were secret names he dared not whisper even in the dark of the back side of his mind. How he *saw*. What he used was only the echo of something greater. How he instinctively *knew* what motions to make in a fight, the inevitable flow of it. That, too, and the images of a past he'd never had, they were there, too. They were all manifestations of a single concept shining in the dark he had avoided, because "it didn't make sense." Of course it hadn't. It was only one, out of an entire universe of things that didn't fit, that avoided neat categorization, whose central ideas, whose basic principles walked among chaos and smiled and bestowed benedictions, but whose import was implacable.

He closed down his mind and walked among symbols of existence within himself. He saw that he could slow Time and perceive better the arrangement of the dance of the glowing parts, that seemed to shine in a dark cavern like golden wires. He had done this before. But only a little. Now he slowed it without stopping, and along one axis, the dance of the wires, the golden worms slowed, slowed, and drifted almost to virtual stop, and there he saw and comprehended that here was the complex symbol of his own identity. And as if along another dimensional line (which he did not try to understand, and in not-trying, saw more of it), there were more Demsings replicated in a line, one after another. He looked closer. No. Not more Demsings. More people. They were not his parents in the flesh: they were further back, different. The process of reproduction was a wall. These were him, continuity, and not-him. And their identities were different, alternating male-female. He moved closer, and manipulated the figure, one part of it, that replicated in all the figures, there were six of them and he was number six, (and there were more out the other side of Time, too, a procession extending into a shadowy infinity as hazy as the bottom of the shaft) and the fragile barrier he had built dissolved before the corrosive power of memory and he saw that they were him and he was they, and in the sudden flood he *knew* who he was and who he had been: Demsing Ngellathy. Nazarine Alea. Phaedrus. Damistofia Arart. Rael. That one. Tiresio Rael. And Jedily Tulilly, the rough clay they had started with. Jedily was just an empty shell, whose contents had been mined out by the others along the chain of personas, and he saw how it was done, the whole thing, how to initiate it, how to control it, what its tradeoffs were. Jedily-Rael-Damistofia-Phaedrus-Nazarine-Demsing, a light was growing inside him as the contents of those personas flowed into Demsing, last of the line and it peaked to a soundless explosion which whited-out everything, and when the radiance faded away, he knew he was the Morphodite, the changer, the immortal shapeshifter, the changer of worlds. He saw how he read the structure of the wave of the present, yes that was exactly what it was, a wave, moving among varied environments, and there were other waves, too, and a medium for them, and another higher-order world in which such waves moved, unthinkable entities moved *there* (not even as the Morphodite had he seen this before). And he saw the simple process by which one controlled those waves, how one searched out and found the key to Change, and moved that key. At the base of every human expression of collective organization, one person rested who defined that thing, and that one person was not the chief, but the bottom. They never knew it, nor did anyone else. Unseen and unknown symbols of power, they moved, serene in ignorance. Their real power in the outside world of appearances was invisible, while the seeming lords of the world of appearances were like little cheap clanking windup toys that crawled, scuttled, or rolled about. Some of them were nothing but apes with big mouths, and dumb little plastic hands that clashed cymbals. They were the least of the least, prisoners of the collective, mere visible symbols of it, powerless and willbereft. Every person. *Every. Each.* Was dualistic—central definer of one thing, slave of another. Humanity was a vast collective network of these threads of causality. Go for the outer symbol, the posturing chief, and you did nothing: the organism could always grow another head, and did. Assassinations were the fulminations of impotent fools, *Bonbinans in Vacuo.*

Rael was the first to use it. Demsing saw that. But Rael had been required to use an elaborate system of computation, cumbersome and Qabalistic. He did not know it, but he was, had been, still deeply in the shadow of Jedily, where they had started the Morphodite, and that elaborate system of computation had been her way. With each version, the process of visualizing and perceiving the Reality and how to manipulate it became more subtle, more abstract. By the time Nazarine had been reached, she did nothing but draw complex abstract ideograms on a piece of paper, and apply rules of Change to them. Like the *I Ching*, but more so. And for Demsing, six generations of the Morphodite now produced the result that he no longer needed outside symbols: he could do it entirely internally, within his mind's eye. Look, and Will it. That was all.

He set up the symbol for all that he had on Thelledy, Galitzyn, Chalmour, all of them, almost off-handedly, easily, tossing it to the change casually, reveling in his ability. And as quickly recoiled from the Answers as though he had been stung, as though a mine had exploded in his face, a rifle butt in the teeth, a rubber hose in the night. He saw Chalmour outlined in radiance like a goddess, glowing threads flowing out of her all over Teragon, enveloping the planet like a golden web, and reaching beyond, into space, into Time. No wonder he had, in the world of appearances, moved to her, become her lover, instinctively. There was nothing like this anywhere in the combined memories of all the creatures the Morphodite had been. Nothing comparable to her. She was unique in Time, a unique nexus of expressions, and now for her to be harmed, injured, killed, or even moved out of her own course in any way, had consequences of such magnitude he had difficulty finding adequate expressions for it. *He* himself had a unique place in relation to her, but he could only move along a narrow path, even with his powers.

These things were never permanent. They constantly reformed, shifted, moved around. The mana passed on. And so, eventually, did Chalmour's mana, her reality as Talisman. Demsing *saw* the net of the golden web unraveling in its own way, the focal points and junctions reforming, shifting, the mana passing on. Chalmour would not always be thus, but throughout her life, she would always be a focal point, an intersection of lines of control.

He saw that the girl was a treasure beyond price, and that she was a key to the Wa'an School, that for now whatever happened to her was to happen to them. He could reach them through her, and Rael's old system of killing the foundation was crude and brutal beyond belief. But because of her interconnected linkages with all the other things she was, the golden web, he could not manipulate the Wa'an School through her without disastrous side effects elsewhere, incredible and explosive consequences. He saw in this why it was so, how they had connected their fate to hers, by the simple and arrogant acts of a few. The coupling in Reality mirrored the coupling which had taken place in the world of bodies. And as they had wounded her, so they had wounded themselves, and the whole order of which Chalmour was center shook and trembled. They sensed it, too. They were deep in the Art themselves, yes, you could approach this through the channel of the Martial Arts. Yes. The result was not as good as his way, not as clear an access to the Center, perception, and Control, but it went further than any other extant system. Demsing could even derive the Grandmaster's name. Telny. She couldn't see it as he did, but she could smell it, could hear the pounding of Destiny coming close with the careless acts of . . . of . . . Yes, his name was Ilyen, and of course, the amateurish hubris of Thelledy. He saw it.

Demsing saw it in the web of what was, in Reality. It was indefinite in some areas, clear in others. It had to be that way. He felt no jealousy, no envy, no sense of property. He felt only concern, for her, for what she was enduring, not the priceless release and gift of the self, the baring of the light that was in us all, but something that worked as a kind of rape, and in many ways was worse than rape, because it was irresponsible manipulation for the sake of the exercise of the power to manipulate, and in that was an echo of all the petty little assholes who had ever jerked someone around. Every tinhorn little straw boss, every desk lifer, every status-dingbat dipshit. And Demsing spoke clearly and ringingly in his private window into the eternity, *It's time we ended this.*

10

If you have to remind others of your authority, then functionally you don't have any—at least anything that will last while your back is turned.

H. C., Attitude Papers

WHEN THEY DID meet, it was under an atmosphere of considerable distrust, only partly alleviated by the admission of Telny, in candor, who she was and whom she represented. She had been required to go one step further, and conduct the meeting with Faren in an office under the ownership of the Water Cabal, with company guards nearby; that she had agreed to this protocol without any hesitation spoke well of time pressures and a bad situation somewhere else, and she had not seemed to care who had seen it. Certainly, to the sharpened senses of the average inhabitant of Teragon, such actions were statements of current conditions that spoke so plainly that the words that went along and rationalized such acts could effectively be ignored.

Faren sat across a low table from the younger woman; and Telny, for all her projection of competence and mature authority, was considerably younger than Faren. She was not intimidated by Telny: she had seen worse, traveling among the stars. Doubtless, Telny was both dangerous and powerful, but to offset that, she was also nothing more, or less, than a variety of local tough, and Faren was not impressed.

Telny said, in a low, slightly hoarse voice with no apparent accent or mannerism, "There are no recording devices?"

"None, as we agreed. They signed a penalty contract with me and lodged it with Klippisch's group, with interest provisions. As tight as the Water Cabal is, and as little as they pay, I regard that as something close to absolute security."

"That was also my assessment. Well, then, to the matter at hand. I will speak plainly and without tricks: we need information on Demsing, and we are willing to pay for it."

"Pay for it?"

"I quite understand that such a situation is analogous to the deplorable practice of paying for sex, when the ideal is that such communications should, in an ideal world, flow freely. But such is the case."

Faren looked away, and then back to Telny. "I have few needs and live a simple and a direct life. What I have is sufficient, as far as money goes. For a long time, Demsing helped in that, but I no longer need it. No money. But I would hear your reasons. That is real exchange, real money. Tell me.

Telny had expected difficulty, but not this kind. *Offworlders!* But she did not hesitate. That was why she, and not someone else, was Grandmaster. *Choose! Right or wrong, but choose!* She said, "Normally when we do surveillance on a person, as we come to know more about the target, a more complete picture emerges. We have done such work, directed at Demsing, but it seems that the reverse is true, and I am now in a difficult position of sensing with all my instincts that things are going wrong, deadly wrong, with an increased risk to myself and the organization of which I am a part. I need hard information before I can proceed."

This was the moment Faren had hoped would never come. For thirty-five standard years she had aged, hoping against hope that this would not be. She had done everything she could to prevent it. Now, what could she tell this "local thug," however self-assured she seemed to be. The universe was full of more fantastic things than this overurbanized planet could imagine, deadly things that made their roughhouse little world look like the bush leagues. Here, they murdered by night. There, they coldly and casually wrote whole planets off, entire ecosystems, erased not peoples, but entire cultural concepts. She knew this well. Nazarine had told her. And could this idiot understand what she was pressing for release? She doubted it.

She said, hesitantly, "Demsing has certain abilities which were hidden from him during the process of growing up. We arranged his life so he would not find them. Some of it he did find, but we had structured him so he would not go beyond imagining that he was just a little better than the ordinary. I spoke with him recently and saw signs that the wall was crumbling. Can you disengage from the situation you are in?"

Telny swallowed, and said, "Yes."

"Then you must do so, immediately, and compensate him, whatever you have to do."

"We are in danger?"

"Not just you. All of us."

Telny said, "We thought we were seeing some of this, but we do not know what we are facing. I cannot direct actions with no more justification than what I have. I believe you. But I need facts. You must reveal what you know, with the same sense of urgency we have, if what you say is all true."

"So you can hunt him all the better?"

"No. We want to negotiate with him directly. A group from Offworld hired us, not through me, to track him. As things have developed, it is becoming apparent that he may be a worse enemy than they. We know something of them, and what they can do. They have money (she said the word with some contempt), but they have little power, now. We have a dossier on Demsing, and the picture that is emerging is that up to now he has been operating at less than optimum, and at that, he equals the better of my field agents."

"At full awareness, which you may have triggered, you will never see the hand that smites you."

"An odd way of putting it."

"He can erase your organization from the face of Teragon and you would never know how it happened and go down fighting phantoms out of your own collective imagination. That's the kind of power he has."

"That's a large claim, but I . . ."

"I have seen him use it, and I have seen the hammer fall across the parsecs on a world neither he nor I ever set foot on. They owned a world; and they fell, nothing went right, a domino effect cascaded around them, and now they are scattered to the worlds. They will never have that power again, nor can anyone else in Time attempt what they did. That's how much power he has."

Telny said, after a moment, "I find that hard to believe."

"So do I. And there's something else about this ability: I think it steadily grows stronger and easier for him to use. That is why we tried to raise him so he would not know it."

"Wait. Demsing was a premature infant when you brought him on-world. We have the records. But you speak of him as if he was, before that. He does not know now, but he acted before. Unravel this."

"Demsing periodically is able to renew his identity by setting off a process of change within his own body. It takes about twenty standard years off his life, his apparent age, when he does it. His earliest identity is known, but his recollections of it are dim, worn out, and the early part of that was erased by the process which was used to create him."

Telny started to protest, but stopped.

Faren continued, "Demsing is potentially immortal. But not deathless: each change is like death. I knew him as his predecessor, and I raised him from infancy. She picked me because she trusted me, and I have carried it out. I failed to prevent what I swore to. We wanted the secret to die with him in this life. We did not know Teragon was such a hell. Instead, it has turned him into something unbelievably deadly. If you have made war on him, and lost track of him, even now it is possible he could be initiating Change, and when he finishes that, *he'll* be gone and you'll have to deal with *her*, and *she* will be the seventh identity that poor creature has inhabited in the last . . . about fifty standard years. Demsing is immortal but has died six times." It all tumbled out in a rush, as if words wouldn't contain it.

Telny exclaimed, "She?"

"It changes sex in Change. Each identity is different, and alternates sexual characteristics. Male. Female. It started as a female. Some lunatic research program to produce a perfect assassin. It escaped their control and destroyed their world, and then hunted its creators down and . . . eliminated any possibility that they could even think that again. I do not understand how it does it, but I have seen it work. Somehow, at full awareness, Demsing can *see* the unseen and unknown chain of micro-causality that connects the parts of the universe, and with that sight, can find the weak link in your chain, and snap it. I knew Demsing as a young woman named Nazarine. She told me. Everything she could remember. At first, it was a killer. It killed the one unknown person who supported a world, an organization. But through each version, it learned, and has become more subtle. Now? I don't even know what Demsing can do, and she who will come after . . . She will do things like . . . leave a water tap running. Move a trash can over a meter to the left. And everything will come unraveled, and you will never see her. I know. This time she will vanish."

"What are we looking for?"

"Demsing, if he hasn't changed. If he has . . . something like an adolescent girl, who might be anywhere from, say, fifteen standard, to maybe eighteen standard. I don't know what she would look like. He had only minimal control over the age rollback, and none over the identity. He doesn't know who he'll become. Only that it will be a girl."

"And she'll know everything he knows."

"Essentially. There is some memory loss in the process as well, but Nazarine had some control over what she lost." She stopped for a moment. "That's what I wanted to prevent. Change. If you've backed Demsing into some corner, and he calls up everything, and does Change, he'll have even more control, and she who is to be will have controls you can't imagine."

"Why are you telling me this?"

"Find him and contact him, promise him anything, but get him to hold off Change until he talks to me."

"What does it want?"

"To be ordinary. To be free of an unspeakable weight. There is no end to the process. Nazarine wanted to forget everything. She hoped going through infancy would erase most of it, and in its life to come, which was Demsing, it would never know, and someday die of old age. That can happen to it if it doesn't change. But she told me that each time, it gets further from being human. Its mind fills with the spectacle of the universe. It becomes a more unique creature. Eventually it will want others like itself, and will find the way to make more. Then it can reproduce. It can't, now."

"The report we have on Demsing states he is sterile."

"With humans. Not with one like him."

Telny looked down at the bare table. She said, "You knew nothing of Teragon, and you brought him here."

"We were looking for a stable life, some place sheltered. We knew it was a city, but not like it was. I lost him early. . . ."

"Apparently we have lost him, too, and we may have given him powerful motivation to do the things you say he can do. To be candid, we took his girlfriend hostage. We hoped to contact him that way."

Faren looked across the table at Telny. "You couldn't know. But they have been killing its lovers and companions and sometimes its adopted children for generations of its life. Nazarine knew all of it."

Telny sat back, and asked, "How can I believe all this? There is nothing like this in any world I know of."

Faren felt her hands shaking. "You people are the most adapted people I've ever seen, but you know almost nothing of the rest of the universe."

"We're not so back-country . . ."

Faren reached under the table, and produced a medallion, and handed it to Telny. It was silvery, heavy, and hard. Platinum. About a kilo of it. "Tell me what this object is."

She looked at it for a long time. "Exquisite workmanship, really nice stuff. I don't recognize it."

"In essence, it's a credit card, and in space, it's good all over the known universe. Bill it to the account of the Prince of Clisp, Planet Oerlikon. It was given to the fourth version by the Prince Emeritus. Take it and give it to Demsing, or whomever you find. It will remember it."

"Why do you have it?"

"Nazarine gave it to me in trust. Besides, it wouldn't spend here. I couldn't use it."

"They gave this to him?"

"Somebody trusted him. Nazarine told me, 'Phaedrus started an orphanage for refugee children, after a war.' "

"You believe that?"

"I believe she had it and used it. I believe things I saw her do. I believe it can Change. I was there. I saw Nazarine change into Demsing. She had been a friend, and when Nazarine ended, it was like something turned out a light. She was talking, and then nothing. It took a long time to turn into Demsing. There was a lot of body mass to get rid of. But I stayed there, through all of it. Awake. And I understand why it fears and hates Change. It is something much worse than death."

"We have a young woman, of about the right age . . ."

"Chalmour?"

"So she says, so we are told, so our reports say."

"I don't think so. Remember, it doesn't have control over who it becomes. That's something wholly under control of the process. It wouldn't do such a deception . . . I don't think."

Telny said, slowly, "If it's done a switch somehow, we've let it into the heart of our operation."

"Not possible. Too many coincidences, too shaky. Besides, I talked with Demsing not long ago. No, it's not Chalmour."

"You're sure?"

"Yes. But whatever Chalmour is, I advise you to treat her well. Demsing wanted her, permanently. There's that; and there is also the idea that he sees something in her we don't. She will be valuable to him. He will not permit another murder. And . . ."

"Yes?"

"I just wanted to say I've never seen Chalmour. The last time I saw Demsing, he told me about her."

"How long does Change take?"

"The time is related directly to the change in body mass; the more it has to lose to reach the new state, the longer it takes. I think it needs at least a standard day to complete even close changes."

"Would Demsing have run a deception operation by you?"

"It's possible, but . . . I don't know. That entity, fully awake, tends to write all of us off once the hunt is up and, judging by the behavior I have seen, it's not entirely wrong to do so. If Demsing spotted you a while back, then he's had time to figure at least part of it out."

"One of our agents. . . . He spotted her some time back. Before Chalmour."

"You have the medallion. And turn Chalmour loose, if you're holding her. Has she been harmed?"

"Yes. No. I don't know."

Faren shook her head, slowly. "You can tell me what you want. That doesn't make any difference; Demsing knows, if he's reached for what he is. He knows." She paused a moment, and then added, "You have heard 'actions speak louder than words'? Very well. Actions leave physical traces, ripples in the fabric of time and space. That is what Demsing perceives. Actions and their echoes. Words, testimony, he knows all of us hedge the truth, lie, make excuses, rationalize, blame, anything to get the judge off our backs. He ignores words entirely and he will come to judge you according to what you did and what you intended and where you were careless and negligent. I have seen! Nazarine was gentle and full of light and love, but she was also implacable, relentless, she heard no pleas, she did know the meaning of mercy. Demsing with the ruthless values of Teragon may well be something beyond anything we could imagine, and if he's changed . . . I must advise you that if you have harmed Chalmour, it would be best if you select a deity and subscribe your heart, because it now owns your fundament."

"Does it have a name, outside its identities?"

"The world where it was made . . . they called it the Angel of Death. The people who made it; they called it the Morphodite."

Telny nodded. "What sorts of capabilities does it have?"

"Assassin, terrorist, master of martial arts which haven't been invented yet, magician, so it seems to us, hypnotist, prestidigitator, student of occult paracausality . . . Nazarine did not seem to be operating at full power. And of course the ability to Change and vanish into the background. It can survive in minimal environments, blend into a background, use others for cover."

Telny stood up, as if suddenly galvanized by a decision. "So. I have decided. I must leave immediately. Like you, I have no recorders nor monitors. But I do have them outside, and I need to get this off right away."

"What will you do?"

"Release Chalmour, of course."

"That is a good place to start."

"Let us hope it is not too late."

"I am with you in that. If you find him as Demsing, send him to me. We may be able to annul the worst of it. He will listen to me, especially if he has activated. He will remember me as Demsing and Nazarine, both."

Telny nodded. "I hope that you are right. I will act on what you have given me, though it contradicts everything I have seen in my life."

Faren said, "Cynicism is a useful tool, but it serves poorly as a religion."

Telny nodded to indicate that she heard, but she did not comment on Faren's remark. Turning away, she left the little office without looking back and made her way through the building, down stairs and through halls, as fast as she could, without running.

Outside, it was Primary-day. The shadows were alive with residents to Telny's practiced eye, and there were a lot of people in the streets, just like Gueldres was supposed to be. About a third of those visible were her own people, and more than half of those invisible were. She set out, reading the activation of the net of secret hand-signs as she walked into the net. It was full of urgency, rippling with potential, but she couldn't wait to shred those things out; in rapid succession she made the hand and gesture motions that would send forth her orders: *On pain of death, release Chalmour immediately, with her own clothing. No surveillance, repeat no surveillance. Put out the word through the net, all receivers, we request parley, will pay indemnities. Demsing to be received no traps no deception. Urgent. I Telny Lossoroch command.*

Around her, the flickering of the net of watchers took the message, reflected it, rolled it around and sent it onward, spreading in ripples out of her sight, to the ends of the world. Gods of Teragon! They'd have her sweeping the floor in a trainee's Chapter House after this. If she survived.

The net was still trembling, flickering, jumping like an interrogatee's smelly hide, still demanding her attention. She sent back, *Report on Galitzyn.*

The net quieted, became still, transparent, and almost winked out of existence. In the silence of the signs that followed, Telny picked up one sender, who spoke for the net. *Galitzyn is gone. Vanished. Nobody saw anything.*

Telny felt a shiver run along her back, something she hadn't felt since she had been a girl in training. How long? Forty years ago? She kept on walking and sent back, *Comply with the order.* And she thought, *I had better alert the whole Order. This might be ugly.*

---

11

*The shells which survive the surf, to lie on the beach for the col-
lector to find, are of necessity the stoutest and the strongest; not
so much the fragile, the subtle, or the evanescently beautiful; and
the softer, more subtle little mollusks who secrete such shells are
even more rarely seen.*

*And so it is with words: words clothe ideas very much after
the fashion of mollusks and seashells, and in our lives as speak-
ers, most commonly, only the industrial-strength words survive,
save on the calmest coasts. With one, as with the other, it is foolish to imagine that what we have found is all that is, or that
what we have found is most numerous, or most important to the
environment of which it is part. Easy it is to understand this of
shells and the sea, harder to see it true of words. And it is good
to remember that in the sea, there are mollusks who have no
shells (Nudibranchs), which correspond to ideas which have no
words.*

H. C., El Torre Quemado

DEMSING STILL INHABITED his private universe in the anteroom
where the shafts converged, looking back to find examples of the
actual manipulative use of the skill his abominable creators had given
him. Seen in the curiously dualistic lifeline of the Morphodite: a personal recollection, as intimate and himself as much as a childhood
memory from here on Teragon, and as close; and a vivid and accurate
account of ancient history, eons back in time. He *was* Rael, and he
wasn't.

Rael took forever to run his interminable calculations, but his results
were fine-tuned and accurate. Demsing looked back to that with a
strange kind of mingled awe and technical criticism, and at the Satan's
Bargain that Rael had made with his creators, too. The next persona,

Damistofia, had used the skill only to *see*, and had not used it fully as an instrument. True, she had defended herself, and she had killed, but that had been tactical defense and passion, and he saw within the system that when you released those drives, there was no result in the macrocosm. None at best, and there were counterproductive possibilities. Passion alone was almost always destructive to the self.

As for Phaedrus, there was a strange character whom Demsing did not entirely understand. What Phaedrus had done had been based on a desire to protect the innocent, and that was well-founded. People who would use terrorism against orphans just to insure they got him, and who used that as an opening statement, would not have hesitated at even deeper turpitude, would not even have blinked at it. Peccant souls! And sick, deeply sick. Why hadn't he looked for the door which would have opened the very jaws of Hell itself upon the perpetrators? Phaedrus had wanted peace deeply.

Nazarine had used it all, and used it well, and had not flinched from the necessity she had found at the end of her segment of the life they all shared. Yes. Kham, Cesar Kham had been the key person, the nobody-who-ruled his own system, and the correct action had been the Zero Option—do nothing whatsoever. But that situation, by the strange, strange logic of the system of analysis they all used, required a validation, an extra push, to become real and powered by Will, and the only sacrifice she had possessed had been herself, and she took it, unhesitatingly. And that with the knowledge that she might end the war with that. That it failed cast no darkness upon the aim she had voluntarily given up her identity for.

What were the courses open to him now?

It was something like the game of chess, with certain modifications: when attacked, one had four choices: to move the threatened piece out of danger, to interpose another piece between attacker and attacked, to attack the attacker by direct assault or by making the consequences of the intended attack too costly, and of course, to do nothing. But with this proviso: all situations are fluid and changing, and the pieces have values which follow no recognizable system. And one other: a decision was called for now and could not be put off, or much more serious things would begin to happen. A balance had been disturbed, and a large mass was now improperly supported.

Yes. Those were the demands of what he saw before him, but there was another element to this, and that was Chalmour.

Chalmour was not the unseen base of any system, at no point in this symbolic plenum did she generate anything by being, as did others. But she connected things and articulated moments of inertia from one system into another, and another. She was a channel, a conduit, and this confronted Demsing and all the pasts who spoke through him with a situation for which his system of perception had no easy answers, or indeed, apparently no answers. He remembered, dimly, how the industrious Rael had come across this possibility when he had explored the boundaries of the field of perception and control, that such a type could exist, a linker, in the corporate systems the Morphodite perceived. Rael's description still rung in his head: stay away. There were equivalent nightmares lurking in the solution to the n-body problem in which n is greater than two, and in fact that was one of the avenues they had used to reach the state of being that was the Morphodite. This was the replicated version of that problem. But despite its complexity, there was one simplicity to the situation now which was easy to perceive, and that was that as far as he could see, there was no way to affect anything outside himself without the shock of the afterwave of the deed passing through the girl, damaging or distorting her beyond repair.

It was not a matter of "fault" and "blame." It was not "cause" and "effect." Those things were illusions the Reality covered its nudity with. She had not put herself in this configuration, and he had not put her there, and indeed, no one had "put" her there: that part of the wave which was Teragon had revealed itself so that she could be no other place, and he Demsing had helped along with all the rest.

He backed out, and re-entered again, beginning now to feel weariness from the continued strain of maintaining the distortion of subjective time necessary to perceive within the underworld inside himself. He knew with ordinary logic that he could only do a timeslip once, meet someone as one identity, go through two *changes*, and meet that person again, so *change* was not really open to him. But there was more to it now than that: *to change at any point even remotely near this point in Time would cost him Chalmour. All lines were blocked.* He could not use *change*, period.

He looked back into the shadows of the personae he had been; Nazarine had lived through such a knot, a place where one couldn't move, and had lived through it by simply waiting it out until the moment came. His grip and concentration began slipping. But he had to extract Chalmour out of the position she was in. And when he tensed the net for the Answer, it flexed instantly into an Answer he couldn't doubt, it came through so clearly: *Only Chalmour can free herself.*

Blocked every way. He let go, and began the long float back to con-sciousness, feeling drained and weak, worn and beaten. It could not be done, directly or indirectly. But he had seen something. Not much, but something. Galitzyn. He could approach Galitzyn-Vollbrecht, and around that nexus, he had a little more room.

Demsing opened his eyes, feeling the weight of his eyelids as an in-surmountable downdrag, his entire body yearning for the hard floor. He was back. Nothing was changed: he was still in the place where the slide-tubes discharged into an anteroom of the glowing shaft into the depths. It was quiet, and the light was dim. He looked wearily into the open, curving mouths of the slide-tubes, all now going up. They were a way out, but not a good way, or an easy one. It would be neither pleasant nor timely to make his way back up those tubes.

Then it occurred to him how much he had missed, concentrating on the things his head had been full of. Demsing pinched himself, to keep awake, and to remind himself of his quite everyday stupidity: *the slide-ways all ended here, an anteroom, and then the shaft. The shaft had to be the only way out. And it had to have some way of controlling descent. Here was the place where the rapid transit began, into the interior.*

And there was something more. *This system of slide-tubes, shafts-down, and all of it could not have been made at any time by the humans who in-habited Teragon.* No one had questioned it, or, if they had, their question had been forgotten in the wash of Time. They had been busy, those early discoverers and colonists, and their descendants, and the immigrants, they had been even busier, and over Time, they simply looked the other way. He slowly got to his feet, forgetting for a moment the fatigue which dragged at him. This was not an end, here, not even a small one; but he could not see how much of a beginning it could be, but when, out of habit, he used his old shallowtrack system, the one he himself had learned to use, he could feel the echoes in it, of something greater than he could see from here. And one other thing: That the answer he was looking for, and the key sequence of acts he needed, lay farther on. The knot unraveled—there.

For a long time, or what seemed to be a long time, Demsing stood in the portal of the glowing shaft, looking down at the curdled, faded, indis-tinct bottom, somewhere out of sight. He went back over his suspicion again; this had to be a drop-shaft into a deeper region, and one that was fairly important, judging by the junction of the slideways. That it had to be, and at one time it would have had to have a means of slowing the descent. It wasn't wide enough for creatures with wings.

But at one time didn't mean, necessarily, now. The machinery could have been turned off, or, more likely, could have simply worn out. He considered the evidence of the small lamps along the way, how some of them were obviously burned out, or broken. All it would take would be one critical component in the braking system of the shaft, and the machinery would fail, and somewhere down there, a body would meet something more solid.

He turned back into the junction chamber and looked for something he could toss into the shaft, but there was apparently nothing, no loose stones, no trash, nothing he could throw. He moved slowly around the walls, looking closely, searching for a loose piece he could pry loose. It was there that he found something else which added to his suspicions: the surfacing of the junction chamber was not made of the concrete-like *Kamen*, but was something different. Harder, slicker, tile-like, but not with a shiny surface. He tapped at a section of the wall; it sounded solid, with a chinky surface sound that suggested something ceramic, or hard stone, and metal, all at the same time. There were no seams or signs of jointing. He hadn't noticed before, because he hadn't been looking for a difference. Everything was made of *Kamen*. But not this. It looked tough, and permanent. Whoever or whatever had made this chamber had intended it to last, and last it had.

Puzzled, he turned back to the portal, to see if there wasn't some clue there he had overlooked.

The walls of the shaft, as far as he could reach around the edge of the portal, seemed to be of the same substance as the walls of the chamber, which he reached by stepping on the inlaid metallic lintel and reaching as far as he could. Disappointed, he stepped back from the edge, and as he did, he heard a low vibration start up from somewhere far below, barely audible, a humming at the very edge of perception, and overhead, the domed roof of the drop-shaft made a sudden, sharp, clicking noise, actually low in volume, but in the stillness, it sounded loud as a shot. There was no echo.

It could not be the wall, or the surface. But it could be the lintel. He stepped on the inlay again, with all his weight, and nothing happened, but when he removed his foot, the same thing happened again. A low vibration starting up and fading, from far below, and a more substantial movement from above, in the dome. The lintel was the activating switch. You stepped on it, and off into the shaft, and that activated the machinery. Both steps, and with the thrust out into the shaft. He took a deep breath, blanked his mind, stepped on the lintel, and off into the shaft, avoiding thinking, except the consideration that if he was wrong, it would end fast at the bottom of the shaft, wherever that was.

He wasn't wrong. As he stepped off, the hum at the bottom quickly ascended into a soft, whining hum of power, and the dome opened up like the petals of a flower, upwards, too quickly for him to see the movement, and his descent was slowed by a surge of air rushing up the shaft. It still worked.

At first, he tumbled violently and dropped faster than he liked, but as he fell, Demsing was gradually able to stabilize himself and control his rate of descent a bit better. He was facing downward into the wind, and could not look back up for long without disturbing his equilibrium, but he watched the walls and managed to find a midpoint where he was reasonably stable and falling controllably fast. Now he was going somewhere.

The shaft was longer than he had imagined it to be; buoyed by the flowing air in the shaft, Demsing fell for what he considered to be a long time, and the humming noise did not get appreciably louder as he fell. The wind around him whipped and tore at him, his face, ears, hands. Whoever had originally designed this mode of travel either did not mind such abrasion, or had some way of avoiding it. Demsing fell on. He felt about carefully for a position which would allow him greater speed, and moved into it, feeling the wind increase.

For a moment, he heard the humming adjust itself to a different rhythm, and with his heart pounding in sudden fear, he felt his speed increase. Damn! It was tracking him somehow, and had decided to give him more speed. Once it reached a steady level, the sense of change stopped, the air flow stabilized, and Demsing fell into the bowels of Teragon, slightly headfirst, the bottom of the shaft still dim and indistinct, hidden behind a veil of thickened atmosphere.

How far did he fall? Demsing had no way of knowing, because his speed of descent was unknown. The nearly featureless walls of the shaft gave no clue, and what light there was seemed to emanate from the walls themselves, an endless cylinder down down down down. By his chronometer, he fell for three hours and more, without a break. Something, he thought between seventy and a hundred kilometers, maybe more. The air was thick and pasty to the touch, and warmer.

Signs that the fall was coming to an end began to appear. He went through a zone in the shaft where the lighting changed from a steady glow to a weak alternation of brighter and dimmer parts, which he sensed as a patterned, regular flickering as he fell past the zone. He opened up a little and slowed himself, and heard the hum increase, to put more air out. There was another clear, featureless section, and then another patterned section, this one different from the first. He still could not make out any structure to the bottom, although he could now see that there was one, a darkness at the far end of the shaft. He felt light-headed and hallucinated; perhaps he should do nothing. The shaft seemed both automatic and responsive. But he opened up to the maximum drag, and after a moment, felt the shaft respond with even more wind. He was definitely slowing, and the bottom was clearly approaching, coming closer, still featureless, and the wind was building to a roar.

The bottom of the shaft was a grating, made of the same material as the walls, which glowed as he approached it, slower than he thought he had been moving, and when his weight touched it, the humming, still sourceless, dropped off abruptly and the air stilled. The shaft was empty, silent, and the silence was louder than the roar of wind had been. He had landed on all fours, and for a long time, he lay on the grating, breathing an atmosphere which seemed liquid and dense. It was distinctly uncomfortable, but for the moment, he thought he could bear it, because wherever he was, he was undeniably there. He had arrived.

12

If one performs a questionable act of bad faith, deception, general wickedness, selfishness or destructive revenge, and then justifies that act by citing some philosophy of Good Intent, what happens instantly is not that by some sort of spurious magic one makes an evil act in the bottom-line real world good, but that one contaminates the philosophy and renders it spurious by one's contemptible use of it. Individually, such acts counted one at a time seem to make little difference, but a lot of them add up, and can in time turn a thing once invented as a good into a powerful instrument of consummate and devouring evil.

H. C., Atropine

ILYEN CAME NO more to Chalmour's cell, a fact which both relieved her and frightened her: the former from direct response, the latter because she wondered, *and after that performance, what other fun and games do they have up their sleeves?* Somebody who was far down in the hierarchy brought her meals, and they did not make small talk when they did. She had time to study this from several sides, indeed she had plenty of time, but since no further interrogations or treatments occurred, she concluded that somewhere, off where somebody made decisions, something had changed about herself in relation to her captors. Something. But what? Very obviously they now had a problem, which she saw immediately: she knew that the Wa'an School had had a long-term interest in Demsing, and that, from little hints she had caught, Thelledy was almost proven to be involved in it from the beginning. At the least, it was suspected. They could, then, expect her to inform various people, Demsing and Klippisch for starters, and from that, inconveniences would certainly result. That was not a cheerful deduction.

On the other hand, the treatment she was now getting argued for something else, quite to the contrary: somehow she had become valuable to them. There had been a shift in values.

There were aspects of this that angered her, and she cultivated that anger. All the responses they had made to her were in relation to somewhere, someone else, not herself, and that was demeaning and degrading. That was the worst part of being a hostage, not any specific treatment, but for the nothingness it implied. That was not how she saw herself, nor had it been the way Demsing had acted toward her. There had been no break between his acts and his words. He made no expectations, required no demands, apparently valued her as she was, although she suspected he saw things in her she could not see herself. No matter, that.

So she examined the possibilities that seemed open to happen to her, and how she might react to them, to increase the price they paid, so that they would understand the most valuable thing she had learned from Demsing: that every person, because each was unique, possessed a unique value, a potential, which made everyone a star, and that no one could be written off. No one.

So it came that she was surprised by what did happen: with no preliminary hints, the flunky who had been bringing her meals appeared with her old clothes, and wordlessly departed, rather pointedly leaving the door unlocked.

She didn't rush. Chalmour took her own time dressing, and when she was ready, she made one last inspection of the room they had held her in. It was empty of anything that was her, her identity. And as she stepped out into the empty corridor, she thought *And so they turn me loose, and even in that they contrive to remind me of what a nothing I am to them, just a tool. They have no more use for me, so I can go. We'll see about that, too.*

Not far off, the corridor deadended, on the left, so to the right was the only way out, and she set off without hesitating. It was an old corridor, because it went through several odd little jags and jogs off in odd directions, as if it had been adapted from sections of older buildings. There was still a sense of being underground, though, and from that she knew she had to find some passage going up. She was not worried about where she came out. They had not moved her long enough to get very far from Gueldres, and she knew her way around.

She found an ancient elevator, which worked, and she stepped into it without hesitating, and pressed the up button, and ascended, and there were no surprises at the top, either. The door opened promptly.

She was in a plain foyer of a building which opened directly on the surface. She could see a street through the front windows. The foyer was finished off with a surface glaze which suggested somewhere in Ctameron, and she was pleased at that: *At least I won't have to fight my way out of Petroniu.*

A single figure stood by the door, backlit and silhouetted by the lighting from the street beyond. The foyer was lit, but not enough. At first, the figure was still, and Chalmour could not make much of an identification, but as she approached the entry, the figure moved, and she saw that it was a woman. An older woman, with careful movements, smooth and dancelike.

This is one of them, too. And her heart sank, but the woman made no move to stop her, or stand in her way. However, as she reached for the pushbar of the door, the woman spoke.

"We don't make many apologies, but this has to be one of them. I am Telny. I ordered this, and my response was in error. An imbalance has been created."

A thousand words eddied within Chalmour's mind, and she found it difficult to choose among them. Finally, hand still on the bar, she managed to get out, "That is understated. In what areas do you imagine such an imbalance?"

"We have inconvenienced you, stolen time which cannot be replaced. Restitution will be made."

With rare restraint, Chalmour said, "I am nobody, but I can easily see that you do not see the real problem. That alone will suffice for me." She surprised herself with the venom in her voice.

Telny's face remained blank. She said, "Nevertheless, according to our statutes and canons, there must be compensation made. Where shall we forward such compensation?"

Chalmour pushed open the door. "Send it to me, in care of Demsing Ngellathy."

"Do you know where he is? We would like very much to arrange a truce." The voice was quiet, controlled, and slightly sad.

Again, thoughts and incomplete retorts swirled in her mind, all of them unsuitable to her purpose, which was to injure, to damage. In the end, she thought nothing and silence might be the best of all. Chalmour walked through the door onto the street outside, and set off in a random direction, never looking back. She did not hurry, but walked purposefully, and after a while, was able to figure out where she was, somewhere in Ctameron on the side toward The Palterie. She assumed she was being followed and further assumed that they could do so without her being aware of it. Nevertheless, she first laid out a decoy course to make it appear she was headed toward her parents' neighborhood, and then altered course to bring her back into Desimetre, to Klippisch's place.

When she reached her destination, Klippisch was in, and pacing up and down in her office, declaiming to an audience of Dossifey and a couple of terrified apprentices. It was a major operation to slow her down. She had reason to be excited: two apprenticemasters gone, and the Mind vanished as well. At the first, Chalmour presented an obvious target, but with some prodding from Dossifey, at last Klippisch slowed down and began listening to Chalmour's tale. There was a lot that Chalmour didn't know, but she described Demsing's suspicions, his acts, and the responses which she knew had occurred. From these pieces, she could build a convincing argument that the disappearances of Thelledy and Galitzyn were connected in high probability.

At last, Klippisch stopped ranting entirely and sat down behind her creaking desk, and remained silent for a considerable time. At last, with a fist propping her head up by the jowl, she growled, "And so where is Demsing now?"

"I don't know. We were below Gueldres, about ten levels down, when we met Tudomany. Then there was the shaft. When they took me, it seemed as if I had gone down a long way, longer than ten levels. I do not know how far that shaft went farther down. I think they were expecting him to come back up, but he didn't."

Klippisch now faced the desk and put both fists on her cheeks, grumbling, "We don't know much about those lower levels. People don't go down there, never have. Would you? There seems to be no end to it, and although it's always been there, there has always been the idea that no one could afford idle curiosity. We found enough room on the surface, and in the upper parts of the underground, to do the things we needed to do—the water extraction plants, the hydroponic compounds, the recyclers. Plenty of room. Too much, even. Almost another planet down there in surface area. And of course people have gone down there and never come back, too. No explanation, no remains, no nothing: just silence. So people stay out. And obviously those people who took you, they knew something about where to go."

"Yes. They knew that part well, but I had the idea that their knowledge was limited, too, that they had gone deeper than most, but not as deep as they could have. Demsing vanishing seemed to mystify them. It was not what they expected."

"I don't know how he's doing it without food and water, if he's looking for a place to hide; but Demsing always was good at doing without in a pinch, so he has longer than most people. Even so, after a while we will have to assume the worst. After all, anybody can have an accident."

"What about Galitzyn?"

"We're out looking for him. Him I'll have over a slow fire! He ran, the rat, but we'll find him, never fear. As for Thelledy, you won't see her again. She's halfway to the other side of Teragon by now—and that Ilyen, too. Sorry you had to put up with that."

"I should have paid more attention to Thelledy's lessons."

"You'd have had to spend a lot more time than you had to stand off something like that; it takes years to learn to override your deepest instincts as they do, and believe me you got off light in that, too. They could have done a lot worse."

"I thought that at the time, but I did not know how far they could go. I don't, now."

"You don't normally see that particular use of skill directed toward females; usually it's used by girls against men, but it doesn't surprise me that they had someone proficient around. Their operatives would have to have something to work against to keep their skill level high, honed. That's a sport you can't practice alone, ha, ha!"

"I want to go looking for Demsing; will you lend me a couple of apprentices?"

Klippisch stopped short and focused on the girl's face. "That would be very foolish, Chalmour. You know where to start, but you don't know where he went, or why, or what might be down there. Under normal conditions, and even under most ordinary emergencies, I don't allow my people any farther down than fifteenth level or equivalent. Besides, they might be down there looking for him as well, and there you'd come with a gaggle of apprentices. . . . Besides, how are you going to track him through those tunnels? I'm telling you it's difficult even for the best trackers, and they know their maximum limitations and hold back."

Chalmour's face was still, but Klippisch knew the girl was deliberately holding it that way. She added, in a softer voice, "Listen. I know how you feel—you must do this. But believe somebody that was good to you: you go down there below the parts we know and that's two of you I've lost."

Chalmour said, in a low tone, resigned, "I'm of no value to you. I was scooped up like a sack of trash, locked up, fed and well-laid at will. Moreover, I didn't escape; they knew how valueless I was and tossed me out when they had done with me. Such a person needs more modest employment than agenting for Klippisch's Group."

"Stop! I'll not have that sort of talk! Not a word. They turned you loose because your value had become a weight they could not bear. They do not ever *let* anyone go. If that had been their intent, they would have had you crawling around on your hands and knees, drooling and grunting and begging for more. And mind, *if* they had found your genetic patterns suitable, they might have made you a breeder, in some underground place they keep for themselves. Don't flinch! There are far uglier aspects of this than mere violence. There are places on this world where corruption runs deep and long in Time, and that Wa'an School is one of them. We know a little about them, but I am certain that what we know isn't even the half of it—or half of a half."

She continued, "And as for your value to me, you have become very valuable indeed, because you have survived what you have. Not many could have walked out of there. I know this because not many do. I was taken once, and I know what they can do. I was ransomed out, and for a year afterwards I had to fight myself to keep from wanting to go back. Do you understand? I wanted to go back. I didn't care. At least you saved enough to hate."

"I have to find him because . . ."

"Because you think that what was saved was something Demsing called out of you, or perhaps put in you?"

It was a rude question, rudely put, and it struck home. Chalmour colored suddenly, her neck and face turning ruddy.

Klippisch said, "I'm accounted good at what I do. And what is that? Running a busload of terrorists? Managing and selling spies and assassins? Wrong, wrong, wrong! What I do is find the best in the human material that sifts through my small grasp, and putting it to the best use. Profit we need and profit we get, but not at the price of throwing out the best we find, or neglecting things that are not apparent on the surface. I want people with self-control, I want people who don't make crummy excuses for behavior that can't be called anything but bad from the ground up, and I damn sure don't want system-riders who con their positions with a hard sell with nothing behind it. This world, like all the rest, is full of those kinds of people, full to the brim. Do you believe me?"

"Yes. I believe that."

"Very well. Then believe me when I say that Demsing is the only person I know who is more fanatic on this subject than I am. Yes, he takes risks, and yes, indeed, when the time comes to be ruthless he is cold as ice. But it's always precisely what has to be done, like surgery, and no more. Whatever happened between you and him happened because what you *are* is intrinsically valuable, even if you can't see it. Do not be taken in by the low estimation of you by criminals, nor overwhelmed by an imagined influence of others. Steer the middle course, and be your own person, your own woman. That you are an apprentice here is a measure of what I could see in you, what I saw in you when we took you in. And the same with him. If it was right, if it is still right, go with it and don't look back."

"If he gets back."

"Yes. If he gets back. That, too."

"How do you know this?"

Klippisch leaned back in her chair, and put her hands behind her head, flexing her sturdy arms. "All of us who have survived are not necessarily old fudds who practice creative obnoxiousness and mutter about the good old days. These are the good old days! Right now, and to the underground of Teragon with the rest of it!"

"Well . . ."

"Besides, I've got work for you. I have Dossifey out looking for Galitzyn." Chalmour looked around the office and suddenly discovered that the room was empty of everyone except herself and Klippisch. "And I've got to be out looking for a new Archive. I need you here, to keep everything connected. There are some operations going on, but they mostly take care of themselves, and they don't need moment-to-moment overseeing. Will you mind the store while I'm out?"

"You'd assign that to an apprentice?"

"You're not an apprentice anymore."

Klippisch knew Chalmour was wavering, probably was settled into it, but she added, "And Demsing; if he can get back, he will. And if he can't, you can't save him. It has to be like that."

"And would he still want me, then?" It was a last resistance, and a last fear, at the very bottom.

Klippisch stood up and looked around to be sure no one was listening. She said, slowly, "Jealousy is the result of insecurity. He does not think that way. There are not many like him. Those kind of men . . . I'll tell you: With those, you can be yourself as you will without fear. That's good. But the price is that they don't accept less than the best, either. But all in all, that's what I'd take a chance on."

Chalmour stood up, and shook herself, like an animal getting over a chill, or perhaps a bad dream, or a sudden pain. "When do I go to work?"

Klippisch nodded and rubbed her hands together. "Now. Come around to this side. I'll call in. Give me your hand." Chalmour extended her hand and Klippisch took it, and, concealing their hands, rapidly spelled out numbers in the hand code to the girl. "You have them?"

"Yes."

"The first one's mine, and the second Dossifey. We both call in often, when we're in this kind of operation. And the third one is yours. These periods are short. But Dossifey should be calling in anytime, now. It's all yours."

"You knew I'd do this. . . ."

"It's the best way. And don't worry. Stay on your feet and don't fall, now. You've made it past the worst part."

13

We imagine that the entire issue of any work of art in any medium lies in the beginning, in the creation. All our mythology supports this, reinforces it. But the real problem, which separates art from artifice, is in knowing when to stop.

H. C., *Atropine*

DEMSING EXAMINED THE bottom of the shaft carefully, everything he could perceive. The air was dense, heavy, sluggish, and hard to breathe. The sides of the shaft were identical to the top. The same material. Whatever, it glowed weakly, but seemed to give off no heat. And in the side of the shaft there was a door, with a metal lever recessed in a streamlined depression. There was nothing that looked like a lock, or any device to prevent entry, so he reached for it, grasped it and turned the lever down, the way it seemed to be intended to move. The lever grated a little inside, but it moved easily enough, and with a push of medium strength, the door swung open.

Into a small room perhaps two body-lengths across, square in plan. Demsing stepped inside and released the door, which closed on its own, latching as it touched. On the opposite side was a door identical to the first. Here, only the ceiling glowed. The room was absolutely plain, without decoration or symbols. He tried the door he had just come through. The handle pivoted down, but felt as if it stopped, momentarily, at a rest or a detent which held it for a moment. Then it released, he pulled it open, and looked out into the shaft and the grating floor. He released it and let it close.

Something about the way it closed and latched: it was not just a door, a security door to bar entry, but something more substantial. It sounded solid, even after all the time . . . He had no idea how long this had been down here. It sealed. He turned to the other door on the far side of the little room, and depressed the lever, and it stopped at a point about halfway down.

At first, nothing happened. There was no sound. But soon Demsing's ears popped as air pressure equalized. The feeling of pressure continued, and his ears popped again, and again. The sensation of breathing syrup lessened, slowly. Here his memories from his other lives did not help him much, but he concluded finally that the antechamber was an airlock. Presumably, beyond this chamber, the air pressure would be similar to the surface.

What surprised him was the soundlessness of the process. He expected to hear machinery, pumps, fans, motors. There was none of this: the air pressure continued to drop, accompanied by the frequent popping of his ears, in total silence. And finally, after what seemed a long time, the handle slipped to its stop position, and the door swung inwards, with only the faintest of sound from its bearings.

A well-lit corridor led off into the distance. Here, all the lighting still worked, although some of the fixtures along the walls were slightly dimmer than the others. *How long?* The air had an odor, but it was very faint, and bore no identity he could recognize. It was neither stale nor musty, but felt fresh and recirculated. The odor suggested . . . machinery, perhaps. Walls, doors, things. He stepped into the hallway, wary as an animal, but there was utter silence. The hall arrowed off into the vanishing point of infinity. Far, far down its impossible length there was a suggestion of something, some detail he could not resolve, but nearby, the hallway was featureless and perfect. And clean.

Demsing was hungry, but he had ignored the pangs for some time. However, he was also becoming very thirsty, and that he could not ignore indefinitely. The fall down the shaft had, in addition to everything else, dehydrated him severely. He hesitated, thinking, *Suppose there's no water down there?* But he set out, not at a run, but with the long stride of a strong walk. There was no water where he was, and no way back up the shaft, unless it could also contrive to blow one back up that distance. He doubted it. And even if it did work in reverse, there was no water there, either. So it had to be forward.

Demsing walked on, but he felt like a burglar who was a long way out of his depth. He had no idea what this enigmatic structure was, had been, could be. *But whatever it was, it had been built to last, and it hadn't been built yesterday, either. It was old; more than old. Ancient.* He could find no mention of this in the myriad things he knew about Teragon. Nothing. It was, in all probability, antecedent to the human settlement of Teragon. There was something else that nagged at him, too: the scale was different, in subtle ways which were not immediately apparent. It seemed, from the size of the shaft, the doors, and the hallway, that the builders were slightly larger than human-size.

Whoever had built it had strange ideas about distances—the shaft, with its impossible long fall, and then the hall, as featureless as the shaft. He walked with a stride that could cover kilometers, but the hall did not change, nor did the end seem any closer. There was only silence, and the lighted hallway. His footsteps resounded normally, but there was no echo, or reverberation. After a time, he fell into the rhythm of walking and forgot about staying alert in the present. He let it take him. And a lot of time passed.

Something began to emerge out of the hallucinatory distance of the hallway, but for a long time he paid no attention to it. He was becoming a little light-headed, and imagined that it would probably amount to nothing more than some sign, which would say something like: NO SMOKING.

It proved not to be a sign, but the first of a series of side portals into other regions. There appeared to be no order in their placement, left, right, large, small. There were no doors. Just openings, which seemed to pass through a maze or baffle. The first one was on the right, and proved to be, miraculously, a kind of sanitary facility. Or at least, so he thought. There were drains in the floor along the wall, and receptacles on the other side, with paddle-shaped levers. He tried one, out of curiosity, and the outlet produced a stream of clear liquid. Water? He smelled it, tasted it, gingerly. Water.

It made some sense. That room was the last before the long walk to the shaft. And again, that nagging sense of scale. The fountain had been higher than a human would have placed it. Well. They breathed air, and they used hydrogen oxide. It had tasted absolutely pure, with no flavor whatsoever, no hint of anything in it. Demsing drank as much as he could hold; he had no idea where he might find more.

Returning to the hallway, he tried the next opening. This one led to a blind cul-de-sac which seemed to have no purpose at all. Just an empty room.

The third opening gave way to a short corridor, and in this one the sound seemed a little close. The corridor ended in a T-junction, with a passage to the right and the left, with no signs. He looked down both. The alternate passages also ended in T-junctions. Momentarily stopped, Demsing made brief trips into each of the four possibilities, and looked down them in turn. Each one appeared to turn into ramps which went up or down at what he considered a fairly steep angle. A maze? In all of them but one, the sound of his passage had a dead, dulled quality. This was subtle, and hard to prove, but one of the ramps up seemed to have more of a feel for space. Right, then left. He walked up the ramp cautiously, listening. The sense of space increased, but whatever the ramp led to, it was concealed behind several turns and landings. The turns were never curved, but had hard edges. At last, after ascending what seemed to him to a position higher than the main hallway, he saw the ramp ahead of him going up into an open space.

He heard no sound, no sense of presence, but Demsing kept to the edge of the ramp as long as he could, risking a glance, but he could not see anything. Whatever this place was, it was lighted in the lower parts, but dimmer above. He could not make out a ceiling, although he could sense one was there. He stood up and walked into it.

For a moment, nothing seemed to register, except the size of the hall. To his left, ramps led up into a slanted area that seemed to rise to impossible distances. But there were no seats or benches. Just oval depressions in the floor at regular intervals. On the right, the entire wall was translucent and glowed with the same light as the dropshaft. Below it, dwarfed by comparison, a bank of consoles stretched across the titan length of the room, along a slightly raised dais, which also had the oval depressions, but only along the edge facing the room. It had the look of an auditorium or a concert hall, or perhaps a council chamber. He walked gingerly up onto the dais.

There was no creature of any sort in this enormous room, whose size eclipsed anything Demsing could remember. The part of his memory he labeled "Nazarine" suggested that it might be as large or larger than some of the environment halls on major spaceships, several cubic kilometers at least. Whoever they were, or where they were, they liked things *big.* They lived underground, but they liked a lot of space.

There was no odor, so sense of presense, no trash, no dust. Everything seemed to have been left just moments ago, but the sense of long emptiness was like that of a tomb.

He approached one of the consoles, and looked at it closely. There were no read-out devices on the consoles. Just banks of what seemed to be oversize beige marbles, perhaps about three or four centimeters across, in recessed receptacles. Some of the consoles had similar arrangements of the little balls, others, different arrays. The consoles which had different arrays had less of them. But nothing anywhere which seemed to function as an indicator. No lights, no meters, no bar graphs, and no space where a screen might be formed.

He wanted to touch the console, if nothing more than to assure himself of its reality, but he held back, half-fearing that they might still be active, like the shaft and the airlock. There was no legend, no symbols. Whoever had once operated these consoles, to whatever purpose, had known what each little ball did. On the other hand, given the impression of overwhelming antiquity, he found it hard to believe that the consoles would still function. Machinery he could believe, but here was something more fragile.

And what had been the purpose of this hall? He doubted that it had been an operational control room. The enormous space for audience seemed to belie that; one would not, he reasoned, conduct operational actions before a large audience, or could he make that assumption? This was something beyond his experience as Demsing.

Demsing called upon his memories from his other selves, shadowy figures which were undeniably himself, but also had, even now, phantom identities of their own. Nazarine, Phaedrus, those two were still fairly clear and distinct. Damistofia was weak and poorly defined. She hadn't lived long enough to stabilize as a unified personality. Rael was there, but only as abstracts. That personality could speak, but its voice was almost gone.

The only one of them who had knowledge of complex machinery was Nazarine, and her knowledge was second-hand, data she had obtained from a teaching program. She knew it, it was fact, but there was no hands-on experience to give it depth. The only thing she contributed was that somewhere on the console there should be either a switch to turn it on and off, or another to activate it, should it be on all the time.

None of them had any experience with aliens who used machines. Nazarine remembered things like gracile dogs, and Phaedrus remembered Bosels, whose intelligence was questionable. They could not help him!

He fell back on the computational system of the Morphodite: Zero. There was no matrix of actions and numbers of people to work with. There was nothing here to work with. Only himself. He would have to disturb this continuum to read anything from it, and without knowledgeable participants, he was casting in the dark.

Stuck.

Demsing shook his head. Not so! When gifts gave out, one still had oneself. Assumption: this is an auditorium. Conclusion: the consoles control displays of information, or entertainment. There are no readouts at the positions: Conclusion: that the wall is the read-out. He looked closely at the consoles, and began to see an order to it. The consoles with fewer controls had the same number of banks as they had fully configured consoles on either side of them. It would take a crew to operate this thing to its full potential.

He touched one of the consoles. Solid and firm. The balls seemed to be in no special arrangement. Start somewhere. He touched one, felt it. What did it do? It rolled, and surprisingly smoothly, with an oily, dampened motion to it, despite the fact that it was dry. A linkage deeper inside? That one did nothing. Another. The same. Nothing. Demsing started going to each one, moving it in turn, fully expecting what he found, that the equipment was dead and still, even though the mechanical part still functioned. Nothing.

The last ball on the lower right only moved one way, horizontally, left-right. To left did nothing, but to right had an immediate effect: above, on the wall, a large hexagonal area brightened. And now the ball moved up and down as well. Up produced a stream of symbols flowing across the bottom of the illuminated panel, constantly changing, urging someone long forgotten to inconceivable actions and responses. The string of symbols moved very fast, but even if they had been still, they would have made no sense to Demsing. He could not determine if they were numbers or letters, or that such a distinction existed in that language. Demsing rotated the ball to the left, to turn it off, as he thought proper.

It did not turn off, but went dark, darker than its surrounding hexagons, and inside the dark field were random points and diffuse curdled smears, each one with a legend beside it, in the same characters as had been in the stream.

Apparently, the ball had to be moved in a certain order. He rotated it again, right, down, then left. The dark display winked out. Rapidly, he went through the same start sequence again, and the same dark presentation appeared. Demsing looked at it for a time, and then, rapidly, he ran down the line of consoles, finding the activation ball-switch, and using the same prodecure, turned all of them on, and it was as he suspected, and the wall filled in with the dark display as he turned each one on. A picture filled in across the wall.

He looked up at it, but he was too close, and the display wall at this distance and angle conveyed no intelligence to him, so he moved farther out, into the gallery, onto the ramp and the implied seats, until he could see it more as a whole.

In a way, it resembled the night sky; points of light on a dark field would describe it. But this resembled no night sky with which he was familiar, and contained objects whose import was not immediately apparent. He was further hampered by the fact that on Teragon few people were interested in the stars and fewer still studied them, so that he actually knew very little about astronomy, or astrophysics. Essentially, the field before him displayed a large mass of stars, surrounded by smaller groups of them, and some individual points by themselves. By each group and by some of the individuals, there was a string of symbols, presumably an identifying tag of some kind.

The large mass, slightly to left center, was itself divided up into different parts. The outer parts were coded in orange, and formed a sphere which surrounded the central parts. The orange part extended out quite far, including several of the outer groups. Deeper inside, there was a blue disk, with recognizable ripples corrugating its surface, clearly a spiral feature. The disk was like a wheel, and faded out in the center. Inside the disk was another wheel in yellow with a conspicuous bulged center, and at the very center, one black spot.

Demsing opened up his memory and reached back for earlier personas, to see if this made sense to them. It did. Nazarine recognized it, and so did Rael, but Nazarine spoke for both of them, a condensation.

You're looking at a projection of the galaxy. Our galaxy. When you look up at the sky at night, the stars you see with the naked eye are all inside that. Then followed a swift image of basic astronomy, recalled and told simultaneously. Demsing was embarrassed to reveal to his former personas how provincial he had become in Teragon.

The little furry spheres are globular clusters. That number seems higher than I recall, but these folk may have better instruments. The larger patches are the irregular satellite galaxies. The two large ones, close in, are the Magellanic Clouds, which are not satellites of the main galaxy, but independent members of the Local Group, which have just made a close open orbit around the galaxy, their closest approach being almost directly over the galactic South Pole. Their suspected orbit is now carrying them away from the galaxy, across the plane of the disk, in the general direction of the Andromeda Galaxy, M31, in the common plane of the Local Group. Teragon is located at that deep red point about in the middle of the blue disk. They have it marked.

The sense of conversation was an artifact of the way he had grown up, walling off the memories, and of the way he had reconnected them to himself. The effect was weak, but definite. And this "voice," although single, held the incommensurable personalities of both Rael and Nazarine.

A map implies scale of operation. This is a galactic scale map. Whoever used to be here navigated or astrogated on a galactic scale, since this display is the basic picture you get when you activate it. It will doubtless show other things.

Demsing had only turned on what appeared to be the lowest operations level of consoles; he had not turned on those which appeared to be supervisory positions. Now he returned to the dais and the center console, and turned it on, the same way.

At first, there was no apparent change in the presentation, but after a moment, he could see a faint silvery trace, linking the Small Magellanic Cloud with the main galaxy. The trace connected the two in a long ellipse which intersected the galactic disk at the location of the red Teragon Marker, passed "underneath," out the other side of the disk, and back to the Small Cloud.

He stepped back into the seats to look at it. *Yes, that's an orbit, all right. The way it's oriented, that would make the motion of the Teragon System quite different from the motion of the stars around it. The only reason this has not been noticed is probably that Primary is so feeble. Get a parsec away from Primary and you wouldn't even know it was there, unless you were an astrogator, looking for it. And nobody does motion studies of white dwarfs. There are too many of them, and they are too faint. Much more exciting stars to study!*

The "voice" continued, *The stars around these parts are mostly disk stars, orbiting the center of mass in what are basically circular orbits with local motions added-on. An orbit here takes about two hundred million years. That orbit displayed up there would be quite a bit longer, I should guess about three times as long if they stick to straight celestial mechanics without drive systems, which we don't know. Give it a period of eight hundred million years, just to be on the safe side.*

Demsing looked at the display for a long time, trying to understand the implications of that map, in an abandoned and empty auditorium, whose owners were not in evidence. It implied a scale of rational thought which could not adequately be understood. He could not grasp it.

That's just an orbit. It doesn't mean necessarily that they actually flew it as presented. Consider this fact. That when the group of stars we now call our own neighborhood was on the other side of the galaxy, in the same orbit, neither human beings nor the bright marker stars we use for astrogation existed.

Demsing let that information flood into him, and went back to the dais, and turned off the consoles, one by one, returning the display to its inactive state, as he'd found it.

He left the empty auditorium without looking back at it, but his mind was full of the enigma it represented, the questions such an artifact raised. This was something so vast that the Morphodite's ability to manipulate societies and certain causal relationships was rendered of less importance than the heartbeat of an insect.

And he still had to find food, and a way out of here, back to the surface.

14

To anyone who might say that they see light at the end of the tunnel, I answer that there is no light there whatsoever, that there is only and solely the darkness. You do not walk into the heart of darkness which is the deception of contemporary life unless you carry the inextinguishable light with you, within you, well-fueled and protected against the downdrafts of the membraneous wings of unnamed and unnamable things. There is no light at the end of the tunnel: remain in light as long as you can. Remain in light. Remain in light.

H. C., 1984

THE HARDEST THING IN LIFE, Demsing thought as he walked through the underground structure, *was realizing what one didn't know.* It was a terror and an unspeakable horror greater than any fear openly acknowledged, and within everyone's deepest secret heart, it was this which aimed and guided the lives of all, even those who claimed bravery. Indeed, those who talked the loudest feared it the most.

The diabolical subtlety of this was most apparent in the lives that all chose to live, finding a structure within which one could seek the narrow excellence. As long as that bubble was never punctured, the assumptions behind it would never be questioned.

He saw it as Demsing-himself, a citizen of Teragon, with its endless transformation into a world of urban gangs—sophisticated and relatively civilized in most cases—and the incredible depth of blindness and ignorance such a habit naturally and easily led them all into. And he also saw it with the continuity of the Morphodite, through all of those-before who he had been, lived those lives. Behind them all loomed another provincial world, Oerlikon, and behind that, still another, and even that one had fallen at the very moment it should have stood and flown, the narrow and ugly dream of narrow and ugly men with their spurious dreams of power and manipulation.

He would have never questioned it, although now he could see the evidence strewn all around the planet, if indeed one could call it that. How had it happened? They had all come there from somewhere else, and they had to come through space. Had they known nothing? Had they covered the viewports up? Were they not curious?

And he saw why Faren had told him nothing, too. That, too. It would have hampered him fatally on Teragon, and above all else she had wanted him to succeed here—that had been her promise to Nazarine. To integrate him completely within the world they had fallen onto, and learn to forget the evil knowledge they had forced somehow onto Rael back in the beginning.

But something about that supposed history seemed to fit into the air of antiquity which invested the corridors and rooms and halls underground. The surface of Teragon had been sealed off from the underground parts, which he now traversed so casually. When they found more tunnels and passages, they wrote them off as someone else's work, and left them in their darkness. Somebody made them. It wasn't important. There was nothing down there. Like that. Teragon was old, too.

So all this had been down there, below, all that time, and how much more time?

Along the main corridor, as he thought of it, he passed other chambers, whose purposes were not immediately apparent. He seemed to be approaching a center of some kind. But there were no signs or symbols on the walls, nor were there any pictures. Whoever these creatures had been, he didn't know much about them, and he thought that they probably would not have appeared human, although the screen on the wall in the auditorium suggested eyes, and a visual band similar to the human norm.

He thought he would have preferred actual ruins, instead of this functioning underground city. Ruins presupposed a lot of things, mostly comfortable to the viewers who came after. But these were not ruins. Nonetheless, Demising walked along the halls and chambers with more confidence. Maybe the machinery still worked, true, but the uncontacted surface and the emptiness worked together powerfully. There was no one here, and whoever they had been, they had been gone a long time. That itself made their achievements more awesome, and Demsing did not touch many things.

Where were they, when they left Teragon? Had this system been falling empty all the way from the Lesser Magellanic Cloud? Or even longer?

There was one thing which had to be true about this place. It was maintained, and that meant that something maintained it. Somewhere there had to be a device, or a control center, completely automated. He did not have quite enough nerve to call it a computer, although one could do so, with a wide range of meaning for that word.

But he was not looking for it. His main concern was to find something edible, if it existed, and then a way back to the surface. And so far, he had found neither.

As he walked through the underground city, Demsing found rooms of different sizes and configurations, but nothing which he could identify as personal quarters, or anything like a market district. He did find more of the consoles with the ball-switches, those in a complex of chambers that were divided up into cubicles, with a console and a hexagonal screen to each cubicle. In each chamber, there was one console of different arrangement, and that one had a different screen, slightly larger, but the shape suggested that when activated, it would display a screen smaller than that of the more numerous type of console. Again, the air of operational control seemed to be absent, here, in these places, and the only purpose Demsing could imagine for them would be some type of school, or training facility. There were no seats, benches, or anything designed to support a buttocks or any analogous structure. It appeared the creatures stood most of the time.

He kept looking. He had found auditoriums, schools, toilets, and water fountains. If they—whatever their configurations—performed these acts, sooner or later they had to eat, and he felt certain that eventually he would find something.

The main hallway he stayed on had increased in size after the auditorium, and somewhat deeper into the complex, expanded to monumental dimensions, gradually becoming taller then wide, and the width opened up to something approaching a hundred meters. This area seemed to be a center of sorts, a place where many passages entered the main one, and some of them were almost as large. He tried to imagine what this place might have looked like in the heyday of the creatures. Obviously, the width was related to the numbers they could expect, since he had found enough of the small rooms and passages to make a rough guess at their apparent size—something a bit larger than human, but not giant. He also had the impression they were stout, or thick, and were possibly thicker-skinned, perhaps with some kind of heavy hide, probably stiff.

As the walls receded to open up into what could only be a square, he began to see water fountains placed along the walls, more and more of them. The ones he tried all worked. Out in the vast open space, there were also a number of enigmatic structures which looked something like the water fountains, but which were separate from the water facilities. The ceiling soared overhead into distances he could not accurately estimate.

The structures seemed to be placed randomly out in the open, and had the paddle-like levers typical of the fountains, but there was no outlet for them. On closer inspection, however, there was a slot below the paddle, which opened into a basin shaped like an abstract design for a seashell. He pressed one.

In strange soundlessness, the slot disgorged a granular meal into the basin. A measured amount. Food? He smelled it, cautiously. The meal had a faint odor, but he couldn't identify it. Some scent, subtly yeasty. It was neither a sweet odor nor pungent. As he smelled it, however, he felt his body respond automatically. His stomach began grumbling, his mouth watered, and he felt an urge to eat the stuff. Hesitating, he tasted it. There wasn't much of a flavor, rather like very bland meal. Demsing reviewed his circumstances, his chances for rescue or escape, and stolidly ate the stuff.

He finished one of the portions off, and sat beside the dispenser to await any effects the stuff might have, understanding that it might have delayed effects hours later when it would be too late. There were no immediate effects, other than a release of the tension he had been feeling, and with no one in sight, Demsing leaned back against the dispenser and drifted off to sleep.

After a time, he woke up and ate some more, this time two portions. The hall remained the same, the lighting did not vary at all. There was no sense of the passage of Time in this place. Demsing had a chronometer, but it seemed to make little difference. He looked at it, but the figures were meaningless.

Now he had time to look around a little more. He climbed up on top of one of the dispensers and looked as far as he could, down the length of hall to either side. Back where he had come from, he could see the hall narrow and, in the far distance, end. Ahead, in the other direction, the hall narrowed a little, and then continued on, with side-entrances that blurred into meaningless detail farther on. There seemed to be no end to it, that way, and there was no horizon, indicative of curvature. He could not accurately estimate the distance. If it was truly straight, it had to end somewhere up there, because it would eventually intersect the surface if it did not end. But he couldn't make an end out in the smudged details near the perspective vanishing point.

Around the edge of "the Square," as he called it, Demsing found chambers with airlocks which were the receiving-ends of dropshafts from somewhere above. Some of these he entered, and tried to activate, but although the automatic pressure adjustment still operated smoothly, he could not persuade the shafts to operate in reverse, and he suspected that they did not.

Continuing his prowling, he also found the entries of drop-shafts to deeper levels, very similar to the one he had entered, and for the first time, he began to feel hopeful he could find an upshaft. They came down those shafts to this level, which seemed important, and they also had many side-passages running off in every direction, so eventually he thought he'd find one. From what he had seen, the creatures seemed to know where everything was without signs.

He stayed close to the square and made careful observations to make sure he didn't get lost, while he explored, and when he didn't find what he was looking for, went back, ate again, and rested. This was how he came to measure time—by "eats" and "sleeps."

During his explorations, which he continued, Demsing found no evidence of anything resembling a private home, apartments, or barracks—anything which could be construed as a living space, private or public. At the end of an inclined side-passage of quite impressive size, he did find a smaller version of the grand square, but other than smaller size, it seemed not to differ at all from the larger one which he was using as a base.

His image of the creatures who made and used this place made a strange picture in many ways. For instance, since he had an idea of their physical limits, but no idea of the details of their appearance or structure, he substituted a figure in his mind's-eye, and played at imagining the squares and plazas, the tunnels, halls and assembly rooms he had found, filled with the creatures, moving along, gathering, eating, drinking. These imaginary projections were brown in color, stocky and barrel-like, with short limbs, and their outlines were blurred and out of focus, so that one could not see details. And he visualized them as being much more communally minded than humans; they would have liked crowds. And one other thing: they didn't sleep. The absence of private rooms

and the unchanging, constant illumination of the underground suggested that.

He was beginning to feel defeated. He had found nothing resembling
an upshaft at all, or a lift, and it was beginning to nag at him. They had
shafts coming down from higher levels, and they had shafts going lower;
they had to have some method of going up, somewhere. In fact, he was
near giving up for a time, when he found the top end of an upshaft almost by accident.

He had missed it by an ordinary mistake: Demsing had been looking
for airlocks as an indicator of the shafts, and just on a chance, had investigated a small side-passage. This one had ended in a large room quite
different from the others he had been in; the creatures seemed to prefer hard, well-defined edges, rather than curving surfaces, and normally
their rooms were square or rectangular in plan. This room was quite different. Circular in plan, it was, in its interior space, a torus, formed by a
smooth-lipped well in the center, and a downward-pointing projection
from the ceiling. The ceiling showed distinct sectioning lines. Here,
then, was the upper end of an upshaft, and it worked the same as the
others. A blast of air, surging up the shaft, propelled the body to the top,
where it would slip over the edge of the lip of the well, onto the floor.

Now that he knew they existed, he redoubled his efforts to find the
bottom end of an upshaft.

One more eat and one more sleep, and he found one, at the end of a
fairly long passage he risked checking out. Like the downshaft he had
come down in, this one was at the end of a long, featureless hall, and
was entered through an airlock. There was no difference from the outside to indicate its status or function, but inside, on the inner door, a bas-
relief circle had been embossed. Demsing locked the pressure doors and
entered the bottom of the upshaft, after the air pressure had equalized.

For a time, nothing happened, and he wondered how they activated
it. He tried jumping; nothing happened. So he began a minute examination of the surface of the tube.

It was hard to see, and he might have missed it, but near the pressure
door of the airlock, there was one of the ball switches. He rolled it a little, experimentally, and found that it only moved one way. He rolled it
to its stop without hesitating.

For a moment, nothing happened, which caused a shock of disap-
pointment and anger to rush through him, but at the moment when he
was starting to move, he heard a soft click from somewhere below the
grating he was standing on, and the blast of air started. Before it took

him, he risked one glance upward, and all he could see was the shaft. Its end was hidden in the soft lighting and the perspective vanishing point somewhere far above.

This was different from falling: in the downshafts, the energy of the falling body had to be braked. Upward, the air blast had both to provide upward motion against gravity, and control the rate. It was not pleasant, and it was very slow starting. After he had found a stabilized position, he was rising very slowly, and he could still see the bottom clearly, when he could clear his eyes in the blast. It was a lot harder than the down-shafts, and Demsing did not wonder that the creatures did not have so many of the upshafts. He glanced at his chronometer, and wondered how long it would take to go up the same distance he had fallen down.

After the journey upshaft, Demsing no longer wondered that the crea-tures of the underworld did not care to go up; it was a long and difficult journey. For the first part, it was slow—not as fast as falling down the downshaft. For another, it went in stages, as if the airlift system some-how wouldn't work so well rising. And that was an experience. When he reached a landing, one of the torus-shaped upshaft receivers, he was dumped over the edge of the well with no ceremony and little braking. Then he had to walk down a short passage to the next stage, enter the upshaft, activate it, and go through the same process all over again, with the certain promise of more bruises at each receptacle. And so it went, through ten stages. Ten more.

By this time, Demsing was both bruised and sore from the landings, and windburned from the air blast coming up the shafts. He picked himself up, and started down the exit passage which would lead to yet another of the upshafts. In all his trips along the passageways, each one had been slightly different. Some were straight, but of various lengths. One in particular had been a long walk. Others went through compli-cated changes in level and direction before reaching the airlock. So he wasn't surprised when he didn't find an airlock right away. There was only one way out of the well, and Demsing followed it, although wearily.

This one was small and narrow, and the poorest-lit passage yet. Many of the small footlights were broken or inoperative, and the passage turned often, sometimes very sharply, and went up, constantly, but oc-casionally at a steep enough angle to make him slow down to catch his breath. Still he went on, doggedly, deliberately shutting his mind out and walking on until he found the next airlock sealdoor, which he really didn't want to find.

Afterward, he could not accurately remember how long he walked up that narrow, twisting passageway. Sometimes he dozed off while walking. But at last he did come to an end of the passage. It was partially blocked by rubble, and almost all the lights were out. The ceiling had fallen in.

Behind him was a darkness deeper than dark. Demsing did not know how long he had been walking. Ahead of him the tunnel ended in a loose mound, although at the top, there was clear space, and some weak light beyond. Lethargically, he cleared a hole he could crawl through, stepped over the rest, and found a door. It was different, but he did not care, and so he opened it, and stepped through, into a wide, polished *Kamen* tunnel, with some metal stairs nearby. He looked back at the door. Someone had painted "DANGER—ROCKFALL" across it.

He was back, on the surface of Teragon.

As it turned out, he had twelve more levels to go before he emerged into the weak light of Primary, still wheeling overhead in its eccentric course, but those he didn't mind, nor did he mind finding himself on the far side of The Palterie. He set out for Desimetre immediately, and was halfway there when he realized that he didn't know if he could find the downshaft he had fallen down again. But that was no matter, seen against what he had done, what he had seen. And what he knew. And what he had to do.

15

*A most neglected component of the study of perception is the con-
sequence of timing: not so much what we come to know, but
when we come to know it. And not only what date, what time,
but in resonance and in cadence with what else is being discovered as well as what is already known. The range of expressions
of this temporal congruence can reach meaningless entropic noise
on the one hand, and on the other, powerful and expressive
music which captures the culmination of a moment, an individual, a culture, or a point of history; for good as well as for evil.*

H. C., Atropine

DEMSING HAD SHED much of his former habit of subtle concealment, and walked openly through Desimetre. It was not so much a
move of carelessness or forgetfulness, but a deliberate stance, which
would certainly produce results of its own, as well as provide himself
with a longer field of view.

Having realized his own layered past, and having come to terms with
it, enabled him to assess considerably better than before, when his perceptions had been colored by his own shadow. What he saw as he
walked was easy enough to pick out of the general pattern: his appearance had been picked up quickly by wide-flung members of the Wa'an
School, and it had been unexpected, but their reaction had been fast, as
he would have expected.

As yet, there had been no response, but they remained alert and followed him closely. It was so easy to pick it up. And as for what they
might do, he shrugged off. He had read them, down there in the underground, basing his input on things he had known, and deeper things he
realized he should have known. It didn't matter much, now, about
them: they were powerless and had let control of events pass to others.
So they watched him, and he thought: *Let them watch.*

When he neared Klippisch's place, on a street in Desimetre that had become more familiar to him than any other place in the imaginable universe, he noticed that the number of watchers increased, but was divided into two cohorts: one converging on him, obviously with himself as the target, not yet of any action, and another, which had been aimed at something else, but whose aim had now been changed. From what? They had been mobilized as a team to take over Klippisch's operation, apparently, but had stopped to wait for the correct moment, crucial to their pattern of thinking, before proceeding.

As he had almost reached the door to enter the building, a woman who had been just a passing figure suddenly turned her full attention on him, and he knew who she was. Not precisely who, but certainly what. This would be the one who was running this operation. What had she been called? Telny? He turned to the woman and stopped.

Demsing saw by slight betrayals within her motions that she had been told what he could become, and was terrified, under the surface layer of effective and ruthless control. He said, "Yes, I am the one you seek."

It seemed to shake Telny, like a gust of wind, which never blew on Teragon but which they remembered in speech forms whose origins had been lost uncounted years, centuries. She came closer, and asked, "Have you recovered your pasts?"

"Yes. I see Faren has told you. It could have been no one else."

"What do you intend to do?"

Now he hesitated. Could he say it, so baldly? He thought not. Telny was not ready yet. He said, "I need to collect a company of friends, so that we all may address ourselves to something greater than the sum of our disputes. Send your people to other jobs. We have no need for them."

"We?"

"You are certainly invited. But not the entire horde out there. After all, they have been set to locate me, and so here I am. They are no longer required, and you will see that your mission has changed."

"You came as yourself!" It was almost accusatory, as if she expected to see the direct evidence of Change, an adolescent girl.

"Well, of course. Who else would I come as?" For some reason this seemed to frighten her even more. He added, "Go ahead—do as I ask."

"On faith."

"Oh faith; I have to show you by example what living for the sure thing alone brings us all."

Telny smoothed her hand through her hair, glanced around, and re-peated it.

Demsing added, "The Klippisch team, as well."

"We give it all up. Do you know that Dossifey caught Galitzyn, and is bringing him here now?"

He lied, "Yes." Then, "I need Galitzyn, too. He is about to become useful, instead of what he has been, a nuisance."

She made another gesture, and almost immediately Demsing could feel the pressure easing off, the watchers dispersing, the net which had been so carefully assembled, now drifting apart. If he could thread his way through this narrow passage, that dispersal would spread through-out Teragon, propagated by the Wa'an School and all its members.

Telny said, "I am Telny. I lead, here. I will take you at your word, al-though I see no evidence of the powers of which I was told."

"The problem with this most difficult art that I was taught, and de-vised in part in an earlier version of myself, is that it cannot be demon-strated convincingly: it can only be used. I do not wish to waste valuable people."

"Surely you could find a target that doesn't matter so much."

Demsing shook his head. "They are all valuable. Priceless, in fact."

"Then you will extract your price for Chalmour?" She had read his answer completely wrong. How could this woman be so effective and still be so dense to what he was trying to tell her?

He said, slowly, "How should I punish you for permitting the one act which put you and your organization within my reach? You are here, and you speak before acting: do you need any more proof? And if there is to be talk of revenges, then let's speak instead of that girl you wrote off and sent against me in Meroe. There was a crime you should feel proper guilt over."

She protested, "That was an internal matter, a routine sanction against insoluble flawing! You have no right to question that, especially since your actions dispatched her!"

"I released her, that is true. That is why I have the right. And that is what I am going to change."

"Then we will have no more control. If we don't have death as a bot-tom line, we can no longer enforce our disciplines."

"When you have to use force, you're wrong from the start, no matter what you say." He turned into the building. "Come inside. We have oth-ers to meet."

Telny, disoriented by the unexpected responses, followed him, saying,

"There is no one here except Chalmour and a scrub team of apprentices under Weenix and Slezer, unwashed recruits from Petroniu and the more disreputable parts of The Palterie."

Demsing entered the office, saying over his shoulder, as if Telny no longer mattered, "They seem to be doing well enough." And he saw Chalmour, behind Klippisch's desk, looking in his direction, but not precisely at him, as if she wanted to see him, and yet wanted not to see him. The apprentices let him pass unchallenged, and he covered the distance, and those few meters seemed to take forever, while she continued to stare at the door, only daring to watch him with her peripheral vision, as he approached the chair, and touched her gently across the back, just below her neck, and he could feel the tension in her, the muscles held rigid, the artificial light of the office making her pale skin even paler. She turned her face toward Demsing slowly, not yet daring to speak, nor would anyone else. Chalmour stood up, turning and suddenly reached for him and grasped him tightly. Demsing enfolded her within the circle of his arms, holding her as tightly as she held him.

Telny said, after a time, "Of course, we regret any events which may have taken place while . . ."

Both of them turned to stare at Telny after her snide reminder. She fell silent, as much from what she saw in Chalmour's eyes as for what she saw in Demsing's. But it was Demsing who spoke for them. "That has no power over me, and you have none over her. Remember that."

"We will see what power we have."

Demsing sighed. "This is tiresome. You will cease such word-bandying or I will write you out of the Teragon that is to be. Understood?" Telny fell silent. He said, "You allowed me to reach Chalmour. That was your mistake. As long as you could reach her before me I could not act on your organization with my skill. But it's too late, now. I can do what I need to, and protect Chalmour, who ties me to you. Test me once more and you yourself will live to see the example you asked for."

Telny could not mistake what he said, or the conviction in his voice. Finally, she said, "Very well. But I will say one more thing. It is my understanding that you have to concentrate on your inner vision in order to see it."

Demsing nodded. "That was true at one time. With each successive version, the routine of separation of perceptions has become less necessary. I can call it up now, just by wanting it. I can see the possibilities even as we talk, and there are many ways to enter that. Many, not just one. Of course, each one has its trade-offs, this, here; that, there: slight change according to the way I approach it. While I have spoken to you in this sentence I have seen fourteen distinct ways to write you and your organization off. It is only because I need you, we all need you, that I refrain from doing so."

Telny, clearly, was not accustomed to this kind of talk, and totally without proof, too. But when it came to testing it with action, something held her back, if for no better reason than to hear what he had to say. She stepped back, conscientiously relaxed; she had performed more interrogations than she could remember in her life, and all the signs of deep truth were on Demsing; it didn't matter if he could do what he said or not, in the abstract: he believed he could do it. More than that: he *knew* he could do it. In many, far too many cases, will and belief were sufficient.

There was a commotion by the door, a spattering of angry words, and Klippisch, Dossifey, and Galitzyn entered the room. Klippisch was still remonstrating with Galitzyn, who was unable or unwilling to argue with her. Dossifey had him tied by the thumbs, behind, and was absentmindedly leading him around like an unwilling specimen of livestock, grinning like an idiot.

When Klippisch saw who was present, she stopped short, breathed deeply, and began again. "Demsing! Where in the hell have you been? We have been ransacking the planet looking for you, and here you are, and you have brought one of those night-crawlers with you!" She referred to Telny at the last.

He answered, "I see Dossifey has located our missing Galitzyn, who might also answer to the name of Pitalny Vollbrecht."

"That, and more he'll answer to," Klippisch exclaimed. "Bad enough he runs off, but now I can't find a replacement anywhere, and the house surrounded with the night-demons." She leered at Galitzyn suggestively, with a glance which promised good. "Slezer has been slack in his interrogations! Some practice he shall have!" She paused for breath, and added, for effect, "We'll use the Mad Dentist Procedure Number Five! Slezer! Bring the leg irons!"

Galitzyn, it was true, had lost considerable color and in fact looked slightly greenish, a pale gun-metal sheen on his skin.

Demsing said again, "I don't think we need Slezer and his hands of thumbs. I think Ser Vollbrecht might be willing to discuss things with us in plain language."

Galitzyn nodded, hopefully, although his smile faded when he looked at Klippisch, who still seemed to want torture, if only in principle.

Telny said, softly, "Klippisch, do you remember that remarkable tale that was circulating, say, about thirty-five standard years ago, about a changeling?"

Klippisch stopped, looked about absently for a moment, and answered, "Yes, I do, now that you mention it. Loose on one of the big ships. But never any more than that."

"Demsing is that changeling."

Galitzyn-Vollbrecht rolled his eyes, and groaned. Demsing said, "Yes, it is true. And for you, Galitzyn, you know what I am. You came all this way to do something with me. And so you know that I have remembered. I remember it all. So ask me openly—what do you want with me?"

Galitzyn looked from face to face, and saw no relief there, not from any of them. Now that it was all out, he had no friends on this feral planet. He said, "It began when Kham failed to return. We were also notified of Palude's suicide. But there was no report, nothing. And no idea of the whereabouts of the Morphodite. On Heliarcos we knew that we had lost track of it in space, and it was only a matter of time until it would appear there. So the Regents . . . closed the whole complex down, and left. To the four winds. The entire facility! Pompitus Hall! The Black Projects were only part—the smallest part, but they closed it all down!"

Demsing asked, casually, "So where are they now?"

"No one knows. They destroyed all the records, closed down all funding, covert links, and ran. They were doing other projects, apparently things like the Morphodite, that they didn't want known in general circulation. They left them high and dry. There is all kinds of trouble out there, on these isolated planets."

He paused for breath, and then continued, "We had to work on the quiet, you understand. All of us who were left behind had to find other positions on Heliarcos, and not all made it. Some became miners, or janitors. It was a hard time."

Demsing said, "Jedily Tulilly sympathizes with your suffering."

Galitzyn said, "We traced you here, to Teragon. We wanted to set things right, and we wanted to ask your help. It was then that we found out that you didn't know anything of your past, and then we didn't know what would happen, if you found out by accident. It seemed worse, in the light of what you seemed to have become. I was sent here to find a way."

Demsing said, "The operations you spoke of: their failure was what Nazarine went through Change to make happen. It has gone too far now to change that."

"We didn't want them salvaged. No. We just wanted you to help us rebuild them. The Regents left us with the bills, and the responsibilities. Their problems are beyond what we can solve."

"We wanted to make sure that sort of thing would be difficult to set up again. The tales of the horror stories will circulate forever. Mankind has another in its pantheon of villains." Demsing finished, sadly. "Those Regents, they should have read more fiction before they started. An ancient tale, 'Frankenstein,' says it all."

"Would you have helped us?"

"Probably not. But I would have answered you directly. You see, when you do one of these operations that I do, you pay a kind of price for it: once set in motion, the consequences can't be redone. The act of alteration makes that sequence immune to further alteration. Rael knew this. I know it a lot better. The continued use of the powers of the Morphodite tends to build a rigid universe with no flex in it. It needs flex. Without that, it breaks. The breaks appear in the macrocosm as destructive natural phenomena. It's like the reverse of magic, in that use of the power builds a universe immune to any power. It becomes locked in. I cannot save you from your own evil. Only you can do that."

"I see. Then you have no further use of me?"

Klippisch barked, "Not so fast. I have business with the good academician Pitalny Vollbrecht about an unexpired contract!"

Telny said, "Your requirements for us are obviously gone. So we would like to be paid."

Demsing said, "There is nothing I can do for you; but there is something you can do for me."

Galitzyn stopped short, struck at Demsing's obvious sincerity. "What do you have in mind?"

Demsing asked, "You have a faculty, back on Heliarcos?"

"Dispersed somewhat, and in deep trouble, but yes."

"All kinds of experts, specialists, scientists?"

"Yes, all sorts. Xenobiologists, Cyberneticists, Natural Scientists, Theorists, Philosophers. . . . Why?"

"We have a grand mystery for them to solve, here, and to assist us to find a way off Teragon. This planet is not a natural object."

Galitzyn looked alertly at Demsing. So did the rest of them. He asked, "What is it, then?"

"It's a spaceship. Totally artificial, inside and out. And older than anything we've run across before. And its owners have vanished without a trace."

*We are vehicles for things which speak through us, and we can
sometimes relate these things to totemic spirits whose symbols are
drawn from exemplars in the animal world: Raven, Eagle, Coy-
ote, Wolf. These are some of the more obvious symbols—but there
are others, equally powerful, who have no symbolic form borrowed from nature.*

H. C., Atropine

THELLEDY HAD TAKEN charge of the team assigned to capture Galitzyn, and she had reported their discovery, expecting to get back,
from Telny, the signal to proceed. Instead, what she got back was an
order to cease and desist, and to disengage immediately. For a moment,
she considered going on without orders. She believed that with a little
extra effort, she could run the offworlder to earth. But in the end, she
backed off and instructed her people to disperse. It was true that if she
disregarded the order and succeeded quickly, there would be no stren-
uous objection, at the least no punishment. But if she had miscalcu-
lated, and Galitzyn remained missing, while she continued, then the risk
started to increase.

When she had seen to it that all her team members were out of the
area, she left, herself, walking quite openly through the streets, going
nowhere in particular.

This had all been easy for a long time, almost a routine operation,
with no contact. Everything had worked within the bounds of the expected. But since the Meroe incident, things had been drifting astray,
none of them going right. Yes, Meroe. That's where they could trace it
from, although the apparent diversion from plan hadn't actually begun
until long after Demsing had returned to Desimetre.

She shook her head. They still didn't know who had actually killed
Asztali, even though Demsing was the most likely suspect. But why kill

her at all? Certainly not for revenge—he already had that, from the Carrionflower. But it was after that, that he had started looking for Vollbrecht, so he got that from Asztali, but how had she known that? There was a slip, somewhere. She had heard or found something she had not been allowed to have, and so . . . they had set her up, knowing that he tended to do things like that when pressed, hard. She would have carried an antidote, obviously, but if the contents had been switched, the injection would have had no effect, and there she would have been. The conclusion was inescapable.

They wanted him to move out of the Meroe area, but no one reasonably expected him to return to Desimetre, and walk almost into the middle of the contact point. And with him asking about Vollbrecht they couldn't risk moving him again. He saw too far.

She had faith in the organization of which she was a part. That was not the question. But there was no denying that things had not worked right since then.

And she was being followed, herself. She had just picked that up, and had not been aware of it. She looked about, but saw nothing out of order. A street somewhere in Desimetre, descending down the slope slantwise, curving, following an imaginary contour. This part of Desimetre was more given to residences, and most of them occupied little courtyards, behind low garden walls. Not a good place for tracking, so whoever it was seemed to have a good grasp on the fundamentals. And who might it be?

They had lost track of Demsing, so he was a possibility. More than just possible, and the thought of that made the skin on the back of her neck prickle.

Thelledy made an effort to maintain her original pace, without revealing her suspicions. But now, she changed the general direction, at an intersection where the street forked, the main channel going off downhill more steeply, and the other, to the left, starting back up the rise. She had some of her own methods of clarifying situations like these.

For a long time, she strolled on, seemingly aimlessly, but there was direction in her way. Near the top of the rise, there was a certain restaurant which had several ways in and out of it, and she knew that she could either lose her shadow there, or confirm who it was. Whoever it was would have to come in close, or lose her, and she thought they might see that. But the sensation continued without a ripple. When she reached the restaurant, she went directly into the cavernous interior, which was broken up into several areas, then up the stairs to the second level, where she faded into the dim background and waited.

She didn't have long to wait. She saw someone come in, just as she had, giving the whole show away by looking around. She sighed. An amateur, at the crucial moment. It was Ilyen. She glanced around the restaurant, and saw that others had seen what he was doing. She made a hand sign, which he caught out of the corner of his eye, looked again, and found her. He smiled sheepishly, and came up the stairs to join her.

She motioned for him to sit, and he did. She said, "Not so good, your grand entrance! Even the proles picked you out."

"Well, by then it didn't matter. It looked like you were headed here, so I thought it would be a good place to catch up with you."

"Such as it is, you have found me."

"Have you given any thought to the general situation we might be in?"

"Relative to what?"

"Specifically, to the fact that we have no idea where Demsing might be, or what he's doing." There was a curious eagerness about him.

She said, "Go on."

"I know where he is."

"He, or someone like him?"

"Demsing. He's at Klippisch's place. I saw him there. Walked in right in the open. Telny was there, and when she gave the signal to disperse, I stayed. He's there all right, and they found Galitzyn, too, so all of them are in one place."

"And you came looking for me."

"Yes. They are all there, talking."

Thelledy studied Ilyen for a long time. Finally, "You are perhaps trying to tell me something?"

He sat back in the narrow chair, and shrugged. "There is an opportunity, there, to accomplish many ends."

"Where is Telny?"

"Inside, with them. Demsing invited her, and she went."

Thelledy turned away. "It's no business of mine, now. Or yours. I can't go back there."

"It wouldn't take long."

"To do what?"

"Settle things with Demsing. This has been going all against us, and that comes from him. We could settle this for all time."

"You're out of your mind. We'd never get in, much less do anything."

"There are no guards; the ways are open."

"What about Telny?"

"Include her with them. It's done, then we negotiate."

"With whom? And for what?"

"Galitzyn and Klippisch." He didn't say for what.

"Why break with the organization?"

Here Ilyen paused, as if collecting his thoughts carefully. He began, "See, the loyalty you mention only works one way. When it comes to it going downhill, then it's excuses. Consider Asztali. . . ."

Thelledy considered, and remembered that Ilyen had been, to use a euphemism, "quite close" with Asztali. "Go on. But I know about that: they had her up for punishment . . ."

"Shuck and jive. You heard it from them. I heard it different. There was no offense, there was no punishment. She was considered expendable, something to buy Demsing to move. All the antidotes in her kit were dummied. How do you like that? You might be next, and over something even more trivial."

"How do you know this?"

"I have it from the ordinance-keeper. Orders from on high, she said, dummy the drug kit. No reason, nothing. But it was obvious they wanted Asztali to fail. She wasn't failing anything, as you have doubtless been told. She was one of the best, and more than a little troublesome to some of the old farts who were catching a free ride. The plan was, he'd trap her, and see who it was, and that would flush him out. Mind, he was hard to follow in Meroe. But nobody imagined he was going to hear 'Vollbrecht' from her. Nobody ever overrode a Carrion-flower before. So he moved more than they wanted."

"So that was why you worked Chalmour over? I kept quiet when you told Telny I gave the order. Yes, I see that."

"I almost blew it, but yes, there's an element of that. But the main thing is that you know, out of this, that you can't trust them anymore. All up and down the line: you provide them with the foundation to act in the first place, and they sell you out cheap whenever they feel like it. Asztali is not the only one."

"Why act now, specifically?"

"Demsing. Telny is going to cut a private deal with Demsing. He's been on to something from the start, and now it's all going to come out. The world is going to change. And the Organization? Poof, poof, piffles: The old ladies get retirement and the operators get retraining. That is, we will graciously be allowed to step and fetchit."

Thelledy listened with shock and disbelief, but there was a certain ring to Ilyen's accusations which she could not deny. It was, she thought, a bad place to be in, because none of the choices looked especially good. If Ilyen was right, and he had assembled a powerful argument, then all the time, the work, the things they had done without, all that would be for nothing, when the new deal was cut. Demsing, Galitzyn, Telny, all in on the new world, and the rest of us cut out of it. And if he was wrong? That line of thought was simply unspeakable. If they were quick, they could probably sell out to Klippisch, but that would only be temporary. The problem with treason is that if you spend it for trifles, then it's gone forever. You had no value to anyone. And it was treason, no doubt about it. The question was, what could they buy with it?

"Why me?"

He did not hesitate. "After it's done, one negotiates, the other signals . . . supporters in other places. And as for why you, it's that we've had you in sight for a long time. We were fairly certain you'd see the worth of our argument, without bolting and blowing the whistle, and so far, you've listened. Haven't you?"

"Yes, but I . . ."

"So go ahead and report it. Then what if I'm right? Then you threw away your only chance, for nothing. Or bow out of it, say nothing, and then I'll do nothing, and what-if?"

Thelledy felt herself under enormous pressure to choose a course and act on it, but there was something murky, concealed about this, too. She thought, not entirely clearly, but accurately enough, that if she was being brought into it this late, it was obvious that she wouldn't rate very highly in the new order, either, and that thought had an air of wistful sadness to it. Things never became easier as one grew older. That was what we all missed about childhood. Things were clear, then.

As if divining her thought, Ilyen added, "I know. There aren't any good choices anymore. Still one must bet on something. You can't just pass, because that's a choice, too."

And she thought that she should negotiate some kind of agreement with Ilyen, as for her place, afterward, but that was a pointless idea. Ilyen was already a traitor. If he broke one loyalty, others would mean even less. And she thought she saw something else, too: that such a plan could only have layers of backup contingency plans behind it. If Ilyen walked out of here alone, she would never leave alive. She risked a glance around the room, at the people she had identified as a random collection of Proles, and saw, at a deeper look, that that was exactly what she had been supposed to see. The room was flickering and alive with an active net.

In the end, it was not fear that decided her, but the simple existence of the network, controlled by Ilyen. If they had gone that far, and were operating clandestinely already at that level, then this had deep roots, indeed, and it might be better to go with it. And as a final aside to her own sense of guilt, she added that she had never cared that much for Demsing, anyway.

"What sort of plan do you have in mind?"

"Knives, front and rear. You to do the back door. I take the front, and wait for you to move. One-two, crossfire. It will have to be fast."

"Fast I can handle. How do I know you'll come in?"

"Because you know one can't do it, and you know I wouldn't ask if I thought I could do it alone. And as far as trapping you, well, there are easier ways of doing that, at a much lower level of loss. Point?"

"Point."

"We finish that, then holdfast. They'll talk."

"You're sure about that?"

"There will be backup from my side. In on signal."

"Now?"

"Yes," he said, getting to his feet. "But one thing more. I want Chalmour for my own purposes, unharmed."

Thelledy shrugged, standing up. "Why not?" Although she did so with a certain fatalism. Already Ilyen's regime looked less attractive than the one he would replace. Perhaps there was a way, too, to line all of them out; yes. There was a way. Once he came in on her entry, there would be no turning back. Tricky, but it would work. A double-cross, and then a quick alibi. She might escape this yet.

You never know when you are going to have to make your stand.
It might be right here, right now. Might not be. Might be never,
you never know.

H. C., Atropine

EVERYONE EXCEPT GALITZYN was surprised at Demsing's announcement. Galitzyn nodded and said, "Teragon has been regarded as suspicious for a long time. Surveys picked up all kinds of things that don't add up, but the trouble is, no one has ever had time to run it down. There is simply too much to do, too many objects to study. But I'll tell you what I know about Teragon and Primary. For one thing, White dwarfs don't have oxygen-atmosphere planets. To get to be white dwarfs, they blow out any planetary systems they might have had. The few which are known possess a few lumps of slag, and the rocky remnants of gas giant cores. Also the orbit of Teragon is odd in two ways, no, three: it doesn't orbit in the plane of Primary's equator, it's in far too close to have the physical features it does, and its orbit is too close to a circle—the eccentricity is so small it can't be measured from outside the system."

He stopped to catch his breath, and then went on, "Primary is odd, too. Primary, judging by its percentages of heavy metals, is an extremely old star, and it has an anomalous galactic orbit. Surveys mark it off as one of the halo stars with an eccentric orbit, tilted so that it intersects the galactic disk. It just happens to be passing through the disk in this era, otherwise no one would ever have seen it. Nobody is studying individual halo stars, and besides, you can't even see a white dwarf much farther off than ten parsecs. I know it's odd. Why do you think Teragon is a ship?"

"Because I found an area, deep under, where the owners used to live. I saw their instruments."

"You weren't hallucinating?"

"There was food and water. I was down there a long time. I could not have lived without those things. There was a large space, like an auditorium, with display consoles, which I turned on. It showed the galaxy, and the outer satellite systems. The orbit for Primary has its far end out at the Lesser Magellanic Cloud."

"But you saw no one down there?"

"No one, no trace, no nothing. They have been gone a long time. Everything works, but the builders are gone. They left no pictures, nothing. I only saw part of it; there seems to be no end to it, and I never saw anything like a control room. It will take years to unravel everything that is down there. But some of the displays show writing, so eventually, someone should be able to wear it down."

"How far down?"

"I'm guessing, but the upper part I explored started maybe seventy-five kilometers down, maybe more. You get there by falling down an air shaft which blows a countercurrent against you. Apparently they thought that was a fine way to travel. I didn't much care for it, but it works."

Demsing turned to Telny. "Do you see, now, why I asked you here? This is an unknown which makes all our wars pointless. We could become one people."

Telny said, "Yes. True, but we could also become a planet of impoverished souvenir-peddlers to the great and mighty folk who'd stop by on the grand tour, all those offworld swells."

"We could learn to use it, instead of riding passively on it. We would be the cutting edge. We already have the basic talent here; we combine and refine. I think, somewhere down in that underground, there is a control room, from which we can fly this world anywhere we want. We could have a real sun, and an outside, instead of this nighted city."

Telny nodded. "I see that well enough. So what do we need them for, Galitzyn-Vollbrecht and his offworlders?"

Demsing answered, "We are street-wise, but we have forgotten much of the whole range of our ancestors. No one here has the background now to comprehend everything down there. We're the most sophisticated, most urbanized people in the human universe, and we're primitives. If we take that underworld without understanding what we have, it will be like handing a piece of fine art to a Barbary ape: we will destroy the record preserved down there, and then each other. The point is to integrate ourselves, and then ourselves with the rest who are out there. Pull together instead of flying apart, each of us alone in our specialist culture. We start that here, on Teragon."

"You argue for peace, not war, but I know you know the value of war, and survival."

"I do. But peace is the way, here. We can have it all, but we have to learn to combine, work together. The universe has become a place with too many unknowns. I did not understand that before, but I do now. It always was that way, but we went our own ways far too long."

Demsing said, to Galitzyn-Vollbrecht, "And this is the place where Pompitus Hall can redeem its reputation, and regain, by your own efforts, not mine, your place." He noticed that Dossifey had not untied his thumbs, yet, and asked him to. Presently, Galitzyn was rubbing his wrists and massaging his thumbs. And considering possible outcomes.

Then he asked Klippisch if he could invite Faren in on the discussion they were having, that it was important that she be here as well.

Klippisch agreed, "Yes. I can see a kind of logic behind what you are saying, but I'd like to hear her speak, too. She's an offworlder as well, but she adapted here. It would be quicker if Dossifey called her." She gestured with her head, and Dossifey faded out of the room, still smiling, to find a communicator out of the office.

Once, when Demsing had let the Morphodite flood into him, and seen how to change causality, he had glimpsed the possibilities of a certain design. Now he saw, with that part of his mind which perceived such things, that this design moved from a possibility to something *between*, a potential. He felt its energy, its *tightness*, its justice, but he also felt the price of activating it. There was a sadness to that. He could see it clearly, but there was no other way. A weight was settling on this room, this time, slow, ponderous, planetary in mass, more than planetary, balancing, shifting, moving. He could feel the weight. Yes. He had moved Dossifey out of the room. When he came back, he would be out of position. He looked about him: *they* felt nothing, they sensed nothing. It needed one more step . . . now. . . .

Demsing motioned to Klippisch that she should assume her rightful seat behind her own desk and preside over the discussions. And she did it, stepping around Demsing and Chalmour, who were still holding each other tightly. Yes. One more block fitted into place. The mass around him he could feel settled more securely. This had happened to Phaedrus, but accidentally. He hadn't had enough knowledge and skill to move it. And just as accidentally, the focus had moved on, later, settling on someone else. That was the way of it. The people who were upholders of their world never knew it, or if they did, they always tried to manipulate it after it had passed on to another upholder. Even now, he wasn't in complete control of it. It settled on him and upon Chalmour, together. Klippisch sat in her chair and pulled it up close to the desk. Yes. Even better.

All this time, Galatzyn and Telny had been talking, in low tones, exploring the possibilities.

Galitzyn caught his attention. "Yes. You say there was no trace of the creatures down there, none whatsoever?"

"None. There wasn't even a scent of them. The place was clean, the air was recycled, everything worked, the fountains still ran water, and the dispensers still made food-stuff. I had no trouble with any of it. But it felt like they had been gone for a long time. I saw no trace of violence or disease; perhaps whatever maintains the underground could have cleaned that up as well, but surely something would have been broken. We're guessing. We don't know, at least until we can get a crew down there working in that auditorium. I had the feeling about that place, that if you could control those consoles, you could eventually bring it all up. The answers are there, just more than one alone could operate. We have to work together."

Galitzyn agreed. "Absolutely. We have some people who can winkle it out. It'll take time to get them here, though. Did you sense any need for haste?"

"None down there. They are gone, so it would seem. But I feel some haste up here, in this world."

Telny said, "I know. I can feel the pressure of it. But I also see that you are right in this. It has to be all of us, doesn't it?"

"If we continue fighting over scraps, the unknown things slink out of the hidden parts of the forest and bite us while we engage each other."

"Well-said, indeed! Often I have said that very thing to my own trainees, but it is hard to get them to see that. *I* forget it sometimes."

Demsing still maintained contact with Chalmour, but he reached forward, and moved a large glass paperweight over a few centimeters toward Klippisch.

Telny, alert to minutiae as ever, saw the action, but saw no reason for it, and that was what set her internal alarms off. An action without a reason was a clear break in the pattern. And what was it Faren had said? Yes: . . . *it would leave a water tap running, or move a trash can over a meter to the left,* and *you would never see the hand that smote you. It would all come unraveled, and you would never see it.* What was Demsing doing?

Was the talk deception, for him to make his random moves in this room, to bring another world-sequence into being? But there was no lie in his voice: he believed deeply in what he had said, here. *I'm seeing him set something up, seeing it happen in front of me, and who knows what re-action he's preparing for?* She thought of moving the paperweight back, but hesitated. *Suppose that's the move I'm supposed to make? Then what?*

But for now he seemed to be satisfied by that move and made no more, and her attention was recalled to Klippisch and Galitzyn, who were still arguing possibilities, and how to bring still others into it. She felt her own control over this world slipping as she stood here, but Demsing seemed satisfied, withdrawn, content. He had brought forth his message, and now was moving into the sidelines, and she didn't un-derstand that, either.

And from Demsing's point of view, each action now caught the on-rushing future into a tightening vise, but it wasn't tight enough yet; like the zen archers of old, he was waiting for the perfect moment of pre-cise tension in the string, the bow, and the sublime emotion of allowing the target to aim him, and the last act which would propel the arrow into Time. Yes, now that he took the burden from its nameless prede-cessor, he felt its power, its inertia, its mass, and its price: as it settled onto him, he felt his visions of himself fading away, an egoless awareness which was the only prelude to action.

They continued to talk, but it was unimportant now, and he only lis-tened, agreeing sometimes, more often saying nothing. He had had to give up this world and its deeds to transform it. The secrets of the un-derground were no longer his. Yes, this was the right way.

After a time, Faren appeared at the door, and came in. She expressed no surprise at seeing Demsing, instead of what he might have been, the nameless girl who would have been roughly contemporary with Chal-mour. Demsing left Chalmour where she was, by the corner of the desk, and as she turned to follow him with her stance, she stepped in front of Klippisch's only route from behind the desk, should threat come through the door.

Demsing briefly hugged Faren, and as she came farther into the room, he turned with her so that Faren was between Telny and himself. Dossifey came back, from the other door, but turned to the window be-hind Klippisch. It was moving into position like something in slow mo-tion, under water, an effortless glide. Then he felt fear, but he shrugged it off. It would be just like Change, wouldn't it? Maybe easier than Change.

He was looking toward Dossifey's door, and he saw it burst open, and behind it, Thelledy with a short, slightly curved blade, held before her like a spear. She was diversion, and Dossifey and Telny moved instantly to break her flight. He did not look back, but he felt the shadow behind him, the ice-bite of the knife, and that would be Ilyen. Too late, Telny realized her mistake and was turning, but Faren was in her way; there was no way she could clear the older woman in time. Klippisch reached for the paperweight, missed it, and lunged for the side, but Chalmour blocked her, too. Dossifey tripped Thelledy, and drew his knife as she fell.

Demsing fell forward, curling as he settled to the floor, to miss Thelledy, and he watched impassively as Chalmour took Klippisch's knife—Klippisch let her have it—and as Ilyen smiled knowingly at her, she deftly grasped his hair with her right hand, and jerked, and as his head came up, cut his throat. Demsing felt Thelledy bump up against him, grow rigid, and then relax.

He felt the weight lift off him, in just the way he had known it would. It had worked.

Faren and Chalmour bent down to him, both of them with eyes wild. It was dim now in the office, dimmer than even the poor daylight of Primary. Only seconds. He saw Telny's face, too, upside down. He said, "This was the only way I could do it. Faren knows what Nazarine told her."

Faren said, "You are Nazarine?"

"Yes, Nazarine, Phaedrus, all of them, Damistofiya, Rael, Jedily. Yes. All, and Demsing, too. They knew, a long time ago, ancient history, human sacrifice, only they couldn't find the right one, and they turned away from the way to find the one. I saw that I could make it all right, here, now, but the price was myself. And at least one more."

He heard Dossifey. "Thelledy's dead. Ilyen soon will be."

Chalmour cried at him, "Why? Why?"

"Had to be. Got worse if it went any other way. Horrors, reduced to rats in the ruins. Now you have a future, Chal'; use it and don't look back. It will work. Telny!"

The upside-down figure spoke, "Here!"

"Take care of Chalmour: she's your life, now. Faren knows. Ask her. Chalmour has the foundation . . ." Demsing thought that it had gotten very dark, and that he was still talking, there wasn't enough time to say what he had to, and besides, he didn't think they could hear him. No, this was much easier than Change. He smiled, and wondered what he would look like when he woke up.

There were five left standing in the office, and they all stood, and reached across Demsing to touch hands. Klippisch, Telny, Faren, Galitzyn, Chalmour, in silence. It was Telny who broke the silence, at last, amid the fearsome scents of violent death and fear still in the air of the room.

"We know what we have to do."

"Let us begin," said Klippisch.

Chalmour bent down and touched Demsing, but did not cry.

Faren said, "He wanted to use his curse and his gift for us, once, instead of against us, to even the balance of all that had gone before. I do not understand the workings of this, but I know how Nazarine saw what could be, and what the price was for actualizing the things that could become. And so here, Demsing, the same, saw what good there was in us, and how to preserve it and strengthen it, before we were swamped by the unknown that has always been all around us, whether we saw it or not. We cannot see it, but we will act it out, according to what was set in motion, here."

Telny stepped forward. "I understand some of these things in a small part, from what I have known. Let us use this well; such as these are unique. As we all are, unknowing."